SelectEditions

SELECTED AND EDITED

SelectEditions

BY READER'S DIGEST

THE READER'S DIGEST ASSOCIATION, INC.
MONTREAL • PLEASANTVILLE, NEW YORK

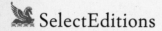 SelectEditions

Vice President, Books & Home Entertainment: Deirdre Gilbert

INTERNATIONAL EDITIONS
Executive Editor: Gary Q. Arpin
Senior Editor: Bonnie Grande

251-268-0101

CONTENTS

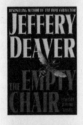

Ghost
Moon

Karen Robards

Run away, Olivia. Run, run away.

She could swear that's what she heard.

Run away. Run.

She told herself it was her imagination. It was the wind, or water lapping at the shores of the lake. The voices could be anything. They certainly did not belong to ghosts. . . .

"Karen Robards is one terrific storyteller."
—*Chicago Tribune*

Prologue

"MOM, I wet the bed." The small, shamed voice and the little hand that went with it tugged Louise Hardin out of a deep sleep. She opened one groggy eye to discover her daughter Melissa standing at her bedside in the darkened room. Behind her the alarm clock glowed the time: 1:00 a.m.

"Mom." Missy's hand tugged once more at the long sleeve of Louise's pale green nylon nightgown.

"Oh, Missy, no! Not again." Louise rolled out of bed, careful not to disturb her husband, Brock, who slumbered peacefully beside her. Brock had to get up early to be at the office. As he said, the rest of them could sleep all day if they chose, but he had to earn a living. Besides, he hated the fact that Missy sometimes still wet the bed. He was a pediatrician, and he tended to take her frequent accidents personally.

"I'm sorry, Mom," Missy offered in a tiny voice when they gained the relative safety of the hallway outside the bedroom. "At least this time I dreamed I was on the potty. It seemed so real. And then I was all wet, and I woke up and I wasn't on the potty at all."

"All your dreams seem so real." If Louise's voice was just a tad dry, she couldn't help it. She was really really tired, and this was getting to be almost a nightly occurrence. As a seven-year-old, Missy was getting her up at night almost as much as she had when she was a baby. Louise had started leaving the hall light on at night because,

in addition to wetting her bed, Missy had suddenly become afraid
of the dark. She had nightmares about monsters hiding in her room
and watching her as she slept. Sometimes she woke up screaming,
and Louise would race down the hall to find her daughter huddled
in the center of her bed with the covers pulled over her head, crying her eyes out. Inevitably Louise ended up bringing Missy into
bed with her and Brock, a practice of which Brock strongly disap-
proved. Louise agreed that he probably knew best—as he fre-
quently pointed out, *he* was the expert—but she could not find it in
her heart to punish her daughter for being afraid of the dark.

The ammonia-like smell of urine struck Louise in the face as soon
as she stepped inside Missy's room. She sighed.

"I'm really sorry, Mom," Missy offered again.

Without a word Louise let go of Missy's hand, closed the door,
turned on the light, and crossed to the chest to extract a clean
nightgown from a drawer. Accustomed to the ritual, Missy had already pulled her wet nightgown off and was in the act of dropping
it on the floor. Lips thinning, Louise moved to her daughter's side
and tugged the dry nightgown over Missy's head. As the gown fell
into place, she reached around behind Missy's neck to free the long,
dark brown braid of her daughter's hair.

"Are you mad at me, Mom?" Missy asked humbly as the two of
them worked together to strip the wet sheets from the bed.

Louise's heart smote her. "No, baby, I'm not mad at you." She
carefully tucked in the corners of the clean sheets that were kept,
along with spare blankets, in a trunk at the foot of Missy's bed.
Smoothing a pink wool blanket over the sheets, she pulled back a
corner. "Hop in."

"Don't tell Daddy," Missy said, obeying.

"I won't." It was a ritual, these words.

Louise tucked the clean, dry bedclothes around her daughter as
Missy snuggled onto her side, a small smile curving her lips.

"Good night, baby." Louise brushed her lips across the warmth
of her daughter's exposed cheek and straightened.

"I love you, Mommy." Missy's voice was already sleepy.

"I love you, too, Miss Mouse. Now go back to sleep." Louise
gathered up the wet bedding and nightgown. She headed toward

the basement, meaning to put the sheets in to wash and thus leave no trace of the night's misdeeds for Brock to discover.

What Louise didn't know was that concealed in Missy's closet behind a double rack of neatly pressed outfits and a mountain of stuffed animals a man listened and waited. He'd thought about running for it when the child had gone for her mother, but he'd been afraid that he wouldn't get away in time, and indeed the little girl and the woman had returned within minutes.

Now he and his little sweetie pie were alone again.

His heartbeat quickened as he waited for the mother to return to her room. When she did, he waited even longer, listening to the soft, light rhythm of the child's breathing.

Finally he eased open the closet door.

The next morning, when Louise went to rouse Missy, her daughter was stretched out in bed as neatly as could be, lying on her back with the covers pulled up under her chin.

"Time to get up, sleepyhead," Louise said. Playfully she jerked the covers down.

In that moment she knew. Praying she was mistaken, she grabbed her daughter by the arms.

Missy's body was cold and stiff.

The child was dead in her bed.

The next week this banner headline appeared in the New Orleans *Times-Picayune*: PROMINENT BATON ROUGE PEDIATRICIAN CHARGED WITH MURDERING DAUGHTER, 7, FOR WETTING BED.

The dateline was May 6, 1969.

GHOSTS. They were everywhere on that steamy summer's night. Their white, misty shapes hovered over the old graveyard that stood sentinel on the bluff beside the lake, played hide-and-seek behind the Spanish moss that dripped from the twisted branches of the bald cypress trees, stretched heavenward above the inky surface of the water. They whispered together, their words falling like drops of water through the mist, almost drowned out by the other, more corporeal sounds of the night. *Run away. Go. Run away,* was what they said. Whether the ghosts were real or the product of atmosphere and imagination, though, who knew? And what difference, really, did it make?

It was hot, still, although it was some ten minutes past one a.m. on August 20, 1999, which was a Friday night or, rather, a Saturday morning. Hot with the thick, damp kind of heat that always lay like a blanket over Point Coupee Parish in August.

LaAngelle Plantation heat. Courtesy of the swampy Louisiana low country to the south and the mighty Mississippi to the east. It came with its own feel, its own smell, its own taste.

She was come home at last, Olivia Morrison thought, inhaling the indefinable aroma of decay, swamp water, and vegetation run amok that she remembered from her earliest childhood. The knowledge both exhilarated and frightened her. Because the truth was that this was, and was not, her home.

"Are we almost there, Mom?" The tired little voice at her elbow was barely audible over the night sounds around them.

"Almost." Olivia glanced down at her eight-year-old daughter with mixed tenderness and concern. Sara looked dead on her feet, her sturdy little body drooping like a wilted flower. Tendrils of jawlength coffee brown hair curled and clung to the moist skin of her neck and forehead. The gingham sundress that had been so pretty and crisp that morning in Houston was now as limp-looking as the child herself. Her dusty black ballerina flats— thriftily bought big to allow for growth—slipped off her heels with every step to slap against the spongy ground. The lace-trimmed white anklets she wore with them were grimy with dirt. They'd walked from the bus stop at New Roads, a distance of perhaps five miles, because nobody had answered the telephone at the Big House when Olivia called, and she didn't have the money for a taxi.

Not that she would have had much chance of rousting out Ponce Lennig and his beat-up Mercury anyway, Olivia thought, lifting strands of shoulder-length coffee brown hair away from her own moist neck. LaAngelle's only taxi service had always been erratic at best. Not that that mattered either, since she was down to her last five dollars and change.

Ponce would have gladly given them a free ride out to the house, but Olivia would have had a hard time confessing just how broke she was. Once upon a time, as Olivia Chenier, spoiled and wild and the youngest of the golden Archer clan, she had been as glamorous and above their touch as a movie star to the people of the town.

Once upon a time. A long time ago. Now she was a dental office manager, barely scraping by. How the mighty are fallen.

No one but Aunt Callie knew she and Sara were coming, and Aunt Callie didn't know precisely when. Olivia couldn't blame any of the family for not being on hand when she called.

She hadn't seen them, any of them, for nine years.

With a twinge of anxiety she wondered how they would react to her return. Her hand tightened around Sara's.

"I think I'm getting a blister," Sara complained.

It was all Olivia could do to suppress a sigh. Sara was not usually whiny or grumpy, but she was rapidly becoming both. And who could blame her? The child had been traveling since seven that morning, first by bus and then on foot.

"Listen, baby, if we keep walking up this path just a little bit farther, we'll go up some steps to the top of a bluff and you'll be able to see the house from there."

Sara's gaze swept their surroundings. "It's spooky here."

"That's just because it's night." Olivia's words were comforting, but she, too, glanced around, almost unwillingly. *Run away, Olivia. Run. Run away.* She could swear that's what she heard, murmured over and over again through the shifting pockets of steam. They should have kept to the road until they reached the long driveway. Taking the shortcut through the woods had been a mistake.

"Aren't you scared?" Sara asked.

"No," Olivia said stoutly, but she wasn't quite sure that she was telling the truth. There was no turning back at this point, though. The road was farther behind them than the house was ahead.

Overhead a pale crescent moon slipped in and out of view. All around them leaves rustled, branches swayed, and twigs snapped as who knew what nocturnal creatures moved about. Not far ahead, atop a kudzu-covered bluff, a long-ago patriarch's marble crypt gleamed faintly through the darkness. Fingers of diaphanous white mist rose above all.

Spooky? Oh, yes. Although she would never admit it to Sara.

"Is that the lake where your mom drowned?"

Trust her sensitive, imaginative child to hit upon the one topic that Olivia really did not want to talk about just at that moment. The death of her mother had been the defining event of her childhood. It had changed her in a moment, like a catastrophic earthquake instantly reshapes the topography of the land. And yet, although the memory of the pain was sharp and strong even so many years later, she could conjure up no memory of how she had learned that her mother was dead or of who had told her. No memories of her mother's funeral, or her stepfather, or the Archer family in mourning. It was as if her memory banks, where the events surrounding her mother's death were concerned, had been wiped clean. All she knew were the bare facts: Her mother had drowned at age twenty-eight in that lake.

The same lake from which voices now seemed to be calling to her.

"Yes." Olivia set her teeth against the sudden stab of loss remembered and ignored the icy tingle of dread that snaked down her spine. She would not give in to the morbid fear of the lake that had been the bane of her growing-up years. After all, she was twenty-six now, a divorced mother who had been the sole support of herself and her daughter for nearly seven years.

"After your mom died, your stepfather kept you here with him until he died, and then his family took care of you until you married my father, right?"

Sara knew the tale well; a somewhat edited and greatly glamorized version of her mother's history was her favorite bedtime story.

"Yes," Olivia agreed. Tonight, walking through the cypress groves that ringed aptly named Ghost Lake, drawing ever nearer to the Big House and the reunion with the Archers that she had both longed for and dreaded for years, her past was no longer a fairy tale. It had suddenly become all too real.

"What's that?" Sara's voice went high-pitched with surprise.

Mother and daughter stopped and exchanged startled glances. For a moment they stood still, every sense alert, as a new and incongruous sound joined the chorus of the night.

"I think it's 'Twist and Shout,' " Olivia said incredulously. After a couple of seconds a reminiscent smile curved her lips. The family must be having a party. Of course, that was why no one had answered the phone when she had called from the bus station. The Archers did things like that. In the summer they had huge outdoor barbecues to which the whole town was invited and came.

The Archers had always been bigger than life, more colorful and exciting than anyone else she had ever known. Since leaving them, Olivia realized, her life had turned as drably brown as an acre of parched land. Now, just as soon as she had set foot on Archer land again, peacock colors began seeping in.

How she had missed their brightness!

"It's a party. Come on, we're missing the fun." She tried to infuse a note of gaiety into her voice and was heartened to see Sara smile in response. Hand in hand they walked forward with renewed energy, buoyed by the infectious beat of the '60s hit.

"Wow!" Sara's reverent exclamation echoed Olivia's thought as they puffed their way up the last step cut into the twenty-foot-high limestone bluff. Once on level ground, they stopped by mutual, unspoken consent to absorb the scene before them.

Flaming six-foot-tall citronella torches formed a picturesque and, as Olivia remembered it, highly effective mosquito barrier around the perimeter of the lush five-acre lawn. Beyond the torches tiny white Christmas-tree lights glittered everywhere. They were wrapped around the trunks and branches of the flowering dogwoods. They were strung through the neatly trimmed boxwood hedges that lined the stone paths leading to the gazebo and, farther on, to the various outbuildings and the Big House. They ringed the rose garden and dripped from the eaves of the gazebo. In addition, the Big House—a twenty-four-room Greek Revival mansion of white-painted brick with a pedimented portico and more than two dozen soaring fluted pillars supporting twin galleries—was lit up like a jack-o'-lantern from within. Its long, rectangular windows glowed softly against the midnight-blue backdrop of the night.

Although dozens of guests still mingled, it was obvious from the stream of headlights moving slowly down the long driveway that the party was beginning to break up.

Once upon a time, Olivia thought, on a night like this, she had worn a short red dress and danced and laughed and eaten boudin until she thought she would pop, and fallen in love. . . .

The spicy scent of the rice and pork sausage that was boudin was in the air, awakening her taste buds along with her memories.

If she could only go back and have it all to do over again, she would do things very differently, Olivia told herself.

A sharp slap on her left forearm brought her startled gaze around and down. "Mosquito," Sara said matter-of-factly.

"Oh." Olivia was thus recalled to the present and realized in that instant that if she could live her life differently, she would not, because living her life differently would mean that there would be no Sara, and Sara was worth far more than the sum of all the things that Olivia had given up to get her.

"Thanks." She smiled at the daughter who looked enough like her to be her own miniature. "Ready to join the party?"

"Are you sure it's okay?"

Typically, when faced with a new situation, Sara's instinct was to hang back. Shy was not quite the right way to describe her, Olivia thought. Cautious was more like it, and reserved.

"I'm sure," Olivia said with more confidence than she felt, and drew Sara with her through the ring of torches. As they walked along the stone path toward the gazebo, Olivia was both pleased and frightened to recognize a familiar figure: her grandfather—or stepgrandfather—to be precise. Even at eighty-seven, as he must be now, he was still taller than the man he was talking to, although he was slightly stooped and thinner than she remembered.

She had been gone too long, Olivia thought with a sharp pang in the region of her heart. Whether he had loved her or not, and Olivia was not sure that he ever had, she realized in that moment that she had always loved him. She was suddenly fiercely glad to have this chance to put things right.

"There's my grandfather," she said softly to Sara, indicating with a nod of her head the old man who had cast a shadow as big as a mountain over her youth. Big John was what nearly everyone called him, including his grandchildren. He'd once stood six feet five and weighed two hundred fifty pounds, which was how he'd earned the name. As head of the family, Big John Archer owned all this— the LaAngelle Plantation estate on which they now stood, as well as the whole town of LaAngelle, practically, where Archer Boatworks was the main employer.

They were nearing the gazebo, and the man Big John was talking to glanced toward them. He had thinning gray hair, a square-jawed, big-nosed face, and a noticeable belly. His gaze drifted over them without much interest and then returned in a classic double take to fix on Olivia's face. She recognized him then, although he was some thirty pounds heavier than she remembered and much balder, too: Charles Vernon, Big John's son-in-law and the town physician. He would be around sixty now. She had always known him as Uncle Charlie.

His arrested expression attracted the notice of two women in the group, and they, too, looked at Olivia. She was still puzzling over their identities when Big John himself turned her way, peering through the darkness to discover what had attracted his son-in-law's attention.

Olivia was surprised that he did not immediately seem to recognize her. Then she realized he was now a very old man, with a very old man's vision. Allowances must be made for that.

She and Sara stepped into the circle of brighter light cast by the hundreds of twinkly white bulbs adorning the gazebo, and immediately their shadows were behind them, long and dark against the velvety grass. Big John's lips parted slightly in response, and his eyes widened. One thin hand lifted, as if to ward her off.

"My God," Big John said in a hoarse voice. "Selena!"

Then Olivia knew, knew the cause of the horror on his face, of his failure to greet her. Instantly she opened her mouth to correct him, to ease his mind of the terrible misapprehension that apparently gripped him, but it was too late. He made a harsh sound. His hand curled into a claw, and he clutched at his chest. Before anyone could react, he pitched forward, tumbling down the steps to land face-first in the yielding cushion of manicured grass.

2

SELENA. He had thought she was her mother. Even as she let go of Sara's hand and flung herself to her knees at Big John's side, Olivia realized that. In appearance she was as much a mirror image of her mother as her own daughter was of her. All three had the same strong, square jaw; prominent cheekbones; straight nose; wide, full-lipped mouth; and large, thickly lashed brown eyes. With figures that could best be described as curvy rather than slender, the Chenier women were not classic Anglo beauties. They were, rather, Cajun beauties, whose looks reflected their rich French-Acadian heritage.

Selena had died at roughly Olivia's present age. Big John would remember her that way. Some trick of memory and/or lighting had made him think that he was seeing her mother again, twenty years after she had been laid in her grave.

Urgently Olivia grabbed his upper arm through the nubby linen of his sport coat, shaking it, only to find him unresponsive. He did not seem to be breathing. *Please. Oh, please.* Terror, sharp tasting as bile, rose in her throat.

"It's me, Olivia," she said pitifully, uncertain whether he could hear her.

"Move!" Uncle Charlie dropped to his knees beside her, unceremoniously pushing her out of the way as he turned Big John onto his back and checked for a pulse. Above them one elderly woman began to scream, while another ran toward the house.

"Oh, please help him!" Olivia watched helplessly as Charlie repositioned Big John's head and jaw and opened his mouth.

"Mom." Standing just behind, Sara touched her shoulder, her voice hushed, scared. "Mom, is he dead?"

"No. No, pumpkin, of course not." She prayed Big John was not, although she was terrified that her words were a lie.

More and more people were crowding around. A man shouldered through them to drop down on one knee on the opposite side of Big John's body from where Olivia crouched.

"What in the name of God happened?" The question, addressed to Charlie, was low and rough.

"Heart attack, I think."

"*What?* What caused it? He was fine. . . ."

"*She* showed up," Charlie said, his head jerking sideways to indicate Olivia. "He took one look at her and keeled over."

Across Big John's body Olivia's stricken gaze met narrowed blue eyes that had once been as familiar to her as her own. His eyes widened as he registered her identity.

Seth.

She must have said it aloud, because he replied with, "Olivia." Just her name, no more, in a tone that was about as welcoming as stone.

"I think . . . Big John thought I was . . . my mother. He looked at me and said 'Selena' and—and just collapsed," she said wretchedly. Tears trickled down her cheeks. Surprised by the feel of their wetness against her skin, she wiped them away with her free hand.

"Have you ever in your life done anything but cause trouble?" Seth's gaze, hard with animosity, held hers.

Olivia felt as if he had slapped her. *Unfair!* she wanted to cry, but her tongue and lips would not form the word.

They both switched their attention to Big John. Charlie was pumping hard, his right hand crossed over his left on Big John's chest, his face red with effort. Seth's strong brown hand moved to grasp the old man's limp paper-white fingers.

"Big John, it's Seth," he said softly. "It's okay. You're going to be okay."

Seth was Big John's oldest grandson, his favorite. If Big John could hear anything in this moment of extremis, Seth's would be the voice that would most comfort him.

"The ambulance is here!" a woman called with high-pitched excitement. People scattered as an ambulance came up the driveway, then pulled off the pavement to bump over the lawn toward them. When at last the vehicle stopped, medical technicians leaped out and hurried toward the victim.

"Stand back, please! Stand back!"

Olivia stumbled to her feet, keeping Sara close to her, making room along with the rest of the crowd as the emergency personnel took over. With the sound of popping buttons Big John's shirt was ripped open, and the paddles of a portable defibrillator were applied to either side of his chest.

"One, two, three—clear!"

The defibrillator did its job, once, twice, lifting Big John's body off the grass.

"We've got a pulse," one of the EMTs cried.

"Let's go!"

With a series of well-coordinated movements the EMTs scooped Big John onto a stretcher, picked the stretcher up, ran the few steps to the open back door of the ambulance, and loaded him inside.

Seth and Charlie ran behind them, sport coats flapping in the breeze. They were joined by a thin sixtyish woman with short, carefully groomed auburn hair. Olivia recognized her as Charlie's wife, Belinda Vernon. She was Big John's daughter and Seth's aunt.

All those years ago Belinda Vernon had disliked her. Swamp trash was what Belinda had called her once, angry over the teenage Olivia's unrepentant attitude after Belinda took her to task for an outfit she was wearing. After that Olivia never again deigned to address her as Aunt Belinda. The few times she'd had to call her something she had simply said Belinda in an insolent way that had only served to fuel the older woman's outrage.

Olivia found herself running toward the ambulance, too, Sara's hand clutched in hers. She caught up with the others just as Charlie jumped in the back with Big John and the EMTs. Belinda clambered up next. Olivia grabbed at Seth's sleeve as he put a foot on the ambulance floor preparatory to heaving himself inside.

"Seth . . ." Instinctively Olivia wanted to go with them.

Seth glanced back at her, his face hard and unwelcoming.

"Stay here," he said shortly. Then he was inside the ambulance, and the door closed in her face.

"Oh, my God. Olivia." A hand curled around her arm, above her elbow, as the ambulance jolted away. Olivia glanced up to discover another familiar face.

"Aunt Callie," she said in what was almost a sob as Seth's mother wrapped her in a warm embrace. Sara was still pressed close against her side, and Olivia put one arm around her daughter's shoulders, holding her close, enfolding her in the hug. Callie had lost a great deal of weight, Olivia discovered. The once sturdy woman felt almost fragile in her arms.

In her invitation to Olivia to come home for a visit, she'd written that she was ill.

"I'm glad you came, Olivia." Although she was clearly upset, Callie managed a shaky smile as they separated. "Oh, my goodness. Forgive me, dear, but I've got to go to the hospital right away. Do you know what happened to Big John?"

"He had a heart attack, I think. At least that's what Uncle Charlie said. It was my fault. He—he thought I was my mother."

"Oh, my goodness," Callie said again helplessly. Her lips trembled. She took a deep breath, seemed to struggle to get hold of herself, and caught Olivia's hand, squeezing it. "Don't blame yourself, dear. Please. You and"—she glanced down at Sara, who was looking up at her with huge, frightened eyes—"your daughter are very welcome. What happened surely wasn't your fault. Big John hasn't been well, and he's been a little unclear in his mind." She looked desperately around. "Oh, my. I have to get to the hospital. Where is that car?"

"This is Sara." Olivia's arm was still around her daughter's shoulders.

"Please, let's head toward the house." With murmured acknowledgments and waves for other guests, Callie herded them forward. After a few moments she managed a smile for Sara. "Hello, Sara. I'm your aunt Callie."

Sara said nothing, just nodded her head and peeped at Callie from Olivia's other side.

"Callie, how dreadful. Phillip just told me that Big John collapsed. Do you need a ride to the hospital?" A tall, slender blonde in perhaps her mid-thirties ran up to them, long-legged in high-heeled black pumps, and placed a hand on Callie's arm. She had rather sharp features that were carefully made up, chic chin-length hair, and wore a simple sleeveless black linen sheath that looked like it had cost the earth. A stocky dark-haired man followed a step behind her, looking agitated. Olivia recognized the man as Seth's cousin Phillip Vernon. He and his brother, Carl—Charlie and Belinda's sons—had once thrown Olivia into the lake, for which Seth had obligingly beat them up. Phillip would be about thirty-four now, Olivia calculated, some three years younger than Seth.

"Oh, Mallory, yes. I do mean to go to the hospital, but Ira's already fetching the car," Callie said, her voice quivering. "I—"

"Olivia!" Phillip interrupted, his eyes widening as they moved past Callie to fix on Olivia's face. "What are you doing here?"

"I asked her to come, Phillip," Callie intervened. "Olivia, this is Mallory Hodges, Seth's fiancée. Mallory, this is Seth's cousin Olivia Morrison and her daughter, Sara."

Seth's fiancée. As they all hurried toward the house and Olivia and Mallory exchanged hasty greetings, Olivia turned the knowledge over in her mind. She had known that Seth had married and divorced, but she hadn't known he was planning to marry again.

"Did my father go with Big John in the ambulance?" Phillip asked as they reached the Big House's wide front steps and began to ascend in a group to the first-floor gallery.

"Both your parents did, and so did Seth," Callie replied, glancing around distractedly. "Olivia—"

A white Lincoln Town Car stopped by the walkway that led from the driveway to the house and honked twice, causing Callie to break off in midsentence and glance toward it.

"Oh, thank goodness! I must go. Olivia—"

Before Callie could finish whatever it was she had been trying to say, she was cut off by a blond sprite in an ankle-length blue cotton nightgown who darted out the front door.

"Nana, what's happened? What's wrong?" The screen banged shut behind the child, the sound as loud as a gunshot. She was about Sara's age and exquisitely pretty, Olivia saw as the girl skidded to a stop at the top of the steps. Her hair came down to her waist, and she had delicate bones and huge cornflower-blue eyes.

"Oh, Chloe, what are you doing up? It's after midnight," Callie said in a despairing voice.

"She ain't never been to bed, though I swear I tried." Martha Hendricks, the family's longtime housekeeper, followed on the little girl's heels. She was fiftyish, clad in a flowered cotton robe and pink terry-cloth slippers, a big-boned woman with a plain round face and an unnaturally black beehive of hair. She sounded harassed. "She saw that there ambulance out of the window, and you know how Miss Curiosity is. Nothing would suit her but that she had to stick her nose in the middle of what was goin' on."

"Oh, dear," Callie said.

The waiting car honked impatiently. They all glanced toward it. At the same time, Martha saw Olivia, and her jaw dropped.

"Well, I never! Miss Olivia!"

"Hello, Martha." Olivia managed a smile. The housekeeper had changed very little. "It's good to see you."

The car honked again.

Callie threw her hands up in the air and glanced distractedly from Chloe to the car. "Oh, goodness, I have to go. Big John's had a—spell, Chloe, and they've taken him to the hospital, and that's where I'm headed. It's nothing for you to worry about. Martha, you and Chloe take Olivia and her daughter in and get them settled for the night. Olivia, we'll talk tomorrow. At least—"

"Oh, my lord in heaven!" Martha said, her eyes round as saucers. "The ambulance— It weren't ever for Mr. Archer?"

"Nana, I want to go to the hospital with you!" Chloe was shrilly insistent.

"Honey, you can't. Hospitals don't allow children. Now, these are your cousins, come to visit, and I need you to stay here and help them feel welcome. Phillip, Mallory . . ."

The front passenger door of the car swung open from the inside as the trio rushed toward it. Phillip and Mallory jumped into the back. Callie clambered into the front seat. The car took off down the driveway while the doors were still closing.

Olivia stared after them, her eyes burning with unshed tears. She should be speeding to the hospital, too.

"Well, we sure ain't doin' ourselves or nobody else any good standin' out here. You better come on in, Miss Olivia." Martha's brisk words brought Olivia back to reality. Even if she were welcome at the hospital, she could not leave Sara on her own among people who were strangers to her.

Olivia took a deep breath, looked up at Martha and Chloe, who stood on the veranda—as the first-floor gallery was properly called— and started to say something to Chloe.

But Chloe spoke first. "If you're my cousins, how come I've never seen you before?" she demanded, scowling down at Olivia and Sara.

"Miss Chloe!" Martha gasped. "Say you're sorry this minute."

There was a moment of silence while the issue hung in the balance. Then, "I'm sorry," Chloe said sulkily.

"Are you Seth's daughter?" Olivia asked in a gentle tone. She held tight to Sara's hand as they began to once again ascend the steps. She could sense Sara's reluctance to continue.

"That's right," Chloe said, still sulky. "But you're not my cousins. You can't be. Phillip and Carl are my daddy's only cousins. So who are you?" Her sweeping glance included Sara in what was unmistakably a condemnation.

"You're right. We're not precisely your cousins." Olivia held on to her patience with an effort. She stepped onto the wide-plank floor, with Sara's hand curled tightly in hers. Everything about the veranda was just as she remembered it, from the weathered gray paint beneath her feet to the white wicker swing and rockers at its far end. Even the pair of stuffed ring-necked pheasants that Charlie, a skilled taxidermist, had hung by wires from the ceiling as a joke years ago were still there. "I guess you could call us courtesy cousins, though, if you wanted to."

"Why would I want to?" Chloe asked.

"Miss Olivia grew up here, just the same as your daddy did," Martha said to Chloe in a scolding tone. "She's your cousin in all the ways that count, and this is her home, same as it's yours."

Olivia smiled gratefully at Martha, then looked at Chloe again. The child was scowling at her. Giving Chloe the benefit of the doubt, Olivia tried to explain the situation in a way the girl would understand.

"Big John had four children, you know—Michael, James, David, and Belinda. Your grandfather was Michael. My stepfather was

James, the second oldest. Your father is the big cousin who looked out for me when I was growing up. Your nana is my aunt Callie, and Big John is my stepgrandpa."

"So what you're saying is you're just a stepcousin," Chloe said. They were entering the house now, with Martha holding the screen door open so that Olivia and Sara could precede them inside.

"That's right," Olivia said with a flickering smile as the cooler air inside the house enveloped her. Apparently Big John had finally sprung for central air.

"So if you grew up here," Chloe insisted, "how come I've never seen you before?"

"Miss Olivia got married and moved away," Martha interjected before Olivia could reply, shooting Chloe a warning look. "And that's about enough out of you, missy, or you'll make me tell your daddy that you were rude to guests."

To Olivia's surprise the threat seemed to work. Chloe was silent. For a moment they stood rather awkwardly in the huge entry hall. As far as Olivia could tell, nothing in the hall had changed from when she was a girl. Same well-polished hardwood floors with the same red-based Oriental runner leading toward the kitchen at the far end of the hall. Same cream-painted walls with the same quartet of mahogany pocket doors opening into living room and dining room and library and office.

Taking it all in, Olivia felt for an unsettling moment as if she had been transported back in time. She'd last seen the entry hall nine years ago, on the night she had the quarrel to end all quarrels with Seth and then eloped with a rodeo circuit rider named Newall Morrison.

"Come on into the kitchen, why don't you," Martha said to Olivia, then glanced at Sara and smiled. "I bet you're thirsty, hon. I've got some soda pop in the icebox. Or maybe you'd rather have a glass of milk?"

Sara shook her head no without replying.

"Doesn't she ever talk?" Chloe asked, frowning.

"This is my daughter, Sara Morrison," Olivia said, addressing Chloe in a slightly stern tone. "Sara, this is Chloe Archer."

"Hello," Sara produced in a rough approximation of her normal voice, although she continued to hang back.

"How old are you?" Chloe looked hard at Sara.

"Eight," Sara said in response to a well-disguised maternal squeeze of the fingers.

"So'm I." Frowning, Chloe continued to look Sara up and down. Clearly unnerved, Sara dropped her gaze to the rug.

Olivia sighed inwardly. "Martha, I think we're just going to go on upstairs. It's late, and Sara needs to get to bed."

"That's probably a good idea," Martha said. "Let's see. Sara can have your old bedroom for tonight, and you can have the room next door to it that used to belong to Miss Belinda. I changed the sheets this mornin' in case anybody needed to stay all night after the party, if you know what I mean."

Olivia nodded. In case anybody got too drunk to make it home was what Martha was really saying. "That sounds fine."

"Miss Chloe, you lead the way, why don't you."

Chloe obeyed, and they all headed upstairs. Family portraits— oils in elaborate gilt frames—marched one after the other up the wall of the stairwell all the way to the ceiling. More examples of Charlie's handiwork were interspersed here and there: a small stuffed boar's head with graying tusks, a horned sheep, a three-point buck.

"Oh, we don't want to forget about your suitcases." Martha paused midway up the stairs and spoke to Olivia.

"There's nothing to forget." Olivia grimaced ruefully. "We left them behind the counter at the bus depot."

"Lands, then, how'd you get . . ." Martha sounded perplexed. Then, with a scandalized gasp, "Never say you walked all the way from the bus dee-poe!"

Olivia nodded ruefully. "I tried to call somebody at the house to pick us up, but there was no answer here. And Ponce didn't answer his telephone, either."

"Ponce has done retired," Martha said. "His son—you remember Lamar?—well, he runs the taxi business now. When he feels like it, that is."

There was condemnation in her voice. Olivia did indeed remember Lamar. Although he had attended the local public high school and she had gone to St. Theresa's, an expensive private school in Baton Rouge, their paths had crossed with some frequency when they were teenagers. Two years older than Olivia, Lamar Lennig had been a good-looking, if sullen, boy. She wouldn't have given him much more than the time of day back then if Seth hadn't caught him hanging around once too often and ordered him to keep away from her. After that she'd gone out with Lamar a few times just to teach Seth that he couldn't run her life. Looking back, Olivia had to admit that Seth had been right. Lamar had been a major-league loser. Just like Newall. Seth had warned her against him, too.

Olivia sighed. "I remember Lamar," she agreed.

"I bet you remember where your room is, too," Martha said with a smile. They were in the upstairs hall now. Olivia nodded and turned left toward the east wing, one of the two wings that had been added to the main house decades after it was built.

Her childhood bedroom was the second on the right. Reaching it, Olivia opened the door and walked inside. It had been redecorated, of course. But the fireplace was still the same, with its small, elaborately carved mantel and creamy marble surround. The windows, the moldings, and the narrow oak floors were unchanged, too.

Just walking into the room that had been hers during her growing-up years brought back emotions so powerful that Olivia felt dizzy. She was suddenly overcome by a long-forgotten memory of her mother bending over her, kissing her good night. The light floral scent of her mother's perfume, the warmth of her lips, the silken brush of her hair against Olivia's cheek—it all came back to her with such force.

The little girl she had once been had felt safe, sleepy, comforted by her mother's presence. She also had been dreading the moment when her mother would turn and go out of the room, because she was scared to death to be left alone in the dark.

Making a great effort, Olivia pulled herself together and focused on the present and her daughter.

"If Sara doesn't mind sharing her bed with me, I think we'll both sleep in here, for tonight at least," Olivia said to Martha. If her voice was a little thin, no one seemed to notice.

"I don't mind." Sara spoke up eagerly.

Martha nodded. "That's fine, then. Chloe's bedroom is next to Mr. Seth's, in the east wing. My room's across the hall from theirs, next to Miss Callie's. I'll scare you two up somethin' to sleep in, then, and we'll see about gettin' your things picked up from the bus dee-poe. Maybe, if I can get Lamar on the phone, he can run them out first thing in the morning."

"Thank you, Martha." Olivia glanced at Chloe, who was still staring at Sara. "Good night, Chloe."

"Good night," Chloe said with reasonable civility, and turned away as Martha grasped her hand. The two of them headed toward the opposite end of the house. When they were gone, Olivia looked down at Sara, who still stood pressed against her side, one hand in hers, one hand wrapped in her skirt, her gaze on the ground.

"You okay, pumpkin eater?" she asked, dropping her daughter's hand to give her a gentle hug.

Sara nodded and hugged her back. "I'm glad you're going to sleep with me tonight."

"You better not hog all the covers." Olivia's reply was deliberately light.

That made Sara smile. "I won't." She moved away from Olivia's side and slowly revolved as she looked around the room.

"What do you think?" Olivia asked, smiling.

"This place is awesome," Sara said. "It's like a mansion."

Compared to their low-rent two-bedroom apartment, Olivia guessed it was.

"See this bed?" Olivia said, crossing to it and throwing herself down on her back, arms spread wide.

Sara nodded.

"This is the bed I used to sleep in when I was a little girl."

A rap on the door caused Olivia to sit up, feeling slightly foolish about being caught in her abandoned posture on the bed. Martha stood in the open doorway, her gaze moving over them indulgently.

"I've brought both you girls nightgowns," she said. "And robes. And toothbrushes."

"Oh, Martha, you're wonderful." Olivia stood up and moved across the room to take the items from her. "Thanks."

Martha smiled first at her, then at Sara. "It's good to have you home, Miss Olivia. And you, too, Miss Sara."

Martha left, and Olivia closed the door. Turning back to her daughter, she found Sara standing beside the bed, wide-eyed.

"She called me *Miss Sara*."

"That's just the way things are done around here. Don't let it go to your head."

Sara wrinkled her nose. "I won't."

Moments later, nightclothes and toothbrushes in hand, Olivia and Sara went along to the bathroom across the hall to wash up and brush their teeth. After they were clean and clad in borrowed nightgowns, they padded back to the bedroom, closed the door, turned out the light, and got into bed.

Olivia meant to wait until Sara went to sleep, then get up, go to the kitchen, and, if there was no news, call around until she found the hospital where Big John had been taken.

"Say your prayers," she instructed Sara, as she did every night. Lying close beside her daughter, with the tiny white lights that still twinkled outside penetrating the curtains, Olivia listened.

"Now I lay me . . ."

She had murmured that same prayer, in that same room, as a child. It was easy to imagine that time had flown backward again, that her mother lay beside her listening to her prayer, and for a moment the illusion was so real that it sent a chill down her spine.

"Are you sad about that old man, Mom?" Sara asked.

Again Olivia forced herself back to the present.

"I'm worried about him," Olivia said. "I'm hoping he'll be all right."

"Should I say a God-bless for him, too?"

"That would be nice."

"God bless that old man," Sara said, and Olivia had to smile.

For a moment Sara was silent. Then she said, "That girl—Chloe—is really mean, isn't she? And she doesn't like us."

"She doesn't know us. Once she does, she'll love us, especially you. I mean, what's not to love?"

"Oh, Mom." Sara giggled sleepily.

"Hush, now." Olivia kissed her daughter's cheek as Sara snuggled close.

"Tell me a story about when you were growing up," Sara begged as she did every night.

"It's too late, pumpkin. Go to sleep."

"But Mom . . ."

"Go to sleep."

Finally the sound of her daughter's breathing told Olivia that Sara had done just that.

Sliding carefully out of bed, she felt for the robe Martha had left her and pulled it on. Then, for no real reason except that it had always been her habit before she went to sleep in this room, she crossed to the long windows that were really more like French doors and made sure they were locked tight. Finally, she turned on the small lamp by the bed so that if Sara awoke, she wouldn't be in the dark; then Olivia left the room. Quietly closing the bedroom door behind her, she headed downstairs.

She was terribly afraid that Big John would die. And if he did, it would be all her fault. She should have stayed away.

AT ONE time in the house's history the kitchen had been three smallish rooms. Remodeled in the '50s, it was now huge, some forty feet long by twenty feet wide. It boasted custom-built cherry cabinets, a massive Sub-Zero refrigerator, and a commercial-looking stove. A long well-scrubbed and scarred oak trestle table in the center of the room provided seating for up to twelve. The far wall was a bank of multipaned floor-to-ceiling windows, which included two French doors that opened onto the lower of the two galleries that surrounded the house.

Olivia walked across the cool, rough-textured brick pavers that tiled the floor. She was heading toward the butler's pantry, which was basically a walk-in food closet with a sink and a telephone, at the far end of the kitchen.

Entering the pantry, Olivia picked up the receiver and dialed Baton Rouge information. At the same moment as the operator answered, the sound of one of the French doors opening caused Olivia to glance around.

"What number, please?" came the tinny inquiry over the wire.

"There's nothing we can do." Seth's voice, sounding the faintest bit testy, was clearly audible through the open door, although Olivia could not yet see him. Callie walked into the kitchen, her face as pale as skim milk. She looked far older than she had outside in the torch-lit darkness, and Olivia once again chided herself for staying away too long. She should have at least visited once or twice over the years—but then how could she have done so without revealing how far down in the world she had fallen?

On her last night at home, when she had screamed at Seth that she was going to marry Newall Morrison whether he liked it or not, he had warned her that if she did, the family would wash its collective hands of her. She would be on her own.

She hadn't listened, of course. She'd been so young, so sure she knew everything about everything.

And dumb, too. Eloping with a man she had known just four months was about as dumb as it got. She knew better now, but of course, now was too late.

In inviting her and Sara to visit LaAngelle Plantation, Callie had written that she'd been ill. Looking at her for the first time under a bright light, Olivia wondered just how serious that illness was. She felt an icy pang of fear.

Behind Callie came a man Olivia did not know. He was about Callie's age, bald except for the short white fringe circling his head just above his ears. His left hand, square and stubby-fingered, rested possessively on Callie's thin shoulder. He was followed into the kitchen by Seth's fiancée, Mallory. Reed-slender, elegant, self-assured, and obviously affluent, Mallory was everything Olivia was not but wished she was. Only after Mallory appeared did Seth come into view, closing the back door behind him and locking it with a click.

A dial tone buzzed in Olivia's ear. Her call had been cut off. Of course—she had never said a word to the operator.

"Oh, Seth, we should have stayed," Callie said reproachfully to her son as the party walked across the kitchen. The bald man pulled out a chair. Callie sank into it as if her legs had suddenly given out, resting her arms on the table and leaning forward on them. The others sat, too, except for Seth, who stopped beside his mother to look down at her.

"Mother, they only let one person at a time into the intensive care unit, and Belinda was there. She's his daughter, remember? And her husband, Charlie, was there, too, as Big John's personal physician. Phillip was in the waiting room. There is nothing any of us can do tonight that they cannot."

Seth, too, looked older in the bright kitchen light, Olivia saw. He was, as he had always been, deeply tanned, but there were glints of silver in the short blond hair above his ears. Tall, broad-shouldered, and lean, he exuded restless energy even at this late hour. There was an air about him of one born to command.

"You do need to rest, Callie." This came from the bald man, who was seated beside Callie and who looked at her with concern.

"I'm not an invalid yet, Ira." Callie glared at the speaker.

"How's Mr. Archer?" This subdued question came from Martha, who had quietly entered the room. In her flowered robe and slippers she looked as at home in the kitchen as a loaf of bread.

"He's had a heart attack, Martha," Callie said.

"Is it bad?" The words came out of Olivia's mouth before she could stop them. Mentally kicking herself, she peeked like a guilty child from inside the butler's pantry. As the eyes of everyone in the room focused on her, she gathered her composure and stepped out into plain sight.

"Bad enough," Seth said shortly, his gaze raking her from head to toe. More than ever conscious of the deficiencies of her appearance, Olivia just managed not to flinch. She would be greatly changed from his memories of her, and the knowledge was humiliating. Nine years ago she had been a headstrong teenager, sexy and flaunting it. Now she was a twenty-six-year-old single mother with five dollars and change in her purse and a lifetime's worth of hard lessons under her belt.

Callie looked at her, her face softening. "Oh, Olivia, come and sit down, honey. What a homecoming for you. But we're so glad to have you with us again!"

Olivia reluctantly approached the table, all too conscious of her borrowed pink bathrobe, bare feet and legs, scrubbed face, and brushed straight hair pushed haphazardly behind her ears. Smiling at Callie, she sat down at the far end of the table.

"Is your little girl—Sara—asleep?" Callie asked kindly. "She's adorable."

"Thank you." Praising Sara was the way to Olivia's heart. "She's a sweetie. And yes, she's asleep."

Seth ruthlessly interrupted this cozy exchange. "You need to go to bed, Mother. You and Olivia can visit in the morning—unless she intends to run off in the middle of the night again?"

This barb, and the look that accompanied it, brought Olivia's chin up. For a moment she was seventeen again and under attack. Then she remembered she was all grown up now and that Seth had no power over her any longer. She smiled at Callie without deigning to answer Seth. Callie returned her smile with a gentle one of her own.

"Mallory, are you ready to go? I'll drive you home," Seth said abruptly, his attention moving to his fiancée.

"Anytime you're ready, darling." Mallory looked up at Seth in a melting way that told Olivia where he would most likely be spending the balance of the night.

The man sitting next to Callie pushed back his chair and got to his feet. "Seth's right, Callie. You need to go to bed."

"If you two don't quit mollycoddling me . . ." Callie glanced from the man to her son in exasperation. Then she looked at Olivia. "Olivia, by the way, this is Ira Hayes, our local sheriff. Ira, this is our own Olivia, come back to us."

"Pleased to meet you, young lady," Ira said with a smile.

"I'm pleased to meet you, too." Olivia returned his smile. From the look of it, Callie had found a boyfriend, and Olivia was glad for her. She hadn't dated much while Olivia had been growing up. Her husband, Michael, Big John's oldest son, had been killed in an accident at the Boatworks twenty-seven years before. She had married again, briefly, but when that marriage ended in divorce, she had moved back to LaAngelle Plantation to make a home for Big John, whose wife was dying, and for Olivia, who had just lost her stepfather, Michael's brother James.

Mallory smiled at Callie and Olivia. "I'll see you tomorrow, Callie. It was nice meeting you, Olive."

"Olivia," Olivia and Seth corrected in practically the same breath. For an instant their gazes locked in surprise, and then Seth looked away.

"Go to bed, Mother," he said brusquely over his shoulder as he ushered Mallory toward the door. Ira dropped a quick kiss on Callie's cheek and followed. They exited, and Olivia, Callie, and Martha were left alone in the kitchen.

Callie sighed, then flashed Olivia a quick smile that did nothing to conceal her exhaustion.

"Olivia, dear, we should have brought you home years ago," she said. "I wanted to, but Big John and Seth said that you'd made your choice, and we had to let you live your own life. You haven't had it easy, though, have you? I can tell just by looking at you that you've had some hard times."

"Hard times are part of growing up," Olivia said lightly. Martha set a steaming cup of coffee in front of her, and with a quick smile of thanks Olivia took a sip.

"But we hate for our children to suffer them." Callie glanced up at Olivia. "And I have always considered you in some fashion my child, dear. Now more than ever."

"Aunt Callie—" Olivia began, then broke off as Callie abruptly rested her head against the back of her chair and closed her eyes.

Martha came swiftly forward. "Can I fetch you something?" she asked Callie quietly.

"I'm all right," Callie said, opening her eyes. Her face was even paler than before. "Martha, would you go get my pain pills, please. I forgot to take the last one, what with everything, and I'm paying for it now."

Martha nodded. "I won't be a minute." She left the room.

Olivia leaned forward, reaching for Callie's hand. "When you wrote to me, you told me you'd been ill," Olivia said. "What kind of illness? What's wrong with you?"

Callie's gaze met hers, the blue-gray eyes calm and steady. "I wish there was some easy way to say this, dear, but there's not. I have cancer. Non-Hodgkin's lymphoma. I was diagnosed two years ago. The doctors said it was slow growing, so I didn't think it was anything to get too excited about. At the end of this past July they told me that the disease had become aggressive. That's when I wrote to you to come home."

"Oh, Aunt Callie." Olivia's fingers tightened around the older woman's. "Are they treating you? What—"

"I started chemotherapy in August," Callie said. She smiled a little. "The regimen is three weeks on, one week off, for six months. It's working, they tell me, so I can't complain."

For a moment Olivia stared at the older woman in appalled silence. Then she burst out with, "I'm so sorry! I'm sorry you're sick, and I'm sorry I stayed away so long. As soon as I saw Big John and you and—and everyone again—I realized how much I had missed you all. But . . . but . . ."

"But you were too proud to come scooting home with your tail between your legs. I know." Callie squeezed her fingers. "It's all right, Olivia. And it's time to put all that behind us. There's a good chance that I'll live a long time yet, the doctor says. But no more family rift! That nonsense has gone on long enough. Whatever happens with Big John—and I pray that he'll be fine—we're all going to be a family again. And I expect you to do your part to make that happen."

Olivia stared rather helplessly at Callie. "Seth said tonight that all I do is cause trouble. I'm almost certain that I'm the reason Big John had the heart attack."

"Nonsense." Callie shook her head at Olivia. "Big John's health hasn't been all that good. The man is eighty-seven, after all. As for Seth, he's had a difficult few years of his own, you know. He's running the Boatworks now, and that's a lot of responsibility. And of course there's Chloe. When that witch Jennifer Rainey that Seth married ran off to California five years ago, she took Chloe with her. Seth was—well, he was upset, to say the least. Then last year Jennifer remarried and sent Chloe back, just like that. She travels a lot with her new husband, she said, and having Chloe with them all the time made things awkward."

Callie paused, again feeling poorly. Before Olivia could do more than squeeze her hand, she rallied and went on.

"Seth had a house in town, but when Chloe came to live with him, he moved back in here so that I could help him raise her.

Chloe has had some difficulty adjusting. Now Seth's planning to get married again, which should give her a little more stability. Except that for right now Chloe doesn't seem to care for Mallory." Callie sighed. "Life is never simple, is it?"

"Never," Olivia murmured with a crooked smile. Callie's revelations about Chloe prompted her to feel a rush of compassion toward the child. She knew what it was like to feel unwanted and how that could make one act out. As the child of her mother's first marriage, left behind with her stepfather and his family when her mother died, she had never quite felt like she belonged in the Archers' privileged world. "Have Seth and Mallory set a date yet?" Olivia asked.

"November sixth. Only ten weeks away. Mallory's planning this big blowout."

The swinging door from the hall opened with a soft sound, and Martha came in holding a small brown vial. "I've got your pills here," she said.

"Thank you, Martha." Callie took the vial gratefully and opened it, shaking two small pink tablets into the palm of her hand. Meanwhile, Martha removed a glass from the cabinet, filled it with water, and brought it back to Callie. Olivia saw that Callie's hand was slightly unsteady as she raised first the pills and then the glass to her mouth. Swallowing and setting the glass back down, she looked at Olivia very directly. "How long can you stay, Olivia?"

"I could only get a week off from work," Olivia said. "And Sara starts back to school in eleven days. But if you want me, I'll come back to visit just as often as I can. I promise."

"If I want you?" Callie shook her head at Olivia. "Honey, of course I do. We all do. With all the twists and turns and barriers and potholes we've encountered along the road, we're family. One thing I've learned since getting sick is that family is all that matters." She took another drink of water, then grimaced. "I think I better take Seth's advice and go to bed now. I'm so tired I can hardly sit upright all of a sudden."

"It don't surprise me none," Martha said, reaching for Callie's chair as if she would pull it back for her. "What with everything that's happened today, anybody'd be plumb wore out."

"Since I've been ill, Martha won't even go to bed until I do. I don't know what I'd do without her," Callie said to Olivia, with a tired smile for Martha.

"I'm going to bed, too." Olivia stood, watching with increasing worry as Callie slowly and carefully got to her feet. Her heart swelled with love and pity and regret. She'd been wrong to let pride keep her away from her family. But until tonight she'd been too young to realize how truly fleeting life was.

The lesson was being taught her with a vengeance.

They parted at the top of the stairs, with Callie and Martha heading one way and Olivia going the other. Even after she was curled up next to Sara, Olivia couldn't get Callie out of her mind. And Big John, too. No matter what anyone might say, the guilt of causing his heart attack would stay with her forever.

Please, God, don't let him die, Olivia prayed. And keep Aunt Callie safe, too.

The fear of imminent loss rose sharply in Olivia's throat and settled like a stone in her heart. For a long time she lay there in the bed that had been hers as a child, weeping silently so as not to disturb her own beloved child, until finally exhaustion claimed her and she fell asleep.

Jeanerette, Louisiana—April 14, 1971. It was the middle of the night, and something was outside her bedroom window. Becca Eppel heard the faint crunch of footsteps in the pea gravel her mother used for mulch around the shrubbery, followed by rustling in the shrubbery itself and then a thumping sound as whatever it was hit repeatedly against the glass. She was too afraid to look. It might be a werewolf or a vampire. She huddled on her side, her knees drawn up to her chest and her back to the window, hoping that whatever it was would go away.

But the thumping continued.

Becca wished she could go to her mother. But her mother was in the hospital having another baby. Number five. Like they really needed more kids in the family.

Thump, thump.

Becca shivered. Mrs. Granger from across the street was staying with them while Mom was in the hospital. Mrs. Granger was about a hundred and smelled like cabbage and hardly ever smiled. No matter how scared she got, Becca couldn't go to her.

Thump, thump.

Becca couldn't stand it any longer. She eased the bedclothes away from her face.

She could see the thing at the window.

Becca's eyes widened, and for a moment she forgot to breathe. It wasn't her imagination at all. Although it was just a black shape, she could definitely make out two pointy ears.

Sylvia. Her cat. She must have slipped out the door. Now she was sitting on the windowsill asking to be let in.

Even as she watched, Sylvia butted her head against the glass.

Thump.

Smiling with relief, Becca got out of bed and crossed to the window. Her bare feet padded silently over the hardwood floor.

She unlocked the window and raised it, then lifted the screen, too, just enough for Sylvia to swarm in along with a breath of relatively cool air. Becca closed and locked the window again, then bent to pick up her cat.

"What a smart girl." Becca stroked the animal, who began to purr, and turned to head back to bed. She wouldn't be afraid with Sylvia to sleep with her, she thought.

She was still smiling faintly when something grabbed her from behind and yanked her back against a strong adult-size body. Hard arms, bare and hairy with gloves on the hands, wrapped around her. A werewolf? No. . . .

Sylvia leaped for safety. Becca tried to scream. As her mouth opened, a sick-smelling rag was clamped down over her face.

Becca never even managed to make a sound.

It had been a long time. Almost two years. Carrying the little girl's limp body to his van, he quivered with anticipation. The last time had been messy, with newspaper headlines and a circus of a trial that had resulted in the girl's father being convicted of murder. Well, he had learned from his mistakes. He should never have taken Missy back to her bed. With this girl he'd do better.

Nobody—except him—would ever see her again.

EVEN after she finally drifted off, Olivia slept fitfully. For a moment or two after she awoke, hazy remnants of the night's dreams floated through her mind. Her mother had appeared in one, sitting in the small wooden rocking chair in the corner of the bedroom, softly singing a lullaby to the little girl, Olivia, in the bed. The smell of her perfume—White Shoulders, Olivia remembered with sudden clarity—had been the most magical thing in the world. But another dream had been terrifying. It involved the lake and a voice calling to her from its depths. *Run away. Run away.* Except for the voice, the details were lost in the mists of sleep.

Olivia rolled onto her back, determinedly banishing the last cobwebs of sleep from her mind. She glanced at her daughter. Sara lay sprawled on her stomach, deeply asleep, her arms outflung and one bare brown foot thrust out from beneath the covers. Olivia smiled. Even when Sara was a baby, Olivia had never been able to keep her feet covered at night.

Olivia crept from bed and was in the kitchen at ten minutes before seven, according to the big clock that hung above the stove. Wide-awake but fighting the incipient pangs of a headache, she turned on the coffeemaker and looked over at the chalkboard next to the telephone for any messages.

There were none, which Olivia supposed was good news.

A knock sounded at the door. Who on earth would come over so early? Still clad in the robe and gown that Martha had loaned her, Olivia hurried to the door, then parted the curtains slightly so that she could check the identity of the visitor.

There, on the wide veranda, stood Lamar Lennig, with Olivia's cheap black suitcase and Sara's cheap red one at his feet. An inch or so less than six feet tall, he was broad-shouldered and muscular-looking in jeans and a white T-shirt. His black hair was long enough so that it curled into small, flat ringlets at the nape of his neck, and his features were bluntly good-looking. As a teenager, he'd been the local hunk, and though he'd never formally been her boyfriend, they'd gone out a few times and messed around a little. All right, more than a little.

Now she found herself embarrassed to see him. Total amnesia on his part seemed too much to hope for.

Seeing no help for it, Olivia opened the door. "Hello, Lamar," she said without enthusiasm.

A broad smile spread slowly across his face, and his eyes lit up with pleased surprise. "Well, as I live and breathe, Olivia Chenier," he said. His gaze ran over her. "Still lookin' babe-alicious as ever, I see."

For Olivia his audaciousness had once been part of his charm. "Thanks for bringing the suitcases," she said, stepping onto the veranda and reaching down to pick them up.

"No problem." Lamar's hands beat hers to the bags. "Nobody told me these belonged to you. I would have been here earlier if I'd known. Like the middle of last night."

His wide grin spoke of remembered intimacy and a continued assumption of familiarity. Olivia didn't like what it implied, but she realized she had truly earned the expression on his face.

He brushed past her to carry the bags inside. "Where do you want me to put these?"

"Right there is fine," Olivia said, following him back into the kitchen and pointedly leaving the door open behind her.

Lamar set the suitcases down near the table and turned to face her. "You planning to stay for a while?"

Olivia crossed her arms over her chest. "A week, probably."

"If you want to go out . . ."

"I doubt I'll have time," Olivia said pleasantly. "My daughter's with me, and—"

"Got a daughter, do you? Left hubby at home?"

"I'm divorced."

That nugget of news seemed to amuse him. Cocking his head to one side, Lamar grinned at her again.

"Hello, Lamar." The unexpected greeting made both of them glance around. Seth had entered the kitchen through the open French door. He still wore the navy sport coat, T-shirt, and khakis he'd had on the night before. Obviously he had spent the night out.

"Mornin', Seth." The grin with which Lamar had teased her vanished from his face as if by magic. He stood straighter, his attitude respectful. "I just came by to drop off some suitcases."

Seth reached into his back pocket and withdrew his wallet. "How much do we owe you?"

"Ten dollars should about catch it."

Seth opened his wallet and extracted a bill, which he held out to Lamar. "Thanks," he said. It was an obvious dismissal.

"Anytime." Lamar accepted the money and his fate with good grace. He turned to leave, casting a crooked smile at Olivia where Seth couldn't see. "Good to see you, Olivia."

"You, too, Lamar."

With a wave Lamar exited, closing the door behind him. Seth looked at her then, his eyebrows lifting questioningly.

"Entertaining already?" he asked, heading toward the coffeemaker. The aroma of freshly brewed coffee filled the air.

"Not at all. I just happened to be in the kitchen making coffee when Lamar dropped off the suitcases."

"I'm sure you'll be glad to get your clothes." He leaned one hip against the counter and looked at her consideringly. "If you're interested, it looks like Big John's going to pull through. They said he's stable this morning."

That got to her, as it was undoubtedly meant to do. She met his gaze with sparks in her eyes. "What do you mean, *if* I'm interested? Of course I'm interested. I always thought of him as my grandfather—just like he's yours."

Seth made a derisive sound. "If you hadn't stayed away for nine years, having you pop up might not have been such a shock."

Olivia's hands clenched by her sides. "Aunt Callie invited Sara and me to come for a visit. She knew we were coming. Ask her. If you and Big John weren't so gall-darned bullheaded, she probably would have told you we were coming in advance instead of planning to spring it on you when it was too late for you to object. Anyway, for years now you—you all—have known where I live. You could have come to see me anytime."

"You were married." Seth poured some coffee into a cup. "What God hath joined, let no man put asunder."

Olivia discovered that she hated him just as much as she always had. "Oh, shut up," she said. Grabbing a suitcase with each hand, she stalked from the kitchen.

By the time she was halfway up the stairs, Olivia could have kicked herself. She had responded to Seth exactly as she would have when she was a teenager. The next time he baited her, she vowed, she would ignore him.

Sara was still sleeping when Olivia entered the bedroom. After unpacking clothes for the two of them to wear that day, Olivia took a shower, washed her hair and blew it dry, put on makeup, and pulled on a pair of cutoff jeans, a lime-green T-shirt, and Keds before returning to check on Sara again. The alarm clock told her that it was eight fifteen. Sara still slept.

Stymied, Olivia headed back downstairs. Faint sounds from the kitchen told her that someone was there. She certainly didn't want to encounter Seth again. Trying to ignore the fact that her temper had cheated her out of her much needed morning coffee, she went out the front door into the enveloping warmth of the day. Just in time to keep it from banging shut behind her, she caught the screen door and eased it closed. No need to alert whoever was in the kitchen to her presence.

For a moment Olivia stood beneath the shelter of the veranda, looking past the fluted columns and hanging ferns at the sun-drenched grounds of LaAngelle Plantation. Past the bluff, she could see part of the lake glimmering silver in the morning light. The ghosts of the night before had been burned away by the rising sun.

Crossing the veranda, Olivia headed down the wide stone steps. The pair of giant magnolias that were the centerpiece of the lawn were as magnificent as she remembered them, with white, waxy blossoms the size of dinner plates bursting through glossy green foliage. The sweet olive and jasmine near the gazebo were in bloom, as was the rose garden. Closer at hand, crimson amaryllis was massed in glorious profusion in front of the neatly clipped thicket of dark green boxwoods that circled the house. The air was redolent with the scent of flowers; just breathing in was a pleasure.

Although the grounds were beautiful, the reminders of last night's party were not. At the far end of the lawn a quartet of workmen, toting black plastic garbage bags, were picking up plastic cups and forks, napkins, and the remnants of balloons.

As Olivia looked around, a peacock came strutting from around the side of the house with his head up and his tail fully extended. All iridescent greens and blues, he was a beautiful sight.

LaAngelle Plantation was just the same as it had always been, Olivia thought as she rounded the side of the house and headed toward the backyard: a place that belonged more to the past than to the present. But on this morning, with the perfume of flowers in the air and her rebellious teenage years a wry memory, that seemed like a good thing rather than a bad one.

A movement of some sort on the very edge of her peripheral vision drew her attention, and Olivia glanced toward the house. A huge white Persian cat was walking delicately along the rail of the upper gallery, its tail waving plumelike through the air. Only at the last minute did Olivia see its goal: Chloe, still wearing her blue nightgown, leaning over the railing at the far end of the upstairs gallery, something cupped in her hands. As Olivia watched, the child let go.

The object plummeted downward, glittering brilliantly in the sun as it fell, and landed in the sweet bush below.

Chloe straightened and saw Olivia at the same moment that Olivia glanced up at her again. Olivia was too surprised to call to the child, or even to wave, and Chloe did not speak, either. Shooting Olivia a baleful glance, she snatched up the cat that had by now almost reached her and disappeared into the house.

Curiosity piqued, Olivia moved to the sweet bush and peered in and beneath it. Its fragile pink flowers and umbrella-shaped foliage concealed an inner hollow that, Olivia remembered from her own childhood, was an ideal hideaway. Stooping, pushing aside the fragrant canopy, she ducked beneath the leaves and looked around. Almost instantly she spotted it: a bracelet. It dangled from a branch just a few inches off the ground.

That was what Chloe had dropped from the gallery. Disentangling it carefully, Olivia ducked out into the sunlight again, prize in hand. Straightening, she looked at it as it lay across her palm.

It was a watch, not a bracelet. A delicate woman's watch, with a platinum casing and a band made of linked diamonds. Olivia wondered where Chloe had found something so obviously expensive, and why on earth she had chosen to drop it into a bush. She tilted the casing into the sun so that she could read what was engraved there: MALLORY HODGES.

Frowning, she tucked the watch into her front pocket. Obviously it would have to be returned, but her every instinct shrank from describing the circumstances that had led her to discover it. Could she simply say that she had found it on the lawn?

Olivia continued along the pea-gravel path that led to the *garçon-nière*, the small two-story frame lodge at the edge of the property that had once housed the single, young adult males of the family and, more recently, was used as a guesthouse. She paused at the perennial garden, admiring the profusion of colorful flowers that bloomed with abandon around the garden's centerpiece, a five-foot-tall marble angel.

Sara's going to love all this, Olivia thought, and then turned back toward the house to see if her daughter was awake yet.

At the back of the house, the driveway widened into a paved parking area. Seth was walking across it toward the stone carriage house that had been converted into a four-car garage at its far end. He had changed into loose khaki slacks and a dark green polo shirt and was busy talking into a cell phone.

If it had not been for the diamond watch in her pocket, Olivia would have given him a wide berth. As it was, she thought crossly, she might as well hand the thing over and get done with it. As Chloe's father and Mallory's fiancé, Seth was the person to whom it should be given. She started walking toward the carriage house just as Seth closed the phone and slid it into a pocket.

"Seth, wait a minute!" she called.

He turned to look at her as she came toward him. "What?" The question was faintly impatient.

"I—I need to give you something." Olivia reached into her pocket and drew forth the watch, which she held out to him. It sparkled in the light.

"Mallory's watch." His tone changed to one of surprise. He glanced at her sharply. "Where did you get this?"

Here was the tricky part. "I found it outside."

His eyes narrowed at her. "It was on top of my bureau not more than an hour ago. Mallory left it in the car last night."

"So what are you implying?" Olivia bristled at the accusation she thought she discerned in the words. The sound of running footsteps distracted her, and both she and Seth looked around to try to identify the source.

"Daddy, wait!" Twin ponytails flying, and carrying a tennis racket, Chloe darted across the pavement toward the garage. She ignored Olivia to address Seth. "Where are you going? You promised to take me over to Katie's for tennis this morning!"

The impatience in Seth's face lessened only slightly as he looked at his daughter. "Chloe, I can't. I—"

"Where did you get that?" Chloe interrupted, her voice suddenly shrill as she spied the watch that lay across Seth's hand. Her gaze shot immediately to Olivia. "Did you give it to him? What did you tell him? Did you make up some big lie about me?"

Olivia's eyes widened. "No, of course not. I—"

"Watch your manners, young lady!" Seth's voice was furious.

"Whatever she told you, it's not true!" Looking appealingly at her father, Chloe was the picture of childish innocence. "Are you going to believe her or me?"

"Chloe . . ."

Before Seth could continue, Chloe's lower lip trembled. "You're going to believe her, aren't you? You always believe everything everyone else says about me. I hate you!" she choked out. Bursting into noisy tears, she ran toward the house, shooting Olivia a venomous glance as she bolted past.

For a moment afterward there was silence as the two adults gazed after the departing child. Then Seth looked at Olivia.

"I apologize for my daughter," he said heavily.

"It's all right." Olivia felt a spurt of sympathy. "My theory is you haven't really put in your time as a parent unless your child embarrasses you thoroughly at least once a month."

Seth closed his fist around the watch in his hand. "My ex-wife spoiled Chloe rotten. Then she married again, and her new husband didn't want a stepdaughter as part of the deal. So she sent Chloe back to me, as if the child were no more than a pet she'd grown tired of. It hurt Chloe badly."

"Your mother told me."

"I figured she would." Seth's expression changed, grew wry. "Now, tell me. Where did you really find the watch?"

Olivia thought the matter over for a moment. "I'd rather not say," she said finally. "I think you should ask Chloe."

"Livvy—" He broke off at the stubborn expression on her face and shook his head impatiently, shoving the watch into his pocket. "I really don't have time for this right now. I have to be at the hospital at nine thirty."

Seth pinned Olivia with an evil look and headed after his daughter. Watching him go, Olivia had to smile. Having Seth stomp off in a temper brought back memories. Years ago she had been the object of his wrath.

He had called her Livvy, as he used to when she was a child. That he could use the nickname gave her hope. It would be nice to be on friendly terms with Seth again. As a little girl, she had thought her big stepcousin hung the moon. Even when she was older, for all she had butted heads with him, she had still admired, respected, and, yes, loved him.

Now they were both adults, divorced, with daughters the same age. For the first time in their lives they were on more or less equal footing. Except, of course, that Seth was rich, successful, and sure of his place in the world. While she . . .

Another car pulled into the parking area. This was a white Mazda Miata, a sporty two-seater convertible with the top down. Mallory, sunglasses in place and a white silk scarf tied around her blond head, was driving.

"Hi!" Mallory waved and got out of the car.

"Hi," Olivia answered with a smile.

Mallory walked toward her. She was wearing a cute little tennis outfit with a tiny pleated skirt. "Have you seen Chloe? Seth asked me to take her to a friend's house to play tennis."

"I think she and Seth are in the front yard," Olivia said.

Mallory smiled. "Here they come."

Olivia looked around to discover that Seth and Chloe were indeed approaching. Seth had his hand on Chloe's shoulder. Chloe, still clutching her tennis racket, looked sullen.

Watching them, Mallory sighed, then, summoning a smile, waved cheerily. Seth waved back. Chloe didn't.

"Honestly, that child," Mallory muttered under her breath, then shot a quick look at Olivia to see if she'd been overheard. Her gaze on Seth and Chloe, Olivia pretended to be deaf.

Seth marched Chloe right up to Olivia. A paternal squeeze of the child's shoulder prompted a barely audible, "I'm sorry."

"That's all right," Olivia said gently, wincing inside at Seth's handling of the situation. Forcing an apology out of an obviously reluctant child would only serve to make her more rebellious, in Olivia's opinion.

Mallory, having the good sense not to comment on the exchange, addressed Chloe a shade too heartily. "Your dad asked me to take you over to Katie's. I called her mother, and we decided that we're going to play tennis, too. Maybe we can work in a mother-daughter doubles match. Wouldn't that be fun?"

Chloe scowled. "Yeah, fun," she said.

The sarcasm was unmistakable, and all the adults present chose to ignore it. Sarcasm beat a tantrum hands down.

"Well, let's go, then." Mallory smiled at Chloe, a mere stretching of her lips that didn't reach her eyes, then smiled at Seth more genuinely. "Don't worry about us."

"I won't." His expression relaxed a little.

Chloe climbed into the passenger seat of the Miata, and Seth opened the driver's side door for Mallory.

"Bye," she said, smiling up at him as Seth closed her door.

Mallory put the key in the ignition, then looked up at Seth, who was stepping away from the car. "Oh, darling, would you mind fetching my watch for me before we go? I'm absolutely lost without it."

Seth flicked a glance at Chloe. "I just happened to have it on me." He reached into his pocket and withdrew the watch, which he handed to Mallory.

"Thanks." Mallory fastened the watch around her wrist. "I should never have taken it off in the car."

Seth's expression changed subtly. "No," he agreed with a glimmering smile, and the way he said it made Olivia wonder what else Mallory had taken off in the car.

"Can we *go,* please?" Chloe's tone was hostile.

"Behave," Seth said to his daughter.

Mallory waved, then revved the Miata to life and headed down the driveway. Seth looked after them for a moment. When the Miata was out of sight, he glanced at Olivia. "I've got to go," he said. "I'll see you later."

Then he, too, got into his car and drove off.

THE Jaguar ate up the miles between LaAngelle and Baton Rouge with no trouble at all. Which was only to be expected for a car with a monthly lease payment of almost seven hundred dollars, Seth reflected. Attracting wealthy buyers was the name of the game for someone like himself who built yachts for a living; an image of success was necessary. But still, the money that he paid out for the car was money he didn't have to spare.

Only no one knew that except himself and Big John and maybe a couple of loan officers down at the bank. And if he had his way, no one else was going to find out. Unless Big John died. Then the cat would be out of the bag, because the estate would be probated and everyone would know that Archer Boatworks had been teetering on the verge of bankruptcy for a long time.

A couple more years of hard work, paired with a little good luck, and Seth figured he could turn the company situation around. Archer Boatworks would be soundly in the black again. The big commercial orders for barges that his grandfather had not wanted him to accept—they were *yacht* builders, Big John argued—were making the difference. If he'd listened to Seth earlier, things would never have gotten this bad, but the old curmudgeon was as stubborn as a mule in a corncrib.

If Archer Boatworks went down, LaAngelle Plantation, which had been in the family for generations, would be taken by the bank because Seth had had to use it as collateral to finance the building of the barges. What's more, one fifth of the town worked for him directly, and the other four fifths of the population owned or worked for businesses that were dependent on the Boatworks for their survival. By Seth's calculations that was almost three thousand people whose lives and livelihoods he held in his hands. That huge responsibility accounted for the eighty-hour weeks he put in and his increasing inability to sleep nights.

Jennifer hadn't been able to take it. When they'd met, at a Mardi Gras party thrown by a multimillionaire whose one-hundred-twenty-foot yacht had been built by the Boatworks, she had thought he was a rich man, too, and a gentleman of comparative leisure. That was a large part of why she had married him, he figured out later. The truth had come as a shock to her, and she had hightailed it out of Dodge as soon as she found a better prospect.

Sometimes, when the burdens of work and family felt as if they might suffocate him, Seth caught himself thinking longingly about just chucking it all, climbing into his Jaguar, and taking off into the sunset. But the price for that freedom would be too high. It would mean letting go of his heritage, letting down the people he loved. He didn't want to do that. Not often. Only sometimes.

Like today.

His daughter was a brat. His mother had cancer. His grandfather was in intensive care. His business was struggling.

Deliberately he thought of Mallory. With her he'd gotten lucky. She was beautiful, educated, with her own solvent real estate business. She loved him. She was going to make a fantastic wife.

Except he wasn't one hundred percent certain that he was in love with her. And Chloe hated her. And Mallory wasn't any too fond of Chloe, either, although she tried to hide it. He couldn't really blame Mallory. Chloe was his own daughter, and he felt like throttling her about half the time.

But he and Chloe were a package deal, for better or worse, and if he didn't love Mallory, then he certainly should, because she was absolutely what he needed in a wife and Chloe needed in a mother. Mallory was stable. Mallory loved the plantation. Mallory was capable and successful and a heck of an organizer.

Maybe that was why over the last several weeks, as preparations for the wedding had moved into full swing, he had sometimes felt like a small corporation caught in the grip of a takeover. Maybe Mallory should knock off trying to organize him. Maybe he wasn't quite ready to marry again after all. Who knew why he felt the way he did? All he knew was that right now his relationship with Mallory was starting to feel like just one more problem.

And now Olivia was home. Seth had been shying away from coming to terms with that. He hadn't really thought much about her in a long time—years. But all he had to do was see her again, and everything came rushing back.

She and her mother had come to live at LaAngelle Plantation when Livvy was a year old. Almost immediately she had started toddling about after him, and he, twelve years old, had been enchanted by the big-eyed chubby little girl.

Then he left for college and grad school and a job away from the family business. By the time he'd come home again, at Big John's request, Olivia had been fifteen and running wild.

Seth had done his best to take her in hand, but trying to control the teenage sexpot that Livvy had become was like trying to hold back the tide. God help him, that last year when she was seventeen and he was a grown man of twenty-eight, sometimes he'd found himself sexually attracted to her, too.

And why not? She'd been mouthwatering in the tight jeans and skimpy tops she'd worn almost as a uniform. Chubby no longer, she had become voluptuous instead. Her hair had been longer then, almost down to her waist, dark and silky straight. With her big brown eyes and pouting lips she'd looked like one of the girls in the Hawaiian Tropic commercials. He would have had to be a eunuch not to notice.

She was thinner and paler now and more subdued. She had obviously learned some hard lessons about life. But to his dismay he still found her sexy as hell.

Add another problem to his list.

Pulling into the parking lot of St. Elizabeth's Hospital, Seth sighed. Right now he had to focus on Big John.

Charlie was waiting for him, leaning against his own leased vehicle, a '99 Lexus. Which, presumably, he really could afford. As Big

John's personal physician, Charlie would have the latest on the old man's condition, but the only reason for him to be waiting in the parking lot was to tell Seth something that he wasn't yet ready to tell the others gathered inside.

Great. Seth parked and got out, his muscles already tightening in anticipation of what he would hear.

Charlie didn't disappoint him. Rumpled and tired-looking, he walked away from his car to clap a hand on Seth's shoulder.

"I'm sorry," Charlie said, "but I've got some bad news."

Was there any other kind? Seth thought.

Not lately. Not for him.

THIS time Sara was awake when Olivia went up to check on her. She was sitting on the edge of the mattress, fully dressed except for her white tennis shoes, which were on the floor. As Sara put on her shoes, Olivia crossed to the windows and drew back the curtains, letting bright sunlight pour into the room.

"It's a beautiful day," she observed, looking back at her daughter. "I went for a walk, and I've already seen all kinds of interesting things."

"Like what?" Sara looked up at her mother.

"A big Persian cat." Sara loved cats, although she'd never been allowed to have one. Their apartment complex did not allow pets. "Some peacocks."

"Peacocks!" Sara's eyes widened. "Really?"

"Mmm-hmm." Olivia smoothed Sara's hair away from her face. "But first things first. To the bathroom with you, miss."

By the time Sara was clean and brushed and they were heading downstairs, it was almost ten o'clock.

"Breakfast," Olivia decreed as Sara reached the bottom, and pointed toward the kitchen.

Callie and Martha were sitting at the table. Both looked around as Olivia and Sara entered.

"Good morning!" Callie greeted them with a smile. Rosy blush and lipstick made her appear rested and deceptively healthy. "Did you two sleep well?"

"I did," Olivia answered, while Sara merely nodded.

"What can I fix you for breakfast?" Martha got to her feet.

"Sit back down, Martha. I'll get it," Olivia said. "Sara only ever eats toast, and I'll have coffee."

"My goodness, you look like your mother," Callie said, smiling at Sara, who was hesitantly approaching the table. "Come on and sit down." She pulled out the chair beside her own, patted the seat, then glanced at Olivia, who was putting slices of bread in the toaster. "Seeing the two of you together sure takes me back. It seems like only yesterday that you were that age, Olivia, and Selena was fixing toast for you."

"My mother fixed me toast for breakfast?" Olivia questioned lightly, pleased to see Sara sitting beside Callie.

Callie laughed. "That's all you would eat—grape jelly on toast with the crusts trimmed off, cut into triangles. Only your mother could fix it to suit you."

"I only like Mom's toast," Sara said shyly. "And I like grape jelly on it, too."

The toast popped up just then, so Olivia missed out on Callie's reply. Spreading butter and jelly, she searched her mind for a memory of her mother doing the same for her but drew a blank. There were so many holes in her memory where her mother was concerned. For the first time it occurred to Olivia that perhaps something was not quite right about that.

"What are you two going to do today?" Callie asked as Olivia carried the toast—crustless, spread with grape jelly and cut into triangles—to the table.

Olivia smiled and sat beside her daughter. "Explore."

"Do you like tennis?" Callie asked Sara. "Chloe's been playing a lot this summer. She's playing right now, as a matter of fact, but she should be back before lunch."

"I've never played tennis," Sara said, consuming a bite of toast. "I think I'd like it, though."

"Sara likes animals," Olivia put in, sipping from a cup of coffee that Martha had set before her. "We're going to go outside and see if we can find that big Persian cat I saw this morning."

"That's Ginger." Callie smiled. "Named for Ginger Spice, actually. Chloe was a big fan of the Spice Girls when we got the kitten, but I think that craze has died out now. Like the Beanie Baby thing. This time next year it'll be gone."

"Oh, does Chloe collect Beanie Babies?" Sara asked excitedly. "I love Beanie Babies."

"Miss Chloe has a whole bookcase full up in her room," Martha put in. "I'd say she has just about every one ever sold."

"Does she have Nip the cat?" Sara was so intrigued that she forgot to eat. A toast triangle hung ignored from her hand.

Callie laughed. "Honey, you'll have to ask Chloe. She probably does. Her daddy's bought her enough of them."

The telephone rang.

"I'll get it." With a quick glance at Callie, Martha pushed her chair back. Getting to her feet, she moved quickly toward the pantry.

"LaAngelle Plantation," she said, then listened. After a minute she looked at Callie. "It's Mr. Seth calling from the hospital. He wants to talk to you."

A worried frown creased Callie's brow at the news. Standing up, she crossed to the butler's pantry and took the phone Martha held out to her. The conversation was brief, but from Callie's reaction Olivia could tell it contained bad news.

She stood motionless for a moment, then turned to find the eyes of everyone in the kitchen fixed on her.

"Big John's had a stroke," she said heavily. "He was recovering from the heart attack well, but now he's had a stroke."

"Oh, no." Olivia's hand flew to cover her mouth.

"Seth wants me to call David and tell him he needs to come home." Callie's voice sounded hollow. "Right now."

"Oh, no," Olivia said again. David was Big John's sole surviving son. He lived in San Diego, where he owned and ran a restaurant. Olivia had always liked him, and he had been kind to her whenever they met. But that was infrequently, because Big John and his third son were like oil and water. They did not mix.

If Seth was asking his mother to summon David *right now,* then Big John must be on the brink of death.

NO MATTER what Martha or Olivia said to dissuade her, Callie insisted on going to the hospital. Olivia was elected to drive her despite Callie's protests that she was perfectly capable of going alone. Sara would stay with Martha.

Olivia wasn't perfectly happy with this arrangement—she didn't like leaving her daughter in a strange environment. But when she left, Sara and Martha were in the kitchen, happily contemplating making peach ice cream with the old-fashioned ice-cream maker that had been in the family for decades.

"I'll be back as soon as I can." Olivia dropped a quick kiss on Sara's cheek on her way out the back door.

"I'll be okay," Sara said. "Don't worry about me, Mom."

"SARA seems like the sweetest little girl," Callie remarked in the car on the way to the hospital. They were traveling south on Highway 415 in Callie's navy-blue Lincoln Town Car, with Olivia behind the wheel. On the east side of the raised two-lane road was a freshwater swamp, where cattails, alligator grass, and marsh elders grew higher than the levee that held back the Mississippi River. "Is she always that good?"

"Sara is a sweetheart," Olivia said with conviction.

"It's obvious you've done a good job mothering her." Callie sighed. "I just wish Chloe had been as lucky. Seth has tried his best, and so have I, but . . ." Her voice trailed off. "Well, I don't guess Jennifer was any great shakes as a mother anyway, so she's no real loss."

"I can't take too much credit for Sara. Even as a tiny baby, she only cried when she needed something. I think being good just must be in her nature."

"She doesn't take after you much, then, does she?" Callie sent her a sudden, teasing smile. "I can remember you throwing some ungodly tantrums when you were a little bitty girl. I used to think Selena was a saint for dealing with you so patiently."

Olivia felt a sudden tightness in her throat as shadows of memories danced along the edge of her consciousness. What stood out suddenly was an overwhelming sense of feeling loved. My mother loved me, she thought. She swallowed, then took a deep breath and managed to say in a near-normal voice, "You know, I don't really remember much about my mother."

Callie glanced at her. "I'm not surprised. You were only six years old when she . . . died."

That brief hesitation did not escape Olivia's notice. There were so many questions Olivia wanted to ask, but this was not the time or the place. If she talked any more about her mother, she feared she would cry.

"Tell me about the plans for Seth and Mallory's wedding," Olivia said. "Is it going to be held at St. Luke's?"

St. Luke's was the Episcopal church in LaAngelle. The Archers had been mainstays of the congregation for generations.

Callie shook her head, smiling. "Mallory's expecting about five hundred guests, so that lets St. Luke's out. It's too small. The ceremony's going to be at St. Bartholomew's in Baton Rouge, and the reception will be held at the Baton Rouge Country Club. Mallory's having a ball planning everything, but I think Seth would prefer something a shade less elaborate. He hasn't said anything, but I know him. He's starting to get nervous."

"Is he?" Olivia smiled, too, at the idea of Seth's suffering from pre-wedding jitters.

"This is hard on Seth, you know." Callie's tone turned suddenly serious. "My cancer, I mean. He's a fixer. Any problem that anybody has, he tries to fix it. But he can't fix this."

Olivia didn't know what to say. Fortunately, the turnoff into Baton Rouge loomed just ahead, and the topic was lost as she concentrated on getting over the long, crowded bridge that spanned the Mississippi River and led into the city.

The intensive care unit was on the fourth floor of St. Elizabeth's Hospital.

"I hope we're not walking into more bad news," Callie murmured, curling a hand around Olivia's elbow as they walked past the busy nurses station.

"Oh, Callie, you shouldn't have come!" Dressed in a celery-green summer pantsuit, her short auburn hair meticulously sprayed into place but her face pale and tired, Belinda Vernon was coming down the hall toward them. Both hands were outstretched toward Callie. Behind her a sign marked WAITING ROOM hung above an open door to the left. Phillip Vernon walked out that door after his mother, spotted Callie and Olivia, and headed toward them, too.

"I had to come," Callie said, embracing Belinda. "How is he?"

"Not good." There was pain in Belinda's voice. "Charlie says all we can do now is pray."

"Hello, Olivia," Phillip said in a subdued tone. Olivia echoed his greeting as Callie and Belinda broke apart. Belinda's gaze then alighted on Olivia, and she nodded without speaking. Civil but not friendly, Olivia thought. Well, she could live with that.

"Mom, it's your turn." Carl poked his head out of the waiting-room door, glancing down the hall toward his mother. Like his brother Phillip, Carl was stocky and blue-eyed with dark brown hair. He greeted Olivia with a quick hug and a smile.

"We can only go in one at a time," Belinda explained to Callie as the group began to move toward the intensive care unit. "It doesn't really matter. Daddy doesn't know anybody anyway."

One of the double doors to the unit swung outward, and Seth walked into the hall.

"How is he?" Belinda asked as he joined them.

Seth shook his head at her. "No change." His glance slid past her to touch on his mother and Olivia, and his lips tightened. "Mother, you shouldn't have come."

"I wanted to," Callie answered with quiet dignity. "Big John is my father-in-law, and he is as dear to me as my own father was."

"You have to think of yourself, Mother." Seth glanced at Belinda. "I know it's your turn to sit with him, but would you mind letting her go in for just a minute so that she can go back home?"

"You go ahead in, Callie," Belinda said. "Seth is right."

Callie allowed Seth to take her arm and escort her to the door. He pulled it open, said something briefly to someone inside, and then, as Callie disappeared within, stepped back out into the corridor.

"You weren't planning on seeing my father, I hope?" Belinda asked Olivia as Seth came toward them. "Since the sight of you is what made him collapse in the first place, I just can't permit it. I'm sure you understand."

Olivia nodded unhappily. She did understand, however unpleasant she might find Belinda's edict.

"That's a little harsh, don't you think?" Carl protested.

"It's all right, Carl," Olivia said.

Joining them, Seth lifted his eyebrows inquiringly as he caught the tail end of the conversation.

"You can't blame Olivia for the old man's heart attack," Phillip added, talking to his mother.

"No, you can't," Seth said, surprising Olivia, who was sure he did blame her for it. He fixed his aunt with a steady gaze. "You know as well as I do that Big John could have had a heart attack at any time. What happened wasn't Olivia's fault."

Olivia sent Seth a small smile of thanks.

"You always did take her part," Belinda said bitterly, and turned on her heel, walking into the waiting room.

"She's upset," Phillip said excusingly to Olivia.

"You wanna go down to the cafeteria, get a cup of coffee while you wait for Aunt Callie to be ready to go?" Carl asked.

Olivia hesitated, then nodded. "That'd be great."

"I'll bring Mother down when she's ready," Seth said. "And when it's appropriate to do so, I'll tell Big John you were here."

"Thank you." Olivia smiled at him briefly, then turned away with Carl. As they walked toward the elevator bank, Olivia could hear the murmur of Belinda's voice. She guessed, without really knowing for certain, that Belinda was talking about her.

That was because of the single word she overheard clearly before moving out of earshot. The word was "trash."

THE big white cat sat on the porch rail, looking at her. The Persian was really fluffy, with big blue eyes. For a moment Sara returned the stare. Then with a flick of its tail the cat jumped down to the floor, heading toward the blue earthenware bowl that held the melted remnants of Sara's peach ice cream. Sara had finished eating it about an hour ago, set the bowl down on the porch floor beside the swing, and forgotten about it while she curled up with a book she had found.

If she could have anything she wanted in the whole world, Sara reflected, what she would wish for first would be a horse of her own. The second thing she would wish for would be a cat. Or maybe she would wish for the cat first. It was hard to say. No, the very first thing she would wish for was that her mom would have lots of money—enough money so that she wouldn't ever have to worry again. Then her mom could buy her the horse and the cat. That would be best of all.

The cat—the real cat—was licking up the ice cream, its little pink tongue moving busily in and out of the pale orange goo. Sara slipped off the porch swing and dropped to her knees on the wooden planks beside it.

"Hello, kitty," she said. She reached out to pet the cat. Its fur was silky soft and thick, and as she ran her hand along its back, the cat began to purr.

"What are you doing to Ginger?" The accusing voice was so unexpected that Sara jumped. Her shoulder hit the swing's metal frame, and it hurt. Wincing, she scooted forward out of the reach of the swing, rubbing her shoulder and looking around at Chloe, who had materialized out of one of the long window-door things that opened onto the big upstairs porch.

"What are you doing to Ginger?" Chloe demanded again.

"Nothing. I was just petting her."

"She's my cat." Chloe took a step forward and snatched Ginger up, cradling the cat tightly in her arms. Ginger suffered this with good grace, merely running her tongue over her whiskers to get at the last drops of ice cream and fixing Sara with an unblinking gaze.

"She's beautiful," Sara said with sincerity, looking at Ginger. "I wish I had a cat."

"Why don't you get one, then?"

"Pets aren't allowed in the apartment where we live."

"You're really poor, aren't you?"

Sara shrugged. She'd never considered the matter in quite that light, but . . . "I guess."

"I could tell from your clothes. They're cheap." Chloe made a face. The cat stirred in her arms, and her hold on it shifted as she lifted it higher and rubbed her cheek against its fur. "Do you like Beanie Babies?"

"I love them." Sara's reply was fervent. "I have almost thirty."

Chloe snorted. "Is that all?" she asked scornfully. "I have all of them. Well, nearly all, except for some of the very rarest ones, like Trap the mouse. But my dad says he'll get them for me when he can find them."

"Do you have the Princess Bear?" Sara asked, awed. "That's the one I want most right now."

"I have two. Want to see them?"

Sara nodded with open eagerness.

"Come on, then."

THE following morning, Sunday, the family went to church. Although she and Sara had been less than regular churchgoers in Houston—the lure of a Sunday morning to sleep in was often just too great to resist—Olivia remembered the Sundays of her growing-up years with fondness. Every week without fail the Archers attended the service en masse. The only excuse was sickness.

"I hate church," Chloe muttered resentfully as the Jaguar nosed toward St. Luke's.

"No, you don't." Callie's response was tranquil. She was in the front passenger seat beside Seth, who drove. Olivia sat with the two girls in back. To Olivia's mingled surprise and relief she had returned from the hospital the day before to find Sara and Chloe playing Beanie Babies upstairs in the gallery. After playing together all day, the girls were now friends.

"Oh, yes, I do." Chloe's expression was mutinous.

"That's enough, young lady," Seth said in a voice that brooked no defiance. Chloe looked like she could explode but said nothing more.

The Jaguar pulled into the parking lot of the gray stone church. As Seth turned the engine off, a man emerged from the white Lincoln Town Car in the adjacent parking space. Olivia recognized Ira Hayes. Dressed in a navy sport coat, red tie, pale blue shirt, and white slacks, he looked much more attractive than when Olivia had first met him in the kitchen two nights before. He opened Callie's door for her and stood waiting. Her smile of greeting was so warm that Olivia realized her aunt must be fonder of this man than she had guessed.

Olivia released her seat belt as Chloe scrambled out the door with Sara right behind her. Olivia's own door swung open from the outside. She glanced up to find Seth holding the door for her. He appeared very distinguished in a light gray summer suit with a white dress shirt and a navy tie. With the sun glinting down on his blond hair, he was—handsome. The realization rattled Olivia. She had never before had such a thought about Seth.

"Are you planning to get out?" he inquired politely, reaching in a hand to assist her to alight. Olivia realized that she had been sitting there staring up at him for several seconds. Flustered, she grasped his hand and scooted out. His hand was warm and strong and far larger than hers. Clasping it made her suddenly very aware of him as a man. It occurred to her that she could be—might be—*was*—attracted to Seth, a mind-boggling thought. What was wrong with her, she asked herself, that out of the blue she was reacting to him this way?

"Seth! Where's Mallory?"

Olivia instinctively turned to look as a woman who appeared to be about forty came up to them. Her gaze was moving with open curiosity over Olivia.

"She's showing houses today," Seth replied courteously.

"That real estate business of hers certainly keeps her busy." The woman made another pointed look at Olivia.

"Yes, it does," Seth agreed. His gaze caught Olivia's, and he smiled. For a moment something almost wicked danced in his eyes. Then he reached out a hand to catch hers and draw her forward. "Olivia, this is Sharon Bishop. She's the new principal of the high school. Sharon, this is Olivia Morrison."

The women exchanged polite greetings, and then Seth and Olivia followed Callie into the church.

"You should have told her I was your cousin," Olivia whispered scoldingly over her shoulder at him.

"She'll figure it out," he said.

St. Luke's was a beautiful church, with high ceilings supported by dark carved beams, walls of rough white plaster, and rows of gleaming mahogany pews. Olivia sat between Sara and Seth. On Seth's other side was Chloe, and next to Chloe was Callie, then Ira. Although Sara and Chloe had originally been sitting together, Seth had shifted his daughter to his other side after the two girls succumbed to a muffled fit of giggles over a dropped hymnal. Olivia silently agreed with him that it might be wiser to separate the children, but sitting so close to Seth did nothing for her peace of mind. With six of them in one pew it was a bit crowded, and her arm brushed Seth's sleeve whenever she moved. She was conscious of his height when they stood up to sing and of the pleasingly deep timbre of his voice. As the service wore on, she grew so aware of him that it was embarrassing. The realization disturbed her, and she forced herself to think about something else. But after a few moments, no matter how hard she tried, Seth—and Seth alone— filled her mind.

Maybe being back in LaAngelle was awakening the old Olivia, she thought. As a teenager, she had enjoyed sex, which was really why she had imagined herself to be so in love with Newall. But then Sara had been born, and before long Newall had left her. Occupied with feeding and clothing and caring for her child, her body had been routinely exhausted.

There was nothing wrong with a renewed interest in sex, Olivia thought. But she needed to choose a more suitable candidate.

Anyone but Seth.

ON SUNDAY night when Seth's gray Jaguar pulled into the parking area behind the house, its lights cutting bright swaths through the darkness, Olivia and the two girls were out in the yard. It was about ten o'clock, which, given the heat of a LaAngelle summer, meant that it was the best time of day to be outdoors.

Armed with mason jars, Sara and Chloe were darting about chasing lightning bugs, which they dropped into the jars to make "lanterns."

The arrival of the Jaguar coincided with an unearthly shriek from Chloe. Stopped in her tracks by the sheer intensity of that scream, Olivia ran to the child's rescue.

"Chloe! What on earth . . . ?" Olivia gasped.

"It's on my arm! It's on my arm!" Clearly panic-stricken, Chloe hopped about, her bare right arm extended out from her body. "Get it off me! Get it *off* me!"

"It's okay. Hold still now, and let me see."

Placing a hand on her shoulder to hold the dancing child still, Olivia grasped Chloe's extended wrist. One of her bugs had escaped from her jar and was now fanning its wings in the vicinity of her elbow.

A relieved smile curved Olivia's lips. She recaptured the bug with a gentle swipe of her hand.

"My God, what is it?" Seth came pounding to the rescue.

"It was on me!" Chloe's voice quivered piteously.

"*What* was on you?" Seth's gaze darted from his daughter to Olivia.

"A lightning bug," Olivia said, the merest hint of dryness in her voice as she opened her palm for just a second so that he could see the evidence in her hand. "Chloe, if you'll give me your jar, I'll put him back in for you."

"That scared me to *death,*" Chloe said, handing over the jar.

"Me, too," Sara said as Olivia unscrewed the lid and scraped the bug off her palm. "I thought a monster had you."

"You mean like a giant frog?" Chloe asked.

"More like a giant lightning bug," Sara said. "Maybe the king of all lightning bugs, who's come down from the sky on this beautiful night to rescue the lightning bugs we've caught and wreak dreadful vengeance on us for catching them." Sara added a delicious shudder, getting into the spirit of the story.

"You're making that up!" Chloe stared wide-eyed at Sara, who giggled. Chloe giggled, too, and then both girls were looking around with pleasurable fear for the imaginary creature.

"Here." Having screwed the lid back on, Olivia passed the jar back to Chloe. "Next time a lightning bug lands on you, just brush it off. You scared me to death screaming like that."

"I guess that makes it unanimous, then," Seth said under his breath as the girls scampered off. "From the amount of noise she was making, I thought she was being murdered at the very least."

"Yes, well, your daughter obviously likes lightning bugs better in a jar than on her arm." The attraction she had felt for Seth earlier had not faded, Olivia discovered as she caught herself measuring her height against his—at six feet two, he was exactly a foot taller than she was—and admiring the breadth of his shoulders and the narrowness of his hips.

"Any problems this afternoon?" Seth asked.

"Chloe's been wonderful all day," Olivia replied.

"I'm glad to hear it," he said.

Olivia changed the subject. "How's Big John?"

Seth slapped absently at his bare forearm—Olivia suspected a mosquito—then glanced at her again. "No change to speak of. He's still unconscious, still on a respirator. Charlie says every day he hangs on, his chances improve, though." His gaze slid the length of her body, which was clad in cutoffs, a red tank top, and her Keds. "You're going to get eaten alive out here, dressed like that."

Olivia shook her head, smiling a little. "Sara and Chloe and I are wearing so much insect repellent that we're slimy with it."

Olivia felt Seth's gaze running over her body. For a second she thought that he was looking at her breasts, and her breathing suspended. Then, before she could be sure, he turned abruptly away, heading toward the parking area. "I've brought David home with me. And Keith. They flew into Baton Rouge this morning and took a taxi to the hospital. They'll be spending the night here. Come and say hello."

"I'm glad David came." Keeping one eye on the girls, Olivia trailed him to the parking area, where the bug light on the far side of the garage revealed Callie just stepping back from an embrace with a tall, well-built man. Immediately Callie turned to another man—shorter, stockier—and hugged him, too.

Seth advanced on the group. "I told you Olivia was home." He spoke to the newcomers as he and Olivia reached them.

The taller of the two men turned to Olivia, smiling. He was about sixty years old and had the wrinkles and jowls to prove it. His hair was still dark and thick, though, and Olivia wondered if it was dyed. This was Seth's uncle David, whom she had met perhaps half a dozen times in her life. Olivia returned his smile.

"Well, hello, Olivia!" David greeted her jovially. "The last time I saw you, you were—what?—twelve years old. At my mother's funeral, I believe it was."

Murmuring assent, Olivia submitted to a quick embrace, and they exchanged air kisses. Then David gestured at his companion. "You remember Keith Sayres, of course?"

Certainly Olivia did. When David brought his live-in companion to his mother's funeral, the explosion had been unforgettable. Big John had nearly gone off into an apoplexy at the idea that his gay son would so publicly flaunt his homosexuality, and Belinda had ranted for days about how reprehensible it was.

Oh, yes, Olivia remembered Keith Sayres.

"How are you?" she said cordially to Keith.

"Worried about David because of his dad, but otherwise fine," Keith replied. "It's a shame that it takes things like this to get families together, isn't it?"

"It certainly is," Callie answered, and then at her urging, they went inside. Left to gather up the children, Olivia finally managed to get them inside as well. Everyone was sitting around the kitchen table when the three of them entered, Sara and Chloe with well-filled lightning-bug lanterns in hand. Declining offers of coffee and cake, Olivia turned Chloe and her lantern over to Martha and took Sara upstairs for bath and bed.

Once Sara was sleeping, Olivia headed for the bathroom for her own bath. The room overlooked the back of the house, and while she was in the tub, she thought she heard one or more cars pull up. Finishing her bath, she put on her nightgown and robe, then peeped out the window and saw that actually three cars were parked in the parking area. One was Mallory's Miata, and she thought the white Lincoln must belong to Ira Hayes, but she wasn't sure about the ownership of the other. The mystery was solved as she headed back toward her bedroom and encountered Carl walking toward her from the stairs.

"What are you doing up here?" she asked, surprised.

"I came up to see if I could talk you into coming down," Carl said easily. "We're havin' a big ole family party downstairs."

He grinned engagingly. Six feet tall, stocky but not fat, with a warm personality, Carl was an attractive man. But getting excited about him posed just about the same problems as getting excited about Seth, Olivia reminded herself. With the addition of Carl's witch of a mother thrown in.

She shook her head at him. "I'm not dressed, and I'm tired," she said. "I think I'll go on to bed. Thanks for thinking of me, though."

After a couple more attempts to persuade her, Carl gave up and headed back toward the stairs. Olivia checked on Sara, then went to bed.

As she drifted off to sleep in the room next to Sara's, a memory of the way Seth had looked at her in the backyard swam through Olivia's head. With a small smile she drifted off to sleep, only to be awakened—after what could have been anything from minutes to hours later—by a piercing scream.

SARA! Olivia came awake instantly, knowing—without knowing how she knew it—that the scream had come from her daughter. Throwing the covers aside, leaping from her bed, she ran for Sara's room.

"Sara! *Sara!*" Flinging open the door, she saw in a glance that the bedside light she had left on was out. She saw, too, that the curtains over one window were slightly parted, allowing a shaft of moonlight into the room. By its light she could see Sara sitting bolt upright in bed, the bedclothes puddled around her waist.

As was her habit, Olivia had checked the window locks before leaving Sara to sleep. Had she not pulled the curtains completely closed again, allowing that shaft of moonlight to enter? She didn't remember seeing light, but maybe the moon just hadn't risen sufficiently then.

"Sara!" Olivia flipped on the light switch by the door.

"Mommy!" Voice shaking, Sara stretched out her arms toward her as if she were a very little girl again. As Olivia hurried to her daughter's side, she saw that Sara's face was as white as a sheet and her dark eyes were huge with shock. "Oh, Mommy!"

They wrapped their arms about each other, and Olivia sat down on the mattress. The clock on the nightstand read 4:28 a.m. Sara's pink Barbie nightgown was damp with sweat.

"There was something—it was standing by my bed!" Sara was nearly incoherent as she pressed her face into the curve between Olivia's neck and shoulder. Olivia tightened her hold as an unexpected chill raced down her spine.

"Something was standing by your bed?" Olivia tried hard to ignore the disorienting sense of having played out this scene before. But she couldn't resist glancing at the rocker in the corner, the rocker where her mother used to sit while she slept. *Why* had her mother sat with her as she slept? Hazy memories teased the outer reaches of Olivia's mind, but she could not access them.

"It had this big, bald head. It was *looking* at me."

"What was, baby?" Olivia concentrated on comforting her daughter.

"The thing by the bed. It—it was wearing something dark, like a cloak or—or something, and when it saw me, it smiled and—and it had fangs!" Sara shuddered. "I think it was the lightning-bug king!" she disclosed with a sob.

Olivia took a deep breath, her sense of horror fading.

"Sara." Olivia kissed Sara's averted cheek. "Baby, I think you just had a bad dream."

Sara shook her head. "It was real. I woke up, and it was standing there. The room was dark—you promised you'd leave a nightlight on, Mom—but it was standing in the light from the window. I could see it. I could see it looking at me, and I could see its fangs when it smiled, and then when I screamed, it disappeared!"

"It was a nightmare, baby." Olivia squeezed Sara tightly and smoothed her hair back from her face. When Sara looked up at her, Olivia gave her a reassuring smile.

"Let me check the light," Olivia said. "I *did* leave it on."

The small bedside lamp was of white china with an inexpensive white pleated shade. Leaning sideways, Olivia reached under the shade for the switch and pressed it. Nothing. Disentangling herself from Sara, she unscrewed the bulb, then raised it to her ear and shook it. The ensuing rattle confirmed what she had suspected.

"The bulb's burned out." Olivia was cheerfully matter-of-fact by this time. The sick dread that had overtaken her when she'd considered the possibility that something—some*one*—actually *had* been in her daughter's room had faded. She put the bulb down. "Let me check the window."

Pulling the curtains apart, she visually checked the latch. It was an old-fashioned brass hook-and-eye latch, and it was firmly locked, just as it had been when she had checked it earlier.

"The window's locked," she said.

"It was just a bad dream?" Sara quavered uncertainly.

"That's what it was." Olivia nodded as she twitched the curtains back into place. "Here, baby, change your nightgown."

"Mommy, can I sleep with you for the rest of the night?"

"Sure thing, pumpkin." Olivia would have suggested it if Sara had not. As a single parent, she worked hard at not being over-protective or overpossessive and not babying Sara too much. But when Sara was sick or upset or they just needed each other more than usual, she let Sara sleep with her. Those were the nights when Olivia slept best of all, because she knew then, with absolute certainty, that Sara was safe.

It had never before occurred to her to wonder why she didn't entirely feel that Sara was safe when she was in her own bed.

There was something about a child's being alone in bed. . . .

"Mom?"

Olivia realized that she had been standing beside the bed staring blankly into space for several seconds. She blinked. "I was just wondering whether we ought to sleep in your bed or mine."

"Yours," Sara said positively, and Olivia didn't disagree. She nodded and held out a hand to Sara, who scooted off the bed.

For no reason except that she just felt she wanted to, Olivia turned the lock on her bedroom door once they were inside. She and Sara got into bed, cuddling together in the middle of the mattress, with the bedside lamp burning brightly.

When Sara was asleep, Olivia switched off the lamp and tried to get back to sleep herself. But the niggling thought remained: *Had* something—or someone—been in Sara's room?

Just before she dozed off, Olivia thought she heard a floorboard creak in the hall. Her eyes popped open, and she was instantly alert. But strain though she might, she heard nothing more. Old houses always had creaks, didn't they?

She lay awake for a long time, listening. Finally, with her arm curved protectively around her daughter, Olivia at last fell into an uneasy asleep.

A LONG time after they were gone, after listening to them enter the room next door and settle down for the night, he took one last peek to make sure the coast was clear and slid out from under the bed.

That had been a close call. He was rusty. It had been a long time. Too long.

Good thing mommies never thought to look in closets or under beds.

That thought made him smile. He felt good. His plan might have been foiled tonight, but his appetite had been whetted.

He would be seeing little Miss Sara again. Very soon.

Grand Isle, Louisiana—July 17, 1974. "Daddy, could you stay in just till I go to sleep, please? If I'm already asleep when you go out, I won't be scared." Maggie Monroe's voice was softly pleading. Dressed in purple baby-doll pajamas, her legs as skinny as a crane's below the ruffled panties she wore and her hair as yellow and frizzy as a dandelion's, she was standing in the doorway of their rented vacation cottage two blocks from the beach. Her father, Vince, was already halfway across the shabby screened porch.

"Gawd-damn, Maggie, you're nine years old. Plenty old enough to stay by yourself whilst I go out for a while. If I'da known you was gonna need a baby-sitter, I wouldn't've taken you on no vacation." He scowled at her and pushed on out the screen door, which banged shut behind him. Maggie stood watching forlornly as he climbed into his bright blue Chevy Impala and roared off.

Oh, why had her mama made such a stink about his never spending time with her anymore? That's what had brought this whole thing on. Mama had screamed it at Daddy in front of the judge at their divorce, and Daddy had called later on the telephone and told

Mama he was taking Maggie somewhere special over summer vacation so they could spend some time together.

Mama had tried to take it back then, but it was too late. The judge had ordered it. So Maggie had to go.

She scurried to the bedroom—there was only one bedroom, so her daddy slept on the foldout couch—and jumped into bed, huddling down and pulling the covers up over her head. The bed smelled musty and sort of like somebody had peed on it a long time ago. So she started imagining, started thinking about herself as a beautiful princess named Allyson who lived in an enchanted castle. It was her favorite fantasy when she was scared or lonesome, and pretty soon, as Princess Allyson, she fell asleep.

Maggie didn't know what time it was when she woke up, but she knew it was a long time later because her dad was home. He'd opened the bedroom door and was now coming to check on her.

"Daddy?" Blinking, she pulled the covers from her face. Her dad swooped down on her, jamming a wet cloth that smelled like gasoline over her nose and mouth. She tried to fight him off, and as she did, she looked up and saw that it wasn't her daddy at all, but a stranger.

Stark terror released a rush of adrenaline that gave her the strength to kick and flail.

It wasn't enough. In less than a minute Maggie's eyes rolled back in her head, and she went limp.

STEALING little girls out of their bedrooms was the best, the ultimate thrill. Inside their own houses they thought they were safe, their parents thought they were safe, and he got off on imagining how horrified the mommies were in the morning when they got up to discover their babies missing.

He chuckled as he drove toward his destination. His toy was locked in a dog cage in the back of the van. From the sounds she was making, she was starting to regain consciousness.

"Mama . . ." she moaned.

Sweetheart, he thought, you won't ever see your mama again.

———————————

WHAT was left of the week passed swiftly for Olivia. An old friend from St. Theresa's came by to reminisce. The rest of the time she spent with Sara and getting reacquainted with her family. One or more of them—usually more—dropped by for dinner nearly every night.

Callie's chemotherapy regimen called for three weeks on, one week off, for six months. Since this was an off week, Callie stayed pretty much close to home, trying to gain back what strength she could. Seth, on the other hand, was hardly ever home. Olivia assumed he was dividing his time between the Boatworks and the hospital, but she didn't know for sure. David and Keith were around, having settled into the *garçonnière* for what David described as an "indefinite period." What that actually meant, Keith said candidly when David wasn't present, was until Big John either died or was pronounced out of danger. Since David no longer participated in the day-to-day running of his restaurant, a lengthy absence would do it no harm.

Chloe was away from the house a lot, involved in her own activities from early morning to late afternoon, and Olivia and Sara spent the days together very happily, exploring outside when the weather permitted, reading when it rained, going into town for an ice cream and to view Olivia's girlhood haunts, and basically just hanging out. Being free to wander and read and talk with Sara was the vacation Olivia needed.

The plan was that she and Sara would return to Houston on Friday. Olivia had bought round-trip tickets on Greyhound that required them to leave New Roads at six a.m. They would arrive back in Houston late that night, and life would get back to normal. With one exception. Now that the connection with her family had been reestablished, and especially given Callie's and Big John's illnesses, Olivia meant to come visit again as often as she could. LaAngelle Plantation was no longer a dream of better times. It was, once again, simply home.

On Wednesday afternoon Olivia and Sara came running back to the house through a sudden rain shower. As they sprinted, laughing, hands clasped, heads ducked against the rain, up the front steps to the protection of the veranda, Callie and Keith called to them. They were seated in the two white wicker rocking chairs near the swing. Fifteen feet above them the pair of ring-necked pheasants that

Charlie had stuffed and hung from the ceiling twenty-five years before still winged their way skyward. On the floor between them there was a big brown cardboard box.

"Come join us, you two," Callie invited.

Olivia smiled assent and headed toward them. Tugging on her mother's hand, Sara resisted. Olivia looked down at her.

"Can I go watch cartoons instead?" she whispered. A big satellite dish behind the *garçonnière* brought three channels of nonstop cartoons into the house, and Sara was in TV lovers' heaven.

"Sure, baby." Olivia let go of her daughter's hand, and with a quick, grateful smile for her mother Sara scampered into the house.

"Looking at pictures?" Olivia approached Callie and Keith. It was fairly obvious, from the snapshots they were passing back and forth, that they were indeed doing just that.

"Oh, Olivia, I kept these for you," Callie said, looking up as Olivia reached her chair. She gestured at the box at her feet. "I thought you'd want to have them someday," she said, then held out a snapshot for Olivia to view.

The picture showed a pretty, dark-haired woman smiling as she crouched behind a cherubic little girl.

On the white bottom border a line was written in small, precise letters, heavily slanted to the right. "Livvy and me," it said, followed by a date: "June 13, 1976."

It was her mother's handwriting. There was a roaring in Olivia's ears. She felt light-headed, nauseated almost, and for a moment she thought she might faint.

"Are you okay, Olivia?" Keith asked with gentle concern.

"I'm fine. I just didn't know that pictures like this still existed. I thought they'd all been thrown away or something." Olivia had taken nothing but a suitcase full of clothes with her when she had eloped with Newall.

"Oh, honey, do you think I would have let anybody throw these away?" Callie asked reproachfully. "They're yours. They've been in the attic all these years. All your things are up there—everything that was in your room the night you left us. I packed it all away myself."

"You did?" Olivia smiled a little shakily at her aunt. "I can't believe you did, after the way I left. But thank you. I think I needed to see them."

"Olivia, why don't you sit down here and go through these with Callie?" Keith stood up, vacating his rocking chair. When Olivia started to protest, he waved his hand at her dismissively. "Do you think I'm going to let *Martha,* fine woman though she certainly is, prepare our meal? When I am a culinary *artiste?*"

He said it jokingly, but Olivia got the sense that he meant what he said. She remembered that he had trained as a chef. Waving her into his chair, Keith disappeared inside. Olivia was left to do something she was not sure she wanted to do: sink down in his abandoned rocker and pore over a box of old photographs, with their accompanying memories of her mother.

And yet, as if compelled to do so, she was already reaching down into the box and picking out a silver-framed five-by-seven portrait. A wedding picture: her mother in a formfitting ivory suit, a bouquet of pink orchids in one white-gloved hand. Beside her stood James Archer, tall and fair-haired and handsome in his dark blue suit. At their feet was plopped a baby in a ruffly pink dress, with a wreath of tiny pink flowers in her dark, feathery hair.

She was that baby.

"Did you know that Selena was working at the Boatworks when James met her?" Callie asked conversationally.

Unable to speak, Olivia shook her head.

"She was. She was from Bayou Grand Caillou, you know."

Callie was frowning at her. Olivia's face was turned toward her, and she could see her aunt perfectly well, but it was almost as if Olivia were looking at her through glass. Olivia continued to rest back in her chair, her hands, limp in her lap, just touching the edges of the picture. She felt strange, immobile, as if even the smallest movement would require too much effort, and she guessed her face must have paled.

"Do you want to hear the whole story, Olivia? Or would you rather not?"

Making a great effort, Olivia moved, glancing down at the photograph in her lap. Her mother looked so young. She knew so little about her.

"Livvy and me." The words written on the back of that snapshot sounded so homey, so cozy. Life with her mother had been cozy. They had shared laughter and warmth and love.

Olivia's heart ached suddenly. Although specific memories were lost to her, the emotions that went with them were coming through loud and clear.

"Of course I want to hear," Olivia said. It was suddenly very important to her that she know everything that there was to know.

Callie nodded, her expression sympathetic. "I never knew your natural father, but Selena always said that he had worked as a shrimper until he was killed in some kind of boat accident a couple of months before you were born. Your mother was left with nothing. She came to LaAngelle because a friend of hers worked at the Boatworks. The girl asked Big John to give her friend Selena Chenier a job, and he did. In any case, James was instantly smitten. He didn't care that she was pregnant with another man's baby; he didn't care that his mother, Marguerite, who was of course Big John's wife, considered her unsuitable. He was head over heels."

Callie shook her head. "I have to tell you that Marguerite and Belinda were not very nice to your mother. I've always thought Belinda was jealous of Selena. She was so young and pretty, you know. So fiery. When she died, James was inconsolable. I really thought he wanted to die, too, so he could be with Selena again. And a few years later he did."

Callie paused, biting her lip guiltily. Her gaze met Olivia's. "Olivia, I always felt that I didn't do enough for you after Selena died. But Marguerite was alive then—your grandmother—and I just couldn't stand up to her. They were too strict with you, and . . . and not very loving, I guess. After Selena— Well, you were the sun and the moon and the stars to your mother. It must have been very hard for you to adjust. Thinking back on it now, well, I feel bad that I didn't try harder to help you, that's all."

"Please don't feel bad." Olivia reached for her aunt's hand. "You were always so kind to me, even when I didn't deserve it."

"I should have done more. I wish now I had." Callie smiled wryly, her hand gripping Olivia's. "That's one of the things about having cancer, you know. It makes you think back over your life, think about what you did and what you didn't do. I should have married again; I should have had more children. And I should have done better by you."

"Aunt Callie . . ." At the regret in the older woman's voice, Olivia's hand tightened around hers. "Sometimes I think things work out the way they're supposed to no matter what we do. If I hadn't run off with Newall, I wouldn't have Sara. And Sara is the best thing that ever happened to me. I don't regret her or anything that brought her to me, not for one instant."

"I'm glad to hear you say that, dear." Callie smiled a little tremulously. Her eyes were bright with unshed tears.

A white Mazda Miata, its convertible top up, burst past the shrouding trees and hedges at the base of the lawn and sped up the driveway with a swoosh of tires. As it passed them to disappear behind the house, Callie blinked, sniffed, released Olivia's hand, and stood up, suddenly brisk. "Well, here's Mallory with Chloe. I think I'll just go in and see how their shopping expedition went. You come on in when you're ready."

"I will." Olivia stayed in her rocker, watching as Callie went inside. Now that she had been given a glimpse into the well of pain and regret concealed beneath Callie's prosaic manner, she could only respect her aunt more. Callie was coping with cancer the way she had coped with every other blow she had suffered in life—by simply keeping on. In Olivia's opinion that was courage.

The rain had stopped, although thunderheads still loomed like purple mountains in the sky. The sound of water dripping from the eaves was soothing. Insects hummed; birds called. The peacocks emerged from the shrubbery near the bluff to pick their way across the grass, no doubt greedy for the worms the rain always forced from the ground in droves. Olivia watched with a feeling of peace. In a moment she would turn her attention to the contents of the box at her side. For now, for just this instant, she was content simply to be.

"I hate you! I hate you! I hate you!" The shriek was followed by the sound of shattering glass. Olivia jumped and looked around in alarm as the screen door burst open and Chloe barged through it, running out of the house as if the seat of her shorts were on fire.

Before Olivia could do anything to stop her, the child flew down the steps and across the lawn, fleet-footed as a gazelle, her long blond hair streaming behind her.

"Chloe Archer, you come back here this instant!" Mallory pushed through the screen door, for once less than perfectly groomed. One side of her chic blond bob was soaked flat and dripped water onto the shoulder of her lavender linen coatdress, which was itself liberally splashed with water. Her face was flushed scarlet, and her eyes flashed fire.

"Chloe Archer!" As the door banged shut behind her, Mallory raced to the edge of the porch to scream after the fleeing child. But if Chloe heard, she pretended not to, disappearing over the bluff as she darted down the steps cut into its side.

For a moment Mallory stood there glaring impotently after Chloe. Then she pivoted on her beige high heels and seemed to become aware of Olivia's presence for the first time.

"That child is the worst brat I have ever seen in my life," Mallory said through her teeth, meeting Olivia's gaze.

The screen door opened again, and Callie came out onto the veranda. Mallory's incensed gaze swung to her.

"Oh, Mallory, I am so sorry!" Callie said, tsk-tsking busily as she walked up to her furious future daughter-in-law. "Oh, dear. Chloe shouldn't have done it, but—"

"But nothing!" Mallory was still talking through her teeth. "She shouldn't have done it, period. She threw a vase of flowers at me simply because I showed her a picture in a magazine of a bridesmaid's dress I thought would look nice on her. That child needs professional help!"

"Oh, Mallory, no. She's just going through a bad time."

Mallory closed her eyes for a moment. She seemed to take a deep breath and opened her eyes again.

"I realize that," Mallory said, and her voice was calmer. "Believe me, I'm trying to make allowances, Callie. I'm trying to be her friend. I just this afternoon canceled a showing of a half-million-dollar property in Baton Rouge so I could take her school shopping. I'm certainly trying, Callie."

"I know you are, dear." Callie sent an appalled eye-rolling look over Mallory's shoulder to Olivia and tsked-tsked some more. "Let's get you dried off. Stepparenting is so difficult."

Callie's eyes met Olivia's again, this time with a silent plea for help. Olivia understood that she was being asked to go check on Chloe, and nodded. Callie looked relieved and ushered a still fuming Mallory into the house.

Olivia carefully put the picture back into the box with the others and headed down the steps. Her movements were reluctant. Chloe wasn't her child, and she *was* difficult. How Callie thought *she* was going to be able to do anything with Chloe when the child's own father, grandmother, and stepmother-to-be couldn't, she didn't know.

Sara had never had a bratty episode in her life. But Olivia had. All at once Olivia remembered the fits she had thrown at her grandmother, at Callie, even at Seth.

Why? Olivia reached the top of the bluff, stared unseeing at the silvery lake, and made a fundamental discovery.

Because she had felt unloved. The truth hit her like a blow. After her mother died, Olivia had never again felt loved.

Chloe was acting out because she felt unloved.

The stone steps cut into the side of the bluff were slick, and she was careful going down them. She smiled wryly. Of all the places for Chloe to run, why did it have to be to the lake?

She could hear the child's gusty sobs before she got there. She'd had an idea where Chloe was, of course. Every child who grew up on this property knew about the overhang. Not quite a cave, it was more of a depression in the face of the cliff. At about five feet deep and maybe six feet wide, it had a craggy, curving roof of rock that soared some twelve feet overhead. What made the spot irresistible were the vines. Tangled tendrils of kudzu stretched over the opening like a curtain, hiding the hollow within. Anyone who didn't know the overhang was there would never have seen it.

With her goal in sight Olivia paused and considered. Approaching Chloe either with sympathy or a lecture was destined to meet with failure. Olivia, therefore, wouldn't approach.

Working quickly, she gathered a small pile of sticks and rocks, then squatted just off the path opposite the overhang and began arranging her trove into a structure.

She also started to sing.

Olivia was *not* a singer, but then this particular application didn't require that she be able to carry a tune. It just required her to attract the attention of one very unhappy little girl.

"Jimmy crack corn . . ." she began softly. She had worked her way through a half-dozen others and was on a lusty chorus of "Zip-a-Dee-Doo-Dah" when a hand tapped against her shoulder.

Olivia stopped singing and glanced over her shoulder in feigned surprise.

"Oh, hi, Chloe," she said, as if she did not notice the child's swollen eyes, tear-wet cheeks, and still trembling lower lip.

"What are you *doing?*" The question was petulant but curious. Chloe's gaze was focused on the small four-walled rock-and-mud structure that Olivia had constructed beside the path.

"Putting on the roof," Olivia replied.

"What is it?"

Olivia scooped up a good-sized glob of mud and patted it down on top of the twigs she had positioned to support the roof.

"A fairy house."

"There's no such thing as fairies." If Chloe's scorn had had weight, Olivia would have been crushed beneath it.

Olivia shrugged, her hands still busy patting mud over the roof. "When I was eight, like you, I used to feel bad sometimes, and when I felt bad, I would build a fairy house, and then I would lie in my bed—I always built the fairy house where I could see it from my bed—and watch for fairies. They always came."

"Fairies?" The single word brimmed with skepticism.

"Well," Olivia temporized, "*something* came. I could see little lights flying all around my house, and going in and out of the windows."

"Lightning bugs!" Chloe pronounced scathingly.

"Maybe," Olivia agreed, finishing the roof. "But I liked to pretend they were fairies."

"It's stupid to pretend."

Olivia shook her head and stood up, surveying her handiwork with pride. A neat little stone, twig, and mud house stood beside the path. "Pretending is wonderful, Chloe. I used to pretend I could fly. I would lie on my back on the grass behind the house and look up at the clouds and pretend I could fly up there." Suddenly Olivia hesitated, shaken, as she realized that she really was unearthing a memory. Her voice softened. "So I could visit my mother in heaven."

How she had wished that pretend game would come true!

"How old were you when your mother died?" Chloe was looking up at her, her tears and anger momentarily forgotten.

"Six," Olivia answered.

"I was six when my mom got married again," Chloe said, and all of a sudden her lower lip started to tremble. "That's how I got to be *here*. She didn't want me after that."

Tears swam in Chloe's eyes. Responding instinctively, Olivia wrapped her arms around the child, hugging her close. Bad move.

Chloe jerked free, glaring at her. "Pretending's stupid!" she said.

Before Olivia realized what Chloe meant to do, she lifted a foot and stomped through the roof of the fairy house. Then she turned and ran back up the path.

At least, Olivia thought, ruefully surveying the ruins of her creation, Chloe was headed in the direction of the house.

It was only when she looked up again that Olivia realized she was alone in the one place on earth she least wished to be: not twenty feet from the edge of the lake where her mother had drowned.

Run away. Its origins were unclear, but the whisper was not, and Olivia blinked as she absorbed what she was hearing. *Run. Run away.*

Olivia stared wide-eyed at the lake for a solid minute before she realized the truth. There were no specters calling out to her from the smooth surface of the water. The words were in her mind. Her fear was speaking.

Run. Run away. A breeze had come up, and involuntarily Olivia shivered. The lake . . . It had always been the stuff of her most terrible nightmares.

But she would not run away from it anymore. It was time to silence that fear once and for all.

Run away, Olivia! Run away!

Taking a deep breath, ignoring the voices, Olivia took one step off the path, then another. Then she was walking determinedly toward the lake, weaving among trees, dodging cypress knees, wading through tangled undergrowth. She meant to stand on the shore, right at the very edge, face her fear.

Olivia! The voice from the lake was shouting at her now, warning her to stay back. Olivia reached the edge of the trees, set foot on the sliver of rocky, muddy beach, and took the final step needed to bring her to the edge of the water.

To her surprise she immediately sank up to her ankles in ooze. As the brackish water rose, lapping at her calves instead of her toes, she looked down in dismay.

Without warning, a hand caught her arm from behind, yanking her violently backward.

Olivia screamed, flailed, stumbled, and would have fallen bottom-first into the muck if someone had not caught her under the arms in the nick of time.

"What the hell do you think you're doing?" It was Seth, she discovered, bending back to look at him from the ignoble position in which she found herself. He was scowling, his thick, straight brows nearly meeting over his nose as his eyes collided with hers.

"What am *I* doing?" Olivia felt her panic dissipate. "What are *you* doing grabbing me like that? You scared the life out of me!"

It was hard to project the true degree of her indignation, she discovered, when her bottom was six inches above the muck and his hands under her arms were all that kept her out of it.

"Didn't you hear me calling you? I yelled, but you kept going like you were in some kind of trance. What were you trying to do?" His tone was so fierce that her eyes widened.

"I was just trying to get over being afraid of the lake," Olivia confessed. "What did you think I was doing, drowning myself?"

She'd meant the question to be humorous, but from the uneasy flicker in his eyes she divined the truth.

"You *did* think that, didn't you?"

His mouth tightened, his eyes darkened, and for a minute she thought he was going to drop her into the goo. Then she was being thrust back into an upright position.

"Next time you plan to go wading, take somebody with you. It's stupid to go walking into the lake alone." He looked down, and his expression became one of angry disgust.

Like herself, she discovered, he was some eight inches deep in slimy mud and water. Unlike herself, he was dressed for work in a navy suit and, Olivia presumed, expensive dress shoes.

"Oh, dear," she said, her eyes meeting his. "I appreciate you coming in after me. I really do."

"Next time I'll let you drown yourself."

Moving carefully as the ooze bubbled and sank around him, Seth lifted a dripping slime-covered foot from the mud, to the accompaniment of a sound like a vacuum seal being broken, and set it down again halfway to shore. With the other foot he was not as fortunate. Lifting it free of the goo, he swore, and Olivia saw as his foot came into view that it was minus its shoe.

"Oh, dear," she said again. His gaze met hers for a pregnant instant, and she began to giggle helplessly. He stared at her without saying anything at all, his expression thunderous. Then he bent, thrust an arm into the muck, and felt around for his shoe. Olivia, meanwhile, squelched toward shore. Clambering onto solid ground, ooze coating her bare legs to midcalf, she turned to observe his efforts. He straightened, shoe in hand, moving with an easy athletic grace despite the impediment of being mired in mud.

"I came down here looking for Chloe," he said, fixing her with a look that dared her to laugh again as he took two long strides onto solid ground. "Have you seen her?"

Olivia nodded. "I *think* she ran back to the house."

Seth made a disgusted noise, dropped his shoe on the ground, and worked his foot back into it. "Apparently she threw a vase full of flowers at Mallory."

"I know."

They turned toward the path, and as they made their way through the undergrowth, Seth automatically reached out to cup Olivia's elbow for support.

"We've got a full house for supper tonight, by the way. Mallory, David and Keith, Charlie and Belinda, Phillip and Connie—Connie's Phillip's wife, I don't think you've met her yet—and their kids, and Carl. Oh, yes, and Ira. No doubt I'm leaving someone out."

"Good God," Olivia said. "Why so many?"

"Charlie wanted to have a family meeting to discuss possible treatment options for Big John. So of course I'm thrilled out of my mind to get home and find that my daughter has disgraced the pair of us again."

"Seth." Olivia turned abruptly to face him. "Does Chloe remind you of anyone?"

One corner of his mouth lifted. "Linda Blair in *The Exorcist?*"

"Seth!"

He laughed. "All right. Who did you have in mind?"

"Me."

His eyes widened. "I'd almost rather have Linda Blair."

"Seth, I'm serious!"

"So am I."

"Fine." Olivia turned on her heel and marched away from him. "If you're too pigheaded to listen . . ."

"Livvy. *Livvy.*" He caught up with her, both hands closing around her upper arms, stopping her. The mud on his right hand was nearly dry, and anyway, she didn't care anymore if his hand was muddy, because she was suddenly too darned mad. He turned her around to face him. "Wait. Tell me. Why does Chloe remind you of yourself?"

"Because she thinks nobody loves her," Olivia said brutally. She'd meant to be more tactful, but her long-simmering sense of injustice chased the tact right out of her.

He didn't like that, she could see. "What do you mean, she thinks nobody loves her? I love her, Mother loves her, and—"

"How does she know that? I've been here a week, Seth, and all I've seen you do is go off to work without so much as a thought for your daughter, and when you do finally see her, you're either fighting with her or telling her to behave. Do you think that feels like love to her? Aunt Callie's good to her, but she's desperately ill. Martha's fond of her, but she's hired help. Mallory—well, I won't even get into Mallory. And her mother—Chloe's mother broke her heart by sending her home to you. The child feels abandoned, Seth. She needs your time and your attention, not punishment."

Anger emanated from him in waves. "You don't know what you're talking about!" he said.

"You just won't listen. You never would listen! You always know everything, and everybody else is wrong, and—"

"Was I wrong about Newall Morrison?"

"Shut up! You just shut up, Seth Archer!" Olivia yelled. Maddened, she jerked an arm free and slapped him full across the face. Horrified at herself the instant after she did it, Olivia stalked away from him, heading for the house. She would go straight upstairs, and with any luck no one would even see her.

The best-laid plans of mice and men . . . The entire company was assembled on the front veranda, enjoying drinks and watching the sunset, when Olivia emerged at the top of the bluff. She hesitated. Her first impulse was to skulk along the hedge until she reached the back door, but someone was bound to see her, and then she would look like an utter fool.

So Olivia walked up to the house nonchalantly, as though she hadn't just had a terrible fight with Seth, as though she wasn't sweaty and angry, dressed in a dirt-smeared T-shirt and grubby cutoffs with drying mud caked midway up her calves. She even managed to fix a pleasant expression on her face as she reached the steps.

"OLIVIA! Just in time for supper." Keith greeted her first with a jovial tip of the half-filled glass he held. Charlie waved. Ira smiled.

Olivia's attention shifted to Callie, who was moving toward her with obvious purpose.

"Chloe came back about fifteen minutes ago. I sent her to her room," Callie whispered as she reached her. "I think Sara's up there with her. Oh, dear, was Seth very mad?"

Olivia answered this with a nod.

"Can I get you a drink, Olivia?" Smiling, Carl came toward her. Olivia shook her head, smiling back. Carl was clearly interested in her as something other than a cousin. It was a pity, all things considered, but she was not interested back. At the moment, especially, all she wanted was to go upstairs.

Shouldering through the screen door, bearing a tray piled high with crackers and grapes and chunks of yellow cheese, Belinda stopped to look Olivia over with disapproval. "Why, you're covered with mud! You ought to go in the back way."

"She's fine, Belinda," Callie reproved, her voice so low that the others wouldn't overhear.

"Oh, look, Mama. There's Seth! I told you he wouldn't be long." Mallory had been sitting on the swing beside an older look-alike blond woman whom Olivia guessed was her mother. Mallory jumped up, moving to the rail and waving, presumably at Seth. Grasping the edge of the screen that Belinda still held ajar, Olivia refused to look around to make sure. She could only hope that the mark on his cheek had faded by this time. What the present company would make of that she didn't even want to guess.

"Why, he's covered with mud, too!" Belinda said loudly, the placement of her body in the doorway preventing Olivia from edging past her. Her gaze, sharp with malice, swung back to Olivia. "Whatever have you two been doing together?"

All eyes turned toward Olivia. Mallory's and her mother's went round as they weighed the evidence on Olivia's legs. Carl, who had almost reached the bottleneck at the door, looked at her mud-covered calves and frowned.

"Making mud pies," Olivia said, smiling sweetly at the gathered company. Then to Belinda she said with just the barest hint of bite, "I really *do* need to take a shower. If you'll just let me by . . ."

There was nothing else Belinda could do but step aside. Let Seth explain later, Olivia thought, and she made her escape.

NOT for anything—not even chicken in sauce piquante, which, from the smell, was what they were having—was she going back downstairs. When Martha came in search of her, she pleaded a headache. Kind Martha brought her up a plate. Sara put in an appearance around tenish, having had supper with Chloe in her room. After Sara's bath and the obligatory bedtime story, Olivia finally went to her room and crawled into bed. She was asleep as soon as her head hit the pillow.

Of course, she dreamed about the lake. She could hear the voice calling to her—*Run. Run away!*—as she stood on the shore, just as she had that afternoon. But in her dream the voice belonged to her mother, a tiny, barely glimpsed figure desperately flailing in the water. As Olivia watched in horror, her mother called out a warning one more time and then disappeared from view. Olivia knew, without knowing how she knew, that Selena had been pulled beneath the surface by some unseen force.

At that point Olivia woke up in a cold sweat. For several minutes she lay without moving, heart pounding, as she convinced herself that she was safe in bed. It was some time before she fell back to sleep.

By morning Olivia had recovered from the dream and was pretty much over her anger at Seth as well. In fact, what she felt most strongly was shame at her own behavior. She'd fought with him just like she had as a teenager. Hadn't she grown up one bit?

She and Sara were leaving for home the next day, she reflected, and she needed to smooth things over with her cousin before she left. But Seth was gone all day, frustrating her good intentions. Since Chloe was confined to her room, with no TV and no playmates allowed, it was clear that he hadn't taken to heart what she'd told him about his daughter feeling unloved and needing his attention.

It was almost eleven o'clock that night, and Sara was already asleep next door when a soft knock sounded at one of the pair of French windows in Olivia's room.

She tensed at the sound, her hands stilling on the blouse she was folding. She didn't like knowing that anybody could get to her room just by walking along the gallery. It made her nervous.

But that was silly. Who would be knocking at her window but family? Moving to the window, pulling the curtain aside, Olivia was rewarded for her fortitude by seeing Seth.

"Come outside. I want to talk to you," he said softly when she pushed open the window.

With only a single glance behind her for the half-filled suitcases that lay open on the bed, she did as he asked. She stepped through the long French window into the soft warmth of the night and followed him to the pair of rockers at the far end of the gallery. When he indicated with a gesture that she should sit, she did so.

"I'm sorry I slapped you," she said abruptly, leaning back in the chair. "I apologize."

"That's a first, coming from you," he said with a laugh, moving to sink down in the other rocking chair. The chair creaked under his weight.

"You're not going to apologize, are you?" she asked.

"What makes you think that?" The question was lazy, teasing almost.

She glanced sideways at him, smiling. "I know you, Seth Archer."

"I know you, too, Olivia Chenier"—the tenor of his voice changed as he added—"Morrison." His opinion of her married name was apparent from his tone.

Olivia sighed. "All right, let's get this over with. You were right about Newall. I was a fool to run off and marry him like I did. I know it. You don't have to keep rubbing my nose in it."

Olivia could feel the weight of Seth's gaze on her.

"If you thought I was rubbing your nose in it, then I do apologize. We all make mistakes." After a long moment of silence he asked quietly, "Was it bad, Livvy? Being married to him?"

Absurdly, the gentleness in his tone made Olivia want to cry.

"Pretty bad," she said in as light a tone as she could muster. "Try to picture never-ending groupies, no money, constant travel from one cheap motel to another while he followed the rodeo circuit. By the time he left me, I had certainly learned my lesson about eloping with strange men, believe me."

"Want to talk about it?" Seth's tone was still very gentle.

Olivia shook her head. "Nope. It's water under the bridge."

"It's not where you've been, it's where you're going that counts," he suggested. That was one of Big John's favorite axioms, and Seth's use of it coaxed a smile from Olivia.

"Exactly," she said. He was still looking at her, but she couldn't read his expression in the darkness.

"I want you to stay here," Seth said abruptly. "*We* want you to stay here. That's what I wanted to talk to you about."

"What?" Olivia looked at him, wide-eyed with surprise.

"I'm offering you a job at the Boatworks and a home here at LaAngelle Plantation for as long as you care to stay."

Olivia was stunned. "Oh, Seth, I don't know what to say. Our home's in Houston now. Sara starts back to school in just a few days, and I have a job that I like, and—"

"Olivia," Seth interrupted. "I can offer you a better job, one that pays more, has a future. For right now I need an office manager. Ilsa Bartlett, who has the job now, is going on maternity leave in two months. I'd like to hire you for that position now. And then later, when Ilsa comes back and you know more about the business, I'll move you into a sales position." He held up a hand, realizing Olivia wanted to interrupt. "Hear me out. The hours would be adjusted so that you could be home when Sara's home. You could drive her— and Chloe if you would—to school in the morning and then leave work in time to pick them up and be with them all afternoon. Yes, I'm including Chloe in that, at least until Mallory and I get married and move back into town. Plus, Mother starts chemotherapy again next week. She needs you here. She wants you here."

"Seth." Olivia took a deep breath. She was stunned. "Oh, Seth, I never thought about staying. I have to think. I— Where would Sara go to school? Where does Chloe go to school?"

Seth smiled. "Right here in town. LaAngelle Elementary. After seeing the results of Grandmother's sending you to St. Theresa's, I thought I might do better to keep Chloe closer to home."

Olivia was surprised by that. An Archer in the local public school. It was unprecedented. Her feelings must have shown on her face, because Seth laughed. "Hey, I may learn slow, but I learn."

Olivia was still trying to sort things out in her mind. "Gosh, Seth, you're asking me to take a big step."

Seth looked away from her, out at the night. "Is there a boyfriend? Somebody you don't want to leave?"

Olivia shook her head, a rueful smile just touching her lips. "Believe it or not, there hasn't been anybody important since Newall. Like you said, I may learn slow, but I learn."

Seth looked at her again. "So what's the problem?"

"Well . . ." Olivia hesitated. "I can't make a decision like this without talking to Sara."

"So talk to Sara." Their eyes met again. "Livvy," he said, "we need you. You need us. Stay."

She wanted to, she realized suddenly. Oh, she wanted to.

"Our bus leaves tomorrow morning at six. Can—can I call you from Houston and let you know what we decide?"

"You're not going to ride in a Greyhound bus all the way back to Houston. What did it take you, something like twelve hours to get here?" Seth stood up abruptly. "If you want to go back tomorrow, I'll fly you there and back in the company Beechcraft."

Olivia looked at him for a moment. Then she said mildly, "The bus isn't really all that bad, Seth."

"To hell with the bus. This is not about the bus." He moved toward her, stopped short, and stood frowning down at her.

Olivia looked up at him, met his gaze, and quite suddenly ceased to breathe. He was close. So close that if she stood up, she would be in his arms. How she wanted to stand up!

"Forget the bus, okay?" His tone was almost rough.

Clinging to the arms of the chair as though she could prevent herself from doing what she suddenly wanted to do more than anything else, Olivia nodded. "Okay."

Seth walked to the rail, leaned both hands against it, and stared out at the night.

Her bond with him spanned a lifetime. He was the big cousin she had always looked up to, bossy and maddening as he could be. She could not spoil their relationship by introducing a sexual element to it. He was too important to her. Besides, he was going to marry Mallory.

"We'll talk tomorrow," he said over his shoulder. "Go to bed, Olivia."

If she wasn't going to make a fool of herself, she had better take some of the best advice she had ever heard in her life.

Olivia let go of the arms of her chair and stood up. "Good night," she said softly to his back.

It was an effort to pull her eyes away from him, but Olivia did it. Then she walked away, along the gallery to her room, and through the French window to safety. She locked it tight, then stood with her back against it for a very long time.

IN THE end the trip to Houston had turned into a family outing, which was probably a good thing, Seth reflected. He was at the controls of a twin-engine Beechcraft on the flight back to Baton Rouge, his mind almost solely occupied with trying *not* to imagine what it would be like to take Olivia to bed. She sat beside him in the co-pilot's seat, wearing a tomato-red T-shirt and a pair of snug white shorts that left the tanned length of her legs bare.

All day long he had wanted her so much that he ached with it, and there was absolutely nothing he could do about it. He was getting married in a little more than two months.

Fortunately, strapped into the seats directly behind him and Olivia were the two best chaperons he could have wished for: Chloe and Sara, both asleep in their seats, lulled by the drone of the engines. Chloe's head lolled sideways onto her shoulder while Sara's rested back against the gray leather seat.

Olivia had insisted on bringing Sara, saying the little girl needed a chance to gather up her personal belongings and say good-bye to her old home. Then she had suggested bringing Chloe as well, and somehow the whole thing had worked out surprisingly well. The girls got along with each other and with Olivia, and Chloe—excited about being included—was on her best behavior.

Behind the girls an enormous fern that Olivia had wanted from her apartment took pride of place. Next to it was a box filled with Sara's Beanie Babies, which the girls had played with until they had fallen asleep. The rest of the gear from Houston was, thankfully, in the hold. Movers were coming next week for the balance.

"Is Sara okay with moving?" he asked Olivia softly, after checking again to make sure the girls really were asleep.

Olivia looked sideways at him. "She's excited, I think, but a little scared, too. It's hard for a child to change schools."

"Did you have much work persuading her?"

Olivia had one leg drawn up under her. She looked tired, faintly rumpled—and simply beautiful.

"I didn't really have to persuade her. It was the possibility of a cat that did it, I think," she said. "We couldn't have one in our apartment. I told her she could have one at LaAngelle Plantation. You don't mind, do you?"

"Livvy, you don't have to ask me. LaAngelle Plantation is your home. Sara—and you—can have anything you like."

Olivia smiled at him. "Sara will be thrilled."

"I've been thinking about what you said the other night," Seth said abruptly. "And I think maybe Chloe does feel unloved. The problem is, I don't know what to do about it."

For a moment she looked at him without saying anything. "Are you asking me for advice? My goodness, this is a first."

"Quit gloating, Livvy. What do you think I should do?"

"Spend time with her. Do fun things with her. Don't just drop her off to play tennis; play tennis with her. Get involved in her school activities. That kind of thing. The key is for you to spend time with her in a way you both enjoy, I think. Let her know you like being with her. Hug her. Tell her you love her. And Seth . . ." She hesitated.

"Hmmm?" He glanced at her questioningly.

She looked at him without speaking for a moment. "Maybe you and Chloe and Mallory should spend time doing things together, too. Fun things. So Chloe can get used to the idea of the three of you as a family."

"Good idea," he said. And he knew it was. But he had trouble picturing himself, Chloe, and Mallory doing anything together that would not end with a tantrum from Chloe and a diatribe from Mallory. Suddenly he realized that he was having trouble picturing the three of them as a family, too.

And that gave him something else to think about all the way home.

THE next month was so busy that Olivia barely had time to catch her breath. She settled into her job at the Boatworks, Sara and Chloe started school, and Callie endured another cycle of chemotherapy. Big John remained hospitalized. Olivia was finally permitted to see him, but since he had not regained consciousness, it wasn't the catharsis she had hoped for. She held his hand, murmured a few words, and then it was time for her to go.

As it became apparent that Big John was going to be in the hospital on a long-term basis, David and Keith had begun dividing the week between their home in San Diego and LaAngelle Plantation. Weekends, which were the busiest time in the restaurant business, were spent in California. Monday through Thursday mornings they spent in LaAngelle or, more properly, at the hospital.

Seth obviously felt that he should be at the hospital more, but his first responsibility was to run Archer Boatworks. As Olivia, with her access to the books, had quickly learned, the business that had provided the family with its comfortable lifestyle for so long had started to deteriorate badly over the last decade or so. With Seth's insistence on taking in commercial work, the company was slowly climbing back. Without him, Olivia realized, the Boatworks would have gone bankrupt long ago.

Ilsa Bartlett, whom Olivia would be temporarily replacing, handled all the routine business of the office, and as she candidly told Olivia, the job was a killer. That relieved Olivia's mind of one worry: that Seth had offered her a position either out of the kindness of his heart or just to get her to move back to LaAngelle.

Carl and Phillip both worked for the Boatworks, Phillip as assistant general manager and Carl as sales manager. As general manager, Seth put in the longest hours. He arrived before seven most mornings and worked until there was simply no work left to be done that day.

Since their trip to Houston, however, Seth had been making an effort to get home no later than seven so he could spend a little time with Chloe before she went to bed. At Olivia's suggestion he also went with his daughter to her classroom on the first day of school—Olivia was surprised to learn that he had never done that before—and attended a midday library awards program a week later to watch Chloe (along with nearly all of her classmates except Sara, the newcomer) receive a medal for reading a certain number of books over the summer. Seeing Sara's downcast face after the program, Seth, all on his own, hit on the perfect way to cheer her up. That evening when he came home, he was carrying two small, exquisitely wrapped presents—one for Sara and one for Chloe. When the girls opened them, searching through layers of tissue paper, what they each found was his business card. Scrawled in Seth's handwriting on the back were the words "Look in my car."

Both girls squealed with excitement and tore out the back door and down the steps to where Seth had left his car.

From the veranda vantage point the grown-ups watched as Sara and Chloe, chattering animatedly, peered through the windows, squealed again, and jerked open the door. Seconds later both girls emerged, each clutching something close to her chest.

"Mom, come look!" Sara called.

Olivia went down the steps to find that Sara cuddled a tiny, fluffy smoke-gray Persian kitten. It had a pink ribbon with Sara's name on it tied around its neck. Chloe was holding an identical kitten, with her name on it.

"Oh, Sara!" Olivia exclaimed, giving her daughter a hug.

"A kitten's what I wanted more than anything else in the whole world," Sara said. She looked up shyly at Seth, who had come up behind Olivia. "Thank you, Seth."

"You're welcome, Sara," Seth said, and Sara smiled at him, her eyes luminous with joy.

Later Olivia thanked him for his kindness.

"You notice I got two," he said, settled on the couch in front of the TV, his arms crossed over his chest as he watched the girls playing with their kittens on the floor of the den. "Absolutely identical so they wouldn't have anything to fight over."

"You did good," Olivia confirmed. She was sitting on the couch, too, at the opposite end. Their gazes met, and she smiled at him, a warm and affectionate smile.

Although Seth was making great progress, Olivia felt, time remained the problem. There was simply not enough of it for all Seth had to do. Besides work and Chloe and Big John, there was Callie. Chemotherapy rendered her weak and ill, and she needed her only child. So did Mallory, who stopped by the Boatworks nearly every day to get Seth's opinion on something concerning the wedding ceremony or reception.

By the end of September, Olivia's routine was firmly established. She rose at six thirty, got herself and the girls up, dressed, and fed, had Sara and Chloe at school by eight, herself at work by eight fifteen, worked until two forty-five, then picked up the girls at three. After that she had her afternoons free for Sara—and Chloe. She supervised homework, arranged play dates, and volunteered to assist with the Brownie troop, among countless other mommy-type activities. For the first time since Sara's birth she had plenty of time to spend with her daughter. Except for her concern for Callie and Big John and the bad dreams that plagued her, she was more content than she had been in years.

The dreams did not come every night. Olivia almost thought it would be easier if they did, because then she would expect them. As it was, there seemed to be no rhyme or reason to it. In them it was always night, she was always standing on the shore of the lake, and her mother was always in the water. Her mother cried out to her, "Run, Olivia! Run away! Go! Run away!" Then Selena would disappear beneath the surface of the water, pulled down by something Olivia could not see.

What made the dreams especially terrible was that each time, some new detail emerged. In one she caught the ripples of something swimming in the water behind Selena as her frightened face turned toward shore; in another she was a helpless observer as Selena sank, only to have one hand break the surface, fingers stretching frantically toward the sky, before it, too, was gone. Each time, Olivia awoke terrified. She would lie in her bed, bathed in sweat, as she reminded herself over and over that it was only a dream.

Or was it? She had never had dreams like this before returning to LaAngelle Plantation. Now they were so persistent and so disturbing that she was beginning to wonder if they were more than just products of her subconscious.

She made up her mind to ask Callie or Seth or someone to tell her in detail about the night her mother died.

Just the thought gave Olivia cold chills. So she put it off, enduring the dreams, telling herself that surely, sooner or later, they would just go away.

The big event in LaAngelle at the end of September was the Fall Festival. Held on a Friday night on the combined grounds of the elementary and high schools, it was a carnival, picnic supper, and dance, designed to raise money for PTA projects. Seth, as one of LaAngelle's leading citizens, had been asked to serve a turn in the dunking booth. He was unenthusiastic, but he knew his duty, so he left home around six thirty wearing swimming trunks and a T-shirt and taking dry clothes with him to change into later when his stint as target ended. Olivia and the girls went with him in the Jaguar. Olivia had agreed to help out at the Cook's Corner booth, where homemade baked goods were for sale.

When her shift was over at eight o'clock, she headed toward the elementary school, where Sara was helping out with the cakewalk. Weaving toward the school through shifting throngs of townspeople, Olivia exchanged greetings left and right but paused only once, to join the crowd at the dunking booth. Seth was seated on the platform yelling good-natured insults at a beefy young man who was getting ready to hurl a baseball at the flat metal disk, which, if struck properly, would drop him into a tank of water. If Olivia was not mistaken, the man throwing the baseball was a Boatworks employee. Seth spied her, grinned, waved—and promptly went down with a gigantic splash. Laughing, Olivia watched as he surfaced, slicking his hair back with both hands and shaking the water from his face.

"Lucky shot!" he yelled after the thrower. He hoisted himself back onto the platform, water streaming from his body. Olivia noted how the wet T-shirt clung, revealing the broad strength of Seth's shoulders and the solid muscles of his chest. Her heartbeat quickened.

She turned her back on the dunking booth and continued walking toward the elementary school. In moments her pulse returned to normal. Her attraction to Seth was pure folly, she told herself. She really needed to start seeing someone. Carl had made it clear he admired her. There were other possibilities, too. Some of the Boatworks employees were available and interested, according to Ilsa.

"Hello, beautiful! All by yourself?" The voice, and the hard male arm that slid around her waist, belonged to Lamar Lennig. He grinned down at her as he held on tight.

"Actually, I'm with the family." Olivia succeeded in twisting free. "I've been working in the Cook's Corner. My shift just ended, and I'm on my way to fetch Sara."

"Let me buy you dinner first." He touched her mouth with a hard forefinger. "For old times' sake."

"No, thanks, Lamar." She shook her head and started to walk away.

"Hey, wait a minute." Catching her arm, Lamar pulled her around to face him. "What do I have to do, get down on my knees and beg?"

"Nope." Without making a big production out of it, Olivia tried to pull her arm free. When he wouldn't release her, she sighed. The only thing to do was very gently set him straight. "Let me go, Lamar. I'm not the girl you used to know. I'm a mother now, a straight arrow, a homebody. I'd bore you to tears in an hour."

"Baby, the way you look, you could never bore me." He moved closer, gripping her other arm as well.

Olivia glanced around. Although literally dozens of people she knew were nearby, the music prevented them from overhearing what was being said, even if anyone was paying attention, which no one seemed to be.

"Let me go, Lamar." The words were a quiet order.

"If you let me buy you supper."

"Thanks, but no." It was a definite refusal.

"Think you're too good for me now, Olivia? I've *had* you, remember? And if I was the daughter of the town slut turned suicide, I wouldn't think I was so all-fired high-and-mighty."

Ordinarily, the reminder that she'd been fool enough to sleep with him would have stung, but she was too stunned by what had come after. She gaped at him soundlessly, her eyes growing huge.

"Get the hell away from her, Lamar." The voice, with its dangerous, quiet threat, and the hands that came down on her shoulders, belonged to Seth. The solid strength of his hands kept her upright, even as she felt the color leach from her face and the world beyond the three of them blur.

Lamar looked at Seth, his expression belligerent. Then without another word he turned on his heel and walked away.

Olivia felt as if she had been kicked in the stomach.

"Seth . . ." she said piteously.

"Livvy." Seth turned her around to face him. "I heard what he said." His voice was grim. He looked quickly around. "We can't talk here." With another glance around he let go of her shoulders and caught one of her hands instead, his fingers entwining with hers. "Come with me."

He led her away from the festival, away from the music and lights and people, around the far side of the school to a gray metal door that led into the gym. The gym was deserted. She followed him across the basketball court to the locker rooms. He pushed open the door marked BOYS and pulled her in with him.

"Give me a minute to get dressed, okay?" With the part of her mind that remained capable of such things, she noticed that Seth was still wearing his soaked T-shirt and shorts and his shower thongs on his bare feet.

"Sit down." He pulled her to one of the long wooden benches with which the room was furnished and gently pushed her down on it. He moved a few paces away and opened one of the long, narrow lockers. His clothes—khaki pants, navy polo shirt, underwear, socks and shoes—were inside.

"Seth."

Bunching his clothes in one hand, he turned to look at her.

"Is it true?" Her voice was thin, high.

"Livvy . . ." He didn't have to say anything more. The answer was written all over his face.

Her eyes widened as if from a blow, and her mouth went suddenly dry. Her chest felt as if it were being crushed by lead weights.

"My God, Livvy, it was twenty years ago." Seth yanked his wet T-shirt over his head, dropped it on the floor, and replaced it with the dry polo shirt.

"He said my mother was a *suicide?*"

"Livvy." He sank down on the bench directly opposite her and leaned forward to take both her hands in his.

"Seth, please tell me. I need to know."

"You don't need to know. You never needed to know." His voice was rough. His eyes were dark with the reflection of her distress.

"Seth . . ." The rest of her plea trailed away unspoken. He knew her well enough. He could read it in her eyes.

"Okay. Okay." He glanced away from her, wet his lips, and looked back. "Your mother apparently just walked into the lake one night. She'd gone to bed earlier. Uncle James had been away for a couple of days, traveling on business. He got home a little after midnight, discovered his wife was missing, and started looking for her. There were a lot of people in the house that night, and everybody eventually spread out to search the grounds. Big John found Selena floating in the lake. Charlie tried to revive her—he'd been at the house with Belinda—but it was too late. Her death was later ruled a suicide."

Olivia held on tightly to his hands. "But why?" she asked. "Why did they think it was suicide?"

His eyes as she met them reflected her misery. "They said she'd been depressed in the weeks before it happened."

"Who said?"

"Charlie. Apparently she was taking some kind of medication."

"But why would she be depressed? What was wrong?"

"Livvy, can't you let this alone?"

"Seth, please."

Seth sucked in a breath, then let it out slowly. "They said she killed herself because she'd been having an affair and Uncle James had found out and was threatening to divorce her."

Olivia cringed. "Who was it? The man."

"I don't know. Hell, I don't even know if there was a man. That's just how the story was told to me."

"Oh, God." That explained it, then. Explained Lamar's remarks and Callie's odd hesitation when talking about Selena's death and even Seth's concern when he saw her walking into the lake.

"I should have been told this a long time ago."

"Why?" His hands tightened on hers. "It's over and done with, and it has nothing to do with you. Nothing to do with your life or the person you are. Nothing at all, you hear?"

He sounded so fierce that she managed a wavery smile for him. "I hear."

"Okay. Good. I'm going to put the rest of my clothes on now, and then I'm going to take you home."

Unable to say more, Olivia nodded.

Seth grabbed his clothes from the bench and headed into the anteroom that held the showers and toilets.

Left alone, Olivia slowly bent almost double, wrapping her arms around her legs and resting her head on her knees. Her head throbbed. Visions assailed her, startlingly real. Her mother—or was it herself?—was walking into the night-dark lake.

She was wearing a nightgown—an ankle-length flimsy white nylon nightgown with wide lace straps—and no shoes. She stepped into the water, and it rose around her, warm and brackish, just as it had the other day when she had stepped in it. Her bare feet sank deep into the mud. Water rose higher and higher, swirling about her as she waded out, wetting her nightgown to the knees, the waist . . .

Suddenly she was no longer a participant but an observer. From the vantage point of the lakeshore she watched her mother flounder and drown, helpless to do anything to alter what was happening. Tears filled her eyes; her grief was suddenly as overwhelming as if she were truly watching her mother drown.

"Livvy?" Seth was back in the room with her.

She heard him say her name, but she was powerless to turn off the grief.

He squatted down in front of her, his hands smoothing her hair back from her face. "Are you crying? Look at me."

She tried to stop. She took a deep gulp of air, but the gulp turned into a sob and the tears continued to flow.

"Livvy." He stood up, his hands circling her wrists, pulling her up with him.

She came to her feet, limp but unresisting. He pulled her against him, his arms closing around her, enfolding her icy body with his warmth.

She buried her face against his chest and cried as if her heart would break.

"Shh. Shh, Livvy. Don't cry. Please don't cry." Holding her tight, he rocked her back and forth.

His murmured attempts at consolation reached her, soothing the raw edges of her grief. Her tears lessened and finally stopped, and for a little while she was content to just rest against him. There was nowhere else on earth where she felt safer, Olivia realized. Nowhere else on earth that felt more like home.

He in turn seemed to be in no big hurry to let her go.

She should unlock her arms from around his waist, ease out of his arms, announce that she was all better now. Instead, she snuggled closer still, savoring the feel of him.

Somehow he must have sensed the alteration in her, because his body changed even as she held him. The muscles of his back tensed, and she could hear the acceleration of his heartbeat.

Olivia felt her own heart speed up. She looked up into his eyes. "Seth," she whispered.

"Olivia." His voice was thick, hoarse. He pulled her up on tiptoe as his mouth came down on hers with fierce hunger. If he hadn't been holding her up, she would have sunk bonelessly to the floor.

"Seth?" The locker-room door swooshed open, footsteps sounded on the tile floor, and Phillip's voice called out urgently, all at the same time.

Seth moved quickly, his head lifting, his body shifting so that his back blocked Phillip's view of her. From Phillip's sudden silence Olivia surmised that he was frozen in shock.

"What is it?" Seth turned his head to speak over his shoulder, his voice remarkably cool.

"God, I'm sorry. I had no idea. . . ." Phillip's voice trailed off, and he took a deep, obviously embarrassed breath. "Your mother's collapsed, Seth. She's been taken to the hospital."

CALLIE was sinking fast. An adverse reaction to chemotherapy had caused her collapse, and the chemotherapy had been, of necessity, discontinued. Her cancer, now overwhelmingly aggressive, invaded her body like a marauding army of killers. Her only hope lay in a bone-marrow transplant or in getting accepted for an experimental treatment. Charlie was frank in saying that she was not an ideal candidate for either. She was already too sick, too weak. Seth refused to accept that verdict. He worked the phone constantly, calling specialists in Boston, in Houston, in New York.

"Son, there are some things you just can't fix," Callie told him gently from her hospital bed.

Seth was an almost constant presence in her private hospital room, and Ira was almost as faithful. Otherwise, people were sitting with Callie in shifts, with everyone from Belinda to Keith to friends taking a turn. Everyone was heartbroken at what was happening, and no one wanted Callie to have to face it alone. Not even for a minute.

"But we don't know that *you're* one of those things that can't be fixed, Mother," Seth replied just as gently. He bent over his mother, taking her hand in his. Frail in her blue hospital gown, Callie clutched his hand tightly.

"Oh, Seth." Callie smiled up at him. "You're a fighter just like your father. That's one thing I never was."

"You are a fighter, Mother. You're going to fight this. And you're going to win." Seth bent down to kiss Callie's thin cheek, and with a quick, unreadable glance for Olivia, who sat in a chair near the head of her bed, he left the room.

Callie's gaze followed him. Then she turned to Olivia, unshed tears bright in her eyes. "That's the worst thing. I know he's going to have a hard time dealing with my being gone, and it just tears me up to think about it."

"Oh, Aunt Callie, please don't talk about being gone like that," Olivia pleaded, reaching for her aunt's hand. "Plenty of people survive cancer nowadays."

"Olivia, honey, I don't think I'm going to be one of them." Callie grimaced and groped for the dial on her tubing that allowed her to self-administer a dose of pain medication. Olivia turned it for her. After a moment Callie took a deep breath and produced a wavery smile. "I can't talk like this to Seth, because it upsets him. He's my only child, my son, and I love him more than anything in the world. But he can't deal with this."

Olivia could find nothing to say, so she simply held Callie's hand. Callie glanced past her out the window, where sunshine poured brightly down from a celestial blue sky.

"You know what I hate? I just hate it like the dickens that I'm going to miss Christmas. The idea that I won't ever see a Christmas tree again—that really bothers me. That's stupid, isn't it? To grieve over a Christmas tree?"

The tears that had been swimming in Olivia's eyes overflowed. Her hand tightened on Callie's. "No, it isn't stupid."

"Now you've got me crying, and I've got you crying, and the upshot of it is going to be that I'll wind up spending some of the most precious hours of my life with a stuffed-up nose and a raw throat." Callie took a deep breath and managed a weak chuckle. "Oh, Olivia, I'm so glad you came home when you did. Your being home at this time has been a blessing to me. It really has."

"I'm glad I came home, too." Olivia could hardly get the words out around the lump in her throat.

"It's going to be all right, honey. You'll see. In the end it'll be all right."

Mallory walked into the room then, carrying a huge bouquet of pink roses in a white china vase, her high heels clicking over the terrazzo floor. Olivia released Callie's hand and murmured a polite greeting to Mallory. As usual, the other woman was perfectly groomed, in a gray silk suit and pearls.

With a quick smile for Olivia, Mallory walked up the opposite side of the bed from where Olivia sat and placed the roses on the bedside table. Their scent perfumed the air.

"How are you doing?" Mallory asked Callie tenderly, bending over the older woman for a hug. The sunlight flashed on her diamond engagement ring, reminding Olivia again that Mallory was going to be Seth's wife. That kiss in the locker room had been an aberration, she told herself, and she would do well to keep that firmly in mind.

"I'm fine," Callie replied, summoning up her usual brisk manner for Mallory. "Now, you just sit right down here and tell the latest news on the wedding. Did you get that caterer you wanted?"

"Well, their estimate was higher than I expected. . . ." Mallory began, availing herself of Callie's invitation to sit.

The three of them chatted about the wedding—which was *not*, at the moment, Olivia's favorite topic—for a little while, and then Ira arrived along with Phillip and his wife. Olivia had seen Phillip at the hospital twice since he had come upon her with Seth. Not by word or glance had he indicated that he remembered anything about what he had seen. Olivia was grateful for that.

"Olivia." Callie caught her hand as Olivia stood up to leave. She was whispering as the others talked among themselves. "Bring Chloe up to see me later today, would you please?"

Looking down at her aunt, Olivia read the clear message in the now faded blue eyes. She nodded as if making a solemn promise, and Callie released her with a tired smile.

When Olivia returned with Chloe, it was just before suppertime. The curtain over the window was closed, and the room was only dimly lit. Callie appeared to be asleep, and Father Randolph, the rector from St. Luke's, was sitting beside the bed. He smiled, coming to his feet and walking over to join them as they stood rather awkwardly just inside the door.

"What have we here?" he whispered, nodding at the object Olivia held in one hand.

"Olivia thought Nana wanted a Christmas tree." Chloe sniffed. "I don't know why. It's not even Halloween yet."

Father Randolph exchanged glances with Olivia. In his eyes she read an exact understanding of the situation.

"It'll make her a wonderful night-light," was what he said. Taking it from Olivia, he set the foot-tall fully decorated artificial pine in the center of the bedside table, moving Mallory's roses to a larger table in the process. Then he plugged in the cord so that the tree was suddenly resplendent with twinkly red and green and blue and yellow lights. Olivia had bought it at a garden-supply center after leaving the hospital.

In the bed Callie stirred, awakened no doubt by their voices, and opened her eyes. Her head turned to the side, her attention apparently attracted by the blinking lights on the bedside table. When she saw the Christmas tree, her eyes widened and she went very still for a moment, just looking at it. Her lips trembled, and then a slow smile stretched her dry lips. Her gaze sought and found Olivia, who was standing with Chloe at the foot of the bed.

"Thank you," Callie said, and then her eyes were all for her granddaughter.

With an effort she hitched herself up a little higher in the bed and held out her hand. "Chloe." Her voice was noticeably weaker than it had been earlier that day.

"Nana," Chloe said on a sob, and then rushed around the bed to take her grandmother's hand.

Olivia and Father Randolph exchanged glances, and together silently withdrew to the hall, leaving the old woman and the young girl to say what would almost certainly be their good-byes.

THE bedside clock read 3:32 a.m. when the dream woke Olivia.

It was not pitch-black inside the room, but near enough to make little practical difference. The pouring rain outside precluded any moonlight from creeping through the curtains.

The dream had come to her the last three nights, each time with increasing intensity, so that she was starting to dread falling asleep. But oddly enough, in the dream, the drowning did not *feel* like a suicide. The emotion that came through was fear, not sorrow. The more she thought about it, the more convinced she grew that what she had been told about her mother's death was somehow wrong.

To make things worse, Sara, too, was having bad dreams. The vampire lightning-bug king was back. One night she had woken up screaming that it was coming to get her. Last night she had dreamed that it was in her room.

Tonight, though, all had been quiet. Except for her own nightmare, nothing had occurred to disturb Olivia's rest. Still, she found it difficult to sleep.

She lay in bed, breathing in and out with quiet concentration, struggling to banish the last fragments of horror.

It did not help knowing that tonight there were only four people in this vast pile of a house: she and Sara in this wing, Chloe and Martha in the other. The house felt empty without Seth and Callie in it.

Suddenly she heard something. Footsteps. She was almost certain it was footsteps on the gallery. Firm, heavy footsteps.

A man's footsteps.

She listened again carefully, straining to hear over the steady rush of the rain.

But try though she might, she heard nothing more.

She lay in her warm, comfortable bed a moment longer, listening so hard that her head ached. Who could be out on the gallery in the middle of the night? Maybe, just maybe, something—someone— really *was* sneaking into Sara's room as she slept. Just considering the possibility made Olivia's blood run cold.

Throwing back the covers, she got out of bed. Leaving the light off so as not to warn away anyone who might still be outside, she crept into the hall and opened the door to Sara's room.

She was safe. Olivia's stomach settled, but she still didn't think she had imagined those footsteps on the gallery.

Closing Sara's door behind her, she returned to her own room, crossed to the nearer of the two windows, and pulled the drape aside. Moving as silently as she could, she unlatched the window, opened it partway, and stepped out onto the gallery.

A rush of rain-cooled air scented with honeysuckle and sodden earth greeted her. Olivia looked cautiously up and down. The gallery was alive with shape-shifting shadows, its far ends obscured enough to conceal all manner of intruders. From somewhere to her right came a series of soft, repetitive sounds, the origins of which were lost in the gloom, muffled almost to the point of extinction by the gentle roar of the falling rain.

She should go back inside right now and lock her window tightly behind her.

She was just about to take her own advice when she perceived that one of the rocking chairs at the far end of the gallery was moving, its rockers grating against the gallery's plank floor.

Someone was in the chair.

She could just make out a dark form blotting out the whiteness of the seat and back and arms of the chair. Thoughts of ghosts and zombies and all kinds of freaky possibilities whirled through her mind, but then she realized that there was something familiar about the sitter's sprawled posture.

"Seth?" she whispered, staring.

There was no answer. The chair continued to move without pause. But somehow she was certain it was he.

"Seth?" She walked toward him. Beyond the porch eaves the rain fell in a dark, translucent curtain. Intermittent gusts of rain-scented air set her blush-pink nylon gown to fluttering about her ankles like wings.

"Seth?" It *was* him. He was staring out into the darkness as he pushed the rocking chair rhythmically back and forth.

Something was wrong. Olivia knew it. Resting a hand atop the chair back, she looked down at him.

"Aunt Callie?" she asked in a dry, constricted voice.

He looked up at her then, his eyes glinting. "Mother died at one seventeen." His voice was utterly calm.

Olivia gasped, her hand flying to cover her mouth.

"Oh, no," she said when she could speak. Tears sprang to her eyes and began to trickle down her cheeks. "Oh, Seth, I'm so sorry!"

"I decided to wait and tell Chloe in the morning." The chair began to move again, back and forth, back and forth, in a terrible rhythm of sorrow and control.

He grimaced. "I stayed until they came to take her away. Walking out of there and leaving my mother in that room with strangers was the hardest thing I've ever done in my life."

"Oh, Seth," Olivia said again, helplessly. She leaned down to hug him, her arms sliding around his shoulders.

"Livvy," he said. Hooking an arm around her waist, he pulled her down onto his lap. She buried her face against his shoulder as tears poured from her eyes like the rain beyond the gallery. She cried for him, because he would not. And for Aunt Callie and herself and Chloe and Ira, and for all the others who had loved Callie Archer and would grieve for her, too.

Seth held her while she cried. She could feel the steady rise and fall of his chest as he breathed, the hard muscles of his arms.

"She talked to me, a little," he said eventually. "Just before she . . ." His voice broke off, and he inhaled sharply. It was obvious that he could not go on.

Olivia lifted her head from the cradle of his shoulder and looked at him. His face was taut with sorrow, but it was his eyes that were the worst. They were dark and liquid, gazing not at her but out into the night, with the glazed look of a creature in terrible pain.

"Seth," she whispered. She kissed him gently, meaning to ease his sorrow. But his reaction caught her by surprise.

He looked full into her eyes, and then he kissed her deeply, ravenously. Her body quickened, throbbed. All thoughts of loss, of grief, of before and after, faded, to be replaced by the now.

Seth was kissing her. There was nothing beyond this.

His mouth lifted away from hers, and he stood abruptly with her in his arms. Carrying her, he walked with long, deliberate strides to the window that she had left open.

He took a deep breath and stopped, looking down into her face. "Livvy," he said, his voice not quite steady. "If you don't want me to make love to you, now is the time to say so."

She lifted her head from his shoulder and met his gaze.

"I want you to," she whispered, her hands tightening around his neck. His eyes gleamed down at her, and the corners of his mouth tightened briefly in acknowledgment.

Then he shouldered his way through her window, took the few strides he needed to cross the room, and laid her down very gently on her bed.

THE few days until Callie's funeral passed in a blur for Olivia. There were phone calls to be made, houseguests to be seen to, and Sara and Chloe to be taken care of, as well as a thousand and one other chores that left her no time to think or feel.

Seth was even busier than she was, and, she suspected, he welcomed the constant activity for the same reason she did: It kept him from having to deal with his emotions. She scarcely saw him, and never alone, which was just as well, because every time she remembered the intimacy of the things they had done together in her bed, she wanted to blush.

Clearly he had put that night behind him. Not by word or gesture did he indicate to her that he saw her any differently than he had before. Once he walked out of her bedroom, it was as though nothing between them had changed.

The hardest thing was watching Seth with Mallory. She was very much in evidence, standing with the family at the funeral home, giving directions to Martha and the other help, and acting as hostess at the house. Olivia seethed with jealousy whenever Mallory was near, and she ached for Seth to wrap his arms around her.

The strain of juggling so many emotional balls must have shown on her face, because on the night before the funeral—it was to be held at eleven o'clock Thursday at St. Luke's—Charlie came up to her as she was refilling the coffee urn in the dining room and asked with some concern how she was holding up.

"You look pale," he said, his hazel eyes kind as they moved over her face. "Are you getting enough sleep?"

Olivia smiled affectionately at him. The short answer was no. So that Chloe would not be alone at night—the time, as she knew from experience, when grief weighs the heaviest—she had set up Sara's room as slumber-party central. Sara and Chloe constructed a tent from quilts, furnished it with sleeping bags, and brought in a TV with a VCR, tapes, books, and snacks. The girls kept her awake till midnight or later every night. After exhaustion finally claimed them, thoughts of Seth and Mallory plagued Olivia. And then, when she finally did manage to fall asleep, her mother's death haunted her dreams, in ever more excruciating detail.

She woke up every night about three thirty a.m., bathed in sweat and terrified. And that wasn't all. One night, just as she was about to close her eyes, she could have sworn she saw the rocking chair in the corner move as if someone were rocking there. Another time, right after the girls had gone to sleep, she'd looked into the gilt-framed mirror that had been hers as a child and gotten the uncanny sensation that the face looking back at her was her mother's.

"No," she said impulsively in reply to Charlie's question, turning to face him and placing a hand on his arm. "I'm not sleeping well. Seth told me not long ago that my mother . . . committed suicide, when I always thought her death was an accidental drowning. I've been having nightmares about it. Seth also said that you tried to revive her the night she died and you'd been treating her for depression prior to that. Is that true?"

Charlie looked taken aback, but he nodded slowly. "I don't know why he told you that. But yes, it's true."

Olivia glanced around as a couple of neighbors wandered in for coffee and dessert. She lowered her voice. "In my dream, when I see the whole thing happening, it doesn't *feel* like she's committing suicide. I think that's what's really bothering me."

Charlie, too, glanced at the people behind them. "If you really want to talk about it, stop by my office next week," he said quietly. "I'll be glad to tell you everything I know."

Olivia nodded and would have said more, but at that moment Mallory appeared in the doorway, her gaze going straight to Olivia, her mouth thin-lipped with rage.

"She cut it up." Mallory spoke under her breath, but her fury was obvious when Olivia, in response to an imperious gesture, joined her in the front hall. At Olivia's questioning look Mallory was more specific. "Chloe took scissors and cut up the dress I bought her to wear to the funeral."

"Oh, no," Olivia said, shocked. "Oh, dear. Are you sure *Chloe* did it? Maybe the kittens clawed it or something."

This attempt to shield Chloe earned Olivia a black look.

"I asked her if she'd tried on the dress yet. She said right to my face that she wasn't going to have to wear it, because she had turned it into rags. I didn't believe her—I thought surely no child, not even Chloe, could be that deliberately destructive—but I went to her closet and looked. She was telling the truth. The scissors were right there on the floor under the dress. She cut it up!"

Olivia sighed. "I'll talk to her," she said. "She was very wrong to do it, and she'll apologize, I'm sure. But—"

Mallory cut her off furiously. "I don't know why I'm even talking to you. The person to handle this is Seth."

Turning on her heel, Mallory stalked away, passing through the open doors into the large antiques-filled living room. Olivia turned and headed in search of Chloe. Martha directed her to the children, on the back veranda just outside the kitchen.

"Chloe, could I speak to you, please?" Olivia called.

Chloe ignored Olivia's summons. Olivia called her again, more sternly this time. Chloe threw her a dirty look, but this time she came over.

"What?" she asked, borderline rude.

Olivia asked her quietly, "Did you cut up that beautiful dress Mallory bought you to wear tomorrow?"

Chloe met Olivia's gaze defiantly. "I told her I wasn't going to wear it, and I meant it."

Seriously concerned by what the destructiveness and defiance of the act said about the little girl's state of mind, Olivia hunkered down in front of her.

"Chloe, honey, why on earth would you do such a thing?"

"That's exactly what I want to know." Seth spoke without warning, making Olivia and Chloe jump. A glance back told Olivia that he was standing behind her, frowning at his daughter, holding the mutilated dress in one hand. One horrified look showed Olivia that the garment had, indeed, been ruined. The black taffeta skirt and white lace petticoat had been cut into ragged strips that fluttered like kites' tails.

"Well, Chloe?" Seth asked.

Chloe crossed her legs in front of her, rested her hands on her knees, and gazed up at her father mutinously. "I don't have to wear what Mallory tells me. She's not my mother!"

"You're right, Chloe. Mallory is not your mother, but that is no excuse that I can see for the deliberate destruction of a perfectly beautiful dress that she gave you." His voice was grimmer than Olivia would have hoped. Chloe was grieving, too. He—they all—needed to take it easy with her.

Chloe glared at him. Then her lower lip began to tremble, and her eyes filled with tears.

"You hate me, don't you?" she cried, jumping to her feet. "Everybody hates me now that Nana is dead! Everybody!"

Bursting into tears, she turned and ran down the back steps, then disappeared into the dark around the side of the house.

"Chloe!" Seth yelled after her. Then, bitterly, as it became obvious that Chloe was long gone, he added, "Damn it!"

He looked at Olivia with a weary sigh. "Should I go after her? Or leave it alone?"

"Go after her."

Seth looked at Olivia for the briefest of moments, then picked up her hand and carried it to his mouth, pressing the back of it to his lips. Before she could say anything, he released her hand, handed her the mutilated dress, and ran in pursuit of Chloe.

HE DIDN'T need this right now. He really didn't. Just getting through this thing hour by hour was taking every bit of fortitude he possessed. He didn't need any more problems.

But as he kept reminding himself, Chloe was only eight years old, and she was grieving, too. Poor little girl. He'd better remember that he was all she had left.

Thank God for Livvy. She was keeping Chloe busy, watching out for her. She was helping him, too. He would be lost if he did not have the memory of their lovemaking to sustain him. Knowing she was going to be there when this was all over gave him a light to steer for through the fog of his grief.

If he could only get through the next few hours, through tonight and his mother's funeral tomorrow, then he could turn his attention to sorting out the rest of his life.

Chloe was huddled on the top step of the gazebo. Seth would never have seen her if she hadn't sniffled loudly as he walked by. He turned his head in response to the sound, and there she was, her arms wrapped around her blue-jeaned legs.

"Hey," he said softly. He wished he had some pet name for her that he could use to kind of warm things up, like he'd heard Livvy call Sara "pumpkin" more times than he cared to count, but he couldn't think of one. "We need to talk."

He climbed the steps and sat down beside her.

Tightening her arms around her legs, Chloe cast him a glance before looking away. But at least she didn't run. In the annals of his relationship with his daughter, that, Seth thought with a touch of gallows humor, was a positive sign.

"Nana told me I should wear my blue dress with the daisies on it to her funeral," Chloe disclosed before Seth could say anything. "She said that it was her very favorite, and if she looked down from heaven and saw me wearing it, that would be like a secret message between us. So that's the dress I'm going to wear, not some stupid fancy black one that *Mallory* bought me."

Seth ignored the belligerence of that speech and the nasty tone in which she said Mallory's name, too. He zeroed in on the really important part.

"*Nana* told you that?" he questioned carefully. "When?"

"When Olivia took me to the hospital to say good-bye. Nana told me to wear my blue dress, and that's what I'm going to do."

"Olivia took you to say good-bye to Nana? When?"

"Sunday afternoon." Chloe shot him a quick, almost wary glance. "Nana said I shouldn't tell you, because it would make you too sad to know we had to say good-bye. But I thought you better understand about the dress."

Seth felt unexpected tears sting his eyes. His throat tightened at the idea of his mother and daughter conspiring to shield him from pain.

"Are you still mad about the dress?" Chloe asked in a small voice.

Seth shook his head. He didn't try to speak.

"Nana said you were going to be really sad after she died. She said that I would be sad, too. But she said she'd still be with us all the time. And she said that if we wanted to talk to her, all we had to do was come outside on a night when there were lots of stars, like tonight, and pick the star that twinkled the most, and that would be her waving at us." Chloe looked up into the sky and pointed. "See that star over there? I bet that's her. I already waved."

Seth looked where Chloe pointed, and saw a large, bright star not too far above the western horizon that did indeed, when seen through tear-filled eyes, seem to blink.

"So don't be sad, Daddy," Chloe said softly, her gaze earnest. "Nana's still with us. We just can't see her anymore."

Seth felt as though a huge hand was squeezing his heart. Here was his little girl, all of eight years old, trying to comfort *him*. He didn't deserve her.

"Chloe," he began. Suddenly the name that he had called her as an always smiling toddler, before things had started going wrong between him and Jennifer, came back to him. "Honey-bug, I love you. I know I don't say it much, but I do. You and me, we're a team. If we stick together, we can get through this thing all right." Seth wrapped both arms around her, pulling her close. Suddenly hugging her didn't seem awkward at all. It felt right.

"Daddy," Chloe said, "you haven't called me honey-bug for a long time."

"I just remembered," he answered truthfully.

The two of them sat together in the moon-washed darkness, talking and looking up at the one blinky star in a star-filled sky.

Crowley, Louisiana—July 4, 1978. Savannah De Hart was too excited to sleep. It was not yet dawn on the morning of the Fourth of July, which was, after Christmas, her very favorite holiday. It was even better than her birthday, because she had to share her birthday with her twin, Samantha. And *this* Fourth of July was special. Yesterday she had been crowned Little Miss Rice at the Old Crowley Rice Society Celebration, and today she would get to ride on the very top of the Rice Society float in the town's parade, wearing her crown and her sash and waving as she passed.

She and Samantha were identical twins, but she could sing and dance a little better than Samantha. That, plus her sparkly personality, as Mommy called it, was why she had won.

Savannah was trying her best to go to sleep. If she didn't, she wouldn't look her best for the parade tomorrow. She lay still, concentrating fiercely on sleep, but finally she couldn't resist taking one more peep at her crown and sash and pageant dress that were all laid out on the chair by the dresser, ready for her to put on for the parade.

There was something in front of the chair, blocking her view. Even as Savannah squinted at it, trying to make out what it was through the darkness, it moved toward her.

"Samantha?" she asked uncertainly, sitting up. But even as she said it, she knew it wasn't Samantha.

She knew, too, that she was in danger, with a dead-on instinct as old as humankind. Terror raced down her spine, and she screamed, only to have the cry immediately choked off by something wet and smelly that was shoved into her face, choking her, at the same time that a hand grabbed the back of her head.

Mommy, she cried, but only in her mind, as she plunged down into a darkness from which there would be no escape.

PICKING victims was both an art and a science, he mused, suppressing the urge to whistle cheerfully as he let himself out the front door of the house—child, crown, sash, and dress slung together in the laundry sack he carried over his shoulder. He'd seen Little Miss Rice at the pageant yesterday, for example, and known instantly that she was perfect for him. Her house was no problem. A five-year-old with a screwdriver could have broken in.

He was amassing quite a collection. There was Becca, who he had to admit was kind of nondescript, because he'd taken her before he'd really known what he was doing. But still, he valued her because she was the first. His muse, if you would. Then there was Maggie, with all that short, frothy yellow-blond hair. And this one, who looked like a little Snow White—she would be the centerpiece, with her crown and sash and dress.

Perhaps, he mused, as, cargo loaded, he drove away down Route 13, he should consider branching out. Go for something a little more ethnic next time.

CALLIE Archer was laid to rest beside her long-dead husband in the family cemetery above the lake. When the time came for Big John to be buried, he would join her there, in the remaining half of the gravesite now occupied by his wife, Marguerite. With the addition of those two the private cemetery would be out of room. The remaining Archers would be buried in the graveyard beside St. Luke's.

Olivia had not been near the place in years. As a child, she had been a fairly frequent visitor, moving from monument to monument, always seeking one particular name. She had never understood why her mother wasn't there beside her stepfather. Once, when she had asked, what they told her made no sense: Her mother had been *cremated*. Now, of course, she understood what that word meant, and she knew, too, with her fresh, terrible knowledge, why it had been done. As a suicide, Selena Archer would not have been permitted to await eternity in hallowed ground.

The pain of that truth was so intense that Olivia immediately strove to banish the thought from her mind.

"Mom, you're squeezing my hand too tight," Sara whispered from beside her, tugging to free her fingers.

"Oh, sorry." Loosening her grip with a quick, apologetic smile for her daughter, Olivia felt some of her pain ease. Sweet Sara, with her wide brown eyes and earnest face, was the present and the future. Olivia's mother belonged to the past and, for today, should be left there.

The Archer family cemetery had been designed to honor the original owner of LaAngelle Plantation, Colonel Robert John Archer, and his wife and descendants. His mausoleum dominated the graveyard. Built of white marble turned creamy yellow with age, it was fashioned like a miniature Greek temple, with an elaborately carved portico, a quartet of fluted columns, and twin life-size marble angels guarding the long-closed door.

The group assembled for the graveside service was considerably smaller than the crowd that had thronged to the funeral service proper in town. St. Luke's had been full to overflowing, but this final farewell was limited to Callie's family and very close friends.

They gathered around the polished walnut coffin, which was covered with a blanket of white lilies; more flowers were massed on the grass just beyond the open grave. Seth and Chloe—he in a black business suit and she in an incongruously cheerful blue dress with daisies appliquéd around the hem—stood hand in hand before the casket. Seth's face was pale and haggard, his eyes red-rimmed, but he was outwardly composed.

Mallory, in a formfitting black knit dress, stood on Seth's other side clutching a prayer book, her engagement ring glinting in the sun every time she moved her hand. Olivia tried not to think about that engagement ring or, for that matter, about the engagement. But the stab of jealousy she felt whenever Mallory leaned against Seth, or took hold of his arm, or tiptoed to murmur something in his ear, pierced even the dark cloud of her grief.

When Father Randolph intoned the traditional " . . . ashes to ashes, dust to dust," Ira burst into noisy sobs and turned away, hiding his face in his hands. Answering tears flowed down Olivia's cheeks. To think that Callie had finally found love again after so many years, only to lose it so soon to death, added another degree of sorrow to her feeling of aching loss. She stood with her head bowed, listening with numb grief until the service ended.

Then she looked up just in time to see, through the film of her tears, Mallory step into Seth's arms, where she was warmly embraced as his head bent over hers.

Obviously Seth didn't need any comfort Olivia might have to offer.

THE following week life at LaAngelle Plantation more or less resumed its usual rhythms. If there was a sense of profound loss in the air, they all labored to ignore it. Meals still had to be eaten, wages earned. Life had to go on.

David and Keith had flown to California immediately after the funeral. They were scheduled to return on Monday afternoon. Chloe was once again sleeping in her own room. Olivia and Sara stayed where they were.

As was her routine before Callie was hospitalized, Olivia got the girls ready on Monday morning and drove them to school, then went on to the Boatworks. Seth had been at work for nearly two hours when Olivia arrived. The door to his office was closed, and she assumed that he was inside, although he could just as easily have been anywhere about the place. She knew he hadn't been sleeping well. Twice since the funeral she had heard him in the wee hours of the morning walking up and down the gallery. She had not gone outside to comfort him. Doing so once had already done far too much damage to their relationship—and her heart.

It felt good to be at work, good to be busy, good to talk to people about the normal everyday minutiae of life. After spending the first hour or so of the workday being very quiet out of deference to the family's loss, Ilsa was, by midmorning, chattering away. Everyone Olivia talked to was pretty much the same way; a few minutes of respectful decorum and then business as usual.

Looking unbelievably slender in a navy-blue skirted suit, Mallory came breezing in about fifteen minutes before lunchtime, carrying an embossed white folder in one hand.

"Hello, Olivia. Hi, Ilsa." Mallory greeted the two women in the outer office with a breezy smile. She leaned a hand on Olivia's desk and asked confidentially, "How's he doing?"

Olivia smiled with as much affability as she could muster. "As far as I know, he's doing fine."

"I'm glad to hear it. The invitations finally came in, and I wanted Seth to take one last look at them before I have them addressed and sent out. I know the timing's a little insensitive, but the wedding's in six weeks. And Callie *did* say she didn't want us to postpone anything because of her." Mallory straightened with a smile, opened the folder, and scooted it across the desk so that Olivia could see. "What do you think?"

Mallory Bridgehampton Hodges
and Michael Seth Archer
Request the Honor of Your Presence
At the Celebration of Their Marriage . . .

Olivia couldn't stand to read any more. She was in love with Seth. The knowledge jumped out at her without warning, and as Olivia absorbed it, she felt light-headed, short of breath.

Oh, no. Oh, no. Oh, no, Olivia thought in a panic, pushing her chair back from the desk. "I'm going to the rest room," she announced, and fled.

When she came back, having bathed her face and held her wrists under cold running water until the light-headedness subsided, Ilsa was alone in the outer office.

"You okay?" she asked with concern. Olivia nodded, sitting back down in front of the computer screen. Ilsa seemed to take her at her word. Still, Olivia was glad of the distraction when Phillip and Carl walked into the office together moments later.

"He in?" Phillip asked, nodding toward Seth's closed door.

Ilsa shook her head. "He and Mallory went to lunch."

"Speaking of lunch"—Carl grinned down at Olivia—"how about letting me buy you a sandwich? Chicken salad's on special at the inn today."

Carl had been asking her out for as long as she had been back in LaAngelle. Olivia just as regularly had turned him down. She started to refuse again, but then she caught herself.

Carl wasn't exactly the man of her dreams, but he would do in an emergency. And this qualified as an emergency.

"Sounds good," she said. He, Phillip, and Ilsa looked equally surprised as Olivia got to her feet.

SETH WAS SEATED IN OLIVIA'S chair behind the computer when she and Carl walked into the outer office. He looked thoroughly put out about something. Maybe—and this was cheering—maybe Mallory had done something to make him cross.

"Did you two have a nice lunch?" Seth asked too politely, his gaze raking Olivia before moving to fix on Carl.

"Very nice." Olivia smiled brightly at Seth as she slipped her nubby gold blazer off her shoulders and hung it in the closet near the door. "So nice, in fact, that we're going to Baton Rouge on Friday to go dancing."

"Oh, really?" Seth's eyes narrowed.

"Hey, hey, hey, that's great! I could've sworn you were gonna say no." Carl was all affable charm as he grinned at Olivia from the opposite side of the desk. Olivia, still standing, smiled back at him, knowing that she was probably making another mistake by encouraging Carl and, at the moment, not particularly caring. Seth, still seated in her chair, did not smile.

"Didn't you have a meeting with a client at one?" Seth's gaze was fixed on Carl now, and there was a definite edge to his voice.

Carl's expression changed ludicrously. "Oh, my God!" He slapped his forehead guiltily. "I completely forgot."

"I gathered that." Seth glanced at Olivia as if he knew precisely where to place the blame—on her. He stood up. "Mr. Crowell waited for about thirty minutes, then stormed out. I don't think we'll be building a boat for him anytime soon."

"Oh, man, I'm *sorry*." Carl groaned.

Seth's gaze shifted to Olivia, his expression grim. "There's a reason lunch is set for *an hour,* from noon until one."

"Does that time limit apply to everyone?" Olivia asked, sweet as pie. "Obviously *you* weren't back from lunch until after Mr. Crowell had left, or you would have taken care of him yourself."

Seth's eyes narrowed. Carl looked horrified. From behind Seth's back Ilsa shook her head in a frantic *no*. But Olivia didn't care if she *was* antagonizing him. Her heart was breaking, it was all Seth's fault, and he didn't care.

Carl rushed hurriedly into speech before Seth could say anything. "I'll call Mr. Crowell back right now and apologize." As he exited, he called over his shoulder, "Thanks for lunch, Olivia. I'll get back to you about Friday."

There was a moment of silence. Then Ilsa ostentatiously turned back to her filing, and Seth, in a carefully neutral voice, said, "Would you come into my office for a minute, please, Olivia?"

"Certainly," Olivia answered as coolly as he had spoken. She lifted her chin and straightened her spine. Seth was politely holding the door open. She sailed by him without so much as a sideways glance. He closed it behind her.

"I don't want you dating Carl," Seth said abruptly, leaning back against the closed door as Olivia turned to face him.

"Oh, really?" she asked. Resting her hip on his desk, she gave her head a toss. "And why is that?"

"Because it will only cause trouble. I have enough on my plate right now without worrying about what's going on with you and Carl."

"I can't go dancing with Carl because it's going to *worry* you?" Olivia couldn't believe it. "Well, guess what? I don't care!"

"I broke up with Mallory today," he said mildly, catching her by surprise.

Olivia's eyes widened as his words penetrated. Her indignation fizzled out like a deflating balloon. "You broke up with Mallory? You broke your engagement?"

"That's what I said." He came away from the door, moving toward her.

"But she had the wedding invitations with her."

"I know. I felt—feel—pretty bad about it, I must admit. But the only alternative was to marry her, and I finally figured out that I don't want to do that."

He was standing in front of her now, not touching her but close, a smile lurking around the corners of his mouth.

Still leaning against his desk, Olivia looked up into his eyes. "And this is supposed to interest me—why?"

This time he really did smile. "I don't know," he said. "I thought we might kind of pick up where we left off."

"Where we left off?" Her heart was thudding in her breast.

"Unless you just went to bed with me to be kind." He picked up her hand and carried it to his mouth. Olivia felt the moist heat of his lips on her skin with every fiber of her being. "*Were* you just being kind to your grief-stricken cousin, Livvy?"

"You're not my cousin," Olivia said fiercely, and threw herself into his arms. Her hands locked behind his neck, and his arms wrapped around her waist.

"No, I'm not, thank God," he said, and kissed her.

The intercom on his desk shrilled, interrupting.

Seth groped for the ringing instrument without releasing her. He punched a button and growled, "What?"

"Mr. Archer, your two-thirty appointment is here." Ilsa's voice sounded as if she were in the room with them.

"Give me one minute." Seth punched the button to turn the intercom off. He found her mouth, kissed her again, then slid his lips along her cheek.

"Seth." Olivia strove to keep a cool head. She was so happy, so deliriously happy, that all she wanted to do was be with him every moment for the rest of her life. But there were difficulties that had to be faced. "Chloe might not like the idea that we're—involved. She likes me now, but . . ."

"Involved? Good word. I like it."

"I think we should be discreet in front of the girls. I . . ."

"Don't worry about Chloe. She likes you. She never did like Mallory. She told me Mallory was only nice to her because she was trying to hook me."

"Chloe has her moments, but no one can say she's not smart." Olivia pulled out of his arms. "You need to get back to work. And I need to go pick up Sara and Chloe. We can talk later."

He put his hands on either side of her face, tilted it up to his, kissed her mouth, and looked down at her consideringly. Then he grinned. "Try to look as grouchy as you did when you came in," he whispered teasingly in her ear. "And remember to tell Carl that going dancing on Friday is out."

Before Olivia could reply, Seth pulled the door open. "Niko!" he said affably, moving around Olivia to shake the client's hand. "Come on into my office, and I'll show you the plans we've drawn up for the *Athena*. She'll be magnificent."

The two men went into Seth's office and closed the door. Olivia escaped with a smile and a quick good-bye for Ilsa, grabbing purse and blazer and hurrying out the door.

SETH got home at a little after five, which was extremely early for him. Olivia was sitting at the kitchen table surrounded by seven little girls in brown uniforms, all busy gluing Popsicle sticks together to make bird feeders.

"Brownie troop," she said by way of explanation as he met her gaze, and she smiled at him.

"Oh," he said, and smiled back. His eyes were dazzlingly blue, she thought, and his mouth . . . She had to fight the urge to stand up, walk to the door, throw her arms around his neck, and kiss him.

Not in front of the girls, she reminded herself.

"Daddy!" Looking up from her bird feeder at last, Chloe greeted him with a smile. "You're home early!"

"Yup." He strolled over to where she was sitting, placed a hand on her shoulder, and looked down at her Popsicle-stick creation. "Great job, honey-bug. Uh, what is it?"

The girls all giggled at his ignorance.

"A bird feeder!" Chloe said indignantly. "Olivia showed us how to make them. We're going to sell them at the carnival."

"Oh." Seth nodded as if he knew just what she was talking about. "Hello, Sara."

"Hi, Seth." Sara awarded him a beaming smile.

"The Christmas carnival at school," Olivia clarified, wiping her hands. "The Brownies have their own booth this year. You know all the girls, don't you, Seth?" Olivia asked casually. To tell the truth, she doubted that he did. In any case, without waiting for his answer, she introduced them, gesturing at each one in turn.

"Katie Evans, Tiffany Holt, Mary Frances Bernard, Shannon McNulty, Ginny Zigler. Say hi to Mr. Archer, girls."

"Hi, Mr. Archer," they chorused dutifully.

Seth smiled and nodded. And looked at Olivia again.

"We'll be finished here in a few minutes. The girls get picked up at five thirty."

"Oh." Seth's eyes met hers. "Where's Martha?"

"Gone to visit her daughter. She'll be back about six."

"I'm going to go up and change clothes," Seth said. "I'll be down again in a few minutes."

"We'll be here," Olivia said, smiling at him again.

"Mrs. Morrison, are we going to paint them today?" Mary Frances asked.

"No, not today. We have to let the glue dry really well first. We'll paint them next week." Seth left the room as Olivia answered. Her gaze followed him until she realized what she was doing. Then she forced her attention back to the girls and their project.

By the time Seth came back downstairs, the bird feeders were lined up on the kitchen counter to dry and the girls were playing in the backyard.

"Where is everybody?" Seth asked, looking around as he came through the swinging door.

"Outside." Olivia was washing her hands in the kitchen sink. He came up behind her, wrapped his arms around her waist, and kissed the back of her neck, which her casual upsweep had bared. A shiver of pure pleasure raced down Olivia's spine.

"You give this place a heart," he said. "I don't think I could face this house right now if you weren't in it."

She turned and saw the pain flare in his eyes.

"Oh, Seth, I know you're hurting," she said. She kissed him softly. "We're all hurting. Everyone who loved your mother. But I know you're hurting most of all. I wish I knew something that would take away the pain."

"Livvy"—he took a deep breath when she slid her mouth across his bristly cheek—"you take away the pain." He kissed her again. When he lifted his head, they were both breathing hard.

"Okay, I think we'd better call a halt," he said after a second, lifting himself away from her with obvious reluctance. He looked at her. "I have a great idea. How about we all—you, me, Sara, and Chloe—go out for pizza?"

Olivia took a deep, steadying breath. Her pulse was racing, but overriding her desire was delight that he had thought of taking Chloe and Sara on an outing.

The smile she gave him sparkled. "That sounds wonderful!"

His eyes moved over her. He didn't have to say it for her to know he found her beautiful. It was there in his eyes.

GOING out for pizza was fun. The four of them sat in a booth in Guido's, which had just opened in a storefront on West Main. The surroundings were spartan, but the pizza—made by the wife of a Boatworks' employee—was great.

Apparently half the town agreed. The place was packed by seven, and people were coming in and out constantly to pick up carryout pizza. Everyone knew Seth, of course, and most everyone knew Olivia. Greetings were exchanged and speculative looks cast their way. She and Seth and their daughters going out for pizza should not have provoked any comment—it was a perfectly innocent activity—but in LaAngelle, given Seth's stature in the community, there was going to be a lot of buzz. Once it was learned that he was no longer engaged to Mallory, the buzz would turn into a roar.

When they got home, Martha was in the kitchen gossiping with Keith. He'd flown into Baton Rouge with David not long before and driven on out to LaAngelle Plantation while David stopped off at the hospital to visit Big John. Martha and Keith had gotten to be good friends over the last few weeks. Like army buddies, they'd shared a lot of KP duties.

As usual, Olivia supervised homework at the kitchen table. By the time the girls had finished, picked out what they were going to wear the next day, and had their baths, it was after ten.

Routines were good, Olivia reflected as she brushed out her hair. They lent an aura of normalcy to day-to-day living, even when the household could never, in the wake of Callie's death, be as it was. She applied a dab of perfume, then went downstairs again. Seth had said he would be waiting in the den. Olivia smiled with anticipation.

He was indeed waiting for her in the den. He was sitting on the yellow chintz couch, talking to David, Keith, and Martha. Taking in this group, Olivia had to smile. So much for being private with Seth. He must have thought the same thing, because when she walked into the room, he looked up, met her eyes, and gave her a rueful smile.

"Oh, Olivia, Carl called for you. Something about Friday. I left the message in the kitchen," Martha said.

Seth's eyes narrowed.

"Thanks, Martha." She was, of course, going to tell Carl that she couldn't go out with him on Friday.

Seth stood up. "If you think he ought to be transferred to another hospital, I have no objection," he said to David. "Charlie doesn't seem to think it's a good idea, though."

"He's not showing any improvement where he is," David said.

"We can talk about it some more tomorrow." Seth shifted his attention to Olivia. "Feel like getting some fresh air?"

Olivia nodded. Out of the corner of her eye she saw Keith look significantly at David. Martha's eyes widened.

"Good night, all," Seth said over his shoulder, and followed Olivia out of the room to an answering chorus of good-nights.

Once outside on the veranda, with the front door shut behind them, Olivia stopped and took a gulp of warm honeysuckle-scented night air. Seth, standing beside her, grinned down at her.

"Think they're talking about us?"

"Oh, yeah."

"It's going to get worse before it gets better. Can you take the heat?"

Olivia shrugged fatalistically. "Considering the alternative is giving you back to Mallory, I guess I can."

Seth turned her around to face him, his hands on her arms.

"By the way, when you talk to Carl, you had better explain exactly why you won't be going out with him, because if he comes sniffing around the front office every day like he has been, I'm liable to break his nose."

Olivia grinned. "Jealous," she said reprovingly. Her arms slid up around his neck.

"Damn right." He seemed suddenly restless. "Want to go for a walk?"

Olivia shook her head. "Not really."

"What do you want to do, then?" He sounded faintly impatient.

"Oh, I don't know. I thought we might go—upstairs." Her eyes twinkled up at him.

They turned as one toward the door and stopped dead, exchanging bemused glances.

"They'll see us," Olivia said hollowly.

Seth ran a hand through his hair in frustration. Then he gripped her hand, pulling her along the front of the house. "I've got a plan."

"What?"

"We'll sneak up the outside stairs and go through the French windows. Come on." Seth pulled her ruthlessly up the stairs behind him, then along the gallery. "Your room or mine?" he asked over his shoulder.

"Mine's locked," Olivia said.

"So's mine." He paused to fish something out of one of the hanging fern baskets. "Yours is closer," he decided.

"What is that?" She gazed at the object in his hand.

"A file. It's been in that basket for decades. I haven't used it often, but when I do, I always put it back. It's pretty handy, actually. You just slip it between the windows, jimmy up the latch, and—presto—you're in." He demonstrated on her window as he spoke. Olivia was appalled at how easily he gained access to her room.

"You mean that thing's been out there all this time?" she demanded as he drew her inside and closed the window behind them. "*Anybody* could have done that! I want those latches replaced with something more modern that can't be jimmied—tomorrow!"

As she considered the possibilities, Olivia's blood ran cold.

"If it bothers you, sure," Seth said, sounding faintly surprised. "It always just seemed kind of convenient to me."

"It would." Olivia was already being distracted by his arms sliding around her waist. Making a mental note to call a locksmith first thing in the morning, she turned her attention to unfastening his buttons.

"LIVVY! Livvy, wake up. Olivia!" His voice was dragging her from the shore of the moonlit lake where her mother struggled in the water. Olivia moaned and flailed.

"Livvy!"

Seth's voice. She would know Seth's voice anywhere. Gasping as though she had run a marathon, she opened her eyes a slit. Seth was leaning over her, his blond hair wildly disordered, five-o'clock shadow darkening his cheeks and chin, his blue eyes narrowed with concern for her.

They had made love. She had fallen asleep. Seth must have stayed with her. As the knowledge that she was sleeping with Seth percolated through her terror-dulled brain, Olivia took a deep breath, and some of the tension in her seeped away.

"Seth," she murmured. Glancing quickly at the clock, she saw that the time was 3:29 a.m.

Seth had dragged her from sleep before the nightmare ended.

"What, baby?" Reaching over, he slid an arm beneath her and pulled her against him. Olivia snuggled close, ending up with her head on his shoulder and one hand splayed across the warm breadth of his chest.

"Talk to me," he said.

She told him everything then: the voices that seemed to call to her from the lake; the nightmare in which something seemed to be pulling her mother under the water; her odd, almost physically ill reaction to her mother's picture; even the face in the mirror that was so like her own but wasn't quite hers. She didn't leave anything out, and by the time she got through, she felt several degrees better.

Seth said nothing for a moment, just lay there with a meditative expression on his face.

"So I'm a total nutcase, right?" she asked.

"I'd say you were more traumatized than nuts," Seth said slowly. "Livvy, I think you ought to talk to a professional about all this. Moving back home after so many years away must have jolted loose all kinds of emotions."

Olivia thought about that for a moment. "Is that what you think is happening?"

"I don't see any other explanation."

Olivia peeped up at him. "You don't think my mother's trying to tell me that her death *wasn't* a suicide?"

One corner of Seth's mouth quirked up in a wry smile. "Livvy, seriously, do you?"

Olivia grimaced. "You're saying it's all my imagination."

"I'm saying you ought to talk to somebody. Get Charlie to give you the name of somebody good."

"Seth."

"Hmmm?"

"I'm glad you were with me tonight. It's been horrible having that dream and waking up terrified and all alone."

Olivia wriggled on top of him and lay there, her chin resting on his chest. Then his arms came around her, and after that neither of them spoke again for a very long time.

AFTER dropping off the girls at school the next morning, Olivia decided on impulse to stop by Charlie's office. Seth's suggestion of seeing a professional had merit. She wanted the name of a psychiatrist—and, she thought, a hypnotist. Perhaps her mother was trying to get a message to her from beyond the grave. Maybe a hypnotist could take her into the dream and elicit information that faded away when she woke up. She had the feeling there was something she wasn't quite grasping, something that was floating maddeningly just beyond her reach.

If so, she had to know.

Charlie's office hours officially began at eight thirty, but Olivia knew he was in when she drove by because his Lexus was parked in the space reserved for his exclusive use. Olivia pulled into the parking lot, got out of the car, and headed for the door. Knocking loudly, she turned the knob and walked into the reception area.

"Uncle Charlie?"

Charlie was nowhere in sight. There was a small bell to ring for service on the counter that separated the reception area from the business office. Olivia hit it twice, then waited.

The reception area, indeed the whole office, was most unusual. Skilled taxidermist Charlie had made use of his talents to enliven corners and other odd niches with his work. Olivia found herself staring at a stuffed black bear taller than she was. It looked so real that she had to resist the impulse to back away from it. Even its eyes looked real. They were, she surmised, plastic.

"Who's there? Oh, Olivia!" Dressed in a white lab coat with a pen protruding from his breast pocket, Charlie looked delighted to see her. "Come in, come in!"

He held open the bottom half of the Dutch door that led into the business office, and Olivia walked inside. Charlie led the way into his private office and settled himself behind his desk, motioning Olivia into a chair. Sitting down, she found herself staring at a huge stuffed bass mounted just above Charlie's head.

"What can I do for you, Olivia?" Charlie asked, surveying her keenly. "That is, I'm assuming this is not a social call."

Olivia shook her head. "Remember the nightmares I told you about? About my mother's death?"

"I do, yes."

"I'm still having them. Actually, they're getting more and more vivid all the time." Olivia looked at him almost pleadingly. "Uncle Charlie, what happened that night?"

He looked at her for a long moment without saying anything. Then he leaned forward, placing his forearms on the desk and steepling his fingers as he looked at her. "There's not a lot I can tell you. I was only there at the end. We'd all been looking for your mother because James was concerned when he came home and couldn't find her anywhere in the house. It was late, after midnight. I forget the time exactly, but late. Big John somehow spotted Selena floating in the lake and started yelling. I came and pulled her out and tried to revive her. It was no use. She was dead."

"Was she wearing a nightgown—a white nightgown, ankle-length, with wide lace straps?" Olivia's question was impulsive. She merely wanted to verify the dream's details.

Charlie stared at her, then blinked. "Why, yes, I believe she was. A white nightgown. Long, because it covered her legs."

Olivia closed her eyes for a moment, then opened them again. "Is there any reason to think that it might not have been suicide?"

"Olivia, I'm sorry, but no. There's no reason to think that."

Olivia sighed. "I guess what I need from you next is the name of a good psychiatrist. And a hypnotist."

Charlie blinked at her. "The psychiatrist I can understand, if you're having nightmares. But a hypnotist?"

"I want to see if there are any details in the dreams I'm having that I'm forgetting when I wake up. I thought maybe a hypnotist could help."

Charlie nodded. He reached for his prescription pad and pulled the pen out of his pocket. Scratching something on the top sheet, he tore it off, then started writing on the second sheet. "A psychiatrist is no problem. I've known John Hall for years. A hypnotist—well, I'll have to look into that. When I come up with somebody, I'll let you know."

"Could you try to find somebody soon?" Olivia hated to be pushy about it, but there was a sense of urgency driving her now. Probably because, knowing Seth, if she didn't fix herself soon, he'd be working on a way to fix her himself.

"Soon as I can, I promise." Charlie pushed the pieces of paper across the desk at her and stood up. "When you call John Hall, tell him I referred you. And the other's a prescription for medication to help you sleep. If you can't beat those nightmares one way, you can beat them another. In fact"—he walked around the desk as Olivia stood up, too—"I think I've got some samples. Go on out to the reception room and I'll bring them out to you."

Olivia did, and he joined her a few minutes later, handing her a small white bottle with a yellow label. "You take two of those at bedtime and you won't have any more problems with nightmares."

"Thank you, Uncle Charlie." Olivia smiled warmly at him and started to pull out her checkbook. He waved her on out.

"You're on the family plan," he told her. "Now, go on to wherever you were going. And let me know how things work out."

Olivia was left with nothing to do but thank him again, put the pills in her purse, and head to work.

It was probably a good thing that Seth was busy with clients all morning, Olivia thought. She had work to do, after all, and he was a definite distraction. She called a locksmith about the French windows, then got busy with the computer. Shortly before lunch a deliveryman walked in carrying a huge bouquet of deep red roses arranged in a tall glass vase.

"These are for you, Mrs. Morrison," he said cheerfully. "Two dozen of the very best. Where do you want them?"

"On—on my desk," Olivia said, trying to hold on to her composure. She bent to sniff the roses. Their scent was heavenly.

"Who—" Ilsa broke off as Carl walked into the office.

"Did you get my message—" Carl began, only to break off as he saw Olivia bending over the roses. "Nice flowers."

The awful thought occurred to Olivia that Carl might have sent the roses. She fumbled for the card, opened it. "Love, Seth."

She breathed an inward sigh of relief. "Thank you," she said to Carl. Ilsa, meanwhile, was eyeing Olivia with open speculation.

"So are we on for Friday night?" he asked. "We'll drive into Baton Rouge for dinner and then go on to—"

Olivia was already shaking her head regretfully, interrupting him. "Carl, I can't."

He frowned at her. "Why not? We had fun over lunch."

Olivia took a deep breath. "We did, but— I'm seeing somebody else."

Carl's frown deepened. "Somebody else? Since yesterday? Who?" His gaze moved suspiciously to the roses.

Olivia could see Ilsa's eyes widen.

"Well, that's it for the morning." Seth walked into the office and stopped, looking from Carl to Olivia to the roses and then back at Olivia again. As their eyes met, Olivia couldn't help it. She had to smile. Seth smiled back at her, then glanced at Carl with disfavor.

"It's you!" Carl burst out, staring at Seth. "You're putting the moves on Olivia. That's low. That's so low! I can't believe you'd do something like that. Mallory—" Carl seemed to choke with indignation.

Seth glanced at Ilsa, whose eyes were now as wide as saucers.

"Okay," he said, looking from Ilsa to Carl again, "here's the deal. You can spread it around the whole company, the whole town, and get this over with. Mallory and I are no longer engaged. Olivia and I are seeing each other. End of story."

Carl's gaze riveted on Olivia. "You're going out with Seth?"

Olivia nodded.

"Well, that's fine, then." Carl didn't sound like he believed it, but at least the words were dignified. His gaze shot to Seth. "Fast work, cuz," he said, and turned on his heel, leaving the office.

Olivia let out her breath on a slow sigh. Her eyes met Seth's.

"I have to drive to Baton Rouge to check on Big John during lunch," Seth said calmly, as if nothing happened. "Want to come with me?"

"I'd love to," Olivia answered.

Seth nodded. "Give me a minute, and we'll go." He walked into his office and shut the door.

Ilsa looked at Olivia. "Wow!" she said.

"I'm crazy about him," Olivia confessed. "Does it show?"

"Like a spotlight in a cave." Ilsa clasped her hands together. "I'm so happy for you. I always thought he was way, way too good for Mallory!"

Seth's door opened again, and Ilsa immediately turned back to the file cabinet. But she sneaked a grin over her shoulder at Olivia as they left.

OLIVIA was just starting to read aloud their nightly chapter of *Little House in the Big Woods* when a knock sounded on Sara's closed bedroom door. She and Sara exchanged a quick glance before Olivia put the book facedown on the bed and went to see who was there.

It was Seth. "Sorry to interrupt," he said. He looked over Olivia's shoulder at Sara, who was tucked up in bed with the kitten nestled beside her. "Hi, Sara." Then, to Olivia in a lowered voice, "Come out into the hall a minute."

"I'll be right back," Olivia said to Sara, and stepped out into the hall, pulling the door almost closed behind her.

Seth slid a hand along the side of her neck and dropped a quick kiss on her mouth. "I just got a call from the hospital," he said. "Big John's having trouble breathing, and I've got to go. David's already there, and Belinda's on her way."

"Oh, no," Olivia said. "Do you want me to come with you?"

He shook his head. "It's better if you stay here with the kids. I just wanted to let you know so you wouldn't wonder where I disappeared to."

Olivia smiled at him, her eyes soft. "I'll miss you."

His gaze moved over her face. "How about if I come and crawl into bed with you when I get back?"

Her smile widened. "That'd be good."

He leaned down and kissed her again, brief and hard. "See you later," he said, and headed down the hall.

Olivia turned and went back into Sara's room. By the time she finished her reading, had a bath, put on her prettiest nightgown, and checked to make sure Sara was asleep, it was after eleven. Seth still wasn't home. As idiotic as it seemed, she was lonesome for him as she climbed into bed. It was amazing how fast she'd gotten used to the feel of his arms around her as she slept.

She was so in love with him it was ridiculous, she thought. Olivia was smiling to herself when she fell asleep.

The sound of the door opening roused her. Whether minutes or hours later, Olivia couldn't be sure. Seth crept quietly into the room, a large, shadowy presence in the dark, closing the door softly, being careful not to disturb her. Olivia cast a glance at the clock: 1:22 a.m.

"Hi," she said sleepily, turning to smile at him. He froze, then, without any warning at all, leaped at her with the agility of a gorilla. Grabbing her head painfully by the hair, he jerked her head back and shoved a soaked, smelly rag in her face.

He was not Seth. He was not Seth!

Olivia's last shocked thought as she choked and tried to fight off the intruder was that it couldn't be happening again.

SHE remembered. She remembered. She remembered being carried like this before, wrapped up like a mummy, unable to move, barely able to breathe. She remembered the icy-cold terror that sent tremors down her spine. She remembered being jostled, remembered the sounds of the night penetrating faintly through whatever it was that was wrapped around her head, remembered the sounds of a man's heavy breathing.

She remembered. Oh, God, she remembered.

This had happened to her before, long ago, when she was a little girl, younger than Sara. Someone had come into her room in the middle of the night and grabbed her, shoving a wet, smelly rag into her face. It had knocked her unconscious, and when she had come to, a woman had been screaming.

Her mother had been screaming. In her mind Olivia could hear her mother screaming as plainly as if it were all happening again, right this very minute. She'd been little, and she'd been lying on the ground inside some sort of cloth bag, and she'd woken up to hear her mother screaming. She crawled out of the bag to see her mother and a man struggling by the shore of the lake. Ghost Lake. The night had been hot and muggy, and fog had been rising like bony fingers stretching up from the water.

She tried to go to her mother, to help her, but her knees wouldn't hold her. Her stomach heaved like she had to throw up.

Then her mother stopped screaming, just like that, like something had cut off the sound. She looked and saw that her mother was in the water now, in up to about her waist, and the man was pushing her face down, holding it under the water.

He was hurting her mother.

She had to save her mother. She got to her feet, grabbing on to the trees for support, just as her mother's face came up, just as her mother seemed to break free of the man and turned, arms outstretched, trying to make it back to shore.

Her mother saw her then and screamed at her. "Run away, Olivia! Run! Run away! Run away!" And then the man caught her mother around the waist and dragged her back out into the lake, and her mother's scream turned into a gurgle as he pushed her face down beneath the water again.

"Run away! Run! Run away!" Her mother's scream echoed in her ears, and she turned and ran, lurched from tree to tree until she got to the path, and then she turned back to look.

Her mother was in the middle of the lake, her face turned toward shore, her eyes wide and terrified, her mouth open as she screamed. She wore her white nightgown, the one with the lace straps that Olivia thought was so pretty. Then the man surfaced behind her, grabbing her around the waist, disappearing under the surface with her, forcing her down.

The last thing Olivia saw was her mother's hand stretching above the surface of Ghost Lake. Then the hand, too, disappeared.

Olivia turned and stumbled along the path through the woods, heading toward the Big House, dizzy and sick and so so scared. He was coming after her; she knew he was.

He was behind her, soaking wet and panting and reaching out for her. Olivia could hear his slogging footsteps, hear his labored breathing, and hear, too, voices coming from the direction of the house. She screamed, only it came out sounding more like a squeak. Then something slammed hard into the back of her head.

When she'd awakened again, it was days later, her mother was dead, and her uncle Charlie was treating her for shock and talking her through the nightmares that plagued her.

And after she'd gotten up, gotten well, life at LaAngelle Plantation had gone on. Day in, day out, for weeks and months and years. She'd had no memory of that night. She had buried it deep inside her mind as too terrible to remember. And gradually even her subconscious had forgotten, until coming back to LaAngelle Plantation had stirred the memories again.

How was it possible that it was happening to her a second time? As the dream coalesced into memory, and the memory solidified enough to be shoved aside so that her mind could function, Olivia realized that what she was experiencing now was no flashback. She had been drugged, taken from her bed, and was now bound and gagged and wrapped in folds of cloth that prevented her from moving. She was being carried over someone's shoulder. A man, from the size and shape of him. He was struggling under her weight. He stepped from gravel to grass, and the sound changed from a crunch to a soft swish.

Where was he taking her?

A horrible thought occurred to her: Oh, God, would he throw her into the lake? It was all she could do not to panic, not to fight, to lay still and quiet and keep her breathing calm. If he suspected she was conscious, he would knock her out again, she was sure, and there would go her last hope, her only hope, of survival.

Breathe in. Breathe out. Keep muscles relaxed.

She heard the faint rasp of metal on metal, and then he turned sideways with her, as if he was having trouble fitting through an opening or a doorway. The side of her head smacked into something hard, and she couldn't help it; she made a sound.

"So you're awake," he said, and the voice was familiar, shockingly familiar, so familiar she couldn't, wouldn't believe it, until he dumped her down without warning on a hard, slick surface and pulled some of the wrapping away from her face.

SETH was tired. So tired he could barely climb the stairs. If he hadn't known Olivia was waiting for him on the second floor, he thought with a faint glimmer of humor, he would have sacked out on the couch in the den.

The events of the last two weeks must be catching up with him, he decided, because he felt totally whacked. His mother's death was a blow from which he was never going to recover. The pain would be with him until he died. Now it looked like Big John was going to go, too.

Tonight's crisis had been some kind of mix-up with the medicines, caught by a new doctor David had insisted take over the case. Charlie hadn't liked the idea, but he was nowhere to be seen at the hospital tonight, and if he was going to make mistakes, he needed to be replaced.

Seth reached Olivia's room, turned the doorknob, let himself in. He could just faintly see her bed by the greenish glow from her clock.

The clock read 1:59 a.m. The bed looked empty.

"Livvy?" he said softly. No answer.

Seth turned on the overhead light.

The bed was empty. The French windows were closed.

He turned on his heel and went next door. There was a lamp on in Sara's room, a little night-light that Olivia allowed to burn all night. By its light, even before he switched on the overhead fixture, Seth saw that Sara's bed was empty, too. The covers had been tossed onto the floor.

Seth's blood ran cold. Even before he awakened Martha, even before he awakened Chloe, even before he rousted Keith from the *garçonnière* behind the house, he knew something was wrong.

Terribly wrong.

While Martha and Chloe huddled in the den, Seth got on the phone to Ira. He wanted the sheriff and his deputies out at LaAngelle Plantation—right now.

UNCLE CHARLIE . . . Olivia couldn't talk, of course, with the gag in her mouth, but her mind shouted his name. She knew him instantly, even through the tan mesh of the stocking he had pulled down over his face. He grimaced beneath the mask and peeled it off, looking down at her almost sorrowfully.

"Well now, Olivia, you've gotten us both in a fine mess," he said. She was in a bag, a white canvas bag, and he began pulling it off her, easing it down over her shoulders, wriggling it out from under her hips. The shiny silver metal surface she was lying on felt slick and cold against her skin. She was bound with duct tape, she saw. The silvery bands were wrapped around her ankles and knees over her pink nightgown and bound her arms to her body.

They were in a crypt. The Archer family crypt. She knew it from the inscriptions on the four tray-size brass plaques set into the marble walls. The plaques commemorated Colonel Robert John Archer, his wife, Lavinia, and two infants. Olivia was close enough to see her own wavery reflection in the brass.

The reflections provided the first horror. They showed her that she was lying on her back on a makeshift tabletop of bright silver metal with scooped-out channels along the sides that looked as though they were designed to catch liquids. Olivia immediately thought of autopsy tables and blood, and she shuddered.

But the real horror looked at her from the corners. Olivia's eyes widened as her gaze moved from one to the other. Three of them. Life-size mannequins of three little girls, each of them dressed with exquisite care, their hair—medium brown, blond, and black—lovingly curled. They were standing upright, their arms slightly bent and held a little away from their bodies. Their skin was the only false note. It had a leathery, thick texture.

"Are you admiring my girls?" Charlie plucked the wadded rag from her mouth so suddenly that Olivia felt as if half the skin of her lips and tongue had been torn away with it. She tried to swallow but couldn't, because her throat was too dry. She coughed, choked, tried again. This time she succeeded.

"Are they—mannequins?" she croaked. Charlie shook his head at her reproachfully.

"No, dear, they're just what they look like. Little girls. Becca, Maggie, and Savannah. I'm particularly proud of Savannah. She was Little Miss Rice, you know."

"Oh, my God." Olivia's stomach heaved. She felt sick, horribly sick to her stomach, and dizzy, too. They were *children*, or they had once been, and her uncle Charlie had . . . "You killed them."

"Yes, well, unfortunately, that's part of the process. You were almost number four, you know. I chose *you* to come after Savannah, but your mother . . . your mother . . ." His face darkened.

"You drowned my mother, didn't you?"

There was a narrow metal cabinet against one marble wall near her head, and Charlie was busy extracting something from it as he talked. He looked at her over his shoulder.

"I knew you would remember sooner or later." His voice was resigned. "I had no choice, you know. I don't know how—she was the only mommy who ever did—but Selena heard me that night. She came running after me as I was walking away from the house, and she wanted to know what was in my bag. Well, it was you, of course, but I couldn't tell her that. So I slugged her and chloroformed her and carried both of you away from the house. It was difficult. The pair of you were heavy. Then she woke up and started to fight me down by the lake, so I had to drop you and deal with her. By the time I was finished, you were hightailing it back toward the house. I knocked you unconscious, but I didn't have time to do anything with you before Big John was on the scene. By the time I got finished dragging Selena out of the lake and doing my bit with CPR, you had managed to get back to the house. I kept an eye on you for a while after that, but except for a few nightmares you didn't seem to remember anything. I don't know if it was because I hit you so hard on the head or because you had hysterical amnesia. Of course, when you came to me this morning and told me you wanted to go see a psychiatrist and a hypnotist, of all things, I had no choice. I knew you would remember sooner or later."

Olivia took a deep breath. It was hot in the crypt, and her body was beginning to stick clammily to the metal on which she lay. But she had to keep her mind clear, had to think. Otherwise, she knew, she was going to die.

"I always thought Big John suspected something," Charlie continued conversationally. "I was already soaking wet, you know, when the two of us went into the water after Selena. I never knew if he noticed or not, but he questioned me pretty sharply afterward. Made me nervous." He chuckled. "I quit collecting after that, you know, and moved my girls up here, just in case he was suspicious enough to really start looking into things. But he never did. I thought he'd put the whole matter out of his mind. Then he saw you again and had that heart attack. He started to babble about Selena to the nurses in the hospital, and I was afraid of what was going to come out. I had to calm the old boy down. Tonight, when I get done here, I'm going to have to take care of him for good. It's a shame. I've always liked him. Just like I like you, Olivia. I wouldn't be doing this if you'd given me any other choice."

He took something else out of the cabinet and closed the door.

"Are you planning to turn *me* into—one of them?" With a nod she gestured at the preserved body of one of the little girls.

Charlie shook his head. "Oh, no. No. You're going to drown yourself in the lake, like your mother. Despondent, I imagine, because you're in love with Seth—Phillip told me that he saw you kissing him, so that will bear that theory out—and he's going to marry Mallory."

"But—but Seth broke their engagement. Yesterday." Olivia was trying to latch on to anything that might change his mind.

Charlie shrugged. "Doesn't matter. Who knows what might drive a troubled young woman to kill herself. After all, you've been having nightmares about your mother drowning in the lake, and just today you came to me and asked me for the name of a psychiatrist. You were depressed, too. I'll swear to it."

He smiled and held up his hand. Olivia was horrified to see that it held a syringe half filled with a golden liquid.

"You needn't be afraid that it's going to hurt. I never hurt my girls. When I'm ready for them to go—I like to play with them for a while first, but all good things must come to an end—I inject them with five grams of sodium pentothal to put them to sleep, then give them fifty cc of pancuronium bromide, which paralyzes all their muscles except the heart, then finish up with fifty cc of potassium chloride to stop the heart muscle itself. They never feel a thing. For you, tonight, I'm going to put you to sleep with the sodium pentothal, then throw you into the lake. You'll die from drowning. The signs will be unmistakable."

"Uncle Charlie—please." Pleading with him was useless, Olivia knew. If the man had an ounce of compassion, she would not now be staring at the near-mummified remains of three little girls. But she had to try. She wanted to live.

A mewling sound from somewhere behind her head made Olivia's eyes widen.

"Oh, now you've woken Sara," Charlie said reproachfully. "She's going to be my number four girl, you know. Wait just a minute while I put her in her cage."

"No! No! No!" Olivia's head slewed around so fast that for an instant it left her dizzy as she strained to see what Charlie was doing. He was moving behind her, out of her line of vision, and when he reappeared, he was carrying Sara, her own sweet Sara, clad in the Cinderella nighty that was her particular favorite. She was obviously groggy, her head lolling against his chest.

"Uncle Charlie, no!" Olivia begged, straining uselessly against her bonds. "Please let her go. Please."

All the terror she'd refused to let herself feel now boiled to the surface for Sara. Her heart pounded. Her breath sobbed in her chest. Her limbs shook.

Please, God, please. Save Sara.

She got a glimpse of her own reflection in the brass plaque to her left. She was struggling, fighting her bonds, her head and shoulders lifting away from the metal. She was struggling so much that it was almost as though she were seeing double, as if there were two of her reflected in the brass.

"Don't you see, Olivia? I'll be giving her a kind of immortality. She'll be a sweet little eight-year-old forever."

"Please don't hurt her," Olivia begged.

"Mommy?" Sara lifted her head from Charlie's chest to blink sleepily at Olivia. "Mommy, what's wrong?"

Olivia's desperation seemed to be penetrating Sara's drug-induced stupor. Sara looked around, blinking, then stiffened in Charlie's arms and began to flail.

"Ah-ah," he said to her. "None of that, now. Let's put you in your nice little cage until Daddy is ready to play."

He walked around the foot of the table, and through another of the brass plaques Olivia saw the reflection of a large dog cage with a padlock on the front. A finger of ice ran down her spine.

"Uncle Charlie, no! Please, no! Sara! Sara!"

"Mommy!"

Again Olivia saw the double images of herself in the brass plaques and saw, too, that one of the images now appeared to be standing beside the table while the other image was lying upon it, still restrained, just as she was. She thought the standing image had a wider jaw, a longer nose—and a white nightgown.

"Mommy! Mommy!"

"Mother, help me!" Olivia cried. She looked wildly around and saw the battery-powered lantern perched on the edge of the table near her feet. She gathered her legs and kicked downward with all her strength—and the lantern flew across the room, although she never felt her bare feet actually make contact. It crashed into the metal door of the crypt, shattering, sending sparks flying everywhere. In the instant before the bulb flickered out and the crypt was plunged into darkness, Olivia saw Charlie whirl toward the sound of the crash, stumble, fall to one knee—and drop Sara on the floor. The blow from the lantern had knocked the crypt door open just a crack. A burst of cool air whooshed past Olivia's face.

"Run, Sara! Run, Sara! Run, run, run!" Olivia shrieked.

Sara ran, scrambling to her feet, bursting through the door, screaming as if all the demons of every nightmare she had ever dreamed were chasing her, as indeed they were. Charlie went after her, shouldering through the door, his big body a ponderous shadow plunging through the night. Olivia lay in her duct-tape prison and screamed, screamed at Sara to run, screamed for help, screamed until her lungs ached and she was gasping for breath.

She screamed until Charlie stumbled back into the crypt. Alone. Sara was safe. Sara had to be safe or he wouldn't be alone. Olivia sagged with relief, thanked God in a rush of dizziness.

She watched as Charlie lurched to the metal cabinet, fumbled with the doors, and removed something from the cabinet.

A second later he was coming toward her. The gray light filtering through the open crypt door showed her the filled syringe in his hand.

Dread iced her veins anew. "Uncle Charlie," she croaked.

He stopped by the table at about her waist level and smiled at her. She could see the gleam of his teeth through the darkness.

"Olivia, dear, what I have here is a syringe filled with potassium chloride," he said almost pleasantly. "If you remember, this is the one that stops your heart."

WHEN the screaming started, Seth was standing on the bank of Ghost Lake near the spot where Olivia had walked into the water that day. He was playing the beam of his flashlight over the lake's surface and praying with all his might.

At first the screams were hardly distinguishable from the cries of predators and prey that routinely split the night. Seth stiffened as the first one reached his ears, and then, as it was followed by another and another, wondered if perhaps something was attacking the flock of peacocks. By the time he knew for certain that they were human screams—Olivia's and Sara's screams—a small figure was hurtling down the trail that climbed the bluff toward the old graveyard. Picking her out with the beam of his flashlight, he ran toward her. He recognized Sara with a rush of both terror and relief. Sara was alive and screaming her lungs out and running as if the hounds of hell were on her tail—but where was Olivia?

Oh, God, where was Olivia?

"Seth, Seth, Seth, Seth!" Sara collapsed into his arms as he reached her, wrapping her arms around his waist. "Seth, he's got Mommy! He's got Mommy!"

"Where?" Seth demanded, even as he bellowed for Ira. He could tell the sheriff was not too far behind him from the bobbing yellow beam of light that labored up the trail in his wake.

"Up there! In the graveyard!"

"Go to Ira. See that light? Run there!" Seth thrust Sara in Ira's direction. Without waiting to see if she obeyed, he took the trail in great bounds, a cold terror driving him.

The screams had stopped.

Up here, in the shadowy sanctuary where his mother lay in her freshly dug grave, where stone angels stood sentinel and the moon and passing clouds combined to give them eerie life, the silence shrieked at him.

"Olivia!" he bellowed. "Olivia!"

"Seth!"

Her voice was faint, muffled even. Seth ran his flashlight around the graveyard, looking everywhere, and almost missed the fact that the door to the mausoleum stood ajar just a little bit.

He sprinted toward it and yanked it wide. It swung open with surprising ease, as if someone had recently oiled the old hinges.

As the crypt was exposed to his view, what he captured with the beam of his flashlight stopped him dead in his tracks.

Olivia was looking at him, her head lifted away from whatever unholy thing it was that she was lying on. Her face was white as paper, her eyes were huge, and she was trussed with duct tape, unable to move. Charlie stood beside her, a hypodermic needle poised to inject just below her ear.

"If you come any closer, I'm afraid I'll have to inject this directly into Olivia's carotid artery," Charlie said, sounding so much like his normal self that Seth had a hard time believing what he was hearing and seeing. One glance at Olivia told him that Charlie was in deadly earnest. "It's loaded with potassium chloride, you see. It will stop her heart within minutes."

Seth took a deep breath. "You don't want to do that," he said calmly. "I love her, Charlie. You don't want to hurt her, because if you do, you'll hurt me. That's how much I love her, Charlie. Enough so that anything you do to her, you do to me."

"I don't want to hurt *you*, Seth, but you see . . ." Charlie paused as the approach of Ira and what sounded like a whole posse of deputies reached their ears.

"Charlie, please."

"They're coming for me," Charlie said. He glanced down at Olivia, then looked at Seth.

"Have somebody check what's in Big John's IV bags, Seth," he said. "I've been keeping him heavily sedated. Once he's not, he should recover."

"The nurses at the hospital already found out. They told David, and that's why he brought in another doctor. Everyone thinks you just made a mistake. It's all right, Charlie."

"Ah, nurses," Charlie said disparagingly. "Mommies! Women! Why can't they just stay little girls?"

He glanced down at Olivia again, hesitated, then turned the hypodermic needle on himself.

"Charlie!" Seth leaped forward, knocking the needle away from Charlie's hand, but it was already too late. The syringe was empty. A little trickle of blood ran down Charlie's neck where the needle had pierced his skin. Charlie sank to his knees, gasped once, then fell forward onto his face.

Ira and his henchmen came bursting through the door then, brandishing guns and flashlights.

"We need CPR here," Seth said, straightening away from Charlie, who no longer seemed to be breathing. He turned to Olivia, who had collapsed limply back against the metal surface she was lying on. "And somebody better call for an ambulance. Charlie just shot himself in the neck with potassium chloride." Then, to Olivia, as he found and unfastened the mesh strap that held her to the table, "Did he hurt you?"

"No." Olivia took a deep, shuddering breath. "Sara?"

"She's safe," Seth said, lifting her into his arms. Two deputies were crouched on the floor giving Charlie CPR, and Seth stepped carefully around them. Another was outside the crypt, talking into a cell phone, presumably summoning an ambulance.

"Call down to the house and let them know we're all right up here," Seth instructed, and the man nodded.

As Seth put Olivia down on the grass just outside the crypt, he heard Ira exclaim to one of his deputies, "Hell's bells, will you come over here and look at this?"

Whatever it was, Seth didn't, at the moment, want to know.

"What is this, duct tape?" Seth asked.

"I think so."

She was shivering, despite the fact that it was a warm night, and Seth guessed that she was suffering from shock. And no wonder. He felt pretty shocked himself, and he hadn't endured anything near what she had. He had only endured the thought that he might lose her. But that, to him, would be the worst thing of all.

"Hold still." Reaching into his pocket, he found the Swiss army knife that Big John had given him years ago and pulled it out. After that it took just a few minutes and some judicious sawing to free her. Gingerly he pulled the tape away from her skin, taking care not to hurt her. When it was off, he chafed her arms and legs to restore her circulation, then helped her to stand up. She leaned against him for support, resting her head against his chest, and he wrapped both arms around her, holding her tight.

"You saved my life," she said. "Thank you."

"I saved my own life," he corrected, pressing his mouth to the top of her head. "I couldn't have lived if you'd died in there."

"Seth, what we've got here looks pretty bad." Ira emerged from the crypt, shaking his head and looking pale. "You need to come take a look."

"Charlie, he"—Olivia shuddered in his arms—"he murdered three little girls. Their bodies are in there. And he drowned my mother. He told me."

Seth looked at Ira, who nodded grimly.

"Sit down here a minute," Seth said to Olivia, and left her on the single step leading into the crypt.

When he emerged, he felt sick to his stomach.

Olivia cast a fleeting look up at him. "Charlie was going to do that to Sara. He was going to do that to me when I was a little girl. That's why he killed my mother. She saved me."

Seth sat down beside her on the step as she told him everything that had happened. In the distance, just faintly, came the wail of a siren. The ambulance itself arrived moments later.

When EMTs came bustling into the graveyard, Seth pulled Olivia to her feet. "Can you walk back to the house, do you think?" he asked.

She nodded.

"Come on, then," he said. "You don't want to see this."

With his arm wrapped around her waist, they moved slowly out of the cemetery and started down the path. Seth was careful to set an easy pace, but Olivia seemed to gain strength as they went. In the places where she had to walk in front of him, Seth looked at her dark, bent head and thanked God that he had her still.

He had thought there was plenty of time for the two of them. But tonight time had almost run out.

They were in the woods now, under the sheltering darkness of the trees. The night was alive with sounds. The rustling canopy overhead blocked the moon, but moonlight filtered through. Barefoot when they had started out, Olivia was now wearing his socks to protect her feet. His shoes were so big she couldn't keep them on.

"Livvy?" They were walking arm in arm, with her leaning slightly against him, moving in the direction of the house. Ghost Lake glimmered off to the right. The stone steps that led up to the lawn were ahead of them.

"Hmm?"

Seth cleared his throat. He was clear about what he wanted to say, but sometimes it was hard to get the words out. "I love you, Livvy."

"I love you, too."

It was as simple as that.

When they reached the top of the stone steps, Chloe and Sara came running toward them, with Martha in hot pursuit. Seth wasn't clear on the time, but it had to be about four a.m.

"Mom!"

"Olivia!"

Both girls flung themselves at Olivia. She hugged them, then wrapped an arm around each as they all headed toward the house, the girls chattering incessantly about their thoughts, feelings, and actions during the night's adventures as they went. Seth didn't really listen, and he didn't think Olivia was listening, either, because all she did was nod and smile.

When they reached the house, Chloe stopped suddenly, which halted the whole group, and looked around, waving.

"What are you doing?" Sara asked, looking around, too.

"Waving to my nana," Chloe said. "See? She's that blinky star there."

Sara squinted up into the star-studded sky. "There's two of them, blinking together."

Seth looked, and Sara was right. There was a binary star winking and blinking at them from high in the western sky.

Olivia was looking, too. "Wave, Sara," she instructed with a smile. "I think one of those stars is Chloe's grandmother, and the other one is yours."

Both little girls waved madly.

"Is it okay to wish on Nana-star?" Chloe asked Seth, a slight frown wrinkling her brow.

"Sure," Seth said. He figured if his mother was now a star, she wouldn't mind being wished on.

"Starlight, star bright, first star I see tonight, I wish I may, I wish I might, have the wish I wish tonight." Then Chloe closed her eyes and scrunched up her face, apparently wishing very hard.

"What did you wish for?" Seth asked curiously when she opened her eyes again.

"I wished that the four of us could be a real family," Chloe said, taking his hand. "Could we, Daddy?"

Seth looked at Olivia over the children's heads. "We could," he said slowly. "If Sara's mom will marry me. Will you, Livvy?"

Olivia met his gaze. Her expression was very solemn for a moment, and Seth wasn't quite sure what to expect.

Then her face broke into a wide smile. "I will absolutely marry you," she said, and walked right into his outstretched arms. As he kissed her, his daughter and hers danced around them, cheering. And two bright stars, bound together for eternity, winked and blinked in the night-dark sky.

KAREN ROBARDS

"I've always written," Karen Robards says during a phone call from her home near Louisville, Kentucky. "I edited the high school newspaper and majored in journalism in college. But it never occurred to me that you could make a living as a writer."

Robards planned to use her verbal skills in the courtroom until she discovered that law school was not her cup of tea. "I read romance novels instead of studying—I'd never read them before, because my mother didn't approve of them—and I started thinking, 'You know, I could write this.' So I took a creative writing course, and the result was my first book." How did she find time to write it while in law school? She laughs. "Well, I *really* hated law school."

To read an exclusive interview with Karen Robards, visit the Select Editions website: 📖 ReadersOnly.com Password: *Life*

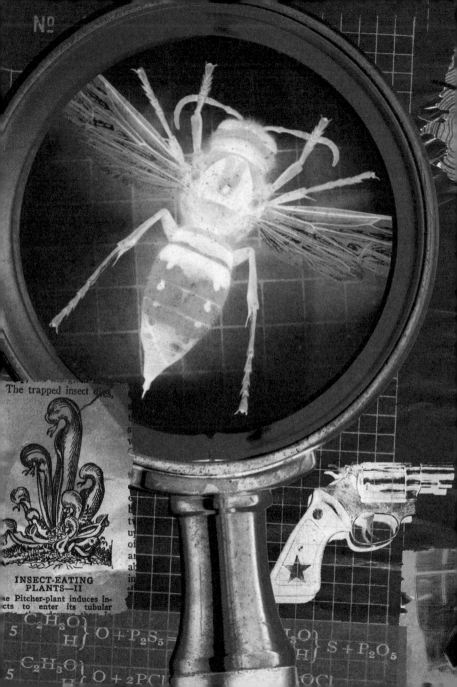

N⁰

The trapped insect dies,

**INSECT-EATING
PLANTS—II**

e Pitcher-plant induces in-
cts to enter its tubular

They call him the Insect Boy,
and he knows insects well.
He knows how they live and die.
He knows how they elude their pursuers.
Above all, he knows how they kill.

ONE

SHE came here to lay flowers at the place where the boy died and the girl was kidnapped.

She came here because she was a heavy girl and had a pocked face and not many friends.

She came because she was expected to.

She came because she wanted to.

Ungainly and sweating, twenty-six-year-old Lydia Johansson walked along the dirt shoulder of Route 112, where she'd parked her Honda Accord, then stepped carefully down the hill to the muddy bank where Blackwater Canal met the Paquenoke River.

It wasn't long after dawn, but this August had been the hottest in years in North Carolina, and Lydia was already sweating through her nurse's whites by the time she started toward the clearing on the riverbank. She easily found the place she was looking for; the yellow police tape was very evident through the haze.

Early morning sounds. Loons, an animal foraging in the thick brush nearby, hot wind through sedge and swamp grass.

Lord, I'm scared, she thought, flashing back vividly on the most gruesome scenes from the Stephen King and Dean Koontz novels she read late at night with her companion—a pint of Ben & Jerry's.

"Hey," a man's voice said. Very near.

Lydia gasped and spun around. Nearly dropped the flowers. "Jesse, you scared me."

"Sorry." Jesse Corn stood on the other side of a weeping willow, near the clearing that was roped off. Lydia noticed that their eyes were fixed on the same thing: a glistening white outline on the ground where Billy Stail's body had been found. Lydia could see a dark stain that, as a nurse, she recognized as old blood.

"So that's where it happened," she whispered.

"It is, yep." Jesse wiped his forehead and rearranged the floppy comma of blond hair. His uniform, the beige outfit of the Paquenoke County Sheriff's Department, was wrinkled and sweat-stained. He was thirty and boyishly cute.

"How long you been here?" she asked.

"I don't know. Since five maybe."

"I saw another car. Up the road. Is that Jim?"

"Nope. Ed Schaeffer. He's on the other side of the river." Jesse nodded at the flowers. "Those're pretty."

Lydia looked down at the daisies in her hand. "Got 'em last night." She looked around. "No idea where Mary Beth is?"

Jesse shook his head. "Not hide nor hair."

"Him neither, I guess that means."

"Him neither." Jesse looked at his watch, then out over the dark water, dense reeds and concealing grass, the rotting pier.

Lydia didn't like it that a county deputy, sporting a large pistol, seemed as nervous as she was. Jesse started up the grassy hill to the highway. "I'll be up by the patrol car."

Lydia Johansson walked closer to the crime scene. The river was deep here and fringed with black willows and thick trunks of cedar and cypress. To the northeast, not far, was the Great Dismal Swamp, and Lydia knew all the legends about that place: the Lady of the Lake, the Headless Trainman. But it wasn't those apparitions that bothered her. Blackwater Landing had its own ghost—the boy who'd kidnapped Mary Beth McConnell.

Lydia couldn't stop thinking about all the stories she'd heard about him. How he'd roam silently through the marshes and woods here, pale and skinny as a reed. How he'd sneak up on lovers parked along the river. How he'd crouch on the shoulder of the road in front of a house and look through the windows, hoping to catch a glimpse of a girl he'd been stalking after school.

Lydia strolled along the shore, stopped beside a stand of tall grass. She noticed that the sedges and cattails and wild rice plants were bending, waving, rustling. As if someone were there, moving closer, staying low to the ground. It's just the wind, she told herself. And she reverently set the flowers in the crook of a gnarly black willow not far from the eerie outline of the sprawled body.

DEPUTY Ed Schaeffer was dizzy from exhaustion. Like most of the deputies in the department, he'd been awake for nearly twenty-four hours, searching for Mary Beth McConnell and the boy who'd kidnapped her. While one by one the others had gone home to get a few hours' sleep, Ed had stayed with the search. He was the oldest deputy on the force and the biggest (fifty-one years old and two hundred and sixty-four pounds). But fatigue and hunger weren't going to stop him from continuing to look for the girl.

The deputy crouched to examine the floor of the woods, then pushed the transmit button of his radio. "Jesse, it's me," he whispered. "I got footprints here. They're fresh."

"You were right, looks like," Jesse Corn said.

It had been Ed's theory that the boy would come back here. Blackwater Landing had always been his stalking ground, and over the years he always came back here.

Ed said, "The trail looks to be moving toward you, but I can't tell for sure. I'm going to see where he was coming from."

Rising to his feet, he followed the footsteps back in the direction they'd come from, farther into the woods, away from the river. After about a hundred feet the boy's trail led to an old hunting blind—a gray shack big enough for three or four hunters. The gun slots were dark, and the place seemed to be deserted. Still . . .

Breathing hard, Ed Schaeffer unholstered his revolver. Did the boy have a gun? he wondered. He felt a flush of panic. He sprinted forward in a crouch to the side of the shack. He pressed against the weathered wood and listened carefully. He heard nothing inside but the faint buzzing of insects.

Before his courage broke, Ed rose and looked through a gun slot. No one. Then he looked at the floor. His face broke into a smile at what he saw. "Jesse," he called into his microphone excitedly, "I'm at a blind maybe a quarter mile north of the river. I think the kid spent the night here. There's empty food wrappers and water bottles. A roll of duct tape. And guess what? I see a map."

"A map?"

"Yeah. Bet it'll show us where he's got Mary Beth."

But Ed Schaeffer never found out his fellow deputy's reaction to this good piece of police work. Lydia Johansson's screaming filled the woods, and Jesse Corn's radio went silent.

LYDIA stumbled backward and screamed again as the boy leaped from the tall sedges and grabbed her arms.

"Oh, Lord, please don't hurt me!" she begged.

"Shut up," he raged. He was tall and skinny and strong. His skin was red and welty—probably from a run-in with poison oak—and he had a sloppy crew cut that looked like he'd done it himself.

His long, dirty nails dug into Lydia's skin painfully, and she gave another scream. He clamped a hand over her mouth.

She twisted her head away. "Don't hurt me! Please—"

"Just shut up!" he snapped. Instinctively she tried to jerk herself free. He wrestled her into the hot grass, and she smelled methane and rotten vegetation. He lost a shoe in the struggle, but he paid no attention and pressed his hand over her mouth again.

From the top of the hill Jesse called, "Lydia? Where are you?"

"Shh," the boy warned, eyes wide and crazy. "Come on, we're getting outa here. Scream, and you'll get hurt bad. You understand?" He reached into his pocket and showed her a knife.

She nodded.

He pulled her toward the river. "Come on."

"Hey!" Jesse cried, seeing them at last. He started down the hill.

But they were already in a small skiff the boy had hidden under some reeds and grass. He shoved Lydia into the boat and pushed off, rowing hard to the far side of the river. He beached the boat and yanked her out, then dragged her into the woods, where he found a path in the underbrush.

"Where're we going?" she whispered, sobbing now.

"To see Mary Beth. You're going to be with her." He clicked his nails together absently and pulled her after him into the woods.

"ED," CAME JESSE CORN'S urgent transmission. "Oh, it's a mess."

"What?" Ed Schaeffer stopped. He'd started jogging back toward the river when he'd heard the scream.

"He's got Lydia. He's over the river and headed your way."

"Damn." Ed thought for a moment. "Okay. He'll probably be coming back here to get the stuff in the blind. I'll hide inside, get him when he comes in. He have a gun?"

"I couldn't see."

Ed sighed. "Okay, well . . . get over here as soon as you can. Call Jim too."

He released the red transmit button and looked through the brush toward the river. There was no sign of the boy and his new victim. Panting, Ed ran back to the blind and kicked the door open. It swung inward with a crash, and he stepped inside fast.

He was so high on fear and excitement that he didn't at first pay any attention to the black-and-yellow dots that zipped in front of his face. Or to the tickle that began at his neck and worked down his spine.

But then the tickling became detonations of fiery pain on his shoulders, then along his arms and under them.

"Oh, God," he cried, gasping, leaping up and staring in shock at the dozens of yellow jackets clustering on his skin. He brushed at them in a panic, but the gesture infuriated the insects even more. They swarmed from the huge gray nest in the corner, which had been crushed by the swinging door when he kicked it in. Hundreds of the creatures were attacking him. Ed raced for the door, ripping his shirt off, and saw with horror masses of the glossy crescents clinging to his huge belly and chest. He screamed.

Run! he told himself. Run for the river, fall into the water, escape from the pain. You'll be all right.

And he did. Crashing through the forest, speeding through the underbrush that was just a hazy blur.

Wait, wait. What was wrong? Ed Schaeffer realized he wasn't running at all. He was lying on the ground only about thirty feet from the blind, his legs not sprinting, but twitching uncontrollably. For a moment he listened to the pulsing drone of the wasps, which finally became a tiny thread of sound and then silence.

 **TWO**

ONLY God could cure him. And God wasn't so inclined.

Not that it mattered, for Lincoln Rhyme was a man of science rather than theology, and so he'd traveled not to Lourdes or to some Baptist faith healer, but to this North Carolina hospital in hopes of becoming if not a whole man, at least less of a partial one.

Rhyme now steered his motorized Storm Arrow wheelchair, red as a Corvette, off the ramp of the van in which he, his aide Thom, and Amelia Sachs had just driven five hundred miles from Manhattan. His lips around the controller straw, he turned the chair expertly with puffs of air and accelerated up the sidewalk toward the front door of the Neurologic Research Institute at the Medical Center of the University of North Carolina in Avery.

Thom retracted the ramp of the glossy black Chrysler Grand Rollx, a wheelchair-accessible van.

"Put it in a handicapped space," Rhyme called, chuckling.

Amelia Sachs lifted an eyebrow to Thom, who said, "Good mood. Take advantage. It won't last." The aide drove off.

Sachs caught up with Rhyme. She was on her cell phone, on hold with a local car-rental company. Thom would be spending much of the next week in Rhyme's hospital room, and Sachs wanted the freedom to explore the region. She was a sports-car person, not a van person. She shunned vehicles whose top speed was two digits.

Sachs finally hung up in frustration. "I wouldn't mind waiting, but the Muzak is terrible. I'll try later." She looked at her watch. "Only ten thirty. But this heat is too much."

Rhyme wasn't paying any attention to the heat. His mind was solely on his mission here.

Ahead of them the automated door swung open. They entered the cool corridor and headed up the hall. Thom joined them at the elevator, and a few minutes later they found the suite they sought.

Rhyme noticed the hands-free intercom. He said a boisterous "Open sesame," and the door swung wide.

"We get that a lot," drawled the pert secretary when they'd entered. "You must be Mr. Rhyme. I'll tell the doctor you're here."

DR. CHERYL Weaver was a trim, stylish woman in her mid-forties. Rhyme noticed immediately that her eyes were quick and her hands, as befitted a surgeon, seemed strong. She rose from her desk, shook Sachs's and Thom's hands, nodded to her patient. "Lincoln."

"Doctor." Months of research had convinced Rhyme that Dr. Weaver's neuro institute set the standard for spinal cord injury research and treatment.

"It's good to meet you at last, Lincoln," she said. "You and I've had some phone conversations about the procedure. So forgive me if I repeat what you already know, but it's important for you to understand what this experimental regeneration and reconstruction technique can do and what it can't do."

"I understand," Rhyme said. "Please go on."

"The nervous system is made up of axons, which carry nerve impulses. In a spinal cord injury—an SCI—those axons are cut or crushed, and they die. So they stop carrying impulses, and the message doesn't get from the brain to the rest of the body. Now, you hear that nerves don't regenerate. That's not completely true. In the peripheral nervous system—like our arms or legs—damaged axons *can* grow back. But in the central nervous system—the brain and the spinal cord—they don't. At least they don't on their own. But there are things that we're learning to do that can help regrowth.

"Our approach here at the institute is an all-out assault on the site of the spinal cord injury. We attack SCI on all fronts. We use traditional decompression surgery to reconstruct the bony structure of the vertebrae themselves and to protect the site where your injury occurred. Then we graft two things into the site of the injury: one is some of the patient's own peripheral nervous system tissue—"

"Because that can regenerate?" Thom asked.

"Yes, yes, obviously." Rhyme frowned at his aide.

Thom was the only one of a half-dozen aides who'd survived more than a few months in the service of Lincoln Rhyme. The others hadn't appreciated his sarcasm and insults and had either quit or been peremptorily fired by Rhyme.

Dr. Weaver continued. "And the other substance we graft is some embryonic central nervous system cells, which—"

"Ah, the shark," Rhyme said.

"That's right. Blue shark, yes."

"Lincoln was telling us that," Sachs said. "Why shark?"

"Immunologic reasons, compatibility with humans. Also," the doctor added, laughing, "it's a damn big fish, so we can get a lot of embryo material from one."

"Why embryo?" Sachs asked.

"It's the adult central nervous system that doesn't naturally regenerate," Rhyme grumbled, impatient with the interruption. "Obviously, babies' nervous systems have to grow."

"Exactly. Embryonic material contains stem cells. Progenitor cells, they're called. They promote growth of nerve tissue. Then, in addition to the decompression surgery and micrografting, we do one more thing, which is what we're so excited about. We've developed some new drugs that might have a significant effect on improving regeneration. Now, the reason that axons in the central nervous system don't regrow is that there are proteins that inhibit regeneration in the sheath around the nerves. So we've developed antibodies that attack those proteins. Those antibodies allow the axons to regenerate. At the same time, we administer a neurotrophin, which encourages them to grow. These are promising new drugs, but they haven't been tried before in humans."

Sachs asked, "Are there risks?"

Rhyme glanced at her, hoping to catch her eye. He knew the risks. He didn't want her interrogating his doctor.

"The drugs themselves aren't particularly dangerous," Dr. Weaver said. "But there are risks associated with the treatment. Any fourth cervical vertebra quad is going to have lung impairment. With the anesthetic there's a chance of respiratory failure. Then the stress of the procedure could lead to severe blood-pressure elevation, which in turn could lead to a stroke. The operation and resulting fluid buildup could cause additional damage."

"Meaning he could get worse," Sachs said.

Dr. Weaver nodded and looked down at Rhyme's file. "You have movement of one lumbrical—the ring finger of your left hand—and good shoulder and neck muscle control. You could lose some or all of that. And lose your ability to breathe spontaneously. And you have to weigh these risks in light of what you hope to gain—you aren't going to be able to walk again, if that's what you were hoping for. Procedures of this sort have had only marginal success with cervical injuries and none at all with a C4-level trauma."

"I'm a gambling man," Rhyme said quickly. Sachs gave him a troubled glance. Because she knew that Lincoln Rhyme wasn't a gambling man at all. He added simply, "I want the surgery."

Dr. Weaver nodded. "You'll need to have a few tests that should take several hours. The procedure is scheduled for the day after tomorrow. I have about a thousand forms and questionnaires for you to fill out." She looked at Sachs. "Are you his attorney-in-fact?"

"*I* am," Thom said. "I can sign for him."

"Fine. Why don't you all wait here? I'll go get the paperwork."

Sachs rose and followed the doctor out of the room. Rhyme heard her asking, "Doctor, I have a . . ." The door clicked shut.

"Conspiracy," Rhyme muttered to Thom. "Mutiny in the ranks."

"She's worried about you."

"Worried? That woman drives a hundred fifty miles an hour and plays gunslinger in the South Bronx. *I'm* getting baby fish cells injected into me."

"You know what I'm saying."

Rhyme tossed his head impatiently. The door opened, and Sachs returned to the room. Someone entered behind her, but it wasn't Dr. Weaver. The man was tall, trim, and wearing a law enforcer's tan uniform. Sachs said, "You've got a visitor."

Seeing Rhyme, the man took off his Smokey the Bear hat. "Mr. Rhyme, I'm Jim Bell—Roland Bell's cousin. He told me you were going to be in town, and I drove over from Tanner's Corner."

Roland was in the NYPD and had worked with Rhyme on several cases. He'd given Rhyme the names of some of his relatives to call when Rhyme was in North Carolina, in case he wanted visitors after the operation. Jim Bell was one of them. Rhyme could see the family resemblance: the same lean physique, long hands, thinning hair, the same easygoing nature. He said absently, "Nice to meet you."

Bell gave a grim smile. He said, "Matter of fact, sir, I don't know if you're going to be feeling that way for too long. We have ourselves a problem." Bell took a seat in a chair next to Thom. "I'm sheriff of Paquenoke County. That's about twenty miles east of here. We have this situation, and well, my cousin— He can't speak highly enough of you, sir. Anyway, this situation . . . I thought I'd come over and ask if you could spare us a little time."

Rhyme laughed, a sound without a stitch of humor in it. "I'm about to have surgery."

"Oh, I understand that. I wouldn't interfere with it for the world. I'm just thinking of a few hours. See, cousin Rol told me all about some of the things you've done in investigations up north. Most of our forensics work goes through Elizabeth City—the nearest state police HQ—or Raleigh. Takes weeks to get answers. And we don't have weeks. We got hours."

"For what?"

"To find a couple of girls who got kidnapped."

"Kidnapping's federal," Rhyme pointed out. "Call the FBI."

"By the time the FBI gets set up, those girls will be goners."

"Tell us what happened," Sachs said. She was wearing her interested face, Rhyme noted with displeasure.

Bell said, "Yesterday one of our local high school boys was murdered and a college girl was kidnapped. Then this morning the perp came back and kidnapped another girl." Rhyme noticed the man's face darkened. "He set a trap, and one of my deputies got hurt bad. He's here at the medical center now, in a coma."

"Are the girls' families rich?" Sachs asked. "Any ransom notes?"

"Oh, it's not about money." The sheriff's voice lowered. "It's sexual. The boy's a stalker. He's been arrested a couple of times."

Rhyme noticed that Sachs was paying rapt attention to Bell. He knew why she was so interested in a case they didn't have the time to participate in. And he didn't like the reason one bit. "Amelia," he began, casting a cool glance at the clock on Dr. Weaver's wall.

"Why not, Rhyme? What can it hurt?" She pulled her long red hair off her shoulder, where it rested like a still waterfall.

Bell continued. "We did what we could. All of my deputies were out all night, but fact is, we just couldn't find a trail." He looked into Rhyme's eyes imploringly. "We'd sure like it if you could take a look at the evidence and give us any thoughts on where the boy might be headed. We're outa our depth here."

But Rhyme didn't understand. He was a criminalist, and a criminalist's job was to analyze evidence to help investigators identify a suspect and then to testify at his trial. "You know who the perp is, you know where he lives. Your D.A.'ll have an airtight case."

"No, no. It's not the trial we're worried about, Mr. Rhyme. It's finding those girls before he kills them. Or at least Lydia. We think Mary Beth may already be dead. See, when this happened, I was thumbing through a book on felony investigations. It was saying that in a sexual abduction case you usually have twenty-four hours to find the victim. After that they become dehumanized in the kidnapper's eyes, and he doesn't think anything about killing them."

Sachs said, "You called him a boy—the perp. How old is he?"

"Sixteen. But to see him, he's big, and his history's worse than most of our adult troublemakers."

"You've checked with his family?" she asked.

"Parents are dead. He's got foster parents. We looked through his room. Didn't find any secret trapdoors or diaries or anything."

One never does, thought Lincoln Rhyme, wishing devoutly this man would fly back to his unpronounceable county and take his problems with him.

Sachs said, "Two victims in two days? He could be a progressive." Progressive felons are like addicts. To satisfy their increasing tolerance for the crimes they commit, the frequency and severity of their acts escalate.

Bell nodded. "You got that right. And there's stuff I didn't mention. There've been three other deaths in Paquenoke County over the past couple of years. We think the perp might've been involved in all of them. We just didn't find enough evidence to hold him."

Rhyme reluctantly felt his mental gears turning, intrigued by the puzzles that the case presented. What had kept Lincoln Rhyme sane since his accident were mental challenges like this. If he'd had to decide between becoming mobile once more and keeping his questioning mind intact, he'd forgo the shark cells and surgery in a minute and choose the brain. Still, the operation, despite the risks, was vitally important to him. It was his Holy Grail.

"Your surgery's not till day after tomorrow, Rhyme," Sachs pushed. "And all you have is a couple of tests before then."

She'd made a good point. He was looking at a lot of downtime before the operation, downtime *without* eighteen-year-old Scotch. Lincoln Rhyme's greatest enemy wasn't the spasms or phantom pain that plagues spinal cord patients; it was boredom.

"I'll give you one day," he finally said. "As long as it doesn't delay the operation. I've been on a waiting list for fourteen months."

"Deal, sir," Bell said. His weary face brightened.

"How long has he been on the run?" Rhyme asked.

"Just a couple of hours," Bell said. "What I'll do is have a deputy bring over the evidence we found and a map of the area."

Rhyme shook his head and frowned. "No, no. We'll come over to the sheriff's department. What's the county seat?"

"Tanner's Corner."

"I'll need a forensic assistant. You have a lab in your office?"

"Us?" asked the bewildered sheriff. "Not hardly."

"Okay, we'll get you a list of equipment we'll need. You can borrow it from the state police." Rhyme looked at the clock. "We can be there in a half hour. Right, Thom?"

"A half hour," the aide muttered. "For the record, Lincoln, I don't think it's a good idea. We're here for your procedure."

"Get the forms from Dr. Weaver. Bring them with us. You can fill them out while Sachs and I are working."

Sachs wrote a list of the basic forensic lab equipment and handed it to Bell. He read it, then said, "I'll work this out. But I really don't want you to go to too much trouble—"

"Jim, I hope I can speak freely."

"Sure, Mr. Rhyme."

"Call me Lincoln," the criminalist said. "Just looking over a little evidence isn't going to do any good. If this is going to work, Amelia and I are going to be one hundred percent in charge of the pursuit. Is that going to be a problem for anybody?"

"I'll make sure it isn't," Bell said.

"Good. Now get going on that equipment. We need to move."

Sheriff Bell stood for a moment, hat in one hand, Sachs's list in the other, then headed for the door.

"Oh, one thing," Sachs said, stopping him as he passed through the doorway. "The perp? What's his name?"

"Garrett Hanlon. But we call him the Insect Boy."

PAQUENOKE is a small county in northeastern North Carolina. Tanner's Corner, roughly in the center of the county, is the biggest town and is surrounded by smaller clusters of residential or commercial pockets, like Blackwater Landing, which huddles against the Paquenoke River—called the Paquo by most locals—a few miles to the north of the county seat.

Nearly all of the residents live south of the river. North of the Paquo the land is treacherous. The Great Dismal Swamp has encroached and swallowed up trailers and houses, snaky bogs have replaced the ponds and fields, and the forests are almost impenetrable. No one lives on this side of the river except moonshiners and drug cookers and a few crazy swamp people. Even hunters tend to avoid the area.

Like most people in the county, Lydia Johansson rarely went north of the Paquo, and she now realized, with an overwhelming sense of hopelessness, that she'd stepped over some boundary into a place from which she might never return—not merely a geographic one but a spiritual one too.

She was terrified being dragged along behind this creature, of course—terrified of the way he looked over her body, terrified that she'd die from sunstroke or snakebite. But what scared her the most was realizing what she'd left behind: her comfortable small life—her few friends and her fellow nurses in the hospital, the pizza parties, the *Seinfeld* reruns, the horror books. She even looked back longingly at the troubled parts of her life—the struggle with her weight, the nights alone, the hours of silence when phone calls from her boyfriend never came. There wasn't a sliver of comfort where she was now.

She remembered the terrible sight at the hunting blind—Deputy Ed Schaeffer lying unconscious on the ground, swollen grotesquely from the wasp stings. Garrett had muttered, "He shouldn't've hurt 'em. Yellow jackets attack only when their nest's in danger." He'd walked inside to collect a map, water, and packs of junk food. He had taped her hands in front of her and flung away his remaining shoe.

Then he'd led her into the woods, through which they'd been traveling now for several miles.

Lydia knew about him, about the Insect Boy. Everybody in Tanner's Corner did. But she'd never seen him up close. She was surprised at how strong he seemed, with taut biceps, long veiny arms, and huge hands. The close-knit brow gave the impression that he was stupid, but she knew he wasn't. He was smart as a snake.

"Where're we going?" she asked.

"I, like, don't want to talk. Okay?"

Little by little, the marshes grew more tangled and the water deeper. Just when it seemed they could go no farther because of the choked bogs, Garrett steered them into a large pine forest, which to Lydia's relief was far cooler than the exposed swampland.

Garrett was walking slowly now, clicking his nails, looking around, as if for pursuers, his head moving in that twitchy way that repulsed and scared her. It was the way psychotic patients on E wing at the hospital behaved.

God, I hate you, she thought.

THE Rollx van passed a cemetery—Tanner's Corner Memorial Gardens. A funeral was in progress, and Rhyme, Sachs, and Thom glanced at the somber procession.

"Look at the casket," Sachs said.

It was small, a child's. The mourners, all adults, were few.

Rhyme's eyes rose above the cemetery and examined the rolling hills—a ridge covered with shade trees, the miles of hazy forest that vanished in the distance. He said, "That's not a bad cemetery. Wouldn't mind being buried in a place like that."

Sachs shifted cool eyes toward him; with surgery on the agenda, she didn't like any talk about mortality.

Then Thom eased the van around a curve and, following Jim Bell's Paquenoke County Sheriff's Department cruiser, accelerated down a straightaway.

As Bell had promised, Tanner's Corner was exactly twenty miles from the medical center at Avery. The WELCOME TO sign assured visitors that the town was the home of 3018 souls, which may have been true, but only a tiny percentage of them were evident on Main Street on this hot August morning. The place seemed to be a ghost town.

"Peaceful," Thom observed.

"That's one way to put it," said Sachs, who felt a sense of unease at the emptiness.

Main Street was a tired stretch of old buildings and two small strip malls. Rhyme noticed one supermarket, two drugstores, two bars, one diner, a bank, an insurance company, and a combination video shop/candy store/nail salon. Everybody sold bait.

Rhyme realized with dismay how out of his depth as a criminalist he was here. He could successfully analyze evidence in New York because he'd lived there for so many years, had walked its streets, studied its history and flora and fauna. But here he knew nothing of the soil, the water, nothing of the habits of the residents, the houses they lived in, the industries that employed them.

Thom parked the van and went through the ritual of lowering the wheelchair. Rhyme blew into the sip-and-puff controller of the Storm Arrow and rolled toward the steep ramp of the Paquenoke County Government Building.

Three men—in jeans and work shirts, with knife scabbards on their belts—pushed out of the side door of the sheriff's office beside the ramp. They walked toward a burgundy Chevy van.

The skinniest of the three poked the biggest one, a huge man with a braided ponytail and a beard, and nodded toward Rhyme. Their eyes—almost in unison—perused Sachs's body. Then the big one took in Thom's trim hair, impeccable clothes, and gold earring. But the men soon lost interest in the visitors and climbed into the Chevy.

Bell, walking beside Rhyme's chair, said, "That's Rich Culbeau, the big one. And his buddies: Sean O'Sarian—the skinny feller—and Harris Tomel. Culbeau's not half as much trouble as he looks. He likes playing redneck, but he's usually no bother."

The sheriff accompanied his visitors up the handicapped ramp. He had to fiddle with the door at the top of the ramp; it had been painted shut.

"Not many crips here," Thom observed. Then he asked Rhyme, "How're you feeling? You look pale."

"I'm fine."

They entered the building. It was dated circa 1950, Rhyme estimated. The halls were painted institutional green and were decorated with photographs of Tanner's Corner throughout its history.

"Will this room be okay?" Bell asked, swinging open a door. "We use it for evidence storage, but we're moving that stuff out."

Boxes lined the walls. One officer struggled to cart a large TV out of the room. Another carried two boxes of juice jars filled with a clear liquid. Rhyme glanced at them. Bell laughed. "That there just about summarizes your typical Tanner's Corner criminal: stealing home electronics and making moonshine."

"Ocean Spray brand moonshine?" Rhyme asked wryly, nodding at the jars.

" 'Shiner's favorite container—because of the wide neck. You a drinking man?"

"Scotch only."

"Stick to that." Bell nodded at the bottles the officer carried out the door. "The feds and Carolina tax department worry about their revenue. *We* worry about losing citizens. That batch there isn't too bad. But a lot of 'shine's laced with formaldehyde or paint thinner or fertilizer. We lose a couple of people a year to bad batches."

"Why is it called moonshine?" Thom asked.

Bell answered, " 'Cause they used to make it under the light of the full moon. They didn't want lanterns to attract revenuers."

The sheriff then explained that he'd called the state police lab and put in an emergency request for the equipment Rhyme wanted. The items should be there within the hour.

Rhyme gazed up at the wall, frowning. "I'll need a map of the area and a blackboard. A big one."

"Done deal," Bell said.

"Then if I could see your senior people in here? For a briefing."

"And air-conditioning," Thom said firmly. "It's not good for him to be in heat like this. We have to cool the room."

Bell said, "Not a problem. I'll take care of it." He walked to the doorway and called, "Steve, come on in here a minute."

An extremely tall young crew-cut man in a deputy's uniform walked inside. "This is my brother-in-law, Steve Farr." Bell gave him the job of finding an air conditioner for the lab.

"I'll get right on it." He turned and vanished into the hall.

A woman stuck her head in the door. "Jim, it's Sue McConnell on three. She's really beside herself."

"Okay. Tell her I'll be right there." Bell said to Rhyme, "Mary Beth's mother. Poor woman. Lost her husband to cancer just a year ago, and now this happens. I tell you—"

"Say, Jim, I wonder if we could find that map," Rhyme said. "And get the blackboard set up."

Bell blinked. "Sure thing, Lincoln. And listen, if we move a little slow for you Yankees, you'll speed us up now, won't you?"

"Oh, you bet I will, Jim."

ONE out of three. One of Jim Bell's three senior deputies seemed glad to meet Rhyme and Sachs. Well, to see Sachs, at least. The other two obviously wished this odd pair had never appeared.

The agreeable one was a thirtyish deputy named Jesse Corn.

One deputy offering the cool reception was Mason Germain, a short man in his early forties. Dark eyes, slicked-back hair, and posture a little too perfect. He wore excessive aftershave—a cheap, musky smell. He greeted Rhyme with a stiff nod. Sachs, being a woman, was entitled to only a condescending "Miss."

Lucy Kerr was the third senior deputy and wasn't any happier to see the visitors than was Mason. She was a tall woman—just a bit shorter than willowy Sachs. Trim and athletic-looking, with a long, pretty face and blond hair done up in a French braid.

Rhyme knew the cold shoulders would be an automatic reaction to the appearance of interloping cops, especially a crip and a woman—northerners, no less. But he had no interest in winning them over. The kidnapper was moving away from them with every passing minute. And Rhyme had a date with his surgeon.

A solidly built deputy—the only black deputy Rhyme had seen—wheeled in a large chalkboard and unfolded a detailed map of Paquenoke County.

"Pin it up there, Trey." Bell pointed to the wall. The deputy mounted the map with thumbtacks and left.

Rhyme said, "Now tell me exactly what happened. Start with the first victim."

Mason said, "Her name's Mary Beth McConnell. She's twenty-three. A grad student over at the campus at Avery. It was pretty early yesterday morning. Mary Beth was—"

"Could you be more specific?" Rhyme asked. "About the time?"

"Had to've been before eight," Jesse Corn offered. "Billy—the boy who was killed—was out jogging, and the crime scene is a half hour away from his home. He had to be back by eight thirty to shower and get to class."

Good, Rhyme thought, nodding. "Go on."

Mason continued. "Mary Beth was at Blackwater Landing."

"What's that? A town?" Sachs wondered aloud.

"No. Just an area a few miles north of here on the river." Mason pointed at the map. " 'Bout two dozen houses, a factory. No stores. Mostly woods and swamp. Way we see it," he continued, "Garrett comes by and grabs Mary Beth. He's going to rape her, but Billy Stail sees them from the road and tries to stop it. But Garrett grabs a shovel and kills Billy. Then he takes Mary Beth." Mason's jaw was tight. "Billy was a good kid. Went to church regular."

"I'm sure he was a fine boy," Rhyme said impatiently. "Garrett and Mary Beth—they're on foot?"

"That's right," Lucy Kerr answered. "Garrett doesn't drive. Think it's because of his folks dying in a car crash."

"What physical evidence did you find?"

"Oh, we got the murder weapon," Mason said proudly. "The shovel. We did the chain-of-custody thing, like in the books."

Rhyme asked, "Did you search the scene?"

Jesse Corn said, "Sure we did. Didn't find anything."

Didn't find anything? At a scene where a perp kills one victim and abducts another, there'd be enough evidence to make a movie of who did what to whom. It seemed they were up against two perpetrators: the Insect Boy and law-enforcement incompetence. Rhyme caught Sachs's eye and saw she was thinking the same.

"Who conducted the search?" he asked.

"I did," Mason said. "I got there first after the call came in at nine thirty. A truck driver saw Billy's body from the highway and called nine one one."

And the boy was killed before eight. Rhyme wasn't pleased. An hour and a half was a long time for a scene to be unprotected.

"Can I ask," Sachs said, "how you know Garrett was the perp."

"I saw him," Jesse said. "When he took Lydia this morning."

"Doesn't mean he killed Billy and kidnapped the other girl."

"Oh," Bell said. "The fingerprints—we got them off the shovel."

Rhyme nodded and said to the sheriff, "And the boy's prints were on file because of those prior arrests?"

"Right."

Rhyme said, "Now tell me about this morning."

Jesse took over. "It was just after sunup. Ed Schaeffer—one of our deputies—and I were at the crime scene in case Garrett came back. Lydia comes round to lay some flowers. I left her alone and went back to the car. Next thing I know, she's screaming and I see the two of them disappear over the Paquo. Ed wouldn't answer the radio, and when I got over there, I found him stung half to death. Garrett had set a trap in the blind."

Bell said, "We think Ed knows where he's got Mary Beth. Ed got a look at a map that was in that shack Garrett had been hiding in. But he got stung and passed out before he could tell us what it was of, and Garrett must've took it with him after he kidnapped Lydia."

"What's the deputy's condition?" Sachs asked.

"Went into shock. Nobody knows if he's going to make it."

So we rely on the evidence. Which was Rhyme's preference—far better than witnesses. "Any clues from this morning's scene?"

"This." Jesse opened an attaché case and took out a running shoe in a plastic bag. "Garrett lost it when he grabbed Lydia."

"Set it over there." Nodding toward a table. "Anything else?"

"Not a thing."

Struggling not to be critical, Rhyme said, "Tell me about these other deaths he was a suspect in."

Bell said, "All in and around Blackwater Landing. Two of the victims drowned in the canal. The medical examiner said they could've been hit on their heads and pushed in. Garrett had been seen around their houses not long before they died, but there wasn't any proof. Last year a girl in her twenties was stung to death. Wasps. Just like with Ed. We know Garrett did it."

"He's a psycho," Mason spat out.

"Schizophrenic?"

Lucy said, "Not according to his counselors at school. Antisocial personality's what they call it. He's got a high IQ. He got mostly excellents on his report cards, before he started skipping school a couple of years ago. Jim has a picture of him."

The sheriff opened a file. "Here's the booking shot for the hornets' nest assault."

The picture showed a thin crew-cut boy with prominent connected brows and sunken eyes. There was a rash on his cheek.

"Here's another." Bell opened a newspaper clipping. It showed a family of four at a picnic table. The caption read, "The Hanlons at the Tanner's Corner Annual Fourth of July Picnic, a week before the tragic auto accident on Route 112 took the lives of Stuart, 39, Sandra, 37, and their daughter, Kaye, 10. Also pictured is Garrett, 11, who was not in the car at the time of the accident."

"Can I see the report of the scene yesterday?" Rhyme asked.

Bell opened a folder. Thom took it. Rhyme had no page-turning frame, so he relied on his aide to flip the pages.

The crime scenes had been very sloppily worked. No soil samples had been taken. There were Polaroid photos revealing a number of footprints, but no rulers had been laid in the shot to indicate size. Also, the report contained only a cursory description of the location and pose of the boy's body. Rhyme could see that the outlining had been done in spray paint, which is notorious for ruining trace and contaminating a scene with undesirable materials.

The friction-ridge—fingerprint—report was marginally better. The shovel had four full and seventeen partials, all positively identified as Garrett's and Billy's. Still, Mason had been careless when he'd worked the scene—his latex-glove prints on the shovel covered up many of the killer's.

The equipment would be arriving soon. Rhyme said to Bell, "I'm going to need a forensic tech to help me with the analysis and the equipment. I'd prefer a cop, but the important thing is that they know science. And know the area here. Anybody come to mind?"

It was Lucy Kerr who answered. "My brother's boy, Ben. He's studying science at U.N.C.—grad school. I'll call him."

"Good," Rhyme said. Then, "Now, I want Amelia to search the crime scenes: the boy's room and Blackwater Landing."

Mason said, "But we already did that. Fine-tooth comb."

"I'd like her to search them again," Rhyme said shortly, then looked at Jesse. "You know the area. Could you go with her?"

"Sure. Be happy to."

Rhyme said, "I want Amelia to have a side arm."

When state law enforcers travel across state lines, they lose their jurisdiction and, usually, their right to carry weapons. Sachs had left her Glock and backup revolver in her Brooklyn apartment.

"Easy," Bell said. "We'll rustle you up a nice Smith and Wesson."

"Let me have some cuffs too," Sachs said.

"Sure thing."

Bell noticed Mason, looking unhappy, staring at the map.

"What is it?" the sheriff asked.

"You want my opinion?" the short man asked. "I don't think we have time for any more searches. There's a lot of territory out there. We've got to get after that boy and get after him fast."

But it was Lincoln Rhyme who responded. Eyes on the map, he said, "We don't have enough time to move fast."

THREE

"WE WANTED him," the man said cautiously, looking around the dusty front yard. "We called family services and asked about Garrett specifically. 'Cause we'd heard about him and felt sorry. But, fact is, he was trouble from the start. We're scared. Scared bad."

Hal Babbage stood on the weather-beaten front porch of his house north of Tanner's Corner speaking to Amelia Sachs and Jesse Corn. Jim Bell and another deputy had been there yesterday to search the house and see if Garrett's foster parents had any idea where the boy might have gone, but they'd been no help. Sachs was here now solely to search his room, but despite the urgency, she was letting Babbage ramble on in hopes that she might learn a bit more about Garrett. She didn't quite share Rhyme's view that evidence was the sole key to understanding and tracking down perps.

But the only thing this conversation was revealing was that Garrett's foster parents were terrified he would return to hurt them or the other children. Hal's wife, Margaret, who stood beside him on the porch, was a fat woman with curly rust-colored hair.

"I never whipped him," the man continued. "But I'd be firm with him, make him toe the line. Like, we eat on a schedule. Only Garrett wouldn't show up on time. I'd lock the food up when it's not mealtime, so Garrett went hungry a lot. And I'd make him clean that pigsty of a room. Those are just things you gotta make children do. But I *know* he hates me for 'em." He nodded to a pile of nails. "We're nailing the windows shut, but if he tries to break in, we'll protect ourselves. The children know where the shotgun is."

He encouraged them to shoot? Sachs was shocked. She'd seen several children in the house, peering through the screen door. They seemed to be no older than ten.

"Hal," Jesse Corn said sternly, preempting Sachs, "don't go taking anything into your own hands. You see Garrett, call us."

"I'd like to see his room," Sachs said.

Babbage shrugged. "Help yourself, but I'm not going in there. Scares me. You show 'em, Mags." He picked up a hammer and a handful of nails and started to pound nails into a window frame.

"Jesse," Sachs said, "cover the approach to the window. I don't want any surprises."

"Sure." And he disappeared into the side yard.

The wife said to Sachs, "His room's this way."

Sachs followed Garrett's foster mother down a dim corridor. "You're really scared he'll come back?" Sachs asked.

After a pause the woman said, "I don't know if he'll come back, but if he does, it'll be trouble. Garrett don't mind hurting people. Once, at school, some boys kept breaking into his locker and leaving notes and dirty underwear and things. Just pranks. But Garrett made this cage that popped open if you didn't open the locker just right. Put a recluse spider inside. Next time they broke in, the spider bit one of the boys in the face. Nearly blinded him."

They paused outside a closed door. On the wood was a handmade sign: DANGER. DO NOT ENTER. A badly done pen-and-ink drawing of a mean-looking wasp was taped to the door below it.

There was no air-conditioning, and Sachs found her palms sweating. She turned on the radio and pulled on the headset she'd borrowed from the sheriff's department. She found the frequency Steve Farr had given her. "Rhyme?"

"I'm here, Sachs. What've we got?"

"I'm about to go in." She tested the door. It was locked. She turned to the woman. "Do you have a key?"

Margaret hesitated, then produced one. Sachs unlocked the door. She motioned the woman back into the living room, then kicked the door in. No sound from the dimly lit room.

Okay. Pistol up. Go, go, go! She pushed inside.

"God." Sachs dropped into a low-profile combat stance, held the gun steady at the figure just inside the door.

"Sachs?" Rhyme called impatiently. "What is it?"

"Minute," she whispered, flicking on the overhead light. The gun sight rested on a poster of the monster in the movie *Alien*. With her left hand she swung the closet door open. "It's secured, Rhyme. Have to say, though, I don't really care for the way he decorates." Then the stench hit her. Unwashed clothing, bodily scents.

"Phew," she muttered. "Place stinks."

"Good, Sachs. You know my rule."

"Always smell the crime scene first. Wish I hadn't."

"I meant to clean it up," Mrs. Babbage said from the corridor. "But I was too afraid to go in. Besides, skunk's hard to get out."

That was it. Crowning the smell of dirty clothes was the scent of skunk musk. Sachs said to the woman, "I'll need time alone here."

She closed the door, looked around, repulsed by the gray, stained sheets, the piles of dirty clothes, the bags filled with the dust of potato and corn chips. The place made her angry, and she wondered why. Maybe because the slovenliness suggested that his foster parents didn't really give a damn about the boy and that this neglect had contributed to his becoming a killer and a kidnapper.

Sachs noticed that there were dozens of smudges and fingerprints and footprints on the windowsill. It seemed he used the window more than the front door, and she wondered if his foster father locked him in at night.

She turned to the wall opposite the bed and felt a chill. "We've got ourselves a collector here, Rhyme."

She looked at the dozen large jars—terrariums filled with colonies of insects that were clustered around pools of water at the bottom of each. Labels in sloppy handwriting identified the species: WATER BOATMAN, DIVING BELL SPIDER . . . A chipped magnifying glass sat on a nearby table, beside an old office chair.

Sachs shivered with revulsion. "I know why they call him the Insect Boy," she said, then told Rhyme about the jars.

"Ah, that's good for us. It's a rare hobby. If collecting coins turned him on, we'd have a harder time pinning him to specific locations. Now get going on the scene."

His voice was almost cheerful. Sachs knew he'd be imagining himself walking the grid—as he referred to the process of searching a crime scene—using her as his eyes and legs. As head of investigation and resources, the NYPD's forensics and crime scene unit, Lincoln Rhyme had often logged more hours on the grid than even junior officers. She knew that walking the grid was what he missed most about his life before he'd been left a quadriplegic since a beam crushed his spinal column at a murder site.

"What's the crime scene kit like?" Rhyme asked. Jesse Corn had dug one up for her to use.

Sachs opened the dusty metal case. It didn't contain a tenth of the equipment of her kit in New York, but at least there were the basics: tweezers, a flashlight, probes, latex gloves, and evidence bags. "Crime scene lite," she said.

Sachs pulled on the gloves as she looked over the room. Garrett's bedroom was what's known as a secondary crime scene—not the place where the actual crime occurred, but the location where it was planned, for instance, or where the perps fled and hid out after a crime. Sachs started her search, covering the floor in close parallel strips, foot by foot, the way you'd mow a lawn. She said, "He's got these posters. From *Alien* movies. And *Starship Troopers*—these big bugs attacking people. Violent. The place is filthy. Junk food, a lot of books, clothes, the bugs in the jars."

"The clothes are dirty?"

"Yep. Got a good one—pants, really stained. They must have a ton of trace in them." She dropped them into a plastic evidence bag. "I've also got a couple of notebooks here." She began flipping through the pages. "No diaries. No maps. Just drawings of insects, the ones he's got in the terrariums."

"Any of girls, young women? Sado-sexual?"

"No."

"Bring the notebooks along. How about the books?"

"Maybe a hundred or so. Books about animals, insects. A Tanner's Corner High School yearbook. It's five years old."

Rhyme asked someone in the room a question. He came back on the line. "Jim says Lydia's twenty-six. She'd have been out of high school eight years, but check the McConnell girl's page."

Sachs thumbed through the M's. "Yep. Mary Beth's picture's been cut out. He sure fits the classic stalker profile."

"The books on his shelf—which ones does he read the most? Start on the ones nearest his bed."

Sachs picked the four with the most well-thumbed pages: *The Entomologist's Handbook, The Field Guide to Insects of North Carolina, Water Insects of North America, The Miniature World.*

"I've got them, Rhyme. There are a lot of marked passages."

"Good. Bring them back. But keep looking, Sachs. He's sixteen. Teenagers' rooms are the centers of their universe. Think like a sixteen-year-old. Where would you hide things?"

She looked in and under the drawers of the desk, in the closet, under the mattress. Then she shone the flashlight under the bed. She said, "Got something here, Rhyme."

"What?"

Sachs found a cheap picture frame containing the cutout yearbook photo of Mary Beth McConnell. There was also an album of a dozen other snapshots of Mary Beth. Most were of her on what seemed to be a college campus. Two were of her in her bikini at a lake. In both the focus was on the girl's cleavage. She told Rhyme.

"His fantasy girl," Rhyme muttered. "Keep going. He may be young and quirky, but he still smells of an organized offender. Even if the girls are dead, I'll bet he's picked out nice, cozy graves for them."

Despite all the time they'd worked together, Sachs still had trouble with Rhyme's callousness. She knew it was part of being a criminalist—the distancing one must do from the horror of the crime—but it was hard for her. Perhaps because she recognized that she had the same capacity for this coldness within herself, that numbing detachment that the best crime scene searchers must turn on like a light switch, a detachment that Sachs sometimes feared would deaden her heart irreparably.

She scanned the room once more. "Rhyme, you know what's weird? He's sixteen and he doesn't have a single *Playboy* or *Penthouse* poster. No rock-musician posters. No VCR, TV, stereo, radio, or computer. Insects—that's all he cares about."

"Maybe it's a money thing—the foster parents."

"If I was his age and wanted to listen to music, I'd *build* a radio!"

Lincoln Rhyme, whose voice was never more seductive than when he was imagining a crime scene, said to her, "Go on, Sachs, get into him. Become Garrett Hanlon. What's your life like?"

She closed her eyes. The best criminalists, Rhyme had told her, were like talented novelists, who imagined themselves as their characters and could disappear into someone else's world.

And she struggled to put aside the person she really was—the cop from Brooklyn who wore her straight red hair long, the former fashion model, the championship pistol shot—trying to become a sixteen-year-old boy. Someone who needed or wanted to take women by force. Who needed or wanted to kill.

What do I feel? She said half to herself, "I don't care about normal relationships. People are like insects—things to be caged. In fact, all I care about are insects. They're my only source of comfort. My only amusement." She paced in front of the jars. Then she looked down at the floor. "The tracks of the chair!"

"What?"

"Garrett's chair—it's on rollers. It's facing the insect jars. All he does is roll back and forth and stare at them and draw them. His whole life is these bugs." But the tracks in the wood stopped before they got to the jar at the end of the row—the largest of them and set apart from the others. It contained yellow jackets. A gray, papery nest was plastered to the side of the jar, and the tiny yellow-and-black crescents zipped about angrily.

She walked to the jar, looked down at it carefully. She said to Rhyme, "There's a jar full of wasps. I think it's his safe."

"Why?"

"It's nowhere near the other jars. He never looks at it. I can tell by the tracks of the chair. And all the other jars have water in them. They're aquatic bugs. This is the only one with flying insects. It's a great idea, Rhyme. Who'd reach inside something like that? And there's about a foot of dirt at the bottom. I think he's buried something in there."

"Look inside and see."

She opened the door and asked Mrs. Babbage for a pair of thick leather gloves. When the woman brought them, Sachs put them on, then wrapped a pillowcase around her bare arm. Slowly she eased the mesh lid off the jar and reached inside. Two wasps landed on the glove, then flew off. The rest ignored the intrusion. Careful not to disturb the nest, she dug only a few inches before she found the plastic bag.

"Gotcha." She pulled it out and restored the lid. She opened the bag and spilled the contents out on the bed: A spool of thin fishing line. About a hundred dollars in cash and four silver dollars. The photo from the newspaper of Garrett and his family a week before the car accident that killed his parents and sister. An old, battered key—no logo, only a serial number. She told Rhyme about this.

"Good, Sachs. Excellent. I don't know what it means yet, but it's a start. Now get over to the primary scene—Blackwater Landing."

"I CAN'T keep up," Lydia told Garrett. "I can't go this fast." Sweat was streaming down her face. Her uniform was drenched. She was dizzy and recognized the first signs of heat stroke.

He glanced at her, eyes on her breasts, fingernails snapping.

"Please," she whispered, crying. "I can't do this! Please!"

"Quiet! I'm not going to tell you again."

A cloud of gnats swarmed around her face.

"Come on," he said. "We're gonna get something to drink."

He led her down a new path, out of the forest. Suddenly the trees vanished, and a huge pit opened in front of them. It was an old quarry. Blue-green water filled the bottom. He stripped off his shirt and bent down, splashed water on his blotched skin to relieve the itching.

She sat down near the edge and splashed water on her face.

"Don't drink it. I've got this." He pulled a burlap bag out from behind a rock. There were bottles of water inside and some packets of cheese crackers with peanut butter. He ate some crackers and drank a bottle of water. He offered her some water. She took it with her taped hands and drank it thirstily.

Refreshed, she asked, "Where's Mary Beth?"

"She's in this place by the ocean. An old Banker house."

Lydia knew what he meant. A Banker was somebody who lived on the Outer Banks, the barrier islands off the coast in the Atlantic. So that's why they'd been traveling east. He probably had a boat that'd take them to the Banks.

She said, "The Outer Banks'll take us a day to get to. More."

"Oh, we're not gonna get there today. We'll hide near here and let the creeps searching for us get past. Then we'll go on to Mary Beth. We'll spend the night."

"Spend the night?" she whispered hopelessly.

But Garrett said nothing more. He started prodding her up the steep incline to the lip of the quarry and the pinewoods beyond.

WHAT'S the attraction of the sites of death? Amelia Sachs asked the question as she stood on the shoulder of Route 112 in Blackwater Landing and surveyed the place where young Billy Stail had died, where two young women had been kidnapped, where a hardworking deputy's life had been changed forever—perhaps ended—by a hundred wasps. Even in the relentless sun and heat the mood of the place was somber and edgy.

Blackwater Landing seemed to be an ill-defined area of several square miles surrounding the swampy inlet where a canal flowed into the Paquenoke River. There were no houses in this immediate area, though Sachs had seen a number of large new colonials as they'd driven here from Tanner's Corner. But Sachs also noticed that this residential portion of Blackwater Landing, like the county seat itself, seemed ghostly and forlorn. It took her a moment to realize why: There were no children playing in the yards even though it was summer vacation. No inflatable pools, no bikes, no strollers.

She examined the crime scene again. Yellow tape encircled two areas. The one nearest the water included a bouquet of flowers. It was where Garrett had kidnapped Lydia, she assumed. The other was a dusty clearing surrounded by a grove of trees, where Garrett had killed Billy Stail and taken Mary Beth. In the middle of this scene were a number of shallow holes in the ground where Mary Beth, an archaeology student, had been excavating arrowheads and relics. Twenty feet from the center of the scene was the spray-painted outline where Billy's body had lain.

A sheriff's department car pulled onto the shoulder, and Lucy Kerr climbed out. Sachs wondered why she'd come. The deputy nodded coolly to Sachs. "Find anything helpful at the house?"

"A few things." Sachs didn't explain further and looked toward the muddy riverbank. "That's the boat he got away in?"

"Over there, yeah," Jesse Corn said, joining them. "He stole it from some folks up the river. You want to search it?"

"Later. Now, which way wouldn't he have come from to get here?"

"Wouldn't?" Jesse pointed to the east. "There's nothing that way. Swamp and reeds. Can't even land a boat. So either he came along Route 112 and down the embankment here. Or, 'cause of the boat, I guess he might've rowed over."

Sachs opened the crime scene suitcase, said to Jesse, "I want some exemplars—samples—of the dirt around here."

"Sure," he said, then asked, "Why?"

"If we can find soil at the scene that doesn't match what's found naturally here, it might be from the place Garrett's got those girls." She handed Jesse a plastic bag. He strode off, pleased to help.

Sachs checked the crime scene case. No rubber bands. She noticed that Lucy Kerr had some bands binding the end of her French braid. "Borrow those?" she asked. "The elastic bands?"

The deputy pulled them off. Sachs stretched them around her shoes. Explained, "So I'll know which footprints are mine."

As if it makes a difference in this mess, she thought. She stepped into the crime scene.

"I can't see the scenario very clearly," she told Rhyme, speaking into her headset mike, as she studied the ground. "Way too many footprints. Must've been eight, ten different people walking through here in the last twenty-four hours. But I have an idea what happened: Mary Beth was kneeling. A man's shoes approach from the west, from the direction of the canal. Garrett's. I remember the tread of the shoe Jesse found. I can see where Mary Beth stands and steps back. A second man's shoes approach from the south. Billy. He came down the embankment. Moving fast, mostly on his toes. Garrett goes toward him. They scuffle. Garrett must've got the shovel away from him. Then Billy backs up to a willow tree. Garrett comes toward him. More scuffling. Then there's the outline of Billy's body in front of the tree. Bloodstains on the ground and at the bottom of the trunk. . . . Okay, I'm going to start the search."

She walked the grid, foot by foot, covering the ground carefully, fighting the dizziness from the heat. But the search was futile.

Next she walked down to the water, searched the small boat, found nothing inside. She asked, "Jesse, can you row me over?"

He was more than happy to. Lucy Kerr climbed into the skiff as they pushed off, and the threesome rowed across the river.

On the far shore, Sachs found footprints in the mud: Lydia's shoes—the fine tread of nurse sneakers. And Garrett's prints—one barefoot, one in a running shoe with the tread that was already familiar to her. She followed the prints into the woods, to the hunting blind where Ed Schaeffer had been stung by the wasps.

"Looks like the scene was swept, Rhyme."

Criminals often use brooms or even leaf blowers to destroy or confuse the evidence at crime scenes.

But Jesse Corn said, "Oh, that was from the medevac chopper to get Ed Schaeffer out."

"But the downdraft from the rotors ruined the site," Sachs said. "Standard procedure is to move an injured victim away from the scene before you set the chopper down."

"Standard procedure?" Lucy Kerr asked abrasively. "Sorry, but we were a little worried about Ed. Trying to save his life."

Sachs didn't respond. She eased into the shed so she wouldn't disturb the wasps that were hovering around a shattered nest. But whatever Deputy Schaeffer had seen inside was gone now.

"Let's get back to the lab," Sachs said to Lucy and Jesse.

They were returning to the shore, when a man lumbered toward them from the brush. Jesse Corn drew his weapon, but before he cleared leather, Sachs had the borrowed Smittie out of the holster, cocked to double action and aimed at the intruder, who froze, blinking in surprise.

Something familiar about him. He was bearded, tall, and heavy, wore his hair in a braid. Where had Sachs seen him before?

It took Jesse's mentioning his name for her to remember. "Rich."

One of the trio they'd seen outside the county building. Rich Culbeau. Slowly she uncocked the weapon and replaced it in the holster.

"Sorry," Culbeau said. "Didn't mean to spook nobody."

"This is a crime scene, Rich," Jesse Corn said. "We're working here. Can't have you in our way."

"I don't intend to be in your way. But I got a right to try for that thousand-dollar reward that Mary Beth's mom's offering."

"Damn," Sachs spat out. Of the major factors contaminating crime scenes and hampering investigations, reward and souvenir seekers are among the worst.

Culbeau looked at Sachs. "I'm not gonna cause any trouble."

"I just want to make sure you don't hurt our chances of finding those women," Sachs added stiffly.

"That's not gonna happen." Culbeau turned and lumbered away.

Sachs spoke into the headset mike again and told Rhyme about the encounter.

He dismissed it. "We don't have time to think about the locals, Sachs. Get back here with what you've found."

As they sat in the boat on the way back across the river, Sachs asked Jesse, "How much trouble's he gonna be?"

"Culbeau?" Lucy Kerr said. "He's lazy mostly. Drinks too much, but he's never done worse than broke some jaws in public."

"What do he and his two friends do?"

Jesse said, "Oh, they don't have what you'd call real jobs. Scavenge and do day labor some. But all three of those boys have money, and that means they're running 'shine."

"Moonshine? You don't bust 'em?"

Lucy answered, "Have to find the still first. Sometimes, down here, you go lookin' for trouble. Sometimes you don't."

Which was a bit of philosophy that Sachs decided was hardly limited to the South.

They landed on the southern bank of the river, beside the crime scenes. As they climbed out, a black motorized barge, forty feet long, eased past them on the canal and headed into the river. Sachs read on the side DAVETT INDUSTRIES. "What's that?" she asked.

Lucy answered, "A company outside town. They move shipments up the Intracoastal through the Dismal Swamp Canal and into Norfolk. Asphalt, tar, stuff like that."

Rhyme had heard this through the radio and said, "Let's ask if there was a shipment around the time of the killing."

Sachs mentioned this to Lucy, but she said, "One of the first things Jim and I did." Her answer was clipped. "It was a negative. And we canvassed everybody who makes the commute along Route 112 here. Wasn't any help."

"That was a good idea," Sachs said.

"Just standard procedure," Lucy said coolly.

LINCOLN Rhyme surveyed the instruments that had arrived from the state police. Wondered what it would be like to close his fingers around an object again. With his left ring finger he could touch and had a faint sense of pressure. But the idea of actually gripping something, feeling its texture, weight, temperature was unimaginable.

In the past he'd experienced despair and denial. Now he was consumed with fury. Here were two kidnapped young women and a killer on the run. How badly he wanted to speed to the crime scene, walk the grid, pluck elusive evidence from the ground, gaze at it through the lenses of a compound microscope, punch the buttons of the computers, pace as he drew his conclusions. He thought again about the operation, about Dr. Weaver's magic hands.

"Would you please plug in the gas chromatograph and turn it on?" Rhyme said to Thom. "It needs time to warm up."

Thom walked to the machine and flicked the ON switch. Then he arranged the rest of the equipment on a fiberboard table.

Steve Farr walked into the office, lugging a huge air conditioner. "Stole it from planning and zoning," he gasped.

Jim Bell came in and helped Farr mount the unit in the window. A moment later cold air was chugging into the room.

A figure appeared in the doorway—in fact, filled it. A man in his twenties. Massive shoulders, a prominent forehead. Six five, close to three hundred pounds. In a high, bashful voice he said, "I'm Ben—Lucy Kerr's nephew."

"Ah, my forensic assistant!" Rhyme said. "Just in time."

Ben glanced awkwardly at the wheelchair. He cleared his throat and swallowed. "Aunt Lucy didn't say anything about forensics. I'm just a student, postgrad at U.N.C. in Avery. Um, what do you mean, sir, 'just in time'?"

"I mean, get over to that table. I've got samples coming in any minute, and you have to help me analyze them."

"Samples. . . . Okay. What kind of fish would that be?"

"Fish?" Rhyme responded. "We're talking crime scene samples!"

The sheriff explained, "Lincoln here's a forensic scientist from New York. He's helping us out."

"Sure." Eyes on Rhyme's legs. Back to the safety of the floor.

Rhyme decided immediately he hated this man, who was acting as if the criminalist were a circus freak. Rhyme wanted desperately to be in his hospital room, awaiting the knife and the shark cells. And part of him hated Amelia Sachs too—for engineering this whole diversion.

"The thing is, I specialize in marine sociozoology. That's the behavior of marine animal life."

Oh, great, Rhyme thought. Not only do I get a crip-phobe for an assistant, but I get one who's a fish shrink. "Well, it doesn't matter. You're a scientist. You've used a GC/MS?"

"Yes, sir," he said. "The thing is . . . Aunt Lucy just asked me to stop by. I didn't know I was supposed to help you. I mean, I have classes—"

"Ben, you have to help us," Rhyme said curtly.

The sheriff explained about the kidnappings and Garrett Hanlon.

"So we need you," Rhyme said. "We don't really have any options here. Garrett's got three hours on us, and he could kill either of his victims at any time—if he hasn't already."

The zoologist looked around the room for a reprieve and found none. "Guess I can stick around for a little while, sir."

"Thank you," Rhyme said.

Ben nodded uneasily and with the grace of a bison walked over to the chromatograph and began studying the control panel.

AMELIA SACHS JOGGED INTO the impromptu lab in the county building, Jesse Corn keeping up the speedy pace beside her. Lucy Kerr joined them a moment later. She said hello to her nephew Ben and introduced him to Sachs and Jesse. Sachs held up several bags. "The evidence from Garrett's room," she said, then held up more bags. "This is from Blackwater Landing."

Rhyme looked at the bags, troubled by the fact that he had to analyze the clues without any firsthand knowledge of the area. "Ben, you have any friends who are geologists?"

"No. They're marine biologists."

"Rhyme," Sachs said, "when we were by the canal, I saw a barge. It was shipping asphalt or tar from some local company."

"Henry Davett's company," Lucy said.

Sachs asked, "Would they have a geologist on staff?"

"I don't know," Bell said, "but Davett's an engineer, and he's lived here for years. Probably knows the land as good as anybody."

"Give him a call, will you?"

"You bet." Bell disappeared.

He returned a moment later. "I got Davett. There's no geologist on staff, but he said he might be able to help. He'll be over in a half hour." Then the sheriff asked, "So how do you want to proceed?"

"I'll be here with you, Ben, and Thom. We're going to go through the evidence. I want a small search party over at Blackwater Landing now, where Jesse saw Garrett and Lydia disappear. I'll guide the team as best I can, depending on what the evidence shows."

"Who do you want on the team?"

"Sachs in charge," Rhyme said. "Lucy with her."

"I'd like to volunteer," Jesse Corn said quickly.

Rhyme nodded. Then he said, "Probably one other."

"Four people? That's all?" Bell asked, frowning. "I could get dozens of volunteers. A hundred men."

"No. Less is better in a case like this."

"Who's the fourth?" Lucy asked. "Mason Germain?"

Rhyme lowered his voice. "What's Mason's story?"

"His attitude?" Bell asked. "That what you're talking about?"

"Exactly. He's gunning for Garrett. Why?"

"Mason worked his way up from dust, an ambitious man in a

town that hasn't got any use for ambition. He just about begged to be lead investigator on that case we were telling you about—the girl who got stung to death in Blackwater. He wanted to get that boy real bad, but he just couldn't make the case against him. When it came time for the old sheriff to retire, the board of supervisors held that against Mason. I got the job, and he didn't, even though he'd been on the force longer."

Rhyme shook his head. "We don't need hotheads in an operation like this. Pick somebody else."

"Ned Spoto?" Lucy suggested.

Bell shrugged. "He's a good man. Sure."

Rhyme turned to Sachs. "Okay, get going. Hold up where the trail stops in Blackwater Landing and wait to hear from me."

The two women and Jesse Corn left the evidence room.

Rhyme eased his head back against the wheelchair headrest and stared at the evidence bags, willing his mind to roam where his legs could not walk, to touch what his hands could not feel.

 *FOUR*

THE deputies were talking. Mason Germain, arms crossed, leaning against the hallway wall beside the door that led to the sheriff's department deputy cubicles, could hear their voices.

"How come we're just sitting here not doing anything?"

"Didn't you hear? Jim's sent out a search party—Lucy, Ned, and Jesse. And that lady cop from New York."

Damn, thought Mason. He hadn't heard it either. Furious that Bell hadn't included him on the manhunt, he stormed up the corridor and nearly collided with Bell himself as he walked out of the storeroom, where that weird guy, the one in the wheelchair, was set up and supposedly helping them with the search.

Bell stopped. "Hey, Mason, I was looking for you. I want you to get over to Rich Culbeau's place."

"Culbeau? What for?"

"Sue McConnell's offering a reward for Mary Beth, and he wants it. We don't need him to mess up the search. I want you to keep an eye on him."

"You musta known I wanted to be in the search party."

Bell looked the deputy up and down. "I can't send everybody. Culbeau's been over to Blackwater Landing once today. I can't have him screwing up the search."

"Come on, Jim. I been after this kid for three years. I can't believe you'd cut me out and hand the case over to that freak."

"Hey, enough of that." Bell lowered his voice. "You want the kid *too* bad, Mason. It could affect your judgment."

The deputy laughed bitterly. "So now I'm baby-sitting a 'shiner."

Bell motioned to another deputy. "Hey, Frank."

The tall, round officer ambled over to the two men.

"Frank, you go with Mason here. Over to Rich Culbeau's. Mason'll fill you in. You got that, Mason?"

Mason didn't answer. He just strode into the deputies' room. Frank followed a moment later. Mason walked straight to his desk, unlocked it, took out an extra speedloader, clipped in six .357 shells. He slipped the speedloader into its leather case and hooked it to his belt. He turned and gestured toward Nathan Groomer, a deputy of about thirty-five. "Groomer, I'm going to have a talk with Culbeau. You're coming with me."

"Well," Frank said, "I thought the sheriff wanted *me* to go."

"I want Nathan," Mason said.

"Rich Culbeau?" Nathan asked. "I brung him in three times for DUI. Him and me are oil and water. I'd take Frank."

Mason looked coldly at Nathan. "I want you."

Nathan sighed, stood up.

Frank asked, "Whatta I tell Jim?"

Without responding, Mason walked out of the office, Nathan in tow, and headed toward his squad car. The two men climbed in. After they'd belted up, Mason said, "Where's your Ruger?"

"My deer rifle? In my truck at home."

"We're gonna go get it."

They pulled out of the parking lot and sped out of town.

Nathan said, "The Ruger. So that's why you wanted me."

"That's right."

Nathan Groomer was the best rifle shot in the department. "So after I get the rifle, we going to Culbeau's house?"

"No. We're going hunting."

LEAVING the county building, Amelia Sachs and Lucy Kerr drove back to Blackwater Landing. Jesse Corn and Ned Spoto, a stocky deputy in his late thirties, followed in a second squad car.

At the ridge overlooking the crime scenes, Lucy and Jesse parked their cars on the shoulder. The four of them then walked down the embankment to the riverside and climbed into the skiff. Jesse rowed them across the river. On the far side they climbed out and followed Garrett's and Lydia's footsteps to the hunting blind, then about fifty feet past it into the woods. There the tracks vanished.

Lucy said to Jesse, "You know the path those druggies scooted down after Frank Sturgis pulled 'em over last year?"

He nodded. "It's the best way to get through this brush and stuff."

"Let's check it out," Ned said.

Sachs wondered how to best handle the impending conflict and decided there was only one way: head-on. "We should stay here until we hear from Rhyme."

Lucy shook her head. "Garrett had to've taken that path."

"We don't know that for sure," Sachs said. "We'll wait."

"PRIMARY scene first," Rhyme called to Ben. "Blackwater." He nodded at the evidence on the fiberboard table. "Let's do Garrett's shoe first. The one he dropped when he snatched Lydia."

Ben picked it up, unzipped the plastic bag.

"Gloves! Always wear latex gloves when handling evidence."

"Sure. Right." Ben shook the shoe, peered into it. "Looks like there's gravel inside."

"Hell, I didn't have Amelia ask for sterile examining boards." Rhyme looked around the room. "See that magazine? Tear out the subscription insert inside. They come off the printing press nice and sterile, so they make good mini-examining boards."

Ben did as instructed. He poured the dirt onto the card.

"Put a sample in the microscope and let me take a look." Rhyme wheeled close to the table, but the ocular piece was too high for him.

"Maybe I could hold it for you to look in," Ben offered.

Rhyme gave a faint laugh. "It weighs thirty pounds. We'll—"

But Ben picked up the instrument and, with his massive arms, held the scope very steady. Rhyme couldn't, of course, turn the focusing knobs, but he saw enough to give him an idea of what the evidence was. "Limestone chips and dust. Run a sample of it through the GC/MS. I want to see what else is in there."

Ben mounted the sample inside the machine and pressed the test button.

A criminalist's dream tool, the chromatograph analyzes compounds such as foods, drugs, blood, and trace elements and isolates the pure elements in them. Most commonly used in forensic science is the gas chromatograph, which burns a sample of evidence. The resulting vapors are then separated to indicate the component substances. The GC is usually connected to a mass spectrometer, which can identify many of the substances specifically.

The limestone in the sample wouldn't ignite of course. But Rhyme was interested not in the rock, but in what trace materials had adhered to the dirt and gravel. This would narrow down the location.

"It'll take a little while," Rhyme said. "While we're waiting, let's look at the dirt in the treads of Garrett's shoe. I tell you, Ben, I love treads. Shoes, and tires too. They're like sponges. Remember that. Dig some out, and let's see if it comes from someplace different from Blackwater Landing."

Ben scraped the dirt onto a subscription card, which he held in front of Rhyme, who examined it carefully. As a forensic scientist, Rhyme knew the importance of dirt. It sticks to clothes, it leaves trails, and it links criminal and crime scene. There are approximately eleven hundred different shades of soil, and if a sample from a crime scene, say, is the identical color to the dirt in the perp's backyard, the odds are good that the perp was present at the scene.

However, in order for it to have any meaning forensically, a bit of dirt from the criminal must be different from the dirt found naturally at the crime scene. So the first step in dirt analysis is to check known dirt from the scene—an exemplar—against the sample the criminalist believes came from the perp.

Rhyme explained this to Ben, and the big man picked up a bag of dirt marked EXEMPLAR SOIL—BLACKWATER LANDING along with the date and time of collection. Ben poured some of this dirt onto a subscription card. He set it beside the dirt from Garrett's shoe.

"Scope them in the comparison," Rhyme said. "See if the color of the unknown sample is different from the color of the known."

Ben mounted the samples in a comparison microscope and looked through the eyepiece. "Hard to say. But . . . maybe there is some difference."

"Let me see."

Once again Ben held the large microscope steady, and Rhyme peered into the eyepiece. "Definitely different from the known. Lighter. And it has more crystal in it. More granite and clay and different types of vegetation. So it's not from Blackwater. If we're lucky, it came from his hidey-hole." The criminalist continued, "When you get the results of the limestone on the GC/MS, run the dirt from Garrett's shoe."

"Yes, sir."

A moment later the screen of the computer attached to the chromatograph/spectrometer flickered. Then a window popped up, and Rhyme maneuvered closer in his wheelchair. He scanned the screen. "Large amounts of nitrates, phosphates, and ammonia."

This was very troubling, but Rhyme said nothing just yet. He wanted to see what substances were in the dirt that Ben had dug out of the treads. Rhyme told Ben to test the dirt now in the GC/MS. And shortly these results too were on the screen.

Rhyme sighed. "More nitrates, more ammonia, more phosphates. Detergent too. And something else. . . . The database has identified it as camphene. You ever hear of that?"

"No, sir," Ben said.

Rhyme looked at Thom, who had been sitting quietly. "Okay, Thom, time for our charts."

The aide wrote on the blackboard as Rhyme dictated to him.

Found at Primary Crime Scene—Blackwater Landing

Limestone dust	Ammonia
Nitrates	Detergent
Phosphates	Camphene

Rhyme gazed at it. More questions than answers. Then his eye fell on the dirt that Ben had dug out of the boy's shoe, and something occurred to him. "Jim!" he shouted. "Jim!"

The sheriff came running in, alarmed. "What's wrong?"

"How many people work in the building here?"

"I don't know. 'Bout twenty."

"And they live all over the county?"

"Yes. Some are from Paquotank, Albemarle, and Chowan."

"I want 'em all down here now. Everybody in the building. I want soil samples from their shoes. And the floor mats in their cars."

Bell retreated. Rhyme said to Ben, "That rack? Over there?"

The zoologist lumbered toward the table on which was a long rack holding a number of test tubes.

"It's a density-gradient tester. It profiles the specific gravity of materials like dirt."

Ben nodded. "I've heard of it. Never used one."

"It's easy. Those bottles . . ." Rhyme was looking toward two dark glass bottles, one labeled TETRA, the other ETHANOL. "You're going to mix those the way I tell you and fill the tubes close to the top."

Ben mixed the chemicals according to Rhyme's instructions and then filled twenty of the tubes with alternating bands of different-colored liquids—the ethanol and the tetrabromoethane.

"Pour a little of the soil from Garrett's shoe into the tube on the left. The soil will separate, and that'll give us a profile. We'll get samples from people who live in different areas of the county. If any match Garrett's, the dirt he picked up could be from nearby."

Bell arrived with the first of the employees, and Rhyme explained what he was going to do. The sheriff grinned in admiration. "That's an idea and a half, Lincoln."

But the time spent on this exercise was futile. None of the samples submitted matched the dirt from Garrett's shoe. Rhyme looked at the clock. Garrett had been on the run for nearly four hours. The criminalist spoke to his aide. "Thom, help us out. Sachs asked for a Polaroid camera. Find it and take close-ups of all the tubes. Mark down the name of each employee on the back of the snaps."

Thom found the camera and went to work.

"Now let's analyze what Sachs found at Garrett's foster parents' house. The pants in that bag—see if there's anything in the cuffs."

Ben carefully opened the plastic bag and examined the trousers. "Yes, sir, some pine needles. Bunch of 'em."

"Good. Did they fall off the branches, or are they cut?"

"Cut, looks like."

"Excellent. That means he cut them on purpose. That purpose may have to do with the crime. And I'd guess it's camouflage." Rhyme continued, "Okay, Ben. Cut a couple of pieces of the pants and run them through the GC/MS."

While they waited for the results, the criminalist examined the rest of the evidence. "Let me see that notebook, Thom." The aide flipped through the pages for Rhyme to see. They contained only bad drawings of insects. Nothing helpful there.

"Those other books." Rhyme nodded toward the four hard-bound books Sachs had found in Garrett's room. One—*The Miniature World*—had been read so often, it was falling apart. Some passages were marked with asterisks, but none gave any clue as to where the boy might have spent time. They seemed to be trivia about insects. He told Thom to put the books aside.

Rhyme then looked over what Garrett had hidden under his bed and in the wasp jar: Money. Pictures of Mary Beth and of his family. The old key. The fishing line. The cash was a crumpled mass of fives and tens, and silver dollars.

"Three-pound-test fishing line," Rhyme commented, looking at the spool. "That's light, isn't it, Ben?"

"Hardly catch a bluegill with that, sir."

The results of the trace on the boy's slacks flickered onto the computer screen. Rhyme read, " 'Kerosene, ammonia, nitrates.' Camphene again. Another chart, Thom, if you'd be so kind." He dictated.

Found at Secondary Crime Scene—Garrett's Room

Skunk musk	Money
Cut pine needles	Unknown key
Drawings of insects	Kerosene
Pictures of Mary Beth and family	Ammonia
Insect books	Nitrates
Fishing line	Camphene

Rhyme stared at the charts. Said, "Thom, call Mel Cooper."

The aide picked up the phone, dialed from memory.

Cooper, who often worked with Rhyme, on loan from NYPD forensics, was one of the top forensic lab men in the country.

Thom pushed the speakerphone button, and a moment later the soft tenor of Cooper's voice said, "Hello, Lincoln. Caller ID says Paquenoke County Government Building. Something tells me you're not in the hospital."

"Just helping out on a case here. Listen, Mel, I need information about a substance called camphene. Ever hear of it?"

"No. But hold on. I'll go into the database."

Rhyme heard frantic keyboard clicking. "Okay, here we go. It's a terpene—carbon and hydrogen. Derived from plants. It used to be an ingredient in pesticides, but it was banned in the early '80s. The main use was in the late 1800s. It was used for fuel in lamps. You're trying to track down an unsub?"

"He's not an unknown subject. He's extremely known. We just can't find him. So trace camphene probably means he's been hiding out in an old building. Listen, Mel," Rhyme went on. "I'm going to be sending you a photocopy of a key. I need you to trace it."

"Easy. From a car?" Cooper asked.

"I don't know where it's from."

"May be less easy than I thought. But I'll do what I can."

When they disconnected, Rhyme ordered Ben to photocopy both sides of the key and fax it to Cooper. Then he called Sachs on her cell phone.

"Which way should we go, Rhyme? We're across the river, but we lost the trail. And frankly"—her voice fell to a whisper—"the natives are restless. Lucy wants to boil me for dinner."

"I've got the basic analysis done, but I don't know what to do with all the data. I'm waiting for that man from the factory in Blackwater Landing—Henry Davett. He'll be here any minute. But listen, Sachs, I found significant traces of ammonia and nitrates on Garrett's clothes and in the shoe he lost."

"A bomb?" she asked, her hollow voice revealing her dismay.

"Looks that way. And that fishing line's too light to do any serious fishing. I think he's using it for trip wires. So go slow, look for traps. If you see something that looks like a clue, remember that it might be rigged. Okay, sit tight, Sachs. I hope to have some directions for you soon."

GARRETT and Lydia had covered another three or four miles. It was noon maybe or close to it, and the day was hot as a tailpipe.

The ground was open here. Broken forests, marshes. No houses, no roads. The paths were like a maze, branching in different directions. It would be almost impossible for anyone searching for them to figure out which way they'd gone.

They walked about a half mile along a narrow path, with rocks to the left, a twenty-foot drop-off to the right, and then Garrett stopped. He stepped into the bushes and returned with a nylon string, like thin fishing line, which he strung across the path just above the ground. It was nearly impossible to see from a standing position. He connected it to a stick, which in turn propped up a three- or four-gallon glass bottle, filled with a milky liquid. Lydia got a whiff of it—ammonia. She was horrified; as a nurse, she'd dealt with alkaline burns. This much ammonia could seriously injure a dozen people.

"You can't do that," she whispered.

"Shut up." He snapped his fingernails. He covered the bottle with boughs, then nodded toward a hill. "We'll stay there. Go on to the ocean in the morning."

Fifteen minutes later they broke from the woods and into a clearing. In front of them beside a stream that had largely been reclaimed by the swamp was an old gristmill surrounded by reeds, cattails, tall grass. One wing of the mill had burned down, and amid the rubble stood a scorched chimney.

Garrett led Lydia into the front of the mill, the portion that had been untouched by fire. He pushed her inside and swung the heavy oak door shut, bolted it. For a long moment he stood listening out the front window, from which the glass was missing. When he seemed satisfied that no one was following, he handed her a bottle of water. She filled her mouth, then swallowed slowly.

When she finished, he took the bottle from her, untaped her hands, and retaped them behind her back.

"You have to do that?" she asked.

He didn't answer, just eased her to the floor. "Sit there and keep your damn mouth shut." Garrett sat against the opposite wall and closed his eyes. They sat this way for a half hour, in complete silence, during which time Lydia became convinced that the entire population of Paquenoke County had abandoned her.

A FIGURE stepped into the room, accompanying Jim Bell.

He was a man in his fifties, with thinning hair and a round distinguished face. A blue blazer was over his arm, and his white shirt was perfectly pressed. A striped tie was stuck in place with a bar.

Rhyme thought this might be Henry Davett, but the criminalist's eyes were one part of his body that had come through his accident unscathed—his vision was perfect—and he read the monogram on the man's tie bar from ten feet away: WWJD.

William? Walter? Wayne?

Bell said, "Henry, I'd like you to meet Lincoln Rhyme."

So this *was* Davett. Rhyme nodded to the man, then said, "This is Ben Kerr, my forensic assistant."

"Sit down, Henry," Bell said, rolling an office chair up to him. The man sat, leaning forward. His posture, his confident eyes coalesced in Rhyme's perception: Davett was charming, decent, and one tough businessman. Rhyme wondered again about WWJD.

"This is about those women who got kidnapped, isn't it?"

Bell nodded. "In the back of our minds we're thinking he might've already raped and killed Mary Beth, dumped her body someplace. We're hoping we've still got a chance to save Lydia. And we have to stop him before he assaults somebody else."

The businessman said angrily, "And his killing Billy—that was such a shame. The boy was just being a good Samaritan, trying to save Mary Beth, and got himself killed." Davett turned to Rhyme. "What can I do?"

Rhyme nodded toward the evidence charts. "We're trying to link those clues to a specific location. Can you help us?"

Davett nodded. "I know the lay of the land well, and I have a chemical engineering degree." He put on eyeglasses and looked up at the chalkboard on the wall. Taking his time, he scanned the list of items found at the primary and secondary crime scenes. "Nitrates and ammonia?"

"I think he left some explosive devices to stop the search party. I've told them about it."

Frowning, Davett returned to the list. "The camphene . . . I think that was used in old lanterns. Like coal-oil lamps."

"Right. So we think the place he's got Mary Beth is old."

"There must be thousands of old houses around here. What else? Limestone dust. That's not going to narrow things down much. There's a huge ridge of limestone that runs all the way through Paquenoke County. It used to be a big moneymaker here. But the phosphate's helpful. North Carolina's a major producer of phosphate, but it's not mined around here. That's farther south. So, combined with the detergent, I'd say he's been near polluted water. Where'd he kidnap the second girl?"

"Same place as Mary Beth—Blackwater Landing." Bell touched the map. "Crossed the river, went to a hunting blind here, headed north a half mile. Then the search party lost the trail."

"Oh, then there's no question," Davett said with an encouraging confidence, looking at the map. "He crossed Stone Creek. Here. See it? Some of the waterfalls there look like beer foam. It starts out near Hobeth Falls up north, and there's a ton of runoff."

"Good," Rhyme said. "Now, once he crossed Stone Creek, any thoughts about which way he'd go?"

Davett again consulted the chart. "Pine needles. There's pine everywhere in North Carolina, but around here most of the forests are oak, cedar, cypress, and gum. The only big pine forest I know of is northeast. Here." He tapped the map. "On the way to the Great Dismal." He shook his head. "Not much else I can say. How many search parties you have out?"

"One—four people," Rhyme said.

Davett turned to him. "What! Just one? That's crazy." He waved at the map. "You should take fifty men, turn them loose around Stone Creek till you find him. You're doing it all wrong."

Rhyme could just imagine what fifty amateur bounty hunters would do in a search like this. He shook his head. "No. All we need is a small search team. A surgical strike. We'll find him."

"Henry," Bell said, "I agreed to let Mr. Rhyme run the show. We're pretty thankful to him."

The sheriff's comment was intended for Rhyme himself— implicitly apologizing for Davett.

But for his part Rhyme was delighted that the man was there. This tough businessman had looked him in the eye and told him he was dead wrong. Davett didn't even notice Rhyme's condition; all he saw was Rhyme's decision, his attitude. His damaged body was irrelevant to Davett. Dr. Weaver's magic hands would move Rhyme a step closer to a place where everyone would treat him this way.

"I appreciate your thoughts," Rhyme said evenly, "but I think we'll have to handle it the way we've started to."

The businessman seemed not to take Rhyme's position personally. "Hey, it's your choice," he said to Bell. "I'd do it differently, but that's what makes horse races. . . . I'll pray for those girls." Then turned to Rhyme. "I'll pray for you too, sir."

Rhyme understood that Davett's last promise was meant sincerely, and literally, and when Davett had left the room, Rhyme said to Bell, "Davett's tie bar. The J stands for Jesus?"

Bell laughed. "You got that right. Henry would drive a competitor out of business without a blink, but he's a deacon in church. The initials stand for 'What Would Jesus Do?' I myself don't have a clue what He'd do. All I know is we better call Lucy and your friend and get 'em on Garrett's trail."

"STONE Creek?" Jesse Corn said after Sachs had relayed Rhyme's thoughts to the search party. The deputy pointed. "A half mile that way." He started through the brush, followed by Lucy and Amelia. Ned Spoto was in the rear.

In five minutes they broke out of the tangle and stepped onto a well-trod path. Jesse motioned them along it, to the right—east.

"This is the path?" Amelia asked Lucy. "The one you thought he'd gone down?"

"That's right," Lucy responded.

"You were right," Amelia said. "But we still had to wait."

"No, *you* had to show who was in charge," Lucy said evenly.

That's right, Amelia thought, then said, "But now we know

there's probably a bomb on the trail. We didn't know that before."

In ten minutes they came to Stone Creek, its water milky and frothing with pollutant suds. On the bank they found two sets of footprints: sneaker prints in a small size but deep, probably left by a heavyset woman—Lydia, undoubtedly—and a man's bare feet. Garrett had apparently discarded his remaining shoe.

"Let's cross here," Jesse said. "I know the pine woods that Mr. Rhyme mentioned. This is the shortest way to get to them."

They made their way across the water, then continued along the trail, surrounded by the turpentiny scent of the air, lulled by the heat and the buzzing of insects.

LINCOLN Rhyme, eyes squinting at the chalkboard, studied the list of items found in Garrett's room. The evidence was inexplicable to him. He glanced again at the insect books. "Thom, could you get me the page-turning frame?" Rigged to an ECU—an environmental control unit—that Rhyme could trigger with his one working finger, the device used a rubber armature to turn pages of books.

"It's in the van. I'll go get it."

He returned a minute later with the turning frame.

"Ben," Rhyme called, "that book on top—the *Field Guide to Insects of North Carolina?* Would you put it in the frame?"

Thom showed Ben how to mount the book, then plugged a set of wires into the ECU underneath Rhyme's left hand. The criminalist read the first page, found nothing helpful. His left ring finger flicked sideways a fraction of an inch. The armature's own finger slid sideways. The page turned.

SURROUNDED by the oily scent of pine, Amelia Sachs and the deputies followed the path through the forest until they came to a steep hill—a series of rocks about twenty feet high. Lucy Kerr was suddenly aware that they hadn't seen Garrett's or Lydia's footprints for a long time. She scaled the incline easily, but at the top she stopped, thinking, No, something's wrong here.

Amelia climbed up beside her, paused. A moment later Jesse and Ned appeared.

"What is it?" Amelia asked Lucy, assessing her frown.

"Doesn't make any sense for Garrett to come this way."

"We've been following the path, like Mr. Rhyme told us," Jesse said. "Garrett's prints were leading this way."

"They *were*. Haven't seen them for a couple of miles."

"Why don't you think he'd come this way?" Amelia asked.

"Look what's growing here." Lucy pointed. "Swamp plants. And look how marshy the ground's getting. We're headed right for the Great Dismal Swamp. There's no cover there, no houses, no roads. The best Garrett could do would be to slog his way into Virginia, but that'd take days. I think we ought to turn around."

She thought that Amelia'd throw a hissy fit, but the woman pulled out her cell phone and made a call. She said into the phone, "We're in the pine forest, Rhyme. There's a path, but we can't find any sign that he came along here. Lucy says it's mostly swamp northeast of here. It doesn't make any sense for him to come this way."

Lucy said, "I'm thinking he'd head south, back across the river."

Amelia repeated this to Rhyme, listened, then hung up. "Rhyme says to keep going. The evidence doesn't suggest he went south."

This was crazy, Lucy thought. Two people who knew nothing of the area telling lifelong residents how to do their job. But she turned and started along the path, leaving the others behind.

Amelia's phone rang, and she slowed as she took the call.

Lucy strode quickly over a thick blanket of pine needles. There was no way Garrett Hanlon would come this way. It was a waste of time. They should have dogs. They should—

Then the world became a blur, and she was tumbling forward, falling hard onto the path and giving a short scream.

"Don't move," Amelia Sachs said, climbing to her feet after tackling Lucy. "Don't move! Ned and Jesse, you either."

Ned and Jesse froze, not sure what was going on.

Amelia found a long stick in the woods, picked it up. She moved forward slowly, slipping the branch into the ground.

Two feet in front of Lucy, where she'd been about to step, the stick disappeared through a pile of pine boughs. "It's a trap."

"But there's no trip wire," Lucy said. "I was looking."

Carefully Amelia lifted away the boughs. They rested on a network of fishing line and covered a pit about two feet deep.

"The fishline wasn't a trip wire," Ned said. "It's a deadfall pit. Lucy, you nearly stepped right in it."

"And inside? There's a bomb?" Jesse asked.

Amelia said to him, "Let me have your flashlight." He handed it to her. She shone the beam into the hole, then backed up quickly. "No bomb. Hornets' nest," she said.

Ned looked. "That bastard."

Amelia carefully lifted off the rest of the boughs, exposing the hole and the nest, which was about the size of a football.

"Man," Ned muttered, closing his eyes, undoubtedly considering what it would have been like to find a hundred stinging wasps clustered around your thighs and waist.

Lucy rose to her feet. "How'd you know?"

"I didn't. That was Lincoln on the phone. He was reading through Garrett's books. There was an underlined passage about some insect called an ant lion. It digs a pit and stings its enemy to death when it falls in. Rhyme remembered the cut pine needles and the fishing line. He figured that the boy might dig a trap and cover it with pine boughs, put the bomb inside."

"Let's burn the nest out," Jesse said. "It's dangerous."

"No," Amelia said.

Lucy agreed with the policewoman. "A fire'd give away our position. Just leave it uncovered so people can see it."

They started down the path once more and covered a good quarter mile before Lucy found it in her to say, "Thanks. Y'all were right about him coming this way. I was wrong." She hesitated, then added, "Jim made a good choice, bringing you down from New York to help out on this. I wasn't real crazy about it at first, but I won't argue with results."

Amelia frowned. "Jim didn't bring us down. We were over at the medical center in Avery. Rhyme's having some surgery day after tomorrow. Jim heard we were here, so he came by this morning to ask if we'd look at some evidence. That's all. You were worried he didn't think you could handle the case?"

Lucy laughed. "I guess I was being paranoid. . . . So, you were over at the medical center. That's where Lydia Johansson works."

"I didn't know," Amelia said.

A dozen memories flooded back into Lucy Kerr's mind. "That's why I'm pretty eager to save Lydia. I had some medical problems a few years ago, and she was one of my nurses. The best."

"We'll get her," Amelia said.

Lucy asked, "That surgery your friend's having? It's for his . . . situation?"

"Yep. But it probably won't do anything. It's experimental."

"And you don't want him to go through with it?"

"I don't, no. It could kill him. Or make him even worse. He could go into a coma. Or lose his ability to breathe or communicate."

"You talked to him about it?" Lucy asked.

"Yes. But it didn't do any good."

Lucy nodded. "I figured he was a man who's a bit muley."

Amelia said, "That's putting it mildly."

THE phone rang, and with a snap of his left ring finger Rhyme answered it.

Sachs's voice clattered into his headset. "We're at a dead end, Rhyme. There are four or five paths here, going in different directions, and we don't have a clue which way Garrett went."

"I don't have anything more for you, Sachs. But the books are fascinating. They're pretty serious reading for a sixteen-year-old. He's smarter than I would have figured. Where are you exactly?" Rhyme looked up. "Ben! Go to the map, please."

"About four miles northeast of where we forded Stone Creek."

Rhyme repeated this to Ben, who put his hand on a part of the map. "I think that's the old quarry," he said.

"Oh, hell." Rhyme shook his head in frustration. "Why didn't anybody tell me there was a quarry near there?"

But of course there was no one to blame but himself. Henry Davett had said that limestone was big business in the area at one time. How else do companies produce commercial limestone? Rhyme should've asked about a quarry as soon as he'd heard that. And the nitrates weren't from pipe bombs at all, but from blasting the rock—that kind of residue would last for decades.

He said into the phone, "There's an abandoned quarry about a quarter mile to your west, Sachs."

A pause. Faint words. She said, "Jesse knows about it."
"Garrett was there. I don't know if he still is. So be careful."

HANDS taped, sitting against the wall, Lydia was terrified. Her captor would pace for a while, look out the window, then squat on his haunches, clicking his fingernails and muttering to himself, looking over her body, then go back to pacing.

They were in what seemed to have been the mill office. From here she could look down a corridor, partly burned out, to another building, probably the grain storage and grinding rooms.

Something orange caught her eye nearby. She squinted and saw bags of Doritos. Also potato chips. Reese's peanut butter cups. Sodas and Deer Park water. Why all this food? How long would they be staying here? Garrett had said just for the night.

Lydia asked, "Is Mary Beth all right? Have you hurt her?"

"Oh, yeah, like I'm going to hurt her," he said indignantly. "I don't think so. The only reason I took her away is to make sure she's okay." Agitated and nervous, he ripped open one of the bags of chips and ate several handfuls, chewing them sloppily. He offered her the bag. "I'll undo your hands if you want some. But I'll have to tape them in front of you."

She shook her head, struggling against nausea.

He drank down an entire can of Coke, ate more chips. Then suddenly he leaped up and crouched close beside her.

Lydia winced as she smelled his body odor. Eyes downcast, she waited for his hands to crawl over her. But Garrett wasn't interested in her, it seemed. He moved aside a rock and lifted something out from underneath.

"A millipede." He smiled. It was long and yellow-green, and he let it climb over his hand. "I like them," he said. "They're dangerous if you try to hurt them. When a millipede is scared, it emits poison and then escapes. A predator crawls through the gas and dies. That's pretty wild, huh?" He watched the millipede making its way toward his elbow.

Lydia felt the horror rising in her. She knew she should stay calm, knew she shouldn't antagonize Garrett, should just play along with him. But seeing that disgusting bug slither over his arm, watching his wet red eyes, she convulsed in panic. The disgust and the fear boiled up in her, and she rolled onto her back. Garrett looked at her, curious what she was doing. And Lydia kicked out as hard as she could with both her feet, catching him squarely in the chest. The kick sent him tumbling backward. He hit his head against the wall with a dull thud and rolled to the floor, stunned.

Lydia struggled to her feet and ran blindly. Hands behind her, still dizzy from the heat and dehydration, she stumbled down a bright corridor. A stairway led to the second floor. She staggered up it, gasping for breath and, not having her hands for balance, bounding off the walls and the wrought-iron railing.

She heard Garrett running through the room below, looking for her. Panic filled her, and she started to regret her defiant escape. But there was no going back, she decided. She couldn't surrender now. She'd hurt him, and he was going to hurt her back if he found her.

The room at the top of the stairs was large, with two huge millstones in the center. The wooden grinding mechanism was rotted, but the waterwheel, powered by the diverted stream, still turned slowly. Rust-colored water cascaded off it into a deep narrow pit, like a well. Lydia couldn't see the bottom.

"Stop!" Garrett cried suddenly. He stood in the doorway.

Lydia jerked in shock.

He stared at her with hatred. "Come on back to the room. I've gotta tape your legs up now."

He started forward.

She looked at his bony face, his angry eyes. Into her thoughts came a burst of images: Mary Beth locked away somewhere. The scuttling millipede. The fingernails snapping.

It was all too much for her. Calmly Lydia stepped out of Garrett's path, past the millstones, and, hands still bound behind her, plunged headfirst into the narrow pit of dark water.

THE crosshairs of the telescopic sight rested on the redheaded cop's shoulders. That was some hair, Mason Germain thought.

He and Nathan Groomer were on a rise overlooking the old Anderson Rock Products quarry, about a hundred yards away from the approaching search party.

Nathan looked at the deputies and the redhead. "Why're you sighting down on Lucy Kerr with my gun?"

Mason handed back the Ruger and said, " 'Cause I didn't bring my binoculars. And it wasn't Lucy I was looking at."

They started along the ridge. Mason was thinking about the redhead. Thinking about pretty Mary Beth McConnell. And Lydia. Thinking too how sometimes life just didn't go the way you wanted it to. He knew he should've advanced further than senior deputy by now. He knew he should've handled his request for promotion differently. Just like he should've handled the first Garrett Hanlon case a lot differently. Now he was paying for those bad choices.

"You gonna tell me what we're doing?" Nathan asked.

"If Jim asks, we were here looking for Culbeau," Mason said.

"And what we're really doing is . . . "

"We're going to get that boy," Mason said. "They're going to flush him for us"—nodding toward Sachs and the deputies—"and you're going to shoot him, Nathan. And kill him dead."

"Shoot him? Hold on there. You're not ramshagging my career 'cause you're hot to get that boy."

"You don't have a career," Mason shot back. "You got a job. And if you want to keep it, you'll do what I'm telling you. Listen, I've talked to Garrett during those other investigations when he killed those other people. And know what he told me?"

"No. What?"

Mason was trying to think if this was credible. "Garrett said he'd kill any law that tried to stop him. Said he was looking forward to it."

"You tell Jim?"

" 'Course I did. But he didn't pay it a lick of mind. See, nobody appreciates the danger like I do. That kid's killed four people so far."

Nathan never even guessed there might be another reason Mason was hot to get that boy. "It's not like I'm a sniper or nothing, Mase."

Mason continued. "You know what the courts are going to do. He's sixteen. They're gonna say, 'Poor boy. Parents are dead. Let's put him in some damn halfway house.' Then he's going to get out in six months, kill some other girl in town who never hurt a soul."

"Thing is, we kill him, we lose any chance of finding Mary Beth."

Mason gave a sour laugh. "Mary Beth? You think she's alive? No way. Garrett raped her and killed her. It's our job now to make sure that don't happen to anybody else. You with me?"

Nathan didn't say anything, but the snapping sound of the deputy pressing the long copper-jacketed shells into the rifle's magazine was answer enough.

 *FIVE*

OUTSIDE the window was a large hornets' nest. Resting her head against the greasy glass of her prison, an exhausted Mary Beth McConnell stared at it. More than anything else in this terrible place, the nest—gray and disgusting—gave her a sense of hopelessness. More than the bars that Garrett had so carefully bolted outside the windows that he had nailed shut. More than the thick oak door, secured with three huge locks. More than the memory of the terrible trek from Blackwater Landing in the company of the Insect Boy.

Garrett had been gone when she'd wakened this morning, groggy and nauseated from the heat. The first thing that she'd noticed was the nest outside the back window, near the bedroom. He'd put the nest there himself, resting it on a forked branch that he'd propped up near the window. At first she couldn't figure out why. But then, with a feeling of despair, she understood: Garrett Hanlon, her captor, had left it as a flag of victory.

She found a rubber band in her backpack and tied her long brunette hair into a ponytail. Sweat trickled down her neck, and she felt a fierce aching of thirst. She was breathless from the stifling heat in the closed room. She thought about taking off her thick denim shirt—she always wore long sleeves when she was on a dig around brush or tall grass (snakes and spiders). But she didn't know when her captor would return, and she didn't want to give Garrett Hanlon any encouragement in *that* department.

With a last glance at the wasps' nest Mary Beth stepped away from the window, then walked around the three-room shack once more, searching futilely for a breach. It was a solid building, very old, with thick-timbered walls. Outside the front window was a field of tall grass that ended in a line of trees a hundred yards away. The cabin itself was in another stand of thick trees. Out the back window she could just see through the trunks to the glistening surface of the pond they'd skirted yesterday to get here.

The rooms themselves were small but surprisingly clean. In the living room were a long brown-and-gold couch; several old chairs around a cheap dining-room table; and another table, on which were a dozen quart juice jars covered with mesh and filled with insects. A second room contained a mattress and an empty dresser. The third room was empty. There were several half-full cans of brown paint sitting in the corner; it seemed that Garrett or someone had painted the exterior of the cabin recently. The color was dark and depressing, and she couldn't understand why he'd picked it, until she realized it was the same shade as the bark of the trees that surrounded the cabin. Camouflage. And it occurred to her that the boy was much cagier and more dangerous than she'd thought.

In the living room were stacks of junk food, but also rows of canned fruits and vegetables—Farmer John brand, which Mary Beth had never heard of. From the label a stolid farmer smiled at her, the image as outdated as the 1950s Betty Crocker. She searched the cabin desperately for water or soda—anything to drink—but couldn't find a thing. The canned vegetables would be packed in juice, but there was no can opener or utensil to open them.

Downstairs was a root cellar that you reached through a trapdoor in the floor of the main room. Earlier, Mary Beth had worked up her courage and walked down the rickety stairs into the low-ceilinged basement, looking for a way out of the horrible cabin. But there'd been no exit, just dozens of old boxes and jars and bags.

As frightened as she'd been with Garrett padding around the cabin yesterday, she was as scared now that he'd forget about her. And she'd die here of thirst.

Outside the window the yellow jackets oozed obscenely in and out of the gray nest.

CHOKING, spitting water, hands still taped behind her back, Lydia found herself in a swampy pool about fifty feet downstream from the mill. She kicked hard to right herself, wincing in pain.

She'd either sprained or broken her ankle on the wooden paddle of the waterwheel as she'd leaped into the sluice. But the water here was six or seven feet deep, and if she didn't kick, she'd drown.

The pain in her ankle was astonishing, but Lydia forced her way to the surface. She found that by filling her lungs and rolling on her back, she could float and keep her face above water as she kicked with her good foot toward the shore. Finally her feet touched the muck of the bottom. Slowly she moved up a steep incline of mud and decaying leaves and staggered into the sedge and swamp grass. She lay down, gasping, and looked around her.

No sign of Garrett. She struggled to her feet, tried to pull her hands apart. But the duct tape held tight. She could see the mill from here. There was no doubt which way to go; she knew where the path was. Move, she told herself. Go, go, go!

Despite fear, despite hopelessness, she started toward the path, limping against the pain in her leg.

IT WAS Jesse Corn who found the bag. "Here! Look here. I've got something. A crocus sack."

Amelia Sachs walked down a steep incline and along the edge of the quarry to where the deputy stood pointing at an old cloth bag.

"Rhyme," Sachs called into her phone, "we're at the quarry. We've got a bag here. What they call a crocus sack. It's an old burlap bag. Looks like there's something in it."

Rhyme asked, "Garrett leave it?"

She looked at the ground. "It's definitely Garrett's and Lydia's footprints. They lead up an incline to the rim of the quarry."

"Let's get after them," Jesse said.

"Not yet," Sachs said. "We need to examine the bag."

"Describe it," the criminalist ordered.

"Burlap. Old. About twenty-four by thirty-six inches. Not much inside. It's closed up. Not tied, just twisted." Sachs eased a corner of the bag down, peered inside. "It's okay. No traps."

Lucy and Ned came down the path, and all four of them stood around the bag.

"What's in it?" Rhyme asked.

Sachs pulled on her latex gloves. "Empty water bottles. Deer

Park. No store price or inventory stickers on them. Wrappers from two packages of cheese crackers with peanut butter. No store stickers on them either. You want UPC codes to trace the shipments?"

"No time. Any idea what was inside originally?" Rhyme asked.

Sachs turned the bag inside out. A few old, shriveled corn kernels fell onto the ground.

"Corn, Rhyme."

The criminalist asked, "Farms around here?"

Sachs relayed the question to the search party.

"Dairy, not corn," Jesse said. "But you'd feed corn to cows."

"Sure," Ned said. "I'd guess it came from a feed-and-grain store someplace. Or a warehouse."

"You hear that, Rhyme?"

"Feed and grain. Right. I'll get on that. Anything else?"

Sachs looked at her hands. They were blackened. She turned the bag over. "Looks like there's scorch on the bag. It wasn't burned itself, but it was sitting in something that was. Charcoal, looks like." She glanced at Garrett's and Lydia's footprints. "We're going after them again, Rhyme."

"I'll call when I have more answers."

Sachs announced to the search party, "Back up to the top." Feeling shooting pains in her knees, she gazed up to the lip of the quarry, muttering, "Didn't seem that far when we got here."

"Oh, hey, that's a rule—hills are always twice as high going up as coming down," said Jesse Corn.

LYDIA was moving as quickly as she could toward the path that would take her to freedom, but her ankle hampered her progress. She paused and looked around. Had Garrett fled? Given up on her and gone to the Outer Banks to be with Mary Beth?

Another thirty feet . . . and there it was—the path!

And then the Insect Boy's hand lashed out from beneath a lush bay tree and snagged her good ankle. Unstable anyway, hands useless, Lydia could do nothing but try to twist to the side so that her solid rump took the force of the fall.

Garrett leaped on top of her, pinning her to the ground, face red with anger. He must've been lying there for fifteen minutes. Keeping silent, not moving an inch until she was within striking distance. Like a mantis waiting for its next kill.

"Please," Lydia muttered, "don't hurt—"

"Quiet." He stared at her as if debating whether to rape and kill her right now. Then he lifted her roughly to her feet and pulled her after him toward the mill, oblivious to her sobbing.

BACK to the insect books, Rhyme decided. The items Sachs had found were common, and nothing could be deduced from them.

Using his left ring finger to tap the ECU controller, Rhyme flipped through the pages of *The Miniature World,* reading the passages Garrett had marked. The information about the ant-lion pit had saved the search party from falling into one of the boy's traps. As fish psychologist Ben had told him, animal behavior is often a good model for human, especially when it comes to matters of survival.

> Praying mantises rub their abdomens against their wings, producing an unearthly noise, which disorients pursuers. . . .
>
> Insects make great use of the sense of smell. For them it is a multidimensional sense. When an ant finds food, it returns to the nest, leaving a scented trail, sporadically touching the ground with its abdomen. When other ants come across the line, they follow it back to the food. They know which direction to go in because the scent is "shaped"; the narrow end of the smell points toward the food like a directional arrow. Insects also use smells to warn of approaching enemies.

But what of all this was revealing to the case? A beautiful green-and-black fly zipped around the room with an unfocused desperation that seemed to match Rhyme's own.

SACHS and the deputies moved slowly as they tried to follow the frail indications of Garrett's passage. And all the while they kept their eyes out for more traps.

They'd left the pines behind. Sachs looked around. Now the trees were what you'd see in a tropical jungle. Lucy said they were tupelo gum, old-growth bald cypress, cedar. And they were bound together with webby moss and clinging vines that absorbed sound like thick fog. There were scummy marshes all around them. The aroma in the air was that of decay.

Finally they stopped at a crossroads, where the path branched out in three directions. As Sachs looked down the choked paths, it seemed impossible that anyone, even Rhyme, could figure out where their prey had gone.

Jesse took a drink of water and said, "You feel different out here. This sounds funny, but you feel that life's different, cheaper. I'd rather be arresting a couple of armed kids on angel dust at a mini-mart than come out here on a call. At least there you kinda know what to expect. Out here . . ." He shrugged.

Sachs's cell phone rang. She listened, nodded, hung up. She took a breath and looked at the three deputies. "Rhyme and the sheriff just heard from the hospital about Ed Schaeffer. Looks like he woke up long enough to say, 'I love my kids,' and then he died. I'm sorry."

Lucy lowered her head, and Jesse put his arm around her shoulders. "What do we do now?" he asked.

Lucy looked up. Sachs could see tears in her eyes. "We're gonna get that boy, that's what," she said with a grim determination. "That all right with you?" she asked Sachs.

"It's fine with me."

LYDIA Johansson and Garrett were back in the mill, in the dark office once again. Lydia sat against the wall, legs splayed. Garrett's eyes were locked on to her body. Her soaked, translucent uniform had ripped open in her fall down the sluice, and Garrett stared with fascination at her bare chest. Lydia eased away from him, wincing at the pain in her ankle, feeling a cold, spidery repulsion. He wasn't just an insect; he was a creature out of a horror book.

"It's your fault you hurt yourself," he said. "You shouldn't've run. Let me see it." Nodding toward her swollen ankle. He sat down beside her. His long fingers—God, they were huge—gripped her around the calf. He studied her ankle. "It's not cut. But it's all black. What's that mean?"

"Might be broken."

He didn't respond. He moved her foot, then froze. His head tilted back, and he inhaled deeply.

Lydia sniffed the air too. A sour smell. Ammonia.

He leaped up. "The trap! They've tripped it! They'll be here in ten minutes! How did they get here so fast?" He leaned into Lydia's face. "You leave anything on the trail? Send 'em a message?"

She cringed, sure he was about to kill her. "No! I swear!"

Garrett continued frantically. "I have to get to Mary Beth."

"I can't walk," Lydia said, sobbing. "What are you going to do with me?"

He hurried to the door, looked outside, returned. He pulled a folding knife from the pocket of his pants. Opened it up with a surprisingly loud click. Turned toward her.

"No, no, please."

"You're hurt. There's no way you can keep up with me."

Lydia stared at the blade, which was stained and nicked. She said a shaky prayer. He came closer.

How had they gotten here so fast? Garrett Hanlon wondered again, jogging from the mill to the stream, the panic he felt prickling his heart the way the poison oak hurt his pale skin. His enemies had covered the ground from Blackwater Landing to the mill in just hours. He was astonished; he'd thought it would take them at least a day, probably two, to find his trail.

Relax, he told himself. After the ammonia bottle had crashed down on the rocks, the police would be moving slowly; they'd be worried about other traps. He probably had a half-hour lead. In a few minutes he'd be in the bogs, and they'd never be able to follow him. Even with dogs. He'd be with Mary Beth in eight hours. He—

Garrett stopped. On the side of the path was an empty water bottle. It looked as if somebody had just dropped it. But nobody ever came here. He picked up the bottle, smelled the inside. Ammonia!

He thought, Oh, no!

A woman's voice barked, "Hold it right there, Garrett." A pretty redheaded woman in jeans and a black T-shirt stepped out of the bushes. She was holding a pistol and pointing it directly at his chest. Her eyes went to the knife in his hand, then back to his face.

"He's over here," the woman shouted. "I've got him." Then her voice dropped, and she looked into Garrett's eyes. "Do what I say, and you won't get hurt. I want you to toss the knife away and lie down on the ground, face first."

But the boy didn't lie down. He merely stood still, slouching awkwardly. He looked utterly scared and desperate.

Amelia Sachs glanced again at the knife in his hand. She kept the sight of the Smith & Wesson on his chest. "Garrett, lie down. Nobody's going to hurt you if you do what we say."

"I got Lydia," Ned Spoto called. "She's okay. Mary Beth's not here."

Sachs said, "Throw the knife over there, Garrett. On the ground. Then lie down."

He stared at her cautiously. Red blotches on his skin, eyes wet.

"Come on, Garrett. There are four of us. There's no way out."

"How?" he asked. "How'd you find me?"

She didn't tell him that Lincoln Rhyme had led them to the mill and the ammonia trap. He had just phoned her as they'd started down the center path at the crossroads. He'd said, "Jim Bell talked to one of the feed-and-grain clerks. Guy told him that you don't see corn used as feed around here. He said it probably came from a gristmill. Jim knew about an abandoned one that had burned last year. That'd explain the scorch marks."

Bell got on the phone and told the search party how to get to the mill. Then Rhyme came back on and added, "I've got a thought about the ammonia too."

He'd been reading Garrett's books and found an underlined passage about insects using smells to communicate warnings. Garrett had possibly rigged the ammonia on a fishing-line trip wire so that when the pursuers spilled it, the boy could smell that they were nearby and he could escape.

After they had found the trap, it had been Sachs's idea to fill one of Ned's water bottles with ammonia and pour it on the ground outside the mill to flush the boy. And flush him it had.

"YOU got a shot? Take it," Mason Germain was whispering.

A hundred yards away from where that bitchy redhead from New York was confronting the killer, Mason and Nathan Groomer were on the crest of a bald hill.

Mason was standing. Nathan was prone on the hot ground. He'd sandbagged the Ruger on a low rise of helpful rocks.

"Mason, the boy's not doing anything."

They saw Lucy Kerr and Jesse Corn walk into the clearing, their guns also pointed at the boy. Nathan continued. "Everybody's got him covered, and it's only a knife he's got. And it looks like he's going to give up."

"He's not going to give up," spat out Mason. "He's faking. He's gonna kill one of 'em as soon as their guard's down."

"Come on, Mason. Lucy and Jesse are six feet away from him."

"Nobody shoots better than you. Take your shot, Nathan."

Mason waited for the booming report of the Ruger. Instead he heard a sigh.

Nathan lowered his head. "I can't."

"Gimme the damned gun."

"No, Mason. Come on."

But the expression in the senior deputy's eyes silenced the marksman, and he handed over the rifle immediately, stood up.

"How many rounds in the clip?" Mason snapped as he dropped to his belly.

"Five. But—nothing personal, Mason—you ain't the best rifle shot in the world, and there are three innocents in the field of target."

Mason knew this. But good shot or bad, he also knew that the Insect Boy had to die and had to die now.

He breathed steadily, curled his finger around the ribbed trigger, and rested the crosshairs on Garrett's face.

The redhead moved closer to the boy, and for a moment her shoulder was in the line of fire. Then she swayed back out of view.

Mason lowered the crosshairs to Garrett's chest. He knew he should squeeze the trigger gently. But, as so often in his life, anger took over. He pulled the trigger with a jerk.

BEHIND Garrett a plug of dirt shot into the air. An instant later the booming sound of the gun filled the clearing.

Sachs spun around. From the delay between the sound of the bullet itself and the muzzle report, she knew the shot hadn't come from Lucy or Jesse but from a hundred yards or so behind them.

Crouching, Sachs glanced at Garrett. Saw his eyes—the terror and confusion in them. For a moment he wasn't a killer or a rapist. He was a scared little boy, whimpering, "No, no!"

The deputies too were trying to spot the shooter. "Who is it?" Lucy Kerr called as they took cover. "Culbeau?"

Another shot snapped past. This one was a wider miss.

"Oh, my God," Jesse Corn said. "Wait, wait. Look, up there. It's Mason. And Nathan Groomer. On that rise."

Furiously Lucy pressed the transmit button on her Handi-talkie and shouted, "Mason, what the hell are you doing? Are you there? Are you receiving? Damn, I can't get reception."

Sachs pulled out her cell phone and called Rhyme. "We've got him, Rhyme. But that deputy—Mason Germain—he's on a hill nearby, firing at the boy. We can't get him on the radio."

"No, no, no, Sachs!" shouted Rhyme. "He can't kill him. If Garrett dies, we'll never find Mary Beth."

Another shot. A rock shattered, spraying them with dust.

Sachs said to Rhyme, "Ask Bell if Mason's got a cell phone and have him call, tell him to stop the shooting."

"Okay, Sachs." Rhyme signed off.

Sachs made a fast decision and tossed her gun on the ground, then stepped forward to stand between Mason's gun and the boy. She stopped breathing. A moment passed. No more shots.

"Garrett, you've got to put the knife down."

"You tried to kill me! You tricked me!"

"No! We didn't have anything to do with it. Look, I'm in front of you. I'm protecting you. He won't shoot again."

Jesse Corn was sprinting through the brush up the hill, waving his arms and calling, "Mason, stop shooting! Stop shooting!"

Garrett studied Sachs's face closely. Then he tossed the knife aside and started compulsively clicking his fingernails.

As Lucy ran forward and cuffed Garrett, Sachs turned to the hill where Mason had been shooting from. She saw him stand, speaking on his phone. Then he shoved it into his pocket and started down the hill.

"What the hell were you thinking of?" Sachs raged as he reached her.

"Saving your ass, lady," Mason replied harshly.

Jesse tried to diffuse the situation. "Mason, she was trying to calm things down, is all. She got him to give up."

But Amelia Sachs didn't need any big brothers. She walked straight up to Mason and said, "I've been doing takedowns for years. He wasn't going to move on me. The only threat was from you. You could've hit one of us."

"Oh, bull." Mason leaned close to her, and she could smell the musky aftershave he seemed to have poured on. "Anyway, I don't know what the hell we need you down here for."

"Mason," Lucy cut in, "we wouldn't've found Lydia if it hadn't been for Mr. Rhyme and Amelia here. Let it go."

"She's the one not letting it go."

"When somebody puts me in the line of fire, there better be a good reason," Sachs said evenly. "And it's no reason at all that you're gunning for that boy because you haven't been able to make a case against him."

"Hey," Jesse called. "There's the chopper."

A helicopter from the medical center landed near the mill, and the medics brought Lydia out on a stretcher; she had a badly sprained ankle. She'd been hysterical at first—Garrett had come at her with a knife, and even though he just used it to cut a piece of duct tape to gag her, she was still very shaken. She managed to calm down enough to tell them that Garrett had Mary Beth hidden somewhere on the Outer Banks. Lucy and Mason tried to get Garrett to say where, but he remained mute and sat, hands cuffed behind him, staring at the ground.

Lucy said to Mason, "You, Nathan, and Jesse walk Garrett over to Easedale Road. I'll have Jim send a car over there. The Possum Creek turnoff. Amelia wants to search the mill. I'll help her. Send another car for us in a half hour or so."

Mason walked sullenly away, gripped Garrett roughly by the arm, and pulled him to his feet. The boy cast a hopeless look at Sachs as Mason led him down the path, followed by Nathan.

Sachs said to Jesse, "Keep an eye on Mason. You may need all of Garrett's cooperation to find Mary Beth. And if he's too scared, you won't get anything out of him."

"I'll make sure of it, Amelia." He glanced her way. "That was gutsy, what you did—stepping in front of him. I wouldn't've done that."

"Well," she said, "sometimes you just act and don't think."

He nodded. "Oh, hey, I was gonna ask—you have a nickname you go by?"

"Not really."

"Good. I like 'Amelia' just the way it is."

For a ridiculous moment she thought he was going to kiss her to celebrate the capture. Then he started off after the others.

Brother, thought an exasperated Amelia Sachs, watching him go. One of the deputies wants to shoot me, and one of them adores me.

SACHS walked the grid inside the mill, concentrating on the room where Garrett had kept Lydia. She found the map that poor Ed Schaeffer had gotten a look at. It showed Garrett's route to the mill, but no places beyond that were marked.

Then Lucy called out from the grinding room. "I've got something." She brought a box over to Sachs. "Found this hidden behind the millstone."

Inside were a pair of old shoes, a waterproof jacket, a compass, and a map of the North Carolina coastline. Sachs also noticed a dust of white sand in the shoes and in the folds of the map.

Lucy started to open up the map.

"No," Sachs said. "There could be some trace inside. Wait till we're back with Lincoln. We lose trace now, we lose it forever." Then she said, "Come on, I want to check out the path he was going down when we stopped him. It led to the water. Maybe he had a boat hidden there. There might be another map or something."

They left the mill and hiked down toward the stream. As they walked, Sachs said, "We ought to send somebody back to that trap—the hornets' nest. Kill 'em and fill in the hole."

"Oh, Jim sent Trey Williams, one of our deputies, over there. But there weren't any wasps. It was an empty nest."

So it wasn't a trap at all, just a trick to slow them down. Sachs reflected that the ammonia bottle too wasn't intended to hurt anybody. Garrett could have rigged it to spill on his pursuers, blinding and burning them. But he'd perched it on the side of a small cliff.

If they hadn't found the fishing line first and had tripped it, the ammonia would have fallen onto rocks ten feet below the path, warning Garrett with the smell but not hurting anyone.

Again she had an image of Garrett's wide frightened eyes.

MARY Beth McConnell stood beside the grimy front window of the shack. She was edgy and faint from the close heat of her prison and from lack of water. She knew she couldn't last more than a day or two in this heat without something to drink. Oh, Garrett, I knew you'd be trouble, she thought angrily. She remembered the old saw "No good deed goes unpunished."

I should never have helped him out. But how could I not save him from those high school boys? She recalled seeing the four of them, watching Garrett on the ground after he'd fainted on Maple Street last year. One tall sneering boy, a friend of Billy Stail's, was about to urinate on Garrett. I *had* to stop them.

But once I'd saved you, from that moment I was yours. . . .

At first, after that incident, Mary Beth was amused that he shadowed her like a shy admirer. Waving hello, calling her at home, leaving presents: a green beetle in a tiny cage, a dragonfly on a string.

But then she began to notice him nearby a little too often. He'd spot her on Main Street and make a beeline to her, glancing at her breasts and legs and hair, rambling on: *"Mary Beth, did you know that if a spiderweb was, like, stretched all around the world, it would weigh less than an ounce? And it's stronger than steel and more elastic than nylon?*

She rearranged much of her life to avoid running into him. But then something happened that would unite her and Garrett far more than she'd ever imagined: She made an important discovery on the banks of the Paquenoke River. Last week, while walking along the Paquo in Blackwater Landing, she'd noticed something half buried in the mud. She'd dropped to her knees and started moving aside dirt. And there it was—the evidence that could prove Mary Beth McConnell's theory, which would rewrite American history.

Like all North Carolinians—and most schoolchildren in America—Mary Beth had studied the Lost Colony of Roanoke. In the late 1500s a settlement of English Colonists landed on Roanoke

Island, between the mainland of North Carolina and the Outer Banks. After some harmonious contact between the Colonists and the local native Americans, relations deteriorated. With winter approaching and the Colonists running short of food, Governor John White, who'd founded the colony, returned to England for relief. By the time he returned to Roanoke, the Colonists—more than a hundred men, women, and children, including Virginia Dare, the first English child born in America—had disappeared.

The only clue to what had happened was the word Croatoan carved in several tree trunks near the fort. This was the Indian name for Hatteras, about fifty miles south of Roanoke. Most historians believed the Colonists died at sea en route to Hatteras or were killed when they arrived.

Mary Beth never thought much about the story until she was studying the Lost Colony at the university. After reading old diaries and journals from the sixteenth and seventeenth centuries, she came to the conclusion that the Colonists had left the word Croatoan to lead off their attackers and escaped not south but west, where they settled along the Paquenoke River, in what was now called Blackwater Landing. There they grew more and more powerful, and the Indians, fearful of the threat, attacked and killed them.

But Mary Beth had never found any proof to support her theory. She'd spent days prowling around Blackwater Landing with old maps, trying to figure out exactly where the Colonists' settlement might have been. Finally last week she made her discovery—what she believed to be evidence of the Lost Colony.

Yesterday morning she had packed up her brushes, her jars and bags, and her gardener's spade and headed off to Blackwater Landing to continue her archaeological work. And what had happened? She'd been kidnapped by Garrett Hanlon, the Insect Boy. Now here she was, alone in this hot, disgusting cabin trapped in a psychotic teenager's love nest. A wave of hopelessness coursed through her. She sat down and cried.

"WE'VE caught him," Rhyme said to Jim Bell and Steve Farr. "That was the bargain. Now I have to get back to the hospital." He was eager to begin preparing for his operation.

"Well, Lincoln," Bell began delicately, "it's just that he's not talking. He's not telling us anything about where Mary Beth is."

Lydia had reported only that Mary Beth was alive and on the Outer Banks.

Ben Kerr stood nearby, beside the computer connected to the GC/MS. He seemed to regret the impending end of his assignment. Amelia Sachs was in the lab too. Mason Germain wasn't, which was just as well—Rhyme was furious that he'd endangered Sachs's life.

Sachs now took up the sheriff's cause. "We found some evidence at the mill, Rhyme. Lucy did, actually. Good evidence."

Rhyme said sourly, "If it's good evidence, then somebody else'll be able to figure out where it leads to."

"Look, Lincoln," Bell began, "you're the only one round here who's got experience at major crimes like this. We'd be at sea trying to figure out what that's telling us." He nodded at the GC/MS.

Rhyme glanced at Sachs's imploring face. Sighing, he finally asked, "Garrett's not saying *anything?*"

"He's talking," Steve Farr said, "but he's denying killing Billy, and he's saying he got Mary Beth away from Blackwater Landing for her own good. Won't say a word about where she is."

"Thom," Rhyme snapped, "call Dr. Weaver at the medical center. Tell her I'll be here for a little longer."

"That's all we're asking, Lincoln," Bell said, relief in his lined face. "An hour or two. We sure appreciate it."

Rhyme asked Bell, "How's Lydia?"

"She's all right. She said that the search party got there just in time. Garrett was about to rape her."

"Okay. . . . Ben, we've got some things to look at."

Ben nodded, pulled on his latex gloves. He then opened the box Lucy had found at the mill and took out the map.

"Let's see if there's any trace in the folds. Open it over a newspaper," Rhyme ordered.

Sand poured out. Rhyme noted that it was ocean sand, the sort that would be found on the Outer Banks. The grains were clear, not opaque, as would have been the case with inland sand.

"Run a sample through the GC/MS. Let's see if there's any other trace that'll be helpful."

Ben started the noisy machine, working it like an expert. As they waited for the results, Ben spread the map out on the table. It depicted the eastern shore of North Carolina. But Garrett hadn't marked any location.

The GC/MS results flashed up onto the screen. Rhyme glanced at it. "Not much help on a specific area. Sodium chloride—salt—along with iodine, organic material. All consistent with seawater." Rhyme asked Ben, "Any other trace in the shoes?"

The young man examined them carefully, even unlacing them, just as Rhyme was about to ask him to do this. This boy has good criminalist potential, Rhyme thought. Probably shouldn't be wasting his talent on neurotic fish.

"Flecks of dried leaves, looks like. Maple and oak, I'd guess."

Rhyme nodded, then looked up at the evidence charts. His eye paused at the references to camphene.

"Sachs, in the mill, were there any old-fashioned lamps?"

"No," she answered. "None."

The criminalist shook his head, said to Bell, "I'm sorry, Jim. The best I can tell you is that she's probably being held in a house near the ocean but—if the deciduous leaves are near the place—not *on* the water. Because oak and maple wouldn't grow in sand. And it's old, because of the camphene lamps. That's the best I can do."

Rhyme was elated that his job was now finished but frustrated that the answer to the puzzle of finding Mary Beth still eluded him. But, as his ex-wife used to say to him as he walked out the door of their apartment at one or two a.m. to run a crime scene, you can't save the entire world. He knew it was time to leave. "I wish you luck, Jim."

Bell said, "Well, I'm going to talk to Garrett again, see if he'll cooperate. Lincoln, you're a lifesaver. I can't thank you enough."

Sachs said to Bell, "You mind if I come with you?"

"Feel free," the sheriff said.

AMELIA Sachs and Jim Bell walked along the blistering sidewalk toward the lockup, which was two blocks away from the sheriff's department. Again she was struck by the ghost-town quality of Tanner's Corner. A coiffed woman parked her Mercedes in an empty row of parking spaces, climbed out, and walked into the nail salon.

The glitzy car seemed completely out of place in the town. There was no one else on the street. Where were the children?

They reached the jail—a single-story cinder-block building—and walked inside. The groaning air conditioner kept the rooms mercifully cool. Bell told Sachs to drop her gun in the lockbox. He did the same, and they walked into the interrogation room.

Wearing a blue jumpsuit, courtesy of the county, Garrett Hanlon sat at a table, across from Jesse Corn. Sachs looked at the boy and was struck at how sad and desperate he seemed.

In a kind voice Bell said, "Did Deputy Kerr read you your rights?"

"Yeah."

"There's a lawyer on his way—Mr. Fredericks. You don't have to talk to us until he gets here. You understand that?"

He nodded.

Sachs saw the one-way mirror. Wondered who was on the other side, manning the video camera.

"But we hope you'll talk to us, Garrett," Bell continued. "First of all, it's true Mary Beth's alive?"

"Sure she is."

"Did you rape her?"

"I'd never do that." Pathos gave way to indignation.

"But you kidnapped her," Bell said.

"Not really. She, like, didn't get it that the Landing's dangerous. I had to get her away so she'd be safe. That's all. I saved her."

"She's near the beach, isn't she? Where exactly, Garrett?"

He looked down at the table. "I can't tell you."

"Garrett, you're in serious trouble, son. You got a murder conviction staring you in the face."

"I didn't kill Billy."

"How'd you know it was Billy I was talking about?" Bell asked.

Garrett's fingernails clicked together. "Whole world knows Billy got killed," he said, his eyes resting on Amelia Sachs.

"We got your fingerprints on the shovel that killed him."

"The shovel? That killed him?" He seemed to think back to what had happened. "I remember seeing it lying there on the ground. I guess maybe I picked it up."

"Why?"

"I don't know. I wasn't thinking. I felt all weird seeing Billy lying there, like, all bloody and everything."

"Well, if you didn't, you have any idea who *did* kill Billy?"

"This man. Mary Beth told me that she was, like, doing this project for school there, by the river, and Billy stopped to talk to her. And then this man came up. He'd been following Billy, and they started arguing and fighting, and this guy grabbed the shovel and killed Billy. Then I came by, and the man ran off."

"What were they arguing about?" Bell asked skeptically.

"Drugs, Mary Beth said. Sounded like Billy was selling drugs to the kids on the football team. Like, those steroid things?"

"Garrett," Bell said, "I knew Billy. He wasn't into drugs."

"I understand that Billy Stail ragged on you a lot," Jesse Corn said. "Called you Bug Boy. You took a swing at Billy once, and he and his friends beat you up bad."

Garrett looked down. "Maybe. But I didn't kill him."

"And Ed Schaeffer died, you know. He got stung to death by those wasps in the blind."

"I'm sorry. That wasn't my fault. I didn't put the nest there. It was just there in the hunting blind. Had been for a long time. I went there all the time, and they didn't bother me."

"Well, tell us about this man you say killed Billy," the sheriff said. "You ever see him around here before?"

"Yes, sir. Two or three times the last couple years."

"White, black?"

"White. And he was tall. About as old as my foster father."

"His forties?"

"Yeah, I guess. He had blond hair. And he was wearing overalls. Tan ones. And a white shirt."

"But it was just your and Billy's fingerprints on the shovel," Bell pointed out. "Nobody else's."

Garrett said, "Like, I think he was wearing gloves."

"Why'd he be wearing gloves this time of year?" Jesse asked.

"Probably so he wouldn't leave fingerprints," Garrett shot back.

Sachs thought back to the prints on the shovel. She and Rhyme hadn't done the printing themselves. Sometimes it's possible to image grain prints from gloves.

"Well, what you say could've happenend, Garrett. But it just doesn't seem like the truth to anybody."

"Billy was dead! I just picked up the shovel and looked at it."

"What about Lydia?" Bell asked. "Why'd you kidnap her?"

"I was worried about her too."

"Because she was in Blackwater Landing?"

"Right."

"You were going to rape her, weren't you?"

"No!" Garrett started to cry. "I wasn't going to hurt her. Or anybody. And I didn't kill Billy! Everybody's trying to get me to say I did something that I didn't!" He gazed at Sachs with imploring eyes.

Bell dug up a Kleenex and handed it to the boy.

The door swung open fast, and Mason Germain walked in. He'd probably been the one watching through the one-way mirror, and from the look on his face it was clear he'd lost patience.

"Listen to me, boy," he began. "You tell us where that girl is, and you tell us now. 'Cause if you don't, you're going to Lancaster. Case you haven't heard about Lancaster, let me tell—"

"All right, that's enough," a high-pitched voice commanded.

A bantam strode into the room—a short man in a gray suit, baby-blue shirt, and striped tie. He wore shoes with three-inch heels. "Don't say another word," he said to Garrett.

"Hello, Cal," Bell said, not pleased the visitor was here. The sheriff introduced Sachs to Calvin Fredericks, Garrett's lawyer.

"What are you doing interrogating my client without me here?"

"He knows where the girl is, Cal," Mason muttered. "He's not telling us. He had his rights read to him. He—"

"A sixteen-year-old boy? Well, I'm inclined to get this case thrown out right now and get on to an early supper." He turned to Garrett. "Hey, young man, how you doing?"

"My face itches."

"They mace you?"

"No, sir. Poison oak."

"We'll get it taken care of. Get some cream or something. Now, I'm going to be your lawyer. The state appointed me. You don't have to pay. They told you you didn't have to say anything?"

"Yes, sir. I said I'd talk to Sheriff Bell here."

The lawyer said to Bell, "Oh, this is cute, Jim. What *were* you thinking of? Four deputies in here?"

Mason said, "We were thinking of Mary Beth McConnell. Who he kidnapped and raped."

"I didn't!" Garrett shouted.

"Shh, Garrett," Fredericks said. To Bell he said, "This interrogation is over with. Take him back to the cell."

As Jesse Corn was leading him out the door, Garrett stopped suddenly and turned to Sachs. "Please, you have to do something for me. Please! My room at home—it's got some jars."

"With your insects?" she asked.

The boy nodded. "Will you put water in them? Please."

She sensed everyone's eyes upon her. "I'll do it. I promise."

Garrett gave her a faint smile before Jesse led him out. The lawyer started after him, but Bell stuck a finger in his chest. "You're not going anywhere, Cal. We're sitting here till McGuire shows up."

"Don't touch me, Bell," he muttered. But he sat. "My Lord, what's all this? You talking to a sixteen-year-old without—"

"Shut up, Cal. I wasn't fishing for a confession. We got more evidence than we need to put him away forever. All I care about is finding Mary Beth. All we know is she's on the Outer Banks. That's a big haystack to find somebody in without his cooperation."

"No way. He's not saying another word."

"She could die of thirst, Cal. She could starve to death."

When the lawyer gave no response, the sheriff said, "Cal, that boy's a menace. He's got a slew of incident reports against him."

"Mostly for truancy. Oh, and for peeping—when he wasn't even on the property of the complaining party, just hanging out nearby."

Bell said, "This incident's different, Cal. We got eyewitnesses, we got hard evidence, and now one of my deputies is dead. We can do to this boy what we pretty much feel like."

A slim man in a wrinkled blue seersucker suit walked into the interrogation room. Thinning hair, a lean fifty-five-year-old face. "I heard enough to make me think this is one of the easiest cases of murder one, kidnapping, and sexual assault I've had in years."

Bell introduced Sachs to Bryan McGuire, the county prosecutor.

"He's sixteen," Fredericks said.

The D.A. said, "Isn't a venue in this state that wouldn't try him as an adult and put him away for two hundred years."

"You're fishing for a bargain, McGuire?" Fredericks asked.

McGuire nodded.

"Of course we're bargaining," Bell said. "There's a good chance that girl's alive, and we want to find her before she's *not* alive."

McGuire said, "We got so many charges on this one, Cal, you'd be amazed at how flexible we can be."

"Amaze me," the cocky defense lawyer said.

"I'll give you first manslaughter for Billy," McGuire offered, "and negligent homicide for Ed Schaeffer."

Fredericks chewed on this. "Let me see what I can do," he said, then vanished into the cell to consult with his client. He returned five minutes later, and he wasn't happy.

"What's the story?" Bell asked.

"He's stonewalling, Jim. He says he's protecting the girl. He says you oughta go look for this guy in tan overalls and a white shirt."

Bell said, "He's making it up."

McGuire slicked back his hair. "Listen, Cal. Get us the girl's whereabouts, and if she's alive, I'll go with reduced counts. You don't, I'll take it to trial and go for the moon. That boy'll never see the outside of a prison again. We both know it."

Silence. Then Fredericks said, "I've got a thought. I had a case in Albemarle a spell back, a woman who claimed her boy had run away from home. But it seemed fishy. She was giving us pretty odd stories and had a history of mental problems. I hired this psychologist, hoping he could give me an insanity opinion. He ran some tests on her. During one of 'em she opened up completely and told us what happened."

"Hypnosis?" McGuire asked. "That recovered memory crap?"

"No. He called it empty chair therapy. It really started her talking. Let me give this guy a call and have him come over and talk to Garrett. The boy might open up. But"—now the defense got to poke a finger at Bell's chest—"everything they talk about is privileged, and you don't get diddly unless I say so first."

Bell caught McGuire's eye and nodded.

The D.A. said, "Call him."

Sachs turned to Fredericks. "What happened with the child? Did he run away?"

"Naw. The mother killed him. Baled him up in chicken wire with a cinder block and drowned him in a pond behind the house. Hey, Jim, how do I get an outside line?"

 *SIX*

ON THE street across from the lockup Amelia Sachs saw Lucy Kerr sitting on a park bench in front of a deli, drinking from a bottle of iced tea. She crossed the street. The women nodded to one another.

Sachs went into the deli and came out a minute later with a beer in a large Styrofoam cup. She sat next to the deputy. She told Lucy about the discussion between McGuire and Fredericks, about the psychologist.

"Hope that works," Lucy said.

They said nothing for a few minutes. A lone teenager clattered past on a noisy skateboard and vanished. Sachs commented on the absence of children in town.

"True," Lucy said. "I think most of the young couples have moved away. Tanner's Corner is not the sort of place for anybody on the way up."

Sachs asked, "You have any children?"

"No. Buddy and I never did. Then we split up, and I never met anybody after that. My big regret, I'll have to say—no kids."

"How long you been divorced?"

"Three years."

Sachs was surprised the woman hadn't remarried. She was very attractive, especially her eyes. When Sachs had been a professional model in New York, before she decided to follow in her father's law-enforcement footsteps, she'd spent a lot of time with many gorgeous people. But so often their gazes were vacant. If the eyes aren't beautiful, Amelia Sachs concluded, neither is the person.

Sachs told Lucy, "Oh, you'll meet somebody, have a family."

"I've got my job," Lucy said quickly. "Don't have to do everything in life, you know." She paused. "Fact is, I don't date much."

"Really?"

Another pause. Then on impulse, it seemed, the policewoman said, "You know that medical problem I told you about?"

Sachs nodded.

"Breast cancer. Wasn't too advanced, but the doctor said they probably should do a double mastectomy. And they did, three and a half years ago. Now I'll meet some nice guy and we'll have coffee or something, but in ten minutes I start to worry about what he's going to think. And I end up not returning his phone calls."

"I'm sorry," Sachs said sympathetically. "You go through chemo?"

"Yup. Was bald for a while. Interesting look." Lucy sipped her iced tea. "Maybe when I'm older, I'll meet a widower with a couple of grown kids. That'd be nice."

She said this casually, but Sachs could hear in her voice that she'd repeated it often to herself. Maybe every day.

"You've always wanted children?" Sachs asked.

Lucy lowered her head. "I'd give up my badge in a minute for a baby. But, hey, life doesn't always go in the direction we want."

"And your ex left you after the operation?"

"Not *right* after. But pretty soon. Hell, I can't blame him. I ended up being different. Turned into something he hadn't bargained for."

Sachs said nothing for a moment. Then she offered, "Lincoln's different. About as different as they come."

Lucy considered this. "So there's more to you two than just being—what would you say?—colleagues?"

"That's right," Sachs said.

"Thought that might be the case." She laughed. "Hey, you're the tough big-city cop. How do you feel about children?"

"I'd like 'em. Pop—my father—wanted grandkids. He was a cop too. Liked the idea of three generations on the force."

"Past tense?"

"Died a few years ago."

Lucy looked at Sachs. "Can he have children? Lincoln?"

Sachs sipped the beer in earnest. "Theoretically, yes," she answered. And chose not to tell Lucy that this morning when they were at the Neurologic Research Institute in Avery, she had slipped out of the room with Dr. Weaver to ask if the operation would affect Rhyme's chances of having children. The doctor had said that it wouldn't and had started to explain about the intervention necessary that would enable her to get pregnant. But just then Jim Bell had shown up with his plea for help.

Nor did she say that Rhyme always deflected the subject of children, leaving her to speculate why he was so reluctant. It could have been any number of reasons: His fear that having a family might interfere with his practice of criminalistics, which he needed to keep his sanity. His knowledge that quadriplegics, statistically at least, have a shorter life span than the nondisabled. Perhaps it was the belief that he and Sachs would hardly be the most normal of parents.

Lucy mused, "I always wondered, if I had kids, would I keep working? How 'bout you?"

"I carry a weapon, but I'm mostly crime scene. I'd cut out the risky stuff. Have to drive slower too. Sitting in my garage in Brooklyn right now I've got a Camaro that'll churn three hundred sixty horsepower. Can't really see having one of those baby seats in it." A laugh. "I guess I'd have to drive a Volvo station wagon."

Silence fell between them—that odd silence of strangers who've shared secrets and realize they can go no further with them.

Lucy looked at her watch. "I should get back to the station house. Help Jim make calls about the Outer Banks." She tossed the empty bottle into the trash, shook her head. "I keep thinking about Mary Beth. Wondering where she is, if she's okay, if she's scared." Lucy paused. "Hope to see you before you leave," she said, and started to walk away.

"I'll be around for a while," Sachs said. "Lincoln's operation is in two days, and he'll have a week or so of recovery."

A car pulled up across the street, and two men got out. Garrett's lawyer, Cal Fredericks, was one, and the other was a heavyset man in his forties. He was in a shirt and tie. His sleeves were rolled up, and his navy sports jacket was draped over his arm. His tan slacks were savagely wrinkled. His face had the kindness of a grade-school teacher. They walked inside the lockup.

Sachs tossed the Styrofoam cup in an oil drum outside the deli, crossed the street, and followed them into the jail.

Inside, Cal Fredericks introduced Sachs to Dr. Elliott Penny. They shook hands. Then Sachs turned to the defense lawyer. "Can I ask you something?"

"Yes'm," he said cautiously. Sachs was, in theory, working for the enemy.

"What's Lancaster?"

"The Violent Felony Detention Center."

"It's juvenile?"

"No, no. Adult."

"But he's sixteen," Sachs said.

"Oh, McGuire will try him as an adult."

"How bad is Lancaster?"

The lawyer shrugged. "He'll get hurt. No getting around that. A boy like that is going to be at the bottom of the food chain. The best we can do is hope the guards look out for him."

"How about bail?"

"There's no judge in the world who'd set bail in a case like this." Fredericks nodded toward Dr. Penny. "No, our best bet is to get Garrett to cooperate, then work out a plea."

"Shouldn't his foster parents be here?"

"Should be. I called them, but Hal said the boy's on his own."

"But Garrett can't be making decisions on his own," Sachs said. "He's just a boy."

"Oh, the court'll appoint a guardian," Fredericks explained. "Don't worry. He'll be looked out for."

Sachs turned to the doctor. "What're you going to do? What's this empty chair test?"

"It's not a test," Dr. Penny explained. "It's a technique that gets very fast results in understanding certain types of behavior. I'm going to have Garrett imagine that Mary Beth is sitting in a chair in front of him and have him talk to her. Explain to her why he did what he did. I hope to get him to understand that she's frightened, that she'll be better off if he tells us where she is."

The lawyer glanced at his watch. "You ready, Doctor?"

Dr. Penny nodded.

"Let's go." The doctor and Fredericks disappeared into the interrogation room.

Sachs hung back, got a cup of water from the cooler. When the deputy at the front desk turned his attention back to his newspaper, she stepped into the observation room, where there was a video camera for taping suspects. The room was empty. She shut the door and sat down, peered into the interrogation room. She could see Garrett in one chair in the middle of the room. The doctor took a seat at the table. Fredericks stood in the corner, his arms folded.

A third chair, unoccupied, sat facing Garrett.

Through the cheap, clattering speaker above the mirror Sachs heard their voices.

"Garrett, I'm Dr. Penny. How're you?"

No answer. Garrett looked down, clicked his finger and thumb.

Fredericks said, "The doctor's here to help you, Garrett. He's going to talk to you and try to find out a few things. But everything you say is going to be just between us. We won't tell anybody else without your permission. You understand that?"

The boy nodded.

"Remember, Garrett," the doctor said, "we're the good guys. We're on your side. . . . Now, see that chair there? We're going to play sort of a game. You're going to pretend there's somebody real important sitting in that chair."

"Like the President?"

"No. Somebody important to you. I want you to talk to that person. And I want you to be real honest. If you're mad at them, you tell them that. If you love them, tell them so. It's okay to say anything at all. Nobody's going to be upset with you."

"Just talk to the chair?" Garrett asked the doctor. "Why?"

"For one thing, it'll help you feel better about the bad stuff that's happened today." He moved the empty chair closer to Garrett. "Now, imagine that Mary Beth is sitting there. And you've got something important you want to say to her. Something you've never said before, because it was too hard or too scary."

"But I don't want to say anything to *her*," Garrett said. "I already told her everything I wanted to say."

"Well, maybe you want to tell her how she let you down. Or made you angry. You can say anything, Garrett. It's all right."

Garrett shrugged. "Can't it be somebody else?"

"Right now let's stick with Mary Beth."

"Okay. I guess I'd say I'm glad she's safe."

The doctor beamed. "Good, Garrett. Let's start there. Tell her that you saved her. Tell her why." Nodding to the chair.

Garrett looked uneasily at the empty chair. He began, "She was in Blackwater Landing and—"

"No. You're talking to her. Pretend she's sitting in the chair."

He cleared his throat. "You were in Blackwater Landing. It was, like, really really dangerous. People get killed in Blackwater Landing. I didn't want the man in the overalls to hurt you too."

"The man in the overalls?" the doctor asked.

"The one who killed Billy."

The doctor looked at the lawyer, who was shaking his head.

Dr. Penny said, "Garrett, you know, even if you did save Mary Beth, she might think she did something to make you mad."

"Mad? She didn't do anything to make me mad."

"Well, you took her away from her family."

"I took her away to make sure she's safe." He looked back to the chair. "I took you away to make sure you were safe."

"I can't help but think," the doctor continued softly, "that there's something else pretty important to say, but you don't want to."

Garrett looked down at his long, grimy fingernails. "Well, maybe there *is* something. But . . . it's kinda hard."

Dr. Penny said softly, "Mary Beth wants you to say it."

Garrett asked, "She does? You think so?"

"I do," the doctor reassured. "Do you want to tell her something about where she is now? Where you took her? What it's like?"

"No," Garrett said. "I don't want to say anything about that."

"Then what do you want to say?"

"I . . ." His voice faded, and his hands were shaking.

Sachs was sitting forward in her chair in the observation room. Come on, she found herself thinking. Come on, Garrett. We want to help you.

Dr. Penny continued, his voice hypnotic. "Go ahead, Garrett. There's Mary Beth right there in the chair. What's that one thing you really want to say to her that you haven't been able to?"

Suddenly, startling both men in the room, Garrett leaned forward and blurted out, "I really really like you, Mary Beth. I think I love you." He lowered his head, his face red as sunset.

"That's what you wanted to say?" the doctor asked.

Garrett nodded.

"Anything else?"

"Well, there's, like, this book I'd really like to have from my house. It's called *The Miniature World*. Would that be okay?"

"We'll see if that can be arranged," the doctor said. He looked past Garrett to the lawyer, who rolled his eyes in frustration. The men rose, pulled on their jackets.

"That'll be it for now, Garrett."

Sachs quickly rose and stepped back into the lockup office. Fredericks and the doctor followed her as Garrett was led back to the cell.

Jim Bell pushed through the doorway. Fredericks introduced him to the doctor, and the sheriff asked, "Anything?"

Fredericks shook his head. "Not a thing."

Bell said grimly, "Was just over with the magistrate. They're gonna arraign him at six and get him over to Lancaster tonight."

"Tonight?" Sachs said.

"Better for him to get him out of town. There are a few too many people around here who'd like to take matters into their own hands. And Cal, you wanta do any horse trading, better get on it now. McGuire's going for murder one."

IN THE county building, Amelia Sachs found Rhyme as ornery as she'd thought he'd be.

"Come on, Sachs, help Ben pack the equipment and let's go. I told Dr. Weaver I'd be at the hospital sometime this year."

"Ben," she said, "could you give us a few minutes alone?"

"No, he couldn't," Rhyme snapped. "We don't have time."

"Five minutes," she said.

Ben looked from Rhyme to Sachs. Then the big man stepped out of the room. Sachs stared at Rhyme with an imploring gaze.

He tried to preempt her. "Sachs, we've done all we can do. Garrett will work out a plea and tell them where Mary Beth is."

"I don't think he did it."

"Killed Mary Beth? Maybe not but—"

"I mean killed Billy."

"You believe that man-in-the-tan-overalls story?"

"Yes, I do."

"Sachs, he's a troubled boy and you feel sorry for him. But—"

"That doesn't have anything to do with it."

"You're right. It doesn't," he snapped. "The only thing that's relevant is the evidence. And the evidence shows there's no man in overalls and that Garrett's guilty."

"The evidence *suggests* he's guilty, Rhyme. It doesn't prove it. Besides, I've got some evidence of my own."

"Such as?"

"He asked me to take care of his insects for him. Doesn't it seem a little odd that a cold-blooded killer would care what happened to some damn insects?"

"That's not evidence, Sachs. It's psychological warfare, trying to break down our defenses. The boy's smart, remember. High IQ, good grades. He's learned a lot from the insects. And one thing about them is that they have no moral code. All they care about is surviving. Those are the lessons he's learned."

"But you should've heard him when he was talking about Mary Beth. He was concerned about her."

"He was acting. What's my number one rule?"

"You have a lot of number one rules."

He continued unfazed. "You can't trust witnesses."

"No, he loves her. He really believes he's protecting her."

A man's voice interrupted. "Oh, he *is* protecting her."

Sachs and Rhyme looked to the doorway. It was Dr. Elliott Penny. He added, "Protecting her from himself." He stepped forward.

Sachs introduced them.

"I wanted to meet you, Mr. Rhyme," Dr. Penny said. "I specialize in forensic psychology."

"What did you mean just then, about Garrett protecting her from himself?" Sachs asked. "Some kind of multiple personality?"

"No," replied the doctor. "But there's definitely some mental or emotional disturbance at work. Garrett knows exactly what he did to Mary Beth and Billy Stail. I'm pretty sure he's hidden her someplace to keep her away from Blackwater Landing, where he probably did kill those other people over the past couple of years. And I think he was planning to rape and kill Mary Beth at the same time he killed Billy, but the part of him that *loves* her wouldn't let him. Yet he still felt the urge to kill her, and so he went back to Blackwater Landing the next day and got a substitute victim—Lydia Johansson. He was undoubtedly going to murder her in place of Mary Beth."

"I hope you're not billing the defense," Sachs said acerbically, "if that's your sympathetic testimony."

The doctor shrugged. "My professional opinion. Obviously I haven't run all the tests, but he exhibits clear dyssocial and sociopathic behavior. He's got a high IQ. He exhibits strategic thinking patterns, displays no remorse. He's a very dangerous person."

"Sachs," Rhyme said, "this isn't our game anymore."

She ignored him, his piercing eyes. "But Doctor—"

The doctor held up a hand. "Do you have children?" he asked.

A hesitation. "No," she responded. "Why?"

"You understandably feel sympathy for Garrett—we all do—but you might be confusing that with some latent maternal sense."

"What does that mean?"

The doctor continued. "I mean that if you have some desire to have children yourself, you might not be able to take an objective view about a sixteen-year-old boy's innocence or guilt."

"I can be perfectly objective," she snapped. "There's just too much that doesn't add up. Garrett's motives don't make sense."

"Motives aren't evidence, Sachs. You know that. Motives are the weak leg of the evidentiary stool."

"I don't need any more maxims, Rhyme," she muttered.

Dr. Penny continued. "I heard you asking Cal about Lancaster." Sachs lifted an eyebrow.

"Well, I think you *can* help the boy," the doctor said. "And the best thing you can do is to just spend some time with him. The county will assign a caseworker to liaise with the guardian the court appoints, and you'll have to get their approval. But I'm sure it can be arranged. He might even open up to you about Mary Beth."

As she was considering this, Thom appeared in the doorway. "Van's outside, Lincoln."

Rhyme glanced at the map one last time and then turned toward the doorway. "Once more into the breach, dear friends."

"I'll help Ben put away the equipment," Sachs announced. "I'll be over to the hospital soon, Rhyme."

But the criminalist had, it seemed, already departed, mentally if not physically, and he said nothing. Sachs heard only the vanishing whine as the Storm Arrow steamed down the corridor.

IN EDDIE'S, a bar a block from the lockup, Rich Culbeau said sternly, "This ain't no game. You listening?"

"I'm listening," Sean O'Sarian said. "I only laughed at the TV commercial. We're going in the back. The door'll be open."

"The back door to the lockup is always locked, and it's got that bar on the inside," Harris Tomel said.

"The bar'll be off, and the door'll be *un*locked. Okay?"

"You say so," Tomel said skeptically.

"It'll be open." Culbeau continued, "We go in. There'll be a key to his cell on the table, that little metal one. You know it?"

Of course they knew the table. Anybody who'd spent a night in the Tanner's Corner lockup had to have barked his shins on that table bolted to the floor, especially if he was drunk.

"Yeah, go ahead," O'Sarian said.

"We unlock the cell and go in. I'm going to hit the kid with the pepper spray. Put a bag over him—I got a crocus sack—and get him out the back. If he shouts, won't nobody hear him. Harris, you be waiting with the truck up near the door. Keep it in gear."

"Where we gonna take him to?" O'Sarian asked.

"The old garage near the tracks," Culbeau said. "We get him out there. I got my propane torch. And we start on him. Five minutes is all it'll take, and he'll tell us where Mary Beth is."

"And then afterward?" O'Sarian whispered.

"Accidents happen," Culbeau said.

O'Sarian toyed with a beer-bottle cap. "This is getting risky."

"You want out? Won't take more'n us two." Culbeau scratched his beard. "I'd rather split the money two ways than three."

"Naw. Everything's fine," O'Sarian said.

"Hold on." Tomel nodded at the window. "That's a pretty sight."

The redheaded policewoman from New York was walking up the street, carrying a book.

O'Sarian said, "I could use a little of that myself."

The redhead walked into the lockup.

O'Sarian said, "Well, that screws things up a bit."

Culbeau said slowly, "No, it don't. Harris, get that truck over there. And keep the motor running."

"What about *her?*" Tomel asked.

Culbeau said, "I got plenty of pepper spray."

INSIDE the lockup, Deputy Nathan Groomer leaned back in the rickety chair and nodded at Sachs. "Hello, miss. Thought you were leaving."

"Will be soon. How's the boy doing?"

"Oh, I dunno. Anything I can help you with?"

"Garrett wanted this book." She held it up—*The Miniature World*. "Is it okay if I give it to him?"

Nathan took it and searched it carefully. For weapons, she supposed. Then he handed it back. "Creepy, that boy is. Okay, slip your weapon in the lockbox there, and I'll let you in."

Sachs put the Smith & Wesson inside. "You want the cuffs too?" She touched her handcuff case.

"Nope. Can't get into much trouble with those. I'll let you in."

RICH Culbeau handed Sean O'Sarian a red-and-white canister of pepper spray. "Aim low 'cause people duck."

"Which of 'em should I take?"

"The boy. The girl's mine," Culbeau muttered.

They dipped their heads as they went past a filthy window in the back of the lockup and paused at the metal door. Culbeau noticed that it was open a half inch. "See, it's unlocked," he whispered. "Now, we go in fast, spray 'em both." He handed O'Sarian a thick bag. "Then throw that over his head."

O'Sarian gripped the canister firmly, nodded at a second bag, in Culbeau's hand. "So we're taking the girl too."

Culbeau sighed, said an exasperated "Yeah, Sean, we are." He closed his big fist around the door handle.

WOULD THIS BE HIS LAST VIEW? Lincoln Rhyme wondered. From his hospital bed he could see a park on the grounds of the medical center—lush trees, a rich green lawn, a stone fountain.

From the bedroom in his town house at 345 Central Park West in Manhattan, Rhyme could see sky and some of the skyline along Fifth Avenue. But the windows there were high off the floor, and he couldn't see Central Park itself unless his bed was shoved right against the pane, which let him look down onto the trees.

He wondered again whether or not the operation would have any success. Whether he'd even survive it. So why was he doing it?

Oh, there was a very good reason. Yet it was a reason that the cold criminalist in him had trouble accepting and one that he'd never utter out loud. Because it had nothing to do with being able to prowl over a crime scene searching for evidence. Nothing to do with his inability to do simple things like scratching an itch. No, it was exclusively because of Amelia Sachs.

Finally he'd admitted the truth—that he'd grown terrified of losing her. He'd brooded that sooner or later she'd meet someone else. It had to be inevitable, he figured, as long as he remained as immobile as he was. She wanted children. She wanted a normal life. And so Rhyme was willing to risk death, to risk making his condition worse, in the hopes that he could improve.

Oh, he knew that the operation wouldn't let him stroll down Fifth Avenue with Sachs on his arm. He was hoping for a minuscule improvement—to move slightly closer to a normal life. Slightly closer to her. In his imagination he could picture himself closing his hand on hers, feeling a faint pressure of her skin.

A small thing to most people, but to Rhyme a miracle.

The door to the hospital room swung open. And Rhyme looked up, expecting to see Dr. Weaver. But it wasn't the surgeon. Sheriff Jim Bell walked in, followed by his brother-in-law, Steve Farr. Both men were clearly upset.

The criminalist's first thought was that they'd found Mary Beth's body, that the boy had in fact killed her. And his next thought was how badly Sachs would react to this news, having her faith in the boy shattered.

But Bell had different news. "I'm sorry to have to tell you this,

Lincoln. I was going to call. But then I figured you should hear it from somebody in person. It's about Amelia."

"What about her? What? Tell me!"

"Rich Culbeau and those buddies of his went by the lockup. I don't know what they had in mind exactly—probably no good—but anyway, what they found was my deputy Nathan Groomer cuffed in the front office. And Garrett's cell was empty."

Rhyme still didn't understand the significance. "What—"

In a gruff voice Bell said, "Your Amelia trussed Nathan up at gunpoint and broke Garrett outa jail. It's a felony escape. They're on the run, they're armed, and nobody has a clue where they are."

SEVEN

RUNNING. Her legs ached. She was drenched in sweat and was already dizzy from the heat and dehydration.

Garrett was beside her, jogging silently through the forest outside Tanner's Corner.

When Sachs had gone into the cell to give Garrett *The Miniature World,* she'd watched the boy's happy face as he'd taken the book from her. And, almost as if someone else were directing her, she'd reached through the bars, taken the boy by the shoulders. Flustered, he'd looked away. "No, look at me," she'd instructed.

Finally he had. She'd studied his blotchy face. "Garrett, I need to know the truth. This is only between us. Did you kill Billy Stail?"

"I swear I didn't. I swear! I saw a man in tan overalls. He killed Billy. I saw him in the bushes, and I ran down the hill. Mary Beth was crying and scared. I picked up the shovel, which I shouldn't've. But I didn't think. Then I took Mary Beth away from there so she wouldn't get hurt. That's the truth!"

"And Lydia," Sachs had persisted. "Why did you kidnap her?"

" 'Cause she was in danger too. Blackwater Landing's a dangerous place. People die there. Disappear. I was just protecting her."

Of course it's a dangerous place, she'd thought. But is it dangerous because of you?

"Lydia said you were going to rape her."

"No, no, no. She jumped into the water, and her uniform got wet and torn. I saw her, you know, on top. Her chest. And I got kind of . . . turned on. But that's all."

Sachs had stared at him a moment longer. Finally she'd asked, "If I get you out of here, will you take me to Mary Beth?"

Garrett had frowned. "If I do that, then you'd bring her back to Tanner's Corner. And she might get hurt."

"We can make sure she'll be safe—Lincoln Rhyme and I."

"You can do that?"

"Yes. But if you don't agree, you'll stay in jail for a long time. And if Mary Beth dies because of you, it'll be murder, same as if you shot her. And you'll never get out of jail."

He'd looked out the window. "All right."

"How far away is she?"

"On foot it'll take us eight, ten hours."

Yes or no? she'd debated furiously, leaning against the bars.

"You're cool. I like you," Garrett had then said—in such a disarming, innocent way that Sachs, lost in the complete folly of what she was doing, had to laugh out loud.

"Wait here," she'd told him, and stepped back into the office. She'd reached into the lockbox, pulled out her gun, and, against all training and sense, turned it on Nathan Groomer.

"I'm sorry to do this," she'd whispered. "I need the key to his cell, and then I need you to put your hands behind your back."

Wide-eyed, he'd hesitated. "This is way past stupid, lady."

"The key."

He'd opened the drawer and tossed it on the desk. He'd put his hands behind his back. She'd cuffed him with his own handcuffs and ripped the phone from the wall.

She'd then freed Garrett, cuffed him too. The back door to the lockup had been open, but she thought she heard footsteps and a running car engine. She'd opted for the front door. They'd made a clean escape, undetected.

Now, a mile from downtown, surrounded by brush and trees, the boy directed her along an ill-defined path. They trotted through the forest for a half hour, until the ground grew soupy and the air became fragrant with the smells of methane and decay. The route finally became impassable—the path ended in a thick bog—and Garrett led them to a two-lane asphalt road. They started through the brush on the other side of the shoulder.

Several cars drove past leisurely. Sachs turned and watched them enviously. On the lam for less than an hour, she reflected, and already she felt a heart-wrenching tug at the normalcy of everyone else's life—and at the dark turn hers had taken.

THEY were at Harris Tomel's house, a nice five-bedroom colonial the man had never done a lick of work to. Unlike Culbeau, whose own split-level he put a lot of time into keeping nice, and unlike O'Sarian, who put a lot of time into picking up waitresses who'd keep his trailer nice, Tomel just let the house and yard go.

But that was Tomel's business, and the three men weren't at his house to discuss landscaping. They were here for one reason only—because Tomel had inherited his father's gun collection.

They stood in the paneled den looking over the gun cases. O'Sarian picked the black Colt AR-15, the civvy version of the M-16. Tomel took the beautiful Browning shotgun with the inlay, while Culbeau chose Tomel's nifty Winchester .30-06.

They packed plenty of ammo, water, Culbeau's cell phone, and food. 'Shine of course. Sleeping bags too. Though none of them expected the hunt to last very long.

A GRIM Lincoln Rhyme wheeled into the dismantled forensic lab in the county building. Lucy Kerr and Mason Germain stood beside the fiberboard table that had held the microscopes. Their arms were crossed, and as Thom and Rhyme entered, both deputies regarded the criminalist and his aide with a blend of contempt and suspicion.

"How could she do it?" Mason asked. "What was she thinking?"

Rhyme asked merely, "Was anybody hurt?"

"No," Lucy said. "But Nathan was pretty shook up, looking down that barrel of the Smith and Wesson."

Rhyme struggled to remain outwardly calm, yet his heart was pierced with fear for her. Lincoln Rhyme trusted evidence before all else, and the evidence showed clearly that Garrett Hanlon was a kidnapper and killer. Sachs, tricked by his calculated façade, was on the run with a clever, dangerous boy who'd murder her in a minute when he didn't need her any longer.

Rhyme knew only that he had to find her as fast as possible.

Jim Bell entered the room.

"Did she take a car?" the criminalist asked.

"I don't think so," Bell said. "No vehicles missing yet."

Lucy said, "Get some dogs, Jim. Irv Wanner runs a couple of hounds for the state police. He'll track 'em down."

"Good idea," Bell said. "We'll—"

"I want to propose something," Rhyme interrupted. "I'll make a deal with you."

"No deals," Bell said. "She's a fleeing felon. And armed."

"She's not going to shoot anybody," Thom said.

Rhyme continued. "Amelia's convinced there's no other way to find Mary Beth. That's why she did it."

Bell said, "You can't go breaking murderers out of jail."

"But she doesn't think the boy's a murderer. Give me twenty-four hours before you call the state police. I'll find them for you. If troopers and dogs get involved, we all know there's a good chance of people getting hurt."

"That's a hell of a deal, Lincoln," Bell said. "Your friend busts out our prisoner—"

"He wouldn't *be* your prisoner if it weren't for me. You never would've found him on your own."

"No damn way," Mason said. "We're wasting time, and they're getting farther away by the minute. I'm of a mind to get every man in town out looking for 'em now. Pass out rifles and—"

Bell interrupted him and asked Rhyme, "If we give you your twenty-four hours, then what's in it for us?"

"I'll stay and help you find Mary Beth. However long it takes."

Thom said, "The operation, Lincoln."

"Forget the operation," he muttered, feeling the despair as he said this. He knew that Dr. Weaver's schedule was so tight that if he missed his appointed date on the table, he'd have to go back on the waiting list. But he pushed this thought aside, raging to himself, Find her, save her. That's the only thing that's important.

Mason said, "How do we know you aren't gonna send us round Robin Hood's barn and let her get away?"

"Because," Rhyme said patiently, "Amelia's wrong. I think Garrett *is* a murderer, and I think he used her to break out of jail. He could kill her at any minute."

Bell paced for a moment. "Okay. You've got twenty-four hours."

Mason sighed. "How the hell are you going to find her in that wilderness? You just going to call her up and ask where she is?"

"That's exactly what I'm going to do."

LUCY Kerr was on the phone at a desk in the office adjacent to the war room.

"North Carolina State Police, Elizabeth City," answered a woman in a crisp voice. "How can I help you?"

"Detective Gregg, please."

" 'Lo?" asked a man's voice after a moment.

"Pete, it's Lucy Kerr over in Tanner's Corner."

"Hey, Lucy, how's it going? What's with those missing girls?"

"Got that under control," she said, reciting the words Lincoln Rhyme had dictated to her. "But we do have a little problem."

Little problem. . . .

"We need a cell-phone trace. Magistrate's clerk is faxing a warrant to you right now."

"Gimme the phone and serial numbers."

She gave him the numbers. "It's a New York number. Party's roaming now."

Pete Gregg said, "You want a tape of the conversation?"

"Just location." And a clear line of sight to the target.

"Oh, here's the fax." A pause as he read. "A missing person?"

"That's all," she said reluctantly.

"Okay, hold the line. I'll call my tech people."

Lucy sat on the desk, shoulders slumped, flexing her left hand. For a reason she couldn't understand, Amelia Sachs's crime had tapped into an anger within her more intense than anything she'd ever felt. White-hot fury at Sachs's betrayal.

"Hello, Lucy," Pete said from Elizabeth City. "You're good to go. When's the subject going to be making a call?"

Lucy looked into the other room, called, "Ready?"

Rhyme nodded.

Into the phone she said, "Anytime now."

"Stay on the line," Pete said. "I'll liaise."

Please let this work, Lucy thought. Please. Then she added a footnote to her prayer: And give me one clear shot at my Judas.

THOM fitted the headset over Rhyme's head. The aide then punched in a number. If Sachs's phone was shut off, it would ring only three times and the pleasant lilt of the voice-mail lady would start to speak.

One ring . . . two . . . "Hello?"

Rhyme didn't believe he'd ever felt such relief, hearing her voice. "Sachs, are you all right?"

A pause. "I'm fine."

In the other room he saw Lucy Kerr's sullen face nod.

"Listen to me, Sachs. You have to give yourself up. I know what you're doing. Garrett's agreed to take you to Mary Beth."

"That's right, Rhyme."

"You can't trust him," Rhyme said, thinking in despair, Or me either. "I've made a deal with Jim Bell. If you bring Garrett back in, they'll work something out with the charges against you. The state's not involved yet. And I'll stay here as long as it takes to find Mary Beth. I've postponed the operation." He closed his eyes momentarily, pierced with guilt. He had to betray her to save her.

"Garrett's innocent, Rhyme. I know he is."

"We'll look at the evidence again. We'll find more evidence. We'll do it together, Sachs. There's *nothing* we can't find."

"There's nobody on Garrett's side. He's all by himself, Rhyme."

"We can protect him."

"You can't protect somebody from a whole town."

"Please, Sachs." Static. Come home, he was thinking. Please. Your life is precious to me. "Sachs, whatever you think about Garrett, don't trust him."

"He's cuffed, Rhyme."

"Keep him that way. And don't let him near your weapon."

"I won't. I'll call you when we have Mary Beth."

The line went dead.

Rhyme closed his eyes, furious that he hadn't gotten through to her. Thom reached forward and lifted the headset off his head. With a brush he smoothed Rhyme's dark hair.

"Damn," the criminalist muttered.

Lucy hung up the phone in the other room and stepped inside. "Pete said they're within three miles of downtown Tanner's Corner. If she'd been on the line a few minutes longer, they could've pin-pointed her down to fifteen feet."

Jim Bell was examining the map. "Three miles of downtown."

"Would he go back to Blackwater Landing?" Rhyme asked.

"No," Bell said. "We know they're headed for the Outer Banks, and Blackwater Landing would take him in the opposite direction."

"What's the best way to get to the Banks?" the criminalist asked.

"They can't do it on foot," Bell said. "They'll have to get a car, or a car and a boat. Two ways to get there. They could go Route 82 south to 17. Or they could take Harper Road to 17. Mason, you take a couple of boys and get over to 112. Set up a roadblock at Belmont." The sheriff continued, "Lucy, you and Jesse take Harper down to Millerton Road. Set up there."

Then Bell called his brother-in-law into the room. "Steve, you coordinate communications and get everybody Handi-talkies."

"Sure thing, Jim."

Bell then said to Lucy and Mason, "Tell everybody that Garrett's in one of our blue detention jumpsuits. What's Sachs wearing?"

Rhyme said, "Jeans, black T-shirt."

Lucy and Mason headed out the door.

A HALF hour later Ben Kerr walked into the lab. He actually seemed glad to be back, though he was visibly upset at the news that necessitated his return. Together he and Thom finished unpacking the forensic equipment while Rhyme stared at the list of evidence found at the mill:

> Map of Outer Banks
> Ocean beach sand
> Oak/maple leaf residue

As Rhyme gazed at the list, he realized how little Sachs had found at the mill. He wished they had more evidence from the scene. Then he recalled something. He glanced at Bell. "Did you say Garrett was wearing a prison jumpsuit?"

"That's right."

"You have what he was wearing when he was arrested?"

"It'd be over at the lockup."

"Could you have them sent over here?" the criminalist asked. "Have them put in a paper bag. Don't unfold them."

While the sheriff called the lockup, Rhyme stared at the map of the Outer Banks of North Carolina. The sheer size of the area was daunting. Hundreds of miles.

GARRETT Hanlon led Amélia from the brush onto an asphalt road. There was a familiarity about it, and she realized this was Canal Road, the one that they'd taken from the county building that morning to search the crime scenes at Blackwater Landing. Ahead she could see the dark rippling of the Paquenoke River.

"I don't get it," she said. "They know we're gone. This is the main road into town. Why aren't there any roadblocks?"

"They think we're going a different way. They've set up the road-blocks south and east of here."

"How do you know that?"

Garrett answered, "They think I'm stupid. But I'm not."

"But we *are* going to Mary Beth?"

"Sure. Just not the way they think."

His confidence and his caginess troubled her for a moment, but her attention slipped back to the road as they continued on in silence. In twenty minutes they were within a half mile of the inter-section where Canal Road ended at Route 112 in Blackwater Land-ing, the place where Billy Stail had been killed.

"Listen," he whispered, gripping her arm with his cuffed hands. She cocked her head but heard nothing. "What?"

"Into the bushes."

They slipped off the road into a stand of scratchy holly trees. A moment later a large flatbed truck came into view.

"That's from the factory," he whispered. "Up ahead there."

The sign on the truck was DAVETT INDUSTRIES. When it was past, they returned to the road.

"How did you hear that?"

"Oh, you gotta be cautious all the time. Like moths."

"Moths? What do you mean?"

"Moths are pretty cool. They, like, sense ultrasound waves. They have these radar-detector things. When a bat shoots out a beam of sound to find them, moths fold their wings and drop to the ground and hide. Magnetic and electronic fields too. Insects can feel them. You know that you can lead some insects around with radio waves? Or make 'em go away too, depending on the frequency?" He fell silent. Then he nodded up the road, toward Blackwater Landing. "Ten minutes, and we'll be safe. They'll never find us."

As they started down the road again, she wondered what, realistically, would happen to Garrett when they found Mary Beth and returned to Tanner's Corner. There would still be some charges against him. But if Mary Beth corroborated the story of the real murderer—the man in the tan overalls—then the D.A. might accept that Garrett *had* kidnapped her for her own good. Defense of others was recognized by all criminal courts as a justification. And the charges would probably be dropped.

And who was the man in the overalls? Had he been the one who'd killed those three residents over the years?

Then something else occurred to her—that Garrett could identify Billy Stail's real murderer, the man in the tan overalls, who by now might've heard about the escape and be out looking for Garrett and for her too. To silence them. Maybe they should—

Suddenly Garrett spun around. "Car, moving fast."

He pulled her into a stand of sedge, pressed her to the ground. *Moths fold their wings and drop to the ground.*

Two Paquenoke County squad cars were racing along Canal Road. Sachs couldn't see who was driving the first one. Lucy Kerr was driving the second car.

The cars skidded to a stop where Canal Road met Route 112. They parked blocking both lanes, and the deputies got out.

"No, no, no," Garrett muttered, dumbfounded. "They were supposed to think we were going the other way—east. They *had* to think that. How'd they figure out we were coming this way? How?"

Because they've got Lincoln Rhyme, Sachs answered silently.

RHYME was once again studying the map on the wall.

"This idea of yours," Jim Bell said, "is a big risk—committing everybody to Blackwater Landing. If they really *are* headed east to the Outer Banks, they're gonna get past us. We'll never find them."

But Rhyme believed his idea was right. Twenty minutes earlier, as he'd stared at the map, he had started wondering about Lydia's abduction. He remembered what Sachs had told him when they were in the field pursuing Garrett this morning.

Lucy says it doesn't make any sense for him to come this way.

And that had made him ask a question. Why exactly did Garrett kidnap Lydia Johansson? To kill her as a substitute victim was Dr. Penny's answer. But he *hadn't* killed her. Or raped her. Nor was there any other motive for abducting her. They were strangers. She'd never taunted him; he didn't seem to have an obsession with her; she wasn't a witness to Billy's murder.

Then Rhyme had recalled that Garrett had willingly told Lydia that Mary Beth was being held on the Outer Banks. And the evidence at the mill—the ocean sand, the map of the Outer Banks. Lucy had found it very easily, according to Sachs. Too easily. The scene, he decided, had been staged to lead investigators off.

Rhyme had shouted bitterly, "We've been set up!"

"What do you mean, Lincoln?" Ben had asked.

"He tricked us," the criminalist had said. "From the beginning." Rhyme explained that Garrett had intentionally kicked off one shoe at the scene when he kidnapped Lydia. He'd filled it with limestone dust, which would lead anyone with knowledge of the area to think of the quarry, where he'd planted the other evidence—the scorched bag and corn—that in turn led to the mill.

The searchers were *supposed* to find Lydia, along with the rest of the planted evidence, to convince them that Mary Beth was being held in a house on the Outer Banks. Which meant that she was being held in the opposite direction—west of Tanner's Corner.

Garrett's plan was brilliant, but he had made one mistake—assuming that it would take the search party several days to find

Lydia. By then he'd have been with Mary Beth in the real hiding place, and the searchers would be combing the Outer Banks.

And so Rhyme had asked Bell what was the best route west from Tanner's Corner.

"Blackwater Landing," the sheriff had answered. "Route 112."

And Rhyme had ordered Lucy and the other deputies there as fast as possible.

Lucy had responded skeptically, "Let's hope you're right."

There was a chance that Garrett and Sachs had already been through Blackwater Landing and were on their way west, but Rhyme didn't think that on foot, and keeping under cover, they could have gotten that far in so little time.

SACHS and Garrett crouched in the bushes, watching a line of passenger cars waiting to get through the roadblock. Then behind them another sound: sirens.

They saw a second set of flashing lights coming from the other— the southern—end of Canal Road. Another squad car parked, and two more deputies got out. Armed with shotguns, they started slowly through the bushes, moving toward Garrett and Sachs.

Garrett looked at Sachs's gun. "Aren't you going to use that?"

"No, of course not," she whispered fiercely, horrified that he'd even consider it. She looked behind her into the woods. It was marshy and impossible to get through without being seen or heard. Ahead of them was the fence surrounding Davett Industries. Through the chain link she saw cars in the parking lot.

Amelia Sachs had worked street crimes for a year. That experience, combined with what she knew about cars, meant that she could break into and hot-wire a vehicle in under thirty seconds.

But how could they get out of the factory grounds? There was a delivery-and-shipping entrance to the factory, but it too opened onto Canal Road. They'd still have to drive past the roadblock. Could they steal a pickup and make it through the fence where nobody could see them, then drive off-road to Route 112?

The deputies on foot were now only two hundred feet away.

Whatever they were going to do, now was the time. They had no choice. "Come on, Garrett. We've got to get over the fence."

"WHERE ARE THEY—THE deputies making the sweep?" Rhyme asked frantically.

Bell was on the phone, standing by the map. He glanced toward Rhyme. "They're close to the entrance to Davett's company."

A secretary stuck her head in the door. "Sheriff Bell, state police on line two."

Jim Bell stepped into the office across the hall and hit the button. He spoke for a few minutes, then trotted back into the lab. "We've got 'em! The police have pinpointed her cell-phone signal. She's on the move, going west on Route 112. They got past the roadblock."

Rhyme asked, "How?"

"Looks like they snuck into Davett's parking lot and stole a truck, then drove off-road for a while and got back on the highway."

That's my Amelia, Rhyme thought.

Bell continued. "She's going to ditch the car, get another one."

"How do you know?"

"She's on the phone with a car-rental company in Hobeth Falls. Lucy and the others are after her, silent pursuit. Another few minutes, and the tech people will have her exact location."

"Good luck," Lincoln Rhyme muttered. But he couldn't have said whether that wish was directed toward predator or toward prey.

YOU drive fast, Amelia, Lucy Kerr thought. Well, so do I.

She was speeding along Route 112, the gumball machine on top of the car spinning madly with its red, white, and blue lights. The siren was off. Jesse Corn was beside her, on the phone with Pete Gregg in the Elizabeth City state-police office. In the squad car directly behind them were Trey Williams and Ned Spoto. Mason Germain and a deputy named Frank Sturgis were in the third car.

"Where are they now?" Lucy asked.

Jesse asked Pete Gregg this question and nodded as he received an answer. He said, "Only five miles away. They cut off the highway, heading south."

Please, Lucy prayed, stay on the phone just a minute more. Amelia, I shared my darkest moments with you. I told you about the surgery, about my shyness with men, about my love for children. I apologized when you were right and I was wrong. I trusted you. I—

Jesse's hand touched her shoulder. "The highway curves up ahead," he said. "I'd just as soon we made that curve."

Lucy exhaled slowly and eased off on the speed.

THE deputies were out of their cars.

The state police had finally lost the signal from Amelia's cell phone but only after it'd been stationary for about five minutes at the location they were now looking at: a barn fifty feet from a house in the woods, a mile off Route 112. It was, Lucy Kerr noted, west of Tanner's Corner. Just as Lincoln Rhyme had predicted.

"You don't think Mary Beth's in there, do you?" asked Frank Sturgis. "It's seven miles from downtown. I'd feel pretty foolish."

"Naw. They're just waiting for us to go past," Mason Germain said. "Then they're gonna go to Hobeth Falls and pick up the car."

Jesse Corn had called in the address of the house. "It's owned by a guy named Pete Hallburton," he said. "Anybody know him?"

"Think so," said Trey Williams. "Married. No connection to Garrett that I know of."

Lucy said, "I think we should hit the barn on foot—fast—from two directions. I'll go in the front. Trey, you take the—"

"No," Mason said adamantly. "I go in the front."

Lucy hesitated, then said, "Okay. I'll go in the side door. Trey and Frank, you're on the back and far side." She looked at Jesse. "I want you and Ned to keep an eye on the front windows and back doors of the Hallburtons' house."

"Got it," Jesse said.

Lucy said, "If they come out driving, just take out the tires. Don't shoot Garrett or Amelia unless you have to. You all know the rules of engagement." She was looking at Mason when she said this, thinking of his sniper attack on the boy at the mill. But the deputy seemed not to hear her. Lucy called in on her Handi-talkie and told Jim Bell they were about to storm the barn.

She clicked off the radio. "Let's move out."

They ran, crouching, using the oaks and pines for cover. Lucy's eyes were fastened on the dark windows of the barn. Twice she was sure she saw movement inside.

"I'm not going to say anything," Mason said. "I'm just going in.

When you hear me kick in the front door, Lucy, you go in the side."

"Let me make sure that door's open."

They dispersed, jogging into position. Lucy ducked under one of the windows and hurried to the side door. It wasn't locked and was open a crack. She nodded to Mason, and he nodded back.

She took a deep breath to calm herself. Another.

Then there was a loud crash from the front of the barn as Mason kicked in the door. "Sheriff's office!" he cried. "Nobody move!"

Lucy kicked the side door. But it moved only a few inches and stopped fast, hitting a large riding lawn mower parked just inside.

"Damn," she whispered, and ran around to the front of the barn.

Before she got there, she heard Mason call out, "Oh, God."

And then she heard a gunshot. Followed by a second one.

"WHAT'S going on?" Rhyme demanded.

"Okay," Bell said. The sheriff stood with the phone pressed against his ear, his other fist clenched. He nodded as he listened. He looked at Rhyme. "There've been shots."

"Shots?"

"Mason and Lucy went into the barn. Jesse said there were two shots." He shouted into the other room, "Get the ambulance over to the Hallburton place. Badger Hollow Road."

Steve Farr called, "It's on its way."

"Is Amelia all right?" Rhyme asked.

"We'll know in a minute," Bell said.

But it felt more like days.

Finally Bell stiffened as somebody came on the line. "He did what?" He listened, then looked at Rhyme's alarmed face. "It's all right. Nobody's hurt. Mason kicked his way into the barn and saw some overalls hanging on the wall. It was real dark. He thought it was Garrett with a gun. He fired a couple of times. That's all."

"Amelia's all right?"

"Garrett and Amelia weren't even there. It was just the truck they stole that was inside. They must've been in the house, but now they've probably heard the shots and taken off into the woods. They can't get too far. I know the property. It's all surrounded by bogs."

Rhyme said angrily, "I want Mason off the case."

Bell obviously agreed. Into the phone he said, "Jesse, put Mason on." There was a short pause. "Mason, what is this all about? Why'd you fire? . . . Well, what if it'd been Pete Hallburton standing there? Or his wife? . . . I don't care. Get in your cruiser and head back here right now. That's an order. . . . I'm not telling you again. I— Damn." Bell hung up.

A moment later the phone rang again. He answered it fast. "Lucy, what's going on?" The sheriff listened, frowning. He paced. "You're sure?" He nodded, then said, "Okay, stay there. I'll call you back."

"What happened?"

Bell shook his head. "She did a number on us—your friend."

"What?"

Bell said, "Pete Hallburton's there. He's home—in his house. Lucy and Jesse just talked to him. His wife works the three-to-eleven shift over at Davett's company, and she forgot her supper, so Pete dropped it off a half hour ago and drove home."

"Were Amelia and Garrett hiding in the trunk?"

Bell gave a disgusted sigh. "He's got a pickup. No place for them to hide. But there was plenty of room for her cell phone."

Rhyme barked a cynical laugh. "She called the rental company, got put on hold, and hid the phone in the back of the truck."

"You got that right," Bell muttered. "She knew we'd have a locator on the phone. She and Garrett waited till Lucy and the squad cars left Canal Road and then went on their merry way."

EIGHT

AFTER the police cruisers had abandoned the roadblock, Garrett and Sachs jogged to the end of Canal Road and crossed the highway. They skirted the Blackwater Landing crime scenes, then moved quickly through an oak forest, following the Paquenoke River.

A half mile into the forest they came to a tributary of the Paquo. It was impossible to go around. Garrett pointed his cuffed hands to a place on the shore. "The boat."

Sachs squinted and could just make out the shape of a small boat.

It was covered with brush and leaves. Garrett walked to it and, working as best he could with the handcuffs on, began stripping off the foliage hiding the vessel. Sachs helped him.

"Camouflage," he said. "I learned it from insects."

Well, Sachs too had used some of the boy's esoteric knowledge about insects. When Garrett had commented on the moths—their ability to sense electronic and radio signals—she'd realized that of course Rhyme would set up a locator on her cell phone. She remembered that she'd been on hold for a long time at Piedmont-Carolina Car Rental that morning. So she'd sneaked into the Davett Industries parking lot, called the rental company, and slipped the phone, playing interminable Muzak, into the back of an unoccupied pickup truck whose motor had been running, parked in front of the employee entrance to the building.

The trick had apparently worked. The deputies took off after the truck when it left the grounds.

Sachs and Garrett now finished uncovering the boat. It was painted dark gray, was about ten feet long, and had a small outboard motor on it. Inside were a dozen plastic gallon bottles of water and a cooler filled with boxes of crackers and chips. Sachs opened one of the water bottles and drank deeply. She handed the bottle to Garrett, and he drank too. He then climbed into the boat.

Sachs followed, sat with her back to the bow, facing him. He pulled the starter rope, and the engine sputtered to life. Like modern Huck Finns, they started down the river, Sachs reflecting, This is knuckle time.

It was a phrase her father had used. The trim, balding man, a beat patrolman in Brooklyn and Manhattan most of his life, had had a serious talk with his daughter when she'd told him she wanted to give up modeling and get into police work. He'd been all for the decision but had said this about the profession: "Amie, you have to understand, sometimes it's a rush, sometimes you get to make a difference, sometimes it's boring. And sometimes—not too often, thank God—it's knuckle time. Fist to fist. You're all by your lonesome, with nobody to help you. And I don't mean just the perps. Sometimes it'll be you against your boss. Could be you against your buddies too. You gonna be a cop, you got to be ready to go it alone."

"I can handle it, Pop."

Sitting in this rickety boat, being piloted by a troubled young man, Sachs had never felt so alone in her life.

"Look there," Garrett said, pointing. "It's my favorite. The water boatman. It flies under the water." His face lit up with unbridled enthusiasm. He looked nothing at all like an escaped criminal, but for all the world like an enthusiastic teenager on a camping trip.

RHYME was furious with himself for not anticipating the cellphone trick. This isn't a game, he thought. Sachs's life is in danger. He couldn't afford to slip again.

A deputy appeared in the doorway, carrying a paper bag. It contained Garrett's clothes from the lockup.

"Good," Rhyme said. "Do a chart, Ben: 'Found at the Secondary Crime Scene—the Mill.' "

"But we've got one," Ben said, pointing to the chalkboard.

"No, no, no," Rhyme snapped. "Erase it. Those clues were fake. If we can find some evidence in his clothes"—nodding at the bag—"that'll tell us where Mary Beth *really* is."

"If we're lucky," Bell said.

No, Rhyme thought. If we're good. He said to Ben, "Cut a piece of the jeans, near the cuff, and run it through the GC/MS."

As the criminalist and Ben waited for the results from the chromatograph, Rhyme asked, "What else do we have?"

"Dark brown paint stains on Garrett's pants," Ben reported.

"Call Garrett's parents and find out what color their house is."

Ben found the number in the folder and called. He spoke to someone for a moment, then hung up. "The house is white, and there's nothing painted dark brown on the property."

"So it's probably the color of the place where he's got her. But keep going. Put on—"

But Ben was already pulling on the latex gloves. "This what you were going to say?"

"It was," Rhyme muttered.

Thom said, "He hates to be anticipated."

"Then I'll try to do it more often," Ben said. "Ah, here's something. Dirt in the cuff." He brushed a small amount out onto a magazine subscription card and looked at it under the microscope. "Nothing distinctive," he said. "Except little flecks of white."

"Let me see."

Ben carried the large microscope over to Rhyme, who looked through the eyepiece. "Okay, good. They're absorbent-paper fibers. Now, that dirt is very interesting. Can you get some more? Out of the cuffs?"

"I'll try." Ben brushed more dirt out onto the card.

"Scope it," Rhyme ordered.

Ben prepared a slide and slipped it onto the stage of the compound microscope, which he again held rock steady for Rhyme, who peered into the eyepiece. "There's a lot of clay. Feldspathic rock, probably granite. Oh, and peat moss."

Impressed, Ben asked, "How'd you know all this?"

"I just do." Rhyme didn't have time to go into a discussion of how a criminalist must know as much about the physical world as he does about crime. "What's *that*?" he asked, nodding at the subscription card. "That little whitish green thing?"

"It's from a plant," Ben said.

Rhyme ordered, "Describe it."

Ben looked it over with a magnifying glass. "A reddish stalk and a dot of liquid on the end. It looks viscous. There's a white, bell-shaped flower. I'm pretty sure it's from a sundew."

"What's that?" Rhyme snapped. "Sounds like dish soap."

"It's like a Venus flytrap. They eat insects."

"I'm not interested in their dining habits," Rhyme said sarcastically. "Where are they found?"

"Oh, all over the place here."

Rhyme scowled. "Useless. Damn." He then looked at Garrett's T-shirt, spread out on a table. There were several reddish blotches on the shirt. "What are those stains, Ben? You game to taste it?"

Without hesitation Ben lifted the shirt and licked a small portion of the stain. "Fruit juice, I'd guess. Can't tell what flavor."

"Add that to the list, Thom." Rhyme nodded at the chromatograph. "Let's get the results from the pants and then run the dirt."

Soon the machine told them what trace substances were embedded in Garrett's clothes and what had been found in the dirt in his cuffs: sugar, more camphene, alcohol, kerosene, and yeast. The kerosene was in significant amounts. Ben added these to the list.

What did all this mean? Rhyme wondered. There were too many clues. He couldn't see any relationships between them. But after a few minutes something came back to him. Something that Sachs had mentioned when she was searching the boy's room.

"Ben, could you open that notebook there, Garrett's notebook?"

"You want me to put it in the turning frame?"

"No. Just thumb through it," Rhyme told him.

The boy's stilted drawings of the insects flipped past: a water boatman, a diving bell spider, a water strider.

Rhyme remembered that Sachs had told him that, except for the wasp jar—Garrett's safe—the insects in his collection were in jars containing water. "They're all aquatic."

Ben nodded. "Seem to be."

"He's attracted to water," Rhyme mused. "And the kerosene . . . Boats run on that, right?"

"White gas," Ben said. "Small outboards do."

Rhyme said, "How's this for a thought? He's going west by boat on the Paquenoke River."

Ben said, "Makes sense. And I'll bet there's so much kerosene because he's been making runs between Tanner's Corner and the place he's got Mary Beth. Getting it ready for her."

"Good thinking. Call Jim Bell in here, would you?"

Bell returned, and Rhyme explained his theory.

Bell said, "Water bugs gave you that idea, huh?"

Rhyme nodded. "If we know insects, we'll know Garrett Hanlon. You got a police boat, Jim?"

"No, but half my people have their own boats, and we could use one of theirs. It won't do us any good, though. The Paquo's got a thousand branches flowing into it. If Garrett's on it, I guarantee he's not staying to the main channel. Impossible to find him."

Rhyme studied the map, following the Paquenoke west. "If he was moving supplies to the place where he's got Mary Beth, that means it's probably not too far off the river. How far west would he have to go to be in an area that was habitable?"

"Have to be a ways. Ten miles or so west." Bell touched a spot.

"That's north of the Paquo. Nobody lives there. South of the river it gets pretty residential. He'd be seen for sure."

"That bridge?" Rhyme nodded toward the map. "The Hobeth Bridge. What are the approaches to it like?"

"Just landfill. But there's a lot of it. The bridge is about forty feet high, so the ramps leading to it are long. You thinking Garrett would have to sail back to the main channel to get under the bridge?"

"Right. Because the engineers would've filled in the smaller channels on either side when they built the approaches."

Bell was nodding. "Yep. Makes sense to me."

"Get Lucy and the others there now. To the bridge. And Ben, call that fellow—Henry Davett. Tell him we need his help again."

Praying, Oh, Sachs, be careful. It's only a matter of time until he comes up with an excuse for you to take the cuffs off him, then to lead you someplace deserted. Then he'll manage to get a hold of your gun. . . . He's got the patience of a mantis.

GARRETT knew the waterways like an expert river pilot and steered the boat up what seemed to be dead ends, yet found creeks, thin as spiderweb strands, that led them steadily west.

"Look there!" He was pointing at a bug skipping over the surface of the water. "Water strider," he told Sachs as they eased past. "Insects are, like, a lot more important than us. I mean, when it comes to keeping the planet going."

Garrett spoke with the verve of a revivalist, his face serious. And as Sachs listened to him, foremost in her thoughts was this: Anyone who could be so fascinated by living creatures and, in his odd way, love them couldn't possibly be a rapist and killer.

Garrett finally steered out of the back routes and into the main channel, hugging the shore. Sachs looked behind them, to the east, to see if there were police boats in pursuit. She saw nothing except one of the big Davett Industries barges, headed upstream, away from them. Garrett eased into a little cove and peered through an overhanging willow branch, looking west toward a bridge.

"We have to go under it," he said. "We can't get around." He studied the span. "That's where they'd be waiting for us."

Garrett beached the boat and shut the motor off. He climbed out and unscrewed the outboard, which he pulled off and hid in the grass, along with the gas tank. He then took the cooler and the water jugs out of the boat and lashed the oars to the seats with two pieces of greasy rope. He poured the water out of a half dozen of the jugs, recapped them, and set them aside. Finally, gripping the boat by the side, he waded into the river.

"Help me," he said. "We've got to turn her upside down. We'll put the jugs underneath. She'll float fine."

Sachs realized what Garrett had in mind. They'd get underneath the boat and float past the bridge. The dark hull, low in the water, would be almost impossible to see from the bridge. Once past, they could right the boat and row to where Mary Beth was.

He opened the cooler and found a plastic bag. "We can put our things in this." He dropped his book, *The Miniature World,* inside it. Sachs added her wallet and the gun. She tucked her T-shirt into her jeans and slipped the bag down the front of the shirt.

Garrett held his hands out. "Can you take my cuffs off? I won't do anything bad. I promise."

Reluctantly Sachs fished out the key and undid the cuffs.

IN WAR, as Mary Beth McConnell had learned in her studies, the Weapemeoc Indians, who were native to what is now North Carolina, used to finish off their wounded adversaries by applying the *coup de grâce*—a blow to the head with a club called, appropriately, a coup stick.

A coup stick is nothing more than a large, rounded rock set in the split end of a stick and lashed into place with a leather thong. It's a very efficient weapon, and the one that Mary Beth was now making was surely as deadly as the ones that—in her theory—the Weapemeoc warriors had used to crush the skulls of the Roanoke settlers as they fought their last battle at what was now called Blackwater Landing.

Mary Beth made hers out of two support rods from an old chair in the cabin and a rock she'd found in the root cellar. She mounted the rock between the rods and bound it with long strips of denim torn from her shirttail. She swung the weapon several times, pleased with the power the club gave her.

She walked to the door, then slammed the stick into it several times near the lock. The door didn't budge. Well, she hadn't expected it to. But the important thing was that she'd tied the rock to the head of the club very firmly. It hadn't slipped.

"THERE'S a boat."

Lucy shifted in the shade of a bay tree on the shore near the Hobeth Bridge, her hand on her weapon. "Where?" she asked.

"There." Jesse Corn pointed upstream. "It's upside down."

"I can hardly see it," she said. "You've got good eyes."

"Is it them?" Trey Williams asked. "Did it capsize?"

Jesse said, "Naw. I got a feeling they're underneath it. We used to do that as kids—we'd play submarine."

Lucy said, "What do we do? We need a boat to get to them."

Ned Spoto pulled his Sam Browne harness off, handed it to Jesse. "Hell, I'll just go out and kick it back into shore."

"We'll cover you," Lucy said.

"They're underwater," Jesse said. "I wouldn't worry too much about them shooting anybody."

"But we're not taking any chances," Lucy said. Then to Ned, "Don't flip it over. Just swim out and steer it this way. Trey, you go over there, by the willow, with the scattergun. Jesse and I'll be on the shore. We'll have 'em in a cross fire if anything happens."

Ned, barefoot and shirtless, eased into the water. Lucy wondered how uncomfortable Amelia Sachs was underneath the boat. Very uncomfortable, she hoped.

Ned breaststroked very quietly out toward the boat. Lucy pulled her Smith & Wesson from the holster, cocked the hammer. Trey was standing beside a tree, holding the shotgun, muzzle up.

The boat was thirty feet from them, near midstream.

Ned was closing the distance quickly. He'd be there in—

The gunshot was loud and close. Lucy jumped as a spume of water shot into the air a few feet from Ned.

"Oh, no!" she cried, looking for the shooter.

"Where, where?" Trey called, crouching.

Ned dove under the surface.

Another shot. Water flew into the air. Trey started firing at the boat. Panic fire. The 12-gauge was loaded with seven rounds. The deputy emptied it in seconds, hitting the boat with every round, sending splinters of wood flying everywhere.

"No!" Jesse cried. "There are people under there!"

"Where are they shooting from?" Lucy called. "I can't tell. Where are they?"

"Where's Ned?" Trey cried. "Is he hit? Where's Ned?"

"I can't see him," Lucy shouted. "Cover me!"

She ran down the embankment. Suddenly, near the shore, she heard a choking gasp as Ned bobbed to the surface. "Help me!" He was terrified, looking behind him.

Charging into the water, Lucy holstered her gun and grabbed Ned's arm, dragged him to the shore.

"Who the hell—" he struggled to say.

"Don't know," she said, pulling him into a stand of bushes. He collapsed, spitting and coughing. He hadn't been hit.

They were joined by Trey and Jesse, both of them crouching, eyes gazing across the river, looking for their attackers.

"They're dead," whispered Jesse, staring at the terrible, ragged holes in the boat. "They have to be."

The boat was easing toward them, half submerged now. It floated into an uprooted cedar extending into the river and stopped.

Pale and troubled, Jesse glanced at Lucy, who nodded. All three of the other deputies kept their guns on the boat as Jesse waded out and flipped it over. The remnants of several shattered water jugs bobbed out and floated leisurely downstream. There was no one underneath.

"They set us up," Ned muttered bitterly. "It was an ambush."

Lucy hadn't believed that her anger could get any more consuming, but it was now. It seized her like a raw electric current. "Okay, here's what we're doing," she said in a low, deliberate voice. "It's getting late. We're going as far as we can while there's still some light. Then we'll have Jim bring us some supplies for the night. We'll be camping out. We're going to assume they're gunning for us, and we're going to act accordingly. Now, let's get across the bridge and look for their trail. Everybody locked and loaded?"

"Yep."

"You bet, Lucy."

"Then let's go."

"YOU came damn close to hitting Ned."

Harris Tomel said, "No way."

But Culbeau persisted. "I said scare 'em, not hit 'em."

"I wasn't going to hit him. I know what I'm doing, Rich."

The three men—Culbeau, Tomel, and O'Sarian—were on the northern bank of the Paquo, trekking along the river.

In fact, while Culbeau was pissed that Tomel had fired too close to the deputy swimming out to the boat, he was sure the sniping had worked. Lucy and the other deputies would be skittish as sheep now and would move nice and slow.

They walked for twenty minutes. Then Tomel asked him, "You know the boy's going in this direction?"

"Yep."

"But you don't have any idea where he's gonna end up."

Culbeau said, "If I did, we could just go there direct, right? Don't worry. We're gonna find him."

They soon came to a bend in the river, and being on high ground, they could see miles downstream.

Tomel said, "Hey, look, a house. Bet they're headed there."

Culbeau nodded. "Bet they are. Let's go."

A MILE downstream from the Hobeth Bridge the Paquenoke River makes a sharp bend to the north. It's shallow here near the shore, and the muddy shoals are piled high with driftwood and trash. Like skiffs adrift, two human forms floating in the water now were eased by the current into this refuse heap.

Amelia Sachs let go of the plastic water jug—her improvised flotation device. Straightening her legs, she found the river bottom only four feet below her. She stood unsteadily. Garrett appeared beside her a moment later and helped her onto the muddy ground.

They crawled up a slight incline, through a tangle of bushes, and collapsed in a grassy clearing. Sachs pulled the plastic bag out of her shirt. It had leaked slightly, but there wasn't any serious water damage. She handed Garrett his insect book and opened the cylinder of her gun, then rested it on a clump of brittle grass to dry it.

She'd been wrong about Garrett's plans for the boat. They had slipped empty water jugs under the overturned boat for buoyancy, but then Garrett had shoved it into midstream without getting underneath it. Then he'd told her to fill her pockets with rocks. He'd done the same, and they hurried downstream past the boat and slipped into the water, each holding a half-full water jug for flotation. With the rocks for ballast, only their faces were above the water. They'd float downstream ahead of the boat.

"The diving bell spider does this," he had told her. "Like a scuba diver. Carries his air around with him." Garrett said that if the police weren't at the bridge, they'd swim over to the boat, beach it, drain out the water, and continue on their way. If the deputies were on the bridge, their attention would be on the boat and they wouldn't notice Garrett and Amelia floating past ahead of it.

He'd been right, and they'd gotten under the bridge undetected. But Sachs was still shocked at what had happened next. Unprovoked, the deputies had fired round after round at the overturned boat.

Oh, Lincoln, she thought, what a mess this is. Why did I do it? She knew she couldn't turn back now. She'd have to keep going, play out this crazy game. "Where do we go now?" she asked.

"See that brown A-frame house over there, near the river?"

"Yes. Is Mary Beth there?"

"Naw. It's empty. But they've got a little trolling boat we can borrow. And we can get dry and get some food."

What did breaking and entering matter after today?

Garrett stood up, then bent down and picked up the pistol. She froze, watching him balance the gun in his hand with a familiarity that unnerved her. Then he handed it to her. "Let's go this way."

Sachs replaced the weapon in her holster, feeling the flutter of her heart from the scare.

They started toward the house. After a moment Garrett muttered, "They're pissed now—the deputies. And they're after us. With all their guns and things. You wanta know something, Amelia? I was thinking about this moth, the grand emperor moth."

"What about it?" she asked, hearing in her memory the shotgun blasts meant for her and this boy. Lucy Kerr, trying to kill her.

"The coloring on its wings. Like, when they're open, they look just like an animal's eyes. I mean, it's pretty cool. There's even a white dot in the corner, like a reflection of light in the pupil. Birds see that and think it's a fox or a cat, and it scares them." He looked behind them again, up the river. "We'll have to slow 'em down. How close you think they are?"

"Very close," she said.

With all their guns and things.

"IT's them." Rich Culbeau was looking at the footprints in the mud of the shore. "And they're only ten, fifteen minutes old."

The men headed cautiously up a path, moving closer to the A-frame. It looked like a nice place, Culbeau thought. A vacation house probably.

The woods ended, and the men saw a large clearing around the house—easily fifty yards, with no cover. The approach would be tough.

"Think they're inside?" O'Sarian asked, kneading his Colt.

"I don't— Wait, get down!"

The three men crouched fast.

"I saw somebody moving around downstairs. Through that window to the left." Culbeau looked through the scope on the deer rifle. "On the ground floor. I can't see too good, with the blinds. But there's definitely somebody there." He scanned the other windows. "Damn!" A panicked whisper. He dropped to the ground.

"What?" O'Sarian asked, alarmed.

"Get down!" Culbeau said. "One of 'em's got a rifle with a scope. They're sighting right at us. Upstairs window. Damn! They've got the whole field covered from here."

"We wait till it's dark?" Tomel asked.

"With little Miss Lucy Deputy coming up behind us?"

"If we shoot," O'Sarian said, "then Lucy and the other deputies will hear. I think we oughta go around the side and try and get inside. A shot would be a lot quieter in there."

"That'll take a half hour," Tomel snapped.

O'Sarian clicked the safety off his gun and squinted toward the house. "Well, I'd say we gotta make it take less than half an hour."

 *NINE*

STEVE Farr led Henry Davett into the lab once again. The businessman thanked Farr, who left, then nodded to Rhyme.

"Henry," Rhyme said, "thank you for coming." He continued, "I've got some more evidence, but I don't know what to make of it. I was hoping you could help again."

The businessman sat down. "I'll do what I can."

Rhyme nodded at the evidence charts on the wall. "Could you look that over? The list on the right." It was the list of evidence from Garrett's clothes from the lockup. "Anything on it seem familiar to you?"

As Davett gazed at it, he said in a distracted voice, "It's like a puzzle."

"That's the nature of my job," Rhyme said.

"How much can I speculate?" the businessman asked.

"As much as you like."

Davett thought for a moment, then said, "A Carolina bay."

Rhyme asked, "What's that? A horse?"

"No. It's a geologic structure you see on the Eastern Seaboard. Mostly in the Carolinas. They're basically oval ponds, about three or four feet deep, freshwater. They could be a half acre in size or a couple of hundred. The bottom of them is mostly clay and peat. Just what's on the chart."

"But clay and peat are pretty common around here," Ben said.

"They are," Davett agreed. "And if you'd found just those two things, I wouldn't have a clue where they came from. But you found something else. You see hundreds of insect-killer plants—Venus flytraps, sundews, and pitcher plants—around bays, probably because the ponds promote insects. If you found a sundew along with clay and peat moss, then there's no doubt the boy's spent time around a Carolina bay."

"What does bay mean? An inlet of water?" Rhyme asked.

"No. It refers to bay trees. They grow around the ponds." Davett rose and walked to the map. With his finger he circled a large area to the west of Tanner's Corner. "You'll find Carolina bays mostly here, in this area, just before you get to the hills."

Rhyme was discouraged. What Davett had circled must have included seventy or eighty square miles.

Davett wrote a phone number on a business card. "I should be getting home," he said. "My family's expecting me. You can call me anytime. Wish I could be more helpful."

Rhyme thanked him and turned back to the evidence charts.

IT HAD taken Rich Culbeau and Harris Tomel twenty minutes of hard scrabbling through the brush to get to the side porch of the A-frame vacation house without being seen.

Sean O'Sarian was waiting back on the path, lying on the ground with his black gun like an infantry grunt, ready to slow up Lucy and the other deputies with a few shots over their heads in case they came up the trail toward the house.

"You ready?" Culbeau asked Tomel, who nodded.

Culbeau eased open the knob of the mudroom door and pushed the door inside, his gun up and ready. Tomel followed. They heard rock music playing and voices upstairs.

The two men moved slowly. Ahead was the kitchen, where Culbeau had seen somebody moving when he'd sighted on the house through the rifle scope. He nodded toward the room.

"Don't think they heard us," Tomel said. The music was up pretty high.

"We go in together. Shoot for the legs or knees—we still gotta get him to tell us where Mary Beth is."

"The woman too?" Tomel asked.

Culbeau thought for a moment. "Yeah, why not? We might want to keep her alive for a while. You know what for."

Tomel nodded.

"One, two . . . three." They pushed fast into the kitchen and found themselves about to shoot a weatherman on a big-screen TV. They crouched and spun around, looking for the boy or the woman. Didn't see them. Then Culbeau looked at the set. He realized it didn't belong here. Somebody had rolled it in from the living room and set it up in front of the stove.

Culbeau peered out through the blinds. "Damn! They put the set here so we'd see it from across the field, from the path, and think there was somebody in the house." He took off up the stairs.

"Wait," Tomel called. "She's up there. With the gun."

But of course the redhead wasn't up there at all. Culbeau kicked into the bedroom where he'd seen the rifle barrel and the telescopic sight aiming at them. And he now found pretty much what he expected to find: a piece of narrow pipe on top of which was taped the rear end of a Corona bottle.

In disgust he said, "That's the gun and scope. Damn! They rigged it to bluff us out. It cost us a half hour. And the deputies are probably five minutes away. We gotta get outa here."

IT WAS dusk. Garrett Hanlon paddled the narrow skiff toward the shore. "We gotta land someplace," he said. "Before it's, like, totally dark."

Amelia Sachs noticed that the landscape had changed. The trees had thinned, and large pools of marsh met the river. The boy was right; a wrong turn could take them into an impenetrable bog.

"I'm a long way from Brooklyn," she said.

He clicked his nails. "And it bothers you not being there?"

"You bet it does."

"That's what pisses insects off the most. Like, it's weird. They don't mind working, and they don't mind fighting. But they get all freaked out in an unfamiliar place."

That's me, Sachs thought. I guess I'm a card-carrying insect.

Garrett squinted through the monotone of dusk. "Up that path. We're going to a trailer I stay in some."

He eased himself into the water and pulled the boat onto the shore. Sachs climbed out. He directed her through the woods and seemed to know exactly where he was going despite the darkness.

"How do you know where to go?" she asked.

"I'm like the monarchs. I just know directions pretty good."

"Monarchs?"

"The butterflies. They migrate a thousand miles and know exactly where they're going. It's really really cool—they navigate by the sun and, like, change course depending on where the sun is on the horizon. When it's dark, they use the earth's magnetic fields."

Garrett continued to lead her through the woods, then down a road. After ten minutes he turned into an overgrown driveway where an old trailer sat in a clearing. In the gloom she couldn't see clearly, but it seemed to be ramshackle, rusted, and overgrown with ivy.

"This is yours?" Sachs asked.

"Well, nobody's lived here for years, so I guess it's mine. I have a key, but it's at home." He managed to open a window, boosted himself up and through it. A moment later the door opened.

She walked inside. Garrett found some matches and lit a propane lantern. It gave off a warm yellow glow. He opened a cabinet in the tiny kitchen, peered inside. "I've got Farmer John macaroni. And some beans too."

He started opening cans as Sachs looked around. A few chairs, a table. In the bedroom she could see a dingy mattress.

Garrett hung pieces of greasy cloth over the windows to keep anyone outside from seeing the light inside. He stepped out for a moment, then came back with a rusty cup, filled presumably with rainwater. He held it out to her.

She shook her head. "Feel like I drank half the Paquenoke."

He drank from the cup, then heated the food on a small propane stove. In a soft voice he sang an eerie tune over and over: *"Farmer John, Farmer John. Enjoy it fresh from Farmer John. . . ."* It was nothing more than an advertising jingle, but the chant was unsettling, and she was glad when he stopped.

He poured the food into two bowls and handed her a spoon. They ate for a few minutes in silence.

Sachs noticed a raucous, high-pitched noise outside. "What's that?" she asked. "Cicadas?"

"Yeah," he said. "It's just the males that make that sound."

"Why do you like insects so much, Garrett?" she asked.

"I don't know. I just do." He scratched one of his poison-oak welts. "I guess I got interested in them after my parents died. I was pretty unhappy. I felt funny in my head. Confused. The counselors at school said it was because Mom and Dad and my sister died, and they, like, told me I should work harder to get over it. But I couldn't. All I did was go into the swamp or the woods and read. For a year that's all I did. Just moved from foster home to foster home. But then I read something neat. In that book there."

Flipping open *The Miniature World*, he found a page. He showed it to her. He'd circled a passage headed "Characteristics of Healthy Living Creatures." Sachs scanned the list of entries:

> A healthy creature strives to grow and develop.
> A healthy creature strives to survive.
> A healthy creature strives to adapt to its environment.

Garrett said, "I read that, and it was like, wow, I could be like that. I could be healthy and normal again. I tried totally hard to follow the rules it said. And that made me feel better. Kind of like the book saved my life. So I guess I felt close to them. Insects, I mean. They taught me all sorts of stuff about life." He grew quiet, then said, "Insects never go away."

"What do you mean?"

Garrett put the book down. "See, the thing is, if you kill one, there are always more. You know reincarnation? Like coming back in another life?"

Sachs nodded.

"That all started because of moths and butterflies. Like, the caterpillar doesn't really die. It just becomes something else. It's sad when people go away. That's forever. If my mom and dad and sister were insects and they died, there'd be others just like them, and I wouldn't be alone."

"Don't you have any friends?"

Garrett shrugged. "Mary Beth. She's sort of the only one."

"You really like her, don't you?"

"Totally. She saved me from this kid who was going to do something mean to me. She talks to me." He thought for a moment. "I guess that's what I like about her. Talking. I was thinking, like, maybe in a few years, when I'm older, she might wanta go out with me. We could go to movies. Or go on picnics. I was watching her on a picnic with her mother and some friends. They were having fun. I watched for, like, hours. I just sat under a holly bush and pretended I was with them. You ever go on a picnic?"

"I have, sure."

"I went with my family a lot. I mean, my real family. I liked it."

"And you thought you and Mary Beth would go on picnics?"

"Maybe." Then he shook his head and offered a sad smile. "I guess not. Mary Beth's pretty and smart and a bunch older than me. But maybe we could be friends. But even if not, all I really care about is she's okay. She'll stay with me till it's safe. Or you and your friend—that man in the chair everybody was talking about—you can help her go someplace where she'd be safe." He fell silent.

"Safe from the man in the overalls?" she asked.

He didn't answer, then nodded. "Yeah. That's right."

"I'm going to get some of that water," Sachs said.

She picked up the cup. She went outside, looked at the rainwater barrel. It was covered with a fine screen. Lifted it, filled the cup, and drank. The water seemed sweet. She listened to the creaks and zips of the insects.

Or you and your friend—that man in the chair everybody was talking about—can help her go someplace where she'd be safe.

The phrase echoed in her head: *the man in the chair, the man in the chair.*

She returned to the trailer, looked around the tiny living room. "Garrett, would you do me a favor and go sit over there?"

He looked at her for a moment, then stood and walked to the old armchair she was nodding at.

She walked across the room and picked up one of the old rattan chairs in the corner. She carried it to where the boy sat and placed it on the floor, facing him. "Garrett, you remember what Dr. Penny was telling you to do in jail? About the empty chair?"

"Talk to the chair?" he asked, eyeing it uncertainly.

"That's right. I want you to do it again. Will you?"

He stared at the chair for a moment. Finally he said, "I guess."

Sachs remembered how the doctor had tried to get Garrett to imagine that Mary Beth was in the chair, and while he hadn't wanted to say anything to her, he did seem to want to talk to *somebody*. Oh, Rhyme, I understand you like cold, hard evidence. But I believe there's more to Garrett Hanlon than the evidence tells.

"Look at the chair," she said now. "Who do you want to imagine sitting there?"

He shook his head. "I don't know."

She pushed the chair closer. Smiled to encourage him. "Tell me."

"Well, I don't know. Maybe . . . maybe my father."

"Your real father?"

Garrett nodded. He was agitated, nervous, clicking his nails.

Looking at his somber face, Sachs realized with concern that she had no idea what she was doing. Nonetheless, she was going to try it. Lincoln Rhyme disparaged her being a "people cop" and warned that it would be her downfall. But for Amelia Sachs the best type of evidence was that found in the human heart. "What was your father's name?" she asked.

"Stuart. Stu."

"You two got along okay?"

"Better than most of my friends and their dads. Their dads were always yelling at them. You know, 'Why's your room so messy?' 'Why didn't you get your homework done?' But mostly Dad was pretty good to me. Until . . ." His voice bled out. "I don't want to tell you."

"Well, don't tell *me*. Tell *him,* your dad." She nodded at the chair. "There's your father right there in front of you. Imagine it."

The boy edged forward, staring at the chair almost fearfully. For an instant there was such a look of longing in his eyes that Sachs wanted to cry. "Go ahead, Garrett. Tell me about him. Tell me what he looked like. What he wore."

After a pause the boy said, "He was tall and pretty thin. He had dark hair. He always wore nice clothes. He didn't even have a pair of jeans. He always wore shirts with collars on them. And pants with cuffs." A faint smile bloomed on Garrett's face. "He used to drop a quarter down the side of his pants and try and catch it in his cuff, and if he did, then my sister or me could have it. On Christmas he'd bring home silver dollars for us, and he'd keep sliding them down his pants until we got them."

The silver dollars in the wasp jar, Sachs recalled. "Did he have any hobbies? Sports?"

"Not sports. He liked to read. History. And stuff about nature."

"Well, imagine that he's sitting there in the empty chair. He's reading. He puts the book down, and he's looking at you. Now you've got a chance to say something to him. What would you say?"

He shrugged, shook his head. Looked around the trailer.

But Sachs wasn't going to let it go. She said, "Let's think about a specific thing you'd like to talk to him about. An incident. Something you're unhappy about. Was there anything like that?"

"Okay, I guess there was something."

"What? Tell him, Garrett."

"Well, that night . . . the night they died."

Sachs felt a faint shudder. "What about that night?"

"See, they were in the car going to dinner. It was Wednesday. Every Wednesday we went to Bennigans. I'd have the chicken fingers. And me and Kaye, my sister, we'd split fries and onion rings."

There was so much sorrow in his eyes, Sachs thought. "What do you remember about that night?" she asked.

"It was outside the house. In the driveway. They were in the car— Dad and Mom and my sister. They were going to dinner. And"—he swallowed—"they were going to leave without me."

"They were?"

He nodded. "I was late. I'd been in the woods. And I'd kinda lost track of time. My father wouldn't let me in the car. He must've been mad because I was late. I wanted to get in so bad. It was really cold. I remember I was shivering, and they were shivering. There was frost on the windows. But they wouldn't let me in."

"Maybe your father didn't see you. Because of the frost."

"No. He saw me. I was right beside his side of the car. I was banging on the window and he saw me, but he didn't open the door. He just kept frowning and shouting at me. And I kept thinking, He's mad at me, and I'm cold, and I'm not going to have dinner with my family." Tears ran down his cheeks.

Sachs wanted to put her arm around the boy's shoulders, but she remained where she was. "Go on"—nodding toward the chair— "talk to your father. What do you want to say to him?"

"It's so cold!" Garrett said, gasping. "It's cold and I want to get in the car. Why won't he let me in the car?"

"No, tell *him*. Tell your father. Imagine he's there."

Garrett looked at the old chair uneasily. "I just wanted to go to Bennigans with you!" he said, sobbing now. "That's all. Why wouldn't you let me in the car? I wasn't that late!" Then Garrett grew angry. "You locked me out! You were mad at me, and it wasn't fair. What I did wasn't that bad. I must've done something else to make you mad. What? Why didn't you want me to go with you? Tell me what I did." His voice was choked. "Come back and tell me. What did I do? Tell me, tell me, tell me!"

Sobbing, he jumped up and grabbed the chair. Screaming in fury, he smashed it into the floor of the trailer. Sachs pushed back, blinking in shock at the anger she'd unleashed. He slammed the chair down a dozen times, until it was nothing but a shattered mass of wood and rattan. Finally Garrett collapsed on the floor. Sachs rose and put her arms around him as he sobbed and shook.

After five minutes the crying ended. He stood up, wiped his face on his sleeve. "I'm going outside," he said, and pushed out the door.

She sat for a moment, then set the alarm on her Casio wristwatch for five a.m. She was utterly exhausted. But as tired as she was, Amelia Sachs didn't lie down on the bed. She shut off the lantern and pulled the cloth off the windows, then sat in the musty armchair. She watched the hunched-over silhouette of the boy, sitting outside on an oak stump and gazing intently at the moving constellations of lightning bugs that filled the forest around him.

She found herself thinking of an empty chair. Not the chair from Dr. Penny's technique, but Lincoln Rhyme's red Storm Arrow wheelchair.

That's what they were doing down here in North Carolina, after all. Rhyme was risking everything—his life, what was left of his health, his and Sachs's life together—so that he could leave the chair behind, empty. Figuratively at least.

And sitting here in this foul trailer, a felon, alone in her own knuckle time, Amelia Sachs finally admitted to herself what had troubled her so about Rhyme's insistence on the operation. Of course, she was worried that he'd die on the table. Or that the operation would make him worse.

But that wasn't why she'd done everything she could to stop him from having the operation. No, no. What scared her the most was that the operation *would* succeed.

Oh, Rhyme, don't you understand? I don't *want* you to change.

I love you the way you are. That mind of yours holds me tighter than the most passionate lover ever could. And if you were like everyone else, what would happen to us? Why would you need me?

Amelia closed her eyes. But it was an hour before the sound of the wind and the cicadas finally lulled her into a deep but troubled sleep.

LINCOLN Rhyme muttered, "I don't believe it."

He'd just spoken with a furious Lucy Kerr and had learned that Sachs had taken several shots at a deputy under the Hobeth Bridge.

"I don't believe it," he repeated in a whisper to Thom.

The best the aide could do was offer, "It's a mix-up. It has to be. Amelia would never shoot at a fellow officer even to scare them."

Jim Bell asked, "You have any more ideas, Lincoln?"

Rhyme nodded at the evidence charts, then reiterated what they knew about the house where Mary Beth was being kept. "There's a Carolina bay near the place. Half the marked passages in his insect books are about camouflage, and the brown paint on his pants is the color of tree bark, so the place is probably in or next to a forest. The camphene lamps are from the 1800s, so the place is old. But the rest of the trace isn't much help. The yeast would be from the mill. The paper fibers could be from anywhere. The fruit juice and sugar? From food or drinks."

The phone rang. Rhyme's left ring finger twitched on the ECU, and he answered the call. "Hello?" he said into the speakerphone.

"Lincoln." He recognized the soft exhausted voice of Mel Cooper.

"What do you have, Mel? I need some good news."

"That key you found? Finally tracked it down."

"What is it?"

"It's to a trailer made by the McPherson Deluxe Mobile Home Company. Company's out of business, but the serial number on the key you've got fits a trailer that was made in '69."

"Tell me, Mel, does one live in these things in a trailer park or drive 'em around like a Winnebago?"

"Live in them, I'd guess. They measure eight by twenty. Not the sort of thing you'd cruise around in. Anyway, they're not motorized. You have to tow them."

"Thanks, Mel. Get some sleep."

Rhyme shut the phone off. He told Bell about what Cooper had found. "What do you think, Jim? Any trailer parks around here?"

"A couple. But they aren't even close to where Garrett and Amelia were headed. Should I send somebody to check them out?"

"No. Garrett probably found a trailer abandoned in the woods and took it over." Rhyme glanced at the map, thinking, And it's parked somewhere in a hundred square miles of wilderness.

MIDNIGHT in the swamp. The sounds of insects. The fast shadows of bats. An owl or two. The icy light of the moon.

Lucy and the other deputies hiked four miles over to Route 30, where a camper awaited. Bell had pulled strings and "requisitioned" the vehicle from a Winnebago dealer. Steve Farr had driven it here to give the searchers a place to stay for the night.

Inside the cramped quarters, the searchers hungrily ate the roast-beef sandwiches that Farr had brought. Then Lucy called in and told Jim Bell that they'd tracked the pair to an A-frame vacation house, which they'd broken into. "Looked like Sachs and the boy had been watching TV."

But it had been too dark to follow the trail, and they'd decided to wait until dawn to resume the search.

Lucy sat down at the table, pulled her service revolver out of its holster. "Steve, you bring what I asked for?" she asked Farr.

The crew-cut young man dug in the glove compartment of the camper and handed her a box of bullets. She emptied the round-point cartridges from her pistol and speedloaders and replaced them with the new bullets—hollow points, which have more stopping power and cause much more damage to soft tissue when they hit a human being.

Jesse Corn watched her closely, then said, "Amelia's not dangerous." He spoke in a low voice, the words meant for her only.

Lucy set the gun down and looked into his eyes. "Listen, Jesse, Amelia's a traitor, and we can't trust her. I saw that look in your face when you saw she wasn't under the boat. You were relieved. I know you think you like her. But she busted a killer outa jail. And if you'd been the one out there in the river instead of Ned, Amelia would have shot at you just as fast." She continued, "And Garrett—that's one sick boy. It's just a fluke he's not doing life right now."

"I know Garrett's dangerous. It's Amelia I'm thinking of."

"Well, it's us that *I'm* thinking of and everybody else in Blackwater Landing that boy could be planning on killing if he gets away from us. Now, I need to know if I can count on you, Jesse."

Jesse glanced at the box of shells, then back to her. "You can."

"Good. 'Cause at first light I'm tracking them down and bringing 'em back. I hope both alive. But that's become optional."

 **TEN**

AMELIA Sachs woke just after dawn. She was in agony—her body's response to sleeping in an armchair. But she felt oddly buoyant. Fierce sunlight streamed through the windows of the trailer, and she took this as a good omen. Today they were going to find Mary Beth, return to Tanner's Corner with her. She'd confirm Garrett's story, and Jim Bell could start the search for the real killer—the man in the tan overalls.

She saw Garrett awaken in the bedroom and roll upright on the saggy mattress. She noticed his skinny frame and worried about getting him some good food—cereal, milk, fruit—and washing his clothes, making sure he took a shower. This, she thought, is what it would be like to have a child of your own.

"Morning." She smiled.

He smiled back. "We gotta go," he said. "Gotta get to Mary Beth. She's got to be totally thirsty."

Sachs got unsteadily to her feet.

Garrett pulled his shirt on quickly. "I'm going outside. I'm going to leave a couple of empty hornets' nests around. Might slow 'em up if they come this way." He stepped outside but returned just a moment later. He left a cup of water on the table beside her, said shyly, "This is for you." He stepped out again.

She drank it down. Longing for a toothbrush and—

"It's him!" a man's voice called in a whisper.

Sachs froze, looked out the window. She saw nothing. But from a tall stand of bushes near the trailer the forced whisper continued. "I've got him in my sights. I've got a clear shot."

The voice was familiar, and she decided it was Culbeau or one of his friends. The redneck trio had found them. They were going to kill the boy or torture him into telling where Mary Beth was so they could get the reward.

Garrett hadn't heard the voice. Sachs could see him. He was about thirty feet away, setting an empty hornets' nest on the trail.

She grabbed the Smith & Wesson and stepped quietly outside. "Garrett," she whispered.

He turned, saw Sachs motioning for him to join her. He glanced to his left, into the bushes, and she saw terror blossom in his face. He cried, "Don't hurt me, don't hurt me!"

Sachs dropped into a crouch, cocked the pistol, and aimed at the redneck as he pushed through the bushes toward Garrett.

It happened so quickly. . . .

Garrett falling to his belly in fear, crying out, "Don't, don't!"

Amelia lifting her pistol, pressure on the trigger.

The man bursting from the bushes into the clearing, gun raised.

Just as deputy Ned Spoto turned the corner of the trailer right beside Sachs, blinked in surprise to see her, and leaped toward her, arms outstretched. Startled, Sachs stumbled away from him. Her weapon fired, bucking hard in her hand.

And thirty feet away she saw the bullet from her gun strike the forehead of the man who'd been in the bushes—not one of the rednecks, but Jesse Corn. A black dot appeared above the deputy's eye, and as his head jerked back, a horrible pink cloud puffed out behind him. Without a sound he dropped to the ground.

Sachs gasped, staring at the body. She dropped to her knees, the gun tumbling from her hand.

"Oh, God," Ned muttered, also staring in shock at Jesse's body. Before the deputy could recover and draw his gun, Garrett rushed him. The boy snagged Sachs's pistol from the ground and pointed it at Ned's head, then took the deputy's weapon and flung it into the bushes. "Lie down!" Garrett raged at him. "On your face! Now!"

Ned did as he was told, tears running down his tanned cheeks.

"Jesse!" Lucy Kerr called from nearby. "Where are you? Who's shooting?"

Garrett glanced at the body, then past it, toward the sound of approaching feet. He put his arm around Sachs. "We have to go."

When she didn't answer, when she simply stared, completely numb, at the scene in front of her—the end of the deputy's life and the end of her own—Garrett helped her to her feet, then took her hand and pulled her after him. They vanished into the woods like lovers hurrying for shelter before a thunderstorm hit.

WHAT was happening now? a frantic Lincoln Rhyme wondered. An hour ago, at five thirty a.m., he'd finally gotten a call from a very put-out drone in the real estate division of the North Carolina Department of Taxation. The man had been awakened at one thirty and asked to track down delinquent taxes on any land on which a claimed residence was a McPherson trailer. Garrett's parents hadn't owned one, so Rhyme had reasoned that if the boy was using the place as a hideout, it was abandoned. And if it was abandoned, the owner had defaulted on taxes.

The drone told him there were two such properties in the state. In one case, near the Blue Ridge, the land and trailer had been sold at a tax-lien foreclosure to a couple who currently lived there. The other, in Paquenoke County, wasn't worth the time or money to foreclose on. He'd given Rhyme the address, an RFD route about a half mile from the Paquenoke River.

Rhyme had called Lucy and the others and sent them there. They were going to approach at first light and, if Garrett and Amelia were inside, surround them and talk them into surrendering. The last Rhyme had heard, they'd spotted the trailer and were moving in.

Unhappy that his boss had gotten virtually no sleep, Thom went through the morning ritual carefully: the four B's—bladder, bowel, brushing teeth, and blood pressure.

"It's high, Lincoln," Thom muttered. Excessive blood pressure in a quad could lead to an attack of dysreflexia, which could result in a stroke. But Rhyme ignored him. He was riding on pure energy. He wanted desperately to find Amelia. He wanted—

Rhyme looked up. Jim Bell, an alarmed expression on his face, walked into the lab. Ben Kerr, equally upset, entered behind him.

"What happened?" Rhyme asked. "Is Amelia all right? Is—"

"She killed Jesse," Bell said in a whisper. "Shot him in the head."

Thom froze, glanced at Rhyme.

The sheriff continued. "He was about to arrest Garrett. She shot him. They took off."

"No. It's impossible," Rhyme whispered. "There's a mistake."

Bell was shaking his head. "No. Ned Spoto saw the whole thing. I'm not saying she did it on purpose—Ned went for her and her gun went off—but it's still felony murder. This is way past us now, Lincoln. I've got to get the state involved."

"Wait, Jim," Rhyme said urgently. "Please. She's desperate now. She's scared. So's Garrett. You call in troopers, a lot more people are going to get hurt. They'll be gunning for them both. I'll—"

Suddenly Bell was jostled aside as a man rushed into the room. It was Mason Germain. "You bastard!" he cried, and made for Rhyme, grabbing him by the shirt. "You freak! You come down here and play your little—"

"Mason!" Bell and Thom started forward, but the deputy shoved them both aside.

"—play your little games. And now a good man's dead because of you! I'm going to kill you. I'm going to—" But Mason's voice was choked off as a huge arm wrapped around his chest and he was lifted clean off his feet.

Ben Kerr carried the deputy away from Rhyme.

"Kerr, let go of me," Mason gasped.

"Calm down, Deputy," Ben said, then looked at Bell, who nodded.

Ben released Mason, who stood back, fury in his eyes, and said to Bell, "I'm finding that woman and I'm—"

"You are not, Mason," Bell said. "You want to keep working in this department, you'll do what I tell you. We're going to handle it my way. You're staying at the office here. You understand?"

"Yeah, I understand." He stormed out of the lab.

Bell asked Rhyme, "You all right?"

Rhyme nodded.

Thom adjusted Rhyme's shirt. And despite the criminalist's protest, he took his blood pressure. "Too high, but not critical."

The sheriff walked to the window and stared outside. "Lord, first Ed, now Jesse. What a nightmare."

Rhyme said, "Please, Jim, let me find them and then give me a chance to talk to her. If you don't, it's going to escalate. You know that. We'll end up with more people dead."

Bell sighed. "You think you can find them?"

"Yes," Rhyme answered. "I can find them."

THERE was no evidence from the trailer, of course. Lucy and the other deputies had searched it, but too fast. The only clues Rhyme had to Mary Beth's location—to where Garrett and Sachs were now headed—were on the charts in front of him: the evidence found in Garrett's room and on the clothes he wore at the mill.

When Rhyme was mired in the denial stage of grief after his accident, he had tried to summon superhuman willpower to make his body move. He recalled the stories of people who lifted cars off children or ran at impossible speeds to find help in emergencies. But he'd slowly come to realize that those types of strength were no longer available to him.

But he did have one type left—mental strength.

Think! All you have is your mind and the evidence that's in front of you. The evidence isn't going to change. So change the way you're thinking.

He went through the charts once more. The key—that had been solved. The yeast would be from the mill. The sugar, from food or juice. The camphene, from an old lamp. The paint on the jeans, from the building where Mary Beth was being held. The kerosene, from the boat. The dirt in the boy's cuffs? It exhibited no particularly unique characteristics and was— Wait. The dirt.

Rhyme recalled that yesterday morning he and Ben had run the density-gradient test on dirt from the shoes and car floor mats of county workers. Thom had photographed each tube. On the back of each Polaroid he had noted which employee it had come from.

"Ben, run the dirt you found in Garrett's cuffs at the mill through the density-gradient unit."

After the dirt had settled in the tube, Ben said, "Got it."

"Compare it with the pictures of the samples you did yesterday."

The young man flipped through the Polaroids, paused. "I've got a match!" he said. "One's almost identical."

"Whose shoes was it from?"

Ben looked at the back of the Polaroid. "Frank Heller. He works in the department of public works. I'll find him."

Ben vanished. He returned a few minutes later, accompanied by a balding, heavyset man in a white, short-sleeved shirt.

"Frank, we need your help," Rhyme explained. "The dirt on your shoes matches dirt we found on the suspect's clothes. Which means he might have the girl near where you live. Could you point out on the map exactly where that is?"

Frank touched a spot. It was north of the Paquenoke, north of the trailer where Jesse had been killed.

"What's the area like around you?"

"Forests and fields mostly."

"One more question. Are there any Carolina bays near you?"

"Oh, you bet there are."

Rhyme put his head back, closed his eyes, slipped into his own world—an orderly place of science and evidence and logic.

Paint sugar yeast dirt camphene paint dirt sugar . . . Yeast.

Rhyme's eyes snapped open. "There a coffee machine here?"

"Coffee?" Thom asked. "Not with your blood pressure."

"No. I don't want a cup of coffee! I want a coffee filter."

"I'll dig one up." Jim Bell left, and returned a moment later.

To Ben, Rhyme said, "See if the paper fibers from the filter match the ones we found on Garrett's clothes at the mill."

Ben rubbed some fibers off the filter onto a slide of the comparison microscope. He gazed through the eyepiece. "The colors are a little different, Lincoln, but the fibers are pretty much the same."

"Good," Rhyme said, his eyes now on the stained T-shirt. "Jim," he went on, "I need you to get something. For a control sample."

"You bet, Lincoln." He fished his keys from his pocket.

"Oh, you won't need your car."

LUCY, Ned, and Trey pushed through a large oak forest. Jim Bell had told them to wait at the trailer and he'd send Steve Farr, Frank, and Mason to take over the pursuit. He wanted her and the other two deputies to return to the office. But they hadn't even bothered to vote on the matter. They'd moved Jesse's body into the trailer, covered it with a sheet. Then Lucy told Jim that they were going after the fugitives and that nothing was going to stop them.

Garrett and Amelia were fleeing fast and were making no effort to cover their tracks. They moved along a path that bordered marshland. The ground was soft, and their footprints were clearly visible, weight on the toes: They were sprinting.

And so Lucy said to her two fellow deputies, "Let's jog."

They continued this way for a mile, until the ground grew drier and they could no longer see the footprints. Then the trail ended in a grassy clearing, and they had no idea where their prey had gone.

"What do we do?" Ned asked.

"Call in and wait," Lucy muttered.

WITH a squeak the door to the cabin swung open. "Mary Beth," Garrett cried. "Mary Beth."

She stood upright against the wall, behind the front door. Didn't say a word. Gripped the coup stick in both hands.

The door eased open farther. Mary Beth stepped toward him and swung the coup stick. But he dropped to the floor just as the rock would have struck him. Reaching up, he grabbed her wrist. His grip was like steel, and she dropped the coup stick.

"No!" she screamed. "No!"

The boy was wild-eyed. There was a grim-faced woman with him, pretty, with long red hair. Her clothes, like Garrett's, were filthy. The woman was silent, her eyes dull.

"They're after us," Garrett said as he pulled the redhead into the cabin and shoved the door closed. "We can't let them see us."

"You bastard!" Mary Beth screamed. "I could've died."

He blinked in surprise. "I'm sorry!" His voice cracked. "I didn't mean to leave you this long. I got arrested."

"Arrested?" Mary Beth asked. "Then what are you doing here?"

Finally the redhead spoke. In a mumbling voice she said, "I got him out of jail. So we could find you and bring you back. And you could back up his story about the man in the overalls."

"What man?" Mary Beth asked, confused.

"The man in the tan overalls, the one who killed Billy Stail."

"But"—Mary Beth shook her head—"*Garrett* killed Billy. I saw him. He hit him with a shovel. Then he kidnapped me."

Mary Beth had never seen such an expression on another human being—complete shock and dismay. The redhead started to turn toward Garrett, but then something caught her eye: the row of Farmer John canned vegetables. She walked slowly toward the table and picked one up, stared at the picture on the label—a cheerful blond farmer wearing tan overalls and a white shirt.

"You made it up?" she whispered to Garrett. "You lied to me."

Garrett stepped forward, fast as a grasshopper, and pulled the handcuffs off her belt and ratcheted them onto her wrists. "I'm sorry, Amelia," he said. "But if I'd told you the truth, you never would've let me out. I had to get back here to Mary Beth."

THE chromatograph rumbled, and everyone in the lab remained still, waiting for the results.

"Okay, here we go," Ben said when the computer screen finally burst to life with the results of the control sample Rhyme had asked Jim Bell to procure. "Here's what we've got: solution of fifty-five percent alcohol. Water, lot of minerals."

"Well water," Rhyme said.

"Most likely." Ben continued, "Then there are traces of formaldehyde, phenol, fructose, dextrose, cellulose."

"That's good enough for me," Rhyme said, then announced to Bell and Mason—who was back in the lab—"I made a mistake. A big one. I saw the yeast and discounted it. I assumed it'd come from the mill, not the place where Garrett really has Mary Beth. But why would a mill have supplies of yeast? You'd only find those in a bakery. Or"—he lifted his eyebrow to Bell—"someplace they're brewing that." He nodded at the bottle that Rhyme had asked Bell to collect from the basement of the sheriff's department. It was moonshine from one of the Ocean Spray jars Rhyme had seen a deputy clear away when he'd taken over the evidence room and turned it into a lab. This is what Ben had just sampled in the GC/MS.

"Sugar and yeast," the criminalist continued. "Those are ingredients in liquor. And the cellulose in that moonshine," he said, looking at the computer screen, "is probably from the paper fibers. I assume when you make moonshine, you have to filter it."

"Yep," Bell confirmed. "And most 'shiners use coffee filters."

"Just like the fiber we found on Garrett's clothes. And the dextrose and fructose—complex sugars found in fruit. That's from the cranberry juice left over in the Ocean Spray jar. Remember you told me, Jim, that's the most popular container for moonshine? Garrett's holding Mary Beth in a moonshiner's cabin, presumably one that's been abandoned since the raid."

"What raid?" Mason asked.

"Well, it's like the trailer," Rhyme replied. "If Garrett's using the place to hide Mary Beth, then it has to be abandoned. And what's the only reason anybody would abandon a working still?"

"Department of revenue busted it," Bell said.

"Right," Rhyme said. "Find out the location of any stills that've been raided in the past couple of years. It'll be an old building in a stand of trees. It's four or five miles from where Frank Heller lives, and it'll be on a Carolina bay, or you'll have to go around a bay to get there from the trailer."

The sheriff left to call the revenue department.

"That's pretty good, Lincoln," Ben said.

Not long afterward Bell hurried back into the room. "Got it!" He circled a spot on the map. "Right here. Head of investigations at revenue said they raided it a year ago. One of his agents checked out the place a couple of months ago. Somebody'd painted it brown, but the place was empty, so he didn't pay it any more mind. Oh, and it's about twenty yards from a good-sized Carolina bay."

"Okay, Jim, I found 'em. Now I want that hour alone with her— to talk her out." Rhyme held Bell's eye. "I know I can do it."

Finally Bell said, "Okay. But if Garrett gets away this time, it's gonna be a full-out manhunt."

"Understood. You think my van can make it there?"

Bell said, "Roads aren't great but—"

"I'll get you there," Thom said firmly. "Whatever it takes."

FIVE minutes after Rhyme had wheeled out of the county building, Mason Germain watched Jim Bell return to his office. Making sure no one else saw him, Mason stepped into the corridor and headed outside into the heat and crossed the quadrangle to a bank of pay phones on the sidewalk. He looked around, and when he saw he was alone, he dropped some coins in, looked at a number on a slip of paper, and dialed.

FARMER John, Farmer John. Enjoy it fresh from Farmer John. . . .
As Amelia Sachs stared at the row of Farmer John cans, her mind was clogged with thoughts of her appalling foolishness. Which had cost Jesse Corn his life. And had ruined hers as well. She was only vaguely aware of the cabin where she now sat, a prisoner of the boy she'd risked her life to save.

"What's that?" Garrett said, leaping up.

Then Sachs heard it too. A car was slowly approaching.

"They've found us!" the boy cried, gripping the pistol. He ran to the window, stared out. He seemed confused. "What's that?" he whispered.

A car door slammed. Then there was a long pause.

And she heard, "Sachs, it's me. Are you there?"

A faint smile crossed her face. No one else in the universe could have found this place except Lincoln Rhyme.

"No," Garrett whispered. "Don't say anything."

Sachs rose and walked to the window. There, in front of the cabin, was the black Rollx van. Rhyme, in the Storm Arrow, had maneuvered close to the cabin—as far as he could get until a hillock of dirt near the porch stopped him. Thom stood beside him.

"Can I talk to you?" the criminalist called.

What was the point? she wondered. Still, she said, "Yes."

She walked to the door. "Open it, Garrett," she said firmly, her eyes boring into his. "I'm going outside."

He looked around the room, then pulled the door open.

Outside, she stood in front of Rhyme. "He did it," she said. "He killed Billy. I got it wrong. Dead wrong."

The criminalist closed his eyes. "Is Mary Beth okay?"

"She's fine. Scared but fine."

"There wasn't any man in overalls?" he asked.

"No. Garrett made that up."

Rhyme saw she was cuffed and noticed Garrett in the window, peering out angrily, holding a pistol.

"And Jesse Corn?" he asked softly.

She shook her head. "I didn't know it was him, Rhyme. I thought it was Culbeau or one of his friends. A deputy jumped me, and my weapon went off. But it was my fault. I acquired an unidentified target with an unsafetied weapon. I broke rule number one."

"I'll get you the best lawyer in the country. We'll get something worked out, Sachs."

"There's nothing to work out, Rhyme. Open-and-shut case." Then she was looking past him, frowning. "What's—"

Suddenly a woman's voice called, "Hold it right there! Amelia, you're under arrest."

Rhyme tried to turn but couldn't rotate his head far enough. He puffed into the controller and backed in a semicircle. He saw Lucy and two other deputies, crouching as they ran from the woods. Their weapons were drawn. The two men used trees for cover. But Lucy walked boldly toward Rhyme, Thom, and Sachs, her pistol leveled at Sachs's chest.

How had the search party found the cabin? Had they heard the van? Had Bell reneged on his deal and told them?

Lucy walked up to Sachs and punched her hard in the face. Sachs gave a faint wheeze at the pain but said nothing.

"No!" Rhyme cried.

Thom stepped forward, but Lucy grabbed Sachs by the arm. "Is Mary Beth in there?"

"Yes." Blood trickled from Sachs's chin.

"Is she all right?"

A nod.

"Does he have your weapon?"

"Yes."

Lucy swore. She called to the other deputies, "Ned, Trey, he's inside. And he's armed." Then she snapped at Rhyme, "I'd suggest you get under cover." And she pulled Sachs roughly back behind the van on the side opposite the cabin.

Rhyme followed the women, Thom holding the chair for stability as it crossed the uneven ground.

Lucy turned to Sachs, grabbed her by the arms. "He did it, didn't he? Mary Beth told you, right? Garrett killed Billy."

Sachs looked down at the ground. "Yes. I'm sorry. I—"

"Sorry doesn't mean a damn thing to me or anybody else, least of all Jesse. Does Garrett have any other weapons in there?"

"I don't know. I didn't see any."

Lucy turned back to the cabin, shouted, "Garrett, can you hear me? It's Lucy Kerr. I want you to put that gun down and walk outside with your hands on your head. You do that now, okay?"

The only response was the door's slamming shut. Lucy pulled out her cell phone and started to make a call.

"Hey, Deputy," a man's voice said, "you need help?"

Lucy turned. A tall, ponytailed man carrying a hunting rifle was trooping through the grass toward them.

"Culbeau," she snapped, "I got a situation here, and I can't deal with you too. Just go on, get out of here." Her eyes noticed something in the field. There was another man walking toward the cabin. He carried a black army rifle. "Is that Sean?" she asked.

Culbeau said, "Yeah, and Harris Tomel's over there."

Tomel was walking up to Trey Williams, the tall African American deputy. They were chatting.

Culbeau persisted. "If the boy's in the cabin, you might need some help getting him out. What can we do?"

"This is police business, Rich. The three of you, clear on outa here. Now. Trey!" she called. "Get 'em out."

The third deputy, Ned Spoto, was crouching behind a tree. He stood up and walked toward Lucy and Culbeau. "Rich," he said, "there's no reward anymore. Forget about it and—"

The shot from Culbeau's powerful rifle poked a hole in Ned's chest, and the impact flung him several feet onto his back. Trey stared at Harris Tomel, only ten feet away. Each man looked about as shocked as the other, and neither moved for a moment. Then there were three sharp cracks from O'Sarian's gun, and Trey fell to the ground, clutching his belly.

"No!" Lucy screamed, dropping the cell phone. Instinctively she lifted her pistol toward Culbeau, but by the time she fired, the three men had gone for cover in the tall grass surrounding the cabin.

It was only a few seconds later that Tomel got his first shot off, taking out the windshield and a front tire of the van.

RHYME felt the instinctive urge to drop but, of course, remained upright in the wheelchair. More bullets slammed into the van where Sachs and Lucy, now facedown on the grass, had been standing a moment before. Thom was on his knees, trying to work the heavy wheelchair out of the depression of soft earth where it was lodged.

"Lincoln!" Sachs cried.

"I'm okay. Move! Get to the other side of the van. Under cover."

Lucy said, "But Garrett can target us from there."

Sachs snapped back, "But he's not the one who's shooting now!"

Another shot missed her by a foot. Thom muscled the wheelchair toward the cabin side of the van. Lucy and Sachs followed the two men to the shadowy area between the cabin and the van.

"Why the hell are they doing this?" Lucy cried. She fired several shots, sending O'Sarian and Tomel scrambling for cover. Rhyme couldn't see Culbeau but knew that the big man was directly in front of them somewhere. The rifle that he'd been carrying was high-powered and fitted with a large telescopic sight.

"Take the cuffs off and give me the gun," Sachs shouted.

"Give it to her," Rhyme said. "She's a better shot than you."

Lucy shook her head. More bullets slapped the van and the porch.

"They've got rifles!" Sachs raged. "You're no match for them. Give me the gun!"

Lucy rested her head against the side of the van and stared in shock at the slain deputies lying in the grass. "What's going on?" she muttered, crying. "What's happening?"

The cover wasn't going to last. It protected them from Culbeau, but O'Sarian and Tomel were moving around the van on each side. In minutes they'd set up a cross fire.

"Lincoln," Thom said, "I'm taking you out of the chair. You're too much of a target."

Rhyme nodded. The aide undid the harness, got his arms around Rhyme's chest, and pulled him out, laid him on the ground. Rhyme had never felt as stabbed by his helplessness as at this moment.

More shots. Closer. Laughter too from the field.

Lucy muttered, "They're almost in position."

"Ammo?" Sachs asked.

"I've got three left in the chamber, one speedloader."

"Loaded six?"

"Yeah."

A shot knocked the Storm Arrow on its side.

Lucy fired back at O'Sarian, but his staccato response with the Colt told them that she'd missed. It also told them that in only a minute or two they'd be completely surrounded.

They'd die here, Rhyme thought. He glanced at Sachs, who was looking at him with a hopeless expression on her face.

You and me, Sachs . . .

Then he glanced at the front of the cabin. "Look," he called.

Garrett had opened the front door.

Sachs said, "Let's get inside."

"Are you crazy?" Lucy said. "Garrett's in this with them."

"No," Rhyme said. "He's had a chance to shoot. He didn't."

The bushes rustled nearby. Lucy lifted the pistol.

"Don't waste it," Sachs called. Just as Lucy rose and fired two fast shots at the sound, the rock one of the men had thrown to shake the bushes and trick her into presenting a target rolled into view. Sachs shoved Lucy aside just as Tomel's shotgun blast, meant for Lucy's back, streaked past, puncturing the side of the van.

"Inside," Rhyme said. "Now."

Lucy said, "I'll cover you. The three of you go together. Ready?"

Sachs nodded. Thom lifted Rhyme, cradling him like a child.

"Go," Lucy said.

Everything blurred as they ran up the few stairs into the cabin. More bullets cracked into the wood of the cabin as they pushed inside. A moment later Lucy rolled into the room after them and slammed the door shut. Thom set Rhyme gently on a couch.

Rhyme had a glimpse of a terrified young woman sitting in a chair. Mary Beth McConnell, he assumed.

Garrett Hanlon, eyes wide with fear, sat holding a pistol awkwardly in one hand as Lucy aimed the gun in his face. "Give me the weapon!" she cried. "Now, now!"

He blinked and handed her the gun. She put it in her belt.

Rhyme stared at the boy's bewildered and frightened eyes, a child's eyes. And he thought, I understand why you had to save him, Sachs, why you believed him. I understand.

He said, "Everybody okay?"

"Fine," Sachs said.

"Actually," Thom said almost apologetically, "not really." He lifted his hand away from his trim belly, revealing the bloody exit wound. Then he went down on his knees, hard.

Sachs, trained in the basic NYPD first-aid course, bent over Thom. He was conscious but pale, sweating fiercely.

She clamped one hand over the wound. "Get these cuffs off me," she cried. "I can't take care of him this way."

"No," Lucy said.

"Lord," Sachs muttered, and examined Thom as best she could.

"How are you, Thom?" Rhyme blurted out. "Talk to us."

"It feels numb. It's funny . . ." And he passed out.

A crash above their heads. A bullet tore through the wall. A shotgun blast hit the door. Garrett handed Sachs a wad of napkins, and she pressed them against the tear in Thom's belly.

"Is he alive?" Rhyme asked hopelessly.

"He's breathing. Shallow. But he's breathing."

Lucy asked, "Why are they doing this?"

Rhyme said, "Jim said they were into moonshine. Maybe they had their eye on this place and didn't want it found. Or maybe there's a drug lab nearby."

"Where's Bell?" Lucy asked. "And Mason?"

"They'll be here in a half hour," Rhyme said.

Lucy shook her head in dismay at this information, then looked out the window, stiffened. "O'Sarian's just found a red can. What's in it, Garrett? Gas?"

The boy was huddled on the floor, frozen in panic. "It's, like, kerosene. For the boat."

Lucy muttered, "They're going to burn us out."

"Damn," Garrett cried. He rolled to his knees, eyes frantic, and flung the door open.

Sachs shouted, "No, Garrett. Don't—"

The boy ignored her. Half running, half crawling, he skittered along the porch. Bullets cracked into the wood, following him. Sachs had no idea if he'd been hit. Then there was silence as the men moved closer with the kerosene.

Sachs looked around the room, filled with dust from the impact of the bullets. She saw Mary Beth, hugging herself, crying. Lucy, her eyes filled with the devil's own hatred, was checking her pistol. Thom was as pale as a sheet. Lincoln Rhyme was on his back, breathing hard.

In a low voice she said to Lucy, "We've got to go get them. The two of us. They're going to set fire to the place in about three minutes. Take the cuffs off." Sachs held out her wrists.

"How can I trust you? You ambushed us at the river."

Sachs asked, "Ambushed? What are you talking about?"

Lucy scowled. "What am I talking about? You used that boat as a lure and shot at Ned when he went out to get it."

"No! *You* thought we were under the boat and shot at *us*."

"Only after you . . ." Then Lucy's voice faded, and Sachs too understood. She said, "It was them—Culbeau and the others."

"And we thought it was you." For a moment Lucy's expression softened, but then the larger betrayal returned to her thoughts— Jesse Corn's death—and her eyes grew angry once more.

Sachs held her wrists out again. "We don't have any choice."

Lucy looked at Sachs, then slowly unlocked the cuffs.

Sachs rubbed her wrists. "What's the ammunition situation?"

"I've got three left."

"I've got five in mine," Sachs said, taking her long-barreled Smith & Wesson from Lucy and checking the cylinder. She looked down at Thom, who was shivering.

Mary Beth stepped forward. "I'll take care of him."

Sachs eased to the door, looked out, deciding what would make good cover and shooting positions. Her hands free again, a hefty gun in her palm, she felt confident once more. This was her world: guns and speed. She said to Lucy, "You go left, behind the van. Keep moving till you get to the high grass. I'm going right. We get into the grass and stay down, move forward toward the forest, flank them."

"They'll see us go out the door."

"They're supposed to. We want them to know we're out there

in the grass. It'll keep 'em edgy and looking over their shoulders. Don't shoot unless you have a clear, no-miss target."

O'SARIAN, with Tomel beside him, was lugging the kerosene can toward the cabin, not paying attention to the front door. So that when the two women charged out, splitting up and sprinting for cover, neither of them got his weapon up in time for a clear shot.

Culbeau, back a ways, must not have been expecting anybody to run out either. By the time his deer rifle boomed, Sachs and Lucy were rolling into the four-foot-high grass surrounding the cabin. O'Sarian and Tomel disappeared into the grass too.

Culbeau shouted, "You let 'em get out. What the hell you doing?" He fired one more shot, then dropped to the earth.

Sachs crawled toward a bit of red color where she'd seen Tomel and O'Sarian a moment ago. The hot breeze pushed the grass aside, and she saw it was the can. She moved a few feet closer and fired. The can shivered under the impact and bled clear liquid.

"Damn," one of the men said, and she heard a rustle of grass as, she supposed, he fled from the can, though it didn't ignite.

Then Sachs saw a flash of light about fifty feet into the field. It was near where Culbeau had been, and she realized it would be the scope of his big gun. She lifted her head cautiously and caught Lucy's eye, pointed to herself and then toward the flash. The deputy nodded, then pointed to herself and motioned around to the flank. Sachs nodded.

But as Lucy started through the grass, running in a crouch, O'Sarian rose and began firing. Lucy dove prone as the dirt kicked up around her, then rose and fired at O'Sarian, a near hit.

Sachs started forward again, toward Culbeau. A moment later she heard Lucy call, "Amelia, he's coming at you."

The pounding of feet in the grass.

Who? And where was he? She felt completely blind, spinning around. Panicked.

The wind parted the grass again, and Sachs saw the glint of the scope. Culbeau was nearly in front of her, on a slight rise—a good spot for him to shoot from. She climbed to her feet and started to run in a crouch. The hillock was still twenty feet away.

But Sean O'Sarian, it turned out, was much closer than that, as Sachs found out when she tripped over him. As she rolled past him, he swung the Colt toward her. She lifted her pistol. They fired simultaneously, both missing. When she rolled prone, he ran in panic.

Before Sachs could fire again at O'Sarian, Lucy Kerr stood and shot him once as he ran directly toward her. The man's head lifted, and he touched his chest. Then he spiraled down into the grass.

The deputy dropped to the ground.

Sachs moved very fast now, toward Culbeau; it was likely that he knew Lucy's position. Five feet. Ready. Move fast. Now! Sachs leaped forward and rolled into the clearing. She went up on one knee, aiming the gun. And gave a gasp of dismay.

Culbeau's "gun" was a pipe from what looked like an old still, and the scope was part of a bottle. The same trick she and Garrett had used at the A-frame on the Paquenoke. Suckered.

THE footsteps were getting closer, powerful footsteps, moving slowly up the wooden steps to the cabin. Rhyme struggled to lift his head from the couch but couldn't.

With a creak the door pushed inward. Rich Culbeau, holding a long rifle, stood in the doorway. He looked at Rhyme and Thom and concluded they weren't a threat. "Where's Mary Beth?" he asked Rhyme.

"I don't know. She ran outside to get help," Rhyme said.

"I didn't see her." Culbeau stepped into the cabin. "You're that fellow from New York. You sure got yourself into a mess here."

Rhyme's eyes slipped to the root-cellar door.

Culbeau started forward. "Mary Beth left, did she?" Aiming his gun at the cellar door, he pulled it open and fired, worked the rifle bolt, fired again. Then he peered into the smoky darkness.

It was then that Mary Beth McConnell, brandishing some kind of primitive club, stepped out from behind the front door, where she'd been waiting. She swung the club, which slammed into the side of Culbeau's head. The rifle fell from his hands and down the stairs into the darkness of the cellar. But he wasn't badly hurt, and he lashed out with a huge fist and struck Mary Beth squarely in the chest. She gasped and dropped to the floor, keening.

From a scabbard on his belt Culbeau took a folding knife and opened it with a click. He moved toward Mary Beth.

"Stop," another voice commanded. Garrett Hanlon stood in the doorway. He was holding a large gray rock in his hand. He walked close to Culbeau. "Leave her alone."

Culbeau stepped back. "Hey, boy, why'd you come back here?" He laughed coldly. "Well, come on, let's get it over with."

Garrett clicked his fingernails twice. Crouching like a wrestler, he pretended to throw the rock several times, and Culbeau dodged. Then the big man laughed again, sizing up his adversary, and swung the knife toward Garrett's belly. The boy jumped back fast, and the blade missed.

Then there was a blur of motion. Mary Beth, still lying on the floor, grabbed the club and swung it into Culbeau's ankle. He cried out as it connected and turned toward her, lifting the knife. But Garrett lunged forward and pushed the man hard on the shoulder. Culbeau was off balance, and he slid on his knees down the cellar stairs. He caught himself halfway down, groped for his rifle.

Rhyme cried, "Garrett, he's going for the gun!"

But the boy just walked slowly to the cellar and lifted the rock. But he didn't throw it. Instead he pulled a wad of cloth out of a hole in the end. And as the first few yellow jackets flew out of the hole, he flung the nest into Culbeau's face and slammed the door shut. He hooked the clasp on the lock and stood back.

Rhyme thought the screams from the basement would last longer than they did.

HARRIS Tomel saw a flash of tan. There, through the crook of a tree some distance away, he could just make out Lucy Kerr's tan uniform blouse. Holding the shotgun, he moved a little closer. It wasn't a great shot, just part of Lucy's chest visible through the crook of the tree. But doable with the shotgun. He sighted and squeezed the trigger.

Damn! The blouse was floating in the air, launched by the pellets. She'd hung it on the tree to lure him into giving away his position. What a nightmare this had turned into.

"Hold it right there, Harris," Lucy's voice called behind him.

He turned to face her, holding the Browning hidden in the four-foot-high grass pointed in her direction. She was in a T-shirt.

"Drop your gun," she ordered.

"I did already," he said. He didn't move.

"Let me see your hands. In the air. Now, Harris. Last warning."

Then he noticed a look of uncertainty in her eyes. She was bluffing. "You're out of ammo," he said, smiling.

The hopeless expression on her face confirmed it.

"But I'm not," came a voice.

The redhead! He swung toward her, thinking, She won't shoot. She's a woman. She's—

The pistol in her hands bucked, and the last thing Tomel felt was a tap on the side of his head.

LUCY Kerr saw Mary Beth stagger onto the porch and call out that Culbeau was dead and that Rhyme and Garrett were all right. Sachs was bending over Tomel's body. Lucy found her cell phone, then called the state police.

The medevac chopper was the first to arrive, and the medics quickly bundled Thom up and flew him off to the medical center. One stayed to look after Lincoln Rhyme, whose blood pressure was edging critical.

When the troopers themselves showed up in a second helicopter a few minutes later, it was Amelia Sachs they arrested first and left hog-tied—hands behind her, lying in the hot dirt outside the cabin—while they went inside to arrest Garrett Hanlon.

 *ELEVEN*

THOM would survive. The doctor at the University Medical Center in Avery had said laconically, "The bullet came and went. Missed the important stuff." Still, the aide would be off-duty for a month or two. So Dr. Cheryl Weaver had arranged for a caregiver from the medical center to help Rhyme.

The case against Amelia Sachs was bad. The county prosecutor,

Bryan McGuire, had already announced that he was going for the death penalty. Good-natured Jesse Corn had been a popular figure around town, and since he'd died trying to arrest the Insect Boy, there was considerable outcry for making this a capital case.

Jim Bell and the state police had looked into why Culbeau and his friends would attack Rhyme and the deputies. An investigator from Raleigh had found tens of thousands of dollars in cash hidden in their houses. "More than moonshine money," the detective had said, then echoed Rhyme's own thought: "That cabin must've been right near a drug factory or something."

Rhyme now sat in the Storm Arrow—drivable despite a bullet hole—in the improvised lab waiting for the new aide to arrive. Morose, he was brooding about Sachs's fate when Mary Beth McConnell appeared in the doorway.

She stepped into the room. "Mr. Rhyme."

He noted how pretty she was, her confident green eyes. He understood how Garrett could have become enamored of her. Like everyone else, Rhyme had been relieved to learn that Garrett hadn't in fact raped Mary Beth.

The girl said to Rhyme, "I just wanted to say thank you. I don't know what I would've done if it hadn't been for you and your friend, that policewoman. Thank her for me."

"I will," Rhyme told her. "Would you mind answering something? I know you gave a statement to Jim Bell, but I only know what happened at Blackwater Landing from the evidence. And some of that wasn't clear. Could you tell me?"

"Sure. I was down by the river, dusting off some of the relics I'd found, and I looked up, and there was Garrett. He was real agitated. He was saying things like 'You shouldn't've come here by yourself. It's dangerous. People die in Blackwater Landing.' He was really freaking me out. I told him to leave me alone. He grabbed my hand and tried to make me leave. Then Billy Stail comes out of the woods. He goes, 'You son of a bitch,' and he starts to hit Garrett with a shovel, but Garrett got it away from Billy and killed him. Then he grabbed me and made me get into this boat and brought me to the cabin."

"How long had Garrett been stalking you?"

Mary Beth laughed. "Stalking? No, no. I was downtown about six months ago and some of the kids from his school were picking on him. I scared them off. That made me his girlfriend, I guess. He followed me around a lot, but that was all. Admired me from afar. I was sure he was harmless." Her smile faded. "Until the other day." Mary Beth glanced at her watch. "I should go. But I wanted to ask you—the other reason I came by—if you don't need them anymore for evidence, would it be okay if I took the rest of the bones?"

"What bones?"

Mary Beth's face furrowed. "The bones I found at Blackwater Landing. I was digging up the rest of them when Garrett kidnapped me. You don't mean they're missing?"

"Nobody recovered any bones at the crime scene," Rhyme said. "They weren't in the evidence report."

She shook her head. "No, no. They can't be gone!"

"What kind of bones?"

"Human bones. I found some remains of settlers of the Lost Colony of Roanoke. From the late 1500s."

"Why do you think it was the settlers' remains?"

"The bones were really old and decayed, and they weren't in a typical Algonquin burial site or a Colonial graveyard. They were just dumped in the ground without any markings. That was what the warriors did with the bodies of their enemies. Here." She opened her backpack. "I'd already packed up a few of them before Garrett took me off." She lifted several of them out, wrapped in Saran Wrap, blackened and decomposed. Rhyme recognized a radius, a hipbone, and several inches of femur.

"There were a dozen more," she said. "This is one of the biggest finds in U.S. archaeological history. I *have* to find them."

Rhyme stared at the radius—one of the two forearm bones. "Could you go up the hallway there to the sheriff's department? Ask for Lucy Kerr and have her come down here for a minute."

"Is this about the bones?" Mary Beth asked.

"It might be."

AMELIA Sachs sat in her cell at the Tanner's Corner lockup. Her heart was numb. Her life, as she'd lived it, was over. Her life as a policewoman, her life with Lincoln Rhyme, her future with children—all that was destroyed. They had got her. Got her for good.

The cell door swung open. A deputy she didn't recognize stood there. "You've got a call." He shackled her and led her to a small metal table on which sat a phone.

She picked up the receiver and heard Rhyme's voice. "That lawyer will be here tonight. He's good. He's been doing criminal law for twenty years."

"Rhyme, why even bother? I broke a murderer out of jail and killed a local cop. It doesn't get any more hopeless than that."

"We'll talk about your case later. Tell me something. You spent a couple of days with Garrett. Did you talk about anything?"

"Sure. We talked about insects, the woods, the swamp."

"I need you to tell me everything he said."

RHYME was alone in the lab. Footsteps sounded. Boots, he decided. He hoped it would be Jim Bell, and it was.

"What's up?" the sheriff asked. "Nathan said it was urgent."

"Come on in. Close the door. But first, is anybody in the hall?"

Bell looked. "Empty." He shut the door, then walked to the table, leaned against it, crossed his arms.

Rhyme turned the wheelchair to face the map of the area. "Our map doesn't go far enough north and east to show the Dismal Swamp Canal, does it?"

"The canal? No, it doesn't."

"I've just been doing a little research," Rhyme said, nodding at the phone. "The canal's part of the Intracoastal Waterway. You know you can take a boat all the way from Norfolk, Virginia, down to Miami and not have to sail on open sea?"

"Sure. Everybody in Carolina knows about the Intracoastal."

"Look at that blue line, Jim, the one between Tanner's Corner and the Paquenoke River."

"You mean, our canal—the Blackwater Canal?"

"Right. Now, a boat could sail up that to the Paquo, then to the Great Dismal and—"

The approaching footsteps weren't as loud as Bell's, and there was little warning as the door swung open. Rhyme stopped speaking.

Mason Germain stood in the doorway. He glanced at Rhyme, then said, "Wondered where you'd got to, Jim."

"Just having a chat with Lincoln here. We were talking about—"

But Rhyme interrupted him quickly. "Say, Mason, I wonder if you could give us a few minutes alone here."

Mason glanced from one to the other, nodded, then left.

Bell frowned. "What's this all about, Lincoln?"

"Could you check out the window, make sure Mason's left?"

Bell walked to the window. "Yeah. He's headed up the street."

"How well do you know Mason?"

"As good as I know mosta my deputies. Why?"

"Because he murdered Garrett Hanlon's family."

"*What?* Mason? Why on earth?"

"Henry Davett paid him to. But I can't prove it yet."

"Hold up," Bell said. "You're a couple of steps past me."

Rhyme said, "It all has to do with the Blackwater Canal." He fell into his lecturing mode. "Now, the point of digging the canals in the eighteenth century was to have dependable transport because the roads were so bad. But as the roads and railroads got better, shippers stopped using the waterways. According to a charming lady, Julie DeVere, at the historical society in Raleigh, the Blackwater Canal was closed just after the Civil War. Wasn't used for a hundred thirty years. Until Henry Davett started running barges on it again."

Bell nodded. "That was about five years ago."

"You ever wonder why Davett started using it?"

"No. But now that you mention it, I don't know why. He's got trucks coming and going to Norfolk all the time."

Rhyme nodded up at the evidence charts. "The answer's right up there. That one bit of trace I never did figure out: camphene."

"The stuff in the lanterns?"

Rhyme grimaced. "I made a mistake there. Camphene *was* used in lanterns. But it can also be processed to make toxaphene."

"What's that?"

"One of the most dangerous pesticides there is. It was banned in the '80s by the EPA for most uses." Rhyme shook his head. "I assumed that because toxaphene was illegal, there was no point in considering pesticides as the source for the camphene and that it had to be from old lanterns. Except we never found any. So I should have started looking for insecticide. And when I did—this morning—I found the source of the camphene."

Bell nodded, fascinated. "Which was where?"

"Everywhere," Rhyme said. "I had Lucy take samples of dirt and water from around Tanner's Corner. There's toxaphene all over the place. The highest concentrations are around Davett's factory—Blackwater Landing and the canal. He's been manufacturing asphalt and tar paper as a cover for making toxaphene."

"But it's banned I thought you said."

"I called a buddy of mine at the EPA. It's not completely banned—farmers can use it in emergencies. But that's not how Davett's making his millions. My friend at the EPA told me about something called the circle of poison."

"Don't like the sound of that."

"You shouldn't. Toxaphene is banned here, but the ban in the U.S. is only on use. It can be made here and sold to foreign countries. It's legal in most Third World and Latin American countries. That's the circle: Those countries spray food with pesticides and send it back into the U.S. The FDA only inspects a small percentage of imported fruits and vegetables, so there are plenty of people in the U.S. still poisoned even though it's banned."

Bell gave a cynical laugh. "And Davett can't ship it on the roads because of all the counties and towns that won't let any toxic shipments go through 'em."

"Exactly," Rhyme said, nodding. "So he reopened the canal to send the toxaphene through the Intracoastal Waterway to Norfolk, where it's loaded onto foreign ships. Only there was a problem. People whose houses butted up against the canal had the right to control who used it."

Bell said, "So Davett paid them to lease their portion of the canal." He nodded with sudden understanding. "And he must've paid a lot of money. Look at all those nice houses in Blackwater Landing and all the nice trucks people are driving around here. But what about Mason and Garrett's family?"

"Garrett's father's land was on the canal. But he wouldn't sell his usage rights. So Davett hired Mason to convince Garrett's father to sell, and when he wouldn't, Mason hired Culbeau, Tomel, and O'Sarian to help him kill the family. Then I'd guess that Davett bribed the executor of the will to sell the property to him."

"But Garrett's folks died in a car accident. I saw the report."

"Was Mason the officer who handled the report?"

"I don't remember, but he could've been." Bell looked at Rhyme admiringly. "How on earth did you figure this out?"

"I talked to Amelia. Garrett told her that the night his family was killed, the car was frosty. He was cold, and his parents and sister were shivering. But the accident was in July. I remembered seeing the newspaper picture of Garrett and his family at a Fourth of July picnic. The caption said the photo was taken a week before his parents were killed."

"Then what was the boy talking about? Frost, shivering."

"Mason and Culbeau used some of Davett's toxaphene to kill the family. I talked to my doctor over at the medical center. She said that in extreme cases of neurotoxic poisoning the body spasms. That's the shivering Garrett saw. The frost was probably fumes or residue of the chemical in the car."

"If he saw it, why didn't he tell anybody?"

"I described the boy to the doctor. She said it sounds like he got poisoned too that night. Just enough to give him MCS—multiple chemical sensitivity. Memory loss, brain damage, severe reaction to chemicals in the air and water. Remember the welts on his skin?"

"Sure."

"Garrett thinks it's poison oak, but it isn't. The doctor told me that skin eruptions are a classic symptom of MCS."

"It's making sense," Bell said. Then, frowning, he added, "But if you don't have any hard evidence, then all we've got is speculation."

"Oh, I should mention"—Rhyme couldn't resist a smile—"I've *got* hard evidence. I found the bodies of Garrett's family."

AT THE Albemarle Manor Hotel, a block away from the Paquenoke County lockup, Mason Germain didn't wait for the elevator but climbed the stairs. He found room 201 and knocked.

" 'S'open," came the voice.

Mason pushed the door open slowly, revealing a pink room

bathed in afternoon sunlight. The African American sitting at the table was lean and with particularly dark skin. He wore a wrinkled black suit. "You'd be Germain?" the man asked.

"Yeah."

When the man withdrew his hand from under a copy of the *Charlotte Observer,* he was holding an automatic pistol.

"That answers one of my questions," Mason said. "Whether you got a gun or not."

"What's the other?" the man in the suit asked.

"Whether you know how to use it."

The man gave a laugh and said, "I'm gettin' the distinct impression you don't much like my kind."

"No, I don't," Mason answered. "But if you know what you're doing, what I like and what I don't aren't the least important."

"That's completely right," the black man said coolly. "So talk to me. I don't want to be here any longer than I have to."

Mason said, "That guy Rhyme's talking to Jim Bell right now. And Amelia Sachs is in the lockup up the street."

"Where should we go first?"

Without hesitating, Mason said, "The woman."

"THE bodies of the Hanlons—where are they?" Jim Bell asked.

"Over there," Rhyme said, nodding to the pile of bones that had been in Mary Beth's backpack. "Mary Beth thought they were the bones of the survivors of the Lost Colony. But I had to break the news to her that they're not that old. They looked decayed because they were partially burned. I knew right away they've been in the ground only about five years, which is just how long ago Garrett's folks were killed. They're the bones of a man in his late thirties, a woman about the same age who'd borne children, and a girl about ten. That describes Garrett's family perfectly."

Bell looked at them. "I don't get it."

"Garrett's family's property was right across Route 112 from the river in Blackwater Landing. Mason and Culbeau poisoned the family, then burned and buried the bodies and pushed their car into the water. Davett bribed the coroner to fake the death report and paid off somebody at the funeral home to pretend to cremate the remains. The graves are empty, I guarantee. Mary Beth must've mentioned finding the bones to somebody, and word got back to Mason. He paid Billy Stail to go to Blackwater Landing to kill her and steal the evidence—the bones."

"What? Billy?"

"Except that Garrett happened to be there, keeping an eye on Mary Beth. He was right, you know: People *did* die at Blackwater Landing. Only it wasn't Garrett who killed them. It was Mason and Culbeau. People had gotten cancer from the toxaphene and died because they started asking questions about why they'd gotten sick. Everybody in town knew about the Insect Boy, so Mason or Culbeau killed that girl with the hornets' nest to make it look like he was the killer. The others they hit over the head and pitched into the canal to drown. People who didn't question getting sick, like Lucy Kerr, they weren't worried about."

"But Garrett's fingerprints were on the shovel."

"Ah, the shovel," Rhyme mused. "I stumbled again. There were only two sets of fingerprints on it."

"Right. Billy's and Garrett's."

"But where were Mary Beth's?" Rhyme asked.

Bell's eyes narrowed. "Right. There were none of hers."

"Because it wasn't her shovel. Mason gave it to Billy to take to Blackwater Landing, after wiping his own prints off it. Mary Beth told me that Billy came out of the bushes carrying it. Mason figured it would be the perfect murder weapon, because as an archaeologist, Mary Beth would probably have a shovel with her. Well, Billy gets to Blackwater Landing and sees Garrett with her. He figures he'll kill the Insect Boy too. But Garrett got the shovel away and hit Billy. He thought he killed him. But he didn't."

"Garrett didn't kill Billy?"

"No. He only hit Billy once. Knocked him out but didn't hurt him that seriously. Then Garrett took Mary Beth away with him to the moonshiner's cabin. Mason was the first officer on the scene. He admitted that."

"That's right. He took the call."

"Kind of a coincidence that he was nearby, don't you think?"

"I guess. I didn't think about it at the time."

"Mason found Billy. He picked up the shovel, wearing latex evidence gloves, and beat the boy until he died."

"How do you know that?"

"Because of the position of the latex prints. I had Ben reexamine the handle of the shovel an hour ago with an alternative light source. Mason held the shovel like a baseball bat. That's not how somebody would pick up evidence at a crime scene. The coroner's report said that Billy was hit at least two dozen times."

His face hollow, Bell asked, "Why would Mason kill Billy?"

"He probably figured that Billy'd panic and tell the truth."

"So how are we going to prove all of this, Lincoln?"

"I've got the latex prints on the shovel. I've got the bones, which test positive for toxaphene in high concentrations. I want to get a diver and look for the Hanlons' car in the Paquenoke. Some evidence will have survived, even after five years. Then we should search Billy's house and see if there's any cash there that can be traced to Mason. And we'll search Mason's house too. It'll be a tough case." Rhyme gave a faint smile. "But I'm good, Jim. I can do it." Then his smile faded. "But if Mason doesn't turn evidence against Henry Davett, it's going to be tough to make the case against Davett. All I've got is that." Rhyme nodded toward a plastic exemplar jar filled with about eight ounces of pale liquid.

"What's that?"

"Pure toxaphene. Lucy got a sample from Davett's warehouse a half hour ago. If we can establish a compositional identity between the chemical that killed Garrett's family and what's in that jar, we might convince the prosecutor to bring a case."

"But Davett helped us find Garrett."

"It was in his interest to find the boy—and Mary Beth—as fast as possible. Davett wanted her dead most of all."

"Mason," Bell muttered. "You think he suspects?"

"You're the only one I've told. I didn't even tell Lucy. I just had her do some legwork for me. I was afraid somebody'd overhear and word would get back to Mason or Davett. This town, Jim—it's a nest of hornets. I don't know who to trust."

Bell shook his head. "How can you be so sure it's Mason?"

"Because Culbeau and his friends showed up at the moonshiner's cabin just after we figured out where it was. And Mason was the only one who knew that, aside from me and you and Ben. He must've called Culbeau and told him where the cabin was. So . . . let's call the state police, have one of their divers come, get those warrants to search Billy's and Mason's houses too."

Rhyme watched Bell rise. But instead of going to the phone, he stepped to the door, opened it, looked out, closed it. Locked the latch.

"Jim, what are you doing?"

Bell hesitated, then stepped behind the Storm Arrow and yanked its battery cable free.

"Jim," the criminalist said, "not you too?"

"You got that right."

Rhyme's eyes closed. "Oh, no," he whispered.

MASON Germain and the sullen black man moved slowly past the window of the Tanner's County lockup.

The man was tall, and by stretching up on his toes, he could look into the window. "She's in there," he said. "She's alone."

"Well, let's go, then," Mason said. He noticed that the man's gun was in his hand, and he hadn't seen him draw it.

THE door to the lockup swung open, and a young deputy walked inside. It was Steve Farr, Jim Bell's brother-in-law. "Hey there," he called to Amelia Sachs in her cell. "I got good news for you. You're free to go."

Sachs noticed two things about him. One was that he wore a Rolex watch, which must have cost half the annual salary of a typical cop in North Carolina. The other was that he wore a side arm. Despite the sign outside the cell area: PLACE ALL WEAPONS IN THE LOCKBOX BEFORE ENTERING.

"Free? To go?"

"Yep. They've decided the shooting was accidental. You can leave." Farr unlocked the cell door and stood back.

Sachs remained seated. "Can I ask why you're wearing your weapon in the lockup?"

"Oh, this?" He tapped the gun. "We don't have any hard and

fast rules about that sort of thing. You're free to leave. Now git your ass outside." Farr pulled the pistol from his holster.

How was it set up? Sachs wondered. Was there someone else outside the door to do the actual shooting? Slowly Sachs stood.

Farr roughly led her to the back door of the lockup, the pistol firmly in the square of her back. He opened the door. "Free to go," he said cheerfully.

She tensed. But then he stepped away from her fast, shoving her outside into the scruffy lot behind the jail. He remained inside.

From nearby, behind a tall bush in the field, she heard another sound. The cocking of a pistol, she thought.

"Go ahead," Farr said. "Git on outa here."

She began to walk forward into the low grass.

"YOU were ninety percent right, Lincoln," Jim Bell said. "Too bad for you I'm the ten percent you missed." The sheriff shut off the air conditioner. "Two families along Blackwater Canal wouldn't grant Mr. Davett easements to run his barges. So his security chief hired us to take care of the problem. The Conklins decided to grant the easement. But Garrett's father never would agree. We were going to make it look like a car crash, and we got a can of that stuff"—he nodded at the jar on the table—"to knock them out. We knew the family went out to dinner every Wednesday. We poured the poison into the car's vent and hid in the woods. They got in, and Garrett's father turned on the air conditioner. The stuff sprayed out all over them.

"The family started twitching and convulsing. Garrett wasn't in the car. He ran up and tried to get inside but couldn't. He got a good whiff of the stuff, though, and he became this zombie. Just stumbled off into the woods. And by the time he surfaced a week or two later, he didn't remember what had happened. So we just let him be. Be too suspicious if he was to die right after the family.

"Then we did just what you figured. Set fire to the bodies and buried them at Blackwater Landing. Pushed the car into the inlet by Canal Road. Paid the coroner a hundred thousand for some ginned-up reports. Whenever somebody would get cancer and start asking questions, Culbeau and the others took care of them." Bell nodded grimly. "And, yeah, we hired Billy to kill Mary Beth, but Garrett got her away before he could."

"And you needed me to help you find her. So you could kill her and destroy any other evidence she might've found."

"After you found Garrett and we brought him back from the mill, I left the door to the lockup open so Culbeau and his buddies could, let's say, talk Garrett into telling us where Mary Beth was. But your friend busted him out before they could snatch him."

Rhyme said, "And when I found the cabin, you called Culbeau and the others. Sent them there to kill us all."

"I'm sorry, but there you have it."

Rhyme shook his head. "Tell me, are the fancy cars and the big houses worth destroying the entire town? Amelia said there are hardly any kids here anymore. You know why? People are sterile."

"It's risky when you bargain with the devil," Bell said shortly. He looked at Rhyme for a long moment, walked to the table. He pulled on latex gloves, picked up the toxaphene jar. He stepped toward Rhyme, unscrewed the lid, and poured the liquid over Rhyme's mouth and nose. The rest he splashed onto the front of his shirt.

The sheriff dropped the jar onto Rhyme's lap, stepped back fast, and covered his own mouth with a handkerchief.

Rhyme's head jerked back, his lips parted involuntarily, and some of the liquid slipped into his mouth. He began to spit and cough.

Bell pulled off the gloves and stuffed them into his slacks. He waited a moment, then walked toward the door, unlocked it, swung it open. He called, "There's been an accident! Somebody, I need help!" He stepped into the corridor. "I need—"

Lucy Kerr's pistol was aimed steadily at his chest. "That's enough, Jim. Just hold it right there."

The sheriff stepped back. Nathan, the sharpshooting deputy, walked into the room, stepped behind Bell, and snagged the sheriff's pistol from its holster. Another man entered—a large man in a tan suit and white shirt.

Ben Kerr too ran inside, ignored everyone else, and hurried to Rhyme, wiping the criminalist's face with a paper towel.

The sheriff stared at Lucy and the others. "Be careful. There was an accident. That poison stuff spilled. You've got to—"

Rhyme wheezed from the fumes. He said to Ben, "Could you wipe my cheek? I'm afraid it'll get into my eyes. Thank you."

"Sure, Lincoln."

The man in the tan suit pulled handcuffs off his belt and ratcheted the loops around the sheriff's wrists. He said, "James Bell, I'm Detective Hugo Branch with the North Carolina State Police. You're under arrest." Branch looked at Rhyme. "I told you he'd pour it on your shirt. We should've put the unit someplace else."

"But you got enough on tape?"

"Oh, plenty. The point is, those transmitters cost money."

"Bill me," Rhyme said acerbically as Branch opened Rhyme's shirt and untaped the microphone and transmitter.

"It was a setup," Bell whispered. "But the poison . . ."

"Oh, it's not toxaphene," Rhyme said. "Just a little moonshine from that jar we tested. Now, could somebody get the AC going?"

AMELIA Sachs had taken three steps into the grass when a man's voice from behind her, inside the lockup area, called, "Hold it, Steve. Put the weapon on the ground. Now!"

Sachs spun around and saw Mason Germain, his gun pointed at Steve Farr's head. Farr crouched and set the gun on the floor. Mason hurried forward and cuffed him.

Footsteps sounded from outside, leaves rustled. Sachs turned back to the field and saw a lean black man climbing out of the bushes, holstering a big Browning automatic pistol.

"Fred!" she cried.

FBI agent Fred Dellray, sweating furiously in his black suit, walked up to her. "Hey, Amelia."

"What are you doing here?" she asked.

"Whatcha think? Lincoln wasn't sure who he could trust and who he couldn't, so he had me fly down and hooked me up with Deputy Germain here to keep an eye on you. Figured he needed some help, seeing as how he couldn't trust Bell or his kin."

"Bell?" she asked, dumbfounded.

"Lincoln thinks he put this whole thing together. He's finding out for sure right now. But looks like he was right, that being his brother-in-law." Dellray nodded at Steve Farr.

"He almost got me," Sachs said.

"You weren't in a single, solitary lick of danger. I had a bead on that fellow from the second the back door opened. He'd so much as squinted at you, he'da been way, way gone." Dellray laughed.

But Mason remained solemn. He said to Sachs, "I'll have to take you back to the cell. You're still under arrest."

"*YOU* killed Billy, didn't you?" Rhyme asked Jim Bell.

But the sheriff said nothing.

The criminalist continued. "The crime scene was unprotected for an hour and a half. And, sure, Mason was the first officer. But *you* got there before he arrived. You never got a call from Billy saying that Mary Beth was dead, and you started to worry, so you drove over to Blackwater Landing and found her gone and Billy hurt. He told you about Garrett getting away with the girl. Then you put the latex gloves on, picked up the shovel, and killed him."

"Why did you suspect me?" the sheriff asked.

"Originally I *did* think it was Mason—only the three of us and Ben knew about the moonshiner's cabin. I thought he called Culbeau and sent him there. But I asked Lucy, and it turned out it was Mason who called her and sent her to the cabin, just to make sure Amelia and Garrett didn't get away again. But then I got to thinking, and I realized that at the mill Mason tried to shoot Garrett. Anybody in on the conspiracy would want to keep him alive, like you did, until you found Mary Beth. I checked into Mason's finances and found out he's got a cheap house and is in serious hock to MasterCard and Visa. Nobody was paying him off. Unlike you and your brother-in-law, Bell. You've got a four-hundred-thousand-dollar house and plenty of cash in the bank. Steve Farr too."

Rhyme continued. "I was a little curious why Mason was so eager to nail Garrett, but he had a good reason for that. He was pretty upset when you got the job of sheriff—couldn't quite figure out why, since he had a better record and more seniority. He thought that if he could collar the Insect Boy, he would be appointed sheriff when your term expired."

"All your damned playacting," Bell muttered. "I thought you only believed in evidence."

"I would've preferred evidence. But sometimes you have to improvise. I'm really *not* the prima donna everybody thinks I am."

AMELIA Sachs, wearing the hand and ankle shackles that Mason insisted on, shuffled from her cell to the interrogation room to meet with the lawyer, who had arrived from New York. He was handsome gray-haired Solomon Geberth. A member of the New York, Massachusetts, and D.C. bars, he had been admitted to the jurisdiction of North Carolina for the single case of the *People* v. *Sachs.*

Lincoln Rhyme sat between Sachs and her lawyer. She rested her hand on the armrest of the Storm Arrow.

"They brought in a special prosecutor from Raleigh," Geberth was explaining. "With the sheriff and the coroner on the take, I don't think they quite trust McGuire. Anyway, he's looked over the evidence and decided to dismiss the charges against Garrett."

He continued. "Garrett admitted hitting Billy and thought he killed him. But Lincoln was right. It was Bell who killed Billy. And even if they brought Garrett up on assault charges, he was clearly acting in self-defense. That other deputy, Ed Schaeffer—his death's been ruled accidental."

"What about kidnapping Lydia Johansson?" Rhyme asked.

"When she realized that Garrett had never intended to hurt her, she decided to drop charges. Mary Beth did the same."

"So he's free? Garrett?" Sachs asked, eyes on the floor.

"They're letting him out in a few minutes," Geberth told her. Then, "Okay, here's the laundry, Amelia. The prosecutor's position is that even if Garrett turned out not to be a felon, you aided in the escape of a prisoner who'd been arrested on the basis of probable cause and you killed an officer during the commission of that crime. The prosecutor's going for first-degree murder and throwing in the standard lesser-included offenses: both manslaughter counts—voluntary and involuntary—and reckless homicide and criminally negligent homicide."

"First degree?" Rhyme snapped. "It wasn't premeditated. It was an accident!"

"Which is what I'm going to show at trial," Geberth said. "The other deputy, the one who grabbed you, was a partial proximate cause of the shooting. But I guarantee they'll get the reckless homicide conviction. On the facts there's no doubt about that."

"What's the chance of acquittal?" Rhyme asked.

"Bad. I'm sorry, but I have to recommend you take a plea."

Sachs felt this like a blow to her chest. Her eyes closed.

The lawyer added, "You have to understand that there aren't going to be any miracles here, Amelia. If we go to trial, the prosecutor's going to prove that you're a professional law enforcer and a champion marksman, and the jury's going to have trouble buying that the shooting was accidental. If that happens, they could convict you of murder one and you'll get twenty-five years."

"If I plead to involuntary, how much time will I do?"

"Probably six, seven years. No parole."

She inhaled deeply. "I'll plead."

Geberth rose. "I'll call the prosecutor now. I'll let you know as soon as I hear anything." With a nod he left the room.

Rhyme said, "Whatever happens, Sachs, I'm not going anywhere. You do some time, I'll be there when you get out."

"Words," she said cynically. "My father said he wasn't going anywhere either. That was a week before the cancer shut him down."

"I'm too ornery to die."

But you're not too ornery to get better, she thought, to meet someone else.

The door to the interrogation room opened. Garrett stood in the doorway. The boy's hands, no longer in shackles, were cupped in front of him. "Hey," he said in greeting. "Check out what I found. It was in my cell." He opened his fist, and a small insect flew out. "It's a sphinx moth. You don't see 'em much inside. Pretty cool."

Sachs smiled faintly, taking some minor pleasure in his enthusiasm. "Garrett, there's one thing I want you to know. Remember in the trailer when you were talking to your father in the empty chair? You said how bad you felt that he didn't want you in the car that night."

"I remember."

"You know now why he didn't want you. He was trying to save your life. He knew there was poison in the car and that they were going to die. If you got in the car with them, you'd die too. And he didn't want you to die."

"I guess I know that," he said. His voice was uncertain, and Sachs supposed that rewriting one's history was a harrowing task and could take a long time.

She looked at the tiny beige moth flying around the interrogation room. "You leave anybody in the cell for me? For company?"

"Yeah. There's a couple of ladybugs—their real name is ladybird beetles. And a syrphus fly. It's cool the way they fly. You can watch 'em for hours." He paused. "I'm sorry I lied to you. But if I hadn't, I couldn't've saved Mary Beth."

"That's all right, Garrett."

He walked to the door, turned, and said to Sachs, "I'll come and, like, hang out if that's okay."

"I'd like that."

He stepped outside, and through the open door Sachs could see him walk to a car. It was Lucy Kerr's. Sachs saw her hold the door open for him, like a mom picking up her son after soccer practice.

"Sachs," Rhyme said. But she was on her feet, shuffling back toward the lockup. She wanted to be away from the criminalist, away from the boy. She wanted to be in the darkness of solitude.

TWELVE

AMELIA Sachs sat handcuffed between two guards on a bench in the Paquenoke County Courthouse, looking absently around her.

Fred Dellray ambled up to her. "Hey there, you want some coffee or something?"

"No, thanks, Fred. Where's Lincoln?"

"Dunno. You know that man—sometimes he just appears. For a man who doesn't walk, he gets around more than anybody I know."

Sol Geberth, in a rich-looking gray suit, sat down on her right. "It's a deal," he said to Sachs. "The prosecutor's agreed to involuntary manslaughter. No other counts. Six years. No parole."

She closed her eyes and felt nausea course through her.

"So?" the lawyer asked. "What do you think?"

Sachs opened her eyes. "I'll take the plea."

THE ROOM WAS CROWDED. Sachs saw Mason Germain, a few of the other deputies. A grim couple, probably Jesse Corn's parents, sat in the front row. She saw only two faces that were, while not exactly friendly, at least not hostile: Mary Beth McConnell and a woman who was presumably her mother. There was no sign of Lucy Kerr. Nor of Lincoln Rhyme.

The bailiff led her to the defense table. He left the shackles on. Sol Geberth sat beside her. They rose when the judge entered, sat down at the bench. After a moment he nodded, and the clerk said, "The people of the state of *North Carolina* versus *Amelia Sachs.*"

The judge nodded to the prosecutor from Raleigh, a tall silver-haired man, who rose. "Your Honor, the defendant and the state have entered into a plea arrangement, whereby the defendant has agreed to plead guilty to involuntary manslaughter in the death of Deputy Jesse Randolph Corn. The state waives all other charges and is recommending a sentence of six years, to be served without possibility of parole or reduction."

"Miss Sachs, how do you plead to the charge of involuntary manslaughter brought against you?"

"Guilty, Your Honor."

"I am hereby sentencing you—"

The red leather doors leading to the corridor swung inward, and with a high-pitched whine Lincoln Rhyme's wheelchair maneuvered inside. Lucy Kerr was behind him.

The criminalist said, "Forgive me, Your Honor. I need to speak with the defendant and her counsel for a minute."

Rhyme carefully steered up to the railing that separated the counsel tables from the gallery. He glanced at Sachs, and the sight nearly broke his heart. In the three days she'd been in jail, she'd lost weight and her face was sallow. Her red hair was pulled up in a taut bun, which made her look severe and drawn.

Geberth walked to Rhyme, crouched down. The criminalist spoke to him for a few minutes. Finally the lawyer rose. He began to speak. "Your Honor, I realize this is a hearing regarding a plea bargain. But there's some new evidence that's come to light. I'd like to make the state aware of this evidence and see if my worthy colleague will agree to consider it."

The judge glanced at the prosecutor and asked, "Well?"

The prosecutor asked, "What sort of evidence? A new witness?"

Rhyme spoke up. "No," he said. "Physical evidence."

The prosecutor said to Rhyme, "Where is this evidence?"

"In my custody at the sheriff's department," Lucy Kerr said.

The judge asked Rhyme, "You'll agree to be deposed?"

"Certainly."

"This is all right with you?" the judge asked the prosecutor.

"It is, Your Honor, but if the evidence turns out to be meaningless, I'll pursue interference charges against Mr. Rhyme."

The judge thought for a moment, then said, "For the record, this is not part of any proceeding. The court is merely lending itself to the parties for a deposition prior to arraignment."

Rhyme parked in front of the bench. As the Bible-clutching clerk approached uncertainly to swear him in, Rhyme said, "No, I can't raise my right hand." Then recited, "I swear that the testimony I am about to give is the truth, upon my solemn oath."

Geberth strolled to the front of the courtroom and asked Rhyme to state his name, address, and occupation. That done, the lawyer said, "Mr. Rhyme, you say you have new evidence that bears on this case. What is that evidence?"

"After we learned that Billy Stail had gone to Blackwater Landing to kill Mary Beth McConnell, I began speculating why he'd done that. And I concluded that he'd been paid to kill her. He—"

"Why did you think he was paid?"

"It's obvious. Billy had no romantic relationship with Mary Beth. He wasn't involved in the murder of Garrett Hanlon's family. So he'd have no motivation to kill her other than financial profit."

"Go on."

Rhyme continued. "Whoever hired him wasn't going to pay by check, of course, but in cash. Deputy Kerr went to the house of Billy Stail's parents and was given permission to search his room. She discovered ten thousand dollars hidden beneath his mattress.

"With Officer Kerr's assistance I did a friction-ridge analysis—that's a fingerprint check—of the top and bottom bills in the stacks of cash. I found a total of sixty-one latent fingerprints. Aside from Billy's prints, two of these prints proved to be from a person involved in this case. Deputy Kerr got another warrant to enter and search that individual's house. Inside the house she found a receipt for the purchase of a shovel identical to the murder weapon. She also found eighty-three thousand dollars in cash, secured with wrappers identical to the ones around the stacks of money in Billy Stail's house."

Rhyme had saved the best till last. "Deputy Kerr also found bone fragments in the barbecue behind that premises. These fragments match the bones of Garrett Hanlon's family."

"Whose house was this?"

"Deputy Jesse Corn's." This drew murmurs from the courtroom.

"Where exactly are you going, Mr. Rhyme?" the judge asked.

Rhyme said, "Your Honor, Jesse Corn was one of the individuals who conspired with Jim Bell and Steve Farr to kill Garrett Hanlon's family five years ago and then to kill Mary Beth McConnell."

The judge leaned back in his chair. "This has nothing to do with me. You two duke it out." Nodding from Geberth to the prosecutor. "You got five minutes. Then she accepts the plea bargain, or I'll set bail and schedule trial."

The prosecutor said to Geberth, "Doesn't mean she didn't kill Jesse. He was still the victim of a homicide."

"Oh, come on," Geberth snapped, as if the prosecutor were a slow student. "It means that Corn was operating outside his jurisdiction as a law enforcer and that, when he confronted Garrett, he was a felon and armed and dangerous. Jim Bell admitted they were planning on torturing the boy to find Mary Beth's whereabouts, and that means that once they found her, Corn would've been right there with Culbeau to kill Lucy Kerr and the other deputies."

The judge's eyes swept left to right slowly as he watched this unprecedented tennis match.

The prosecutor: "I can only focus on the crime at hand. Whether Jesse Corn was going to kill anybody or not doesn't matter."

Geberth said to the court reporter, "We're suspending the deposition. This is off the record." Then to the prosecutor, "What's the point of proceeding? Corn was a killer."

Rhyme joined in, speaking to the prosecutor. "You take this to trial and what do you think the jury's going to feel when Mr.

Geberth shows that the victim was a crooked cop planning to torture an innocent boy to find a girl to murder?"

Geberth continued. "You don't want this notch on your grip. You've got Bell, you've got his brother-in-law, the coroner . . ."

Before the prosecutor could protest again, Rhyme looked up at him and said in a soft voice, "I'll help you."

"What?" the prosecutor said.

"You know who's behind all this, don't you? You know who's killing half the residents of Tanner's Corner?"

"Henry Davett," the prosecutor said. "I've read the filings."

Rhyme asked, "And how's the case against him?"

"Not good. There's no evidence. There's no link between him and Bell or anybody else in town. He used middlemen."

"But," Rhyme said, "don't you want to nail him before any more people die of cancer? Before more children get sick?"

"Of course I want to."

"Then you need me. You won't find a criminalist anywhere in the state who can bring Davett down. I can." Rhyme glanced at Sachs. He could see tears in her eyes. He knew that the only thought in her mind now was that, whether they sent her to jail or not, she hadn't killed an innocent man.

The prosecutor nodded. Quickly, as if he might change his mind, he said, "Deal." He looked at the bench. "Your Honor, in the case of the *People* versus *Sachs,* the state is withdrawing all charges."

"So ordered," said the judge. "Defendant is free to go."

"I DIDN'T know whether you'd show up," Rhyme said, surprised.

"Wasn't sure I was going to either," Sachs replied.

They were in his hospital room at the medical center in Avery.

"You know, Sachs," Rhyme said, "when I heard you'd busted Garrett out of detention, it half occurred to me you'd done it to give me a chance to rethink the operation."

A smile curved her lips. "Maybe there was a bit of that."

"So you're here now to talk me out of it?"

She rose from the chair, walked to the window. "No. I'm here to be with you now and to be in the recovery room when you wake up."

"Change of heart?"

She turned to him. "When Garrett and I were on the river, he was telling me about something he read in that book of his—*The Miniature World*. It was a list of the characteristics of living creatures. One of them was that healthy creatures strive to grow and to adapt to the environment. I realized that's something *you* have to do, Rhyme. You need to try this."

After a moment he said, "I know it's not going to cure me, Sachs. But what's the nature of our business? It's little victories. That's all I'm after here. I'm not climbing out of this chair. I know that. But I need a little victory."

She bent down, kissed him hard.

A nurse appeared in the doorway. "I need to take you to pre-op, Mr. Rhyme. You ready for a ride?"

THE two women sat side by side in a thick shaft of sunlight. Two paper cups of coffee were in front of them, perched on an orange table. In the distance they could just hear the tinny, forced dialogue of a soap opera. A distant page for a doctor. A chime. A laugh.

"You all right?" Amelia Sachs asked Lucy Kerr, who sat subdued.

The deputy hesitated, then finally said, "Oncology's on the next wing over. I spent months there. Before and after the operation." She glanced at Amelia. "He'll be all right, you know. Lincoln."

"No, I don't know," Sachs responded.

"I've got a feeling."

"Appreciate that," Sachs said.

"How long do you think it'll be?" Lucy asked.

Forever. "Four hours, Dr. Weaver was saying."

Someone walked past, then paused. "Hey, ladies."

"Lydia," Lucy said, smiling. "How you doing?"

Lydia Johansson. Sachs hadn't recognized her because she was wearing a green robe and cap. She recalled Lydia was a nurse here.

"You heard?" Lucy asked her. "Jim and those other deputies getting arrested. Who would've thought?"

"Never in a million years," Lydia said. Then the nurse asked Lucy, "You have an oncology appointment?"

"No. Mr. Rhyme's having his operation today. On his spine."

"Well, I wish him all the best," Lydia said to Sachs.

The big girl continued down the corridor, waved, then pushed through a doorway.

"Sweet girl," Sachs said.

"You imagine that job, being an oncology nurse? When I was having my surgery, she was on the ward every day. Being just as cheerful with the terminal patients as she was with the ones in remission. More guts than I have."

But Lydia was far from Sachs's thoughts. She looked at the clock. It was eleven a.m. The operation would start any minute now.

THE prep nurse was explaining things to him, and Lincoln Rhyme was agreeing, but they'd already given him a Valium, and he didn't really have a clue what the young woman was saying.

Then an orderly arrived and wheeled him from pre-op into the operating room itself. Two nurses made the transfer from the gurney to the operating table. One went to the far end of the room and began removing instruments from the autoclave.

"It's pretty funny," he muttered to a nurse who was standing next to him. She turned. He could see only her eyes over the face mask. "They're operating on the one place where I need anesthetic. If I had my appendix out, they could cut without gas."

"That's funny, Mr. Rhyme."

He laughed briefly, thinking, So, she knows me.

The anesthesiologist came in and ran a needle into his arm, prepared an injection, fitted it into the tube connected to the needle. She was an Indian woman and had very skillful hands.

"When I inject this," she said, "I'm going to ask you to count down from one hundred. You'll be out before you know it."

He watched her slip a tube of clear liquid into the IV. She turned away to look at a monitor. Rhyme began counting. "One hundred, ninety-nine, ninety-eight, ninety-seven . . ."

The other nurse, the one who'd mentioned him by name, crouched down. In a low voice she said, "I'm Lydia Johansson. Jim Bell and Henry Davett asked me to say good-bye."

"No!" he muttered.

The anesthesiologist, eyes on a monitor, said, "It's okay. Just relax. Everything's fine."

Her mouth inches from his ear, Lydia whispered, "Didn't you wonder how Jim Bell found out about the cancer patients?"

"No. Stop."

"I gave him their names so Culbeau could make sure they had accidents. Jim's my boyfriend. We've been having this affair for years. He's the one who sent me to Blackwater Landing after Mary Beth had been kidnapped. I was bait. I went to put flowers down and just hang out in case Garrett showed up. I was going to talk to him and give Jesse and Ed Schaeffer a chance to get him—Ed was with us too. Then they were going to force Garrett to tell us where Mary Beth was. Nobody thought he'd kidnap me."

"Stop," Rhyme cried. But his voice came out as a mumble.

The anesthesiologist said, "Been fifteen seconds. Are you counting? I don't hear you counting."

"I'll be right here," Lydia said, stroking Rhyme's forehead. "A lot can go wrong during surgery, you know. Kinks in the oxygen tube, administering the wrong drugs. Who knows?"

"Wait," Rhyme gasped as he saw the operating room go gray and then black.

THIS really was one of the prettiest places in the world, Amelia Sachs thought. For a cemetery. Tanner's Corner Memorial Gardens, on the crest of a rolling hill, overlooked the Paquenoke River, some miles away.

She stood in a small cluster of people beside an open grave. An urn was being lowered by one of the men from the mortuary. Amelia Sachs was next to Lucy Kerr. Garrett Hanlon stood by them. On the other side of the grave were Mason Germain and Thom, with a cane. Thom wore a bold tie with a wild red pattern, which seemed appropriate despite this somber moment. Black-suited Fred Dellray was there too.

There was no minister to officiate, so the mortuary director glanced at the people assembled and asked if anybody wanted to say something. And as everyone looked around, wondering if there'd be any volunteers, Garrett dug into his baggy slacks and produced his battered book *The Miniature World.*

In a halting voice the boy read:

"There are those who suggest that a divine force doesn't exist, but one's cynicism is truly put to the test when we look at the world of insects, which have been graced with so many amazing characteristics: wings so thin they seem hardly to be made of any living material, wind-speed detectors that keep flies grounded in any breeze powerful enough to harm them, a stride so efficient that mechanical engineers model robots after it, spiderweb strands so light and strong that scientists cannot come close to duplicating them, and, most important, insects' astonishing ability to survive in the face of overwhelming opposition by man, predators, and the elements. In moments of despair, we can look to the ingenuity and persistence of these miraculous creatures and find solace and a restoration of lost faith."

Garrett looked up, closed the book, clicked his fingernails nervously. He looked at Sachs and asked, "Do you, like, want to say anything?"

But she merely shook her head.

No one else spoke, and after a few minutes everyone around the grave turned away and meandered back up the hill along a winding path. As they crested the ridge that led to a small picnic area, Sachs recalled Lincoln Rhyme's voice: *That's not a bad cemetery. Wouldn't mind being buried in a place like that.*

She paused to wipe the sweat from her face and catch her breath; the North Carolina heat was relentless. Garrett, though, didn't seem to notice the temperature. He ran past her to the parking lot and began pulling grocery bags from the back of Lucy's Bronco.

This wasn't exactly the time or place for a picnic, but, she supposed, chicken salad and watermelon were as good a way as any to remember the dead.

Whisky too, of course. Sachs dug into several shopping bags and finally found the bottle of Macallan Scotch, eighteen years old. She pulled the cork stopper out with a faint pop.

"Ah, my favorite sound," Lincoln Rhyme said.

He was wheeling up beside her, driving carefully along the uneven grass. The hill down to the grave was too steep for the Storm Arrow, and he'd had to wait up here on the crest. He'd watched from the hilltop as they buried the bones that he'd identified—the remains of Garrett's family.

Sachs poured Scotch into Rhyme's glass, equipped with a long straw, and some into hers. Everyone else was drinking beer.

Garrett was carefully setting out food and drink and napkins on a bench in the shade of a tree.

"How are you doing?" Sachs asked Rhyme in a whisper. "And before you grumble at me, I'm not talking about the heat."

He shrugged—this a *silent* grumble by which he meant, I'm fine.

But he wasn't fine. A phrenic nerve stimulator pumped current into his body to help his lungs inhale and exhale. He hated the device, had weaned himself off it some years ago, but he needed it now. Two days before, on the operating table, Lydia Johansson had come very close to stopping his breathing forever.

In the waiting room at the hospital, after Lydia had said good-bye to Sachs and Lucy, Sachs noticed that the nurse had vanished through the doorway marked NEUROSURGERY. Sachs asked, "Didn't you say that she works in oncology?"

"She does."

"Then what's she doing going in there?"

"Maybe saying hello to Lincoln," Lucy suggested.

Then Sachs had thought, Lydia would know about new cancer diagnoses among residents from Tanner's Corner. She then recalled that somebody had given information to Bell about cancer patients—the three people in Blackwater Landing that Culbeau and his friends had killed. Who better than a nurse on the onco ward?

Sachs had mentioned this to Lucy, who pulled out her cell phone and made an emergency call to the phone company, whose security department did a down-and-dirty pen-register search of Jim Bell's phone calls. There were hundreds to and from Lydia.

"She's going to kill him!" Sachs had cried. And the two women, one with a weapon drawn, had burst into the operating room just as Dr. Weaver was about to make the opening incision.

Lydia had panicked and, trying to escape or trying to do what Bell had sent her for, ripped the oxygen tube from Rhyme's throat before the two women subdued her. From that trauma and because of the anesthetic, Rhyme's lungs had failed. Dr. Weaver had revived him, but afterward his breathing hadn't been up to par and he'd had to go back on the stimulator.

Which was bad enough. But worse, to Rhyme's anger and disgust, Dr. Weaver proved to be as "muley" as he was. She refused to perform the operation for at least another six months, until his breathing functions were completely normalized.

Sachs sipped more Scotch now as she watched Garrett shovel chips into his mouth, then run into the grass. She asked Lucy, "Any word from the county?"

"On being his foster mom?" Lucy shook her head. "Got rejected. The being single isn't an issue. They have a problem with my job—cop, long hours. Garrett's being set up with a family up in Hobeth. Good people. I checked them out pretty good."

Sachs didn't doubt that she had.

"But we're going on a hike next weekend."

Nearby Garrett eased through the grass, stalking a specimen.

When Sachs turned back, she saw Rhyme had been watching her as she gazed at the boy.

He said, "If you were going to say something to an empty chair, Sachs, what would it be?"

She hesitated for a moment. "I think I'll keep that to myself for the time being, Rhyme."

Suddenly Garrett gave a loud laugh and started running through the grass. He was chasing an insect through the dusty air. The boy caught up with it and, with outstretched arms, made a grab for his prey, then tumbled to the ground. A moment later he was up, staring into his cupped hands and walking slowly back to the picnic benches.

"Guess what I found," he called.

"Come show us," Amelia Sachs said. "I want to see."

JEFFERY DEAVER

© JERRY BAUER

Are there any similarities between Jeffery Deaver and his popular forensic sleuth, Lincoln Rhyme? "Well, I do sit around a great deal," replies the author, who puts in long hours of researching, outlining, and writing to produce his mysteries. But otherwise, he says, "most of my characters have nothing to do with me or people I know or have known. I create characters that serve my story."

Just how well Deaver and his characters serve his stories is evident from the great success of his many best sellers, including *The Coffin Dancer, The Bone Collector,* and, most recently, *The Devil's Teardrop.* A Chicago native, Deaver divides his time between homes in Virginia and California.

To learn more about Jeffery Deaver and *The Empty Chair,* visit the Select Editions website: 📖 ReadersOnly.com Password: *Life*

Hawke's Cove

Susan Wilson

When I went to
Hawke's Cove, I was
desperately unhappy.
My husband was gone,
my future unimaginable.
I went there to heal
and wait.
A mysterious stranger
eased my waiting.
He was my constant,
my anchor. . . .

Prologue

IF YOU asked, no one could quite remember when he first appeared in Hawke's Cove. After nearly fifty years it seemed as though Joe Green had always been a part of the scenery, whether driving down Main Street in his beat-up old pickup truck or sitting at the counter in Linda's Restaurant with the rest of the old men, drinking endless cups of coffee and telling Down East stories peculiar to whiskery old men wearing stained work pants and suspenders.

Heard about Lucius? Found him doubled up in the gutter, right out there, in front of the coffee shop. Asked him, Lucius, what's the matter? He says, Get me up, Joe, I'm ruptured. So I help him home like he is, bent half over like a tree in a windstorm. Next day I see him in the hardware store, big as life and fit as a fiddle. So I says, Hey, Luke, thought you were ruptured. Well, Joe, he says, heard it snap, felt it give. But weren't no rupture. Just my galluses givin' way.

For Hawke's Cove, this was a knee-slapper.

Although Joe Green had done about every kind of job, most remembered him as the milkman. Oh, like most, he'd done time scalloping. Spent a couple of seasons on Pete West's fishing boat, but never took to it. Liked working with warm-blooded animals better, he said, than handling cold fish. Now he took tickets at the movie theater they built in Hawke's Cove in the '60s. Been there long enough for most schoolkids to think he'd always stood at the white double doors of the Elm Theater in his crumpled blue seersucker jacket and white slacks in the summer and the heavy fisherman's sweater and wool trousers when the wind off the water blew in the unheated foyer.

Ask anyone about him, and most would say he was a hard worker. A nice guy. Ask them who he was, and most would shrug and say, Why, just Joe Green. Came here long ago and made a life.

And except for one person, no one knew who he really was.

One

Charlie—1993

CHARLIE Worth leaned back in his ergonomically correct desk chair and shot a wad of paper at the wastebasket with an over-the-shoulder hook shot. He missed, and the crumpled memo joined a flock of others surrounding the metal can. This presidential-vacation thing was getting out of hand. Priscilla the Killer kept coming up with more and more stupid angles to write about, and this one was worse than the suggestion about interviewing people in Kennebunkport to see if they could give the people of Great Harbor any good advice vis-à-vis presidents on vacation.

Charlie was determined to be the only feature writer not camping out in Great Harbor for the proposed visit. Besides, he kept pointing out, the Clintons would probably choose Martha's Vineyard. Heck of a lot better golf to be had there than anywhere near this hole-in-the-wall vacation destination. Now, if the Clintons did go to the Vineyard, maybe he'd tag along. At thirty-nine, there were few places Charlie hadn't been to during his journalistic career: Beirut, St. Petersburg when it had been Leningrad, and London as a correspondent for the Boston *Globe.* He'd been to most every Caribbean island, Belize, and rugged Alaskan camps while he'd done a five-year stint as a travel writer. Craving a settled existence, Charlie had given up the travel for a once-a-week byline, sacrificing adventure for a stable home. After eighteen months, though, he found himself daydreaming of chucking the whole security thing and following in the footsteps of the great travel writers, immersing himself in some rare culture, then writing a best-selling memoir.

But even as he played with the notion, Charlie knew that one thing kept him close to home. His aging parents.

He got up, heading toward the coffeepot. As luck would have it, Priscilla St. Lorraine was on her way to his cubicle and caught him before he could take a quick right into the men's room.

"Charlie, have I got a story for you!" She launched into something about an old plane wreck discovered in the waters off Great Harbor during a routine aerial survey prior to the potential visit by the President and his family. It was only when she told him where the plane had been barged that his interest was piqued.

Hawke's Cove.

WHEN Charlie was little, maybe eight or nine, he and his older sisters had found a shoe box filled with photos. Most were of their parents and quasi-familiar adults, looking odd in their old-fashioned hairstyles and out-of-date clothes. Three or four of the pictures had an ocean background. One very old sepia print was of a young woman in a hat, a barn behind her, the doors half open.

"That's Gran the first year she lived at Hawke's Cove." Vangie had come upon her children, the scattered pictures surrounding them on the worn Oriental carpet. She sat beside Charlie and began gathering up the photos. As she collected them, she began to tell Amanda, Julie, and Charlie who was who. Charlie vividly remembered the feel of her thick auburn braid touching his cheek as she reached past him to pick out one photo. A thin bearded man stood holding one end of a line of fish. A crew-cut heavier-set man stood at the other. They both wore pleased grins.

"Who's these guys?" Charlie asked.

"Who *are* these guys." The correction purely reflexive. "That's Ernie Dubee." She tapped the crew-cut man's face. "He was our police chief in Hawke's Cove."

"Who *is* this one?" Charlie touched the face of the other man.

"That's Joe Green. He worked for me on the farm in Hawke's Cove." Something in her voice made all three children look at her just in time to see a small private smile tease her lips.

That was the first time Charlie would hear about Hawke's Cove and the time his mother spent there during the war.

"So, Mom, what do you remember about Hawke's Cove?"

Evangeline Worth smiled spontaneously at the name. "I remember how the air smelled in the morning, the feel of the wet grass on my bare feet. I remember how brilliant—"

"Mom, I asked you, not Evangeline Worth, 'Poet to the People.' Just tell me."

"Tell you what? Stories? You've heard all of them."

"No. Actually, I need to know if you remember a specific incident. A plane crash."

Vangie was glad this conversation was taking place on the phone. That way the sudden shaking in her hands wouldn't frighten Charlie into thinking she'd developed a tremor. "What plane crash?"

She knew, even before Charlie began to tell her. She knew that the Hellcat had been found. As he told her about the presidential vacation and the sonar survey, she felt her mind wander back over half a century. Her mouth twitched in a little self-derisive smile. After this long, which secret needed the most safekeeping? Did it really matter anymore where Joe had come from? What mattered was only that he'd come and her life had been sweetened.

Vangie

VANGIE forced herself to finish doing the dishes after Charlie's call. Last dish put away, she began to pace around the house where she and John had raised their children, had lived for most of their married life in relative contentment. She touched things here and there—Amanda's wedding picture and the Mexican clay horse Julie had brought back from her foreign-exchange year.

Vangie found herself in the bedroom she had shared with John. She stared at the bed, barely ever disturbed with her solitary occupation of it. Since John had gone to the nursing home following his last stroke, she still kept to the same side of the bed she had slept on for fifty-seven years. She ran a finger along the edge of John's bureau, clucking at the dust she could now see only in bright daylight. John's things on the bureau were where they had been for years: the little Devonware dish where he'd placed his cuff links and change; the bone-handled brush, long since out of use. In the home he had a bedside stand with a deep drawer where she kept his shaving things and glasses. There was little else he had need for. Every day she went and shaved him, fed him his lunch, and filled his ears with news about their children and grandchildren. How much of her one-sided conversation he understood she had no idea.

At the foot of their bed was her cedar-lined hope chest, which held blankets and baptismal dresses. Every day John had sat on it to put on his socks and shoes. She opened the cover, releasing a faint whiff of mothballs. Her fingers touched the hard cover of her journal, finding it exactly where she had placed it so long ago.

Vangie closed the lid of the chest and sat on it. She held the composition book in her lap, marveling that every day John had sat on top of her most dangerous secret, blissfully unaware that hidden beneath him lay a piece of herself that he could never have imagined possible, and which would have altered their lives irrevocably had he ever known of it.

She hadn't opened the diary since the day, more than forty years earlier, she had placed it in the chest. Vangie opened the book, fearing a little that it would crack, but the binding held.

Two

Hawke's Cove

APRIL 17, 1944 Yet another stormy day. It seems as though April's lyrical attempt to cleave to the nursery rhyme has been successful. I certainly hope the May flowers live up to the challenge. Ted Frick, who came to see about getting the electricity on out here, says tomorrow should be better. Ted's lived here in Hawke's Cove all his life, "so far," he says with a chuckle.

I feel as though I've lived here a whole lifetime, except that my "lifetime" has been made up of a patchwork of almost thirty summers. I lived each winter in anticipation of returning to Hawke's Cove. Even as a little girl, counting the weeks, then the days, until my parents would put me on the train from Boston to Great Harbor, confident Gran would be there waiting for me.

Although I see to electricity and make blackout curtains and sign up for my few ration coupons, I don't know if I'll see this war to the end here. If the war ever ends. No. I can't let myself think that. I should strike the thought out, but this is a journal meant for private thoughts, not edited for public consumption.

I wait, and the waiting reminds me of pregnancy without the hope, and pregnancy reminds me of death.

I found a pair of John's dungarees and a plaid work shirt in his bottom drawer, the mustiness pungent in them. I'll wash them tomorrow, weather permitting. I wish they had smelled of John. I came to Hawke's Cove partly in the belief little here would remind me of him. But everything conspires to make me think of my husband, still in England, still training for the inevitable. To be sent into combat. If he knows where or when, he has been remarkably circumspect. His letters tell me little.

When I was a girl, spending summers here with Gran and my cousins Frances and Steve, we used to put sachets of lavender in our drawers to keep away the summer musty smell, that faint woody odor released when a drawer or closet was opened. A summer smell—old farmhouse and salt air.

Maybe Ted is right about tomorrow. The sun broke through the clouds just as a plane from the naval air station in Great Harbor passed overhead. I went outside, shaded my eyes, and watched as the single-engine fighter plane nosed its way higher and higher, tucking itself back into the cloud cover to disappear from sight.

APRIL 18, 1944 Well, Ted was right; after last night's heavy rain and wind the storm has blown out, and today has been partly sunny, jacket cool, but softer than any yet this spring. For a long time after coming home from the Laundromat, I stood daydreaming on the dunes. Maybe I should get a dog. Something slightly floppy with puzzled brown eyes. "But what would we do with a dog in the city?" I can hear John's voice clearly. Poor John. He's never understood my love for this place. He finds the locals dull and ignorant. His words, not mine. I met Mrs. Frick today, and she's neither dull nor ignorant. Plainspoken, that's what I'd call her. Describes herself with pride as a lifer.

I had just put my basket of wet clothes in the back seat of the car and gone to treat myself to a grilled cheese at the Rexall. The marbleized gray counter was a bit sticky, even after Sam Moore swished a damp cloth underneath my elbows. After I ordered, I got off the stool and loitered over the magazines while I waited for my lunch. Suddenly I was bumped from behind by a woman looking over the card selection.

"Oh, I beg your pardon." The woman blushed. "I'm Judy Frick. You're Florence Bailey's granddaughter, aren't you?"

"Yes, Vangie Worth. Your husband is doing the work out at my place?" I don't know why I asked; I certainly had heard Ted speak of his wife, Judy.

"That's right. I've heard you're staying on after the season."

"I don't know. Depends." I had no need to say what on. "I'm about to have lunch. Join me?"

Maybe I'm simply starved for conversation, but I really liked meeting Judy. We lingered over two cups of tea—long enough for me to be late getting my clothes hung, and I ended up having to leave them on the line overnight.

I'm getting better about going into town. People like Judy know who I am, in that way of small places, but not much more than that. Generally, the older year-rounders recognize me only when I mention my grandmother. They remember her having grandchildren come spend the summers, but not us in particular. Those my age are gone, most of the men overseas like John. Besides, I don't want people to know my story—not yet. I couldn't bear it. It's enough they simply think I'm here waiting out the war. As best I can, I avoid conversations that might lead to those perfectly understandable questions about children, like, when are we going to start a family? *Start a family.* Sounds like gardening—starting seeds. I started a seed that took root and grew for a long time, almost to harvest. I think maybe someday there'll be a poem filled with that metaphor. But not yet.

Thankfully, Judy nattered on about other people. She charmed me with her observations about everyone who lives in Hawke's Cove. There isn't a soul she doesn't know or have an opinion about. Everyone she mentioned has an attribute attached. "Fair," "deliberate," "cagey," "bad news." I wonder what adjective Judy will use for me.

When we finally left the Rexall, Judy pointed down toward the harbor. "I hear they lost a flier last night."

I could see the little flotilla of lobster boats heading out of the harbor, the larger naval cutter waiting in the cove.

"I saw a plane just at sunset. I wonder if it's that one."

"Suppose it might be."

"Do you think they'll find him?"

Judy shrugged. "They'll try." There was a touch of resignation in her voice, as if she didn't expect success.

Getting home, and despite the lateness of the afternoon hour, I left my basket of wet clothes beside the clothesline and walked along the worn path to the dune overlooking Bailey's Beach. Judy Frick's referring to me as Florence Bailey's granddaughter had brought the old woman so clearly to mind.

Gran, the daughter of well-to-do Bostonians, fell in love with Henry Bailey of Hawke's Cove. Meant for cotillions and social philanthropies, Florence defied her parents and settled here to farm. Her defiance did not exclude her from their love, and when they died, Gran inherited a comfortable nest egg that enabled her to send not only her own children to good schools but me as well.

Even at the height of the Depression she was able to keep two men employed on the farm, although the trade-off was to let the farm buildings run down. She no longer ran the place as a farm a few years before she died, claiming she was too tired to keep watch over hired men anymore. The little room off the kitchen was empty for the first time in my memory the year I was eighteen. Looking back, I suppose that my education came at the expense of the hired men. When Dad died, I know she provided my mother with my full tuition to Smith College.

So clearly is Gran in my mind that coming back along the path, I half expected to see her under her broad-brimmed gardener's hat, seated in her Adirondack chair, drinking bootleg Scotch.

I hung out my clothes, looking up now and then at the search planes hovering about, still looking for the missing pilot. With the naval air station only a few miles away, we see so many trainees crisscrossing the sky, a noisy reminder of the war. The sad fact is that they are mostly boys now, boys with a man's duty strapped on like their parachutes.

APRIL 19, 1944 I slept poorly last night. My thoughts dance from John—glad he's still safe on some English base—to the condition of this house, until, finally, they light on my grief. Sometimes I am able to press the thought of the baby out of my mind with diligent focus on some problem: How big should I make the garden? Should I buy a pig, like Ted Frick suggested? Something to eat my leftovers and ultimately to provide food? Having come here to be solitary, I am cursed by being alone with my thoughts. Yet I don't want to go home. My surroundings there are much too familiar, reminiscent of other times. Of being pregnant. There I ate the strawberries I craved. In this store I bought a layette. Boston seemed filled with pregnant women, and I wonder how that can be. All the men are gone. John is gone. He left for England so soon after we lost the baby, I confuse the events. I had hoped that Hawke's Cove, Gran's farm, would remind me only of summer and youthful fun. I would plant a garden and write poetry. I had forgotten that it was here, in Gran's old spool bed, that our child was conceived.

Looking for gardening tools, I went into the barn today for the first time since I've been back. I found some bits and pieces of useful tools, but scarcely anything whole. An iron rake with a broken handle, a dented hoe. I do find a box of hand tools—hammers, wrenches, and a variety of screwdrivers. The only other thing remotely useful in the barn is a bicycle. Two, actually. They rested against the stall wall, coupled like two beasts. I extricated one, an old Schwinn, and decided to take it to the Sunderlands' for repair. In these days of gas rationing, when every decision to drive is weighed against patriotism, it will be nice to have locomotion without guilt or fear of running out of coupons.

It rained again in the night, and the clothes hang limp on the line. A patch of blue "big enough to mend a sailor's breeches" offers hope that the day will eventually be sunny. Our faithful southeasterly breeze caught the sleeve of John's plaid shirt, draping it gently over the shoulder of my blouse.

I DROVE ALONG THE SHORELINE to the Sunderlands' tumbledown house overlooking Dwight's Cove. The house is surrounded by the detritus of modern life: automobile hulks, all manner of metal scrap, tires, wire, batteries, and wood. As long as I've come to the Cove, long before the War Effort required salvage, the Sunderlands' property has looked the same. Only now they are legitimate scrap dealers and are making a tidy profit from the business. And as long as I can remember, they could fix whatever mechanical problem you might present to them.

What a pair they are, as alike as twins. Somewhere in their middle sixties, they are always referred to as the Sunderland boys. Born and brought up in Hawke's Cove, the only time they've ever left was to serve in the army during the Great War.

When I got there, they were arguing about fixing a motor. Jake approached as I got out of my car and helped me get the bike out of the back seat, nodding all the while to my litany of what needed to be done. "Chain, oil, wheels need straightening . . ." Howard came along, nodding in the exact same way as his brother even before he heard what I was saying.

"Dontcha worry." Jake, his pique at Howie dissipated, slapped his brother on the shoulder. "Howie here'll do it. He's got a way wi' bikes."

"Good. I don't have a phone, so just let me know when it's done when you see me." I started to get back into the car.

"Naw. We'll deliver it to ya. No chaage," Howie offered. As he stepped back to open my door, I noticed a yellow life raft lying in the tall grass behind him. Most of the air had oozed out of it. Jake saw my glance. "Found it washed up this morning. Musta belonged to the flier gone down. No sign a him, though."

"Poor guy. Wonder what happened." I left my car and walked over to where the rubber raft lay on the bent grass.

"Probably got dumped out. Seas were still rough yestahday. Woun't wanta be out in a little raft like that nohow."

I shivered at the thought of being thrown into inhospitable April water. I'd been in Hawke's Cove too many summers not to know of drownings and to learn respect for a contentious sea. Fishermen and children drowned, and now this anonymous pilot.

"Any rate, the navy's coming by to get the raft. We're hopin' they'll leave it once they've taken a look."

Something caught my eye as I turned to acknowledge Howie's remark, a slice in the side of the raft. I bent over and poked my finger into the two-inch cut. "Did you see this?"

Jake and Howie nodded. "Yeah. Might be he gave up."

"Gave up?"

Howie shrugged. "You know. . . ." He drew a finger under his chin like a knife. "Quick death's better'n a slow one."

The day was still warm by the time I got home, so I left the clothes on the line and treated myself to a cup of tea and the seed catalogue, to pick out what I'm going to grow.

Immersed in my task, I have nearly left the clothes too long again. The wind has just begun to take on the evening's dampness; the ethereal wisps of fog that sometimes blow in off the water look like ghosts. I like the image, and maybe I'll use it sometime in a poem. This is all well and good, but I'd better put this journal aside and bring the clothes in.

The oddest thing. John's clothes are gone.

APRIL 20, 1944 Well! Ernest Dubee certainly was more amused than alarmed at my theft. He hasn't changed much from when we were teenagers and he was one of the few townies I knew. Still fair-haired, although it's cropped military short. He's either outgrown or trained himself out of his adolescent pudginess. Although his dad was the police chief when we were growing up, the title more honorific than official in this one-cop town, I am a little surprised to find Ernie in the role.

"I expect it's some vagrant in need of a change of clothes who swiped your husband's things. Probably halfway to Boston by now. I don't think you need to worry." Ernie scratched a few notes on a report form. "Depression sent a lot of men to wandering."

"Ernie. It's not that I'm worried about the vagrant. I just want the clothes back." I was seated on the other side of the large table he uses as a desk. Ernie's mongrel eased its way out from under the table and sniffed at me.

"Pal, get over here," Ernie ordered, and the dog sighed itself back down under the table. "Maybe you should get a dog, missus."

"Only if it's a loaner. I can't have a dog back in the city."

"Pal, you wanta go live with Mrs. Worth?"

Pal raised his eyebrows but was otherwise noncommittal.

"Hey, Ernie, what's with the 'missus'? We've known each other since childhood."

Ernie didn't answer, only shrugged and smiled, and I felt a little embarrassed that I had called him Ernie.

When I left the police station, Judy Frick was just coming down the sidewalk. I must have looked upset, because she stopped and grabbed my arm. "What's the matter, Vangie? You look worried."

"Nothing important. Someone stole John's clothes off the line."

Judy fairly strong-armed me toward the coffee shop. "Let's get a cuppa and you tell me everything."

For one instant I thought she meant the baby. I don't know why that should pop into my head, but in the next instant I knew what she meant and, in my relief, blurted out, "No, come to lunch instead." And in the next heartbeat wished I hadn't. I'm really not ready for confidential chats yet.

WE SAT in the Adirondack chairs, remnants of lunch on the ground beside us, the April sun soaking us in unseasonable warmth. I had made lemonade from lemons Judy brought. I use so little of my sugar ration that I could make the batch nice and sweet.

Judy is about forty-five and plump in a nice maternal way—no bones, just soft places to cry against. I don't know why I write that; I didn't have the urge to cry today.

I did end up doing some confiding. "I don't know how committed to get to this place, Judy. I mean, John could come home, and we'd go right back to Boston."

"I don't think there's much chance of the war ending before you get a garden planted, grown, and harvested, my dear. Get at least that much done, and you can justify being here."

She's placed a finger on my anxiety. I want the war ended so John and I can heal. Still, I do need to prove that I wasn't out of my mind to come to Hawke's Cove. I'm not just hiding; I'm working. So what if the only poetry I make is by planting seeds.

Then I mentioned my second plan. "I could raise a cow or a pig. Make some use of the land for the effort."

"Right. 'The War Effort,' all caps. Don't you hate it?"

"Yes. But you were lucky, weren't you? Ted didn't have to go."

"Teddy did." Judy slowly folded her hands in her lap. "I lost my son to this war."

"Oh, I'm so sorry, Judy. I didn't know."

"How could you? You aren't from here. You don't have a clue who in Hawke's Cove has been affected by this thing. You come here from the city thinking it's untouched by the outside world."

The sun backlit Judy Frick, and I held a hand up to shade my eyes. I couldn't read her expression and felt as if I'd crushed the life out of a good new friendship by my assumptions.

"Judy, I'm sorry. I assume too much."

When I offered sympathy, she rebuffed it. "Teddy was the first from here to die. This town grieved with me. At first I couldn't stand the attention, the overwhelming compassion. Then the next boy died, and Hawke's Cove grieved for his family too. I realized then that they had been the Cove's boys too. My grief was Hawke's Cove's grief. You see, Vangie, we're only a few hundred here in Hawke's Cove. No one's problems—or joys—go unshared."

I reached across the chasm between the chairs and took her plump hand. She squeezed mine, and I knew that she had chosen to keep the nascent friendship alive.

MAY 1, 1944 I'm not being a very faithful journalkeeper. Perhaps it's the wonderful spring air, keeping me outdoors and at my garden; what energy I have left for writing, I devote to letters to John. I try so hard to keep them newsy and light. It would do no good to burden him with my anxieties. He is foremost of those anxieties, but how do I tell him that? Neither one of us writes with any depth. It seems to me that we have held each other at arm's length ever since losing the baby.

I find that there are some things that I can't put into a letter, yet I need to put down on paper. I've told myself that this is the time to really work on my poetry. I need to harness my thoughts and observations and whittle them into verse.

I had dinner last night with the Fricks. Ernie Dubee was there, brave extra man to my war wife.

At first I thought it was out of deference to me that there was little talk of the war beyond the usual complaints of shortages and black-market coupons. Then I realized that it was Ernie they were being careful around. At an age when all of his peers are fighting overseas, Ernest Dubee remains at home. He is a double hostage in that he performs essential war work, policing this small place, and is the sole provider for his elderly mother.

It's been a long time since I've been out in company. I had almost, out of habit, declined Judy's invitation—except that I realized it appealed to me. A shared meal (I brought a green-bean casserole), a card game. It's been five months since all of it happened—the baby's death and John's abrupt shipping out. Even yesterday I couldn't have imagined ever laughing out loud again. But I never stopped tonight, what with silly stories and bad jokes.

I don't believe it's in my nature to be sorrowful. I have always been the cheerful one, the one my parents called their joker. I wonder, am I to be permanently changed by this? Will the person I was ever come back?

I stood out on the back porch for a little while after Judy and Ted dropped me off. Early peepers keep the night from being totally quiet. I had left my bicycle out, and it is overcast enough for me to think it might rain, so I put it in the barn. The strangest thing. I had just the tiniest sense of not being alone in there. Had I heard something, or was it a wafting warm odor that sent a little alarm through me? The moon above the overcast is full, and there was enough light to see shadows, yet nothing moved.

I shake off my suggestibility but do lock my doors tonight. Upstairs, I indulge in the kerosene heater to warm my bedroom before turning in.

IT IS now well past midnight, and the oil lamp casts shadows in the kitchen as I write this. I tried to sleep but woke up cold, a cold that seems to come from within. I have been so long without another human body to warm me that I am incapable of producing my own heat even with three blankets piled on top. I miss

John most at night. I wonder if I will ever sleep beside him again.

He didn't wait to be drafted. He volunteered a few weeks after Pearl Harbor. I was so angry. Not that he'd joined up. It had become unthinkable that one wouldn't join up. I was angry because he did it and *then* told me. I would have wanted him to wait until fall, and I accused him of going in the spring to avoid having to go to Hawke's Cove for vacation. "There's a war on, Evangeline. We can't be particular. You could take on some war work yourself, not spend the time on the beach."

When John came home that first time, fresh from boot camp, I thought he looked like a stranger. The wool of his uniform was hard, and I remember a moment's hesitation before I embraced him. Even then I knew his experiences in the war would separate us. I would be unable to imagine his life, and he would be unable to share it. But then, here, on last summer's leave, I got pregnant, and suddenly my experience was vastly different from anything he could imagine. It made me less impatient with him.

There is another awful thought, too awful to bear recording, but I will. I never meant to become pregnant. I did not greet the news joyfully despite John's rapture. It meant putting aside my own plans. I wanted to finish my graduate work; I wanted to keep teaching. Selfish. When John, right here in this room, suggested making a baby, I was speechless. As usual, he made an airtight case for why we should, and we did. Even as we made love, I was calculating my cycle, hoping it was the wrong time. It wasn't, and I got pregnant immediately. Once again John's plans had prevailed. Then, magically, I began to want the baby. Everything else receded in my life, and I acknowledged to myself that John was right, though not out loud to him. So now, sometimes, I wonder if John thought I didn't hold on to her well enough.

It is so still, even the peepers have quieted. I can hear the bell buoy on Hawke's Shoals. Too erratic to use as a sleep inducement, nonetheless I begin listening for the bell. I count the moments between clangs. Six . . . three . . . seven beats.

MAY 3, 1944 I went to visit the Ruths today. Ruth Banks and Ruthie Jones. Two elderly ladies with a passion for gardening. They were great friends of Gran's, and I feel bad about not visiting them sooner. I've been here exactly six weeks today.

When I got to their cottage overlooking French's Hole, they were fussing about a theft. A wool blanket with Ruthie Jones's initials monogrammed on it was stolen from their line, where she'd hung it to air out. The incident was too close to mine, and I told them about the theft of John's clothes. We clucked about the state of things, but I'm a little more concerned.

I stayed to tea, and we sat in the rose garden on the white-painted wrought-iron benches set there. Ruth Banks is proud to say she and Ruthie have been together longer than some marriages, and I can see equal amounts of irritation and patience keeping them housemates for so long. Some people say that one of them was married and the other jilted by a lover, but I suspect those stories are made up in that artful way this community protects its own.

When I left, Ruthie Jones handed me a massive bunch of daffodils. I placed them in my carry basket, and as I pedaled along the dirt track that runs along the fence line and across the field toward home, the bouquet bounced out, strewing yellow flowers all along the track. I squatted down and duckwalked, gathering the flowers against the crook of my arm, glad no one was around to see me. As I stood up, I saw him. Rather, I saw John's plaid shirt as it disappeared into the thick scrub at the perimeter of the field.

"Hey!" I called out. "Stop!" I was too far away to catch up even if I had had the temerity to actually run after the thief. I'll talk to Ernie and let him know that this character is alive and well and living in the woods.

My garden seems to be doing well. I got in the lettuce and squash yesterday, and my starter cups are showing optimistic little shoots already. I've been cautioned about having too many tomato plants and about having a proper deerproof and rabbitproof fence. I suppose I'll have to ask someone to come do that for me.

Ted has been very diligent about seeing to my electricity. The electric company will be out early next week about hooking me up to the wires Ted has run throughout the house. Ugly knob-and-wire crawling along the walls and across the ceiling, ending in a fuse box now sticking out of the wall on the cellar stairs. He put in an extra circuit for when I invest in a Frigidaire. Right now the icebox suits me for the little I keep in it.

I GOT a letter from John. Roy Tingley in the post office winked as I went to my postbox, so I knew something beyond my mother's weekly plea to abandon my solitude lay in wait for me.

I went into the little park that overlooks the harbor to read it. The onionskin paper is so insubstantial; it moistened quickly from the heat of my hand. The letter tells me very little, and the censor edits so much, but John mentions mates and pints, so I know he's still in England. He signs his letter, as he always does, *"I love you. I miss you. Your husband, John."*

Not once, not in any of his letters, has he mentioned the baby. I don't know why. Is it so I won't become upset? Or is it simply no longer important in his life because his life is so far away?

MAY 10, 1944 I met him today. The man in John's blue-and-red shirt. I had gone down to the beach for the first time this year. The water is far too cold to swim in, but the air is warm, and I wore my bathing suit. I dozed, but the sound of footsteps telegraphed through the sand beneath my left ear. When I sat up, there he was.

"You're burning."

I knew instantly that he was right, and in the second instant that he was wearing John's clothes. "Where did you get those clothes?" We faced each other across my beach blanket.

"Sears Roebuck." He answered without missing a beat, and I felt my face redden. Of course. There was nothing unique about John's shirt or trousers. Half the men in Hawke's Cove wear them. Except John's plaid shirt has a frayed pocket where time and again he'd caught his pen. This man's shirt had no such pocket, only an un-faded patch where a pocket had been.

"I'm sorry. It's just . . . " I really didn't know what to say.

"It's okay. Your husband's . . . ?" The suggestion of a question was open-ended enough for just about any answer, and it was easy for me to tell him about the theft of John's clothes.

"I don't know why I'm so upset about it. They were old clothes, and John, well, he won't be wearing them anytime soon."

I'd slipped my beach coat over my sunburn. Feeling a little less vulnerable, I introduced myself. "I'm Vangie Worth."

It was odd, how he said his name. As if, after I gave him mine, he couldn't remember that he should tell me his. Almost as an afterthought he said, "Joe. Joe Green." As if saying it for the first time. I wonder if he's a shell-shock case, although his eyes don't have any of that vacancy to them I've seen in others who come back mentally wounded. No, his blue eyes were lively and seemed pleased to meet mine. "Maybe, Mrs. Worth, you're upset about the clothes because they were a part of your life before the war. Something left over from a happier time."

I know Ernie will be displeased with me, but I don't think Joe Green is our man. I rather like him.

MAY 13, 1944 I am restless. Despite hours in the garden, biking to town, and long walks, I am antsy, as if I am expecting something. Someone. Maybe I mistake boredom for anticipation. But I have enough to do. How can I be bored? I fill my days with household tasks, read up on canning and pickling in optimistic preparation for my harvest. Sometimes the feeling of waiting forces me out and I walk for hours. Today I left my usual shoreline route and went up through the woods, then over the array of pastures tied together by ancient tracks—deer, cow, and human. One track leads into another, and I follow them all.

If I had the stamina to continue west, eventually I would reach the single-lane bridge cast across the salt marsh that attaches us more firmly to Great Harbor. Traditional debate centers on whether Hawke's Cove is a peninsula or an island. Some traditionalists declare the marsh in flood qualifies as surrounding water. In either case, the bridge is what gives Hawke's Cove its independence.

When we discussed this question at cards the other night, Ted said that there are old-timers who have never crossed the bridge. Never felt the need to. I scoffed at that as legend.

Home from my long walk, I stand out on my back porch and wait. I am not afraid, just waiting. Waiting for John to come home. He never said we'd try again for a baby. I cast about in my memory, tracing back every sentence he uttered as I lay there in the hospital bed. Did he ever say, "When I come home, we'll try again"? I don't remember.

It will be better when I have electricity. I'll have the radio then to block out the silence that nurtures my waiting.

MAY 14, 1944 I saw Joe Green again. I was prowling along the beach, collecting sea glass for my jar, when I found his footprints ahead of mine. I had the advantage of him. He was leaning against that big rock you can get to only at low tide. For a few minutes he was unaware of me, deep in thought. He smoked a cigarette, inhaling slowly, letting the smoke drift out of his mouth as if reluctant to let it go. He stubbed the half-smoked cigarette out against the rock and carefully replaced the stub in the packet. This action brought me into his view, and he smiled as if he was expecting me.

I smiled in return, waved, and headed toward him. Joe isn't exceptionally tall but is rather thin. He wears a beard, which is unusual these days. Could it, like his thinness, be due to some circumstance beyond his control? I have the urge to feed him.

"I'm sorry. I didn't mean to disturb your solitude."

He pushed himself away from the rock. "It's a welcome interruption. I'm not always my own best company."

As naturally as that we fell into step, continuing along the shoreline, just above where the incoming tide licks at the wet sand. He saw that I was collecting sea glass and spotted a few bits for me, placing them into my hand. We spoke of neutral things: the weather, the particular beauty of the seascape today. Neither of us asked questions, yet in that twenty minutes I learned enough about Joe Green to be content. He is amusing, he can identify certain small birds from a distance, and he can make a flat stone skip seven times before sinking. I don't really need to know where he's from or what he does. He's simply a nice guy. He is not wearing John's clothes. I don't know what he learned about me.

Joe and I had come to one of the deer paths that meander up to the woody perimeter of the headland. "Thanks for sharing your walk with me. I must leave you here," he said.

I put out my hand, and he held it in his for perhaps a fraction longer than need be, but I felt no need to pull it back.

As I turned toward home, I happened to glance behind and saw that Joe Green was also looking back toward me from the deer path. We waved again, smiling at the coincidence.

I know that I will not share this little moment with anyone. The last thing I want to do is bring down on my head the well-meaning censure of Judy or Ernie. Or John.

MAY 19, 1944 It seems odd to be writing in my journal in daylight, but the rain keeps me indoors, and I have no taste for housework. My bread is still in first rise. I tease it into rising faster by lighting the heater side of the stove and setting the bowl of raw dough on the drainboard. The warmth clears some of the dampness out of the kitchen.

What news shall I record here? When I look back on these days, I'll want to be reminded of the details that make up a life. That the towel covering the dough is blue and white, that the bowl the dough rises in is one my grandmother received as a wedding present.

I went to church yesterday for the first time since I've been back. The tiny clapboard-and-shingle St. Luke's hasn't shown much decline since I attended there as a girl, flanked on the one side by Gran in her starched cuffs and collar, her straw hat with its indomitable silk flower pinned on. My cousins Frances and Stevie on my other side. Even on the hottest days Fran and I wore harsh little Sunday dresses our mothers had sent along with us, white gloves, and black Mary Jane shoes. Those childhood Sundays came to mind whenever I touched the time-darkened wood of the pews and felt the oversoft kneeler beneath my knees.

I was surprised to see Joe Green there. I don't know why, except that I had never seen him in town before. He had knotted an unfashionably narrow tie under the collar of the shirt that looked like John's. He was one pew ahead of me, and when he raised his head from prayer, I noticed that his maple syrup–colored hair was just a little too long and crept over the collar of his shirt. He seemed deep in private prayer through most of Mr. Cummings's sermon.

My dough is ready to be punched down for the second rise. I get three loaves out of it. Wednesday is a bake sale for the St. Luke's Ladies' Society. I suppose I should bake a pie for them.

IT'S BEEN ON MY MIND LATELY to do something more productive with this place than just gardening. Sylvester Feeney put something in my head the other day when he delivered my milk. I came upon him standing in my yard, one hand punched into his side, the other hand gripping the bottle rack with my one quart of milk poking out of it. He was in deep contemplation of the barn. His old dobbin shook her harness at my approach, and he turned to take the empty bottle from my hand. "You oughta do somethin' with it." He handed me my full bottle of milk. "You gotta nuf land for a couple of milkers."

"I don't know how long I'm staying." I handed him money for the milk. "Besides, I don't know anything about cows."

He climbed back into the driver's seat and clucked to his horse. "Might be I could rent the space if you go back to the city."

And so, when the rain let up, I went into the barn. Two box stalls—filled with the odds and ends of accumulated junk, scrap wood, and rusted tools—are aligned on the left wall. An empty space, probably storage for a cart or feed, is on the right. There is something churchlike about a still barn. Dim with the thin gray light of this rainy afternoon, the hushed space above my head was disturbed only by the dash of swallows swooping up and out of the open hayloft doors. The loft goes from the midpoint of the barn toward the back and is reached by a wooden ladder nailed to it. I remembered the games of hide-and-seek my cousins and I played in here, climbing among the boxes and barrels I know to be still up there, as we ran barefoot through the hay.

There are puddles here and there on the barn floor. What counts, though, is how dry it is in the loft. It might be too wet up there to keep hay.

However, I didn't get a chance to find out, because as soon as I put my hands on the rungs of the old ladder, I heard a car pull up. I was a little embarrassed to greet Ted and Judy Frick with mud on my hands, and it is only as I write this that I wonder how I had come to have muddy hands. I had only touched the ladder.

The rain has intensified, putting off the electrical work. That's what Ted came out to tell me. I made tea for us, and they stayed nearly to suppertime. Judy suggested that it might be "prudent" to get a telephone hooked up, what with my "being out so far." I know she means prudent in light of the vagrant thief being in the area, but somehow I'm less worried about him lately.

MAY 20 (5:30 A.M.) I woke up thinking I had heard a cry. Not a baby's cry, but an adult's cry of anguish. Startled upright, the sound only in my head, I suppose I must have made it.

MAY 22, 1944 Ernie played host tonight for cards. Judy and Ted picked me up. Ted's still being apologetic for the delay on electricity, but I assure him I do not hold him responsible.

Ernie took me aside after the game. "Met a guy out at the sand-pit. Looks like he's been living rough for a few weeks. Told me his name was Joe Green. Might be he's wearing John's clothes."

I shook my head. "No. I thought so, too, when I met him. But he's not. Besides, John's clothes wouldn't fit him."

"Looks to me like they didn't fit any too good."

"He's all right, Ernie."

Ernie kept his skepticism to himself. "He's looking for work. I told him to go see the Ruths. They've always got odd jobs."

"Thanks."

"What for?"

"I don't know. Being a nice guy instead of a hard-nosed cop."

Ernie's fair skin reddened under the compliment.

"SO WHAT was Ernie so intent on?" Judy asked the question the moment Ted shifted into third gear.

"He's met a fellow he thought might be the thief," I said.

"Is he going to arrest him?"

"No, Judy. He's just a guy down on his luck. Ernie sent him to see the Ruths about work."

"You should hire him, Vangie." Ted put his oar into the conversation. "If Ernie thinks he's okay, it would be a good idea to get some help, even if it's just to get the fence built before you lose more of your vegetables to rabbits."

I couldn't naysay that and didn't try. I had them drop me off at the foot of my drive. The night is mild and moonlit. I don't know;

maybe I should hire Joe Green. Except that I have little money to offer, only my cooking and the hired man's room off the kitchen.

As I write this, I balk at complicating my solitude with someone. Facing someone over a dinner table, making general conversation, caring whether another person likes my meat loaf or is just being polite. I'm not sure I'm up to it yet. Equally, I'm not sure if John would approve. He was not happy that I made the move to Hawke's Cove from Boston. His last two letters have not chided me, but before that every one he wrote contained his disbelief that I would continue to stay away from our friends and families. I haven't the heart to tell him again that it was for those very reasons I needed to get away.

Before I went into the house tonight, I paused. I could hear the waves, kicked up by some unseen storm. Compelled, I left the porch and followed the path to the beach.

The moon illuminates the cresting waves so that white lace ribbons come toward me, curl over, and disappear. I think that it is finally time to write poetry again. This thought cheers me. I haven't written any since last summer. Somehow, being filled with the expectation of a child overshadowed my poetic urges.

As I come back up the path and through the vine-held stone wall, the cockeyed barn holds my attention. Dark bulk against a darker sky, it seems all the more like the crooked man's crooked house. Sylvester Feeney's suggestion keeps coming back to me, and now it occurs to me that Joe Green might fix my barn.

MAY 25, 1944 In the crazy way of coincidences, Joe showed up at my porch door just as I was wondering how to find him. Since seeing him in church, I've caught sight of him only twice in town. Once at the market, where he was buying a loaf of day-old bread, the second time as he was walking along Seaview. I offered him a ride, but he declined, claiming to be walking for pleasure.

He's accepted my meager offer of twenty a month, room and board. The Ruths sent him my way after hiring him for a once-a-week lawn cutting. "The ladies thought you might need some work done." Does everyone in Hawke's Cove think I need help?

I invited him in for lunch, which he ate like a man forcing himself to slow down. I made him another ham sandwich and gave him some of the strawberry rhubarb pie meant for the church bake sale.

After lunch we carried our cups of tea out to the barn to have a look around. Joe cast about, poking a nail into a beam, knocking on the walls. He scuffed a bit of the damp hay off the floor, then, handing me his cup, he swung himself nimbly up the ladder. Not to be left behind, I set the cups down and clambered up. Joe gave me his hand as I crested the top rung. "The roof is in better shape than you'd think. The few holes I can see can be patched, although I'd recommend a whole new course of shingles. Won't be worth doing unless you make the investment."

"You're a carpenter, then?"

"Not by trade. My father taught me a great deal."

"He was a carpenter?"

"No, just a follower of a carpenter's philosophy." He didn't elaborate but quickly slipped down the ladder. Grateful to be wearing slacks, I followed more slowly. Joe Green stood open-armed at the bottom of the stairs, as if to catch me should I fall.

I remember as a kid being fascinated by the word "enigma." Well, Joe Green is enigma personified. I asked when he wanted to move into the back room, expecting him to say at the end of the week. Instead he asks if right now is okay. I expect him to fetch things from his current situation, and he doesn't. Clearly Joe Green is a man unburdened by possessions.

Joe seems so comforted to be here. He took a long time in the bath, then apologized for it. I half expected he'd shave the beard off with John's old straight razor I'd put out for him, but he came out of the bathroom with it neatly trimmed instead. He readily helped dry the dishes and is inordinately pleased to have been given borrowing rights to my small library. As if, having fed his body, I had also fed his mind.

Already I feel my hermit's life getting away from me. I had to plan a meal for tonight instead of heating some soup. I write in my journal now in my bedroom. The oil lamp is smoky, so I trim it and am left with a little oval of yellow to write this by. John looks at me from the photo on my nightstand. Do I detect disapproval? Evangeline, he seems to say, what have you done?

JUNE 3, 1944 Tonight I sit at the kitchen table. The hanging kerosene lamp throws too much heat. I feel myself perspire under my hair, and I lift it off my neck and ponder cutting it off. I wonder what John would say coming home to a bobbed wife. Then again, he's never said much about my hair. I used to have him brush it, but it never felt as sensuous as I had hoped. He was as matter-of-fact about it as washing the car. John's sensuality is in his work, ever so delicately marking on his sketches where a door or window will go, seeing the finished design in his mind. I would not call John a passionate man. Knowing no one else, I assume he is a good lover. He is always careful of me, careful of my pleasure. But his passion lies in his work.

I lift my hair away from my neck, twisting it into a knot, but the loose pieces tumble back down. Joe has come in and offers to chip some ice and pour us lemonade. We go out to the porch.

The lemonade glass feels moist in my hand as we sit out under the stars, letting the cool sea breeze work its magic. We are silent for a time. Then Joe starts pointing out constellations. "Cassiopeia, the Big Dipper, Andy Hardy."

"Hey," I say, and he laughs.

In pointing out the stars, Joe leans close enough for his beard to touch my cheek. I don't move. I don't know if he is unaware of it or not. I am aware of nothing else. But I don't move.

"Just checking to see if you're paying attention," he says, and then stands up.

I HEARD him early this morning. A crying out like a warning. It was like the cry I thought I had once made.

JUNE 8, 1944 So much has happened. The Allied Forces invaded Normandy two days ago. John is out there somewhere. I know that without any word. It is the not knowing *exactly* where that is so hard. I wonder if he went with the first wave to land on Omaha Beach, or has he been one of those dropped by plane? Forty-eight hours ago I was living in a temperate zone of concern. I worried and prayed. But now I am terrified. Ever since the news broke, I have been sick to my stomach.

JUNE 10, 1944 Roy Tingley at the post office gently suggested that it might be some time before I got another letter from John, or before mine reach him. Still, I bend to the task of writing him, filling my letters with the bland mundanity of everyday life. *The garden grows well. The Ruths send their regards. Judy Frick sprained her ankle last week. Joe Green has begun work on the barn.* I casually mention Joe's presence in my life, as if it doesn't count. But it does.

JOE and I drove to the Sunderlands' today to borrow pump jacks. Joe graciously declined to drive. "Happy to be a passenger, Mrs. W." He calls me that to keep our relationship businesslike, but it sounds almost affectionate, not deferential.

The Sunderlands wouldn't hear of payment for the use of their equipment, so I wandered down to the beach while Joe helped them load their ancient dump truck with various bits of scrap destined for the War Effort.

As I came back up the path, a little hidden from their sight, I could hear Jake's voice. "You stayin' with Miz Worth?"

"I am."

"Nice lady. Her grandmother Florence was a nice lady too."

Howie chimed in. "Miz Worth can do with a man about the place. That husband a' hers weren't much in the way of keepin' the place up. Dun't think he much likes it here. City boy, you know."

"Well, I don't know Mr. Worth, except that he's over there, so I'll keep my own counsel."

Sunderland boys liked that response. "Yeah, do no good to speak ill of someone in it."

I could tell by the expression on Joe's face that he knew the expected response was to speak of his own experience. To explain in a word or two why he was here. He gave them—and me—nothing.

I announced my return with a hallo. "Job all done?"

"Could use help other end," Jake said to both of us.

I nodded my okay, but Joe shook his head. "If it's all the same, fellas, I plan to get started on the barn today. I need to get a good start on it before the real hot weather sets in."

"What ya gotta do is lift 'er up with them jacks, butcha gotta be careful ya dun't tip 'er over."

"Naw, Howie, that old barn'll cave in fore she tips over." Jake demonstrated the collapse, his hands backed together into a V.

As we were getting back into the car, I spotted the raft still lying on the long grass. "So the navy did leave that with you?"

"Navy ain't been by yet. Guess they don't care. 'Sides, finders keepers. Sea law." Howie gave the raft a proprietary kick.

"Sunderlands found that on their beach," I said to Joe, who was very quiet in the car seat next to me, lost in his own thoughts.

Before going home, we headed into town to pick up a few things at LaRiviere's Market. Joe seemed a little tense, and I wondered if the conversation at the Sunderlands' had upset him.

Just as we came out of the market, I saw Ernie charging toward his police car. He saw us on the same side of the street and came toward us. "Joe Green."

Joe didn't respond, only stood still as I kept moving to meet Ernie.

"Vangie, can I borrow your hired man for a couple of hours?" He motioned to Joe to come over. There was an obvious hesitation before Joe stepped out of his self-imposed suspended animation.

"The Collison twins have gone missing, and I could use a little help locating them. Would you be willing, Joe?"

Joe nodded. "Sure."

He handed me the grocery bag and followed Ernie to his car.

When he got home, Joe told me that the boys had managed to get themselves buried alive in the sandpit. They'd rigged up a breeches buoy over the deep pit using some stolen wire and a couple of turnbuckles nailed to opposing trees. The whole pit is about a hundred feet across and probably thirty or forty feet deep. The town has gotten all of its sand for icy roads and cement mixing from this hole in the ground for decades. It's not the beach sand type of sand, but that nasty yellow dirt that sticks to the seat of your pants and never washes out. Joe came home covered, and I despair of getting it out of the knees of his only decent pair of work trousers.

The good news is, Ernie and Joe found the boys in time.

JUNE 11, 1944 It was my turn to host the card party. It was a little difficult, trying to figure out what to do about Joe. I felt awkward about leaving him out, and equally awkward about including him in a rather fixed group after dinner.

Judy and I cleared the table, stacking the dishes in the sink. Joe stood up to hand me a plate and excused himself. "It's been a pleasure meeting you. I bid you good night."

"Joe," Ernie said. "Sit for a hand or two, won't you?"

Joe looked at me, and taking permission from my surprised smile, nodded. "I'd like that."

We played hearts for a while, then switched to cribbage. The conversation this time did come around to the war. We all believe the invasion will hasten the end. I hear myself speak of it dispassionately. "The Germans surely can't resist this massive an attack."

Ted gripped his cards in his hand without looking at them. "An awful thing, all those men lost."

"I suppose it comes down to sacrifice. National sacrifice, personal sacrifice." Once I had said the word "sacrifice," the room fell silent. The truth is, I thought not of John, but of our child. Judy and Ted certainly thought of their son. Perhaps Ernie was thinking of himself. I couldn't even imagine what Joe was thinking.

"Fifteen for two." Joe ended the silence.

Long after I waved the Fricks good night, Joe leaned against Ernie's car. I went to bed, too tired even to go out with them to say good night. Sometime after I had drifted off into that first heavy sleep, I was awakened by their voices.

"Don't get me wrong. I'm happy in my job. I draw a good salary, have the respect of this community . . ." Ernie's voice trailed off.

"Did a lot of your friends go?"

"Yeah. All of them. I mean, this is a small place. There were probably only twenty of us of an age to go."

"So you stand out."

"Yeah. Something like that."

"And everyone tells you you're doing essential war work, how can the town survive without you, et cetera, et cetera."

Ernie chuckled. "Exactly."

"They're right."

"I know."

"Doesn't make it any easier, though."

"Nope."

I closed my eyes and tried not to eavesdrop any longer. I must have succeeded, because I heard nothing until a leadfooted seagull landed on my roof and started mewing this morning.

JUNE 16, 1944 It's finally gotten really hot. Well into the eighties! I went to the beach right after lunch.

Joe continues hard at work, digging a trench, preparing to set up the pump jacks that he will use to support the barn while he builds a new foundation. He says we will begin to realign the whole building, forcing it out of its seventy-year slump. Joe seems utterly confident that he will be able to carry this off without either dropping the barn or dying in the effort. I felt guilty for skipping off to the beach while he labors on a Sunday. Coming up behind him as he was digging, I startled him.

"Hey, don't do that to a guy!"

"Come to the beach."

He looked back at his work. "How about in half an hour?"

"I left John's bathing trunks on your bed." He didn't argue with me this time, as he has consistently at any suggestion of borrowing John's clothes. He's already spent the pay I advanced him on a Montgomery Ward order, so at least he's got a change of clothes.

It was much more than half an hour later when he finally came to the beach. I was just about ready to leave when I saw him, John's little-used trunks loose at the waist, but good enough. He stripped off his shirt and plunged into the calm water of the cove. He burst to the surface, shaking the drops from his face, then threw himself backward into the water. The sight of his enjoyment made me go back in. It's been a long time since I swam with someone.

Joe and I swam in tandem, not racing exactly, but I think we both enjoyed showing off our form. We climbed out of the water, our suits stuck to us like seaweed, and we pulled at them, laughing at the slightly embarrassing sound of the suction.

There is a strange intimacy in swimming.

I toweled off and pulled on my terry cloth robe. When Joe dropped his towel and bent to pick up his shirt, I couldn't help but notice scarring all along his back, as if he'd been burned or badly abraded. He quickly pulled on his shirt. To thwart my curiosity about his back, he called attention to his hands.

"Oh, Joe. We should have gotten you work gloves." His hands were blistered from the rough handle of the shovel.

Back at the house, I got down the peroxide, Vaseline, and gauze. I poured peroxide over his hands as he held them over the sink. He was stoic for a minute, then danced around the cracked linoleum, waving his tortured hands and making us both laugh.

We sat down, and I took his left hand in mine and began gently working the Vaseline into the four blisters at the base of his fingers. When I turned his hands over to wrap the gauze, I noticed for the first time that the backs of his hands were mottled, like his back, with evidence of healed burns.

We fell silent as I bent over his right hand. The joking subsided, and I concentrated on my work. Over and over I stroked the jelly, smoothing it, taking off the excess.

"I think that's enough, Mrs. Worth." Joe's voice was soft, unsettled, and I quickly tied off the bandage.

THIS afternoon I went to Great Harbor with Judy. We shopped, and after lunch we treated ourselves to a Bogart movie. It was hopelessly romantic, and I loved it. It was very late by the time Judy dropped me home. I stumbled up the back porch steps and into the dark kitchen. I felt for the matches but could find none.

"Damn it." I stubbed my toe on the table.

"Wouldn't you like some light?" I was startled by Joe's voice coming out of the darkness behind me.

Suddenly the kitchen was flooded with electric light.

"Welcome to the twentieth century, Mrs. W."

I clapped my hands together with the same enthusiasm with which I had applauded the end of the movie as the houselights came up. I have electricity. Gran would be so pleased.

JUNE 23, 1944 Joe has been with me a month. In that time he has fixed the other bike, serviced the car, dug out the foundation of the barn to ready it for lifting, built a fence around my garden, planned a fence for the pasture, and kept me company.

He has served as a distraction from my dark thoughts, reminded me what joy there can be in cooking a good dinner for someone who works hard. Given me someone else to think of when I can't bear thinking of John anymore.

JUNE 25, 1944 The wildest thing. In raising the barn Joe has found a store of bootleg whisky. I knew about the rumrunners of Hawke's Cove in the eighteenth century, but this stash is more recent. I suspect it comes from my grandfather's reprobate brother, Ralph, the black sheep of the family. He'd modified a lobster boat to no known fishing specification and taken to long, unaccompanied jaunts, setting out when most boats were coming in. After that Ralph did a bunk, with only a postcard years later to say he was still alive. No one ever heard from him after that card.

Now I guess we know why he disappeared. Clearly he'd bitten off more than he could chew, judging by the quantity of whisky lying at the bottom of a pit suddenly exposed by the work Joe has done. Maybe he stole it; maybe the revenuers were hot on his trail. Whatever the case may have been, Uncle Ralph vanished.

"Well, what do I do with it?"

"Only one good suggestion comes to mind with twenty-five-year-old Scotch whisky." Joe had a glint of mischief in his eye.

"Drink it?"

In the end, it seems best to leave the whisky where it is for the time being. The pit itself is roughly four by six, maybe three feet deep. The flooring of the barn serves as the pit's ceiling and seems in no danger of collapse. Joe suggested the hole might actually have once served as a slave hole during the days of the Underground Railroad. Imagine lying in that claustrophobic place wondering if the next daylight would bring freedom or capture.

JULY 3, 1944 My little electric lamp lights my journal as I lean against the nightstand to pen these thoughts. John's face in the photograph seems less dark beneath the incandescent bulb, almost cheerful. Maybe I think he seems cheerful because, for the first time in nearly a month, I feel cautiously optimistic. I got a letter from him yesterday. He's all right. My prayers are answered.

Roy Tingley fairly beamed as I collected the frail envelope out of my box. A single sheet so thin it is translucent. John's upright architect's handwriting is barely marred by the censor.

Dearest Evangeline,

I'm safe and unhurt. I know you'll have been wondering, so I'll say that right off. Since landing here, we've marched for days across this once beautiful land. There are still farms and vineyards that at first sight seem untouched. Then you see the house has only one side left standing and the dogs have been shot. Many of my companions are the same men I started out with, and we count ourselves very lucky. We make slow progress and mostly we complain about our feet. I'm all right otherwise. How are you? There is a Red Cross station here and they will post this for me, so I must end here. We are moving again. I hold you in my heart. I love you. I miss you.

Your husband, John

I was still sitting on the green bench that overlooks the harbor, the envelope in my hand, when Joe came up to me, a bag of groceries in his arms. "Is he all right?"

"He says he is."

"Good. That's good, Mrs. W." Joe set the bag down and sat beside me on the park bench. We were quiet for a moment, staring out toward the harbor.

"He tells me nothing. He never tells me if he's scared or whether he is in danger."

"What do you tell him?"

"Well, I tell him what I'm doing with the farm, and what my daily life is like. I tell him I miss him."

"Do you tell him you worry about him? That you're scared?"

"No. Of course not. I'm careful not to tell him anything which will worry him about me."

Joe had the good grace not to point out the obvious. As soon as I said it, I knew what the point was. "Oh."

"Mrs. W., he's doing the best he can. There are things he's witness to or participant in which he will never tell you. Please don't expect him to."

A moment later Joe stood up, picked up the groceries, and walked off, leaving me to reread John's letter and wonder of whom had Joe spoken—John or himself?

JULY 4, 1944 We had a big picnic today. All the Fourth of July trappings: potato salad, coleslaw, hot dogs, and lobster. Most of Hawke's Cove turned out for the Great Harbor parade. It was wonderful, all the patriotic good cheer of small-town America as *The Saturday Evening Post* likes to portray it. Hawke's Cove's selectmen piled into the horse-drawn carriage with Great Harbor's selectmen, all of them tossing hard candies to the children waving their little American flags. I am hopelessly attached to such events.

I had thought about not going to this long-standing traditional event. Many of the people there would be Boston folks who come to Hawke's Cove for the summer. There might be someone at the picnic who knew I lost the baby last December. It would be unbearable to have some old summer friend come up with well-meaning condolences and lay bare my secret to these new friends who know nothing about it. Especially Judy. I should tell her, I know. But the more time goes by, the harder it is to say anything.

I told Joe I wanted to stay home and work in the garden, but he talked me into going.

"You have to come, Mrs. W."

"Joe, I don't, but you go. You'll love it. Lots of food and games."

"Exactly the reason you should be there." He handed me the basket with three blueberry pies in it. "I'll bring the car around. You make sure you've got a sweater for when it cools off."

I stood there, big wicker basket clutched in two hands, feeling my reluctance ebb.

We played baseball. We ate and swam and ate again. No fireworks this year. Instead we lit a huge bonfire. Only our faces were illuminated by the golden red light that towered above us for a little while before collapsing. We circled the fire, those of us who stayed late, whose obligations on the morrow didn't preclude watching it die to the last ember. I found myself flanked by Ernie and Joe, all of us silent. The rowdy mood of earlier in the day had drained away, leaving us contemplative. Pal cast his eyes toward

Ernie in a plea to go home. Ernie snapped his fingers at the dog and bade us good night. The fire had dwindled to a bed of ash.

Joe was still beside me, seated on the sand. "I offered to stay and bury the coals. If you want to take the car home, I'll walk."

"No. I'll help you."

I spread the bits of charcoaled lumber out with an iron rake while Joe fetched seawater in two buckets. He doused the ashes, and I raked until there was no longer any steam coming from the embers. It took Joe only a couple of minutes to cover the spot with sand. Tomorrow it will look as if nothing had ever taken place.

I was a little chilled. Joe had sent me back into the house to get my sweater before we left. I was glad of it now and struggled with cold fingers to button it.

Joe pointed to my cardigan. "You're all wrong there." Gently he undid the misaligned buttons and rebuttoned them.

He is such a sweet man. The way he has begun to take care of Gran's place, the way he already knows more people in town than I do, the way they all cheered him on during the baseball game—it is obvious he has come to love Hawke's Cove. I wish John could come to love it. Maybe someday after the war John will come, the scales will fall from his eyes, and he, too, will love this place.

JULY 10, 1944 I see that I am getting less and less reliable in journalkeeping. I would make excuses, but that's silly. I am, after all, the only one reading this.

Did I mention the whisky? Yes, I did. Well, we decided to move it from the pit to the cellar under the house. Mainly because it'll be easier to get at. I haven't been down in the cellar in many, many years, and it lived up to my expectations of cobwebs and clutter. It smells vaguely of apples. In the north corner is a root cellar accessible to the outside by way of a wooden hatch. This is where we've stacked the sixteen boxes of booze. Joe started singing that awful drinking song about ninety-nine bottles of beer, and I threatened to clock him with one. He switched to "Onward, Christian Soldiers." His voice is so nice I let him go through all of the verses.

Sometimes I feel so settled here, as if there is no other life to return to. The city and my mother, my friends—they all seem part of another life. Just being here, able to swim or walk or dig in my garden or play cribbage with friends, has been healing. When Joe comes in and stands at the sink washing up, he brings in the scent of useful work, of the lubricating oil he squirts on the tools he uses. Generally he trails in dirt too. I chide him, and he jollies me back, and I know that this is the best place for me to be.

JULY 16, 1944 I have waited a day before trying to write this. I am so filled with emotion I am numb from the surfeit. I can no longer feel. As soon as I can feel again, I will know how to behave. Now I am just moving from one minute to the next, from kitchen to parlor to porch. No matter where I am, the letter containing my new reality follows me. It sits on my bureau, the simple declarative sentences announcing my husband's disappearance written by formula. Nothing new here for the army. Just substitute "John Worth" for yesterday's name and send it off. Only they don't send them. That's how you know how serious it is. Two young officers in dress uniforms come and stand in front of you in the garden. They have brought Judy Frick, knowing that a woman alone needs a woman at a time like this. Missing. Accept our regrets, Mrs. Worth. Everything is being done that can be done. Off they go, relieved to have gotten it over with.

I don't let Judy touch me at first. She knows from experience there's nothing angry about my refusal to be embraced just then. She knows I'll let her hold me in a little while.

Ted has followed in their car, and he comes over to me. They really want me to go in, but I refuse. "I'm okay. I'm fine." Judy takes my hand and squeezes it gently. Ted pats my shoulder. I thank Judy for being there and assure her I'm all right. I wave gamely at their departing car.

I look for Joe. There he is, waiting to see if I want to lay my head on his chest and weep. I cover my face with my hands, but the tears do not come. I will not let them.

Joe cares for me as if I were a child. He carries me into the parlor and tucks my grandmother's old afghan around my legs just as if I were ill. First he brings me a cup of tea. Then he gives me a shot of the twenty-five-year-old whisky. That helps to stop the trembling.

Then he sits beside me on the davenport and puts his arm around my shoulders. He says nothing, and there is a great comfort in that. Eventually he goes into the kitchen to make me lunch.

"Joe, you don't have to do this."

"Yes, I do. Today I take care of your blisters."

"I don't understand."

"You can take a day off being the caregiver. Let me take care of you."

JULY 27, 1944 For the first few days after John was listed missing in action, I couldn't make myself leave the yard. What if they needed to find me to tell me it was all a mistake? Or that he's been found alive and well, or that he . . . ?

Joe has thrown himself into the last of the foundation work under the barn. He's jacked it into alignment and built piers out of bricks. Now all he needs to do is fill in the trench. I sit and watch him for hours.

At the end of the week Ernie, Judy, and Ted showed up to play cards. "It's our turn," was all Joe said, and I saw complicity in Judy's eyes. In view of Judy's own grief, I am reluctant to share mine with her. How can mine compare, how can I go to her for sympathy when her loss is so much greater? So final. If— No, I cannot write those words. Right now I still am allowed to hope. So I turn only to Joe for comfort. I don't weep or even speak, but he tolerates my silences.

This is the second week. I went to church on Sunday with Joe. After the service the minister, Mr. Cummings, wouldn't release my hand until I agreed to let him come and visit me.

"I feel as if I had some terminal illness, the way people are being so kind, so sympathetic." Joe and I were sitting at a table in Linda's Restaurant, having breakfast.

"No, you're wrong." Joe handed his menu back to the waitress. "People empathize with you. Admire you, even. 'This horrid thing has happened to Evangeline Worth; see how well she's handling it. Maybe we can handle our own bad news as well.' "

"I'm not handling it all that well, Joe. You know that."

"Yes, you are. You're doing fine."

THIS MORNING JOE CALLED ME out to the barn. He'd finished filling in the trenches around the perimeter—wheelbarrow after wheelbarrow of stone and dirt dumped and tamped and now seeded. I admired his work and followed him into the barn. In the early morning a soft light comes in from the opened stall windows and the hayloft. In that light I could see that all the junk was gone. The two box stalls are completely empty and ready for livestock. The space against the wall opposite the stalls has been converted into four milking parlors. The loft is filled with bales of straw for bedding, and newly built shelves hold shiny new milk cans and pails, an optimistic vision of a bovine future for my grandmother's barn.

"This is the best part." Joe took my hand and led me to the double doors, one of which has sat open in the same position since I was a child. Joe pulled the door gently, and the two halves joined in a marvelous symmetry.

It occurs to me to wonder what Joe has done with the collection of trunks and boxes stored in the loft. He's probably just left them alone. I'm not sure what I expect to find in those trunks. Most likely just Gran's collection of old quilts.

JULY 28, 1944 I woke up irritable. It was a nice change from sad. I tried to work out my crankiness on housework, storming through the downstairs with broom and mop. I got to the kitchen, and Joe had trailed in barnyard mud yet again. "Try using the mat!"

"I'll take my boots off. I'm sorry." Wisely he went to see Sylvester Feeney about our cow-buying expedition next week.

Alone at last, I sat on the back porch steps and let my irritability mount. It peaked at Joe's forgetting to stop at the post office yesterday afternoon, and valleyed when I looked at the securely closed barn doors. Then I thought about the trunks. No better time than the present, I thought, and stood up.

The air in the loft was warm. Hay dust sparkled in the sunlight. On the far wall I saw the two trunks I remember being there since my youth. The ghostly voices of my childhood companions echoed once again as I see us playing hide-and-seek up here.

One of the trunks is a round-topped steamer; the other, a simple black rectangle with travel decals pasted all over it, a record of Gran's European tour. My father used it to go to college.

I opened the steamer trunk first. As I expected, there are a half-dozen ancient quilts wrapped carefully in sheets. I refolded the quilts in opposite folds to help preserve them. This left the grand-tour trunk. In it, my father's clothes. I know that they are his, because his varsity sweater lies on top.

I took out everything to look at. Woolen trousers, white shirts, a narrow tie that I think I remember. I dig deeper and come up with his graduation gown and cap.

I dig still deeper and find the Ruths' missing blanket.

"Mrs. W.!" I hear Joe calling, a note of concern in his voice. "Vangie?" He is in the barn now, the worry exposed by this use of my first name. He has never called me Vangie before.

"Up here."

He knows. Even before he sets foot on the ladder, he knows I have discovered one of his secrets. When his head crests the coaming of the loft floor, he sees me with the blanket in my hands.

"You should have told me."

"Yes, but I didn't, and then too much time went by and I couldn't. I stayed here in your barn. I took the blanket to keep warm. I took your husband's clothes so that I wouldn't be naked."

My Joe, my friend, had been the vagrant thief. "Why?"

"I was desperate."

"Why were you desperate?"

"I can't tell you."

My anger is volcanic. I spew it in gobs of words that come from some renegade part of my mind. "You take my kindness and throw it back in my face. You must be laughing at me every day. 'Mrs. Worth, ha ha. I stole her husband's clothes and blithely lied about it. I stole her kindness, I stole her trust, I stole her . . .' " I paused for breath. I'd almost said *heart*. He had stolen my heart. With each raging phrase I stepped closer to him. "My husband lies dead in some French forest and you make me care what happens to you. It isn't right. You've lied to me all along."

I struck him. Over and over. I pummeled Joe Green's chest

because he had lied to me, because my husband was missing, because my baby was stillborn and Joe Green had no knowledge of her. Because I'd known all along he'd been the one who'd stolen the clothes and he'd made me want to be wrong. I pounded until at last he took my wrists in his hands. I could feel our pulses together.

"Your husband isn't dead."

He waited until I dropped my resistance, then let go of my wrists. "You must believe me when I tell you I only did what I had to in order to save my own life. I never thought for a moment it wasn't wrong. That surviving itself was wrong. Then I met you and lied from the very first moment. Of necessity. There hasn't been a day yet when I haven't regretted it. Please don't ask me any questions which will force me to lie to you again."

I stood with my hands at my sides, the hayloft suddenly suffocating. I couldn't answer him, and he took this as mistrust.

"Mrs. Worth, the barn is done. So when you say why I've left, you could also say I've done one good thing for you."

All of my anger was gone. I watched as he turned toward the ladder, and suddenly the realization washed over me. I cannot bear another loss. I don't think I could bear to go back to my solitude.

"Joe. Don't go."

He did not look at me, only stood there with his back to me, his shoulders perfectly straight. "Are you certain?"

"Yes."

He turned around and came back to circle me with his arms. I laid my head on his chest. His cheek rested on my head, and he rocked me back and forth. I clenched the fabric of his shirt, John's shirt, in my hands, determined not to lose him too.

AUGUST 2, 1944 Well, we have three cows. Not exactly a herd, but Mr. Feeney says they're enough to qualify this place as a farm. We drove to Tylerville on Thursday to attend the auction there. Joe was reluctant to go. It was only when Sylvester Feeney described Tylerville as "the back of beyond," and not exactly a watering hole for anyone besides farmers, that Joe acquiesced.

We drove up in Mr. Feeney's truck with the six-cow trailer rattling along behind us. I sat wedged between the two men and, given

I know Joe a little better, leaned right against the centrifugal forces as Mr. Feeney barreled down impossibly twisting back roads. Miraculously, we arrived at the auction barn alive. The barn is actually a cinder-block single-story building with big double doors at both ends and high rectangular windows all along the side. It looks WPA-built. We had passed a camp for conscientious objectors, and I wondered if they had been put to use building it.

Inside was an arena with an auctioneer's podium at one end, surrounded on three sides by wooden bleachers. Wedged once again between my two companions, I looked around at the lineup of farmers, each man's face stamped with the years of his profession. Deeply lined, roughened by the sun and wind, ubiquitous cigarette dangling from rubbery lips. They all were of an age when they should have been able to let their sons take over. Instead they continue as they have all their lives, hoping their sons will come back.

Joe was looking around as well. I wondered if he felt awkward being the only young man present, if the old men wondered about him. He caught me looking at him and smiled.

"Maybe if you limped a little?" I said.

"How do you know what I'm thinking?"

"It's what I'd be thinking. Is this why you were reluctant to come?" Another forbidden question.

"No."

Our whispered conversation was interrupted by the entrance of the first of the milk cows.

"Keep your hands down." Mr. Feeney shifted his unlit cigarette into the other corner of his mouth. "Let me do the bidding here."

I've made an arrangement with Mr. Feeney. I buy the cows, and he buys my milk. He gives me a good price on silage, and I sell him the cows at what I bought them for if I leave Hawke's Cove in less than a year. He's careful, then, about selecting my cows. His criteria are mysterious, and cow after cow is brought before the auction block and nary a nod from Mr. Feeney. I grow restless after seven good milkers come and go, and head off to the ladies' room. The acoustics allow me to hear the bidding as I wash my hands at the sink. "Lot number thirty-four sold to bidder one-oh-three." That's us. I own a cow! Then I own two more, a cow and her calf.

It's been a long time since I've owned any animals, and I quickly run outside to examine Bessie, a black-and-white guernsey. The second cow is a brown-and-white jersey we dub Mom, and her calf, Baby. I can't see the difference in any of them from the sixteen or so that have gone before.

"Pedigree," is all Mr. Feeney says.

Joe and Mr. Feeney loaded the "herd" into the trailer while I watched. Joe got kicked in the knee, but no permanent damage done, he says, although he's still limping a little. Given our earlier conversation, I wisely forgo pointing out the irony.

AUGUST 7, 1944 I never knew cows were so regimented. I thought that they simply chewed their cud and otherwise hung around. Not so. These cows demand to be fed at precisely six a.m., expect to be milked, and moo plaintively if not taken care of immediately.

Joe is so good. He's up and out there taking care of business before I can pull myself out of bed. He never complains, not even joking. Sometimes I think he actually *likes* the work. He bought a soft horse brush at the hardware store yesterday and spent an hour going over the cows as if they were pets.

I shouldn't be surprised. He treats me like a pet, always taking my emotional temperature. Stopping what he's doing to suggest a walk or bike ride if he catches me staring off into space. He refuses to take a day off. "And just what would I do with the time?"

"Go into Great Harbor and see a film? Go to the beach for the day?"

"I have no desire to do the first, and I like the beach when everyone else has left for the day."

We do go nearly every nice day. Usually around three o'clock or so. He's done with the sweaty chores, as he calls them, and I've puttered around sufficiently to fool even myself into thinking I'm productive. I pack up a light snack—whatever fruit is available, a box of crackers. A Thermos of lemonade or just cold water. Nothing fancy.

I notice that Joe is careful about the sun on his back. He never works bare-chested, even on these dog days. I expect one of the reasons he prefers the beach late is to keep the direct sun off those still healing burns. I haven't yet asked how he came to have them. His wall goes up almost visibly anytime I come near asking him those kinds of questions. He is a deeply private person.

AUGUST 15, 1944 It has been a month. A month since the letter was handed to me. A month and no word. I lied to myself: It would only be a few days . . . weeks . . . I would hear something. Now should I tell myself it will be a few months? Years? Ever?

I worry out loud only to Joe. Only Joe hears me pace the floor in the night. Only Joe finds me staring off into space, my hands in the soapy dishwater. Only Joe knows that I never cry.

AUGUST 16, 1944 Our weather has been nearly perfect—sunny days and misty nights. My garden is doing well. The tomatoes are still green, but I've picked all of the peppers, zucchinis, and beans. Summer squash grows with abandon.

Our days have become very cow-oriented. Sometimes we talk as we milk. Often, though, we speak only to the cows, shushing them with soft voices. The rhythmic pulling and pushing on the full udders, the sound of the milk as it dashes into the buckets, our foreheads pressed against the firm sides of the cows, leaves us a little sleepy with the meditative effect.

I have a radio, a brand new Philco. After dinner we listen to the news. Joe is so tired now he usually falls asleep despite valiant efforts not to. I confess I like watching him sleep.

Some nights we sit on the back porch steps and share a sip of the bootleg Scotch or a beer. Most nights I go out with Joe when he does his final check on the girls. Once in a while we go for a night swim. Tonight there was an air-raid drill. We heard the firehouse horn bleat its coded warning. The few lights we could see along the arms of the cove blinked out. It is a dark night, and we'd found our way to the beach with a flashlight. We didn't dare return until we heard the all-clear, so we stayed in the water, drifting away from the shore on the quiet waves. The air was cooler than the water and felt like silk. It was so dark I couldn't see Joe. I felt his wet hair bump against me as he drifted by.

"Did you shut the lights off before we came down?" Joe knows

I am less careful about electric lights than I was about oil lamps.

"I hope so."

"Let it be on your head if the Japs take Hawke's Cove."

I splashed water in the general direction of his voice, but the only response was the sound of his dive. Suddenly he had me by my legs, flipping me into the dark water.

We are given immunity in the darkness. An immunity against being old before our time, against grief, and against solemnity. Just for a little bit. We played. His hands went around my waist and then let go, as if he was suddenly aware of what he was doing.

AUGUST 17, 1944 The night air is silky and cloudless. The early crickets are tuning up, a prelude to fall. Tonight I can hear the waves as I sit here in my room. I am filled with a nameless want. No. I'm not honest even on my own page. I know what it is. I have not been touched in so long—I have not wanted to be touched in so long—that I thought I never would again. But I do want it. I find myself thinking the most inappropriate thoughts, thinking about Joe. I tell myself it's proximity, it's natural curiosity. I think of his hands, long and elegant and so different from John's square, capable hands. I think of them touching my waist. I think of them . . .

I must stop this nonsense. It is wrong.

AUGUST 19, 1944 Judy and Ted think Joe has been discharged. The Sunderlands claim they know for sure he's 4-F, although they couldn't say why. The Ruths hazard the opinion that Joe is a conscientious objector. Ernie never says what he thinks.

I watch Joe when he doesn't know it. Sometimes his naturally mild expression hardens against some interior pain, and I know that whatever the genesis of his being here on my farm, it has a bitter taste. When he first came, he was consistently cheerful. As we've grown accustomed to each other and he's seen some of my drearier moments, he's allowed himself the luxury of being quiet. Of having reflective moments unassailed by my interfering. I let him be. These pensive moods never last very long.

This morning I went out to the barn to find him sitting on the milking stool, his hands still, his cheek pressed against Bessie's side.

He didn't hear me come in, though Bessie swung her head around to see. Joe patted her nose and began milking.

"Hi." I came up behind him. Some impulse made me lay my hands on his shoulders. I could feel the muscles work as he milked.

If he had shrugged or spoken of neutral things, I would have dropped my hands. He did neither, only leaned against my touch.

He still calls me Mrs. W. As long as he does, the borderline is safe. We acknowledge the barrier.

AUGUST 21, 1944 If I hadn't needed the preserve jars, it would never have happened. If I hadn't decided to go with Joe instead of sending him alone to town. If I hadn't been greedy for his company, he wouldn't know this about me, and I wouldn't now have to suffer his feeling more sorry for me than he already does.

Mrs. Sutton had only heard of my being pregnant, not of my loss. She sometimes plays bridge with my mother but left for Florida before I was due. She is one of the few people we know from Boston who spend time in Hawke's Cove. She is not a close friend. I can barely write this.

It was the way it happened that keeps exploding in my mind. I have this impression of a tottering female, perched on impossibly high heels, hands waving in the air.

"Vangie. How's the baby!" She came clattering toward us as we left the hardware store. "Was it a boy or a girl? How wonderful. And this must be John. Still not overseas?" Words fell from her red lips like rain—no, like hail. The assault was unstoppable.

A wall of numbness shut out her voice. I went deaf, although I could see her lips moving and knew that she was exposing my secret to the world. To Joe.

I don't remember Joe's getting me into the car, although he says he fairly strong-armed me away from Mrs. Sutton. He said nothing as he took me home. Instead he took my left hand in his, holding on to it even as he passed the car through its gears. It was only midafternoon, but Joe poured me a glass of the bootleg Scotch. Then another. Until the numbness was replaced by sleep.

When I woke, he was sitting there in the room, on the edge of the bed. I don't know if he'd been there the whole time—by now the sun was quite low—or if it was the feeling of his weight on the bed that awakened me. All I know is that I was glad to see him, glad of his touch as he brushed the hair away from my eyes. "You know, Joe, Scotch isn't a cure."

"No. But it can make things go away for a little while." His voice was a raspy whisper.

"You speak as one who's had to make things go away."

I crawled out from under the afghan with which he'd covered me and sat beside him. Joe took my hand in his and stroked my knuckles with his thumb. Soothed by his touch, I began to talk.

It was the first time I have spoken of Molly as someone who had actually been part of my life. Not just the lost baby, the stillborn. The child I had named. Molly Anne or Charles—those were our names for our unborn child. The child we never considered ever losing. It was only when John showed surprise at my wanting to put a name on the grave of an unbaptized fetus that I realized he didn't understand the depth of my loss.

"By the time they realized I would never dilate enough, it was too late. They cut me, but she was already dead, strangled. It was likely, they told me, that she wouldn't have survived anyway. She was too early. So that was that. Tough luck, try again. Except that John ran away. No. I don't mean that. He was shipped out before I got out of the hospital."

Joe snugged the afghan around me to warm my shivering.

"He came to see me, as he did every day just after breakfast. They gave him compassionate leave, and he had a few days home with me before going back to base. But then he'd gotten his orders. Joe, the grief was washed off his face by the excitement of going overseas. He couldn't even wait until I was discharged.

"I was still being sedated. I was groggy when he came in and told me. I don't recall the time between his telling me he had to go and his leaving. It seemed like minutes, although I know it was a couple of days. I don't even remember if we said we loved each other. It has been as if I lost them both.

"It was the expectations of other people which finally drove me here, where no one knew of my loss. At home they expected me to weep, then get over it. I've done neither."

"Not wept?"

"No."

"Why?"

"I wish I knew. I wish I could. It's as if some spigot is turned off too tight."

"Or maybe if you cry, you'll feel as though you *have* gotten over it."

I nodded. "Sometimes I feel as though I need to remember every detail, no matter how painful, in order to make her real. You see, otherwise I might convince myself it never happened, that she had never been. I don't want to do that."

"You'll never lose her entirely." Joe pressed a soft, comforting kiss on my forehead and stood up to leave, pausing a moment in the doorway. "And you haven't lost your husband. He will come home to you. There is no doubt in my mind."

AUGUST 22, 1944 I really don't blame Joe for telling Judy about the baby. At least he had the sense not to call her on the telephone. The party line is a notorious well for gossip. I didn't know he had spoken to her until she walked into my house this afternoon and put the kettle on. I was shelling peas at the kitchen table.

"Joe did the right thing telling me. You're not to get angry at him." She stood, hands on her hips, daring me to disagree. "He was concerned for you. I think you scared him a little, closing down like that. Of course, he would fall on that man's remedy of Scotch to cure you. Lucky he didn't kill you."

"Well, it got me past the worst." I got up and took down two teacups from the shelf. "The truth is, I'm glad he told you. I regret I haven't been more honest with you."

"Look, Vangie. We all have things bottled up inside which aren't always for other people's consumption. Don't waste time regretting not telling me. This is how you need to deal with your grief. I know. When Teddy died, I closed the door to his room and wouldn't let even Ted in there. I thought if I could keep it exactly as he had left it, he would somehow still be there. We all do inexplicable things to help ourselves get through. Then with John going missing, well, you don't have to say anything about that either. Unless—" and here she squeezed my elbow to better hold my eyes—"unless you need to. Then you mustn't hesitate."

Judy finished her tea in two quick swallows and went on her way. I waved to the departing car, then hunted down Joe Green.

"Mrs. Frick made me promise not to get mad at you."

Joe was on a ladder, replacing a hinge on the barn door. "Can you keep that promise?" He didn't look down as he asked his question, just kept turning the screwdriver.

"I really don't have a choice." The ladder wobbled a little. I stood at the bottom and lent my weight to hold it steady.

Done, he came down and took me by the shoulders. "Mrs. Worth, we always have choices. Are you angry with me or not?"

"No." I sighed. "No, I'm not angry with you, Joe."

TONIGHT we were able to pick up the classical station out of Boston clearly. They had a broadcast of Verdi's *Aida*. We took our coffee into the parlor. Joe sat beside me on the davenport. We listened, the music creating private imagery for us both.

"I've always loved that opera," I said.

"Yeah. I'm a big fan of my namesake's work."

When I gave him one of those perplexed looks he knows how to get out of me, he laughed. "Giuseppe Verdi. The Italian Joe Green." I responded with a playful poke in his ribs, and he got off the davenport to check on the girls.

I was still sitting there when he came back in. "Good night, Mrs. W.," he called from the kitchen. I didn't hear him move to his room, and I knew that he was waiting. I went to the Philco and shut it off, watching as the light from the tubes faded slowly away. Then I went into the dark kitchen, knowing he was still there.

It was as if we stood in a shimmering, beautiful bubble. We could only step to its center; if we backed away, the bubble would burst. So gently, honorably, we kissed good night.

I sit here now and write those words and tell myself it was a chaste kiss. A kiss between friends. Nothing more.

AUGUST 25, 1944 I fill my days with gardening. Weeding, harvesting. I boil and steam, cut and mash, and fill my preserve jars.

I've put up strawberry jam and blueberry preserves, pickles and relishes, stewed tomatoes and sauce. I've canned a cellarful. I'll give some to my friends at home, who still think I'm quite mad to be here playing at farming. I'll prove them wrong. Joe thinks I should enter some of my better stuff in the fair. Maybe I will.

He's frantically getting the rest of the barn roof shingled. The hurricane season is upon us. I can see him from my kitchen window, nailing course upon course of dark gray asphalt shingles.

In between shifts of preserves I went out this morning and handed him shingles. I could tell this was one of those days when his inner devil was plaguing him. Yesterday he had whistled in time with the hammering of the nails, sometimes forgetting himself and singing a line or two from some song or other. Today his shoulders were rounded, and he moved more slowly.

"Want some help?" I called from the ground.

He peeked over the edge of the roof at me and nodded. "What about your canning?"

"It can wait. You look like you could use company."

"Can't argue with that."

With Joe on his knees and me just to his left, handing him shingles, we sidled along the roofline in a bizarre line dance. The barn roof is gently pitched, so it isn't particularly tricky to stand on once you get yourself up the ladder. However, taken with the rhythm of the work, I got a little careless and almost lost my balance. Joe caught my leg, and I grabbed his shirt collar, hauling myself back.

"You saved my life." Even though I said it to be funny, it came out sounding sincere.

"And you saved mine."

We haven't repeated our good-night kiss. We carefully part company now.

JOE'S gone off to check on the Ruths. Ruth Banks fell yesterday and she's confined to the couch for a while. Ruthie Jones is such a helpless little thing that it seems prudent to check in on them once a day. "Here comes our boyfriend!" they chortle whenever Joe drives up. He must have been a good son, the way he treats them as if they are his maiden aunts. I send them some sweet pickles.

We claim to have found Ruthie's blanket in the woods and suggest that a mischievous dog has been the culprit. Isn't it fortunate there are no holes? I say it was filthy and that I washed it before bringing it back. No harm done. Their gratitude is embarrassing, and they mention it every time I see them. I have never lied well. I wonder why I feel like the guilty party. I'm just the accessory.

I've decided to enter my "New York Style" dills in the Great Harbor fair.

LABOR DAY, SEPTEMBER 4, 1944 Here I sit on a hot September Labor Day, glass of lemonade in my hand, journal on my lap. I linger in Hawke's Cove to imagine goals kept out of reach by the war. We live in the present; the future depends on too many variables. For the present I will keep cows and finish the garden off for the year. I'll cover my plot with seaweed to nurture this sandy soil for next year. That's as far ahead as I dare plan.

I won an Honorable Mention for my pickles. Joe encouraged me to try but then wouldn't come with me.

"You've got to come, Joe. It won't be any fun without you."

"You are too kind, but no. I don't like fairs."

"What don't you like about them?"

"Crowds."

"Oh." I got it then. It was the same reluctance he showed in going to Tylerville, until he was assured it was a backwater. Crowds. Crowds of soldiers and sailors.

While I digested all this, he watched me. He must have seen the doubts in my mind, because he touched my face. "I can't go."

"How long to do you think you can get away with never leaving this peninsula?"

"For the rest of my life." There was no joking lilt in those words. Only a calm resignation. Not unhappy. Simply fact.

SEPTEMBER 9, 1944 Through the post office windows I can see little brown cardboard squares like a tic-tac-toe board—the closed boxes of those who have gone home. I have never experienced this phenomenon before. As a girl, I always assumed that Hawke's Cove closed up after the summer folks leave, like school at the end of a term. But far from slowing down, it seems to abound in activity: potluck suppers for social and charitable reasons; the bridge club starts up again after a summer's respite. The Hawke's Cove Civil Defense is looking for members, and Joe joins. Twice a month he gets to make sure blackout curtains are pulled and headlights masked. I've taken up with Great Harbor's Red Cross chapter. I help put together ditty bags for servicemen and hand out juice and cookies at the blood drives.

The war goes on and on, a permanent fixture in our lives. There is no word on John. I tell myself that no news is good news.

SEPTEMBER 17, 1944 (4:30 A.M.) I heard Joe again in the night crying out, then making a weeping sound. Tonight I went down when the sound didn't stop. I was torn—should I wake him, or should I let him fight whatever devil plagues him in his sleep?

Then I heard him say my name. "Vangie." It was distinct, and I thought he must have woken and heard me.

"I'm here, Joe." The moon lay across his sleeping form, and I could see that I was mistaken. He opened his eyes to the sound of my voice. I looked at his confusion.

"What's the matter?" He moved to sit up.

"You were crying." I touched his cheek where I could see moisture reflected in the moonlight. "I came to wake you."

Joe looked at me in surprise. "I was dreaming."

"I know. Then I heard you say my name, and I thought you were awake." I sat beside him on the low squeaky cot. "Do you want to tell me about it? About your dream?"

He had rubbed away the telltale moisture with an embarrassed swipe at his eyes. "No. I don't think I can remember it."

"It helps sometimes, Joe. It helps to say them out loud."

"You've heard me before?"

I nodded. I felt a little like being caught out as a voyeur.

"I really don't remember it."

"Is it the same one every time?"

"I'm always falling into an abyss, reaching for someone I have no hope of grabbing. I pull my hand away empty. Then I scream."

It was chilly in his room. I must have shivered, because Joe put his arm around me. It would have been so easy to lie down next to him. Instead I stood up. "Good night, Joe."

"Good night, Mrs. W."

SEPTEMBER 23, 1944 The Ruths stopped by today with Ruth Banks's nineteen-year-old niece, Jean. She's a nurse cadet, training in Boston. Doing things most of us would be too squeamish to do. She told me that her patients are almost all men sent home from overseas to receive medical care. Her bravado weakened a little when I asked her whether all her men recovered.

"No. Some die despite our best efforts. Many others go to a rehab hospital. You know, amputees and paraplegics."

"So the men you see receive honorable discharges and go home when they leave the hospital?"

"Not always. Those whose injuries aren't maiming generally go back if they are listed as fit for duty."

"So even if John was found, if he was sound, he'd go back?"

"Umm. I don't know, Mrs. Worth. I don't know what they do with POWs."

"POW?" I hadn't thought that John might be held prisoner. Knowing what we do about Nazi camps, I felt a physical tightening around my heart. I have always pictured John simply separated from his men, making his way across France or wherever. I never thought he might be a captive. "I don't know that he's a POW. No one has said that. If he's a POW, wouldn't I be notified? Aren't POW names released to the Red Cross?"

"I don't know."

Joe came in just then, the screech of the screen door cutting off the conversation. Ruth Banks accepted his kiss on her wrinkled cheek. "Jean, let me introduce Joe Green."

Joe turned to shake Jean's hand. "Pleased to meet you. Your aunt's spoken of you often and with pride."

Jean looked up at Joe with an obvious coquettishness, which was quickly replaced by a look of recognition. "Don't I know you?"

Her slightly rude examination of his face washed the smile off Joe's face. "No, I don't think so."

"I do, though. In the hospital. Have you ever been in—"

Joe cut her off. "No. Never."

"I'm sure I've seen you." Jean was persistent, and I could see that this was a trait that probably served her well in her field but was quickly wearing thin in my kitchen. Both Ruths looked a little embarrassed.

Joe had turned his back and was washing his hands at the sink. "I can assure you we've never met before." He stuffed the hand towel over the drying bar and darted out of the kitchen.

With a stubborn tilt to her head, Jean kept at it. "I never forget a patient. I think I had him on the burn ward last year."

I remembered the shiny patches of pink on Joe's back and hands. "I think he would remember being in the hospital if he had been, Jean. You don't forget something like that. Besides, I'm certain he would remember you."

It came out more catty than I meant it, and they left shortly thereafter, warm tea still in the bottom of their cups.

OCTOBER 1, 1944 Joe and Ernie went fishing and brought home sixteen flounder. I took their picture with my Brownie, each holding an end of the string from which hang these ugly flat fish with both eyes on the same side of their heads.

I've been snapping pictures with abandon lately. I had forgotten that I brought the camera with me and only discovered it tucked on the shelf in my hall closet. I've taken pictures of my farm and the cows. I caught Joe out by the barn yesterday, surprising him into a self-conscious smile.

It's nice that Ernie and Joe have become chums. All of Ernie's pals are overseas or dead, and Joe has only me to keep him company otherwise. We had a fish fry tonight, just the three of us. There was so much fish left over that I sent Ernie home set for at least one more meal, for him and his mother, and he promised to deliver another plateful to the Ruths. My house still smells of fish, and I boil apple peelings and cinnamon.

OCTOBER 5, 1944 After lunch today we took a walk to the beach. The cows followed us as far as the pasture goes, then lowed gently as we moved out of sight and down the wooded path. The beach was quiet beside a calm sea. The fall sun struck sparkles in the deep blue water, and in the distance the horizon looked ruffled in that peculiar mirage that occurs when the sea and sky meet.

As Joe and I stood on the dune overlooking Bailey's Beach, a squadron of Hellcats, F6F fighter planes, flew overhead in a noisy display. Joe studied the squadron. He stared with such intensity that I touched his arm. He didn't seem aware of me or that I had touched him. He continued looking at the squadron until they flew out of sight. For the first time since I've known him, he allowed the unhappiness to show, which before I had seen only when he thought himself alone.

"Joe?"

"I'm sorry." Casting off the gloom with an observable effort, he smiled at me and walked toward the path.

"Joe, wait." I trotted to catch up with him. "It helps to talk. It helped me to tell you my story. About Molly."

"I asked you once not to ask me questions I could not answer. I will not put you in an indefensible position of knowing too much."

"I just want you to know that when you're ready, I'll listen. And there is nothing you can say which will make me think of you differently. Or feel differently."

"Mrs. Worth, there you are wrong."

"Joe. You've called me Vangie before."

"I called you from a dream. It was a dream."

We have skirted around each other all day. I went to a Red Cross meeting, and when I got home tonight, he had gone fishing. He still isn't back, and it's past eight.

OCTOBER 7, 1944 I biked to the post office this afternoon and saw two naval officers leaving Ernie's office, readjusting their caps to the specified angle. That reminded me that I wanted to invite Ernie and the Fricks to dinner on Saturday, so I headed across the street. The door to the police department office was wide-open, and I walked in. Ernie's back was to the door, and as I stepped into the small office, he covered his face in his hands.

"What's the matter, Ernie?"

"Oh, Vangie, I didn't hear you come in."

Ernie walked to his desk and fussed with some papers on it, dropping a file folder on top of a glossy photo. "So, what brings you here? Another unexplained theft?"

"No. A dinner invitation."

"Joe'll be there?"

"I expect so. Why?"

Ernie thumped his knuckles against the file folder. "You saw the navy in here?"

I nodded.

"They're looking for a deserter."

"Not Joe."

"Ruth Banks's niece claims to have seen the pilot of that missing Hellcat in your kitchen."

"Oh, Ernie."

"Vangie, you might mention to Joe that they were here."

Some instinct made me take Ernie's hand off the file folder, and I picked up the glossy studio photo of a naval officer that lay beneath it. A beardless Joe Green. I had to ask. "Ernie, would you have warned Joe yourself if I hadn't walked in here?

"I don't know." He didn't look at me.

I laid the photo back down on the desk.

Ernie laid the folder back on top of the photo. "No. I do know. I would have told him."

The two-mile bike ride never seemed so long. I felt as though I could have run faster. It was past five when I got home. No sign of navy jeeps in the drive. None had passed me. Either they believed Ernie or they were taking their time.

Joe was in the barn, mucking, and the practical side of me left him to finish the job while I threw Spam into a frying pan with left-over potatoes. If he had to go, he would go fed.

I called him in to eat before he began milking. I said nothing while he ate, only watched him until he realized that I wasn't eating. He looked into my face and read there the obvious worry.

"Vangie, what is it?"

"The navy is looking for you."

Joe carefully laid his knife and fork across his plate and went to rinse them off. "I'll be in the barn. The cows need milking."

"No!" The kitchen chair fell over in my haste to get to him. "Okay, you'll be in the barn. But Joe, you'll be in the whisky pit."

"Please, no more hiding. I'm tired."

"Please, Joe. Please. For me. I can't lose you too."

WE HAD to move Bessie to get Joe into the pit. As Joe eased himself in, I heard a car come into the yard. He reached up and touched my face. "You don't have to lie for me."

I took hold of the hand that touched my face and kissed his fingers. "Shut up and let me do this the way I want to."

I scattered a little straw over the plank cover as he lowered it. Then I went out to meet the M.P.s.

They were cordial enough for military police, calling me ma'am. My lies were believable. "My handyman left a few days ago. Said he wanted to move on. Didn't say where." They had me look at the photo. "Oh, no, that isn't my handyman. Joe's much older."

They seemed satisfied. Then one of them saw my clothesline. "If your handyman quit a while ago, whose clothes are those?"

"My husband's."

"And where is he?"

"I wish I knew. He's missing in action."

"I'm sorry, Mrs. Worth. I had no idea." To his credit, the young M.P. seemed genuinely sorry for his brash questioning.

The second, somewhat older, M.P. had no such compunction. "If your husband's overseas, why did you wash his clothes?"

"That, sir, is none of your business." Leaving them to think I had some war-wife fetish about my husband's clothing, I shook their hands and walked back into the house.

OCTOBER 10, 1944 I have spent the last forty-eight hours leaving Hawke's Cove. I am now hurtling back to Boston on the train from Great Harbor. My possessions are packed in my father's trunk. I will not be back anytime soon. I have not allowed myself to think, to feel. Wisdom would dictate that I not write down what has happened. But my heart demands that I do. For the second time in my life I feel the need to not let something get away from me.

As soon as the M.P.s left, I went into the barn and released Joe from the pit. He settled down to milk Bessie. I grabbed a pail and stool and went to work on Mom. For a long time the only sound was the dash of warm milk into our pails. I couldn't see Joe on the other side of the wall separating the stalls, but I could hear his sigh every time he stopped milking.

Finally, "My name is Spencer Buchanan."

I held still.

"I am a deserter."

I pressed my forehead against Mom's side and waited.

"When I crashed into Hawke's Cove, I thought that it was an act of divine retribution, that I was going to die. When I didn't, I realized that true divine retribution was in living."

"Retribution for what, Joe?"

He stood and brought his pail over to the worktable. "Murder."

I lifted my pail and brought it over to him. He poured out the milk from our buckets into the milk can.

"Joe, war isn't murder."

"I shot down my own man."

"Surely it was an accident."

"Yes. That's exactly what everyone said. The navy exonerated me. An unfortunate accident of war."

"But you're not satisfied with that?" I pulled myself up on the worktable and sat watching Joe pace back and forth.

"No. You see, the sin is that it meant nothing to me. I had become so used to war and death. I barely knew the kid. I couldn't even remember his name. Then I was shot down and sent stateside to heal. Jean Banks did nurse me, and I was deemed fit to return to active duty. After I had healed, they sent me to Great Harbor's naval air station to await new orders. I hadn't flown for a long time, so I took the Hellcat out to get some practice.

"It was only as I was back in the air again that the significance of my sin came to me. It wasn't in killing him; it was in forgetting him. When the Hellcat's engine seized, I thought, 'Aha! God has found me out for the sinner I am. Good. How can I live with myself, knowing how hard I've become, how little life means to me? I deserve to die.' Except that, in the end, I survived.

"When I crawled up onto the beach at the foot of your property, the only thing I was certain about was that I wasn't going back. I'd done my bit, and it had utterly corrupted me."

"Joe. You're one of the gentlest men I know. You were in a horrible situation—"

"Vangie, don't. You can't explain it away. Any more than you can explain wanting to put a headstone on your child's grave." He took my hands and gripped them until they hurt.

"Joe." I lifted my hands to his face, smoothing his hair away from his brow, needing to touch him.

He held my face in his hands. "Vangie, you're crying."

I wiped my cheeks in utter surprise. "So I am."

We both wept then. I wept for Molly and for John. I wept for this man, for who he had been as Spencer Buchanan and for the Joe Green of now. We wept for each other, and then we kissed, and it was like drinking passion. We clung together there in the soft warm light of the barn, and our clinging became love.

Not one word passed between us. The hay in the loft served as our couch, and afterward Joe covered us with one of the quilts from the trunk. We dozed, then woke, and made love again, this time lingering over it like an expensive meal.

Sometime around dawn I heard the cows shift restlessly in their stalls, waiting for Joe. I felt him leave our nest, stooping over me, carefully pulling the quilt up over my bare shoulders, whispering for me to stay put. I must have dozed again because suddenly he was back and beside me in the hay.

The third time we made love, the sun coming through the cracks in the loft doors brightened the hay into a yellow glow. I took in the deep blue color of his eyes, the pink scarring on his back, and breathed in his scent. Then he asked me, "Will you regret this?"

And I answered, "Never."

Joe went to move the cows from the little paddock next to the barn to the big pasture for the day. Dressed, I slipped down the ladder and heard Sylvester Feeney's truck outside. I bumped the barn door open with my shoulder to greet him, hoping the flush of inappropriate happiness wasn't too obvious.

It wasn't Sylvester, but two army officers who were getting out of a jeep. I stopped somewhere between the open barn door and them. I thought, army. Not navy. Would the army be looking for Joe too? They stepped toward me, hats under arms, and I knew that it wasn't about Joe they had come. "Mrs. Worth?"

They came toward me with the news that my husband had been found.

It IS hardest of all to write this. Joe vanished. He must have seen the soldiers. I ran into the barn to see if he'd slipped into the whisky hole, but it was empty. I called his name, and when he did not answer, I knew. I knew that the choice was taken from me. The decision to stay with Joe or to go to John. Joe had made my decision for me. An act of love. Throughout the last two days I have struggled to accept his gift. I am grateful and hurt. And angry. Angry that he assumed there was a decision to make.

I filled the last hours of my life in Hawke's Cove preparing to leave. I called Sylvester Feeney to tell him I was going home, to arrange for the sale of the girls.

I let myself be held by Judy, who wisely said nothing but made herself useful in getting the details of my departure worked out. She never asked about Joe, only said she'd make sure he was all right when he got back.

She simply knew he'd come back once I was gone.

I didn't, of course, tell her about us.

I slept only a little, listening for Joe to come back. Hearing only the bell buoy on Hawke's Shoals.

My LANDMARKS are beginning to appear as we speed along the track. I am almost home. My mother will meet me at the station and take me home to my empty flat. I'll wait for the phone call that will tell me my husband has arrived and where he is. I'll go to him then. I'll bring him home. We have another chance.

When I went to Hawke's Cove, I was desperately unhappy. My baby was dead, my husband gone, my future unimaginable. I went there to heal and to wait. Joe Green eased my waiting, affected my healing. He was my constant, my anchor. What I have had in Hawke's Cove will always be with me. As Molly will always be with me. As Joe Green will always be with me too.

Three

Vangie—1993

EVANGELINE Worth closed the black-and-white composition book and held it for a long time in her lap. She fished around in her cardigan pocket for a hanky and touched at the corners of her eyes. She remembered so distinctly the pull of that train as it left Great Harbor, the pull on her heart as she left Joe Green behind.

After a few minutes she got up. The reflected light of the lamp on her bureau wobbled as she pulled open her underwear drawer. Beneath the folded undergarments was a brown envelope, addressed to her and postmarked "Hawke's Cove, October 13, 1944." Inside the envelope was a handkerchief monogrammed SJB. Cached between the neat folds were two metal rectangles embossed with his name: Buchanan, Spencer J., and his numbers. His first letter and these dog tags had come in this envelope, and into it she had carefully hidden every one of his subsequent letters in their nearly fifty years' correspondence. In this way they had stayed alive to each other.

If you had been my wife, you would have gotten these at my death. You saved my life, but it is as Joe Green, not Spencer Buchanan I live.

Vangie went into the kitchen and heated water for tea. She hadn't read the early letters in a long time. She'd never read them boldly, like this, spread out on the kitchen table. These letters had been read slyly, sometimes one staying tucked in her pocket for hours before an opportunity to savor it arrived. It was a dangerous game they played. A plain white envelope dropping through the mail slot onto the floor along with bills and magazines.

She could only picture Joe as she had known him; she couldn't remember John as he had been. The inexorable progression from youth to age had erased each preceding stage as completely as an eraser blurs a chalk line. When she thought of her husband now, she saw only the old man he'd become.

It was the last good reason never to see Joe again. Without the blindness of daily contact, their individual changes would be a shock. She still imagined dark hair the color of maple syrup; perhaps he still envisioned auburn curls loosened from her old-fashioned braid.

That one passionate night would simply have faded into a sweet memory had he not sent that first letter. Their correspondence had kept love alive even as the passion of the early letters, like the passion of early love, evolved into loving devotion.

She let the tea bag steep as she lifted the first letter from the pile on the table.

Charlie

"MOM, do you think I could talk with your friend Judy?"

"Charlie, Judy's been in a retirement home for two years. You remember, I told you she moved in after Ted passed away. I'm not sure how she is." Vangie tapped her temple.

Charlie shrugged. There was so much he didn't pay attention to as his mother nattered on about her elderly friends, people he didn't know. "Well, I need to speak with folks who'd have been there."

Charlie noticed that his father's head jerked a little, as if John was waking from a nap. He patted his father's arm. "How about that guy, the policeman."

"Ernie spends winters in Florida. Doesn't come back till May."

John Worth rolled his head a little to the left. Vangie daintily wiped his chin with a tissue and spooned another mouthful of mashed peas toward him. Sometimes she had to take his chin as you would a reluctant baby. This time he opened up easily.

"Well, how about that farmer— What was his name? Joe?"

Vangie was beginning to regret ever telling Charlie about her friends in Hawke's Cove. "Charlie, drop it for now. We'll talk about it later."

"Mom, why don't you come with me?"

Vangie held the spoon in mid-flight toward John's closed mouth. She let the thought ripple through her like a chill. Then, "I can't leave your father." She lowered the spoon. "Can I, John?"

Charlie was always amazed at his mother's tenacity. She insisted that there was nothing wrong with his father's mind, that the stroke had affected only his body. If you wanted to get Vangie Worth's dander up, talk in front of John as if he weren't there.

Charlie loved his father but had a hard time keeping up both ends of a conversation and rarely visited unless his mother was there. "Tell your dad about your trip, your story, your friends. . . ." Charlie would start a monologue, looking at John Worth, at his father's unsteady head and dangling hands, but telling his anecdotes to his mother. Sometimes he would sit in his car in the parking lot of St. Elizabeth's Home and force recollections of his father to mind so that he would remember how his father had been before and thus open up a little with him as he was now.

A late-in-life son, he had still been taught the important boy things by his dad. How to pitch a knuckleball, how to be a good Red Sox fan, how to drive. How to be a decent man. John Worth may have been strict, but he was quick to praise and slow to anger. Sometimes Charlie reviewed this litany as he climbed the steps of the building, making himself be a good son.

"Mom, it'll only be a couple of days. That's why he's here. To give you a break."

"Charlie. You know better than to talk like that. I don't need a break, and I don't need to go to Hawke's Cove."

John's good left hand suddenly flew up, striking the edge of the tray where it stuck out over the table attached to his chair. The remnants of lunch splattered Vangie.

He had meant to touch her.

John—1993

IT WAS Hawke's Cove that came between us.

My fault really. I couldn't hide my disdain at the sight of the ugly farmhouse. For all of Evangeline's rapture about the beauty of the place, what she showed me was a huge disappointment. Cedar shingles so old they looked like loose teeth clinging to the sides. The trim paint had long ago faded. No gutters, no amenities. Beyond it the decrepit barn, sagging on a misaligned rock foundation.

I'd reserve judgment until we got inside. Who knew? Maybe it had a charming interior.

It was neat and clean inside, but this house had never qualified as charming in its life. Wallpaper of an insignificant yellow in the kitchen, a peculiar blue on the walls in the room Evangeline quaintly referred to as the parlor.

Evangeline looked at me. I pulled on a smile, but those perceptive green eyes had seen my distaste. "It's a bit different than I had imagined." Wrong words. I was still newly wed enough to want to please her, so I grinned. "It's great, Ev. Simplicity itself."

"John. Sweetheart. You don't have to love it right away." She kissed me. "Just eventually."

Later, sitting in the inefficient kitchen as Evangeline fried some chicken in a deep cast-iron pan, I sketched. Take out the wall here, replace the huge combination range with a modern electric stove and the soapstone sink with a real countertop and a double-sink unit, maybe bump out an ell as a breakfast nook. My doodling caught Evangeline's eye, and she didn't smile.

"I like it the way it is."

"Just some thoughts on paper, darling. It's what I do."

"It's mine. You can't change it."

I folded the paper and put it aside. When I took out the trash, I saw it crumpled up and lying on top.

EVANGELINE Bailey had caught my eye for the first time on the arm of another boy. I'll never forget it. She was dressed for the Fall Cotillion in a stunning pale green dress. She reminded me of Vivien Leigh, auburn hair rolled under.

She was a senior at Smith, majoring in English literature; I, a graduate student at Harvard, in my last year of architectural school. The Fall Cotillion was held at the Tremont hotel, and in those days anyone who could rustle up a tux attended this first major intercollegiate social event of the year.

As soon as I could, I tapped Evangeline's partner's shoulder. He was gracious, affecting a faux European bow as I took his girl's hand. "John Worth," I said. I felt myself bow slightly and was immediately embarrassed at the imitation.

"Evangeline Bailey." She curtsied in neatly playful response, and my embarrassment faded.

I liked the feel of her in my hands. She was a good dancer. I greedily asked for the next dance. She said yes. I asked if I might write to her. She said yes. I let go of her at the end of the evening and asked if I might kiss her. And she said yes.

EVANGELINE and I corresponded. Her letters were full of snippets of her poetry. I complained she had never sent me a whole poem, but she replied that she hadn't yet finished one worth reading.

It was our luck to have been young adults in the midst of the Depression. A generation before us had enjoyed easy privilege, riding on a false and treacherous wave. We were more circumspect, building up a lifelong habit of denial and economy. At school we worked to receive scholarships. Many of us worked hard at after-hours jobs to keep our places at college. When I asked Evangeline if I could call her, I was already toting up how much I would need to earn beyond my weekly salary, as gofer in a local architectural firm, to afford a long-distance call.

The next time I was able to see her was just after the semester break. The dawning of 1935 seemed to be a heralding of a new hope in a hopeless world. Although the European tribulations distracted us, I paid them little mind beyond their use as a political or philosophical topic during late-night conversations with my fellows. We all sounded as if we were remote from it, as we were. None of us were yet soldiers. I paid more attention to the WPA, wondering if my untried talents would fit in there.

In Northampton, Evangeline worked hard on writing the perfect poem. We wrote to each other almost daily, and on paper our nascent passion was flourishing. I went up again late in February. I had saved enough to spend the night in a cheap rooming house. Now we had the whole weekend to see if this correspondence of ours was translatable into conversation and more.

THE air was cold but dry, the day windless, so we walked out of doors for hours, her arm linked through mine. She wore a little beret, and I kidded her that she looked like a little French girl.

"Nonsense. I've never even been to France. I just happen to like this hat." She skipped ahead of me on the sidewalk. All day long each new expression charmed me, and I fought not to reach for her. Finally she slipped her arm from mine and took my hand in new intimacy. "Show me your room," she said.

"I don't think that would be a good idea."

"The sitting room in my dorm isn't private. And I'm cold!"

She wanted privacy. Against my better judgment and with a conspicuously beating heart, I led the way.

I felt like a thief, letting us into the musty hallway. I had been cautioned about guests, but it was midday and no one was home. I gestured to the sitting room with its overstuffed Victorian furniture and heavy claw-footed tables. Evangeline shook her head no. She did not touch my hand again as we crept up the stairs.

In the room I pressed the door shut until I heard the latch click, then offered the single straight-backed chair to her, but Evangeline sat on the bed. I sat on the chair, but after a few minutes I moved to sit beside her on the bed.

We were young. We were full of ourselves. We leaned into each other and kissed. Then kissed some more. I told myself she couldn't possibly know what such kissing was doing to me. Finally I pulled away. "We should go before the landlady gets home."

I know my voice was husky, but I was surprised when she echoed me in a similarly thickened voice. "Yes, we should go."

It would have been the moment to abandon all ethics, to cave in to a mutual passion that seemed less and less sinful as the moments went on. But we didn't give in. I didn't press her, because I knew right then that I wanted her as my wife. She needed to want me as a husband.

Once the idea of marrying Evangeline got into my head, every thought centered on seeing her, being with her. I had ambition. I had a reasonably certain future as an architect. Providing I got a job soon, as a junior draftsman, I could support us comfortably enough. We would live in romantic poverty as I rose in the ranks and Evangeline wrote poems. In five years we'd have a home, children. Oh, I had it all mapped out. An affliction of my profession, drawing out plans.

I knew that she had feelings for me. Evangeline was affectionate, even passionate. She never mentioned other boys.

ALL the way on the train to Northampton I kept one hand on the letter tucked into my pocket. It was mid-May, the end of term. Evangeline would graduate the next Sunday, and I would receive my master's at Harvard's commencement on the same day.

This trip to see her was unexpected. We had planned to see each other in Boston the week after our respective ceremonies. But now the whole world seemed to open to me like the pages of a book to which I knew the ending. I had called and told Evangeline to meet me at the station and be wearing her best dress.

I saw her from the train window as it pulled into the station. Just as the first time I'd seen her, she was wearing green. A pale blue-green dress with a belted waist showing off her figure. The watery color set off her red-brown hair, and I thought she looked like a Monet. She saw me through the gritty window and waved.

"I was so surprised to hear from you. Is everything all right?"

I kissed her a long time in greeting, holding her against me.

"Couldn't be better." I fought not to blurt out my good news. "I'm taking you to dinner."

I waited until the fresh strawberries and cream had been set before us. "Give me both your hands."

I gathered her two hands together and leaned forward. "I've been offered an entry-level position at Darling and Geer."

She smiled broadly, but I could see she didn't understand what this meant for her.

"It's entry level, as I say, but I'm guaranteed to rise quickly." My words were coming out more quickly than I had rehearsed, so I pulled the formal letter out of my breast pocket and handed it to her. I wanted her to read it for herself.

She smiled again and handed it back to me. "I am so happy for you. It sounds exactly like what you wanted. Good for you!"

"Good for us."

"Us?"

I still held her left hand. "Marry me, Evangeline."

There are so many imperfect moments in our lives. Moments that we edit to convince ourselves that they were perfect. This memory has never needed any polishing. It was perfect. Evangeline gave me both hands. And said yes. "Are you certain, John?"

"You are the only woman I have ever loved. I can't imagine life without you." The words flew out of my mouth like those of a dime novel character's. But I would never take them back. They were then, and now, the truest words I have ever spoken.

THE first time Hawke's Cove came between us was almost immediately after my proposal. It seemed that she planned to spend the summer there, with her doddery Gran and younger cousins, as she had always done. It took some persuading to convince her we needed to plan a wedding. I didn't want to wait until fall.

"John, I told you I always spend summers at Hawke's Cove."

"Well, now I'm going to be in Boston, starting a new job. I need you with me." I played the pathetic lover card. "I'll miss you too much to do a good job. Don't you want to be with me?"

"Of course I do. Why don't you come weekends?"

"I can't afford to do that. Not yet." In my mind Hawke's Cove seemed like a likely summer resort for an established architect, not a dogsbody like me.

In the end, we compromised. She went for two weeks in July. I avoided going at all.

We married in January of 1936, a beautiful winter wedding, where I met her grandmother for the first time. Florence Bailey was still pretty energetic at that time. She pulled me down into a headlock of an embrace. "You treat my granddaughter well, young man. She deserves it." I assured her that it was my only goal.

Evangeline sneaked away for a week's visit to Hawke's Cove that following summer, but did not go again. Her grandmother suffered a stroke just before Easter 1937. The family moved her to Boston to live out her days with them. Then, in 1939, she passed away.

When she left the farm to my wife, I was a little excited. I expected something with airy ceilings and wraparound porches. When I finally saw the place, I understood why Evangeline's cousins hadn't protested. Who in their right mind would want to take possession of a charmless, antique wreck of a farmhouse?

IT SEEMS AS THOUGH THE progression toward war shadowed my progression toward success. I got my first big promotion, and Hitler invaded Czechoslovakia. Evangeline published her first poem, and the Nazi war machine moved inexorably forward. Paris was invaded, and I received an important design assignment. I was making good money. Evangeline was happy taking graduate courses at Wellesley and being a teaching assistant in modern poetry. The Japanese bombed Pearl Harbor, and I signed up.

Despite the horror of the world situation, Evangeline and I managed to have five happy years. Two or three times in those years I acquiesced and went with her to Hawke's Cove. I tried hard to like it, but I don't swim and hate sitting on a hot beach. But it was the house I most despised. Evangeline was stubborn about it, belligerent almost in her refusal to have me do something with it. However, soon enough we were distracted by the war.

By some twist of military planning I spent the first two years of the war close enough to home to make good use of weekend passes. With the draining away of young men into the war, opportunities opened up for Evangeline, and she took a teaching position as assistant professor of poetry at Northeastern University.

In June of 1943 I got an unexpected leave. Over the past few months I'd been thinking about starting a family. We'd touched on the subject once or twice. Evangeline wasn't ready the first time I mentioned it; she was finishing up her graduate work. The second time, just not interested. "Not yet, John. Not yet." That was eighteen months before, and now, despite her career and her success at placing poetry in literary journals, I thought the time was right.

It was inevitable that I'd be shipped overseas. It was possible, perhaps probable, that I'd be killed. I could leave Evangeline a widow, or a widowed mother. When I asked myself which was better, I came up with mother. At least she would have some part of me to hold. Besides, what woman doesn't want to be a mother?

I surprised Evangeline by coming home, and was surprised in turn to find her packing for Hawke's Cove.

"Sweetheart, I told you I was going to the farm to meet my cousin Fran. We've been planning it for a year."

"Of course. I shouldn't have bothered with getting leave."

"Oh, John. Don't be a child. You'll come, of course." Evangeline pulled my dresser drawers open and began taking out my casual civilian clothes—dungarees, a couple of flannel shirts, and my rarely wet bathing suit. "John, this will be great. You remember Fran. You liked her very much when you met her at the wedding. She's only east for a week before heading back to California."

I swallowed my annoyance and smiled at her. Giving in graciously on this would earn me consideration when I offered her my own wish.

THE farmhouse was no more charming to me this time than it had been in the past. It had been a rainy spring, and the feeling of damp was pervasive. Fran would join us the next day.

"But for now I have you to myself!" I reached across the bed in her grandmother's room to snag her and pull her down. We wrestled until we broke apart in laughter. "Let's make a baby," I said before I could govern my mouth. I had thought to broach the subject in the car on the long drive but lost my nerve. Somehow I believed that the whole subject was a woman's province.

"What?" Evangeline sat up. "A baby? Why now?" She got off the bed and walked to her grandmother's vanity table.

"Ev, we've been married seven years; we're not getting any younger. I don't want to be too old to play baseball with my son." I began to list the reasons. Even as I did, I could see the debate in her eyes. Why now? Why during this war when anything could happen?

So I told her. "If anything happens to me, I want to know you've got something of our marriage besides memories." I took the brush out of her hand and stroked her hair the way she liked me to. "Is it so wrong to want to leave you with my child?"

She didn't answer with words, only a little sound that might have been acquiescence. Or defeat. I lifted her from the boudoir chair and carried her to the bed.

As I had hoped, once she was pregnant, Evangeline embraced the idea.

I never loved her so much as when she was pregnant. Other

men's wives looked like whales; mine was graceful and blooming. I came home as often as possible, always amazed at the ensuing changes week to week.

Our baby was due in March. We lost her in December. Evangeline blamed herself, but of course I didn't. I'm not sure I convinced her of that, that in no way did I think her responsible.

It is all a blur to me. The doctor coming to me in the waiting room. Evangeline was so doped up I'm not sure she understood that I had received my orders to go. She lay there, pale against the pillow.

"Evangeline, I got my orders. I have to go before you're released. I wish I could go home with you, but I can't." She looked at me with unfocused eyes, and as I leaned over to kiss her forehead, I prayed then and there that I be returned to her soon.

I know I angered her when I questioned the placement of a headstone with a child's name on it. It just didn't seem right. That I'd had to have that conversation in a censored letter made it seem all the more harsh, I know. Our letters in those first few weeks were terse, as if we'd never written to each other before. I suppose it was understandable; we hadn't had time to grieve together. How do you grieve on paper? I thought it best we simply get on with getting over it. No sense in bringing it up every letter.

I WAS one of the survivors of the ill-fated glider drop. Assigned to a battalion making its way across France, I was sent with ten others to reconnoiter a village. I was the lieutenant, the one responsible for carrying out the mission.

I have not looked back on what happened in almost half a century. But it doesn't fade, the memory. The ambush, the sight of my men shattered in front of me. The sound of their grunts as bullets tore through their bellies. I found cover enough to return fire. It was the first time I had fired my weapon at a human being.

I fired again and again. A kind of tunnel vision afflicted me, and the only thing I was aware of was the crowns of their helmets barely visible over the burrow I had somehow not seen as we walked upright through the fields toward the village, as if we had been tourists, not soldiers. There were two of us left of the ten, me and a boy who hunkered down behind me, sharing the cover of rock and brush. He fired his rifle over my shoulder, so close to my ear that it has had ringing in it ever since. Then he stopped firing and slowly sank into the fetal position against his mortal wound. I stopped firing long enough to hear German voices all around me. I put my hands in the air and gave up. I gave up because I wanted to survive to go home to Evangeline.

The memories all blur into one image, that of walking. For days, weeks, we walked, my captors and I. Through fields and burned-out farms, fording rivers and beating our way through old-growth forest. Eventually we joined a battalion, and I was added to a group of Americans headed for a POW camp. We were loaded into a canvas-enclosed truck—tightly packed, stinking, nervous. Mostly silent. I entertained myself throughout the interminable ride with thoughts of Evangeline. We were in one of three trucks, a small convoy of prisoners. Every now and then we could hear the drone of airplanes and the thud of bombs. Closer, the sound of shelling. Just before dawn the truck in front of ours was hit by a shell. The remaining two trucks skirted the smoking remains and sped down the road. Through the slits in the canvas we could see the burning wreckage and hear the cries of the dying Americans.

A big redheaded private sitting next to me began to rock. He repeated over and over, "I want to go home." The man on his other side quietly put an arm around the big soldier's shoulders. "I want to go home too, sonny. We will. You just bet we will."

The next day we were finally allowed out of the trucks. A POW camp had been arranged at the site of a bombed-out factory. There might have been a hundred of us. Food was sparse and unpalatable. I ate because I would die otherwise, and I was determined not to do that. I consoled myself with the thought that Evangeline would come to know what had happened to me. Perhaps we could even get letters to each other. If the Germans would give me a piece of paper, I would write and tell her how much I love her, how thoughts of her had kept me alive. How we would try again for a baby. That, if she really wanted to, we could spend time in Hawke's Cove. I kept my sanity by formulating plans for our future.

THE RUMOR WENT THROUGH the makeshift barracks, unstoppable. American forces were nearby. They just had to find us. Someone who spoke a little high school German had heard. Indeed, the Nazis seemed anxious. More guards were on than normal. We'd been in the prison for over two months, and even the big redheaded private looked fragile. None of us had the strength to walk the length of the building without sitting down to rest halfway.

After a day of listening to the shells exploding in the near distance, we began to expect our Nazi guards would execute us in preparation for abandoning the prison. Instead they herded us into an interior room. We barely fit. Then they sealed the metal door and left us. I don't know how long we stood there, no light at all, trapped in the small room, listening to the sound of bombing around us and the soft whimpering of grown men beside us. We stood for days. Some died and, packed as we were, did not fall.

Asleep and awake, I thought of Evangeline, promising her I would not die. That I would come home.

I DID come home. Emotionally wounded but grateful. The Allies came and opened the door. I had survived, and the only thing I wanted was to go home and begin again with Evangeline.

Except that she was different. Somehow, in some subtle way, my wife had grown away from me. Not cold or distant or unloving. Simply slightly different.

We tried hard to put our war years behind us. I could not speak of what I had seen, and Evangeline did not speak often of what she had, except in the most anecdotal and mild way. I knew she had bought three cows; I knew that she had won a ribbon for her preserves. She spoke of playing cards with the Fricks, people who remained in our lives via Christmas cards and occasional visits to Boston. I asked for little else from her. I suppose, in some ways, I discouraged her.

I was plagued for a long time with a deep sadness that stalled my ability to keep moving. So unlike myself. Before the war and, especially, after it I was driven to achieve my goals. So when I felt the walls close in on me, I turned snappish at my wife. Evangeline would ask me to tell her what was bothering me. "It helps, to speak about it, John. I know. When I could finally speak of the baby to"—she took a swallow's worth of hesitation—"to Judy, I felt better. Not less sad, just better for having said her name out loud."

"Darling, there is nothing to discuss. You know that. I would prefer it if we never spoke of any of it." I meant both our experiences. We shoved the war into a box and went on with our lives.

We were fully engaged in pulling our lives back together in those first couple of years. I was doing well at the firm; Evangeline was working on her dissertation. We wanted to try for another child.

We had Julie in 1947, followed closely by Amanda in 1949. In 1954 I decided to take the plunge into my own firm. In all that time Evangeline hadn't spoken of going to Hawke's Cove. I diligently paid the taxes on the property, but not once did she suggest we spend any time there. So it seemed a brilliant idea to sell the farm and use the proceeds as seed money to strike out on my own.

"Sell it? My grandmother's farm?" Evangeline was four months pregnant with the surprise of our midlife, Charlie. "I don't know, John. Why not just mortgage the property?"

"Ev, we haven't been there since the war. It would be far better to convert it into cash. I have this perfect opportunity to enter into a business debt free. We never use the place; it's probably tumbled to the ground by now. Put sentimentality aside, Evangeline."

If I expected her to argue, she didn't. Neither did she smile. I had won my point, but I never knew at what cost.

If perfect happiness eluded us, we had enough of imperfect happiness. It all went by so fast. The business was everything I hoped for, except that it was all consuming. Every day was a balancing act between clients, subordinates, and family. Too often family lost out. If Evangeline and I never recaptured the closeness of our days before the war, I could only blame myself for being a harder, less fun-loving man, preoccupied with his career. I wonder if the war changed me, or was I always destined to be so dour?

I would watch my children playing hopscotch in the driveway. How often did I watch Evangeline jump from block to block with her arms straight out from her sides and the girls teasing her about stepping on a line. I watched them. It never occurred to me to join them.

"IT'S IN THE TOP DESK DRAWER, left side." Evangeline was in the kitchen, phone to her ear, shouting at me to pull a manuscript out of her private desk. Her editor was on the phone. I remember everything about that moment. How the October sunlight was golden through the last of the maple leaves in the yard in Cambridge. How I missed Julie, off on her school trip. I could hear Amanda's music on the record player, a young Elvis Presley.

"Honey, can you get it for me or talk to Meagan while I find it?"

"I'm looking. . . ." I rooted around in the desk drawer. She had said left drawer. I was certain she had said left. I closed my hand on a photograph. A young, handsome, and bearded man dressed in clothes I remember owning. I recognized the barn as the one at Hawke's Cove. The man was looking at the camera with a mixture of surprise and pleasure at being photographed. I flipped the photograph over. "Joe Green October '44." I closed the left-hand desk drawer and opened the middle one, where the manuscript lay.

I handed Evangeline the manuscript pages, and she bent over the counter, phone under her chin. She'd already published one volume of poems, and this was to be her second.

Rootless, I walked upstairs. I could hear Evangeline's good-natured laughter as she worked with her editor.

What good would it have done to hand the snapshot to her and say, "And who is this and why do you have this in your most private drawer? Who is Joe Green, and why does he look at the photographer with such love?" What good would it have done? It explained a little the thin wall between us that had been there since she put her arms around me in the VA hospital. It explained a little her acquiescing so easily to selling the farm. I knew that I should be happy about that, as if there had been some competition I had won.

I put the photograph back in Evangeline's drawer.

MY DEAR wife of fifty-seven years has just left me sitting here, fed and wiped and remembering. When she mentioned that place, Hawke's Cove, I saw the look on her face. One instant of sweet temptation.

It was Hawke's Cove that came between us.

Four

Charlie

As IT turned out, the Clintons had decided on Martha's Vineyard, and the advance teams quickly deserted Great Harbor and dashed all hopes of booming tourism for the little towns in the area. Thus it was with no trouble at all that Charlie booked himself a room at the Seaview Bed and Breakfast in Hawke's Cove.

He followed the owner up the narrow and steep stairs to the front bedroom.

"The best part of this room is this." Mrs. Smith threw open the French doors, which led out onto a tiny balcony.

After his hostess left the room, Charlie went out on the balcony and was swept away by the view.

The Seaview was well named, and the whole of the cove was laid out in front of him, shimmering in the late spring afternoon. A single sail was etched against the horizon, then disappeared over it as if Columbus had been wrong. Beneath Charlie the beach road followed the curve of the bay, defended by the seawall that held back the threat of erosion. Charlie thought how spectacular a storm would be, beating the water over the top of that wall, and he could imagine how impressive the sound of the surf.

He shook himself out of his reverie and went back inside to change into jeans and polo shirt. Afterward he fished out his notebook and smiled in satisfaction. It had taken only three phone calls to get information about the missing pilot. Spencer Buchanan had been a twenty-nine-year-old navy pilot who had been sent home after being wounded in the Pacific. He'd been one day away from returning to active duty. Thirty-nine kills to his credit. Looking at the war through the eyes of someone who had been too young for Vietnam but old enough to watch television news, Charlie could imagine that this Buchanan guy might have gone AWOL with good reason. Thirty-nine kills. Maybe he figured he'd done his share.

Charlie did the math on the back of the notebook. If the guy bailed out and came ashore, today he'd be almost eighty, or dead.

He just needed proof that Spencer Buchanan had indeed died. Or had not. In the first instance, he'd write an oh-what-a-pity-prime-of-life kind of story. If it went the other way, well, he'd figure out how to address that unlikely scenario should it arise. Charlie flipped the notebook onto the bed. Enough story. There must be someplace close by to get a decent cup of coffee.

He hooked a left off the porch of the Seaview and headed toward the harbor. Two commercial fishing boats were tied up to the pier, and Charlie could see the salvaged Hellcat floating on a barge next to them.

The old travel writer in him reared up as he wandered along the seafront. His mother's stories had centered so often on the farm that he'd never imagined the beauty of Hawke's Cove's waterfront. Here were buildings not only unchanged since the nineteenth century but, even better, ungentrified. He liked the slightly run-down look of the waterfront's working marina. Cracked pavement, not cobblestones, meandered between the lanes coming up from the harbor and onto the main street.

He stopped at Linda's Restaurant to get a coffee to go. Only a few patrons sat at the counter. Grizzled old men in work clothes. The day's paper was broken into segments and spread down the length of the counter; wordlessly they swapped sections. Charlie leaned against the counter casually while waiting for his coffee.

"How're the Red Sox doing?" he asked the man holding the Sports section.

"Good enough for spring training."

That seemed to close the traditional masculine conversational gambit, so Charlie opened his other one. "Interesting about that Hellcat, isn't it?"

The man nodded and went back to his reading. Charlie had just about written off getting any more response when the man said, "I remember when it went down. I was a boy, but I went out lookin' fer it with my uncle on his lobster boat."

Charlie sat on the stool beside his new friend. "What became of the pilot? Did they ever find him?"

"Dunt know. Dead acourse. Sunderland boys found his life raft floating empty."

"About the time the pilot crashed, did anyone show up here? I mean, did any stranger show up and stay?"

"We always had a lot of strangers show up. Some left, some stayed." He looked at Charlie. "Still do."

"Well, I'm doing a story on the Hellcat. Kind of a human-interest angle. What if the guy came ashore and stayed? Made a life."

Charlie's new friend chuckled. All down the counter the men laughed. Sitting on the end stool, though, one man wasn't laughing. A pair of blue eyes studied Charlie. "What's your name?"

"Charlie Worth."

"Well, Charlie Worth, it makes an interesting story." The blue-eyed man got up and walked toward the men's room. As he passed by, he clapped Charlie on the shoulder. "Good luck with it."

CHARLIE walked across the street from the restaurant and sat on a bench to drink his coffee and think out his next move. As he did, a blue Mazda pulled up in front of Linda's Restaurant. A tall, slim woman got out, and Charlie admired her over the rim of his cup. Dressed in city chic, she wore her dark hair in a French braid. He couldn't tell how old she was from that distance—thirty or forty. A woman, not a girl. She went into the restaurant, and Charlie was tempted to go back in. Before he could talk himself into it, the door opened and she came out with the blue-eyed man who'd asked his name. They looked at Charlie as they stood beside the car, their equal movements defining them as father and daughter. Then in an identical manner they both waved a greeting toward him. Taken by surprise, Charlie raised his hand in self-conscious response.

CHARLIE got up earlier on Saturday morning than he had for years. Waiting for breakfast, he settled into the B and B's porch rocker with a cup of coffee and the paper and squinted against the rising sun breaking into shards against the choppy cove. At this hour the only traffic along the roadway that separated the B and B from the seawall was the occasional pickup truck. A dark spot in the sky caught his eye. An osprey working the shoreline rose straight up, beating his wings like a swimmer treading water.

Distracted away from the paper, Charlie gave up and simply enjoyed the view. It puzzled him—why hadn't his family ever come here? He knew that his parents had sold the farm before he was born. Still, they could have come and stayed in a rooming house. He shook his head against the thought; he could not picture his father in a rooming house under any circumstance. But Charlie knew that although his mother had never come back to Hawke's Cove, the place lived on in her psyche.

The smell of bacon set Charlie's stomach juices flowing, and he stood up to go back in, but the sight of a jogger running at a decent clip along the seawall made him pause. The jogger began to slow as she saw him on the porch. He smiled as he recognized the woman with the blue Mazda. "Morning!" he called out.

"Nice one," she responded. Then, to his surprise, she paused on top of the seawall, still running in place. "You're the columnist Charlie Worth, aren't you?"

It didn't completely surprise him to be recognized. He'd had his picture beside his column now for a couple of years. "Yeah, that's right. You've read my stuff?"

"Nope." Her braid swished from side to side as she kept running in place. "I've read your mother's." Then she was back in forward motion, leaving only the impression of an encounter behind her.

AFTER breakfast Charlie went down to the dock where the barge loaded with the hulk of the F6F Hellcat was tied up. The harbormaster, Steve West, sat in an office stuck out on the end of the pier. Charlie's sudden appearance at that office's door was not unexpected. Since the Hellcat had been raised, there had been a lot of faces peeking in, curious about this artifact from a time long gone.

"Can I ask you a few questions?" Charlie introduced himself to Steve and then jumped into his prepared list of questions. "When they raised the plane, did they find any remains of the pilot?"

"Nope. No sign of anybody."

"Sharks get him?"

Steve chuckled. "Maybe. Though there aren't too many man-eaters in these waters. I think he just went the way of so many lost seamen. Sea doesn't always give up the bodies. Just happens."

"So you think he just got tired and floated away?"

"Be my guess."

Charlie leaned against the doorjamb of the tiny ten-by-ten office. "Can I show you a picture?"

Steve reached for the glossy military photo. "So what was the guy's name?"

"Spencer Buchanan."

"And you think maybe he's still alive? Living here?"

"That's the line I'm taking." Charlie let Steve hang on to the picture for another minute before asking, "Any ideas?"

Steve shrugged. "Well, not really."

"Are you sure?" Charlie had detected a little hesitation.

"He doesn't look like any old guy I know, but he resembles a guy I grew up with who was killed in Vietnam. Scott Green."

Charlie wrote the name on his pad. "One more question. Has anyone been by to see the Hellcat who's been particularly interested in looking at it?"

Steve laughed outright. "Yeah, every man who ever dreamed about flying and every small boy who makes model airplanes."

"Okay. Has there been anyone clearly not interested?"

"Well, probably the only old-timer who hasn't shown up is Joe Green. Scott's dad."

Maggie

MAGGIE Green finished signing checks, still unused to stopping at the *n* and not continuing on with the hyphen, then "Shofsky," as she had done for six years. When she had finally convinced Ethan that theirs was not a successful marriage, he had come back with the accusation that she had been the uncommitted one, not even taking his name completely. Maggie shook that memory out of her thoughts and stacked the bills neatly to go to the post office.

She could hear her father in the kitchen, on the phone with Ernest Dubee in Florida. Every year Ernie went to Key West, and every year he invited Dad to go. He always asked and Dad always said no. Dad would have been hurt not to be asked, and Ernie would have collapsed from the shock if Joe Green had ever said yes.

Thank God he hadn't gone. It had been so wonderful to come

home when things had gotten ugly with Ethan. Her parents had separated several years after Scott died. Her mother had begged Joe to leave Hawke's Cove. She couldn't stand being in such a small place where everyone knew her pain. Her emotional pain eventually became physical pain, and she slid into a hypochondriacal maelstrom out of which she now tormented her second husband. Maggie could take her mother only in small doses, and although Denise lived much nearer Boston, Maggie fled to Hawke's Cove and Joe. There they were, both marriage failures, or as she sometimes kidded, matrimonially challenged.

"Great. We'll see you when you get home." Joe hung up the kitchen phone and began to make a pot of coffee.

"So Uncle Ernie is on his way home?"

"Yup. Doesn't seem possible another winter's gone. Maybe I'll go with him next year."

"Right. And I'll win the lottery." She slapped her father's shoulder in comradely fashion. Everyone knew Joe Green couldn't leave Hawke's Cove. Limited agoraphobia. He roamed these sixteen square miles easily enough, but he couldn't cross the bridge. "I've been thinking about inviting that Charlie Worth guy to dinner. You being an old friend of his mother's and all."

"Leave me out of it. You want to have a date, you don't need an old man around."

"Dad. Not a date. Don't you want to meet him formally?"

"No."

If Maggie was mystified by her father's reluctance to meet with the son of his old friend, she kept it to herself. What didn't surprise her was her own interest in meeting Charlie Worth, admitting to herself that it was his mother she was most interested in. One of Maggie's treasured possessions was the framed poem Evangeline Worth had sent to her parents celebrating her birth.

From the time she had discovered a volume of Evangeline Worth's poems squirreled away on the living room bookshelf, Maggie had adored her poetry, especially "Hawke's Cove Remembered." *Mystical night of sand and sky . . . speak to my heart of the passion of place.*

As an adult, Maggie recognized that the passion of place was not

Hawke's Cove, but that passionate plane where physical and emotional love exist, and the place Maggie seemed to be just one side of or the other.

MAGGIE waved to friends in front of the hardware store as she made the turn to park in front of the post office. It's what she liked best about being here, even if it was only a couple of days a week. Someone to wave to. As a cardiac care nurse, Maggie pulled three twelve-hour shifts a week at Mass General. That left four days to be home. By sharing a condo with another divorcée, she kept expenses down enough to justify living in two places.

Maggie dropped her handful of envelopes as she got out of her car. When she bent over to retrieve them, her purse tipped, spilling out all the change she'd tossed into it over the past week. "Damn." She squatted down to pick up the money. A pair of running shoes appeared in front of her, and she lifted her head to see whose they were.

Their owner squatted beside her, gathering up the loose change and handing it to her. "I think that's all of it. No, wait." He reached down, snagging another quarter. "I'm Charlie Worth. But then you already know that."

Maggie extended her hand. "Maggie Green." She noticed his eyes widening at her name. "Yes, Joe's daughter."

"Hey, I'm doing a piece about Hawke's Cove, and I wonder if you'd be willing to talk with me?"

The fire horn blasted its noontime alarm, startling Maggie. "I'm going to miss the window! It closes at noon on Saturday!"

Charlie

MAGGIE'S sudden flight left Charlie on the sidewalk wondering exactly what it was he was going to ask her, but certain that the first question was if she'd join him for lunch.

Returning triumphant from the post office, Maggie readily accepted his invitation and then led him across the street to Linda's Restaurant.

"This is the first time you've been here, isn't it?" she asked.

"Yes. Though I've been wondering why that's true. It seems as though we should have been here as children. This place was very important to my mother. She just left and never came back."

"Did she ever say why? I mean, clearly the place loomed large in her poetry, especially her third volume."

Charlie felt himself grow a little warm. "You know her stuff pretty well."

"Oh, yes. I love it. It's so full of emotion. Longing, fear, loneliness, and waiting. And it can be so sexy too."

Now Charlie felt a full-bore blush rise above the collar of his polo shirt. "I hate to say that I've read so little of it. I suppose I'm embarrassed. A mother isn't supposed to write sexy poetry at seventy-something." He pulled the conversation back to living in Hawke's Cove. "So, you live here full-time?"

Maggie shook her head and told him about her living arrangements. "But I could be happy staying put here. It was a great place to grow up. Of course, when my parents split, I ended up living in Quincy. I went to high school there. But in my heart I was always a Cover."

The waitress brought them their lunches. Maggie poured oil and vinegar over her garden salad and raised a professional eyebrow at Charlie's hamburger and fries.

Charlie sprinkled salt on his fries. "Your parents divorced after your brother died?"

"A year or so after."

"I'm sorry." Charlie knew that sounded as if he were sorry for her long-ago losses, but in fact, he was sorry that he was revving up to be a reporter. He liked Maggie Green. He took advantage of a large bite of hamburger before asking his next question. He chewed, but before he could swallow, Maggie caught him with a question of her own.

"So, tell me about your story. What have you found out?" Maggie pulled aside the curtain to get a look at the Hellcat. "I hear you're trying to find the pilot." She looked back at him with innocent curiosity.

"Nothing much. My leads are all fifty years old."

"You should talk to my dad. He was here then."

"I'd love to talk with him." Charlie felt that evil blush grow again, this time the blush of duplicity. He would never have made a good investigative reporter.

AFTER lunch they walked over to the pier and the Hellcat. With tacit permission from Steve West, they climbed onto the barge and walked around the hulk.

"Can you tell anything from looking at it?" Maggie asked.

"No. No skeleton sitting in the cockpit, leather jacket and rakish scarf around his neck."

"So what if this guy did make it to shore? Why would he stay in Hawke's Cove? It's pretty limited."

"That's probably why he did. If he did. And we have no proof anyone did." Charlie reached out a hand to Maggie, helping her off the barge. "It's a dumb story, but it's gotten me here."

"I'm glad it did." Maggie didn't let go of his hand until both feet were firmly on the pier.

"Maggie, I have a photo I'd like to show your dad."

"Show it to him at dinner tonight. That's an invitation."

"Great." Charlie felt himself grin. "Thanks."

Five

Joe

SOMETIMES the urge was so strong in him to call her. "Hey, do you remember that night we stood under the stars and I taught you the names for constellations? Our bodies so close, yet so innocent. Do you ever think about the time in the barn when I held you in my arms and you leaned on me? Angry at me. Needing me. And Vangie, do you recall how our fingers intertwined long after our bodies had separated?" But he never called.

Trouble was, he had too much time on his hands. The job at the movie house only filled his nights. His days he filled with what was at hand, tinkering in the house and pottering about the yard. With Maggie's return, the empty house seemed oppressive as she dashed off to this local meeting or that class in some fad du jour. When she was in Boston, it was easier because he had nothing to compare his idleness against.

Joe heard the Mazda crunch up the clamshell driveway. Peeking out of the parlor window, he watched his daughter bound up the front steps and knew that Maggie was bursting with some news.

"Hi, Dad!" She breezed by him, throwing her bag on the chair. "Guess who I had lunch with?"

Joe smiled and pretended to ponder a list. "Well, I ate tuna in the kitchen, so I know it wasn't me. I give up. Who?"

"Charlie Worth."

Joe felt a frisson of anxiety. He studied Maggie's face for suspicion and saw none, only a brightness, a high color to her cheeks that he hadn't seen for a long time.

"I invited him to dinner."

The dread shivered through him.

JOE Green sat on the single park bench that overlooked Hawke's Cove's waterfront. Fishermen lined the twin jetties, casting into the channel, hoping to catch something. Watching the fishermen, Joe thought wistfully of Ernie. Fishing was fun for him only when Ernie was around. On countless dark nights they stood side by side in their waders, casting into the invisible ocean, waiting for that telltale tug on their lines.

Sometimes he and Ernie said very little to each other those nights. But when they needed to talk, they could, and Joe just wanted someone there he could talk to if he wanted. Vangie. He should talk to her. He didn't even know her number. What would he say? "Hey, call your kid off"? No. This was his legacy. His secret. Not theirs. They had another one.

The F6F bobbed from side to side on the barge. The single engine was black with corrosion, so that none of her identifying marks were clear. She had been a stranger plane to him, and he couldn't remember the numbers, only the feel of her in his hands. The smell of burning oil as her engine caught fire.

Sitting in the warm April sunlight, Joe forced himself to conjure the spine-jarring belly landing on the hard water. He remembered pulling up slightly so that the tail would slice through the water first, the nose slapping down a moment later. He closed his eyes and saw himself hauling out the life raft and inflating the Mae West. It was dusk. Soon it would begin to rain, and the longest night of his life would commence.

"Dad?"

"Mags. Hi." Joe was glad of the interruption, afraid of where his thoughts had been going. "Sit down for a minute."

"Can't. I've got a lasagna to put together, and I want to make homemade bread for tonight."

"Getting a little fancy, are we?" Joe glanced sideways at his daughter, amazed as always to see what a lovely woman she had become. Tall, self-assured, stylish without being a slave to it, Maggie Green-without-the-Shofsky was his finest achievement. Surviving achievement. "What's this Charlie guy like?"

"Very articulate, good sense of humor."

"Sounds like his mother."

"I don't know, Dad. You can be the judge of that tonight."

And how will you judge me tonight? Will you ever see me the same again?

"See that plane down there?"

Maggie nodded, following the line of his pointing finger.

"Well, there's something you should know about."

Maggie placed one hand on her father's shoulder and squeezed. "Dad, why don't you tell us both at dinner tonight? If I don't get home right now, we won't eat until midnight."

A reprieve. "Okay, it'll keep." *It's kept a long time already.*

I SIT here on this park bench where I can see the hulk of the plane that brought me here. The midafternoon sun is warm on my neck, and my beautiful daughter is on her way to get the food she will feed to the son of the woman I have always loved.

Sometimes, when I let myself indulge in the solipsistic feast of memory, the overwhelming sensation is that of falling. All of my life, it seems, has been one fall after another. I fell into working for Sylvester Feeney. I fell into despair when Scott was killed. I fell from the sky. I fell in love. Some people plan their lives, or at least follow some outline. Not me. I simply fall.

Right now I feel as though I'm falling down a bottomless pit; there is no hope of knowing where I will land once Charlie Worth and Maggie Green make the inevitable connections.

IT WAS my first flight since the accident. Accident. What a gracious word for a graceless event. It was my first flight after I shot down my own wingman in a moment of complete inattention. He shouldn't have been where he was. He shouldn't have crossed in front of me in the sun. He shouldn't have . . . But he was a kid, we used to say, still wet behind the ears. The war was old by that time, and the pilots they sent to us, in unending replacement, were nervous, untried. But I wasn't. I was the old man; gramps, they called me. Twenty-nine years old. I'm seventy-eight now, and I feel less old than I did then. I was hardened, experienced, and callous. I fired at the shape in front of me. Act first; ask questions later.

My initial reaction to my mistake was not regret, but anger. "You idiot!" I screamed over the radio. Within seconds the Zero I had expected was behind me and I was hit. That's all I remembered.

I woke up in pain, and the physical pain was the only preoccupation I had. I didn't think of the kid or of my mistake until late one April afternoon as I sat in the solarium of the hospital. My burns were nearly healed, relatively minor compared to so many of my fellow patients. My back was still tight with second-degree burns, but my hands were unbandaged and almost free of pain. At the end of the week I was due at Great Harbor for a few weeks of practice before heading back into action.

"Lieutenant Buchanan?" A man and a woman came toward me. They looked to be about my parents' ages, mid-fifties. They both wore the same expression of grief and high expectation. The man introduced himself, but I didn't catch his name. His voice was timorous. The woman examined my face as if trying to memorize me.

It was too much of an effort for me to stand up, so I just offered my hand. They blinked hard at the sight of my scarred hands, the healed patches shining against the unburned skin. The man touched my hand gently without gripping it.

"You were with our son when he died."

I felt myself falling. "Your son?" I'd been with so many who had died. How was I to separate their son from all the others?

"He was killed in the same mission you were wounded in."

Suddenly I realized which of the many boys they meant. The sense of falling spun into my gut until I folded my arms across my stomach and pressed against the nausea.

"Will you tell us a little about how he died?"

I realized they had no idea; no one had told them.

"I'm so sorry for your loss." I couldn't tell them anything.

"Was he brave?" The man spoke, his tremulous voice low.

I leaned toward him. "He died bravely."

"Thank you." A tear rolled down the woman's cheek.

"I'm so sorry." I couldn't look up at them, to make eye contact, knowing my culpability.

They left without another word, and I wondered what possible benefit seeing me could have been to them. I understand better now. Since Scott.

I TOOK the Grumman F6F Hellcat out on that April morning to get some flight time in. I headed north, then east, planning a leisurely circuit that would put Hawke's Cove beneath me. The little town looked like a Monopoly board laid out. When the mild Atlantic sun forced me to squint, I remembered the blinding Pacific sun. It brought back the enormity of my sin. My sin was not so much the accident of killing the boy, but the fact I had not *regretted* it. I still could not think of his name. I had become so inured to death, to causing death, that I had turned into a monster.

I started shaking up there in the April sky. Shaking with an ever deepening fear that I had become so corrupted that there was no hope. It hadn't occurred to me to ask for forgiveness, either from God or those parents.

My mind and my heart were racing, and at the same time I was paying attention to the gauges and dials, to the feel of the unfamiliar plane in my hands. The oil pressure dropped to zero, and I saw the nose of the plane with its trail of black smoke. I laughed. How perfect. God was in charge now. I would surely die.

I did all of the responsible things for a pilot in this position.

Turned off the engine, radioed my location, attempted to glide toward those soft ocean swells in the hope that I wouldn't explode into pieces on impact. I did a pretty good job of it. The plane floated long enough for me to get the raft out and inflate it and my vest. I was bleeding from where my head had hit the windscreen, but I wasn't even dizzy. I paddled a distance from the plane. Slowly she filled with water and disappeared beneath the waves.

The storm earlier in the week had blown out, but the waves still echoed its strength, and I had to keep paddling to prevent myself from being pulled out to sea. I could see land, a dark rim in the distance. It was already dusk. I knew that within a few minutes no search planes would be able to spot me. So, an instant death is too much to ask for, I thought. A fitting punishment. I pulled hard on the oars. As I pulled, I prayed. "One more chance, please, God. One more chance."

I couldn't fight the exhaustion anymore, and I know that I dozed even as I paddled. The sound of waves breaking startled me out of my stupor. I made a nearly fatal mistake as I stood up to see if I could make out landfall. A wave caught the raft and flipped it over. I was tangled in its lines and forced underwater. Thrashing, I found my knife and attempted to cut myself free of the lines. My frozen hand slipped, and I gashed the raft. As the air softened the buoyancy of the raft into a deadweight, I began to accept my death. Suddenly it was easier to die than to fight. Suddenly it seemed a better choice than to live knowing my guilt.

But the human need to survive was stronger. With numbed hands I found the line and this time made a clean slice. My vest brought me back to the surface only to be battered by another wave. This one, though, brought me close enough to shore to feel sand beneath my feet.

I collapsed on the hard white sand of the beach. The name came to me then; the boy's name that had eluded me for weeks. Joe Green. As I slipped into a deep sleep, I remembered his face and his voice and the fact that we called him Giuseppe Verdi as a joke. The last thing I said to him came to me as unconsciousness washed over me. "Hey, Giuseppe. I'll buy you a beer after this run."

"You're on, Lieutenant. You owe me." He climbed into the

cockpit with a jaunty wave made of sheer bravado. His voice, like his father's, was tremulous. The kid was scared. *You owe me.*

Spencer Buchanan fell into the sea. Joe Green climbed out.

I WOKE half a day later to brush the sand off my face and review my options. No. I never did. I simply knew I wasn't going back. I crept off the sand and into the woods and found a new life. I found Vangie. The tumbledown barn seemed a perfect place to hide. I hid and I watched. There she was, standing on the back steps of her kitchen porch, as if waiting for someone. I heard a sigh, a sound of contained unhappiness. I'd watch from my hiding place and wonder who it was she sighed for. I stole food from her garbage pail. I stole her husband's clothes. And I listened to her melancholy, stealing her privacy.

During the day I kept to the woods, sometimes slipping into town to spend a dime for a loaf of day-old bread, buy cigarettes. I had about fifteen dollars in my wallet when I crashed. I buried my uniform and I.D. papers, sticking my money in the pocket of John Worth's jeans. I wrapped my dog tags in my handkerchief and hid them in the barn, where I could retrieve them if I changed my mind about what I was doing. To prove who I really was.

When Vangie offered me a job, I felt as though I had been reprieved. The Ruths sent me to her.

"You go see Mrs. Worth. She could do with some help. Don't let her tell you she doesn't." What wonderful old biddies they were.

"The barn needs work." Vangie seemed to be waiting for me. As if she'd planned on my coming.

BLANCHE DuBois said it best: "I have always depended on the kindness of strangers." Or something like that. It seems I have been dependent for most of my life on the silence of others.

Ernie Dubee looked the other way when I appeared in his town. He had every reason to be suspicious of a stranger in this small place, but something, some humanity in him, kept him from pursuing it with me. He's never asked. I've never told. We were the same, both kept on this peninsula by the hand of God. The difference between us: He was born here and I was reborn.

I cried as I forged stolen baptismal records, giving the newborn Joe Green an identity. The son of an Episcopal priest, I forged my father's signature, aware of my cruelty to my parents, equally certain I could not go back.

The milkman, Sylvester Feeney, must have had his doubts. Able-bodied young man shows up from nowhere. He never cared. As long as I gave him a day's work for a day's pay, Sylvester was happy. He hired me after he bought Vangie's cows.

Judy Frick certainly must have entertained notions about me. The only indication I ever got from her that she knew something about me was the day she told me to marry Denise. "You can't spend your life waiting for someone who will not come back."

"I don't know what you mean."

"She's gone, Joe. And you'll never leave. You deserve a life, and Denise will make one with you. It might not be the one you wanted, but it's better than lonely bachelorhood."

Of course, Judy was wrong about making a life with Denise. I simply made her miserable. When she begged to take a vacation, I couldn't. She had been so young when we got married; I'm sure she thought she would be able to cure Joe Green out of his never leaving Hawke's Cove. Judy was right about one thing. I never have set foot off this peninsula. I never left to see my son off to war. I never left to bring his body home. And I would not leave to save Denise's sanity.

When Scott died, Denise wanted to move off the peninsula she had lived on all of her life. I wouldn't.

"Please, Joe. I can't stay here another minute with everyone touching me and telling me how sorry they are."

I should have pulled her close and rocked her, but I couldn't. The grief I felt had lodged itself firmly in my sternum and would not budge. I couldn't speak for the pain. My wife crawled into bed and developed the first of her imaginary illnesses.

Judy was a great comfort to me, organizing food deliveries and physically hauling Denise out of bed to dress for the funeral. She held me against her soft maternal breast while I cried, and I gave her the view of my grief I was unable to share with my wife.

"Do you want me to call Vangie?"

The sudden interjection of her name surprised me into pulling away from Judy. Oh, to have Vangie with me now, to share this horrible thing with her. To feel her comforting arms around me. The temptation was great. But I shook my head; it would not have been fair to her to put her in that position. "I'll write to her, Judy. I don't want her to have to feel like she should be here."

"She'd come, you know."

"I don't want to put her in an awkward position."

Judy nodded and handed me a tissue. "It needed asking."

I sent a letter to Vangie expressing my agony in a way I couldn't with anyone else. Deliberately I sent it after the funeral so that she wouldn't have to struggle with deciding to come or not. It would have been more than I could have borne to have her within reach and not touch her. I don't mean sexually. That part of our passion was so unexplored that it seemed something I have imagined. No, I needed her loving touch, the touch she had given me when nursing my blisters or coming up behind me as I milked. The touch we gave each other when words were useless.

Writing that letter, for all its single dimension of words on paper, I was closer to Vangie than I had ever been with my wife.

DO I regret doing it? Deserting? That's the word I avoid even to myself. *Desert.* No. A long time ago I stopped thinking about it. I justified my action to myself. I did my service. Over and over until I lost my humanity. Oh, I do sometimes wonder what might have been had I gone back. If I had survived another tour. I once toyed with the idea of the priesthood, following in a two-generational tradition. My experience, though, had divorced me from ever feeling I could follow that path honestly. My liberal arts degree might have led me to teaching. Maybe I would have become a journalist like Charlie.

Yeah, sometimes I wish I had my freedom. More so now than when I was young. I'd like to go with Ernie to Florida. Except that I've played this role of agoraphobic for so long I'm not certain I can leave. But if I did leave, I would go to Vangie.

I INTENDED to go with Scott to the bus station. I went to the filling station and gassed up the car. I ran a wet rag around the dusty interior and toyed with the idea of washing it. Scott always took care of the car, from the time he could earn a couple of bucks doing it for me. I see him now, all shaggy fair hair, dirty T-shirt hanging out over tattered bell-bottoms. In my mind's eye his sister comes from somewhere to my right, calling out in sibling mockery, "Can't get me!" Scott snaps the hose toward her, and she hops out of range only to come back for more. She adores her older brother. It is plain on her freckled face.

When Scott was born, I thought that I'd been forgiven. He looked at me with those muddy unfocused eyes, and I was sure that I saw the face of a benevolent and forgiving God. Why, maybe he was the reason I'd made the decision I had. Maybe I had been intended all along to be this child's father.

If he was the reason I had deserted, he was also the real reason I married his mother, Denise. She was very pretty, very young, and I was susceptible.

"I don't mind, Joe. I want to love you." She kissed me hard, her tongue playing lightly over mine, her hand on mine to take it to her breast. The oldest trick in the book.

I don't blame her. I mean, for leaving me, or trapping me. The daughter of a fisherman and his common-law wife, she looked at me as security and stability. Besides, she loved Hawke's Cove, and I never expected that she would want to leave.

After Denise told me she was pregnant and Judy told me to marry her, I began to tell myself that what had happened between Vangie and me was the result of being young, emotionally needy, and sexually deprived. I tried hard to diminish in my heart what had happened. Time would have covered up the memory eventually. Except that we wrote to each other, keeping what we had together alive through our words. We wouldn't let it go.

Denise couldn't compete. And she knew it.

SCOTT washed the car before he left. Maggie, no longer freckled, brought him lemonade. At some point, just after he'd enlisted, he'd had all his fair curls cut off. He looked like a stranger. He didn't threaten his sister with a dousing, and for the first time I felt the conviction that he was to be my ultimate sacrifice.

Tomorrow we would take Scott over the bridge to Great Harbor and put him on a bus. I would put him on a bus to his future. This immoral war would finish the job the other one began.

I leaned against the oak tree. I had tried to talk him out of enlisting. His number was high enough he might never have been called. He was doing well at college; he didn't need to enlist.

"Dad, it's my decision. Just because you sat out your war . . ." He pulled himself back. When I think of this conversation, I only hear his voice. I could not look at him. Once again I was falling out of the sky.

WE WERE a silent group, the four of us driving to Great Harbor. In some acknowledgment of his manhood Scott sat in the front, his mother in back beside an uncharacteristically quiet Maggie.

As I drove around the bend in the road and straightened the car toward the causeway and the bridge, I felt the unrelenting weight of choice. The emotional weight became physical, and as the bridge to Great Harbor drew closer, I began to panic.

March 21, 1967
Dearest Vangie,

I could not take him across. I stopped the car and got out. Scott followed me. "I can't go, son. I can't. . . ." There was absolutely nothing I could say that would explain my behavior. I let them think it was the agoraphobia. My children have accepted that I don't leave Hawke's Cove. They have never asked why. Scott didn't ask me now, even as I abandoned him to his fate. I couldn't tell them that it was fear of being recognized. Fear that some cop would stop me and discover I have no driver's license, no identification. Nothing that tells people who I am. That I don't exist. It wasn't really that. What I couldn't tell them was my deep conviction that Scott was my sacrifice for living so well.

There, on the side of the road, Scott let me hug him close. "I'll be fine, Dad. I'll call. You just keep the kid out of my room."

He got into the driver's seat. I walked over to the window and took the last look of my son's face I would ever see. "I love you, Scott. I'm proud of you."

I don't know if I really said that. I sit here now and think that maybe if I had gone across, he would still be alive.

I SIT here. An old man on a green park bench looking out over his past. I don't indulge all that often.

The sun is nearly down, and I'm cold now. But I sit here still, reluctant to leave my memories. I'm glad Maggie ignored my wishes and invited this young man home. Vangie's son.

Six *Charlie*

CHARLIE found the Seamen's Home in Great Harbor without difficulty except that he passed the entrance twice, not believing that the imposing white mansion was actually a nursing home. Built as a hospital, it had survived incarnations as a private school and a hotel. Now the place had been turned back to its original purpose, offering assisted living on the first floor. The second and third floors represented increased degrees of skilled nursing, culminating in hospice care on the fourth floor.

On the way Charlie had entertained himself with thoughts of Maggie, partly to close off the dread he always felt in going to a nursing home and partly because she was pleasant to think about. He liked her, liked her style and her wit. Especially, he liked that they had a common bond; after all, their parents knew each other, at least they did once.

Charlie was involuntarily drawn into making comparisons with his father's nursing home. A brick building with the institutional atmosphere of a nineteenth-century mental hospital, St. Elizabeth's was clean and the care adequate, but the odor of depression filled the halls. By contrast this place was sweet smelling; an open window overlooking Great Harbor's port let in the April afternoon. The receptionist directed Charlie to Judy Frick's room.

Judy had been a resident here since shortly after Ted died. A couple of heart attacks had slowed only her body down, not her spirit, and she still doled out advice and opinion to her visitors.

"Mrs. Frick?"

"Charlie Worth. Come in!"

Charlie bent down and kissed the papery cheek, letting her hold his hand. "You remember me, then?"

"Charlie, I admit you've grown up a little since I saw you last, but you haven't changed. You still look like your father."

The Fricks had come to Boston every couple of years. The last time was before his father's first stroke.

"Besides, my boy, I may be ninety-two, but I haven't lost my marbles yet. Your mother told me you might come by. Chasing some mystery."

"So she told you I'm trying to locate the pilot of the Hellcat."

"She said you were assigned a wild-goose chase."

Charlie smiled. "Nonetheless, may I ask you a few questions?"

"Shoot."

"How easy would it have been for a man to show up in Hawke's Cove and fit in?"

"Easy enough."

"I thought New Englanders were supposed to be crusty."

"You're a New Englander. Except that you're a reporter. We keep to ourselves, right? I see the skepticism in your eyes, thinking, Not really. We're nosy. Well, we fuss over everyone's problems if they can't keep their problems to themselves. I mean, a man works hard, causes no one any trouble, keeps his own counsel, no one faults him for it. We might wonder, but we don't ask. That's how it could be done."

"So you think that this guy did come ashore and stay."

"The ultimate wash ashore. Ha. No. I don't." Judy got up and fussed a bit with her African violet. "If such a thing happened, I'm sure that he would have kept going."

"According to the navy report there was a brief investigation following the pilot's disappearance because a young nurse claimed to have seen him. In Hawke's Cove. The pilot, Spencer Buchanan, was deemed AWOL. Pretty serious offense for wartime."

"Spencer Buchanan." Judy pinched three dead leaves from the plant. "Nice name. But doesn't ring a bell."

"I have a photo; would you look at it?"

Judy took the black-and-white studio portrait of the missing pilot, an unsmiling young man in full-dress uniform. She pushed her glasses back up on her nose and held the picture out. "How old-fashioned he looks. How young."

"Do you recognize him?"

"No."

Judy

ANYONE with eyes in his head could see that they were in love. The way they looked at each other, all moony-eyed. Not that I'm sayin' they did anything wrong. No. Just that they were both young, healthy, and desperately alone.

I'm also not sayin' that I know for sure that Joe Green is the AWOL pilot. But he did just sort of show up, never spoke of his war experience, and, except for those scars on his back, was pretty fit. Vangie showed up with scars too. It took me a long time to figure her out, but I knew that there was something eatin' at her. Course, eventually it all came out.

When Joe Green appeared—yeah, that's exactly what he did, appeared—everyone kinda took to him. Quiet, polite. I think he appealed to every woman who had a son gone.

Oh, yeah. Joe and Vangie, it was as plain as the nose on your face that they were in love. And fightin' it! When she finally broke her silence about her dead baby, Joe nursed her like she was sick. Gave her too much whisky and put her to bed. Sat there all day, he told me, just watching to make sure she was breathing. I know he didn't realize just how much he was telling me. That he was watching her out of love. She scared him. Her grief scared him.

I always felt a little guilty, later, I mean, when my initial reaction to John's disappearance was *at least she has Joe.* I didn't know John then, and it seemed natural that Vangie would end up with Joe. Funny how it is, you just link people. Abbott and Costello, Tracy and Hepburn. Joe and Vangie. It seems to me that you go against nature when you try to link up the wrong people. Like I did to Joe and Denise. Yes. I take full responsibility. Course, she's the one who got pregnant. And he's the fool who fell for it.

In my own defense I still believe that he needed to settle down and find a home. He couldn't keep living in Syl Feeney's spare room. Denise was a Cover. Born and bred.

The day she sprang her delicate condition on him, I thought, well, Vangie's home and settled and living the life she chose long before Joe Green arrived. She'll never come back, and he ain't leavin'. Most men would've left Hawke's Cove by this time. The postwar boom was in full swing, jobs everywhere, a lot more interesting and better paid ones than as Syl Feeney's milkman. He wasn't going to, though. I knew it even if Denise didn't.

So now Vangie's son is in town and asking questions. Nice young man, though he's not so young as they were then. I wonder if Joe is the pilot. We talked a little bit about war when Scott joined up. Joe was beside himself. That would have been the time to tell me if he'd ever been in active duty. Said not a word about himself, only fretted about the boy fighting in a war that seemed so wrong, misguided.

Then Scott was killed, and I thought Joe Green needed Vangie. He admitted to me he heard from her; she told me they wrote. I told them both news about the other because I never lost touch. Vangie'd be hungry for news of Joe. But she wouldn't look at pictures. Said she wanted to remember him exactly as he was.

He said the same thing.

When I told Vangie that Joe was getting married, I saw her go pale. Then she smiled and agreed with me it was the best thing for him. "He'll be a wonderful husband." That's what she said, but she couldn't hide the hard swallow she took before she said it.

Of course she couldn't've abandoned John Worth. He was her husband, and in those days that was that. There were times, though, over the years, when I think she might have done it. Left John. He wasn't easy. She always claimed being a POW had hurt him in ways that couldn't be explained. Called it his darkness. Wouldn't talk; kids made him nervous. Wouldn't ever come to Hawke's Cove. John really hated the farmhouse. Vangie explained that he wanted to start his own firm; they needed the cash.

I think that was the hardest news I ever brought Joe. "Vangie's selling the farm." I was going to suggest he buy it, but the look on Joe's face stopped me.

"Sell Bailey's? That can't be her idea."

"John's starting his own business."

"I see." Without another word he got up from my porch rocker and walked home. I didn't see him for a long time after that. Denise got pregnant with Maggie not long afterward. I half believed that some secretly held hope had been demolished and Maggie was his second attempt at making a life with Denise.

Denise was well on her way to becoming a hypochondriac by this time. Every time I saw her, she listed her aches and pains like an old woman. Trouble was, she was a victim of her own designs. How could she expect a man in love with another woman to love her?

Oh, yes. Denise knew about Vangie. Oh, nothing concrete, nothing she could get alimony with. She just knew, as a woman does, that his heart was not hers. She saw his eyes light up when I gave him some news. I saw her jaw clench.

"Judy, can you do me a favor?" Joe always had time for a cup of coffee, pausing on his route to keep me company.

"Sure, what?" I don't know what I expected.

"I think it's best if you don't mention Vangie in front of Denise."

I'll say this for him, he was sensitive, kind. Being a man, he thought that if Denise didn't hear about Vangie, she'd forget about her. Ha.

Charlie

"MOM?"

"Charlie, hello. How's your project going?" Charlie could hear the water running from the kitchen sink. "Did you see Judy?"

"Yes. Yes I did."

"How is she?"

"Pretty good. She's a little frail, but her mind's clear." Charlie thought he heard a little "humph" over the staticky connection. He stood still on the porch of the Seaview Bed and Breakfast and hushed the hum in his cell phone. "She sends her love."

Leaving the Seamen's Home, Charlie thought about asking his mother if she maybe wanted to move Dad here. He balanced the pros and cons. Pro: nice surroundings, lovely view. Con: no one lived here; how would Mom come every day? The cons evolved into a daydream, and before he could govern his imagination, Charlie had Vangie uprooted from her home of fifty years and ensconced in Hawke's Cove, where he would be a good son and visit her every weekend. Charlie allowed himself to imagine Maggie as a prominent feature in his daydream. He liked her, this athletic, rather matter-of-fact woman. It had been a long time since he'd met anyone who interested him beyond one shared meal. Too much effort had to go into peeling away the layers of someone else to get to the substance; too much effort had to go into protecting one's own layers. Only twice had he liked a woman enough to let her get past his protective bonhomie. The first time was when he was a student at B.U., but graduation had sent them in opposite directions. The second time, two years ago, had ended when she balked at a deeper commitment. He'd been hurt and now worked hard at resisting the urge to go through the effort ever again.

Until today. Maggie Green had chipped a little at his resistance.

Charlie pulled his thoughts back into line. "Mom, how come you never brought us here?"

There was no immediate answer. Then, "I wanted to, Charlie. Very much. But I couldn't." Charlie's phone was suddenly perfectly clear, and the note of old pain carried over the airwaves.

"Why not?"

"Don't be a nudge." The pain was replaced by annoyance.

"I met a fan of yours."

"Of mine? Who?"

"Maggie Green." When she didn't say anything, Charlie added, "Joe Green's daughter."

"I know whose daughter she is. I didn't know she was a fan."

"Has all of your poetry books and still keeps the poem you wrote for her over her bed."

"Is she living in Hawke's Cove now?"

"Part-time. With her dad. I'm having dinner with them tonight."

"With Joe?"

"Are you all right, Mom? You sound funny." The hum distorted what she said next. Charlie asked her to repeat it.

"Okay, Mom. No problem." He filed her request in his mind and then broached the subject he'd intended to discuss all along. "I showed Judy the photo of the missing pilot, Spencer Buchanan."

"Did she know him?"

"She said no, but I think she was lying. She said something else which would indicate she did recognize him. 'How young he looks.' Mom. I've got nothing concrete, but I've got a pretty good hunch Joe Green is the guy. Am I right?"

"How would I know?"

"Steve West says the photo looks like his son, Scott."

"What does Maggie say?"

"I haven't shown it to her yet. I'm bringing it tonight."

There was a long silence, and Charlie wondered if his phone had quit. "Mom?"

"Please don't."

"So, I'm right, aren't I?"

"Charlie. Let it rest. Let us all rest with our secrets. What good, except for a five-paragraph story, is this thing to you?"

Charlie sighed and couldn't answer.

Vangie

April 18, 1993
Dearest Joe,

By the time you get this letter, you will have met Charlie. I'm taking the coward's path here, not having called to warn you. I thought about it, about calling. I called directory assistance and got your number. Wrote it right here in my address book, listing it as casually as any other. I have spent the last few days reading the chronicle of our relationship, my diary and your letters. The early letters were passionate, powerfully felt, driven by a need to preserve the new—forbidden—love. As time went on our love solidified into trust. Whatever happened, we had each other. Never absent in thought and heart. Eventually, as if we had lived our lives together, we achieved that quiet friendship of complete understanding. But I have always missed your touch.

So now I sit here, staring out at the empty bird feeder in the backyard and thinking of what you will tell Charlie and Maggie.

I think you will tell them the truth. And by telling them your truth, you will tell them mine.

Joe, the one thing I have never told you is that once I very nearly came to you. I enclose here that letter, the one I wrote but never sent, because for a long time after the event, I wasn't reconciled to its conclusion. I sent another one instead. I remember it being very chatty and bland. Your next letter asked what was wrong. I had to let a whole month go by before I could answer. By that time I had regained my equilibrium and my grip on the life we both agreed to live. The only reason I send it to you now is because I would hide nothing from you.

And I might yet come.

July 17, 1968
Dearest Joe,

I nearly came to you today. I got as far as the bridge, and I stopped. All I had to do was cross that single-lane wooden bridge to change our lives irrevocably. Do you realize that not once in all these years have we ever discussed changing our minds?

I have believed you to be a lifeline should I need one. It has been implied any number of ways in your letters. I very nearly took hold of that lifeline today and hauled myself ashore.

Where you and I have always been circumspect is in our portrayal of our spouses, though we both suffer from contentious marriages. I know you are unhappy with Denise. There, I've said it. Your unhappiness shows in those tightly constructed sentences that leave her out of your life.

John and I are often at odds: he is critical; I am stubborn. We argue about the children, his hours, my housekeeping. We are seldom cruel, often silent. What touches off a skirmish? Today he simply complained he didn't have an ironed shirt. I was in the middle of a stanza. He often does that, makes a comment on something undone while I'm stealing a little time to write.

In my anger I snatched the shirt in his hands and in so doing knocked my jar full of sea glass onto the floor. It smashed, and bits of rare blue and, rarer still, rose-colored glass flew under the desk and into the carpet and across the room. Pieces you had helped me to collect. The lovely rounded edges of glass worn frosty by the sea mingled with the shards of ordinary glass from the jar. I wondered how I would ever separate them.

John and I looked at each other, and it seemed as though if one word was spoken, too many would be said. I grabbed my keys and purse and walked out of the house. I hurried, desperate not to hear his voice calling me back, drawing me back into my role as mother and wife. I drove away from my life. When I pointed the car northeast, I knew that I was going to you.

I tried to think only of those months on Bailey's Farm when you and I danced around our feelings, pretending to ourselves that we felt only friendship. I wanted to be angry enough at John to justify this desertion. Instead I grew angry at you.

You never let me make the choice, Joe. You made it for me, and I resent it. But we both know it was the right choice. By the time I got to the bridge, I knew that I couldn't cross it.

I have never hated my life enough to change course. Even during the bad times, I have kept true to that decision. As have you.

Sometimes life is one shattered illusion after another, and it is the illusion of ourselves that is the most fragile. As long as we stay apart, we can depend on the purity of our illusions. I will never pick up your dirty laundry; you will never see my sagging breasts. Our relationship is immune to the mundane realities of a physical presence. We have not grown old and crabby, nor has the precious fact of our love been lost in the frets and annoyances of life lived together. We can hold it like a jewel, our ordinary lives a foil around it.

Seven

Joe

JOE stared at the face in the bathroom mirror. He had most of his hair and all of his teeth, and was pleased that he carried maybe only twenty pounds more than he did as a young man.

Yet so little remained of the smooth-faced young pilot who had crawled onto the beach. Only the deep blue of his eyes was the same. He had nothing to fear from a fifty-year-old photograph.

Joe could hear voices downstairs. That slightly forced volume of new acquaintances, polite phrasing.

At some point this afternoon Joe had stopped being nervous—at least about being found out. He admitted a little excited nervousness at meeting Charlie Worth properly. He knew him well already. He'd watched him grow up through Vangie's letters. Known about his successes and failures, his love life and his peripatetic career. Knew his mother saw Charlie as gentle, funny, a good man. Joe knew that Charlie was Vangie's son, and there was so much he wanted to ask him. Did his mother still wear her hair long, gathered into a loose twist against the back of her head? Did she still like to play cribbage? Did she ever talk about those times? About him?

Joe hesitated at the top of the stairs, his right hand touching the bannister, taking an unconscious comfort in the solidity of it. Then he heard Maggie calling him.

THEY were in the kitchen, where Charlie was uncorking the bottle of Chianti he'd brought. The mingled odors of lasagna and homemade bread lay as a backdrop to the scene. As Joe came into the room, Charlie offered him a glass of wine and then his hand. Joe took one, then the other. "Welcome, Mr. Worth. I'm so glad you found us."

"Well, if Maggie hadn't dropped her purse . . ."

"Hey. I was going to call you anyway." Maggie lifted her glass toward the doorway. "Let's go sit."

"I think your investigation would've led you to us in any case."

"You're right. You've been on my list of people to talk to."

Joe nodded and led the way back to the living room. He waited to see where Charlie would sit, then took the Boston rocker near the fireplace. "So what have you learned?" He lifted the Chianti to his lips, using the action to cover his sudden anxiety.

"Not as much as I had hoped. Well, actually, I never expected to find anything. It was a lark; come here and write a nice little quasi-travel piece with the Hellcat as the center."

"But something changed."

"Maybe." Charlie licked his lips.

Maggie shared the couch with Charlie, leaning with her elbows on her knees. They bumped hands as they both reached for the dip, apologizing with a smile. "So what have you heard?"

"It's less what I have heard and more what I'm just guessing at. Nothing really. Nothing substantial."

"Dad, you were going to tell me something about the plane this afternoon. What was it?"

Pretending to struggle getting salsa on a chip, Joe didn't reply.

"Dad? Do you know something about the crash?"

The dip slipped off the chip, and Joe put a soggy nacho in his mouth. "Oh, no. I really don't. I was going to tell you about the efficiency of the Hellcat in war."

Mercifully, the oven buzzer sounded, and Maggie excused herself, leaving Joe and Charlie to poke around for a new topic. "So, ever fish?"

Charlie shook his head. "Not really. My dad took me trout fishing a few times when I was a kid." He set his empty glass on a coaster and raised his forefinger at Joe. "You're the one."

Joe felt his fingertips grow cold. "The one?"

"Yes, in the snapshot of two guys and a line of fish."

Joe hoped his relief didn't show. "Ernie Dubee and me. I remember your mother taking that snapshot. She still has it?"

"I expect she does. I remember it in a box of a million others."

"How is your mother?" *Don't tell me about her age or infirmities; just tell me she is well and happy.*

"Sassy as ever."

It was the perfect response, and Joe laughed with joy. Now he could say her name out loud. "Vangie and I worked hard on that farm. Did she ever tell you?" *What did she say about me?*

"Yeah. You featured prominently in a lot of her stories."

Joe felt the cold leave his fingertips. "Did I?"

Maggie came into the living room to call the two men in to dinner. In an old-fashioned gesture Charlie offered his arm to Maggie. "She always made this place sound so magical. I still don't know why she never came back."

Joe followed them into the dining room, grateful they couldn't see his face and know that he knew the answer.

Vangie

THE new marbled black-and-white notebook had an inviting heft to it. It was exactly the kind Vangie had used—one hundred pages, wide-ruled—for years. Usually she scratched out new poems in these books. Today she began a new journal.

APRIL 18, 1993 After I went to the nursing home this afternoon, I bought this notebook to use as a journal. I feel a little silly. What have I got to record except the exceedingly routine patterns of old age? But a journal is also a recording of thoughts, emotions, and memories, and I am filled with those. After coming home, I wrote to Joe. Somehow the very act of mailing the letter was high drama. It is the first time we face the possibility of including others in our secrets. Is the game up?

It's eight o'clock. By this time Joe and Charlie have met. Joe's daughter will serve them a meal, and Charlie will ask questions that don't seem important, then piece together the whole. It is possible that by the time Charlie sees me next he will know everything.

The nursing home today seemed particularly pungent. A thin layer of cleaning solvent rode the breeze as the aides pushed past me, linen carts piled high with sheets. The first time I went to the veterans hospital to see John, it, too, was potent with the scent of disinfectant. I was shaking with nerves. I didn't know what to expect from John or from myself. So much had happened. To both of us.

The ward I was directed to seemed endless; narrow iron beds flanked the walls. Men with unspeakable wounds called out greetings as I walked the gauntlet of hospital beds. Lost among the acres of cots, John lay somewhere in this place. It seemed the cruelest taunt to make me search for him, after all the waiting and not knowing.

"Mrs. Worth?" An orderly touched my elbow. "Your husband is in ward three. He's waiting for you."

THAT day I went to find John in the VA hospital, I was still alive with feelings I thought would never dull. Would I never be done with grieving? For Molly. Then the missing John. Now Joe.

Now I know that some grieving happens before the real death. Every day I grieve a little for John, missing the husband who opened his arms to me from his hospital bed so many years ago. So very happy to see me. I sat and held this skinny, frightened man, so haggard I might not have recognized him had he not been watching for me. We gripped each other and wept. I wept a little for the fact that the woman John held was not the same woman he had left behind. No longer the woman he thought I was.

"Evangeline, you will never know how you kept me from giving up. Knowing I had you, had you to come home to, I kept going when it would have been easier to die."

I wept because for the rest of my life I would have to pretend to be that woman.

He came back from the war a defeated man. Those months in a German concentration camp had reduced him in ways that went deeper than the physical changes. He needed constant reassurance, needed, in those first few months, to know I was there in the house with him at all times. Or if I went out, exactly when he could expect me back. He needed my devotion. I loved and cared for him through all those months of regeneration, but I thought of Joe and missed him horribly.

John would say I seemed distracted. Was I upset about anything? I'd just say I was worried about him.

There is so much I haven't recorded. Events and occasions that were every bit as important as those seven months in Hawke's Cove. My whole life.

Joe

"THEN Vangie says, 'Drink it?' " Joe leaned back in his chair. He was telling Charlie and Maggie about the whisky pit. "I wonder if that booze is still there in the root cellar. No one but summer people or renters have used the place since . . . since it went out of your family's hands. No one's been in it in years."

Charlie sat forward. "Could I see it?"

"The Scotch?"

"No, the farm. Bailey's Farm."

"Sure. When?"

"I'm leaving tomorrow."

"Why not go out on your way home?"

"Will you show it to me, Joe?"

Joe nodded. "Sure. About nine?"

It was quite late. They had never left the dining room, content to keep the cluttered table under their elbows. Maggie had outdone herself, completing their dinner with a simple dessert of vanilla ice cream and California strawberries.

"Maggie, that was wonderful. I hope that I can do the same for you when you're in town."

"Is that a date?"

"Could be. How does your schedule look?"

Joe stood up and collected the dessert dishes, giving Maggie and Charlie privacy to complete this date business without his supervision. He carefully rinsed the glass bowls. What will Vangie think, their children dating? She'd think it was something out of Shakespeare or a Greek comedy. Joe played a little with the possibilities and found himself chuckling out loud.

"What's so funny, Dad?"

"Oh, Maggie, life is full of sweet irony." Handing her the dish towel, he pretended to need the bathroom.

Charlie

"I REALLY like your father." Charlie took the wet pan from Maggie and rubbed the damp dish towel around the inside.

"Well, I'd like to meet your mother."

"You know, the next time your father comes to see you, we should get everyone together."

"Oh, Charlie. That's not possible."

"Why?"

"My dad's an agoraphobic. He never leaves Hawke's Cove."

"How long has he been like that?"

"Forever. As far as I know, he's never ever left. Not even as far as Great Harbor."

"Really. I thought agoraphobics couldn't leave their homes."

"No. Not always. Those are severe cases. Dad's just this side of eccentric."

"So he was born here?"

Maggie swished the sponge around the inside of a serving dish. "No. But he's lived here all his adult life. I know that much."

Too many pieces were falling into place for Charlie. He stood behind Maggie at the sink and kept silent for a minute.

"I'd still like to meet your mother."

"She'd love to meet you, Maggie. I'll bring you by before we go to dinner on the twenty-fifth. Okay?"

"Great. I'd love that."

Charlie flopped the dish towel around the inside of the bowl. "Funny, don't you think, how she never came back."

"I don't think so." Maggie fished around in the dishwater for the last pan. "I think it makes perfect sense."

"How so?"

"Charlie, hasn't it ever occurred to you that they were two adult people living in the same house under difficult circumstances. And that, well . . . fill in the blanks."

"No, Maggie. My mother was a married woman, devoted to my father." Charlie shook his head in rejection of the notion, all the while letting it sift down to where he knew he'd always wonder.

"Who was, as you've said, missing."

"Maggie, I really don't think anything happened."

"Charlie, I'm not suggesting malfeasance, just the logical culmination of a deep friendship."

"So why didn't they keep in touch?"

"They have. They've been writing to each other for years."

"How do you know?"

"My mother found her letters to my father."

Charlie felt a strange feeling in his intestines. "Love letters?"

"Loving enough that she left him." Maggie sighed. "Charlie, I'm sorry. Dad doesn't even know that I'm aware of it. And I'm really just guessing. I don't know for sure. Only that Mom found some letters, and it was their last big argument."

"Maggie, I don't know what to say."

"Don't say anything. My mother would have left my father anyway. She just needed one good reason." Maggie let the water run out of the sink and dried her hands. "I have to make a phone call. Why don't you go sit with Dad. Unless you're ready to leave?"

"No." Charlie was still thinking about what she'd said. "No, I'm not ready to go." As he walked by her, Charlie impulsively touched Maggie's cheek, making her blush a little.

JOE was sitting outside on the porch. *"Shhh."* He held one finger to his lips. "Listen, Charlie."

Charlie had already picked out the distant sound of a bell buoy marking the channel more than a mile away. The random rhythm of the hammer striking the bell reached them, the sound unobstructed by gentle hills and stubby trees.

"Your mother used to call that her lullaby bell. She'd count between chimes until she fell asleep. On a calm night like this she could get to ten, maybe fifteen."

"She wrote a poem about a bell buoy." Charlie sat on the porch rail, facing Joe Green in his porch rocker.

"Sing to me of faraway places . . . where my love might be . . ."
Charlie smiled. "Yeah, something like that."
"And lulled, I'll dream of a time . . . when he will sing to me."

Joe

Dearest Vangie,
  I have just seen your son out to his car. Well, not exactly. I shook his hand at the doorway and let Maggie walk out with him alone. She stood a long time by the car, and I worried that he was telling her something. But she came back into the house, all private smiles, and kissed me good night. She hasn't done that in a long time. I may be deluding myself, but there's a certain spark between them. I am absolutely certain I do not imagine it.
  You are anxious to know whether or not I told them the story. I have not. Charlie is indeed hunting down Spencer Buchanan, but he is considerate and never asked a question I couldn't answer honestly. We actually veered away from the topic early on in the evening and never got back to it. He never even produced the

photo he's been showing around town. Claimed to have left it in the B and B. Thus I am certain he is onto me.

I told them stories, Vangie. I told them about fixing the barn and finding the Scotch, about the cows and the Fourth of July. I pulled out stories about the Ruths and the Sunderlands. I told them all kinds of things except that I am he whom Charlie seeks. I told them everything important to me except that you and I . . . we are, well, what we are to each other.

Imagine my joy at speaking your name out loud. Imagine the pleasure at hearing your words through your son's voice.

I overheard Maggie telling Charlie about my "agoraphobia." Something occurred to me then that had never crossed my mind before. If it hadn't been for you, I might have given myself up and taken my punishment. But I stayed here in Hawke's Cove because I never gave up hope that someday you would come back.

JOE hurried to get to Bailey's Farm before Charlie did. He wanted a few minutes on his own to get past the changes that others had wreaked on the place. Parking his truck, Joe got out and assessed the yard. The place had been left derelict, abandoned by the last owners against back taxes or a contested will, Joe couldn't recall which. The back porch screen was ripped open, and the shutters on the kitchen window hung askew. Leaving it till last in his survey, Joe finally looked at the barn. He smiled in self-satisfaction. His foundation work had survived. One door was open, and Joe gave it a gentle push. After fifty years the door swung easily to meet its mate.

When Charlie pulled up to the house, Joe was sitting on the back porch steps. He stood up as Charlie got out of the car, flourishing the keys he'd gotten from the real estate agent.

"Shall we go in?" Charlie held the screen door open.

Joe hesitated a little. Charlie saw his hesitation and put out a hand to steady him.

HE KNEW exactly what he'd write to Vangie. "You wouldn't believe how unchanged it all is. It was modernized in the '50s, deserted in the '70s, and now the old place has regressed to the

'40s. The linoleum in the kitchen is a different pattern, but cracked in the same places. What must have been new wallpaper thirty years ago is faded into a pale yellow nearly the same shade as the kitchen always was. Ditto the blue paint in the parlor. Of course, everything seems smaller than memory. And empty. No voices echo."

Charlie had brought breakfast in a paper bag. He and Joe leaned against the sink and sipped lukewarm coffee out of paper cups and ate homemade sugar doughnuts from Linda's Restaurant.

"Want to look around?" Joe brushed crumbs from his shirt and put the lid back on his coffee.

Charlie led the way. They wandered around the first floor, then up to the second. Joe said nothing, pointed nothing out. He let Vangie's son take in the old empty house without annotation.

"Well, I can see why Dad had no use for the place. Yet at the same time I can see why Mom did. Yin and yang." They were back in the kitchen. "Can we look at the barn?"

"Sure." Joe left his coffee cup on the counter.

The stalls were cluttered with junk; cobwebs hung thick above their heads. But the light was the same, the dust motes swirling as the two men moved toward the ladder to the loft.

"It looks just like it did the first time I saw it." Joe kicked at a pile of newspapers. "Full of junk and swallow nests."

"Tell me about coming here, Joe."

"Well, your mother wanted to get this barn straightened up. She was alone, and I needed a job."

"No. I mean about coming to Hawke's Cove."

"What do you want to know, Charlie?"

"Joe, I want to show you something." Charlie went out the open barn door to his car and returned with a glossy photo of Spencer Buchanan. "I had one of the guys at M.I.T. play around with the photo. I realized no one would recognize the guy in a 1942 photo, so I had him computer-age the image. This is what Spencer Buchanan would look like if he had survived and was alive in 1993. If he'd spent most of his life working outside. If he hadn't died in a plane crash."

Charlie handed Joe a computerized image of himself.

"When did you get this?"

"Last night. Before I came to dinner. They faxed it to me."

"Have you said anything to Maggie?"

"No."

"Thank you."

"You should tell her, Joe. She needs to know."

"She'll know soon enough."

"No, Joe. I'm not writing this story. I can't."

Joe felt himself sag. "You don't have to protect me."

"Some things should stay undiscovered. Not like the Scotch."

Through the open barn door they could both see Maggie's car pull up beside Charlie's.

"I'll tell Maggie." Joe handed the copy back to Charlie. "Can I tell you too?"

Charlie shook his head. "No. I don't need to know. Just tell me one thing, Joe. Did my mother know?"

Dear Vangie,

What could I say? Everything that has defined my life suddenly condensed into one word: yes or no. The guilt, the shame, and the love I feel for you. Charlie was asking for all of it.

I am by nature a runner. I run from the painful things in life. I ran away from the truth that I killed that boy. I ran away the day you knew John was alive. By failing to cross the bridge, I ran away from my son. I wanted to run away from Charlie. But Vangie, I'm too old and there's nowhere left to go.

I ran from you that day not because I didn't want you to have to choose, but because I was afraid you wouldn't choose me.

Eight

Vangie

JULY 27, 1994 From where I sit, a little trapped by the old Adirondack chair, I can see the path to the beach. If I block out the new addition, I can almost cast myself back to my grandmother's time. The teenage voices laughing this morning were not my cousins', but my grandchildren's. The adult voices admonishing them to hurry and get dressed not my grandmother's, but my daughters', anxious with the momentous occasion of their only brother's wedding.

The path is still sandy. I haven't tried to follow it, except in memory. It winds down along the pasture and through the trees that seem exactly the same. Up and over the dune, and there you are. Charlie tells me that he's found out the cove wasn't named for some prerevolutionary family named Hawke, but for the ospreys that lived here in abundance then.

They say that with all the recycling there is very little sea glass left to gather anymore. That what you find is mostly white or brown. I would like to walk the beach again and see if this is true. John swept up my sea glass and threw it away. He thought he was doing me a favor, cleaning up my broken jar. Maybe I'll attempt to get down there later, after I've rested and recorded these events.

When Charlie brought Maggie home that first time, I was nonplussed. I had not expected her to look so much like Joe. How Joe must have looked at forty. Charlie offered to let me see the computer photo, but I wouldn't.

They bought Bailey's Farm together. Maggie and Charlie. They've brought it back to life; beyond the new paint and repairs, they have filled it with love. When I watch them, their fingers touch, they glance at each other as if needing constant renewal from the source. I watch with a jealousy they cannot imagine.

I like to think that Maggie and Charlie fell in love right here, at Bailey's Farm, when she met them that afternoon. I like to think that the spirits of the long-ago Joe and Vangie breezed through them and opened their eyes to each other. Full circle. That they might finish what we never could.

Charlie relayed my message to Joe. And Charlie relayed one back to me when he got home that Sunday. "Mom, he told me to take your hand like this . . . and tell you that for him, too, not a day goes by he doesn't think of you."

I KNEW his voice the minute I heard it. He called me that afternoon, just after Charlie had gone home. I knew it was Joe, even though the slight raspiness of age laces his soft voice. "Vangie."

"Joe," I answer, and hear the age in my own.

We are not the same people, but it doesn't seem to matter. The first call has undone the self-inflicted prohibition against calls. We talk often; embarrassingly high phone bills are now part of my life. At first we spent a lot of time reminiscing. That didn't last long; there were too many other things of interest to discuss. Politics and movies and opinion.

Then, when it became obvious our children were "getting serious," it was the future we reviewed. We both admitted an unreasoning fear they'd break it off and we'd be on opposite sides of a fence. But they didn't. Yet we have never met face to face.

It would have been easy; I could have gone anytime with Charlie. But John began to fail. I have long since forgiven myself for the infidelity of the body; I could not, in these last months, commit the infidelity of the mind. When there was no comfort left for him except my being with him, to leave would be unforgivable. For the same reason, Joe did not come. He would have broken out of this prison of his own choosing to be with me, but I would not let him. I owed John that much. Even after John died last month, I could not fly off to meet Joe. There was so much to take care of.

I am so nervous about seeing Joe—not about the changes time has made in him, but in me. Before I came out here in the yard to wait, I stood in front of the pier glass in my grandmother's bedroom and stared hard at the old lady reflected there. I stared long enough that the soft edges hardened and she stood up taller, her hair darkened, and her eyes grew sharp. Until the real Vangie looked back at me, the Vangie Joe Green will expect.

Everyone has gone to the rehearsal. Because it is Maggie's second and because this is a late marriage for Charlie, the whole thing will be simple. Still, they need to practice. In my role as matriarch I need no rehearsal, and am glad for the few hours alone. Here.

Someone will come back to take me to the big family dinner in Great Harbor's fanciest restaurant. Denise will not be there, bitterly angry at Maggie for loving my son. Maggie says never mind. Eventually she'll get over it. I admire Maggie's courage.

No one has said if Joe will come. He still hasn't left the Cove despite, as he puts it, the weight of a lifelong lie having been removed. I didn't ask him when we spoke last night. I called a few minutes after I arrived at Bailey's Farm with Julie and her family. Things were pretty chaotic, and we only spoke for a minute.

Our first local call, Joe kidded. While everyone bustled around bringing in luggage, we spoke of inconsequentials. I told him the trip was fine. Can you believe it, the bridge is now two lanes! Stopped in Great Harbor to see Judy, still going strong!

Then, when left suddenly alone in the kitchen, "I can't wait to see you." Kids. We behave like kids.

By the time we got into Hawke's Cove last night, it was too late and, even in July, too dark to see much. I was up early this morning to get a good look. I think I felt as much excitement about seeing my house as I do thinking about seeing Joe. I was so afraid Charlie and Maggie had changed the place so much it would bear no resemblance to my memory. Charlie assured me over and over that they had kept the "integrity" of the place, and he was as good as his word. Except for the addition, of course. They've enlarged the kitchen into one of those great rooms, which serve as living room and dining room and gathering place. Above it, two more bedrooms. It is not without perfect irony that I approve of the remodeling. Essentially the same remodeling John wanted to do and I refused to have done—our first wedge.

Charlie led me to my old room, my grandmother's room. It's clean and fresh and just the same as I remember it, except that the old spool bed is long gone and the new one is bigger and an unremarkable pine. As I lay there last night, I could hear the bell buoy on the shoals ringing out its erratic warning. The sea was calm, the chiming spaced out in long intervals. I lay awake a long time.

I tiptoed out of the house at dawn to stand alone in my yard and see the changes time has brought. Not many really. The winter pasture, as Joe warned me, has reverted to woodlot. My garden is all lawn now, not even a depression to mark its location. How many yards of topsoil must that have taken?

Pulling my housecoat belt tighter, I went into the barn. No bovine perfume lingers behind. Only cars and their particular odors. But the ladder is still there. The wood rung beneath my hand is smooth from wear, from generations of farmers climbing up and down to feed their stock. From children's bare feet, racing up to play hide-and-seek. Joe, sheltering there in the loft. My foot, as I come down the ladder toward the rest of my life.

I wonder if I could still climb up there. I am wondering this still when I hear Julie calling everyone to breakfast.

AFTER breakfast Maggie took me by the arm and gently walked out with me, ostensibly to have a prenuptial chat with her mother-in-law-to-be. Pretending to want the lowdown on her intended's bad habits. They've been living together in their new Beacon Hill flat, so I think she pretty much has his bad habits figured out. However, I went along with her ruse, and we came out to the Adirondack chairs.

"Hope this weather lasts through tomorrow."

"Oh, Maggie, it will. You and Charlie don't need to worry. Look, not a mare's tail in sight. Red sky last night too."

"Vangie, I really love him."

I smiled at her. "I know you do, honey. And he loves you very much. You've been the find of his life."

She licked her lips, dry with nerves. "Vangie, all these years you've been the only person to know who my father really was."

"No, Maggie. You knew. Maybe not his name, but you know perfectly well who he is."

"Point taken." Maggie sat forward on the edge of the green chair. "May I ask you something?"

I wondered what tipped her off. "Go ahead."

"You and my father were lovers."

"That's not a question."

Maggie said nothing.

"Will my answer change your opinion of your father?"

"No."

"Of me?"

She hesitated, then smiled. I am still amazed to see her father's smile on her lips. "No."

"Yes. For one . . . beautiful . . . night. The next morning I learned that John had been found."

"Oh, Vangie." Maggie reached across the space that divided us and gathered my hands in hers.

"Consider it the luckiest break in your life. If things had played out differently, you and Charlie would have been siblings."

Maggie's laugh, like her smile, recalls her father.

After she leaves me sitting here, I think that I have misspoken. What we had has certainly lasted more than one beautiful night.

I MUST have dozed. The light has changed. My journal is upside down on the ground beside my chair, my pen beneath it. I lean forward to pick it up, and that's when I see him. A dark-haired man, coming up the path with a young man's stride. I think, How odd. He's still wearing John's clothes. As he gets closer I see that, of course, he isn't. Plaid shirt and black Dockers, recent vintage. I have mistaken a baseball cap for dark hair. As Joe gets closer, I edge my way out of the deep Adirondack chair and stand up to meet him. There is an exquisite moment when we both pause, just far enough away from each other that the work of time is muted.

"You are as lovely as I remember." Joe touches my face with gentle fingertips.

We kiss in the way of old friends, then stand a long time just holding each other. The body never forgets, and his scent is as familiar to me as if I had breathed it in every day of my life. There seems to be nothing left to say, as if the letters have said it all for us and now we need only to hold each other. To be together.

It is so temporary. We have no idea how much time is left to us. Tomorrow we will see our children married and we will dance together at their wedding. We will toast their future with seventy-five-year-old Scotch.

For us, it will have to be enough.

SUSAN WILSON

Martha's Vineyard occupies a magical place in Susan Wilson's heart. As a child, she spent lots of time on this island off the coast of Cape Cod and now lives there full-time with her husband and two daughters. While writing *Hawke's Cove,* which is set on an imaginary island, she drew on what she loved most about the Vineyard. "I tried to imagine what it was like fifty years ago," she said.

Wilson decided to write this romantic story because, as she put it, "I have a soft spot for unrequited love." Still, she is quick to admit that *Hawke's Cove,* her second novel, is not based on her own experiences with romance. In real life Wilson and her husband fell in love as teenagers and have been happily married for close to twenty-six years.

To learn more about Susan Wilson and *Hawke's Cove,* visit the Select Editions website: ReadersOnly.com Password *Life*

The Color of Hope

Susan Madison

A Victorian vacation house
on the beautiful coast of Maine.
Sailboats on the bay. A happy
family enjoying the simple
pleasures of summer. It all
seemed so perfect.

Amazing how quickly things can change.

CHAPTER ONE

ALL her life Ruth Connelly had feared death by water.

Once, standing as a child at the sea's edge, foam covering her feet, she had been filled with the sudden knowledge of terror, clear and sharp as the knife her parents sliced bread with.

She held their hands as water heaved away from her and lunged back again, heavy with intent. Wrinkles of water, glinting where the sun caught them. Diamond fingers, beckoning . . .

Terrified, she tried to move away, out of its reach, but they urged her forward. Go on, don't be frightened. It won't hurt you. Unconvinced, she pulled at their hands, but they held her tight, stepped nearer themselves. It's the sea, they said in high, bright voices. Come on, honey, the sea.

Pebbles shifted under her toes. Slippery. Cold. The ground gave way. She stumbled and fell. Mommy! Daddy! She heard them, miles above her, laughing. She tried to stand, but an unexpected wave slammed into her, glassy and green, determined. Daddy! She screamed again, and the sea poured through her, swamped, deluged her. The gasp, the choke, clutching at green, at water, which slid through her fingers. She remembered it still, salt stinging in her eyes, burning the back of her throat. She would never forget the purity of her panic, the premature step into adulthood as she sensed something of which she should not yet have been aware: Death. Oblivion. Nothingness.

You were only under the water for a second, her father soothed as he swung her up against his chest.

It was a second that would last a lifetime.

All her life she had feared death by water. All her life she had imagined that the death would be her own.

STANDING on Caleb's Point, the low bluff that marked the ocean-most edge of their property, she looked down at the scene of that unforgotten moment. Beyond the fallen boulders was a tiny strip of sand—small pebbles, really. A beach, nothing to be frightened of. But all these years later, Ruth still feared the sea. At some instinctual level she knew that it would destroy her if it could. And yet she loved this place. Up here, with the murmur of the waves, the honey-colored air, the waving grass, she found solace. She had come here so often during the years of her growing up. She did the same now as an adult, a mother, a wife.

The point pushed out into water dotted with lobster-pot buoys. Arms of green woodland curved around the horizon on either side, trees falling down to narrow shorelines of rocks scarred by winter tides. The woods were broken here and there by the shingled roofs of summer cottages. Further out, in the open channel, the gray gran-ite hump of Bertlemy's Isle rose from the water like a turtle shell, crowned with a small stand of spruces. Tomorrow, as always, the four of them would sail out there to celebrate Will's fourteenth birth-day. She grimaced, thinking that they needed something to celebrate.

Hawkweed leaves scratched the back of her thighs as she lowered herself to sit on the ground. Behind her a boulder reared out of the earth; the rain-formed dip at its center provided a toehold for rein-deer moss and asters, blue iris. Ruth leaned against it and closed her eyes, smiling as she remembered how, as a little girl, Josie had be-lieved that the boulder was a pixie's garden. She sighed. It was so peaceful up here. No arguments. No bickering. No tension. Maybe she should get one of the local carpenters to make a bench so she could sit in comfort.

Every time they came up to Maine from their Boston apartment, she toyed with the idea of moving here permanently. Paul already held a part-time visiting professorship at Bowdoin College; surely he would find it easier up here to finish the book he was writing. The children, it went without saying, would be ecstatic. What held her back were her own needs. She could probably find work with one of the legal firms in Portland, but she had worked too hard to want to start again at the bottom.

She stared at the distant whale shapes of Mount Desert Island on the horizon. Triangles of white sail were scattered across the water, heading out to sea from the little yacht club in Hartsfield. One of them belonged to the children. Could they see her up here? She waved, just in case.

At her back, higher up the slope, were the pinewoods. Spruce, pine, balsam, hemlock. The hot resin-scented air always recalled the simplicity of summer days when she was still just a mother and not a lawyer as well. Picnics under the trees. Hide-and-seek. Swimming in the pond. Where had it all gone? Time had rushed by, leaving her to wonder what had happened to the chirping voices of her children, to their unconditional love, their trust. The slipperiness of pine needles under her feet, the taste of crab cakes and fresh-made brownies. She had been happy then. Glad to subsume ambition in the treasure of her children. Will, with his freckled face and cowlick; Josie, her hair tied back in pigtails, smiling. They had filled her world. Often, overcome by a rush of love, she would squeeze them close and murmur, "I love you. I *love* you," pressing the words into the nutty fragrance of their hair, breathing them in while they squealed and wriggled and said they loved her too. They would always love her.

Will had not changed much since then, but Josie had grown so secretive, so distanced from them. Ruth knew this was only to be expected, part of her daughter's reach toward adulthood. But even so, Josie's hostility was hard to live with.

She got to her feet, brushing at her shorts. Her spirit sagged. Time to go back into the real world. She took the forest trail that led down through moss and fern, blueberry and wild ginger, past the boulder from which Josie, playing king of the castle, had fallen and torn open a gash above her eyebrow that required six stitches. Halfway down the hill the trail forked—one path leading further into the woods, the other descending sharply toward the back of the house, passing the wild cranberry bog and the freshwater pond.

The boundaries of their property were wide—though, strictly speaking, it was not their property but hers alone, deeded to her by her parents. There was hardly a square yard that did not hold special memories, her own as well as those of the people who had lived here down through the generations.

"That's where Grandma's wedding hat was blown into the pond, isn't it, Mommy?"

"That's where Great-grandmother was stuck in the bog."

"Over there's where Great-uncle Reuben fell off his horse 'cause he was drunk."

One day Josie's children, and William's, would listen to the same stories and, in their turn, pass them on.

As she came out of the trees, the house stood before her: Carter's House. Foursquare, white clapboard, wraparound porch, shingled roofs and turrets. It had been built more than a hundred and fifty years earlier by her seafaring great-great-grandfather, Josiah Carter, who spent thirty years on the China run. He had worked his way up from ship's boy to owning his own clipper, probably indulging in more than a little piracy on his way to fortune. A prodigious womanizer and a legendary drunkard, it was said that Josiah would drink until reason left him and then spy all manner of wonders: frozen demons in the rigging, angels setting the sails. On the day when God himself admonished him from among the shrouds to forswear the demon drink and the loose living, he accepted the inevitable and made his last voyage. Having found himself a virtuous wife, he purchased a large acreage of fields and wooded hillside above the village of Sweetharbor, built a cedar-lined house, and filled it with the spoils of his voyages.

Succeeding generations had cared lovingly for the place. There had been some modernization, of course. Ruth's grandfather had brought in electricity. Her father had installed central heating and glassed in the two side porches, but in its essentials the house remained very much as old Josiah had left it—still smelling of cedar, still full of the curiosities he had brought back from distant shores.

"I'M NOT coming tomorrow," Josie said.

"Of course you are," said Ruth.

"I have better things to do, thanks, than go off on some stupid kid's picnic."

"I'm not a kid," said Will.

"What kind of better things?" Ruth asked.

Josie looked belligerent. "I said I'd drop by the Coombs'."

"Who're they?"

"You wouldn't know them, Mom. They're only year-rounders, not worth your while cozying up to." Josie had been working on one of her canvases; there was a smudge of blue oil paint on her face and more on her fingers. Her contempt was infuriating.

"I want you to come with us," Ruth said. "It won't be the same without you. Besides, it's your brother's birthday."

"So what?"

"So he'd like to take the boat out one last time before we go back to the city." Ruth began spreading chocolate butter frosting on the cake she'd made earlier in the afternoon. "We all would."

"Not me. I don't care if I never set foot on a boat again."

"That's nonsense. You were out sailing yesterday. I saw you."

"Only because Will forced me."

"If you don't come, you'll ruin Will's day."

"Will, do you really want to listen to Mom and Dad scream at each other all afternoon? I sure as hell don't."

"Thank you, Josephine."

Will, the peacemaker, flashed his dental braces. "I'd really like it if you'd come, Jo-Jo, but you don't have to."

"Don't call me Jo-Jo."

"Josie, then."

Will was always so equable, so reasonable. Like his father used to be, Ruth thought. She slapped at his wrist when he snuck a finger into the bowl of frosting.

"Count me out," Josie said.

"Aw, c'mon," said Will. "It'll be cool. Besides, it'll be our last chance to go out in the boat."

"Jeez, you are such a wimp. You and your dumb braces."

Ruth felt her temper rise. Will was sensitive about the ironwork on his teeth. "That's enough out of you, young lady," she snapped. More than enough, to tell the truth. She tried to tell herself that her daughter had been zapped by adolescence, that inside she was a mass of bewildered hormones, but it did not help much. "You're going to come—and you're going to behave yourself."

"How come we have to go to this geekfest at the Trotmans' first?"

"I told you why. Because Ted Trotman wants me to come."

"Since when do we all have to kiss Ted Trotman's ass?"

"Don't use language like that in this house. Ted has sent a lot of business my way. Besides, he's asked someone specially to meet me. I can't just not show up."

"Jeez, Mom, why do we always have to do *your* stuff? Like, we're supposed to show up at some nerdy party, but you couldn't come to the school exhibition that had *three* of my paintings, as if you cared, and you missed Will's game—"

"I explained why I couldn't come, Josephine. I can't just take time off whenever I feel like it."

"Dad seems to be able to manage it."

"Dad doesn't have the demands on him that I do."

"You mean he's not as interested in making money."

Ruth put down the frosting knife. "You know why I—"

"Don't say it, Mom," Josephine said loudly. "*Please* don't tell us you're only working your buns off for *our* sake."

"Why not?" Ruth's face flushed with rage. "It's the truth."

"Mom," Will said, changing the subject, "why can't we live here all the time? I mean, we're year-rounders, really. Grandad was the local doctor for years. You and Dad are the first Carters not to live up here all the time."

"First off, we moved down to Boston when I was little. After that we only summered here, so I don't think we count as year-rounders, especially since your dad's from California. And second, he and I had to go where the work was."

"You could have found something here if you really wanted," Josie said. "Anyway, if we go to the Trotmans', you know Dad'll drink too much."

"Yeah," said Will.

"And if he does," Josie said, "we shouldn't be going sailing."

"If we're going out on the boat, obviously your father's not going to drink too much," Ruth said. "I don't know why you're making such a fuss. All your friends'll be there. You used to enjoy those parties, Josie."

"Before I discovered what a *murderer* Ted Trotman is."

"How do you figure that?"

"All those companies he's on the boards of? They're releasing dangerous toxins directly into the environment. And he's got interests in the Amazon destroying thousands of square feet of rain forest every day."

"He probably doesn't even know."

"Everybody knows. And he's just had that *gross* deck built out of Honduran mahogany. He should be in jail."

Looking at her daughter, Ruth felt a kind of anguish. Under the tan Josie's face was pinched. Was she experimenting with drugs? With boys? Yesterday she had been so exasperating that Ruth had threatened to send her off to one of those attitude-adjustment schools for wayward kids. She had meant it as a joke, but right now it seemed like a darn good idea.

"What is all this, Josie? Some garbage you've picked up from your Save the Entire Universe group?"

"Typical of you to mock something you know squat about," Josie said scornfully. She tugged a drawer open.

"Are you looking for something?" Ruth said.

"No."

"If you want something to do, you could go down in the basement and put the clothes in the dryer for me."

It seemed to be the cue Josie had been waiting for. She turned. "God, I *hate* the way we live," she said. She pressed her long hair back behind her ears, exposing turquoise studs, which set off the gray of her eyes.

Ruth's heart sank. Please, not another argument about the rain forests and tuna fish and the Silent Spring, all of which Josie seemed to think was personally due to her mother. "Which particular aspect of it do you have in mind?"

"Like why can't we hang our clothes outside, like the year-round people do? The Hechsts or the Cottons."

Ruth made a face. "Feel free to use the clothesline, Josephine.

You'll find clothespins in the basement. Or perhaps you'd rather protect the environment and carve your own."

"Yeah, great," said Will, trying again to ease the tension. "You could sell them door to door. Like those guys who come around with onions and stuff. Gypsy Josie."

"Shut up!" Josie yelled, as though she were in kindergarten instead of pushing seventeen. Her face went red.

"Shut up yourself."

"Be *quiet,* both of you."

Josie frowned. "And there's another thing."

"I don't want to hear it," Ruth said.

"See what I mean?" Josie said. "You never talk to me." She touched her ear studs with long paint-stained fingers. "I want to leave school."

"Don't we all?" said Will.

Ruth sighed heavily. "Not this again, Josie. I've already told you what a ridiculous idea that is."

"I mean it, Mom. *Really.*" Josie's voice rose. "I want to leave high school right now and go to art school instead. I want to paint. It's all I ever wanted to do, right from when I was a little kid."

Ruth drew a deep, exasperated breath. "For the hundredth time, you don't have the slightest idea how difficult it is to make a living as a painter."

"If you *looked* at my work, you'd know I could make it."

"There's no way I'm allowing you to leave high school without graduating." Ruth could feel her own voice rising. "If my parents had allowed *me* to leave school—"

"It's *my* life we're talking about here," Josie said angrily. "I don't need a high school diploma. All I want is to be a painter."

"What you do with your life once you've left home is your business," Ruth said coldly. "But while you're in my care, Josephine, the answer's no."

"Screw you!" Josie shouted. She slammed out of the kitchen, managing to catch with her bare foot the base of one of the two Chinese porcelain vases on either side of the hall stairs. It toppled and rolled down onto the broad pine planking; a large triangular chip broke from the rim.

"Josie!" Ruth was furious. She picked up the chip. "Damn it. Can't you be more careful?"

The depth of her own rage surprised Ruth. After all, the vase could be mended. Nor was it simply frustration over her deteriorating relationship with her daughter. More than that, the broken vase seemed symbolic of a rupture she only partially understood—yet another rip in the fabric of their lives.

Josie walked away without responding. Ruth ran out into the hall to find her halfway up the stairs. "Josephine!"

The girl stopped, her shoulder blades defiant. "What?"

"The very least you could do is apologize."

"Sorr-ee, Moth-er," Josie said with singsong insolence.

Ruth bounded up the stairs faster than she would have thought possible and grabbed hold of her. "How dare you," she said, shaking the girl. Josie turned her face away. "How dare you speak to me like that after damaging my property through sheer carelessness."

Josie smiled contemptuously. "That's the trouble with this family," she said. "Objects matter more than people."

"You're talking crap."

"Am I?"

Josie's eyes were blank with hostility. And something else. Uncertainty, maybe even fear. Which was fine by Ruth. Uncertainty was good. Fear was better. She opened her mouth to argue, then closed it. The wall between them seemed all of a sudden too high to climb.

"It's not because it's an *object* that I'm upset," she said wearily. "What bothers me is that it's that particular object. Great-great-grandfather Carter brought it back in his boat from China."

"I said I was sorry, didn't I?"

Paul came into the hall with the newspaper in his hand. He stared up at them over his reading glasses. "Josephine," he said, "don't be so discourteous. Can't you see it's not the vase she regrets? It's the way you've violated the spirit of the house."

"The spirit of the house?" sneered Josie.

"That's what I said. Now apologize to your mother."

Josie muttered an apology, then marched up to her room.

"Jeez," Paul said. "What did we ever do to deserve this?"

His support was more than Ruth could have hoped for, and she was grateful. These days she felt she seldom had it. She put her hand on his arm. "Thank you, darling," she said.

He looked down at her and patted her hand absently.

"Do you think I should give up my job?" she said. "Maybe the price is higher than I realized."

"Get real, Ruth. You'd hate that. The time when they really needed you is long gone."

"I suppose so, but—"

"And we've grown accustomed to the money you make."

"So you think I should go on working?"

"As with so much in this family, it's your decision, Ruth."

"Sometimes I wish you'd just put your foot down."

"You'd stamp on my instep so hard I'd be on crutches the rest of the year." Paul made a face. "Besides, don't you think it's a bit late to go back to being a mommy?"

LIKE all the Trotman parties, the Labor Day weekend cookout was an elaborate affair. Mindy's from Augusta had been called in to handle the catering. In addition to two barbecue pits, with piles of charcoal-broiled ribs and racks of lamb, there were long flower-decked tables containing local crab and lobster, sushi, and tortillas.

It was one of those rare Maine days when the temperature hits the nineties and everyone was bathed in a light sheen of sweat. This would be the last party of the season. Tomorrow the summer visitors would begin heading back to New York City, Boston, and Philadelphia. School would be starting, university semesters getting under way.

People drifted languidly across the well-watered gardens. Even the rocks between the sculpted shrubs looked as though they had been set in place by the Trotmans' world-famous landscaper. Standing on the huge new deck—Honduran mahogany, right? Or was it Peruvian?—Ruth knew she preferred the more rugged look of the land around her own cottage.

"Ruth, I've been looking for you!"

She fixed a smile on her face and turned. Ted Trotman, dapper in madras shorts and a polo shirt, was coming toward her, accompanied by an older man. "Ted," she said warmly, "wonderful party."

"I want to you to meet Phil Lavelle, who's driven up from Brunswick specially to meet you."

"Hi." Ruth put out her hand and shook the beefy paw that Lavelle extended. He was short and fat, in white shorts and a baseball cap. At least he was not wearing it backward.

"Ted's been talking up a storm about you," he said.

"With good reason." Ruth eased back her shoulders, knowing she looked good in her beige linen shorts and navy halter top.

"I'll leave you together." Trotman patted Lavelle on the shoulder. "Watch out, Phil. She's sharp as an ice pick."

"So"—Lavelle hoisted a plump buttock onto the deck rail— "Ted's obviously hooked."

"He gives us a lot of business."

"Persuade me that I should too. What can Landers Keech Millsom do for *me?*"

"For a start, we aren't generalists." Ruth loved moments like this, playing the fish, reeling him in. "We specialize in mergers and acquisitions, debt refinancing, contract negotiations. We help clients identify market position and form strategic alliances."

"I do like the fact that so many of your partners serve on the boards of public and private companies."

"Company policy," Ruth said. "Doing so gives us a unique insight into management perspectives, and that can help us on the shop floor as well as in banking and government circles. Now, when I was looking into the background of your firm, I noticed that you were involved in some fairly complex union negotiation that didn't work out as successfully as it should have." She smiled.

Lavelle removed his cap, wiped an arm across his forehead. "Tell me about it."

For ten minutes she outlined an alternative strategy. She could see him wondering why his legal advisers had not come up with the same idea, and wincing as he contemplated the money his company could have saved. By the time their glasses were empty, he was sold. When they shook hands, he told her that he would phone to make a lunch date. When he did, she would be prepared. He would see just how secure his interests would be, once he had placed them in the capable hands of Landers Keech Millsom.

When he had moved off, she stood looking at the crowd of guests. Will was playing Frisbee with his friend Ed Stein and one of the Trotmans' golden retrievers. Josie was standing with her friends Tracy and Shauna. When she moved her head, the sun caught the shining highlights of her hair, somewhere between clear honey and maple syrup.

In spite of herself Ruth smiled, remembering a rare moment of empathy with her daughter. Last fall Josie had dyed her hair a raw bright orange. Running out of the bathroom, she had collapsed dramatically against the kitchen table. "I can't go to school like this," she said. "I'd rather *die.*"

Ruth had soothed and comforted, all the while trying not to laugh, and eventually had gone down to the nearest drugstore to buy another shade of dye. The next day Josie had come from school carrying a sheaf of white freesias. "Thanks, Mom," she had said, "thanks for coming to the rescue last night."

"They're beautiful, Josie." Ruth had admired the delicate white blooms on their thin green stems.

"They're my absolute favorite flower." Josie had sniffed the overwhelming fragrance. "Don't they smell fantastic?"

"Just wonderful, sweetheart." Ruth had hugged her tightly.

As Ruth recalled the moment now, Josie looked up and caught her mother's eye. She scowled and turned away. Don't do that, Ruth wanted to call. You cannot imagine how much that hurts.

STANDING in the shade of a juniper tree, Paul watched his wife and wondered if she had impressed the fat little man from Boston in the white shorts. She was good, no question about it. No wonder Bob Landers kept increasing her bonus.

Chris Kauffman strolled into sight, at his side the young woman who had taken the Prescotts' cottage for the summer. He and Ruth had been lovers for a brief few weeks last year, both of them left temporarily spouseless in the city. Several people had made sure Paul knew about it.

Jeez, it was hot. The ice in Paul's glass had melted. He swallowed the last drops, throwing back his head. He had never let on that he'd heard about Ruth's affair. He guessed it would mortify her.

Besides, there'd been an episode on his side too. There were ups and downs in every marriage. How could there not be?

A pleasant alcohol-induced blur sat inside his head. Lovely day. Reasonable job. Pretty wife. Beautiful children, even if Josie was sometimes a pain. On the whole, a good life. He pushed himself away from the tree. Time to get another drink.

RUTH stowed thick sweaters in a duffel bag. She packed the birthday food she had prepared for Will, who had fairly sophisticated tastes: chicken legs baked in satay sauce, cold cooked lobsters, a ginger-and-lime dressing for the avocado. She added local raspberries, plates, forks, plastic glasses, a bottle of chilled wine, cans of Diet Pepsi and Sprite. Finally she slipped the chocolate cake into a Tupperware container, hoping it would not look too battered when they finally ran up onto the stony beach of Bertlemy's Isle.

Josie came in and flung herself around the kitchen. "You don't like me much, do you?" she said suddenly.

The words pierced Ruth. "What a terrible thing to say."

"But it's true, isn't it? You'd never send Will away to one of those boarding school–type places, would you?"

"That was just a—"

"I saw the way you looked at me at the Trotmans'."

"And I saw the way you looked at *me*," said Ruth. "As if you hated me."

"Maybe I do."

Ruth was suddenly close to tears. "Well, I don't hate you." She held out her arms. If only Josie would run into them, the way she used to. "I *love* you."

"Yeah. Sure."

Ignored, Ruth let her arms drop. I love you, she had said and meant it. Yet Josie was right: She did not *like* Josie much. Not the alienated Josie she had been this summer. But it makes no difference, she wanted to say. Love is the important thing, and the love was still there.

"Would you love me no matter what I did?" Josie asked.

"Of course I would. You don't turn love on and off. How would you feel if I accused you of not loving me?"

"Who says I do?"

"Josie!" Ruth felt lost. Was her obviously unhappy daughter simply looking for reassurance? Was she trying to explain why she was so much at odds with her family this summer? In her ears glinted the earrings Ruth had bought for her last Christmas, small silver rectangles with a copper heart set in the middle. Was it a signal of some kind that she should have chosen to wear those particular earrings? And if so, what was the message?

"If you didn't love me, I wouldn't blame you," Josie said. "Parents get stuck with their kids, don't they? The same way children don't get to choose their parents. Just because they live in the same house doesn't mean they have to like or love each other, does it? I mean, why should they?" She looked at her mother with careful indifference.

"I can only assure you that I—and your father—love you and Will more than we can possibly say. Surely you know that."

"You'd give your life for Will, wouldn't you?"

"Of course."

"Would you give your life for me?"

"Of course I would." Trying to lighten the conversation, Ruth added, "Let's hope I never have to."

AT COLLEGE Ruth had made herself learn to swim, and she had found that this eased her terrors. Nonetheless, as the four of them walked in single file along the catwalk, she felt the old anxieties surge. The sea was her enemy; it would destroy her if it could.

As they climbed aboard the *Lucky Duck,* the thirty-five-foot wooden-hulled sloop Paul had bought ten years earlier, Ruth shaded her eyes and looked apprehensively at the sky. The motionless heat had given way to sudden gusts of wind, and rain was on the way.

"Don't worry, darling." Paul put his arm around her shoulders. "The worst we'll get is a bit of a blow."

"Which is fun, right?" Will reached for the cooler and the picnic basket. "It's a perfect day for sailing, isn't it, Dad?"

"You bet. Absolutely."

"Okay." Once she and Paul had become engaged, Ruth had

forced herself to crew for him, summer after summer, until she was pretty competent around a boat. But she was always going to be a fair-weather sailor.

As they cast off, Josie produced her Walkman and slipped on the headphones, blotting her family out in a manner that proclaimed she was only here because she had been forced to come. They got up a fair speed once they reached open water. Ruth sat back in the cockpit with her eyes closed, listening as Paul and Will discussed tomorrow morning's race. "If we come in among the first three," Paul said, "I'll be happy."

"I want to do better than that," said Will. "Last race of the summer, Dad. You and me, we gotta really go for it."

"The *Duck* doesn't stand much chance against the Steins' new boat," Paul said.

"We could beat them. Mr. Stein only bought the boat because Ed nagged him. He doesn't know port from starboard."

"Ed's pretty good, though."

"Yeah, but not as good as we are. Team Connelly," Will said. "We're the ones to beat."

Josie pulled off her headphones. "Fat chance," she said. "Sam Hechst could run rings around you. And with me crewing for him, that's exactly what he'll do."

"In his dreams," said Will.

"Sam Hechst?" Ruth said. "Is he related to Gertrud and Dieter?"

Josie sighed heavily. "He's Dieter's nephew, Mom. Surely even you know that." She spoke to her brother again. "First three? You'll be lucky to be in the first ten."

"Wanna bet?"

"Yes, Josephine," Paul said. "Are you prepared to put your money where your mouth is? Twenty bucks says we beat you."

"You're on!"

"Loser buys lobsters all around," said Will. "Okay?"

"Okay, you greedy little dweeb."

Ruth smiled sleepily, warmed by the fine salt-flavored air. Below her the water chuckled and splashed against the hull. The sun was hot on her shoulders. This was how it should always be. Just like this.

CHAPTER TWO

"WE'D better get started back," Paul said. In the last hour the weather had taken a sharp downturn, and out to sea the water was unpleasantly choppy. Thunderheads were piling up along the horizon; the sky had turned a dark purplish color.

"Okay." Will started packing away the remains of the food. "Great picnic, Mom," he said. "Thanks." He and Josie stowed the stuff in the dinghy, which they'd used to row ashore Bertlemy's Isle. Small waves slapped ill-temperedly at the sides of the sloop and set the dinghy rocking. Water was breaking high up the shallow beach.

Will pointed. "Some storm brewin'," he said, sounding passably down east.

"Ayuh." Sister and brother grinned at each other.

Getting into the dinghy, Ruth envied them their insouciance, their familiarity with the water. In a small boat she always felt vulnerable. The sea had only to reach out and grab hold of her.

Paul waded in and shoved them off, then scrambled over the stern. The children rowed the dinghy to the sloop, a hundred yards offshore. A mile away the afternoon's regatta slipped toward the harbor.

Even as they prepared to cast off, the gusting wind changed, blowing straight toward them, off the land. The squall was closer now, and the seas were running heavier.

Paul spoke, his voice calm. "Okay, crew, shorten the sail."

"Right." Will grinned. Gray water raced past the hull.

"Put your safety harness on first. You too, Josie. We'll set the small jib and put two reefs in the mainsail."

"Aye, aye, sir."

"Ruth, go below and make sure everything's secured."

She stumbled down the companionway, hating this, wishing it were over. Having checked that there was nothing loose in the cabin, she stood on the bottom step and looked forward across the deck to where Josie and Will were struggling to control the flogging canvas. It began to rain, blinding sheets of water flying horizontal to the sea.

With the sails set, the children clambered into the cockpit, sliding their safety harnesses along the jackstay. Josie took the wheel while Paul went up on the foredeck and got the anchor up. "Bring the life jackets," he yelled over the buffeting wind.

Ruth fastened her own life jacket and brought the other three up into the cockpit. Overhead, the clouds were now the color of coal, and visibility was down to no more than a few yards. Whitecaps rolled relentlessly across the sea, each one slamming against the hull. Paul and the children fought their way into their life jackets against the rolling pitch of the boat.

"Okay, the anchor's up," Paul said. "Let's do it."

Wind filled the sail as he reefed it in. As they moved off, Ruth took the wheel, feeling the deck buck beneath her feet, forcing herself to stay calm. Below, the sea sucked greedily at the boat.

"The wind's still straight off the shore," said Paul after a while. "Even if we try tacking, we're not going to go anywhere. I'll put the engine on. We'll have to motor-sail home."

"Aw, Dad," said Will, his cheeks reddened by the wind and the salt spray. "This is fun."

"Yes." Josie was animated by the scent of risk. "Let's not use the engine."

"We have to. There's not enough sail up."

Paul turned the key in the ignition. The engine coughed, sputtered, died. He tried again. Ruth fought rising panic. He tried once more, and this time the engine caught.

Ruth could see he was relieved. Paradoxically, this made her more frightened. Moving close to him, she caught the smell of wine on his breath. "Damn it, Paul," she said angrily, keeping her voice low, "how much have you had to drink?"

"Only some of the wine you packed to drink to Will's health."

"Some? Most, if we're being honest. How much at the Trotmans'?"

"Not a lot." He grinned. "But they do make strong martinis."

The boat heeled violently to port, and all four of them grabbed onto anything solid they could find. "Clip on, kids!" Paul shouted, and added brusquely, "You too, Ruth."

"How long before it calms down?"

"What the hell does it matter?"

"How long, Paul?"

He shrugged. "I don't know. Half an hour, tops." He did not hide his irritation at her question.

Half an hour? Ruth hoped nobody realized how scared she was.

They motored for a while, parallel with the coast. Through the drumming rain the sky was nighttime dark. Over to starboard Ruth saw the lights of a lobster boat. "Look," she said. "Couldn't we attract their attention? They could give us a tow or something."

"For God's sake, woman. We don't need a tow," Paul said.

"Are you sure?"

"I'm sure. And will you, for Pete's sake, let go of my damn arm."

Ruth was cold, wet, and frightened. "Don't talk to me like that! You bring us out here when you're completely smashed and—"

"You're being a pain in the ass," Paul said angrily. "Did it ever occur to you that—"

"Shut up! Shut up!" Josie screamed at them. "Can't you two stop quarreling for even five minutes?" Her face, screwed up against the rain, was full of animosity.

Exasperated, Ruth turned on her. "Shut up yourself!" she shouted. "You self-righteous little prig."

"You make me sick," Josie said.

Ruth did not reply. They were not making much headway, and although he would never admit it, Ruth could see that Paul was growing concerned. There was already a five-foot swell, and she knew that the seamanlike thing to do would be to head further out to sea and ride the storm out. But when Paul suggested it, she said, "No! For God's sake, let's get home."

"We'll have a hard time. The best thing we can do is either ride out the weather or head around the coast to Ellsport." As he spoke, the boat smacked heavily into the trough of a wave and Ruth shrieked, clapping her hands to her mouth.

"Knock it off, Ruth, *please,*" Paul said. "It's just a bit of a blow. Happens all the time in these waters."

"Why don't we put out to sea?" Will asked. "Wait it out."

"I already said we should. But your mom apparently knows best and thinks we should head for shore."

"You're the skipper," Josie said. "We should do what you think's best—which everyone except Mom knows is putting out to sea."

Ruth wanted to scream at them to get her home, get her off this quivering, heaving, dangerous vessel. Her lips were trembling. "I'd . . . I'd rather get back, if we can."

"Then Ellsport it'll have to be," Paul said.

"Da-ad," complained Josie.

"We can make it." Shouldering Ruth aside, Paul took the wheel and bore away to starboard, heading parallel to the shore up the coast. The wind's scream died down, and the smashing of the waves seemed milder. For a while they motored in comparative quiet.

Then there was a sudden clunking sound from somewhere under the boat. The engine stopped dead. Without power the boat veered around, and the fierce weather caught it again.

"What the hell was that?" Paul said.

"Did we catch a trapline?" asked Will.

Paul leaned over the rail on one side. "I'll check."

"There's netting floating around." Josie hung over the stern.

"Some amateur fisherman, I'd guess, cutting his net loose." Paul steadied himself with a hand on Josie's shoulder. The boat wallowed heavily, clumsy as a walrus, and he clenched his fists with frustration. "Damn it all to hell!"

"What's happened, Paul?" Ruth said. "Can it be fixed?"

He laughed a little grimly. "Not in these conditions."

"So what now?"

Paul glanced up at the sail. "I don't know."

"You don't *know?* Paul, you're supposed to be the damn expert. How can you be so irresponsible? I don't know why you ever brought us out in these conditions."

"Shut the hell up, Ruth." Paul turned away and spoke to the children. "What do you think, kids? More sail?"

"Wind's awful strong," Josie said.

"Unless we head out to sea," said Will.

They all stared at Ruth. Tears gathered in her eyes and mingled with the rain, warm against her cold skin. She felt excluded by the other three. The wind howled around the sails, and the sheets were thrashing back and forth, cracking like whips.

"Dad," Will said suddenly, "we're getting close to shore."

They had been drifting with the current. Under these shallow waters was a slew of hidden rocks and shoals. As though to prove it, there was a second thunk beneath them, much more severe than the last. All four were thrown heavily against the cabin bulkhead.

Josie screamed, clutching at her left arm. "My wrist!" Her face screwed up with pain. "Mom, I think it's broken!"

From somewhere beneath the boat came a noise like a giant chewing glass. "Paul!" Ruth moved toward Josie. "What's that?"

"Sounds like we've been holed," Paul said. "Take the wheel, Ruth, while I try to see what the damage is."

Josie was sobbing. "My wrist, it really hurts."

Ruth knew that a more competent mother would have found something—a knife, a flashlight, anything—and tried to splint the wrist. What were they going to do if the boat capsized? Josie would not be able to swim. "Don't worry, Josie," she said. "It'll be okay." She did not believe it.

They were not moving at all, though the wind tore at the sails. Waves bore down in solid ranks, knocking them further onto the rocks. With every wave the boat reared out of the water and smashed down again.

"The cabin's full of water!" Ruth screamed. Her knees faded under her. She tasted salt at the back of her throat.

Paul was back in the cockpit, looking distraught. "Oh, God," he moaned. "My beautiful boat."

"Guess we're out of the race tomorrow," said Will.

"Which makes Sam and me rich." Josie gave a crooked smile.

"Great. Lobsters all around." Will looked at his father's face and stopped grinning. "What now, Dad?" he asked soberly.

"Better get into the dinghy. Get away from these rocks."

"But won't—" Wind snatched the words away from Ruth.

"Now!" Paul pushed her roughly to the rear of the cockpit. He ordered Will down the ladder and motioned Josie after him.

"I can't, Dad," Josie said. She was holding her injured wrist at an odd angle against her chest. It took much longer to lower her down than seemed reasonable. All the time, the sea hammered at the hull.

"I'll give you a hand," Paul told Ruth.

"But shouldn't we stay with the boat?"

"Do it," he snapped.

She tried to follow his orders. Standing with one leg over the stern rail, she saw her children below, their white faces upturned in the near dark. The tiny craft pitched on the black water. Fear locked her legs. "I can't," she said.

"Come on, Mom. Come on, it's okay. You'll be okay, I promise." Will's voice was gentle, calming.

Paul was behind her. "You'll be okay, Ruth," he said. "I'm right here. I'll steady you. Just get in the damn dinghy."

The sea reached up toward her. "I can't, Paul. I can't."

"Ruth, get a grip, will you? Jump. We don't have much time." He reached into his back pocket and brought out his cell phone. "Do it, Ruth."

The boat lurched; the beaten timbers shrieked. Water poured up from the cabin into the cockpit. Paul pushed her, and screaming, Ruth fell toward the sea before landing awkwardly in the bottom of the dinghy. Her right knee flamed with pain. Above them the stern of the boat lifted with the sea—four, five, six feet above their heads—before five tons of wood and metal came crashing down inches away.

Ruth saw Paul's hands on the rail as the stern lifted. He dropped toward them and scrambled to untie the painter. The dinghy swirled away into the gloom. A mighty wave suddenly swelled out of the black sea and caught the underside of the dinghy, lifting it endways so that it stood almost perpendicular, tipping them out, thrusting them down under the surface. Ruth heard Josie's shriek of agony as the force of the water caught her damaged wrist.

Ruth's head was full of blinding pain. The cold was unbelievable. It forced the air out of her lungs. She broke the surface, choking. She could see neither of her children. "Will!" she shrieked. "Will!" Frantically she reached out, felt something under her fingertips, reached again and caught the webbing of Will's harness. She pulled it close. "Will. Thank God."

Paul was beside her, his hand strong over hers on the safety rope. "The coast guard—I got through. . . . They're on their way."

They heard a scream. "Dad! Mom! Help me! I can't hold on." In the near dark Ruth could see her daughter's terrified face, white against the thrashing sea. Her mouth was open, a dark circle against her pale skin. And then she disappeared.

"Josie! Oh, God, *no!*" Desperately Ruth lunged toward the space where Josephine had been. "Josie, where are you?"

The sea crashed down, forcing Ruth below the churning water. Fighting her way upward, she yelled again, but the only answer was a whack and groan as the boat crashed on the reef. She and Paul and Will clung to the safety ropes around the dinghy, shouting Josie's name.

"She can't have gone. She can't." Paul took a deep breath. "Hang on, Jo!" he shouted. "Hang on."

Ruth felt consciousness fading. The bone-chilling cold was creeping toward her brain. How long could they endure it? Will already seemed to be unconscious. Clumsily she wound his harness strap around her wrist. "Josie," she screamed. "Come back, Josie!"

"Josie!" Paul yelled. "Can you hear us? Answer me, Jo."

Ruth began to shiver, huge tremors running through her body. "She's gone. She's not here. Oh, Paul, where's she gone?" My girl, she thought, my beloved daughter. Images fluttered about in her head like tattered rags. It can't be—the unthinkable. She can't be dead. Not my Josie. It isn't true. It isn't . . . "Josie, come back!"

Afterward none of them knew how long had passed before they heard the throb of a helicopter overhead. For all of them the only reality was that Josie had vanished. Paul kept repeating like a mantra that she had her life jacket on, she couldn't drown, the helicopter would find her, she would be picked up.

"We're going to be all right," Paul said, but Ruth knew that was a lie. If Josie had . . . Her mind could not take in the fact. . . . If they lost her, nothing, ever, was going to be all right again.

NEWS of the accident spread quickly. The Connellys' friends came by, urging them to say if there was anything they could do to help. But time pressed, and they had no choice but to take up again the rhythm of their lives back in the city. The year-round people were more practical. There was scarcely a family that could not tell the story of a lost lover, a father who had never come home.

There were flowers: bunches of hydrangeas and pots of geraniums. But mainly they brought food. Paul and Ruth would get up to find the back porch covered with casseroles. Every day Gertrud Hechst came to the house, carrying a dish of her home-cooked specialties—dumplings or a sauerbraten or a blueberry pie—and stayed to sweep the porches, scrub the kitchen floor. Their nearest neighbors, Ben and Marietta Cotton, the brother and sister whose forebears had lived on the point for twice as long as the Carters, dealt with other practicalities. Ben chopped wood for the winter, while his sister dusted, washed, made coffee—all kindnesses performed without words.

Ruth was aware of their presence, their compassion. For the most part these were people still living the same hardscrabble lives as their parents and grandparents, and she was grateful for a generosity some of them could ill afford. Nonetheless, they seemed inhabitants of a world to which she no longer belonged. Each day, she went through the motions of normality. She got up, showered, dressed, drank the coffee that someone—Marietta? Gertrud?—put in front of her, but could not have said at any moment what she was doing.

Her whole being was concentrated on two things. First, on keeping hold, in whatever way she could, of her sanity. Second, on the certainty that somewhere Josie was still alive. She spent hours up on Caleb's Point, a pair of field glasses around her neck, scanning the ocean for the sight of a white arm, a piece of wreckage to which her daughter might be clinging. She went down to the shoreline and clambered over rocks and boulders, searching wild-eyed, her body bruised from falling, her emotions wound tight. A branch of bleached driftwood, a tangle of seaweed, and her heart jumped. Josie! My darling—unconscious, maybe, but alive. She took the car along the coast and doggedly searched the beaches and coves until her tearless eyes were raw with looking.

She refused to accept that her search was futile. The coast-guard cutters had swept up and down the coastal waters a dozen times, to no avail. From Portland up to the Canadian border, locals had been alerted, fishing boats had been asked to keep a lookout, pleasure craft warned.

As the days passed and there was still no news, Paul phoned Will's school principal. Mr. Fogarty, expressing his deep sympathy, suggested that Will come back to the city; he was sure that Will would be welcome to stay with the family of his best buddy, Ed Stein.

"I agree with him," Paul said. "I've called Carmel Stein, okayed it with her."

"It's not okay with me." Will stared at his mother, hunched with misery in the kitchen. "Don't make me go. Tell him, Mom."

"I think your dad's right," Ruth said expressionlessly. "You shouldn't miss school."

"But I want to be *here*." Will was trying not to cry, his freckled face flushed, all his ebullience vanished. "She's my sister."

"Oh, Will." Ruth got up and put her arms around him.

He turned his head into her breast. "Don't send me away, *please. Please*. If it hadn't been for my birthday—" He began to sob.

With a terrible anguish Ruth looked at Paul. "Will, it's not your fault," she said. "It's absolutely not."

"It's nobody's fault," said Paul, his voice dead. "Ruth, it would be better for him not to be here."

Paul had given up on Josie, she could see. Too exhausted by grief to argue, she turned away. "I promise we'll call you, Will, the very minute there's any news."

"But I want to—"

"You can come right back as soon as . . . as she's home."

Recognizing that arguing was futile, Will gave in. "Okay," he said quietly. He stood up, looking at them both. In his eyes Ruth saw that he too had accepted the truth she herself refused to concede: Josie was lost to them.

TWO weeks after the accident someone pounded at the front door. It was early. The turning leaves were netted in sea mist that would not burn off the horizon for another couple of hours.

In the kitchen Ruth felt her body swell with anticipation. "They've found her," she said. "Paul, she's home!" She stumbled down the hall and flung open the door.

"Miz Connelly?" The man on the porch tipped his cap.

"Yes." Ruth looked beyond him. "Where's my—"

She heard Paul's footsteps behind her on the pine planking and his voice, desperate. "What've you found?"

"Coast guard, sir, ma'am. Lieutenant Edwards." The young officer pulled something from a zipped navy carryall. "Do you recognize this?"

Paul's hand sought for Ruth's. "It's her life jacket," he said. "Josie's. It's got her name printed on it."

"It was found washed up almost at the border with Canada."

Ruth took it from him. "No," she said. "Please. No."

It was waterlogged, the red canvas torn by the pounding of the sea. The weight of it in her hands finally put an end to the hope that had sustained her over endless hours of searching. Something broke inside her, and she pressed the ripped, stained jacket to her chest as though she might squeeze one last precious drop of Josie from it.

Paul wept, pressing his fingers against his eyes. Ruth knew she ought to hold her husband, comfort him, but she was too immersed in her own pain. When Paul put his arm around her, she moved away.

"They'll find her," the officer said in a low voice. "Might not be for a while. Tricky waters around here, as you'll be aware, Mr. and Miz Connelly." He did not add what they all knew—that occasionally bodies never did show up.

Ruth watched the coast-guard vehicle drive away. She looked at the field grass that spread down toward the sea, the bright flowers dotting it, the lichen-yellowed rocks emerging from ancient earth. "I will never come here again," she said. "Never."

She stepped off the porch and walked away from her husband, toward the pond behind the house. Hands tucked under her arms in an attempt to ease the pain that constricted her chest, she paced its perimeter. Never again. There would be no more memories attached to this house, to the woods, the pond.

Every summer Paul would tow a wooden raft out to the center of the pond and tether it there; from it, both children had learned to swim. As she walked the reedy borders, the mental snapshot of her daughter's sunburned body as she dived from the raft was so clear that Ruth almost expected to hear the splash and the sound of Josie's laughter.

She picked up the trail and followed it through the woods up to Caleb's Point. In these woods, on this bluff, Josie had been happy. How long had she struggled, choking as the sea rushed in? Had she known which was her last gasp? Had death come as a relief? Had it been the cold that killed her? Ruth thought of the girl's body lying deep below the surface of the sea. She shivered.

Was there any pain worse than this loss? Not able to forget the hostility between them over the recent summer weeks, her mouth loosened and twisted. Death had come so suddenly, there had been no time to explain that it would not always be like this. No time, either, to describe the never-ending ache of parental love or the way in which it saturated the heart.

SHE lay on her side in bed, staring at the round shadow of the lampshade on the wall. The room was scented by two sandalwood chests, which had come from China a hundred and fifty years ago. Through the open windows she could hear the sea, gentle now, no more than a whisper down on the shore. Josephine. My child, my firstborn. Her heart felt as though it were made of lead, heavy as a coffin.

Paul came out of the bathroom, and she listened to him moving about the room. Heard his bare feet on the hooked rugs, the soft thud as he dropped the towel on the floor. The bed dipped as he climbed under the covers. She felt the long weight of him as he stretched out beside her. He tried to put his arms around her. "We'll get through this, Ruth," he whispered.

She whipped around. "Don't touch me," she said.

He raised himself on his elbow. His eyes were red, and she guessed he'd been crying. "Ruth," he said sadly, "I understand how you feel—"

"You don't understand anything," she said. "Nothing."

"We have to support each other. No one else can."

"If you hadn't been drunk . . ."

His body stiffened. "Yes. If I hadn't—what, then?"

"You'd have been more careful."

"You mean I wouldn't have allowed a storm—freak storm—to catch us, is that what you mean?" He was using his pleasant voice, the soft professorial one that screwed her up inside.

"You'd have left Bertlemy's Isle before it started. You'd have taken more notice of the weather."

"You're telling me that if I hadn't drunk three martinis, we'd still have Josie?"

"And most of the wine."

He sighed. "If you hadn't forced her to come," he said, ticking the points off on his fingers. "If you had let us ride out the storm at sea. If you hadn't been knocked down by a wave when you were a kid . . . What the hell good are 'ifs,' Ruth?" His face softened, and he tried to pull her close.

Again she twisted savagely away. "Don't touch me. Just don't."

CHAPTER THREE

THE medical examiner came up from Bangor to hold an inquest. The verdict was death by cause or causes unknown. A few days later they held a short service in the little Episcopal church in Hartsfield. "Not a funeral," Paul explained to Will, who had traveled up from Boston with Ed Stein and his parents. "Because there's no . . . no body."

"That means she could still be alive?" Will's voice shook.

Paul held his son. "The area's been thoroughly searched."

"But suppose someone picked her up," Will said stubbornly. "A Libyan tanker. Or—or a fisherman from New Brunswick."

"They'd have contacted the coast guard."

"Maybe she's lost her memory."

Paul squeezed Will's shoulders. "I don't think so," he said quietly.

A plaque was placed on the Carter tomb in the graveside next to the church. Ruth stood between her husband and her son, pinched and silent. Beside her, Paul wept. Will carried a sheaf of white freesias, his face wet with tears. Ruth felt detached from it all, as though her capacity for emotion had been destroyed.

AFTER Paul went back to Boston with Will, Ruth made an appointment with Dee's Realty in Sweetharbor. As she walked along Old Port Street, people came up to her, faces she half recognized, and murmured softly of how sorry they were, what an exceptional person Josie had been, so concerned, so thoughtful of others. Ruth heard them, smiled acknowledgment, took nothing in. Their words seemed meaningless. Josie was dead.

Dee's Realty was housed on the second floor of a weathered shingled building opposite the 7-Eleven. Belle Dee, a tiny energetic woman with close-cut blond hair, shook hands with Ruth and poured coffee for them both.

"I heard what happened," Belle said. "I'm just so sorry. What a terrible thing to—"

"We don't expect to be using the house for some time," Ruth interrupted. "I'd like you to take over the maintenance of it."

"Maintenance?"

"That is what you do, isn't it? One of the services you offer?"

"Yes, but—"

"Then please give me the paperwork. I'll fill it out and return it," Ruth said.

Belle put down her cup. "Will you be back next summer?"

"I doubt it." Ruth felt very small and cold.

"Then have you considered renting? Our books are full of people anxious to rent for the summer."

"I don't want strangers in my house," Ruth said.

Belle Dee foraged for paperwork in the drawers of her desk. "Mrs. Connelly—"

Ruth took the papers and stood up. "It was good to talk with you," she said, then turned on her heel and went out.

Later that day, driving away down the track, she did not look back. Behind her, Carter's House stood mellow in the sloping autumnal sunlight, the black shutters fastened across the windows incarcerating her memories. An era was ended. That part of her life was over.

MOST weekends that fall Paul and Will drove up Route 1 to Sweetharbor. Father and son were building a bench as a kind of memorial to Josie. Paul tried to get Ruth to come with them, but she always refused, shaking her head, not meeting his eyes.

"It's a great bench, Mom," Will told her, having just returned from Maine. "Dad's carved the middle of the back into the shape of a heart. He's really good."

"You're not bad yourself," Paul said, ruffling his son's hair. "Will's a killer with the sanding machine. Smoothest wood I ever did see."

"You should see the way Dad shapes the slats," countered Will. "I gotta admit I'm impressed."

Ruth looked away, hating them for being so contented with each other. Hating them, too, for being able to return to Carter's House when she knew she never would.

Once the bench was finished, Paul had a brass plate set into the top rail engraved with Josie's name and the dates of her birth and her death. Ruth would not look at it. The finality of that second figure was too much for her.

Again she refused to go to Maine, so Paul and Will drove up without her. At Carter's House their neighbor Sam Hechst was waiting for them. Between the three of them they heaved the bench into the back of Sam's pickup and took it up to Caleb's Point.

"I never realized how heavy teak is," said Will.

"That's because it's durable," Paul said. "Hope we didn't use the wrong kind, like Ted Trotman did for that deck of his."

"We'd have got it from Josie if we did."

"Tell me about it!"

They poured concrete and set the bench fair and square, facing out to sea. They bolted it down and, when it was ready, rubbed linseed oil into the wood until it gleamed.

Finally Sam touched a finger to his fur-lined cap. "Guess I'll leave you two," he said. "You'll want to be alone to do your grieving."

"Thanks, Sam." Paul shook his hand. But when the old Chevy pickup had banged away into the distance, he could not grieve. He gazed bleakly at the gray winter water of the sound. Was it his fault that Josie had died? Could he have done more, saved her life? He would never know. The wind blew in off the sea, cold and salty, and tears ran down Paul's face, but his heart was empty.

"It's okay, Dad," Will said. He slipped his hand into his father's, his own eyes full of tears. "We'll be okay."

"I hope so."

"I kinda wish Mom would talk about it, though."

"Not talking is her way of handling it," Paul said. He reached over and touched his son's shoulder. "You miss Josie?"

"Of course I do. She was my . . . She was my friend as well as my sister." Will bit his lip. "Yeah, I miss her lots."

"Me too. All the time."

"Dad . . ."

"Yeah?"

"Do you think she could be . . . I mean, sometimes I really wonder if she's out there somewhere, still alive."

"Oh, Will, I wish I thought she was, but she's not, son. We just have to accept it. She's not."

"I guess you're right."

They drove back to the city without mentioning Josie's name again.

"I didn't feel a thing," Paul told Ruth later. The two of them were in the living room together but, as always these days, apart—Paul on the sofa nursing a glass of wine, Ruth at the table. "The bench was there for her, *because* of her, and none of it made any sense at all."

"I can see that," she said, not looking up. The Tiffany lamp shed jeweled light onto her office papers.

"I put my arm around Will's shoulders, and he burrowed his head into my jacket, like a puppy. We just stared at the ocean."

"He used to burrow like that when he was a little boy."

"I know." Paul was silent for a long moment. Then he went on. "I couldn't cry. I mean, there were tears running down my face, but they were tears of cold, not of grief. I haven't cried since the memorial service."

"I don't want to think about it, Paul."

"Ruth, I . . ."

Ruth gazed at him expressionlessly, then returned to her papers. She would not look back. She had found a way to manage. She worked late most evenings and came home too tired to talk, with a legitimate excuse for going early to bed. On weekends she brought work home, crowding out the spaces where Josie might have lurked.

She fulfilled her maternal duties, made sure Will had clean clothes, that he got to his extracurricular classes on time, but her real life was lived at work. Often, reluctant to return to the aching spaces of her home, she would call to say she could not get away from the office, and remain at her desk.

On the nights when she did come home, she would prepare

supper for Paul and Will, sit with them while they ate it, saying little or nothing. Her appetite was minimal: Swallowing food was too keen a reminder that her body needed fuel to keep it functioning. It seemed wrong that she was alive when Josie was dead.

TOWARD the middle of October, Bob Landers came into Ruth's office. "Do you know what the time is?" he asked.

"No." She looked up blindly, then glanced at her watch. "Goodness, is it really eight?"

"Ten after. You're working too hard, Ruth."

"Probably." She glanced down at the papers spread over her desk. "But there's a lot to do."

"Ruth," he said, "it's time to call it a day." He leaned over and swept her documents into a heap. "I know you have good cause, but recently you've been looking extra stressed, and I'm not the only one who's noticed it."

"Did you come to complain about something I've done, Bob?"

"Quite the opposite." He looked at her affectionately. She and Bob went back a long way, to college days, to before she began dating Paul. "In fact, I should have mentioned sooner what a fine job you did of bringing Phil Lavelle on board."

"Thanks." That summer day at the Trotmans' party came back to her, when Josie—belligerent, feisty—had been so much alive.

"You're doing me a lot of good in the firm," he continued. "You're more than justifying my choice. Frankly, at the time, some of the others thought you were too young to be promoted to partner."

Ruth forced herself to speak. "I wish."

"Now listen, Ruth. I'm going to say what I came here to say. Unweighted. Unloaded. Then you go home and think about it. No obligations attached, no strings. It's entirely up to you."

"Intriguing."

"As you already know, some time in the new year the McLennan Corporation is scheduled to fight an antitrust infringement case through the British courts. The hearing's supposed to last about three weeks but might take six, and during that time we're—LKM, I mean—going to need someone on the ground over there."

"I can't appear in a British court."

"I know that. You'd be an adviser. Nobody knows McLennan's affairs as well as you, and you've always got along well with him. In fact, he specifically asked for you to be part of the team. On top of that, although I'm not in the business of providing my partners with therapy, I have the feeling it might do you good to get away."

"I'm a married woman. And a mother. I can't just take off."

"I'm aware of that fact, but Paul's around a lot of the time. And it might not be that long."

"It's tempting," Ruth said slowly. A breathing space—it was exactly what she needed. "I'd have to talk to Paul, of course."

"Do that. Take a while, consider the angles."

"YOU should go," Paul said.

"But am I being unfair, leaving Will? I don't want to upset him. It's barely six weeks since . . ."

"You could take him with you. Put him in school in London for a month. It'd be a real experience."

"It's an idea, but I'll be up to my eyes with work. Not that Will's any trouble, but he'd be an extra consideration." Paul was raising sardonic eyebrows, and she said, "Do I sound horribly self-absorbed?"

"You could say that." His lip curled contemptuously.

"Look, if you disapprove, why are you urging me to go?"

"Because it's obviously what you want to do."

He was right. The thought of getting away had a kind of comfort about it. Somewhere new. A fresh start. "I have to say . . ."

"So you'd better go, hadn't you?"

His voice was so inimical that sudden tears came into her eyes. She turned away so that he would not see them. What had happened to them?

When she suggested that he come to England with her, Will was adamant that he did not want to.

"You might make some new friends," she said.

"I've got enough already," he said. "Besides, I just want to go on the way I am now." He looked at her with a carefully neutral expression on his face. "Do you have to go, Mom?"

"I don't *have* to, but it's an honor to be asked. It'd certainly be a good career move to go."

"Right."

"Would you rather I stayed here, Will? Because if so, I'll tell Bob Landers I can't do it."

"Hey, good career moves don't happen that often, do they?" The effort he was making wrenched Ruth's heart.

"If you don't go, you won't be able to bring us back some of that nice warm British beer," Paul said.

"Or a deerstalker hat," said Will. "With the earflaps? So you gotta go, Mom. I really want one of those."

Hugging him, Ruth asked, "Will you miss me?" and realized that the moment to turn down Bob's offer had passed.

FOR Thanksgiving the Connellys flew to California to stay with Paul's brother, Luke, in La Jolla. All three adults spent the vacation trying to build new memories, giving Will—and themselves—a fresh book of experiences. They ate seafood at Antony's and toured Universal Studios. One day they crossed over the border to Tijuana, where, in a small back street, Will bought Ruth a silver ring with money he had been given for his birthday, and Ruth found Paul a leather belt with a turquoise as big as a golf ball set in the buckle. They drove up to Carmel, around Seventeen Mile Drive, listened to seals bark offshore at Point Lobos. At Pebble Beach, they drank coffee and watched the sun make rainbows in the sea spray.

But however much she tried, nothing soothed the raw edges of Ruth's damaged heart. She smiled for Will's sake, sang along to the car radio, but all the time the absence of Josie throbbed inside her like an abscess waiting to burst.

Despite Will's pleas that they spend Christmas at Carter's House, they remained in Boston. Will came down with a chest infection that kept him out of school for several days, and Ruth frantically juggled her schedule so as to be home earlier and leave later. She was leading a team handling a complicated bank merger against a background of dissent from a coalition of consumer-rights groups while trying to find time to submerge herself in the McLennan merger plans.

The night before she left for England, she said to Paul, "You're sure about this? Me leaving you and Will?"

"Absolutely," said Paul. Avoiding her eyes, he said, "Actually, it couldn't have come at a better time."

"What's that supposed to mean?"

"I've been thinking for a while that we need some space."

The word filled her with dread. "Space?"

"The time away from each other will do us both good."

"What are you saying?"

"For God's sake, Ruth." Impatiently he shook his head. "With you gone, at least we'll both have a chance to think things through."

"You mean our marriage?"

He avoided her gaze. "Ruth, we aren't connecting anymore. Sometimes I wonder if we ever did, even before the accident."

"How can you say that?" she said. "Something like that was bound to throw us off course. We had a good marriage. We still can." Even as she spoke the words, she was not sure that they were true.

"I don't know who you are anymore," Paul said wearily.

"I'm the same as I always was."

"Oh, no. No, you're not."

Tears gathered at the back of her throat. If she gave in to them, she might drown. Instead, she stiffened her shoulders. "Are you saying that you want a trial separation?"

"Sounds good to me," he said.

"Thank you, Paul. That is so exactly what I needed right now."

"I'm sorry." He did not sound it. "I know my feelings aren't of much concern to you, but it seemed better to get it out in the open before you left."

She did not answer him. There was nothing she could say.

CHAPTER FOUR

THE McLennan Corporation provided Ruth with a luxurious apartment in Chelsea. There was a small balcony overlooking the Thames, and she sat there sometimes, bundled up against the cold of a London January, watching the play of light on the water, drinking her morning coffee before setting off for the corporation's offices. Big barges drifted past on the tide; tourist boats chugged up toward Greenwich. She put Paul's last words out of her mind. If she was to carry out the task she had been sent here to do, she could not afford to indulge in worries about her relationship with her husband. Instead, she found that away from Boston she could begin to let her memories unclench, to allow her thoughts to stray to Sweetharbor and Carter's House. And to Josie, a little girl falling from a boulder, in the Beetle Cat with her brother, opening her stocking on Christmas morning with her face alight with wonder.

Ruth had been afraid she would be lonely in England, but she found that she was simply on her own. She found it liberating. As the days unfolded one after the other, she began to see that Paul was right: This intermission was exactly what they had needed. The McLennan case had already generated a ton of paperwork. Despite that, Ruth made one rule. The case could have her for the rest of the week, but Sundays were hers. She took buses from London out to Cambridge, to Oxford, to Canterbury. She stood beneath Gothic roofs, walked through ancient cloisters, and marveled at the history that flowed past her in a constant stream. It was a world away from the life she was used to.

Her evenings were spent catching up with all the ramifications of what was an exceedingly complex piece of litigation, involving McLennan subsidiaries not only in England but also in France, Spain, and Germany. Two weeks after her arrival, following extensive meetings with the European teams, the Office of Fair Trading, and representatives from the Competition Commission, they seemed to be making no headway at all.

Ruth telephoned Dave McLennan in Boston. "The Germans think we should settle," she told him.

"Toss that."

"I agree. So far there's been no abuse of market power, and I can't see that there ever will be. The CC doesn't have a leg to stand on. Wish you were here, though, so you could tell them yourself."

"Tell you what. I'm going to Frankfurt at the end of the week. I'll come via London. Set up a meeting, will you? Thursday at eight."

"Eight in the morning? The French team's going to love that."

"In that case, make it seven thirty."

"Dave!"

Thursday morning Ruth found herself seated at the handsome zebrawood table that dominated the boardroom of McLennan (London) Corporation. The entire cast of lawyers and advisers was there. Dave McLennan stared pugnaciously at them.

"I understand there's disagreement about how best to proceed." He paused. "I want you to know, right up front, I think we should tough it out. Ruth, perhaps you'd give us your views on the matter."

Ruth had already made her views very plain but was happy to do so again. "I . . . that is, we—Landers Keech Millsom—believe that it's premature at this point to settle. Quite apart from the question of establishing precedent, we think we stand an excellent chance of prevailing if we go the distance."

Nick Pargeter, the English lawyer, nodded. "So do we. Frankly, I can't understand what the problem is." He was the most elegant man Ruth had ever met: His suits were beautifully cut; he had the kind of English hair she associated with gentlemen's clubs.

"But what happens if we lose?" said one of the gray-haired, gray-suited Germans.

"This is the problem." One of the Frenchmen nodded. "In such a case we could be looking at a disaster."

"I don't need to tell you, gentlemen," said Ruth, "that there are basically two ways to fight any case. When the facts are on your side, plead the facts. When they aren't, plead the law. In this case the facts are our best ally."

"What do you mean?" It was the gray German again.

"Herr Jacob, as I've said before, in order to prosecute us successfully in an antitrust action, the commission must show there has been an abuse of market power. We believe the present market is simply too volatile for that claim to stand up to the court's scrutiny."

"As we've repeated from the beginning," said Pargeter.

"Then why are they bringing this case in the first instance?" demanded the Frenchman.

"Nick, do you want to explain?" said Ruth.

Pargeter gave an exaggerated sigh. "Ms. Connelly has told you that the market is volatile. That's because new players are coming in every day, including the Japanese and your own compatriots, Herr

Jacob. So no one can claim a controlling share, because no one knows for sure how big the market actually is."

"That might change in two years," Ruth put in. "But as matters stand, the prosecution is whistling in the dark."

"Whistling in the dark?" The Frenchman frowned.

"Flying a kite. Um . . . hasn't got a leg to stand on." Pargeter's mouth curled as he tried to suppress laughter.

"I assure you," Ruth said, "that LKM doesn't offer its advice lightly. Perhaps you recall *Texaco* v. *Pennzoil?*"

The French team shook their heads.

"Remind them," said McLennan impatiently.

RUTH'S absence panned out conveniently for Paul. Even before Bob Landers's offer, he had arranged a sabbatical semester in order to make a final push on his book. With any luck he would be able to deliver it to his publisher by the end of the month. And he could spend the rest of his time with Will.

Without Ruth's wounded presence casting a blight over the apartment, he found himself regaining some of the former *joie de vivre* that had vanished with the death of his daughter. It was not that he wanted to play down her loss; it was simply a recognition that life had to continue without her and, given that fact, that there was enjoyment to be squeezed from it. He put his relationship with Ruth on hold: It was, he decided, the best way to handle it.

One night, as he watched the late movie, he heard Will moaning in his bedroom. Quietly opening his door, Paul saw that the boy was asleep but tossing restlessly, the sheets kicked down, his pillows on the floor.

"Wake up." Paul put a hand on the boy's shoulder. "It's okay. You're all right."

Slowly Will opened his eyes, the shreds of the nightmare still clinging to his expression. "I dreamed I was— That we were drowning." He grabbed Paul's hand so tightly that the joints cracked. "We were out in the boat, and the sea came. . . ."

"Shh." Paul sat down. "It was just a dream."

"She swam away," Will said painfully. "She said if it wasn't for my birthday, none of this would have—would have happened. I could see her, Dad, her face disappearing under the water, and she was saying it was my fault she was drowning."

"Will, you weren't responsible for the storm or anything—"

"I *was*. If I hadn't wanted that stupid picnic . . ."

"An accident like that, any accident, can happen anytime. And usually it's nobody's fault." Paul could see the luminous hand of Will's bedside clock. "Look, Will, it's nearly two in the morning. Want to come and keep me company in bed, the way you used to when you were little?"

"I'll be okay, Dad."

"Are you sure?"

"Sure."

Paul bent to pick up his son's pillow, and as he did so, something fell onto the floor. He picked it up and put it beside Will's head. A cuddly bear with a spotted bow tie and big brown eyes of glass. He frowned. "Isn't that— Wasn't that Josie's?"

"Yeah. Uncle Luke brought it back from England."

"Where did you get it?"

"From Carter's House. After the accident."

"Will, it's not going to be easy to get over losing Josie. It'll take time. You know that, don't you?"

"That's what the guy at school said."

"Which guy?"

"The school shrink. I—I went in to see him the other day."

"Did you?" Paul hoped his voice sounded sufficiently casual, though he could feel the thump of his heart. Was his son so unhappy that he voluntarily went in to see the school counselor? Oh, Will, Paul thought. What can we do to help you?

When Ruth next called from London and asked how Will was, Paul said forthrightly, "Not good."

"What is it?" she demanded. "What's wrong?"

"He's having nightmares about drowning."

"Oh, no. I hoped that after all this time . . ."

"And I've noticed he's not eating well."

"You're making sure he takes vitamin supplements?"

"Yes, Ruth."

There was a pause. "Paul, should I . . ." He could hear Ruth's reluctance in her hesitation. "Come back? I can, if you think it would be best. I mean, it would be really difficult, but—"

"I can't see the point." Frankly, Paul was happier alone in the apartment with Will. Ruth's absence made things easier all around. At least for now. "It's not as if we can do much to help Will."

"So we just go on showing that we love him."

"I do that," Paul said sharply. "All the time."

"Me too."

Paul did not respond.

"WILL and I went up to Carter's House for the weekend," Paul said, telephoning from Boston the next week.

"Oh?" Ruth closed her mind. She did not want to hear about it.

"Didn't go in, of course. Just looked around outside, made sure everything was shipshape. Went up to the point, checked out the bench. By the way, Mrs. Dee says there's mail in the house."

"I told her not to forward it," Ruth said. It would be letters of condolence for the most part. She was still not ready to read the polite regrets of other people. "How's the book coming?"

"The publishers had a few queries, and one chapter has to be rewritten, but otherwise they're pleased."

"I'm so proud of you, Paul. I'll be able to tell people I'm the wife of a published author."

"That'll be almost as good as having a wife who's a partner in a prestigious law firm."

His tone was cool, but Ruth let it pass. "Paul, I—"

"Here's Will."

"Paul . . ." But he was gone.

"Hi, Mom."

"Hi, honey. How're you doing?"

"Fine."

"Fine fine or *really* fine?"

"Really fine, Mom."

"You sound tired."

"You'd be tired too if you had an English teacher like I've got. What an ass-kicker."

"That's no way to talk about Miss Carling, William."

"That's Marling, Mom. If you'd made it to the parents night last semester, you'd know what I mean."

"Sorry." Why had she missed the evening? Ruth tried to remember. "I'll be back soon, hon, very soon. Promise. I really miss you." Her voice skipped a beat, broke.

"Hey," said Will, awkwardly, "don't go all weepy on me."

She tried to laugh but could not.

"I'm being a good boy and drinking my milk." As always, he tried to lighten the atmosphere, scared by the intensity of adult emotions. "And I promise to quit smoking, cut down on the booze, and flush my stash down the john, okay?"

This time she managed to laugh. "Okay."

Putting down the receiver, she thought she had never been lonelier.

A FEW days later Nick Pargeter called her. "They've given in!" he said, his tone exultant. "We are talking total capitulation."

"What?" Ruth had gone to bed around two, after working the entire evening on one clause the OFT seemed to find particularly difficult to accept. And it was now—she glanced at the alarm clock beside her bed—barely seven o'clock. "Who's capitulated?"

"The commission, blast their eyes," said Nick. "I had a letter this morning. They've agreed that there's no case. We're off the hook."

"That's *great!*"

"Just a couple of days to sort out the nitty-gritty, and after that we can all go home."

"Hey, Nick, do we make a great team or what?"

Ruth felt light-headed with euphoria. She could not remember when she had felt so good. They had won! Landers Keech Millsom would be delighted.

"Ruth, have dinner with me tonight," Pargeter said. "To celebrate. A decent meal and a bottle of bubbly are more than our due."

"All right," Ruth said. "On one condition."

"Name it."

"You don't invite Herr Jacob along too."

He laughed. "I may be an uptight Englishman, but I do have some notion of what constitutes a good time. And it does *not* include Herr Jacob."

Later, over excellent food, they talked about everything except the case. For each of them the next project already loomed. But first there was time for this interlude. "I'm going to miss you," Nick said regretfully. He raised his glass. "Not many lady lawyers are as sharp and as funny as you."

"Thank you."

"And beautiful." He surveyed her from under half-closed lids. "Why did you become a lawyer?" he asked.

"There's a question." Thoughtfully she sipped her wine. "Why does anyone do anything?"

"There's an evasion."

She sighed. "I guess I wanted to change the world. Don't we all, when we're young?"

"I can't remember that far back."

"I did, though. And instead, I went into corporate law. It wasn't the money that tempted me; it was the prestige, the chance to show that I was better than most."

Pargeter poured her another glass of wine, and she raised it to her mouth, thinking back to her determination that somehow she would make a difference. "Yes, I decided on law because I wanted to right wrongs, make the world a better place for the little people. I remember being appalled in school at the way the law could be subverted."

"It's the same in this country."

Ruth laughed. "My daughter used to get all fired up about the unfairness of things." It was the first time she had thought of Josie without pain. "*She* was sixteen. . . ." The words slipped out before she could stop them.

"Was?"

"She died. Last year."

"My dear, how perfectly awful for you." He put a hand over hers. "What happened?"

"It was a sailing accident." The sound of the wind in the sails and the crash of the waves came back to her with a vividness that was almost unbearable.

"Was anyone to blame?"

"Blame?" She stared at him, her eyes suddenly filling.

"Ruth, I'm sorry. I shouldn't have asked."

"We were caught in a squall," she said painfully. "My husband wanted to ride it out, but because I was frightened, I wouldn't agree. I wanted to get home. We drifted onto the rocks. . . ." It was something she had never admitted before. "I guess if anyone is to blame for my daughter's death, I am." She could feel his emotional withdrawal. He had expected a mild flirtation with a colleague over a bottle of Bordeaux, and instead, he had been drawn into something private and desperate. She looked at her watch, said lightly, "Good grief, is that the time? I still have to pack. Would you mind, Nick, if we broke this up now?"

PAUL met Ruth at the airport. Despite the heavy workload of the past weeks, her time away had smoothed the lines of stress. She looked younger, more carefree, and—to his distress—much more vulnerable, more like the girl he had fallen in love with.

How well he remembered other comings together after separation, when he would feel his heart soar with the sheer joy of seeing her. He put his arms around her.

"Where's Will?" she said.

"He had to stay after school. Basketball practice."

"I can't wait to see him again."

They walked together to the parking lot, and Paul backed the car out and made his way onto the highway. He asked about the windup of the McLennan case, and she told him some of the details. Finally she said, "I'm bushed." She yawned and leaned her head against the back of the seat.

He felt sick. What would she say when he told her? He glanced at her and noted the familiar line of her jaw, the little mole just below her left ear. She had once been so dear to him. And now? There was a void where love used to be.

When he let her into the apartment, she looked around appreciatively. The furniture was polished, the rugs vacuumed; there was a vase of white freesias on the coffee table. "Wow! You must have paid Bess extra," she said.

"Bess is off sick. I found someone in the yellow pages."

"It looks great."

"Will and I decided it was that or jumping out the window before you saw what it looked like."

"Bess won't have to clean for six months."

Paul went into the kitchen. "Coffee?" he called. His hands were damp with sweat.

"I have to take a shower before I do anything else."

IN THE shower she closed her eyes as the water fell over her shoulders. It was so good to be back. Despite the awkwardness, there was still so much between them. It had been a long time since they'd made love, far too long. It was her fault, she knew that. She was ready to acknowledge how wrong she had been. The separation had made her realize how much Paul meant to her. Above all, she wanted to tell him that it was not his fault that Josie had died.

She came out of the shower with a towel wrapped around her and said without preamble, "Let's go to bed."

"What?"

"Paul, I want to make love with my husband again."

"Ruth, I . . ."

"I've missed you so much."

She came toward him, put her arms around him. She let the towel slip, stood on tiptoe, and kissed him, pressed closer. "Paul," she murmured, "don't you want to?"

"I do, but . . ."

She stepped back. "But what?"

"Not now."

"Then when?"

He looked at her hard, and she could see the shine of tears in his eyes. "I don't know."

She turned away. "I feel like such a fool," she said.

In silence she went into the bedroom. When she came back, fully dressed, he was drinking coffee, staring at the table. "Okay," she said. "Let's talk."

He drew a deep breath. "I'm . . . I'm moving out, Ruth."

"You mean, leaving us?"

"Not Will. Just you."

"You don't want to give us a second chance?"

He shrugged. "Ruth, we just don't seem to have anything in common anymore."

"That's a pretty poor reason. Especially after nearly twenty years together."

"It's the main one I have."

"Is this all because of the . . . what happened?"

"Let's face it, Ruth. Things weren't going right before that."

"Nowhere near wrong enough for you to just pick up and go."

"You don't begin to understand my feelings. Maybe that's what was wrong with us in the first place: an inability to see the other's point of view."

"We didn't start out like that, Paul."

"We changed somewhere along the way. When you joined LKM, you became a different person. Your work always seemed to be more important than we were."

"That's so unfair," Ruth said furiously. "I *had* to work."

"And since the accident, you've put such a distance between us that I don't see how we can ever cross it."

"Don't say that, Paul," she begged. "Please don't."

"We've been apart for—what?—nearly four weeks. And I'm afraid I've enjoyed it, being on my own with Will. It's been such a relief not to be shut out by the person I'm supposed to be closest to."

"I've changed. The time away helped me see things much clearer."

He shook his head. "I've changed too. I loved you once. Maybe I still do. But every time I think about us, all I can remember is you ignoring me, keeping me at arm's length."

"You're right. I know that now; I didn't before. Oh, Paul . . ." She was crying. "Don't go. Please don't."

"We want different things now," he said quietly.

Ruth wiped her tears with the back of her hand. "I suppose that means there's another woman?"

"Ruth"—he reached over and put a hand over hers—"there isn't."

"Then why?"

He spoke very deliberately. "I need to talk about Josie."

She flinched. "I can't, Paul. Soon, maybe, but not now."

"That's why I have to go."

"Have to?"

"Oh, Ruth." He shook his head. "Perhaps it's my fault you've become what you are now."

"Someone you don't want . . ."

"Someone so hard that you'd need a shovel to find the person underneath." Paul stood up. "The truth is . . ." He hesitated. "The truth is, I'm more comfortable when you're not here. I can cope better on my own."

She gazed at him in disbelief. "That is such a hurtful thing to say." Tears began to roll again down her cheeks, and for a moment she was on the verge of flinging herself into his arms, begging him to change his mind. Then she remembered how he had looked when she stood naked in front of him. "If you're leaving, better do it before Will gets back," she said.

CHAPTER FIVE

HE LEFT before Will came home from school. His bags had been packed and stowed in his car. Sitting in the driver's seat, he leaned over and opened the glove compartment, where he kept a photograph of Ruth. She gazed at the camera, laughing, eyes squinched up against the sun. Clear gray eyes, just like Josie's. Every time he looked at her, he saw his daughter again. God, they were so alike.

Suddenly he was weeping. A grown man sitting in his car, sobbing. What would people think if they saw him? What did he care what they thought? He smudged the tears away and stared into the bleak concrete space of the underground parking lot. If she came down now, if the door of the elevator opened and she came toward him across the oil-stained concrete, asked him to stay, he knew he would.

He turned the key in the ignition, floored the accelerator, gunned out of the parking space and up to street level. Across town a sterile new apartment waited for him.

AFTER so many weeks in the anonymity of Chelsea, Ruth had looked forward to being among her own things again, sitting in a familiar chair, picking books out of bookcases, cooking in her own kitchen. Instead, she moved about the big apartment in a daze. Jet lag made her brain feel sluggish; she could scarcely keep her eyes open.

She sat down on one of the two broad window seats and stared unseeing at the traffic in the street below. All she could think of was that Paul was gone. In the days ahead she would probably learn to paper over the wounds, but for now there was only an agonizing sense of loss.

Much later she heard Will's key in the lock. "Mom!" he said, his face alight. "You're back."

"Did you think I wouldn't be?"

"Of course not."

She hugged him, held him tight. When she finally let him go and looked at him properly, she was alarmed. In the few weeks she had been away, he had changed. He looked ill. Exhausted.

Sitting with a coffee in the kitchen while he drank most of a quart of milk straight from the carton, she said carefully, "Your father has moved out."

He wiped his mouth with the back of his hand. "Where to?"

"I don't know." Before he left, Paul had said something about leaving his new address on the bulletin board in the kitchen.

Will's eyes widened. "You mean, like, moved *out?*"

"Yes."

"Are you upset?"

"We've been married for nearly twenty years." She got up and hugged him again. "Honey, I'm really sorry."

"It's not your fault."

"I sort of think it is. Or *he* does, which comes down to the same thing."

Will scratched at the waxed surface of the milk carton. "Do you still love him?"

"Of course I do."

He bit his lip. Her chest ached with the realization that he did not want her to see how upset he was. "I don't see why he's all of a sudden got to go," he said.

"I think he's realized he's happier living on his own."

"What about me?" His chin trembled. "I'm his *son.*"

She started to weep. "Ah, Will. Sweetheart."

"We had some good times together while you were in England," he said. "I thought he loved me."

"He does. He does. His leaving has nothing to do with you."

"First Josie, now Dad," he said unsteadily. "Why does stuff like this happen? What did we do?" He began to sob. "What else is going to happen to us, Mom?"

"Nothing, Will, I promise you. This is as bad as it gets. From here on in, it'll start getting better." She put her arms around him again and held him close. "And maybe, after a while, Dad'll realize it's more fun living with us than on his own."

"He said we'd rebuild the boat," Will said. His body shook. "He said it'd be our spring project."

"It still will be. Just because he's—he's living somewhere else doesn't mean he's stopped being your dad."

The two of them swayed together, mother and son, until Will wiped his face on his sleeve and said, "Don't cry, Mom." He put his hand up and curved it around the line of her jaw in an oddly adult gesture. "We'll be okay."

SUDDENLY there was such a rush of work that she barely had time to scramble through the days. Coming home exhausted at night, she would find messages from Paul on her answering machine. She did not return the calls. She was running on autopilot, juggling home and work, aware that home was coming off second best. The successful outcome of the McLennan antitrust case was seen as a triumph for her; people began to drop by her desk to ask for her advice. Bob Landers hinted at further promotion.

Her initial concern about Will's health abated somewhat. She put his paleness down to the fact that he was growing too fast. He seemed to be getting taller by the day: sleeves halfway up his arms, pants way above his ankles. She told herself, too, that the alterations in his behavior were simply his way of coping with the stresses to which he had been subjected.

Almost overnight he had become difficult and uncooperative. His response to her grew increasingly hostile. She tried to adjust to life without Paul, make things easier for him, but he offered her no help.

She came home after work one day to find Will watching a rerun of *Star Trek* instead of doing his homework. Buttered popcorn was spilled over the scatter rugs. She had spent the afternoon with the board of a Texas company whose executive had seemed incapable of grasping even the most basic procedures of corporate taxing, and her patience had worn very thin indeed.

"Will," she snapped, "what the hell's all this mess?"

"What?" He looked about him. "Guess I must have knocked the pan over."

"Well, clean it up. And turn off the set. You know the rules: No TV until your homework's done."

"This is educational," he said.

"Don't be ridiculous, Will." She picked up the remote control and snapped off the set.

"Don't *do* that," he shouted.

"Don't try to kid me that Mr. Spock is educational."

"But it's the one where they go back in time to the '20s." He grabbed the remote and flicked on the TV again.

"Will," she said, "turn it off."

"I want to watch it. You don't care about anything except yourself, do you? No wonder Dad left."

"That's enough," she said, her voice rising.

He stood up and strode menacingly toward her. "Well, it's true. You know damn well I'm right."

"Don't use that kind of language." Ruth bent and pulled the plug. "And go do your homework."

"Lousy bitch."

She grabbed his arm. "I *will* not be spoken to like that," she said furiously. Looking at his sulky, belligerent face, she felt as though her life were falling into ruin.

Will slouched grumpily to his room and emerged only when she knocked at the door to say supper was ready. Slumped in his chair, he stared at the vegetable lasagna she had prepared and pushed his plate away.

"Aren't you hungry?" she asked, concerned.

"Starving, but that looks disgusting." He reached for the bread basket and lavishly buttered a roll.

"Will," she said, "it took me ages to make that last night, when I had plenty of other stuff to do for the office. Now eat."

"I'll throw up."

"Eat it," she shouted. "Eat it, Will, or I'll damn well take a spoon and feed you myself."

He stared at her. "What did you say?"

"I said I'd feed you, Will, just like I did when you were a baby. And I mean it. I'm sick and tired of your behavior. Have some consideration for me, will you? I know you miss your father. We've had a terrible, terrible year—"

"It's not *my* fault he went."

She had been here before. She had seen that same look of hostility in Josie. She had felt the same dislike flowering between them. She shut her eyes and counted to ten. "I can't go on like this, Will. I just can't cope with the way you act, as though you can hardly bear to be in the same room as me."

"Maybe I can't."

"Then perhaps you'd better go live with your dad."

He threw his knife down on the table. "Everything *sucks!*" he shouted. *"Everything."*

"Tell me about it, William. I've got feelings too," Ruth said. "I'm hurting inside, just like you are. I understand how you feel. I honestly do." She drew in a deep ragged breath and covered her face with her hands. She began to weep.

Will seemed bewildered. "Hey, calm down, will you?"

"Please stop taking everything out on me. *Please.*"

"Look, I'm sorry. . . ."

"I'm doing my best. You may not believe it, but I am."

"Okay. I'm sorry." He reached for the pasta and took a large helping. "All right?" He dug his fork in and began to eat.

"I ASKED you to take the laundry out of the machine and fold it," Ruth said one evening about a week later. The two of them were living in an uneasy partnership. Explosion was never very far from the surface, but Will was obviously trying to be less surly.

"I know you did." He was lying on the sitting-room couch. "I was too tired when I came back from school."

"You were too tired last night to put the dishes in the dishwasher. Have you done your homework?"

"Not yet. Because I'm pooped."

"You weren't too tired to go up to Sweetharbor with your father last weekend."

"We didn't go in the end. We stayed in his apartment instead, took it easy. Watched football on TV."

"At your age you shouldn't be tired."

"What do you expect, with schoolwork, team practices? And the band's taking up all my slack."

"Maybe you should drop the band for the moment."

He stared at her. "No."

"Is it just that you're trying to do too much? Or is there something else wrong that you're not telling me?"

He did not answer for a while. Then he said reluctantly, "I haven't been feeling real good lately. I keep throwing up. And I get these pains in my joints."

Ruth's heart began to beat faster with anxiety. Was he doing drugs? "I heard that your friend Dan Baxter has a drug problem."

"So what if he has?"

"William, I promise I won't be angry if you tell me you've been trying stuff out."

"I haven't."

She shook her head. "But you look terrible. You've got shadows under your eyes, and you don't eat."

"Read my lips, Mom." He closed his eyes wearily. "I do not have a drug problem, okay? Dad says I'm growing too fast, that's all, and he was just the same."

It would have to do for the moment. Exhausted, Ruth went back to preparing for the next day's work.

The following morning she went into Will's room to hurry him along for school and found him still under the covers. That was all she needed. She looked impatiently at her watch.

"Come on, Will. Up, up, up. We're running late."

"I don't think I can get out of bed," he said.

"We all feel like that sometimes," she said.

"I mean I *can't* get up."

She laughed. "If this is a way of skipping the math test, forget it," she said, pulling at his covers. "Come on, guy."

"Mom, I mean it. I just . . . I feel too weak."

He seemed serious. Ruth felt his forehead. "You don't have a fever," she said.

"Honest, Mom. It's not the math test." His eyes were suddenly frightened. "I . . . I don't know what it is."

Ruth looked at him, biting her lip. Dare she leave him alone? She could rush into the office, cancel her lunch date, get back at noon. But if he really could not get out of bed . . .

She called her assistant. "I'm going to be late, Marcy."

"Nothing serious, I hope," Marcy said.

"My son's not well. Get hold of Jim Pinkus, will you? See if he can reschedule my ten-o'clock appointment."

"What about your lunch date with Baker Industrial?"

"Might not be a bad idea to call Petrinelli's assistant, just in case. Maybe reschedule. Make up some excuse."

When she went back into Will's room, she was fighting panic. Seeing him lying there, trying to smile, his face almost as white as the pillow, it was hard to disguise her fear.

"I'm going to run you to the clinic, Will."

"Aw, Mom."

"We need to get this dealt with, whatever it is. Here, let me help you up." She slid an arm around his shoulders and tugged him into a sitting position. She had not realized how thin he was. She swung his legs sideways, so that by pulling him forward, he was standing. He stood, already a head taller than she was, smelling of boy sweat and cigarettes—she had guessed for some time that he was smoking—and slept-in sheets. She wanted to kiss him, tell him she loved him. When had she last done that except in the most mechanical way?

While he showered, she phoned the HMO, then left a message on Paul's machine, asking him to call her, adding that it was about Will. She did not want to admit it to hersellf, but she was afraid that if he thought she was calling on her own behalf, he might not call back.

By the time she had finished her calls, Will was back in his room, a towel around his waist.

"Are you okay to get dressed by yourself?"

"Think so. I feel a little better." He sat down on the edge of the bed and closed his eyes. "Sort of, anyway."

"How about breakfast? There's cereal, eggs."

"I'm not real hungry, Mom." He reached for a shirt. The bones of his arms pushed against the skin, almost fleshless.

My God, Ruth thought, can he be anorectic? It was supposed to be a disease that mainly afflicted girls, but it would explain the weakness, the tiredness. Maybe even the pains in his joints.

As she drove across town to the clinic, it seemed as if every light turned red as she approached it and every bus in town deliberately stopped in front of her car to slow her down. Breath plumed from the pedestrians on the sidewalks, not one of them aware of her need to get where she was going as soon as she could. Her thoughts churned, panicky, terrified.

Anemia. Anorexia. Anemia. Anorexia. One or the other. They were not life-threatening diseases. They could be cured. Hang on to that. Call Bob Landers tomorrow, dump the job. She would do anything. Will was ill, he was collapsed in the back seat, but he was going to be all right.

Greg Turner, the pediatrician, was waiting for them. She watched his expression change as it fell on Will. He pushed up a sleeve and examined Will's skin, asked if he had any pain. Will mentioned his stomach. The doctor's fingers probed gently, withdrawing when Will winced.

He looked at Ruth. "I want him down to the hospital," he said. "I want some tests done."

"What is it?" She stepped closer. "Is it something serious?"

"Ruth"—Greg took her hands in his—"I wouldn't presume to make a diagnosis yet. Now, I've called an ambulance—"

"Ambulance?"

"To take him in. You can ride along with them."

Ruth looked at her son. He gave her a ghostly grin. " 'S okay, Mom. Chill out."

PAUL found Ruth alone in a waiting area, cut off from the busy passages by a half wall full of houseplants. She was sitting with a magazine on her lap and her eyes closed. He took a moment to watch her. She was much too thin, her body angular under her fashionable short-skirted suit. She looked so frail.

He called her name, and she opened her eyes, rising to her feet. When he spread his arms, she stepped inside them. "I'm scared," she said.

"What the hell is going on, Ruth?"

"I can't really take it in, Paul, but they're running all sorts of tests. It's something . . . something bad." Out in the peach-colored passage beyond the planter, a woman walked by holding the hand of a kid around eight or nine years old. The child's eyes were hollow, its skull naked except for a fringe of pale hair. It was impossible to tell whether it was a boy or a girl.

"What kind of bad?"

For answer, she began to sob. "They're talking about . . . They've done blood tests, and I overheard one of the technicians saying it could be—" She seemed too frightened to pronounce the word.

"What, Ruth?" He shook her impatiently.

"Cancer. Leukemia." The word barely made it through her lips.

"My God. You sure they were talking about Will?"

"I—I don't know, Paul," she said. Tears filled her eyes but did not fall. "Help me, Paul."

He drew her down to sit beside him. "Leukemia? Oh, God." He took her hand, squeezed it. The word spelled a horror he felt too drained to contemplate. Leukemia meant blood drives and donor appeals and television documentaries. Leukemia meant pain and little kids dying.

Ruth shivered. "I should have seen it, Paul. I was just too damn busy, ignoring all the signs. I knew he didn't look good. He was so tired all the time, but I was too wrapped up in my work, my stupid *job!*" Ruth screamed out the last word. She tore herself out of Paul's half embrace. "I'm a lousy mother who never deserved to have children in the first place."

He shook her. "Stop it. Stop, Ruth. We don't even know for sure what's wrong with him. Maybe Greg Turner was just playing it safe, sending you down here."

Someone joined them. A doctor. Under his white coat he wore an oxford shirt and a paisley tie. "Hi, I'm Mike Gearin. Staff hematologist. Sorry to keep you waiting."

"What's . . ." Ruth swallowed. "What's wrong with my son?"

"Well"—the doctor looked down at his notes—"I'd prefer not to discuss it until we can give you a firm diagnosis, but at this stage it does look as though your son has a serious blood disorder."

"Oh, God," whispered Ruth.

"Which blood disorder?" Paul said.

"He's being checked out by experts: A hematologist. An oncologist. A urologist. A neurologist." He curved his mouth into the shape of a smile, although it was like no smile Paul had ever seen. "Nothing but the very best. We've done the blood work, and now we have to wait for the results of the other tests. If there's something there to find, we'll find it." But his eyes said that something already had been found.

IT WAS almost six o'clock when Dr. Gearin reappeared. This time he asked them to follow him to a small side room, which held a low couch and two chrome upright chairs. One of them was already occupied by an older doctor, who stood up and held out a hand. "Good to meet you both," he said. "I'm Dr. Caldbeck, chief of hematology."

Dr. Gearin took the other chair. He had a very direct gaze; his bright brown eyes gave him an eager and hopeful air. "Well," he said, "there's no point trying to soften the blow for you. As we suspected, William is seriously ill."

"It looks like ALL," Dr. Caldbeck said. "Acute lymphoblastic leukemia."

Ruth felt as though she were suspended by a fraying rope over a deep ravine. There was no ground under her feet, only black chill space. "Leukemia's almost incurable, isn't it?" she asked.

"By no means. ALL is extremely responsive to therapy, and we are constantly expanding our understanding of the disease, which means the chances of recovery keep on improving. These days we expect cures in eighty percent of the cases."

"Are you absolutely certain of the diagnosis?" Paul asked.

"As sure as we can be, I'm afraid. The blood work we've done seems fairly conclusive. After we've seen the results of the bone-marrow aspiration, we can begin treatment."

"What are his chances?" Paul asked. "That's the only thing we can take in right now."

"Much depends on the patient himself and his response to treatment," Dr. Caldbeck said, "but ALL is very sensitive to chemotherapy, which uses drugs to kill the rogue cancer cells."

"But there's a downside to it, isn't there?" Paul said.

"The use of high-dose chemotherapy to kill the cells destroys the bone marrow," Gearin said quietly. "If the loss becomes critical, we have to find a healthy donor and infuse bone marrow from him or her into the patient."

Ruth's head seemed to be full of drifting clouds through which she could dimly perceive Will floating away from her until he was no more than a speck in the distance. Her jaw trembled. She stared dry-eyed at the two doctors, their words running around her head. Bone-marrow transplant . . . chemotherapy . . . How did any of it connect with Will, funny Will, whom she had known deep down was not well, but for whom she had simply not found the time?

"I'm cold," she said. "I'm so cold."

"Take my coat." Paul draped his jacket around her. "Will's going to be all right. You heard what the man said. Eighty percent of the cases are cured."

"Which means twenty percent aren't."

"Don't talk like that," Paul said. "Don't even think it."

They went through more details, but Ruth could not concentrate. Dr. Gearin's mouth opened and shut. Words she did not want to hear: nausea, hair loss, ulcers. My poor Will, my poor boy. She wanted to be anywhere but here, with her child lying deathly sick among other sick children. The thought of Caleb's Point came to her. Brightness of sun on sea. Clearness of wind in the pines. Where had it all gone, her treasures: children, husband, home? What fool's gold had she traded them for?

SHE called Bob Landers at home.

"Ruth," he said, "I heard you didn't come in this morning, but don't worry. Jim Pinkus handled the Phillipson meeting just fine. Jake's kicking up his usual—"

"I'm resigning, Bob."

"You're what?"

"From the job, from the partnership."

"Resigning? For God's sake, why?"

"I'm phoning from the hospital. Will has just been diagnosed with leukemia."

"Oh, my God, Ruth, how appalling. I'm devastated. But I'd urge you not to do anything drastic."

"I have no choice."

"We'll grant you an extended leave of absence. Quite apart from anything else, there's the health insurance benefits."

"I hadn't even thought of that." The future stretched ahead, bleak and cold.

"Don't resign, Ruth. Not yet. That way, if and when—"

"Bob, Will is seriously ill. He may . . ." Her voice trembled. She could not say the word. Eighty percent survive; twenty percent do not. The figures pulsed like neon signs in her brain. One in five does not survive. . . . "By the way, don't worry about the Phillipson negotiations. Jim knows what our strategy was going to be."

"As if any of that matters now."

"Not for me, but it does for you." She put down the phone.

At last they were allowed in to see Will. He was in a glass-fronted room off the corridor leading from the nurses station. More peach-colored paint, some pictures on the walls, a clothes locker. He was lying on a bed, wearing a loose green hospital gown. He looked exhausted, ancient, as though his boy's body had been invaded by an old man. An IV drip led from a plastic bag of clear liquid to the vein inside his elbow. Behind him was a tall table holding a tangle of tubing, a box, and a monitor. Lines of electronic green marched across its screen.

Seeing them, he smiled, trying, as always, to break the tension with a joke. "Hey, I was beginning to think you folks had gone on vacation."

"Oh, honey . . ." Ruth took his hand, and he winced.

"Careful, Mom. I've had so many needles stuck in me, bet I look like a pincushion."

"You look fine," Ruth said. "Just fine."

The lost look on her face sent a shiver of pain through Paul's heart. He could feel her fear, and he knew she wanted to say more. Knew that, like him, she wanted to look into his blue eyes and say, Yes, you look fine, my beloved son, my special Will. You have never ever looked so fine as in this moment, when you must know there is something terribly wrong with you and you try to reassure your parents, even though it is they who should be reassuring you.

CHAPTER SIX

"WE'RE proposing six sessions of in-hospital chemotherapy," Dr. Gearin told Paul. "Each treatment will mean several days here. In between, Will can go home, providing certain rules are observed, to give his blood time to recover."

Paul was angry. Bitterness crept along his veins, corroding his ability to function. Aggression bristled under his clothes. The sight of Will imprisoned between the metal sides of a hospital bed was bad enough. Far worse was watching the vitality drain out of him, knowing that all day, every day, plastic tubes were delivering a massive dose of drugs. And pushing this sports-loving boy down linoleum corridors in a wheelchair set up a silent scream inside him. "How long will that take?" he asked.

"We can never be entirely certain," the doctor said. "Many weeks, probably. What we're hoping is that the drugs will send the disease into quick remission. Once the cancerous cells have been eliminated and only healthy ones are being produced, we cross our fingers and hope that the disease doesn't recur."

"Remission isn't the same as cure?"

"It's a temporary cure. Recurrence is always a possibility."

Paul looked down at his hands. The anger fizzed inside him. "Have you got children, Doctor?"

"Yes."

"Then you'll understand how frustrated I feel over all this."

"I'd be exactly the same in your place. The children in my care make me feel so humble. A few days on the ward, and you realize that true courage isn't about fighting wars and slaying dragons; it's about facing long odds with dignity and pride."

"I appreciate that, but why Will?" Paul said helplessly.

"It's unfair, we both know that, Professor Connelly. But if it wasn't Will, it would be someone else asking the same question."

"I guess." Paul sighed. "What makes it even worse is that Will just . . . He just takes it all."

THE chemo left Will too weak and disoriented to do much for himself. When he came home between sessions of therapy, Ruth found herself having to care for him in the same intimate fashion as she had when he was still a baby in diapers. He who had grown into self-reliance was forced to revert to dependency. She could only guess how much he hated it.

Along with the drugs needed to fight the disease, he was taking medication designed to combat infection, which often made him nauseous. His skin broke out into rashes and boils. He developed ulcers in his mouth and throat, making swallowing extremely painful. Ruth knew that accompanying all this was the fear he must be feeling. He was too old, too intelligent, not to be aware that the discomfort he was enduring would not necessarily cure him. His heavy eyes, his lethargy, his wounded skin wrenched her. She had to clap her hands over her ears to hide the sound of his retching. Her heart felt as if it were slowly being flayed.

Each trip back to the hospital was traumatic for them both. It was not just the smells and the prospect of pain. There was no way to avoid seeing the ghostly army of hairless children, whose treatments were further advanced, whose naked white skulls gave them the appearance of creatures from outer space.

What made the return visits even worse was Will's dislike, bordering on phobia, of needles. The pain made him scream aloud. Sometimes his arm swelled up like a balloon. After one particularly harrowing session he wept.

"I don't want any more treatment."

"Hold on, honey. It's not for much longer," Ruth said. Even worse than the sight of his pain was her inability to stop it. It should be *me,* she wanted to shriek at the nurses. Let me suffer, not him. Not him.

"I'd rather die now than have to go through that again." Tears rolled slowly down his white face. His bloodless lips quivered.

"Well, I'm not going to let you," Ruth said.

When he had fallen into a doze, Ruth went to the hospital washroom. One of the other mothers came in—a too thin, bubbly blonde, who always looked dressed up for a night out on the town.

"You're Mrs. Connelly, aren't you?" The woman smiled.

"Yes. Ruth. And you're Michelle's mom." Eight-year-old Michelle was on her third cycle of chemo, and it was known on the ward that she was not likely to survive for very much longer.

"Lynda Petievich. Will is a lovely kid, so patient. He spends hours playing silly games with my Michelle, even though she's so much younger."

"She's such a pretty child."

"Shoulda seen her when she still had her hair." Lynda's face melted like wax, and anguish darkened her eyes.

Ruth reached out and took her hand. "I'm terrified too, Lynda. And every day, when I see you and Michelle and all the moms and dads, I feel truly humbled." She glanced down at her creased jeans. "And you always look so glamorous too."

"That's for Michelle's sake," Lynda said. "Before she got sick, I used to slob around like we all do, but I want her to know that she's worth taking trouble over."

"We've all seen the way she lights up when you appear. It's like having a movie star visit."

"C'mon!" Lynda laughed. "But thanks anyway for saying it."

"RUTH . . . it's Paul." He hated talking to the machine but plowed ahead. "Now that Will's back home, I'd like to come see him if—"

She picked up. "Hi, it's me."

"Can I come over tonight?"

"I'll tell Will. He'll be glad to see you."

"It'd be nice to see you too," he said awkwardly. "Maybe we could have a drink or something. I'll bring a bottle of wine." He felt absurd, being so hesitant about it. She was still his wife, after all. There was nothing strange about the two of them sharing a glass of wine.

When he arrived, he gave her a hug and handed her the bottle and a package.

"What's this?" She fingered the pretty giftwrap.

"Well, either you stand there guessing, or you open it and see. Ninety-nine percent of people polled favored the latter option."

Inside a wad of tissue paper was a necklace. Four little wooden hearts strung on a leather lace. Her face lit up. "How lovely, Paul. Where did you find them?"

"Would you believe I made them?"

"As a matter of fact . . ." She smiled at him. "Yes, I would."

"Since Will and I made Josie's bench, I've been working with wood. I brought some tools down from Carter's House."

"They're lovely," Ruth said. "Unusual." She ran a finger over the delicate carving. "Thank you so much."

Paul drew the cork and poured them each a glass of wine. "May I say, Mrs. Connelly, you're looking particularly good tonight."

"Thank you."

"Where's Will?"

"In bed. It hasn't been a good day for him—a lot of nausea."

"I'll go and visit with him awhile."

He went down the passage to his son's room, thinking, She didn't put the necklace around her neck. Probably thought it wasn't sophisticated enough for that dress she was wearing. Four hearts. One for each member of the family they used to be.

He knocked at Will's door. "Can I come in?"

"Hi, Dad."

Paul went in. "How're ya doin', son?"

Will lay back against his pillows, his face pale and weary. "Okay, I guess."

"I brought you a new tape. Nobody I ever heard of, but they're supposed to be good."

"Barenaked Ladies. Neat." Will picked it up, tried to produce enthusiasm. "Ed hasn't got this one yet."

"Anything I can do for you, son?"

"Actually, Dad, I'm almost too tired to talk. But . . ."

"But what?"

"I'd kind of like it if you—if you'd read to me, like you used to when I was a kid."

"Be my pleasure."

"I really wanted to read, but my eyes gave up on me."

"You can get tapes of books, you know," Paul said. His throat ached with unshed tears. "I'll bring some next time I come."

"Great." Will closed his eyes.

"What shall I read? Poetry, history, philosophy, religion?"

"Actually, I'm halfway through this vampire book."

"Vampires? Give me a break."

"It's neat, Dad. This vampire falls in love with this beautiful girl, whose brother's murdered by—"

Paul groaned. "I just remembered there's something else I'm supposed to be doing."

Will laughed—a quiet, weary sound. "I'm on page fifty-seven. You'll love it when you get into it."

WILL was back in the hospital for the next in his series of treatments. Arriving to spend some time with him, Ruth heard voices through the open door of his room. Peeking through the half-drawn blinds that covered the corridor window, she saw Michelle sitting on the edge of the bed. The little girl had Will's hand on her knee and was painting his nails with colored polishes. Her face was very serious. "It's gonna look so pretty, like a rainbow," she said.

"Hey, Michelle," Will said. "You know guys don't usually wear nail polish, don't you?"

"Course I do, silly." Michelle screwed the cap onto a tiny bottle of bronze and picked up another. "This one's Inca Gold. My mom wears this when she and my dad go dancing."

"Do they do that a lot?"

"Every Friday. My mom's got these gowns she made herself. She made me one, and one for my sister, Kelly, too."

"What color is Kelly's?"

"Kind of shiny bluey, to match her eyes. And mine's pink."

"To match *your* eyes?"

"Nobody has pink eyes," said Michelle sternly. "It's pink 'cause that's my favorite color. My mom mostly wears green 'cause that's what she was wearing when my dad fell in love with her. Where did your mom and dad fall in love?"

"I don't know," Will said. "Maybe at our house in Maine. It's called Carter's House."

"Why?"

"Because it was built by somebody called Carter. My great-great-great-great-grandfather, I think."

"What's it like?"

"It's painted white, and there's the sea in front," Will said. "All the rooms smell of pine trees and salt, and everybody's happy there."

Ruth felt a knife twist in her heart. They should have spent last Christmas at Carter's House, as he had begged to do. But Josie was up there—what was left of her.

"The sun always shines, and the birds sing," Will said.

"All the time? Even at night?"

"Specially at night."

Michelle regarded with satisfaction the golden nail she had just painted. Her tiny fingers clasped Will's rough boy's hand. "I bet you never had a manicure in your whole life, did you?"

"Boys don't have manicures."

"Kelly's practicing on my dad."

"You tell Kelly she can practice on me anytime she likes. She's kinda pretty."

"She's *real* pretty," corrected Michelle. "Go on about the birds at night. Do they keep you awake?"

"There's this special cap I wear," Will said. "I pull it down over my ears if I want to sleep."

Michelle touched the pink gingham mobcap she was wearing to hide her naked skull. "My sister made this."

"It's cute," said Will. "Think she'd make one for me?"

"No, 'cause you'd look *stoopid,*" Michelle said. "Now, what shall we do for the last nail? How about purple?"

Ruth walked into the room. "Looks like somebody's been getting the beauty treatment."

Will splayed his hands girlishly across his T-shirt. "Whaddya think?"

"Truly gorgeous," Ruth said.

"I feel like a drag queen."

"What's a drag queen?" asked the little girl.

"You don't want to go there," Will said.

"Hi, Mrs. Connelly," said Michelle.

The little girl's cheeks were unnaturally swollen, puffed out with the drugs she was taking. Her face was chalky white, except for around her eyes, which were set deep into their sockets. She looked very frail. "I love your hat, honey," Ruth said. God, how difficult it was to behave normally, faced with such sadness.

"My sister made it. Will wants one, but he'd look *stoopid*."

"I don't know. . . ." Ruth smiled as Michelle began to pack her nail polishes into a pretty bag patterned with bluebells. "Are you going to stay a bit?"

"I gotta go see Billy. He's feeling bad today."

Ruth stood at the door and watched the child walk away down the corridor. From behind she looked like any other little girl, skipping occasionally to catch up with herself.

WHEN her son's second round of chemo was finished, Ruth telephoned Paul. "Now that Will's back home again, it would be good if you'd sleep over every now and then," she told him. "I've got a hell of a job to do with him so sick, and you should be helping too, for his sake as much as for mine."

"I know that," he said. "But I—I'm looking at a hectic schedule this semester."

"You can change things around if you want to, Paul. Think of our son. If you were a fourteen-year-old kid, imagine how you'd feel if you were throwing up all the time. Imagine being unable to control your body and needing someone to clean you up. Think how you'd have hated it."

The picture she painted made him uncomfortable. Perhaps he hadn't been doing as much as he should. Even though he often dropped by to see Will, drove him to the hospital, spent time with him—hours, even—took him out when he felt well enough, it was not the down-to-earth, nitty-gritty stuff she was talking about. "Okay." He sighed inwardly. If Will needed him, then he must do whatever was best. "I'll work out some kind of a schedule so I spend more time with you."

"Not with me, Paul, with Will. If you prefer, I can make arrangements to be out of the apartment while you're there."

"Ruth . . ." He hesitated. "Just tell me what you want me to do."

"I'd like you to spend at least three nights a week here in the apartment. There's no need for us to overlap—"

"Ruth . . ."

"I can go and stay with the Steins."

"That won't be necessary, unless you want to."

"Of course I don't."

"When would you like me to start?"

"Today's Thursday. How about next Tuesday?"

He turned the pages of his diary. "That looks fine. Uh, Ruth . . . Are you . . . Are you seeing anyone?"

Her voice could have formed ice cubes in a heat wave. "You've forfeited any right to ask that kind of question."

"That means you are," he said.

"Why should you give a damn?"

"I'm still your husband. You're the mother of my son. I still care about you both."

"Even though you chose to walk out. Are *you* seeing someone?"

"There's someone I see occasionally, since you ask," he said deliberately, though it was not really true. "Nothing serious."

"I'll assume you'll be unaccompanied when you come."

"I'm not a complete jerk."

Almost in a whisper he heard her say, "I never thought you were."

ON TUESDAY evening Ruth found herself taking extra trouble with her appearance and opening a bottle of expensive wine she had picked up.

"Will went to bed early," she told Paul when he arrived. "I don't think you should wake him. He's sleeping very badly these days." She handed him a glass of wine.

"I spoke to Gearin," Paul said. "They seem optimistic."

"That's good."

They sat in the living room without speaking until Ruth, for something to say, said, "Are you going up to Sweetharbor anytime soon?"

"Maybe next weekend. Why do you ask?"

"The agent rang. She thinks someone's been in the house."

"I don't know what I could do about it that she can't."

"I guess she wants one of us to check that nothing's been stolen." He leaned over and refilled his glass, offered her the bottle.

She shook her head. Sitting together like this, the way they had so many evenings before, was a painful reminder of what they had lost. That she should be trying to make conversation with her own husband cast a shadow on her heart. "I think I'll go to bed." She stood awkwardly, wondering if she ought to kiss him, thinking how absurd this was—the two of them in the home they had shared for most of twenty years, and she did not know whether she should kiss him good night. In the end, she smiled briefly and left the room.

Paul switched on the TV, surfed the channels, settled down to watch an *Inspector Morse* episode he'd seen at least four times before. He was dozing to the staccato theme music at the end of the show when he heard Will's voice. "Dad . . ."

Will was standing by the living-room door. His skull gleamed white above his bony face.

"Will. Hi, son." Ruth hadn't warned Paul about the hair loss, and he did his best not to look surprised.

Will came in and sat down on the sofa beside his father. "What're you watching?"

"Some British thing. *Inspector Morse.* Ever seen it?"

"A couple of times."

"What do you watch these days?"

"*South Park. The X-Files.* All those nature programs. There was one about whales the other day."

"I saw that." Paul faked a double take. "Love the haircut."

"Thanks for pretending you didn't notice."

"And did you know you've got a diamond stuck in your ear?"

"It's fake," Will said. "Mom and I went and had it done. I thought I'd spend a couple years nagging her, but she just said okay. What do you think?"

"Cool."

"And we bought a hat, but you can still tell I'm bald."

"Have to say, it's kind of startling, first glance. For a moment there, thought I was watching Kojak, not Inspector Morse."

"Hey, Dad, aren't there famous bald guys other than Kojak?"

"Got to be. Just give me a moment, and I'll come up with someone. How about Shakespeare?"

"Doesn't count. He had hair on the sides."

The two of them laughed. Paul spread his arm across the top of the sofa, and Will snuggled in close. He picked up the remote and pressed it. "Hey, look. Clint Eastwood, in *Unforgiven*. Ever seen it, Dad?"

"Of course. It's one of those films whose sum is greater than its parts," Paul intoned solemnly. "A comment, if you like, on our contemporary culture, which manages to—"

"Cut it out, will you, Dad? Let's just enjoy the movie."

They sat together in companionable silence, Will held close by his father's arm.

IN EARLY May, Will returned to the hospital for his final dose of chemotherapy. As Ruth pushed him down the corridor, they both automatically glanced into Michelle's room, only to see another child lying on the bed.

"Oh, Mom, I hope she hasn't . . . isn't . . ." Will grabbed her hand.

Ruth found one of the nurses and asked where the little girl was. There was no need for an answer: The expression on the woman's face was enough. Will began sobbing, his thin shoulders heaving. "No. Oh, no," he said. "No. Please no."

"Will . . ." Ruth put her hand on her son's shoulder. There was nothing she could say. "When?" she said softly to the nurse.

"Two days ago. It was very quiet," she said. "We all knew it was coming."

"That doesn't make it any better when it happens."

"I know. But it helps some if you're prepared."

Ruth raised her head and stared at the woman. "Can anyone really be prepared for the death of an eight-year-old?"

The nurse looked away uneasily. "Her mom and dad were there, and grandparents. And her big sister. She just kind of smiled at them all and closed her eyes and didn't open them again."

"It's not fair," Will said, his voice breaking. "She was only a little kid."

Ruth could think of nothing to say that would comfort Will. When he had settled in his room and Dr. Gearin arrived to examine him, she walked to the phones and called Lynda.

NEXT day Ruth spent some time deciding what to wear to say good-bye to Michelle. Somber colors seemed wrong. In the end, she chose a daffodil-yellow suit with a green silk scarf—the colors of spring, the colors of hope. She drove to the address Lynda had given her and was surprised to find what seemed to be a hall attached to the back of a restaurant called The Old Warsaw. The place was packed with people and noise and laughter. There was a long table covered in platters of food and another stacked with bottles of wine and vodka. Someone handed her a glass, and she pushed her way through the crowd toward Lynda, who was standing at the end of the room with her husband. A large portrait of Michelle stood on a table, draped in long curling strands of pink-and-white gift ribbon and surrounded by soft toys. Rainbow-colored balloons hung from the walls, and vases of pink rosebuds were set all around.

"We're having a party to celebrate her," Lynda said, hugging Ruth. She wore a dress the color of strawberry ice cream. "We said our own private farewells at the church this morning, but Michelle always planned to have a party when she was better—and this is the party she would have had." Tears tumbled down Lynda's cheeks, but she kept on smiling.

"Michelle would have loved it," said Ruth, looking around.

We did not do this for Josie, our daughter, our sister, she thought. Instead, we bottled it up, kept it inside. How sterile the Maine service had been, with the autumn leaves falling and the arctic wind scything through our bones.

THAT evening Paul planned to produce his textbook orders for the fall semester. He was hoping to be done in time to watch the game on TV. He made himself a gin and tonic and had just taken the first sip when the telephone bleeped. He picked up. "Yes?"

"Paul?" The voice was so faint he hardly recognized it.

"Ruth, is that you? What's wrong?"

"It's Will," she managed.

"What?" She stayed silent. He could feel the disorienting fog of panic creeping along his veins. "What's happened?"

"I came home to find a message from Dr. Gearin. He wants me to call him as soon as I can, and—and I don't think I can face any more bad news on my own."

"I'm on my way," Paul said.

In their apartment, he dialed Gearin while Ruth watched, her eyes wide with apprehension. Behind the doctor he could hear the noises of the hospital, the squelch of rubber soles on polished floors, a baby crying. "It's Professor Connelly," Paul said. "You asked us to call you."

"Yes. Absolutely. I wanted you to know the good news."

Paul hardly dared hope. "Does that mean what I think?"

"The leukemia's in remission. The last tests we did showed no traces of the disease. The cancer cells have gone. He's cleared. For the present Will is cancer free."

"Oh, God."

"Of course we'll be keeping a close eye on him. We can't be completely sure that the cancer will stay in remission. We just have to keep praying it will. And there are many, many cases where it has."

In other words, it's gone away, Paul thought, but maybe only for the moment. We will never be able to sleep easily again. He did not say this aloud. Ruth had carried a heavy burden, and he was not about to add to it. "I can't tell you how grateful we are for everything you've done."

"It's almost as wonderful for us when this happens as it is for the parents," Gearin said.

"Thank you, Doctor. Thank you so very much." Paul slammed down the phone and gave Ruth a two-hundred-watt smile. "He's beaten it, Ruth! The cancer's gone."

"He's going to be okay." She collapsed onto the sofa and began to cry. "Oh, Paul, I can't believe it," she said. "I just can't."

"Me neither." He sat down beside her, seized her face between his hands, kissed her wet cheeks, her closed eyes, her mouth.

She leaned against him, her head on his shoulder. "I tried to believe that he would be cured, but I was still terrified he wouldn't. All these months—looking at him, wondering how much more suffering he had to go through. And now he's cured."

"Cured . . ." Paul pressed her against his side, refusing to remember Gearin's qualified approval of the term.

CHAPTER SEVEN

WILL picked up his life again, gradually going back to school for the last days of the semester, and Ruth was able to return to the office. Surveying the crowded city streets, noticing as though for the first time the flowers in the Public Garden, she realized how narrow her existence had grown.

As long as Will stayed well, they could look to the future. Yet she knew that she would watch him, listen for him, worry about him every second of every day. One cough, and she would see his death.

When she asked him what he wanted for his fifteenth birthday, he did not hesitate. "I'd like to go up to Carter's House. We haven't been there for ages."

"Oh, Will. I . . . I can't."

"Why not?"

"Because ever since . . . since . . ."

"Since Josie died."

"Yes. If I go up there, I'll see . . . her everywhere."

Suddenly Will exploded. "Josie, Mom. Her name's Josie. *Josephine*. Why can't you ever say it? She's got a right to be talked about. You've just shut her out of our lives, and it's not fair. That's why Dad left, because he couldn't stand the way you keep pretending that she never existed. I'll bet we all think about her every day and miss her and want her back and . . . and . . ." He was crying now, harsh boyish sobs that erupted from his thin chest with the force of cannon fire. "She was my sister. Why can't we talk about it, instead of acting like nothing ever happened? Because it *did* happen, Mom."

"Yes. I—"

"Josie drowned, and she's gone, and we *aren't* normal." He sobbed harder. "We *can't* be normal ever again."

"I guess . . ." She paused, trying to put it in terms he could understand. "I guess I saw it as a sign of strength that we'd carried on as before."

"But Mom, I *want* to talk about Josie. I want to talk about Dad leaving, too, and . . ." He rested his forehead against the wall and shook his head. "I even went and had a Coke with that dorky boyfriend of Josie's, just so I could talk about her."

"Rob Fowler?"

"Rob, Bob, whatever his stupid name is." Will glared at his mother accusingly. "At least he *listened*."

"You make it sound like a bad thing that we've managed to continue, when actually it's just the opposite." When he left the room, Ruth said aloud, "Isn't it?"

A COUPLE of weeks after the summer vacation had begun, she came home from work to find Will's friend Ed Stein in the kitchen. "Hi, Mrs. Connelly," he said.

"Hello, Ed. How're your mom and dad?"

"Just fine." He glanced across at Will. "By the way, we're leaving tomorrow for Maine, and they wanted to know whether Will could come up, spend some time with us."

"I wonder what on earth could have put that notion into their heads." Ruth glanced sharply at Will.

"I did, Mrs. Connelly." Ed's gaze was one of limpid innocence. "It'd be really great for me if Will could join us."

"I don't think so," Ruth said brusquely.

"Why *not?*" demanded Will.

"Any particular reason, Mrs. Connelly?" Ed was polite but determined.

"Ed, Will's still recovering from a serious illness. He's got to take things easy."

"Where would be easier than up at Sweetharbor, Mrs. Connelly?

No homework, no classes, no freaks on the streets. No pollution."

"Is this a prepared speech or just off the top of your head?" Ruth laughed. "Though you do have a point."

"Well, I'm *going*." Will shouldered out of the kitchen, followed by Ed, who turned at the door and smiled. "Don't worry, Mrs. Connelly. My mother will call you tonight."

"I'M STILL not clear on this letter from the FTC, Ruth." Jake Phillipson leaned forward. With his head of thick white hair and small black eyes he looked more like a polar bear than the CEO of a powerful electronics corporation.

"What don't you understand?" Behind his head the city burned in the summer heat. The parched urban landscape was coated with a metallic sheen, sunlight bounced off brown reflective glass in the surrounding buildings. Ruth thought of Will. At least he was out of this, safe in Sweetharbor.

"What legal force does it have? What if the Washington people change their minds?"

"Jake, it's the Federal Trade Commission's way of saying that they'll waive the formal process of scheduling an exemption hearing. It means you're home free. You can go ahead with your acquisition."

"I'm not sure I'm comfortable with that," Phillipson said. "After all, it's only a letter. Is it binding?"

Ruth nodded. "Absolutely. The federal court of appeals ruled that these comfort letters have the force of law."

"Okay. But I want a letter from you personally, Ruth, stating that in your professional opinion we are legally justified in going ahead."

"I'll have it FedExed to you this afternoon," she said. They were twelve floors up, with the windows shut, but she could still hear the clamor of a police car and the insistent honks as frustrated drivers leaned on their horns. Sweat beaded her forehead. She pushed her fingers through her hair and smiled at Phillipson. "It's all going very smoothly, Jake. Don't worry."

"I try not to." Phillipson pushed back his chair and stood up. "By the way, how's that boy of yours doing, Ruth?"

A smile lit up her face. "He's in remission, Jake. He's so well, in fact, that I've let him go up to Maine for the summer." She glanced at her watch. "I'll be heading there myself for Labor Day weekend. It'll be his fifteenth birthday."

A MONTH after Will had left for Maine, Ed's mother, Carmel Stein, called Ruth at her office. "Now, you're not to panic, Ruth, but Will's been running a fever."

"No."

"Not a very high one, Ruth."

"No," moaned Ruth. "Please . . ." Blackness filled her.

"We took him straight down to the hospital in Hartsfield, but they didn't seem too worried. Paul said—"

"Paul?"

"He was here. He said—"

"Paul was staying with you?"

"He's come up a couple of times to visit Will, yes."

Ruth was silent.

"But anyway," Carmel said, "everything's fine now. Paul said I shouldn't worry you, but I thought you should know."

"I'll get his doctor to give Hartsfield a call," Ruth said, fighting terror. She had read so much about Will's illness, but now none of it remained in her head. Running a fever—was that significant? Anything had been significant when he was sick. But he was not sick; he was in remission.

"He's eating well," Carmel said, "running around with Ed, just a normal kid enjoying the summer. He's absolutely fine, Ruth. I wouldn't even have called you if it wasn't for his medical history."

Ruth felt nauseous. "Thanks, Carmel. I'll get back to you."

Not again. Please, not again.

She telephoned the hospital in Boston. She called Paul's apartment. She went to a meeting with one client, had lunch with another, attended a conference of partners when she got back. She took notes, made points, but Will was the only thing she could concentrate on. In the end, she lifted the phone and punched in Lynda Petievich's number.

"It's probably nothing," Lynda said. "Hey, I'm not a doctor, but a fever could be nothing more than too much sun."

"You're probably right."

"I'd like to tell you not to worry, but whatever I say, you will. For years you'll worry. That's what being a parent is about. Even when they're not sick, you worry. What're they doing? Why are they late? You know how it is."

"It's the price you pay," Ruth said. "I never thought about it like that. The price for creating a life. It's like a scream, waiting at the back of your throat." She remembered that last summer up in Maine. If only it were possible to return to the innocent days before the accident. If only . . .

THE waves grabbed at her. She tried to get out of their reach, but she could not move. The water glittered cruelly, sharp as razor blades. Terrified, she watched it lap at her knees, her waist, her throat. One roaring green wave detached itself from the rest and slammed against her, covering, devouring her.

She woke sweaty, buried under a tangle of sheets. The panic clung even when she flicked on the light, went into the kitchen for a glass of water, found a book.

It was futile to try to reinvent the past. Nothing would return any of them to that shining summer that had ended so abruptly. She had been heedless of life's lavish prodigality then. Sitting at the kitchen table, she shivered, although the trapped heat of the day hung heavily in the air. Of all the abundance she had once possessed, Will was the only thing left.

She dressed quickly, flung things into a bag, found her keys. Out in the street the night air was almost cool.

She was able to make good time up the Maine Turnpike. On Route 1 hers was almost the only car on the road. Memories flooded her. Of journeys up here with her parents, back when everything was still fresh and full of hope. Of her grandparents—small, courteous, a galaxy away from her, filtered by the space that hung like a curtain between the generations. What did they know of her life? Or she of theirs? And yet the house linked her to them. She was aware of time stretching back to an unimaginable past and leading forward into the unknown.

She stopped for breakfast in Sweetharbor, parking the car behind the little convenience store. The past came flooding in on her.

Josie's presence was everywhere, woven into the fabric of Main Street: the doughnut shop, the sidewalk where she'd tripped and twisted her ankle, the all-season Christmas shop where every year the children had been allowed to buy something new to dangle on the tree they would pick out in the woods when Christmas came around. It was easier than she had expected: Time had stroked smooth the edges of her loss.

Down on the quayside, where the lobster boats bobbed on the swell, she looked in the window of the little craft shop. The display featured brilliant batiked silk, carved wooden bowls, photograph frames.

"Mrs. Connelly?" The voice was deep and warming.

She looked up to see a tall, bearded man.

"Sam Hechst." He held out a hand, and she took it.

"You're Dieter's nephew?"

"That's right." He wore jeans and a denim shirt with the sleeves rolled up. "Are you all up here?"

There was no reason he should know Paul had left them. "I'm just visiting my son; he's vacationing with friends up here."

"You're not staying at Carter's House?"

"No." Ruth swallowed. "Josie—my daughter—I'm sure you heard that she drowned last summer. Our house is too . . . I can't bear to be there."

He glanced at her, indicated the Cabot Inn across the way. "Would you— Do you have time for coffee?"

"That would be nice," she said.

In the dining room of the inn, they found a table by the window that gave onto Old Port Street. When the waitress came over, Sam asked for coffee while Ruth ordered breakfast.

"You said you were visiting your son."

She looked at her plate. "He's been very sick with leukemia."

"I'm so sorry. I didn't know."

"No reason why you should."

"Except that up here everyone knows everyone else's business. Is he better?"

"For the moment. With any luck, for good."

"But you're not opening up Carter's House?"

"No, I . . . Too many ghosts. Too many memories."

"Of Josephine?"

"Of . . . happiness."

"Mrs. Connelly. Ruth. If memories are all you have, then you should glory in them." His dark eyes moved over her, soft as molasses. "You should go back to your house. I'm sure the memories you have of your daughter are good ones."

She nodded. "Yes. Most of them." She drew in a breath. "There was something on her mind that last summer. She seemed to turn against me. One of the worst things about her death is that we never had the chance to put it right."

"Perhaps you should just think of all the good things. For instance, she was a remarkably talented painter."

"Yes."

"She also had a very strong personality." He smiled.

"Yes, indeed."

"But she had a sorrowful soul."

"Sometimes I think I never really knew her," Ruth said simply. "Do you have any idea why she was troubled?"

"I've come to the conclusion—though I'm by no means the first or the most qualified to do so—that all creative people are born a couple of skins short. They feel more, so they suffer more. Fear more. The compensation, of course, is that they also delight more."

"In what?"

"Everything," he said simply. "Higher highs, lower lows. It goes with the territory."

"Are you creative too?"

"I'm a competent craftsman, nothing more. Josephine had the makings of the real thing."

Ruth looked out at the busy street. "Which makes her death even more of a waste."

"Nothing is ever wasted. Who knows what will come out of the experiences you've undergone. There was a song my uncle used to sing in the war: *Keep right on to the end of the road.* That's what we all have to do. Keep right on to the end."

"I'm not sure I agree with the sentiment."

"What else is there to do?"

"If my son had died of leukemia, I'd certainly have killed myself."
Spoken over the banalities of maple syrup and fried bacon, the
matter-of-fact words seemed overly dramatic.

"That would have been the end for you," he said calmly.

"Would you call that giving up?"

"That would depend." He glanced out at the street, then turned
his direct gaze on her. "Your son is cured?"

"Yes."

"Definitely?"

Her mouth moved in a wry smile. "As definitely as it's possible to
be with this kind of disease."

"That's good. That is so good to hear."

DRIVING to the Steins' cottage, she passed the turnoff to Carter's
House. Wildflowers nodded along the sandy track that ran toward
the meadow. Butter-yellow sunshine glowed where the trees broad-
ened out. Would she drive down it ever again? Maybe. But not yet.

Carmel Stein and the boys were sitting on the porch. The dogs
lay at their side, panting in the heat, tongues lolling. Both boys were
in Bermudas and sea-stained Top-Siders, looking so normal, so
quintessentially boylike that Ruth laughed aloud.

She got out of her car and ran toward them.

"Mom!" Will jumped up.

"You should have telephoned, Ruth," said Carmel.

"It was a sudden decision. I woke in the night and started worrying, but I see there was no reason to. Will looks great!" In the
weeks he had been up here, his pale face had acquired a light tan.
Now that he was able to eat properly, he had put on some weight.

"Mom, look at this." Will took off his baseball cap. His scalp was
covered with a fine fuzz of hair.

"What about it?"

"Think I should shave it?"

"That's got to be up to you, hon."

"I kind of like the image," he said seriously. "Especially since
people think I did it on purpose, you know?"

"It's dramatic, I'll give you that."

"And my ear stud—it's not gonna look the same with hair."

"You should go with what feels good," Ed said.

"That's cool," Will said. A choice, after so many months without one, clearly appealed to him. "Mom, we gotta get down to the yacht club. We'll see you later, okay?"

"Will, I thought I should take you back to the city."

"What, *now?* I don't want to go home yet, Mom."

"You had a fever," Ruth said. She could not stop looking at him, the fresh growth of hair, the tanned face. There were new muscles under his T-shirt. Nobody could tell he had ever been sick.

"*Everyone* had a fever that day, Ruth," said Carmel. "The temperature was practically in the hundreds. Even Cool Hand Ed had a fever."

"It's true, Mrs. Connelly. Sweat poured off me. Thought I'd melt into a little wet pool." Ed looked at his friend. "You should leave Will here, where I can keep my eye on him."

"Yeah," said Will. "One day he'll make someone a very good mother."

"Get outta here," Ed said.

"I still think you should come home with me," said Ruth. "After all, the summer's nearly ended."

"Which is why it'd be *mean* to make me go back to the city before I have to. And there's my *birthday*. You promised I could have it up here. And you have to admit I look really good, don't I? It's *better* for me to be up here."

Ruth held up both hands in mock surrender. "Okay, okay. You convinced me."

"Yo!" The two boys gave each other a high five.

CHAPTER EIGHT

RUTH went up to Maine again for Will's birthday. Early in the morning she slipped out of the Steins' house. The sky was gray, heavy with clouds. Between tree trunks the sea gleamed like pewter. Walking along the familiar lanes, she found it hard to believe that twelve months had passed since Will's last birthday. And Josie's death. For the rest of their lives the two events would be irreversibly linked. She took the trail behind Carter's House up to Caleb's Point and sat on Josie's teak bench. She ran her hand over the carved heart. She touched the brass plaque with her daughter's name and dates on it. Green now, with verdigris. JOSEPHINE CARTER CONNELLY. She sat and gazed out at the glittering waters of the sound. Trees, water, rocks, sunshine. Elemental things. In the dip of the boulder the miniature garden flourished. She had expected to feel disturbance, but strangely, she felt peace.

The Steins threw a lunch party for Will, and at dinner that night at the yacht club, Will was strong and shining.

When they were eating the birthday cake Ruth had ordered earlier, Will leaned toward her. "Thanks for being here, Mom," he said quietly.

"You don't think I'd miss your birthday, do you?"

"Except it's not just my birthday. It's also the day that—"

"That Josie died," she said steadily.

He looked down at his plate, pushed the cake around with his fork. "All day long I've been thinking about her."

She sighed. "Me too, Will. Josie's part of us; she always will be. It's taken me too long to accept what you said: that she has a right to be remembered."

Both of them were silent for a moment.

THE fall semester began, and Will had to work hard to catch up on his missed schooling. He played hard as well.

"It's the band, Mom," he said when Ruth told him not to overtire himself. "This gig that Stu's father fixed up for us . . ."

"The Kiwanis dance thing?"

"Yeah. It's the week after Thanksgiving, and people are *paying* to hear us, so we gotta be good."

"Can I come?"

"*You?*" His expression was horrified.

"Yes, William. Me, your mother."

Will sighed. "It's just— You'll be kind of old."

"Thank you very much, William. What's the average age of a Kiwanian? I wonder."

"They're putting this dance on for disabled kids, not adults. Anyway, we don't play your kind of music."

"How do you know what my kind of music is?"

Will rolled his eyes heavenward. "Okay. I guess you can come if you really want to. Ed's mom will be there. Just don't do anything that'll destroy my rep, okay?"

"Like what? Dance naked on a table?"

"Like . . . *kiss* me or something stupid like that."

ONE night in October, Ruth was awakened by a sound. She lay under the covers, still half asleep, and heard Will retching in the bathroom. Instantly she was wide-awake, reaching for her robe. She stumbled out into the passage. Will had left the door ajar, and she could see him hunched over the pedestal.

"What's wrong?" she said. Her face felt stiff, sodden with sleep. Inside her ribcage her heart thumped with rediscovered fear.

Will flapped an arm at her, wanting her to go away, but she stayed leaning against the wall until he had finished.

"What's wrong?" she said again, when he had rinsed out his mouth and washed his face.

"Nothing, Mom." He grinned shamefacedly. "I went out with the guys after school, pigged out on fries and a couple of Cokes. Guess they didn't mix."

"Are you sure that's all it was?"

He shrugged. "Course."

In the morning he seemed fine, though Ruth examined his face minutely, looking for—for what, exactly? He looked well, the last of the summer's tan still warm on his face. She tried not to worry. Kids threw up all the time, especially if they ate too much junk food. It was nothing.

A COUPLE of weeks before Thanksgiving, she came back from the office to find Will asleep on the sofa in the living room. Ed was sitting next to him, watching TV with the sound turned down.

"What's going on, Ed?" she said quietly, dumping her bag on the table. With her head she motioned him into the kitchen.

"I came back with him, Mrs. Connelly. They asked me to."

"Why? What happened?" Bubbles of alarm popped along her veins.

"He was throwing up this afternoon."

"Oh, Ed . . ."

"Don't worry, Mrs. Connelly. We had to eat this really gross fish thing at lunch. A couple of the other kids were barfing their guts out too, but they told me to come home with Will in a cab because of him being sick earlier."

"Thanks, Ed. You're a star." Both of them knew she was thanking him for more than his company on a cab ride.

"So's Will."

"I know that."

When Ed had gone, Ruth went into the living room and looked down at her son's sleeping face. Try as she might, she could see no sign that he was sick. A little pale, perhaps. She clasped her hands together and raised them to her mouth, pressing back dread.

ON THANKSGIVING Day, Will complained of an earache. His summer tan had faded, and he was looking pale. Fiercely questioned by Ruth, he admitted that he had been feeling tired lately, that he'd thrown up a couple more times recently.

"Why didn't you *say?*" Ruth tried to cram the panic back inside. "I wish you'd told me."

"It's stupid. I feel like I'm making a fuss."

"Of course you're not. You've been *ill*. We'll need to keep tabs on you for a while yet."

"I'm okay. Just this earache."

"I'll give you a painkiller for the moment," Ruth said.

When Paul arrived for dinner, Ruth did not tell him about Will's earache. But watching her son picking at the elaborate dishes she had prepared—sweet potatoes baked in molasses, potatoes roasted with onions, green beans sautéed with garlic—Ruth realized she would have to face the truth.

While Paul stacked the dishwasher, she went into Will's room. He was lying on his bed. "Show me your arms," she commanded. "Your legs."

There were bruises around his elbow joints, purple blotches

behind his knees. Watching her face, he said defeatedly, "It's come back, hasn't it?"

"Don't be ridiculous, Will," she said. "We won't know anything until we've had you checked out."

"It's back." He turned his face to the wall.

"It could be anything, Will," she said. "The treatment—the chemo—all those drugs are bound to undermine you."

"I was fine during the summer."

"And you'll be fine again."

"Yeah. Right," Will said bleakly.

If it's back, Ruth thought, if the mutant cells are once again ravaging my child's body, there is help at hand. Radiotherapy. A bone-marrow transplant. We have options; we have chances. "We'll have the doctors look at you." She sat down on the bed and cradled his head against her chest. "Oh, Will," she said, "I love you. You know that, don't you?"

He nodded, his head moving against her. "But I can't stand it, Mom," he said. "I mean it. I'm not going through all that again. The needles. Aching all over. Wanting to throw up all the time. If I have more treatment, it'll all be for nothing in the end."

Ruth put her arm around his shoulders. "You're wrong. Life is good, Will. You have to go on believing that."

"Not for me. Not if I'm sick again. I'd rather die."

"Don't." Savagely she pulled his face toward her, ignoring his cry of pain. "Don't *say* that, William. Not ever. You're going to live. We don't even know there's anything wrong."

"Don't we?" He stared into her face, and the territory behind his eyes was the bleakest of landscapes.

THEY waited in a small room with a low ceiling. It was not the room that had become so familiar during Will's previous illness, and Ruth wondered if it had been chosen in order to avoid dredging up memories. There were two armchairs upholstered in brown cor-duroy, separated by a square wooden coffee table. To one side was a love seat upholstered in contrasting beige. There was a picture on the wall of mountains covered in snow. Through high windows she could see the sky.

Drs. Caldbeck and Gearin came in, looking subdued. "Professor Connelly. Mrs. Connelly." They shook hands before sitting down and opening the files they carried.

"We're very disappointed," Dr. Caldbeck said. "After such a prompt remission we hoped for better results."

"Did you stop treatment too soon?" Ruth asked bluntly. The confusion and fear she had felt the first time around had temporarily vanished. She was not going to give in, nor allow Will to do so.

"I don't think so. His blood was clear; the disease had gone. We certainly wouldn't want to feed high doses of powerful drugs to a healthy body."

"What are his chances?" Paul asked. "Last time you told us eighty percent of cases like Will's end in a cure. What's the percentage now that the disease has recurred?"

Gearin answered. "Somewhat lower than eighty. I can't pretend otherwise. And as you know, the blood samples we took from you both, and from Professor Connelly's brother in California, were not a match, so a bone-marrow transplant is not an option. We have every hope, though, that we'll be able to find the successful combination of other treatments."

"How can I hope?" Ruth said. "More importantly, how can *he* hope? He went through all that horror for *nothing*."

"Not for nothing. You have to believe us," Caldbeck said. "Since Will's form of the disease is proving resistant to the standard drugs, we think we should move to the next level of therapy, and this time combine chemo with radiotherapy. Radiotherapy isn't as painful as chemo, but the side effects are much the same. Luckily they're mostly temporary."

Ruth held the sides of her chair. If it was like this for her, what must it be like for Will? "We're doing the right thing, aren't we?" she said, suddenly doubting her convictions.

"The maintenance of life is what we dedicated ourselves to when we became doctors," said Caldbeck.

"Whatever the cost?"

Gearin stepped in. "When one of our patients comes back, like Richard who came in last week, clear of the disease, healthy, to tell us he's getting married next month, then I *know* we're right. And hard though it is to believe, there's an increasing number of people like him walking around. People we can point to and say, it may be hard, but it works."

FIVE days later Will was given his first dose of radiation. The dim room and the brooding shapes of the equipment produced a malevolent atmosphere made all the worse by the silence. Ruth held her son's hand as he was lifted onto a vinyl-covered table, and she then stepped back as they began to wrap him in sheeting, almost like a mummy. Packs of lead shielding designed to prevent unnecessary incidental radiation leaned against his unresisting body like ramparts against the cancer-destroying lights. Even his face was covered.

The table slid slowly into the dark cavern of the machine. Oh, William . . . What was he thinking, alone, inside that steel casing?

One of the technicians approached. "It looks worse than it really is, Mrs. Connelly," she said. "Honestly, they don't feel anything, and it doesn't last too long." She glanced across at the sinister glow inside the machine and added, "Poor kid."

Because his immune system was low, Will had to spend two weeks in the hospital. His needle phobia made each jab an ordeal. Standing by and watching while the nursing staff dug needles into his flesh, trying to find a place to draw a sample, became almost as painful for Ruth as it was for him. That is my son's body, she wanted to shout. Leave him alone. Hurt me instead. I cannot bear the agony of helplessness.

She wanted to tell him not to try to be brave, but she recognized that maybe his pride was the only thing he felt he had left. She took refuge in aggression.

"Should he be mingling with the other children?" she asked sharply, standing at the nurses station. "He's susceptible to infection. He ought to be kept in isolation."

"Mrs. Connelly, I don't think you can assume—"

Her fist thumped. "My boy needs every chance he can get if he's going to beat this thing."

"It's not hospital policy."

"Maybe I should speak to the hospital administrator."

"He would agree with us, Mrs. Connelly."

"Well . . ." Ruth tapped a restless tattoo on the counter and moved away. She was behaving badly—she knew that. But last time she had trusted the doctors, and they had let her down.

She looked at Will through the window along the corridor. He saw her and waved, beckoned her to the door. "I don't think I should come in," she said.

"Why not?"

"I'm worried about infection."

"You know what, Mom?"

"What?"

"You sound like you've lost it."

"NEARLY Christmas," Ruth said. "Got any ideas about it?"

"Plenty. Or just one, really. But you won't go along."

"Try me."

Small spots of color stood out on Will's cheekbones. "I want to go to Carter's House."

"I know, but . . ." Her whole being rebelled at the thought.

He turned his head away, and her heart clenched as she saw the shiny scalp under his thinning hair. "Funny, isn't it?" he said, his voice scarcely above a whisper. "I've heard you telling Dr. Gearin that you'd give anything in the world if it would save my life."

"And I would, baby. You know I would."

"Then why can't you give me what I want most?"

She was cut to the quick by the truth of what he said. "It'll be darn cold up there at this time of year."

"It's heated, and we can have fires. There're masses of wood stacked under the porch and in the barn. Ed and I were over there during the summer."

"Let me think about it," she said.

But the more she considered it, the more Ruth knew she could not go back to the house. She circled around the problem, seeking a compromise. It came to her the next day.

"Suppose we had Christmas up in Sweetharbor, but not at the house."

Will's face drooped. "What would be the point?"

"Suppose we stay at the Cabot Inn?"

"A hotel? For Christmas? No, thanks." He looked at the wall behind her. "It wouldn't be the same."

"William."—she stepped toward him and gently stroked his hair— "I want to make you happy, truly I do. I know how you want to go back to Carter's House, but I'm simply not ready yet." She pressed a finger against her lips. "When I came up to visit you in the summer, I thought I could, but when it comes to the crunch, I have to be honest. To go back would take more strength than I have."

His eyes were huge, luminous with suffering. He gave an immense shrugging sigh, flexed his mouth. "I guess the inn wouldn't be too bad. Not as good as Carter's House, but okay."

"I'll call, then."

When she put down the phone, Will said, "What about Dad?"

"He can come," she said lightly, "if he wants to."

HE HARDLY ever saw her now. They passed each other in the hospital corridor, bumped into each other in the parking lot. That was it. Nothing deliberate about it, just the way things were. When she looked at him, Paul wasn't even sure she saw him.

He nerved himself to pick up the phone. "Want me to come by, give you a break?" he asked.

"It's up to you. It would help Will, I guess."

"You're important too, Ruth," he said quietly.

Her tone softened. "Thank you, Paul."

"Will mentioned you were going up to Maine for Christmas. Staying at the Cabot Inn."

"That's right." She waited a fraction too long, then said unwillingly, "Look, Paul, I'm not sure about this, but Will would like you to join us."

"Gee, you really know how to make a guy feel welcome."

"A guy who walked out on us, Paul."

"Ruth—" he said. "I wish we could go back." He was almost sure it was the truth. "You're still the one I want to be with. You and Will."

"Too bad you didn't think of that before you left."

I wish we were working things out together, he wanted to say. I wish we could share our pain. But he had to accept her hostility. Will was what mattered, not her, not him. "You haven't let me help with Will this time around."

"You haven't asked to."

"I'm asking now."

She sighed. "Why don't you join us for Christmas, Paul."

CHAPTER NINE

PAUL picked them up from the apartment, and they drove up to Brunswick, hardly talking. In Portland they stopped for coffee, which they drank quickly, standing by the car, stamping their feet, their shoulders hunched against the cold. Ruth and Paul avoided each other's gaze.

As they headed north on Route 1, the harsh reality of a Maine winter enclosed them. On either side of the road the land lay leaden under thick steel-gray clouds. Trees crowded the edge of the road, so dark a green they were almost black, bent under the weight of the last snowfall. Fog pressed down on them, and although the roads were clear between the piled-up banks of snow, visibility was low. The snow tires thrummed against the damp road.

For the last of the drive Paul sat in back with Will; every time Ruth glanced in the rearview mirror, they both seemed to be asleep. But as they approached Sweetharbor, Will sat up. Ruth turned off the highway and began to negotiate the narrow lanes. When they passed the snowy turn down to the Hechsts' house, he said, "Can we stop at Carter's House, Mom? Please?"

"Good idea," Paul said. "Check the place out."

"Just look, no more than that," Ruth said, her voice unsteady. To come here at this special time of year with her estranged husband and her sick son was an experience she shrank from. "Just look."

She reached the turnoff. The track was covered in snow, but they were able to bump along until they came out of the trees.

"Oh," breathed Will. "Look at that, will you?"

The house and barn glowed in the last of the winter daylight. The sun hung low in the misty sky, indistinct and hazy, as though submerged in dry ice. The flat pasture was a thick pale blue, and beyond it the spined spruces stood black and cold.

William sighed with pleasure. He squeezed his mother's shoulder. "It looks just great. Can I get out?"

"If you want," Ruth said. "Just make sure you've got your—" But he had already opened the door and jumped into the snow. They watched him struggle toward the house, whooping faintly with joy, tumbling and dragging himself up again.

"Will he be okay?" asked Paul.

"Tomorrow he'll be bruised and his joints'll ache, but the hell with that. It's so good to see him happy."

"He looks like one of Santa's little helpers in that ridiculous woolen hat. Where'd he get that?"

"Some girl at his school knitted it for him." Ruth put a hand to her face. Her throat was thick.

As though he understood what she was feeling, Paul said, "We can't worry about the future."

Ruth said softly, "I'm so afraid he's not going to make it." The scene was like a Wyeth painting—the white snow, the boy, and beyond him the dark-shuttered house closed around its battalions of ghosts, its shriveled memories.

"I can't possibly reassure you." Paul took her hand. "I can't wave a magic wand and make it all better for any of us."

"I know that."

"Let's at least try to enjoy the next few days. Give Will the best Christmas we can."

"Yes."

THE following morning Will and Ruth went out into Old Port Street and walked along the waterfront, bent against the wind. The sky was overcast, the light dull, but the pure cold of the wind on Ruth's face was invigorating. Her sense of constriction lifted, as it always did when she was up here.

Overnight the temperature had plummeted. In the harbor, water slapped hard at the wooden pilings of the dock and dashed itself repeatedly against the tumbled rocks of the bay, sending up clouds of spray. Seagulls swooped beyond the squat fishing boats, diving for scraps, squabbling over bits of refuse.

Ruth shivered. "Doesn't it look chilly?"

"The water's always cold up here," said Will. He had his hands plunged into his pockets. A thick lumberman's cap was pulled down over his head. "Even in summer."

"Want to go to Don's Donuts?" Ruth asked.

"Okay."

Ruth brought two coffees and a doughnut over to the narrow table by the window. "There you are. Apple cinnamon. Josie's favorite," she said.

"No, Mom," Will said patiently, "it wasn't."

"Yes, it was."

"Maybe when she was, like, fourteen," he said. "Later she liked the chocolate ones much better."

"Did she?" Ruth frowned. "Are you sure?"

Will smiled slightly and rubbed at the steamy window. "Looks pretty, doesn't it?"

"All dressed up for Christmas."

Lights were strung across the street and around the eaves of the buildings. Snow lay piled up at the edge of the sidewalks. The shops were draped with tinsel and plastic likenesses of Santa Claus on his sleigh. In the city they might have looked tacky; here she could not imagine it any other way.

When they had finished their coffee, Will walked back to the hotel while Ruth went into the drugstore. As she was choosing gift-wrap, someone said, "It's good to see you again."

"Mrs. Hechst . . . Trudi!" Ruth exclaimed. "How are you?"

"Just fine." Gertrud Hechst examined her with large pale eyes. "And you, Ruth?"

"I'm doing okay." Ruth nodded her head.

"I'm glad you have come back here for Christmas. Carter's House full again: This is good."

"We're actually at the Cabot Inn. Will wanted to come, and I couldn't face opening up the house. So we compromised."

"Such a compromise." The broad, round face was suddenly creased with concern. "I have heard that William is not well."

"He's very *un*well." Ruth tried to smile but could not quite make it. "And very happy to be up here again."

"But he should be in his own home at Christmastime." The older woman suddenly took Ruth's arm. "I have an idea. Ruth, why do you not bring your family to us for dinner on Christmas Day?"

"What a kind thought," said Ruth, somewhat taken aback.

Trudi smiled delightedly. "A good idea, yes?"

Ruth shook her head. "Thank you, but we couldn't possibly intrude on you. And—" And besides, we hardly know you, she wanted to add, although they had been acquainted all their lives.

"The more the merrier—isn't that what they say? Especially on Christmas Day. *We* should like it very much."

Josie's voice came back to Ruth: *To you the year-rounders are just specimens, like something in a museum.* "All right," she said suddenly. "Thank you, Trudi. I'm very touched."

Crossing the road, she thought about this small community that had always played such an important part in her life. Ruth knew almost nothing about the people who inhabited it. *Knew* them, yes. Stopped and chatted if she met them. Bought lobster from them or raspberries, took jars of their preserves home to the city. But who they were, what their background was, she had little idea. Summer people did not really care about year-rounders.

ON CHRISTMAS Day they drove along the snow-thick lanes to the Hechsts' big weathered house. The sky was dull again, the trees beaded with fog. They pulled up by the wicket gate, and the dogs began to bark, the sound echoing, thrown back to them by the mist. Lemon light spilled out onto the snow as the genial figure of Dieter Hechst stood in the doorway. "Happy Christmas," he called. As Ruth reached the top of the steps, he took her hand in both of his. "Welcome to our house."

"It's so kind of you to have us."

"It's good of you to join us." Dieter was a handsome, placid man with a direct gaze. "Trudi is some pleased."

Ruth heard him greeting Paul and Will as she passed into a small cloakroom area, hung up her coat, and went in to where Gertrud stood waiting, a flowered shawl pinned across her shoulders. The wood-lined living room was a single large space stretching the length of the house, the ceiling crossbeams carved and painted in red and green. Bookshelves covered one wall, and beautiful objects were set about: a large swan made of paper, hand-painted plates, carved angels with shining faces. And everywhere there were candles, dozens of them, on the floor, on the polished surfaces. A Christmas tree stood between the windows, unornamented except for small creamy candles set into holders. Through the window Ruth could see the ruins of Gertrud's summer garden, and beyond it a snow-covered salt marsh, faintly indigo in the winter light.

There were other people already seated on the deep sofas on either side of the woodstove: an elderly lady, a man in a Scandinavian sweater, a woman with the same round face as Trudi's. The long room was full of fragrances: woodsmoke, roasting meat, wine and spices, candle wax.

Ruth opened her mouth in surprise and delight. "How beautiful!" she exclaimed softly. "How lovely."

As though in a dream, she saw Will's face, its angularity softened by the light from the candles, saw Paul greeting the other people. "This is wonderful," he said. "Merry Christmas to all of you."

They were introduced to one another: Dieter's mother, Trudi's sister and her husband. Mugs of mulled wine were passed around, hot and spicy. Ruth followed Trudi into the kitchen. It was large and warm, full of freestanding pieces of unpainted polished pine. A big table stood piled with plates and pitchers, a platter of cheeses, stollen, chocolate-covered stars fragrant with anise. "Can I help?" she said, and hoped she did not sound too wistful.

Gertrud was busy lifting the lids of various pans and sniffing the contents. "Mmm," she said. "This sauce is *good*. Taste that." She held a spoon toward Ruth.

"What is it?"

"For the turkey. Wine, a little Cointreau, other things."

"Delicious." Ruth sat on the edge of the table, swinging a leg. "This is so kind of you, Trudi. Inviting us to join you."

"We are glad to have you."

How generous she was. How warm. Ruth recalled the way she had come to help in the sad days after Josie's death.

Trudi said, "What exactly is wrong with Will?"

Ruth clasped her arms. "He has leukemia." The word sounded sharp and jagged in this warm room.

"Oh, my dear, that is terrible."

"We thought he'd recovered, but it's come back."

"The poor boy. From the way he behaves, you would hardly know he was sick. You must be a very special person, Ruth."

"Me?" Ruth laughed a little sadly. "I don't think so."

"Yes," insisted Trudi. "To have such wonderful children is an achievement. Josie too was very precious. There was a lot of you in Josie. I saw it often when she was here."

"I neglected her. Emotionally, I mean."

"Josie was not neglected in any sense."

"*She* thought so. We argued all the time. Especially that last summer, before she . . . before the accident."

"This is so normal, Ruth. So usual. Josie was growing up; she had found her own path to follow, and it was different from yours. That is all."

Was she right? Paul came into the kitchen carrying a supermarket carton, which he left on the table. Ruth pulled out bottles of wine, Swiss chocolate, a honey-roasted ham, a whole Camembert. "I believe she hated me."

"Ruth, you must not say such things," Trudi insisted, opening the oven to look at the turkey. "Josephine always spoke of you with admiration and with love."

"Did she?" The thought was comforting. Ruth wished it was true.

"Listen to what I tell you: Good children come from good parents. You must believe that."

"Oh, Trudi . . ." Ruth held back sudden tears.

Trudi turned and saw the things Ruth had put out on the table and held her hands up in surprise. "What is this?"

"We couldn't come unless we brought some things with us."

"Such gifts," said Trudi. "So much. Cheese and wine and . . ." She smiled at Ruth, her broad face flushed. "Thank you." She bent down to look in the oven again. "I think this bird is telling me he is ready for the table."

It took them more than two hours to do justice to the feast. The turkey was moist, the cranberry-and-orange relish outstanding. There were piles of moistly golden corn bread; a dish of sweet potatoes puréed with butternut squash; red cabbage cooked with onion and apple; wild rice; roasted potatoes; homemade sausages.

Paul and Dieter's brother-in-law engaged in a heated debate about the United States' role in Latin America; old Mrs. Hechst reminisced about Sweetharbor in bygone days. Will sat with a small smile on his face, watching them all but saying little. He was pale.

There was a lull in the conversation as they finished their coffee. Dieter threw more wood on the stove, and Trudi went into the kitchen and came back with a tray of glasses and a pitcher of eggnog. "In a minute we shall sing together," she said. "But first everyone must make a toast, and I will start. Here's to family." They raised their glasses. "How lucky we are to be together."

"Here's to Christmas," Dieter said.

"To friends," Trudi's sister said.

"To music and laughter," said Trudi's sister's husband.

"To roast turkey," Paul said, patting his stomach, and everyone cheered.

Will lifted his glass. "To Josie. To my sister." He looked at them with sparkling eyes. "I just wish she was here."

As the others raised their glasses to Josie, Ruth knew with sudden piercing clarity that she *was* there. The conviction was so strong she almost voiced it aloud. She had a vision of future Christmases, family gatherings, and someone telling the story of Josephine Connelly, drowned in the cold waters off Caleb's Point. Josie would become another Carter legend—always young, always beautiful. She would take her place alongside drunken preacher Downey and Great-great-grandmother Carter slowly sinking in the bog. There would be continuity. Even long gone, Josie would always be part of this place.

Ruth caught Will's gaze and smiled, wondering who those families would be. Not Carters, she thought. Maybe not even Connellys.

Oh, Will . . . my child, my beloved son.

IT WAS impossible to ignore the fact that Will was not thriving. Just before the Easter weekend Dr. Gearin called Ruth into his office. She knew already what she would hear.

"Will's last CBC was discouraging," he said. The doctor's brown eyes were dulled by the difficulty of what he had to say. "There's been no improvement in his blood count for some weeks. Quite the opposite, in fact."

"What does this mean, exactly?"

"We're always hopeful. We never know what might lie around the corner in terms of treatment breakthroughs."

"But if there isn't a breakthrough—"

"Then, yes, things are looking less good than we wished."

Ruth had tried to pretend away her doubts and fears. Now hopelessness ran along the narrow byways of her body, saturating her with grief. Rocking forward, she gasped. "How can I stand by and watch him die?"

"It hasn't come to that yet, Ruth. Not anywhere near it. Since we haven't found a bone-marrow match in the immediate family, our best hope now is to find a nonrelated donor."

"It's not going to make any difference in the long run."

"It's not like you to be so defeatist." Gearin's voice was deliberately contemptuous. "If you want Will to pick up the vibes from you, then you just go right ahead and make it even worse for him. Maybe you should change to another specialist—"

"What?"

"I don't think I can work with someone who's only concerned with her own thoughts and feelings."

There was a silence. "You're right, of course," she said.

"Good." His smile was sad. "We're now going to undertake a serious search for a nonrelated donor. There is a worldwide register of three million names, so there's a good chance we might get lucky and come up with a match for Will's tissue type."

Unspoken inside Ruth lay the knowledge of how much higher Will's chances would be if Josie were still alive. The likelihood of sibling blood marrows being a match for each other was infinitely greater than anyone else's. Numbness filled her. "He keeps telling me to leave him be, to let him go quietly."

"I know it's tough on him, Ruth, but he's got one more dose of chemo. Let him take that, then convalesce at home. We'll build his strength and pray for a donor."

She managed to move her lips. "And if we don't find a match, how long do we have?"

"I can't say. The desire to live is always a determining factor. I'd say—I'm sorry, Ruth—six months, perhaps more. The human spirit so often confounds us."

"You're telling me that's the end of the road?"

Gearin was silent. Then, very slowly, he bowed his head.

A MONTH later Ruth stood by Will's hospital bed. He lay asleep, flat on his back, arms mottled with bruises. So thin, she thought. So pitifully thin except for his face, which was unnaturally swollen by the drugs. He has almost left us, almost slipped away. What right do I have to try and tug him back? Sunlight slanted through the window and lay across his chest. She had scarcely had time to notice that summer had come once more.

He opened his eyes, curved his lips into a smile. "Hi, Mom."

"Hi, darling."

"The answer's no."

"How do you mean?"

"I know what you want."

"I want you well again. I want you fit. I want you . . ."

"I know all that. They didn't find a match, did they?"

"Not yet, darling."

"Not ever, Mom. Get real."

"You can't be—"

"Even if they find a match, I don't want any more treatment."

"You've said that before."

"And I'll keep on saying it until you believe me. I'm not a child anymore; I know how I feel about things."

"Will, you have to look beyond the short term."

"Short term's all I'm gonna get."

"Don't *talk* like that."

"It's true. And I've had it, Mom. I'm tired. Let me go. Don't make me feel bad about it."

"Letting go is not on the agenda, William. Just try to be brave a little while longer."

"I'm sick of being brave. The only thing I want now is to go back to Carter's House with both of you. You and Dad. I'm tired of hospital rooms and IV poles and guys in white coats, Mom."

"Look, Will. You're very sick. The hospital in Hartsfield isn't set up for specialized care."

"I don't care," Will said stubbornly. "It'll be the last time."

"Don't *say* that!" Ruth yelled. "Just don't *say* it."

Wearily he turned away from her.

CHAPTER TEN

"I'LL go up, Paul. Open the house, get it ready."

"Can't the agent do that?"

"It's more than just dusting and pulling back the shutters. There are preparations I'll need to make. Organizing a bedroom for Will, setting up my computers. I thought I'd put him in the room next to the one you used as your study."

"He'll like that. It looks over the pond."

"There'll be other things to deal with. Part-time nursing care to arrange if he . . . needs it. Emergency equipment. Stuff he'll want brought up from the apartment."

"How long will you stay?"

"As long as it takes," she said bluntly.

"Ruth . . ." Paul's voice twisted. "You don't think . . . He's not really going to die, is he? Up there?"

She was silent. Then she said steadily, "I'll ask Dieter Hechst to give me a hand with moving furniture, anything that needs doing."

"I'll come too—if you'll let me."

"Will would be so happy if you would."

"And you?"

"Me too."

DRIVING up, she could think only of the house waiting for her. For nearly two years it had been left alone. Did she have the courage to disturb the ghosts that flitted like moths through the deserted rooms?

On either side of the road out of Sweetharbor, the fields were brilliant with harebells and daisies. At the turnoff to Carter's House she rolled down the windows, letting in the smell of the ocean. There she saw the sunlit house waiting for her, patient and unchanging, as it had waited at the start of every summer of her life.

For a while she sat in the car, hearing the sea-sigh from below the meadows. She remembered the fevered days following the accident, how she had searched up and down the coast, the salt-wet rocks, the smell of seaweed, the sickening lurch between hope and despair. Eventually she got out of the car, walked slowly toward the porch. Resolutely she took the steps two at a time, put the key in the door, and let herself in.

She had expected stuffiness, the smell of disuse, perhaps a sense of grievance. She had certainly expected pain. What she felt instead was a deep sense of peace. Every smell, every sound was familiar. There was a sense of someone having just left the room, a lingering odor of recent coffee, a cushion dented as though newly leaned against. Furniture was polished; there were even flowers—ironically enough, a vase of freesias—on the Oriental chest. A gauzy light filtered through the blinds. The old house shifted and creaked, its timbers spreading like the branches of a tree to the sun's warmth outside. She walked through the empty spaces, feeling as though she were her own ghost, insubstantial, etiolated.

She could not believe that she was here again. That she could stand upright under the wooden ceilings and not be struck down with anguish. The living room was more or less as it had been when they left after the accident. The piano was open, as though someone was about to play. She pressed a few keys and was surprised to find it still in tune. On the stand was a song sheet—"Mr. Tambourine Man," an old Dylan song she remembered from college days. *In that jingle-jangle morning I'll come following you.* . . .

As she had feared, everything was a reminder of Josie: the chipped Chinese vase, the piano she had loved to play, books she had been reading that final summer, one of her paintings given pride of place on the dining-room wall. Ruth had thought the memories would be impossible to cope with, but to her surprise they were not. Time had gentled them.

She went out through the long French windows, around the back of the house, to where the trail began. The path was overgrown, fallen branches obscuring the way. She climbed up to where the trees opened out. The round tops of Mount Desert Island were faint against the sky. She stood on the edge of the bluff, looking out at the sea spread before her, falsely unthreatening. She sat down on the bench: Josie's bench.

She lifted her face to the skies, closed her eyes. Silence, broken only by the gently deceptive murmur of the ocean, the whisper of the pines behind her. She was filled with a sense of Josie's presence. She is here, she thought, her spirit, close by this bench that had been built for her, placed here overlooking the sea she had loved. Where else would a drowned ghost go except back to the place where it had been happy?

Eventually, wearily, she got to her feet. It was time to return, to prepare for Will's arrival. As she turned to leave, she saw something glinting in the grass at her feet. People had been up here, picnicking maybe, dropping trash. She picked it up. It glittered in the sunlight, metallic. An earring.

"Oh, God!" She spoke aloud, her heart hammering. "Josie!"

The only answer was the throb of the sea. She sat and examined the earring. It lay in her palm like a precious insect, long-legged, steel-shelled. She turned it over. Silver. Square, inset with a tiny copper heart. Exactly like the ones Josie had been wearing on the afternoon she drowned.

Rationalize this, she told herself. Be logical. The earring was not, could not be, Josie's. She would surely have seen it last summer. Someone must have dropped it—a courting couple, a hiker. Someone had sat on Josie's bench. It was simply a coincidence.

SHE had just stepped into the hall when the telephone rang. "Mrs. Connelly? It's Belle Dee, checking that everything's all right."

"The house looks very well cared for. Thank you."

"If you need help in any way, you only have to call."

"It's all under control. Thank you especially for the freesias in the living room. They were my daughter's—"

"I'd like to take credit, Mrs. Connelly, but I can't. We have to be careful, as I'm sure you appreciate, so we never leave flowers. Our clients may have allergies."

"How strange. I wonder where they came from."

"I'm sure there's a simple explanation," Mrs. Dee said. "In the meantime, if there's anything I can do, let me know."

In the living room the white flowers in their stoneware vase seemed too fragile, too few, to have filled the house with their perfume. She touched the trumpet-shaped blooms and heard Josie's voice again: *My absolute favorite flower.*

In the evening cool she sat out on the porch with a glass of wine and a letter opener. Better late than never, she thought, slitting open envelopes mailed almost two years ago. "Deepest sympathy." "Such a lovely girl." "You must be so bereft." "We knew her well." Josie opened in front of her like a blossom unfurling in sunshine, a friend to people she had not met. "Much missed." "Lighted up our home." "So much talent." Josie, her daughter and yet to other people something more than that—a presence, a person. Ruth wiped her eyes. Many of the letters were from local people she barely knew.

One envelope was stiffened with board. Carefully she drew out a charcoal sketch of a young girl, head bent, holding something in her hand—a flower, a paintbrush, hard to say which. Ruth drew in a sharp breath.

The turn of the neck, the shape of an ear half hidden by hair. Josie. My lost Josie. Seeing her again at this distance in time was almost like seeing a stranger. She turned the sketch over and saw a penciled note: "I thought you would like this. Annie Lefeau."

The name meant nothing to her, did not sound like a local family. She went into the house and propped the sketch up in the kitchen, where she could see it whenever she lifted her head from the sink.

The next morning Ruth braced herself, took a deep breath, and put a key into the lock, turned it. Josie's room. Shut up since the day she died.

The smells came at her: oil paint, old polish from the sanded boards, tired patchouli-scented air. Mrs. Dee had been given instructions: No one was to go into this room. Nothing had been touched for two years. Jeans still lay crumpled on the floor; a hairbrush had been flung on the bed. There was a spill of cassette tapes on a bureau top, open magazines, crumpled tissues. Dust lay over everything. There were dead moths, cobwebs, and the desiccated bodies of spider-wrapped flies.

Ruth had never pried into her daughter's private possessions. Now she did not hesitate. The table under the window was covered in a dusty mess of papers; she picked up and examined each one. Most were reminders to call someone, pick up more suntan lotion, borrow a book from the tiny Hartsfield library. There were several scribbled phone numbers.

She could not see Josie's painting equipment, expensive, top-of-the-line stuff, which she thought had been carried up from the side porch after the accident, but canvases were stacked against one wall: A portrait of Dieter and Trudi Hechst, done in American primitive style. An abandoned boat. A forest, thin trunks gilded with sunshine, and a man somewhere in among them—half person, half tree, solemn, hieratic. Josie had been sixteen when she painted these, but there was already a maturity of execution, a clarity of vision. Ruth wondered why she had not noticed it at the time. Why she had not truly believed in her daughter.

On the shelf were books, a Bowdoin College mug holding a silk rose, a carved duck, the whorls of the wood melting naturally into the curves of wing and breast. She turned it over and saw the initials S. H. burned into the wood. *Sam Hechst.*

Returning it to the shelf, she wondered where Josie's purse was. Josie had not known she would never come back from the birthday picnic, which meant that it should have been on the table or tossed on the bed. It would have held money, personal items.

Money—the thought triggered another. Ruth hurried down the passage to the walk-in linen closet and felt around behind the storage bags for the winter bedcovers. In the prudent Yankee tradition of her forebears a contingency fund had been hidden there for as long as she could remember. Last time she looked, the box had contained five hundred dollars.

Now, when she drew it out and opened the lid, it was empty.

Empty!

Only Josie would have known where the box was kept, only Josie would have gone straight to it and tidily replaced it.

Ruth shut the closet door. Looking up and down the passage, she smiled. "I know you're out there," she said aloud. "I *know* you are."

And it was not just Josie's ghost, not some spirit being, but the living Josie. It was impossible. Ruth knew that. And yet the thought refused to go away.

SHE was drinking coffee in the kitchen when Sam Hechst rapped lightly on the open door and came in. "My aunt tells me you need some help," he said.

"That's right. Want some coffee?"

"Good."

They sat on either side of the table, taking stock of each other. Ruth started to speak, but he interrupted her. "Something's happened. Do you want to talk about it?"

Ruth's hands shook; she pushed them into the pockets of her shorts. "The thing is, there are . . ." She stopped. "I know it sounds crazy, but I think, unbelievable or not, that . . . that Josie's still alive." He drew in a breath, and she held up her hand. "Don't say anything until I've finished." Carefully she enumerated her reasons. They seemed fragile, untenable, but she hurried on.

When she had finished, he asked, "If Josephine survived the storm, why do you think she didn't come home?"

"Maybe she didn't want to."

"Why not?"

"I'm not sure. Over these past months I've realized how little I knew about her, what she thought about, what her hopes were." Ruth thought of Annie Lefeau. "Even who she spent time with."

"Isn't that natural? How *could* you know? When you were that age, did you tell your parents everything?"

"No, but—"

"Secrecy is an essential part of growing up."

"I tried to be a good mother," Ruth said anxiously. "I thought I was. But now I can see I didn't give her *time*."

"Nobody could have given Josephine enough time."

"Do you really think that?"

"I told you before, people of her sensibilities, their highs are so high, their lows so low. They want everything *now;* they want everything perfect. It makes them difficult to live with. You can't blame yourself for that."

"There's something else," she said. "It's become all the more important that I find her. My son is . . . He's . . . The disease came back."

"This is terrible." Sam took her hand and held it lightly. "I had no idea, Ruth."

"Time's running out for him. Our last hope is a bone-marrow transplant, but we can't find a match for his tissue. If Josie is alive, there's a possibility that Will could be saved."

He gripped her arms, not moving toward her, just holding her. "Can I do anything at all to help?"

"I'm wondering if you have any idea where she could have gone when she . . . If she . . . After the accident. She seems to have talked to you more freely than she did to me."

"Well, we did talk a lot. And yes, she did fantasize about running away from home. About living with 'real' people, by which I think she meant people concerned about the environment, people who helped others, who made a living using their hands."

"Unlike her parents."

"Perhaps." He smiled. "She had this romantic idea of joining a commune." He tightened his grip on Ruth's hand. "If—if—she survived the accident, maybe she saw it as an opportunity to prove she could earn a living from her painting."

"By allowing us to believe she was dead?" Ruth was horrified. "I can't believe it."

"If you're determined to look for her, I can tell you several places she might have gone. Communes—they're kind of an outdated concept, but they do still exist. I guess artists' colonies might be a better phrase."

"I'd be grateful for any information at all."

AWAY from the coast, Maine changed—no longer the guidebook fantasy but a place undeveloped, almost primitive. Along the endless, deserted roads Ruth passed mobile homes, abandoned wooden buildings, faded FOR SALE signs. She was heading for the tiny hamlet of Colbridge. "There's a sort of collective," Sam Hechst had told her. "Artists and craftspeople marketing their work while the summer lasts. Josie came with me once, when I was dropping off some carved pieces. She liked the setup they had."

Colbridge was set around a triangular village green. Ruth parked in front of a gray house and got out. This far from the coast, the air was windless and dusty. The heat leaned on her, inescapable. She climbed the shallow wooden steps and pressed the bell. After a while the front door opened, and a man looked out at her through the screen door. Ruth could smell the unmistakable scent of marijuana.

"Yes?" He had very short hair, dyed an improbable yellow, and several silver rings in his ear. His T-shirt and cutoffs were splattered with clay.

"My name's Ruth Connelly," she said. "I'm looking for my daughter, Josephine."

"What makes you think she could be here?"

"She came visiting a couple of years ago and liked it. I thought she might have come back here."

"Ah. Let me guess," he said. "She left home, right? Hasn't been in touch since?"

"Something like that." Ruth showed him a photograph.

He scrutinized it briefly before shaking his head.

"Are you sure?"

"Definitely. Ever thought that she might not want to be found?"

"I'd like her to tell me that herself," Ruth said steadily.

As SOON as the telephone chirped, Paul knew it was Ruth. "Hi!" he said. "How's things?"

"Fine. How's Will?"

"Okay, I guess. Anxious to be out of the hospital. Looking forward to seeing you." He waited a fraction. "So am I."

"Are you?"

He didn't answer—the pause between the two of them lengthening but not uncomfortably. "Where are you?" he said. "I tried ringing the house a couple of times."

"I've stopped for coffee in a little town called Sawton."

"Of all the godforsaken places . . . What are you doing up there?"

"I'm—I'm looking for something."

"Looking for what?" He eased the phone against his jaw.

"I don't want to talk about it."

"Okay. Ruth . . ."

"Yes?"

"What are you wearing?" It was what he used to ask when they were courting. Did she remember?

"Green linen slacks, a white T-shirt. And this carved necklace somebody made me. Four hearts strung on a leather lace."

"Are you really?" he whispered.

"Yes, really," she said, and he heard the smile in her voice.

RUTH spent the night at a fine old Victorian house that had been converted to a B&B. She was tired after a long and disappointing day. She had stopped at more galleries and craft centers than she could remember, but nobody knew Josie's name, nobody recognized the girl in the photograph. Time after time she had psyched herself up to speak with total strangers. "Do you know this girl?" And always she had drawn a blank. In a craft shop on the other side of Skowhegan, the woman in charge had looked at the photograph and opened her mouth to speak. Then she put the picture down and began to rearrange pottery bowls on the shelf beside her.

"Yes?" Ruth had said urgently. "You've seen her?"

"I'm afraid not," the woman had said.

"But you looked as if you recognized her."

"I was mistaken."

Now lying in a strange bed, remembering the last time she had searched for her daughter, Ruth was thankful that she was stronger, more able to cope with despair. After breakfast she set off again through the familiar countryside—the cranberry bogs, the gun shops, the pulp trucks thundering by. Signs selling ANTIQUES, NEWTIQUES & COLLECTIBLES. Signs advertising LIVE BAIT AND CRAWLERS. Abandoned cars. Christmas tree farms.

Toward the end of the afternoon she found herself driving into Millport, a small town set far up one of the many inlets off the coast. She passed a social services center, a nursing home, little cafés offering crab cakes and lobster rolls, a garage offering exhaust tune-ups. Further on, a hand-lettered sign pointed down a short dirt track to Annie's Gallery.

Annie.

Could that be . . . Was it possible that this was the same Annie who had sent her that sketch of Josephine nearly two years ago?

Ruth drove down the track and parked. The store was clapboard-sided, with modern bow windows that held none of the usual cute tourist-tempting artifacts: no dungareed dolls in lace-edged caps, no carved wooden sailors. There were paintings, a wooden bowl of bird's-eye maple, and pottery pieces with subtle glazes.

Inside, the floors were wooden and bare, the glass shelves carefully lit. A woman sat behind a table laden with glossy art books. She was in her mid-thirties, wearing a low-cut black top and a floor-length skirt of Indian cotton. A long braid of bright red hair hung over one shoulder. "Can I help you?" she said.

"Are you Annie?"

"That's right."

"Annie Lefeau?"

"Yes."

"I'll just look around." Ruth walked slowly between the intricately carved wooden boxes, the baskets made from local materials and vegetable dyes. At the end of the gallery one of the walls was covered in textile hangings. The other two held paintings.

They were mostly local scenes: seascapes, rocks, boats, weathered houses with the wide gray sky of a Maine winter behind them. At first glance they seemed not much more than standard tourist bait, a reminder of a good vacation in a magnificent landscape. Until you looked closer. The fishing boats were not pleasure craft, but year-round working boats, oil-stained and dirty. The houses were shabby, their lines plain and workmanlike. A graveyard, a boat turned upside-down, an abandoned anchor on an empty shore—the artist had used them to point up the reality of a community on the edge of losing its culture. The paintings were bleak and powerful.

One in particular caught her eye, a marble headstone leaning against the sea wind, its white surface pitted with salt. Patches of lichen burned like orange suns against the carved words: DEATH IS SWALLOWED UP IN VICTORY. As though to emphasize the point, withered leaves lay piled at the foot of the stone, and among them a single white flower.

Ruth made her way to the front of the gallery. "I'm interested in the paintings you have in the back," she said.

The woman looked up. "Any one in particular?"

"There's one of a gravestone. I can't see a signature, though."

Annie smiled. "It's great, isn't it?" Getting up, she led the way to the end of the room. "I love that juxtaposition of life and death, the promise of springs to come."

"Is the artist local?"

"At the moment, yes."

"Is it a woman painter?"

Annie turned, her gaze suddenly wary. "Why do you ask?"

"Perhaps I'm reading too much into it," Ruth said, unnerved, "but it seems to have a woman's perspective about it."

Unexpectedly, Annie laughed. "Yes, the painter is a woman."

"What's her name?"

"All the paintings are signed." Annie stroked the auburn braid on her shoulder and narrowed her eyes like a cat.

Ruth could feel currents of emotion washing about her but was unable to determine what they were. Anger? Anxiety? She squinted at the bottom-left-hand corner of the picture. She could just make out the letters J. O.

J. O. Excitement swelled inside her. "What do the initials stand for?" she asked.

Annie stared at Ruth. "Janie O'Donnell," she said. "You seem to be a lot more interested in the painter than in the picture. I'd like to know why."

The two women faced each other. Finally Ruth said, "Because I think they may have been painted by my daughter."

"Oh, God." Annie paled. "You're Mrs. Connelly."

"How do you know that?"

"I'm . . . I was a friend of Josephine's."

"You sent me a drawing of her . . . after the accident."

"That was before . . . Yes, she drowned. That's why I sent you the drawing."

"Maybe she didn't."

Annie Lefeau's eyes widened. "What makes you say that?"

"Have you seen her, Ms. Lefeau? I've been searching all over. Up and down the coast. Inland. Asking everybody."

"Why do you think she's alive?"

"Instinct. I'm running on blind faith, nothing else." Ruth took a step closer. "Do you know where she is?"

"No." Annie shook her head violently from side to side.

Ruth clenched her jaw to prevent angry words escaping. Writing out a check, she said curtly, "Perhaps you'd wrap the painting for me." As she opened the door, she turned. "I know my daughter painted this," she said quietly. "And I know she did it recently."

Sitting in her car, Ruth removed the wrapping from the painting and looked at it more closely; then she stared at her watch. Four thirty. Just across the road she had noticed a place called the Docksider Diner. She drove over and parked in the lot behind it. Inside, she ordered an iced tea and sat by the window, watching.

After a while she asked for the check, paid it, then sat a while longer. At five fifteen Annie Lefeau appeared, driving a dirty green Camaro. She turned left. Hurriedly Ruth stood up.

She drove fast along the road Annie had taken. Before long she saw the Camaro, three cars ahead of her. Shortly after that a sign indicated a right turn, and Annie swung off, followed by one of the cars behind. And Ruth. Keeping back now, she trailed the cars along the rural road.

Annie turned off into a driveway in front of a one-story house. Ruth continued up the road a way, then found a place to pull off. She turned off the engine and waited fifteen minutes before driving back again to the house.

Pressing the bell, she pulled the screen door open. Ms. Lefeau came to the door almost immediately. "What are you doing here?" she said.

"I have to speak to you."

"I already told you, Mrs. Connelly, I don't know where your daughter is."

"And I think you're lying, Ms. Lefeau. I *must* find her—"

"I suppose you want her to come home with you? So her stepfather can go on abusing her?"

"*What?*"

Annie held up her hand. "Don't pretend you didn't know."

"So she *is* alive?" Ruth put a hand against the doorpost for support, afraid she might otherwise fall.

The other woman moved back. "Don't think I have any intention of helping you find her." She tried to push the door shut, but Ruth crowded after her.

"I don't know what Josephine's told you," she said, "but there is no stepfather. Nor was she ever abused by her father."

"How do you know that?"

"Because . . ." Ruth stopped. "Because I know my husband."

"I wonder how many other wives have said that."

"Ms. Lefeau—Annie, I love Josephine more than I can say. If there's anything I can do to make up for what she perceives I've done to hurt her, I would willingly do it. But that's not the only reason I'm here. My son, William— Please let me come in."

"Why should I?"

"Because I don't think you're in possession of all the facts. May I please come in?"

Reluctantly Annie motioned Ruth to go ahead of her into a pleasant sitting room, where antique furniture had been skillfully combined with modern glass and wood. In front of a fieldstone fireplace, filled with an elaborate arrangement of dried flowers and whitepainted twigs, she faced Ruth nervously. "Go ahead," she said.

"For a start, whatever she may have told you, Josephine was a much loved child. She was not abused by anyone in her family. I don't believe she was abused by anyone at all, not in the way you think. As you're aware, there was an accident and Josephine was lost. We've mourned her ever since. It's only in the past few days that I've begun to believe that perhaps she survived and, for reasons I can only guess at, didn't want to come home. My son is desperately ill with leukemia, and we've been unable to find a bone-marrow match for him. His sister might be able to provide that match. You can see how important it is to locate her."

"This is terrible." Annie Lefeau bit her lip. "How can I believe you?" she said.

"How can you not?"

"Dear Lord, I—I don't know what to do."

"Ask yourself why I should come after you like this, Ms. Lefeau, if I wasn't desperate. Josie's blood might possibly save her brother's life." Ruth seized the other woman's wrist. "You do know where she is, don't you? You do know she's alive."

Annie drew in a deep breath. "Yes. Yes, I do."

"Where is she?" Ruth said, scarcely able to breathe.

"I'm so sorry, Mrs. Connelly. Truly I am. I never did think she was telling the whole—"

"Where is she?"

"She's been—she's been living here, right here with me."

Blindly Ruth reached for an armchair and sank into it. The room began to waver and dim.

"She'd been into the gallery a couple of times, you see, and we'd talked about a lot of things. She was so passionate, so . . . strong. When I read about her death in the papers, I was devastated. That's why I sent you that sketch. And then, later, I—I . . ."

"You what?"

"One afternoon, about a year ago, someone came in, and when I looked up, it was her. I could hardly believe it." Annie shook her head, still incredulous.

"What did she say?"

"I can't really remember; I was so taken aback. But while we were talking, she told me she'd been sleeping in her car, some old rust bucket she'd picked up. I offered her a room, and she's used this house as a base ever since."

"Why didn't she . . ." Ruth cried. "One phone call . . . She can't have hated us that much."

"I thought so too—until she told me that story about her step-father."

Ruth saw the deep hurt inside the other woman. "Josie *is* my daughter," she said gently. "Please, Annie, tell me where she is."

"She trusts me. I just can't betray her."

"Then tell her that Will needs her."

"I can't even do that. She's taken off again. She'll call eventually, but I don't know when."

A choking despair swept over Ruth. To have come so close to her daughter only to lose her again. . . . She buried her face in her hands.

WHEN the telephone rang, he was watching some crap on the TV, not really watching, just thankful to have the bright images to focus on rather than the thought of his son's white face. He reached over and lifted the receiver. When he heard her voice, he hit the MUTE button on the remote. "Ruth, did you find what you were looking for?"

"Almost," she said.

"Want to tell me about it?"

"Paul, it's about Josie. She's alive."

"Ruth—" He wished he was with her, could hold her in his arms and gently explain how life didn't work like that. Drowned daughters didn't just show up after two years, however hard you might desire them to.

"You don't believe me, do you?"

"Where is she?" he asked gently.

"I think," Ruth said, and he could tell she was choosing her words with extreme care, "I think she needs me to find her."

"I worry about you, Ruth."

"Thank you for thinking of me."

"You wouldn't believe how often I do." Putting down the phone, he thought, I'm falling in love with her all over again.

WILL seemed in much worse physical shape than when Ruth had last seen him the week before. The pallor of his drug-swollen face and the gray shadows under his eyes belied the temporary animation he displayed as he moved heavily from room to room, checking the house out, making sure that everything was as he had remembered.

"It's great," he kept saying. "It's so great to be back."

"I've put you downstairs."

"But I wanted to be in my own room."

"I thought you'd like to be able to step directly onto the porch. I've brought all your things down from upstairs."

"But I—" He was about to protest some more, then saw her face. With an effort he said, "Thanks, Mom."

They walked together down the passage to the kitchen. "Where did that come from?" Will asked, nodding at the sketch of Josie tacked to a cupboard door.

"Someone gave it to me."

"You've changed, Mom. A year ago you wouldn't mention Josie's name, let alone have her picture up."

"I chose the wrong way to come to terms," Ruth said. "I finally realize that." Should she tell him now or wait until he was rested from the journey?

Will sat on the edge of the table. "It's going to be great to sleep in a proper bed, instead of that hospital thing with sides like a crib." He stood up again. "Mind if I go down to the shore?"

"Just don't overtire yourself."

From the front porch she watched him walk slowly and with obvious effort across the meadow toward the stony strip of beach.

"Fog's coming in," Will said, looking out into the darkness.

"Which means it'll be cold tonight," said Paul.

"I like the way it wraps itself around the house. Sort of like a blanket."

"What do you say we start a fire?"

"Great idea. There's wood on the side porch."

Paul fetched the big two-handled wicker basket from the hearth, and together they filled it.

The small effort of gathering the logs seemed to completely exhaust Will. Once the fire was going, he sat in front of it, holding his hands to the flames. They seemed almost transparent, as though the life force was inexorably being extinguished. For the first time since the second onset of his illness Paul was truly frightened. "How about a game of Scrabble?" he said.

"Okay." But once they had started, Will couldn't concentrate, his eyes drooping, so deeply sunk that the reflection of the flames in the hearth scarcely reached him.

When Will had gone to bed, Paul sat opposite Ruth, watching the firelight play on her hair.

"What's wrong?" Ruth smiled at him.

"You look so pretty," he said.

"Me? Oh, sure."

He lifted her hand. "You're still wearing your wedding band."

"That's because I'm still married."

He slipped an arm around her shoulders and felt her yield into the curve of his body. Then the telephone rang, and she pulled away, suddenly frantic, scrambling for the receiver.

Annie Lefeau was on the other end of the line.

"Janie—Josephine—called me this morning," Annie said. She sounded tense. "I told her about her brother being sick. She was terribly upset. She was crying and sobbing on the phone."

"Did she say where she was?"

"No. She was calling from a pay phone. I told her about the bone-marrow thing too, that it was Will's last chance."

"Did you tell her I love her?"

"She knows that, Ruth. She said she'd be in touch."

"That's all?"

"Yes, Ruth, that's all."

"I'M STARVING," Ruth said when Will appeared in the kitchen the next morning. "Are you up for breakfast at the Cabot Inn?"

"What about Dad?"

"He's gone down to take another look at the *Duck*."

"We were going to try and rebuild it," Will said. "Before . . ."

"You still could."

The hotel manager was standing by the reception desk when they came in, and at Will's request he seated them at a table overlooking Old Port Street. Will stared out the window. "I really wish we lived here all the time," he said. He gazed at his mother over the rim of his glass of milk.

"I'm thinking," Ruth said slowly, "that maybe we should." Striving hard for cheerfulness, she smiled.

"If we did, what would happen with your job?"

"I'd probably try to find something closer to home."

"Really? Honestly?" He sighed with pleasure.

"Will"—Ruth leaned across her coffee cup—"I don't know if this is the right place or time to do it, but there's something desperately important I have to tell you."

The joy ebbed from his face. "Is it about my cancer? 'Cause if so, don't worry. It doesn't bother me anymore. It did at first, dying and stuff, but I'm okay about it now. I really am." He looked directly at her.

She shook her head. "No, Will. It's . . . It's about Josie."

"What about her?"

"She's alive," Ruth said.

Eyes wide, he stared at her. "Don't, Mom. Please."

"Don't what?"

"Dad told me you'd got this idea that . . ." He looked down at his plate. "C'mon, Mom. Let it go. She's dead."

She reached across for his hand and saw him force himself not to pull away. "Will, believe me. It's true. I've spent the past week looking for her, and I finally found where she's been living for the past year." Ruth described what she had learned from Annie Lefeau.

"But she'd have called us. She'd never have left us hanging like that. Never in a million years. Is this Lefeau woman playing with a full deck?"

"I think so."

"Oh, Mom . . . Are you *sure?*"

"I'm sure. Annie's coming to visit this afternoon. You can talk to her yourself."

ANNIE Lefeau arrived at four o'clock. She had piled her auburn hair on top of her head and anchored it insecurely with colored combs. She seemed less austere, the lines of worry smoothed from her face.

She shook hands with Paul and greeted Will with delight. "I'm so happy to meet you," she told him. "Your sister talked about you a lot."

"You really know her?"

"I really do. She's something special." Reaching into the leather pouch slung over her shoulder, Annie took out a package. "I brought you this."

"Thanks," Will said. He undid the wrapping to reveal a small picture of a freckled boy leaning against an upturned boat and laughing. He stared down at it. "Hey, it's me."

"Josie painted it on your birthday last year," Annie said softly. "She kept it in her room."

"Oh, Mom . . ." Blindly Will passed the little painting to his mother.

"It's beautiful." Ruth showed it to Paul.

"You have a talented daughter, Professor Connelly."

"*Have?* Are you really sure, Ms. Lefeau?"

She drew in a deep breath and clasped her hands together in her lap. Looking above their heads toward the sea, she said, "I need to tell you the truth."

"Which is what, exactly?" Paul said.

She took another breath. "I . . . uh . . . own a cabin in the woods, down by the shore, around the coast a ways from here. It's a sort of extra studio. If I'm working on a painting, I sometimes stay there overnight. It's kind of primitive, but there's packaged food and cans, a sleeping bag. Even rainwater from an old cistern." She leaned toward Paul and Ruth. "After the sailing accident, a week or so after Josephine's disappearance, I went down there to work on a canvas and she was there. I couldn't believe what I was seeing. She was dead. I'd read the papers, I'd sent you that drawing, and yet there she was."

"Josie?"

"Yes."

Ruth looked at Paul and then back at Annie. "Go on."

"When I first saw her, she looked like a wild animal," Annie said. "Hair straggling over her face, bruises everywhere, a filthy strip of something tied around her wrist. She was feverish, rambling. She told me that when she was swept away, the current was much too strong to swim against. The sea was crashing over her; she was choking, certain she was going to die. And then she found herself flung forward by a wave, and before she was sucked back, she realized there were rocks under her feet. The third or fourth time she was washed up, she managed to grab onto a spar of rock. It took her nearly two days to make her way to my cabin."

"But I don't understand." Ruth pressed her hands against her temples. "Why didn't you let us *know?*"

"She was raving, pleading with me not to tell anyone. In the end, I agreed. She said hysterical things. That you wouldn't miss her. That you didn't care about her. I moved her back home with me so I could take care of her while I decided what to do. We had so many arguments those first few days. Finally she said she'd call you. When I came back the next day, she'd gone. I thought she'd returned to Boston."

"And when you saw her again, what did you think then?" Paul asked coldly.

"I . . . I don't really know. I was so happy to see her safely back." Annie fiddled with the combs that held her hair back from her face. "I've behaved so . . . terribly badly."

"Yes, you have," Ruth said.

"So has Josie," said Will.

One phone call, Ruth thought over and over again. How different our lives might have been.

THAT evening they lit another fire and played cribbage with the ivory-inlaid set that had belonged to Ruth's grandmother. Will found it difficult to concentrate.

Ruth put her hand on his. "She'll come," she said softly.

"I wish she'd hurry up," he said fretfully. His breath rattled inside his ribs. The firelight threw long shadows across his face as he put down his cards. "I'm tired. I'll go to bed, guys, if you don't mind."

"That's okay, son."

"I'll come and tuck you in," added Ruth. The bedtime ritual of childhood seemed to calm him a little.

"Ten minutes," he said.

Later, having kissed him good night, Ruth was about to close his door behind her when Will called out. "Mom!"

"What, sweetheart?"

"Are you angry with Josie? For not getting in touch."

Ruth wondered what she should say. "I—I don't know."

"Because I am."

"I think we have to concentrate on the future."

"When she comes, wake me up."

"I will."

"Even if it's late?"

"I promise. Okay?"

"Okay." He smiled the gaunt smile she had grown used to. He lifted his arms. "Mom, give me a hug."

"As many as you like." Tears pooled behind Ruth's eyes as she walked back across the hooked rugs and put her arms around her son. His bones felt as fragile as breadsticks, as though they would snap under the slightest pressure.

Will pushed his nearly naked head into her shoulder, snuggling like a puppy. "I love you, Mom."

"And I love you, William. Oh, with all my heart."

In her head she heard Josie's voice again: *Would you love me, no matter what?*

Would she? Could she?

Before getting into bed, Ruth stood at the balcony rail. A bright sliver of moon hung against the intense lavender of the summer sky, its fragile reflection floating on the black glass of the deeper water beyond the bay. She could hear the ocean sigh at the foot of the pasture. Across the sound, lights flickered among the branches of the firs on the shore.

Josie would come.

She would come. For Will's sake she had to.

CHAPTER ELEVEN

FOG crept in again during the night and lay heaped across the front pasture. The house felt damp, as though the pale sea mist had seeped in through the screens.

Will spent the morning walking slowly from room to room, as though, if he tried hard enough, he could force his sister to materialize at the kitchen table or on the living-room couch. "When do you think she'll get here?" he asked, standing at the windows, gazing into the fog.

"Soon." Ruth hugged him carefully. There were bruises on his neck and down his arms.

"But *when? How* soon?"

The hours went by, and Josephine did not appear.

Around noon Carmel Stein called. "What a dreary day," she said. "Why don't you bring Will over for lunch?"

"Let me just check with him," Ruth said.

She found him huddled miserably on the porch, gazing toward the invisible sea, his hair and clothes pearled with mist. "Want to go over to the Steins'?"

"We have to stay here," he said. "In case she comes."

"But—"

He turned his face to her, his eyes like those of a trapped animal.

Shaken, she went to the phone. "We can't make it today," she lied. "Maybe another time."

Ruth made sandwiches, but Will barely touched his. The seconds, the minutes sluggishly changed into hours.

As the afternoon began to fade, she found him lying on his bed. "I thought I'd drop by the Cottons'," she said. "I bought Marietta some peanut butter cups. I know she likes them. Josie used to take them to her."

"You've never done that before."

"Maybe I should have," Ruth said. "Want to walk down to their house with me?"

"Marietta'll be some glad," he said in the voice he kept for Maine, an attempt to belong to the place he loved best.

"Come with me, Will. We won't be long."

Paul was at the edge of the woods, chopping logs from a fallen sapling birch. His face was flushed. Seeing them coming, he stopped and wiped his forehead with his arm.

"Getting ready for winter already, Dad?" Will asked, giving his ghostly grin.

"Can't start too soon," Paul said.

"We're going to visit the Cottons," Ruth said.

"Mom, maybe I'll stay here. In case there's a phone call."

"I've got my cell phone," Paul said gently to his son. "You can sit and talk to me, and we'll hear if anyone telephones."

THE Cottons' house stood lower down on the same inlet as Carter's House. It was painted the same red as Ruth's barn, its weathered woodwork picked out in white.

Ruth banged at the door, but it seemed the Cottons were not home. She sat on the porch and waited for a while, enjoying the solitude. On the rough grass behind the house, laundry was pegged to a clothesline, billowing with the breeze off the water. She remembered Josie demanding to know why she too didn't hang laundry out, and Ruth could not recall her response. Something to do with not having enough time. Back then, time had constantly slipped past her, carried away on a tide of meaningless duties. Now, with every second precious, she saw how important it was sometimes to do nothing except appreciate the privilege of being alive.

Eventually she wrote a note, using large plain letters. Ben Cotton's old eyes might not be able to make out her normal script. She said that she hoped Marietta's arthritis was better now and that she would drop by again soon. She found a rock to weight down the note on the box of candies, then set off through the woods.

The fog had finally begun to roll back. Wisps of it clung to the trees like cotton candy and then were suddenly gone. Where the trail forked, Ruth hesitated. I'll only stay a couple of minutes, she promised herself. Just a few minutes.

Up on the bluff a breeze blew fitfully off the sea. She stood behind the bench, tracing the letters of her daughter's name: Josephine Carter Connelly. The sea was the color of the lead foil that used to line the big wooden teaboxes in the grocery in Hartsfield when she was a child. A steady certainty possessed her. Today Josie would come home. She knew it as surely as she knew that tomorrow the sun would rise.

Images of Will's and Josie's childhoods crowded into her mind, and suddenly, despite herself, despite her defiant optimism, she was overtaken by a tide of grief. Confronted by the indifferent sky, the unfeeling sea, she could not hold her tears.

"Don't cry . . ."

The voice behind her was so low she thought she must have dreamed words into the sound of the wind.

"Mom . . ."

Slowly she turned. For a moment she wondered whether she was seeing real flesh and blood. "Josie . . ." she whispered.

"Mom . . ."

"Josie!" Ruth held out her arms, and her daughter came running, and the two women wrapped themselves around each other, clinging tightly, for moments that seemed to last forever.

The swell of love inside her threatened to break through the frail barriers of her body as she drew into herself the youthful scent of skin, the smooth slide of hair. "I love you," she murmured, her lips fierce against her daughter's cheek. "I *love* you."

"Mom," breathed Josie. "Oh, Mom."

"We've missed you. *Missed* you, Josie, more than—"

"So have I."

"How I've longed . . . ached to . . ." Ruth stopped. What she wanted to say was beyond words. She held her daughter away from her. "You look so . . ." The long-legged slimness of girlhood had given way to feminine curves. Josie had cut her hair short. Her eyes were older, wiser. "Josie," Ruth said softly.

"What?"

Ruth laughed. "It's so good to be able to say your name . . . to have you here. Shall we go tell the rest of the family you've come home?"

Josie did not move. "Mom, please forgive me."

"Forgive? You're back now. That's all that matters."

"Please, Mom. We have to talk about this."

"Will's desperate to see you. And your father . . ."

"I don't want to see them until we've discussed this, Mom. Why didn't I call? That's what you want to know, isn't it?"

"Now isn't really the—"

Josie's gaze was direct, anxious. "You can't push the question away, Mom. It lies at the heart of everything."

"Okay. You're right." Ruth was terrified of reacting wrongly, of scaring Josie away again, yet at the same time there were important things to say. Behind the flame of love renewed lay something more complex—the need to understand. "I've learned so much about you that I didn't know—how compassionate you are, how thoughtful of others. Yet to the people who ought to matter most in the world . . ."

"You don't know how many times I wanted to call you." Josie's voice briefly failed, and she cleared her throat. "Not at first. But then the longer I left it—what would I say? After what I'd done, how could I expect to come back into your lives? I guess I was afraid."

Fog lay at the far edge of the sky. Below them the sea moved slowly. Josie walked to the edge of the bluff and looked down at the rocks. "I've thought about it so often. At first I was just mad. At you, mostly. Then I was hurt. When I washed up on the beach, coughing up seawater, aching all over, I felt such hurt."

"But why?"

"Because—" She turned, tried to laugh. "It sounds so petty. Because you'd called out for Will, but not for me."

"He was younger, smaller."

"I know. I guess I wanted to punish you."

"It's enough that you're back. I don't need to know."

"You *have* to know. Because I want to tell you that I realize now there was nothing to punish you for. It was just . . . I didn't appreciate how lucky I was to have you for a mother." Josie shook her head. "I admired you for being made a partner, for doing so well. And at the same time I wanted you to be home in an apron, baking cookies." Josie gave a laugh that was almost a sob. "It's only recently I've begun to see that I was so hard on you."

"Josie, you don't have to— I was also hard on you."

"But Mom, don't you see? You set standards for me—for all of us. I see that now." Josie ran her suntanned fingers through her hair. "I just couldn't see it before. After the accident I thought . . . I thought you probably wouldn't mind that much, the way things were between us. And you were going to send me off to one of those behavior-modification places."

"I never meant it, not for a single moment."

"And you were refusing to let me leave school, and then the last thing I heard, when that wave crashed over us, was you yelling for

Will, not for me." Josie began to cry. "Mom, I'm so ashamed of myself."

"Sweetheart, it's all right."

"It's *not*. All I thought about was my own feelings. I didn't give a damn about anyone else's."

"Everything I know about you, Josephine, everything I've come to realize, has made me so proud." Ruth tilted Josie's face and wiped the tears from her cheek. "I only wish I could be as proud of myself." They were both silent for a moment. "Losing you . . . I didn't handle it well. Dad and I split up."

"It's my fault," sobbed Josie. "You guys were so close. Oh, Mom . . ."

"Hush," said Ruth. "I love you more than I can say, Josephine. I always have. I always will, whatever you do. You're my child. It's a bond that can't ever be broken."

"I realize that now."

"If you hadn't left the earring," Ruth said, "even now, I'd never have thought for a minute that you were still alive."

"Which earring?"

"The one you put right here for me to find. One of the pair I gave you—silver, with a copper heart in the middle. You remember, you were wearing them when you—"

"I've still got them. Both of them."

"But it's because of the earring that I first started to—"

"It wasn't mine." Josie clutched at her mother's hand. "I used to go into the house from time to time. I took my painting gear away. And some money. The contingency fund. Sometimes I'd play the piano, sit, and just wish that we . . ."

"Oh, Josie," Ruth said softly.

"And I used to call Mrs. Dee, pretending I wanted to rent the house, to find out if you were coming back."

"We were here at Christmas."

"But not at Carter's House."

"No. I—I wasn't ready for that."

"Oh, Mom, what have I done to you?"

Ruth squeezed her daughter's hand. "Come on, darling, let's go find the others."

They began to walk down through the woods. Consumed with love, Ruth luxuriated in the newfound details of her daughter: the strong line of her back, the way her long legs strode down the trail, the toss of her hair. Everything is going to be all right now, she thought. We can go back to being a family again.

Skirting the cranberry bog, Josie stopped. "How sick is Will?"

"He's going to die," Ruth said. "Unless we find a tissue match so he can have a bone-marrow transplant. He'll be so happy to see you, Josie."

"Mom, I never said this, but . . . I love you so much."

"And I love you."

For a long, deep moment they held each other's gaze. What is she thinking? Ruth wondered. The young woman in front of her was Josie, and yet not Josie. There was a distance between them made up not of antipathy now, but of time. They would need time to learn each other again.

When they emerged from the woods, Will was standing at the edge of the pond, staring toward the trees, as though he already knew that his sister had returned. He began an awkward limping run toward them, arms outspread. "Josie!" His face seemed to be one enormous grin. "Josie, Josie, you're back."

Ruth saw Josie's shock at the sight of her brother and how fear drew the color from her face as she kissed his pale cheek. "You've grown," she said.

"It happens," Will said.

"Where'd you get the ear stud?"

"Mom bought it."

"C'mon," Josie said, digging into herself for the strength not to exclaim over Will's appearance. "Get real. Ruth Carter Connelly bought her son an *earring*?"

"It's true."

"You aren't going to believe this, but I've really missed you."

Will sighed. "It's been so great not having a big sister to boss me around, but I could get used to it again."

"Did you get the picture of you I painted?"

"Ayuh. And I hate to admit it, but you're some good."

"Think so?"

"Know so." Will put out his hand, and Josie took it tenderly in hers.

"Mom," Josie said, "I'll come see Dad in just a minute." To Will she said, "How about a walk down to the shore?"

"Great." Clumsily Will turned. Every movement seemed to hurt him. "You'll have to go slowly, though."

HE RAN across the rough grass of the pasture. He could see them standing by the water's edge, facing each other. As he came closer, the breeze carried toward him a sound he barely recognized. His son, angry? Yelling at his sister?

"Not fair!" Will was shouting.

"I know that—"

"We thought you were dead."

"I'm sorry."

"Sorry's not good enough." Will was weeping now. "So you were going to make them pay—that's so horrible, Josie. And me, what about me? What did I ever do to you?" Will's thin body twisted as the sobs were wrenched from his chest. "Why'd you let me think you were dead?"

"I couldn't have told you and not them."

"The whole time I was sick I worried about you not being around and what it'd do to Mom and Dad if I wasn't either."

Josie too was crying. "Will, you're not going to—"

"I hate you, all right? I hate you for what you did." Will knuckled the tears from his eyes. He bent down and picked up a driftwood branch and threw it into the water. As it floated away, he said quietly, "Which doesn't mean I don't love you too."

"Oh, Will . . ." Josie put her arms around her brother and rocked him against her chest.

After a moment Paul cleared his throat.

Josie broke away from Will and looked up. "Dad."

He stared at her. It really was her, standing below him, hair riffled by the wind lifting off the water—his daughter, his Josie, his little girl. Restored to life.

"Dad," she said again, "I'm home."

He held his arms wide. A pulsing rush of joy filled him as she ran toward him and flung herself into them. "Josie," he said. He felt her heart leaping against his. "Oh, God. Josie . . ."

"Dad, I'm sorry, I'm sorry." Josie wept.

He held her tighter, never wanting to let her go again. Tears ran down his face, dropping into her hair.

"I *love* you," he whispered, but could not have said whether he spoke the words aloud or simply felt them.

That evening he couldn't take his eyes off his daughter as they sat around the dining-room table. Celebrating, Ruth had taken the heavy silver-gilt candlesticks from the cupboard, unlocked the glazed commode, and taken out the best crystal. The return of the prodigal daughter. She who was lost is found again.

She'd changed so much. Her hair was cut close to her head and dyed a dark brown; her face was thin, the bones much more clearly defined. How slight she looked. How beautiful.

Josie was talking to Will. "So this total jerk asks me to paint a mural around his indoor swimming pool. Offers a small fortune."

"How much is that?" asked Ruth.

"Enough to live on for a month or two. Anyway, he says he wants something to remind him of his mother, who's originally from Greece, right? So I spend hours and hours painting this scene with olive groves and grapevines and, like, the Acropolis in the background. You never saw anything so Greek in your life. Took me weeks. And then, when I'm finished, know what he says?"

Will shook his head. "What?"

"He says, I don't see my mom. Didn't I tell you I wanted something to remind me of my mom?"

"So what did you do?"

"Told him I hadn't realized he wanted his mother scoping out the poolside shower. And anyway, since he hadn't given me a picture, how did he expect me to know what she looked like?"

Listening to her, Paul realized that they were a family again. It felt strange and yet entirely natural. "What did he do then?" he said.

"He finked out. Refused to pay me. Said I hadn't carried out the commission. Then I found out he does that all the time. Wanna know what I did?"

"What?" said Will.

"The guy spends half the year in Pacific Palisades, right? So next time he was out in California, I got into his house—"

"Broke in, you mean?" Will's eyes were round.

"Sort of. Then I painted the entire mural white. Two coats."

"Takes guts to obliterate a piece of work like that," Paul said.

"It was the principle of the thing, Dad. I didn't see why he should have something for nothing. Annie Lefeau told me he did the same thing to a woodworker she knows. And a small local builder. How're they going to get justice?"

Where had Josie learned how to force her way into someone else's house? What other dubious skills had she picked up in the time she had been away from them? Where had she been? There was so much Paul wanted to know. He glanced across at Ruth, wondering if she, too, felt this. He poured more wine. He tilted his glass to Josie in a toast. "To you, darling heart. You don't know how happy we are to have you home."

PAUL lay listening to Ruth in the bathroom. It had become a nightly routine for him to lie there imagining her undressing, recalling the way she bent to remove her clothes, the line of her leg, her full breasts. It was a kind of self-inflicted torture. He knew precisely how she would look lying in the tub, the way she would reach for the towel when she was through, the smell of her warm skin.

What would happen if he went in to her once she had gotten into bed? If he slipped under the covers? Maybe she wanted him to do that. Maybe she was waiting for him to make the first move.

He switched off the lamp and lay on his back under the thin summer quilt. The uncurtained window was a rectangle of silvery blue against the larger darkness of the room. A scrap of tissue-thin moon hung in one corner of the sky.

He was half asleep when he heard quiet footsteps across the wooden floorboards. Before he could sit up, the quilt was gently pulled back and Ruth slid in beside him.

"Ruth . . ." He opened his arms, and she came into them, tucking herself in close as she had always done. She was naked, still damp from the bath, and holding her, he recalled all the years of their marriage, all the nights they had gone to sleep curled together like this. She placed a hand on his chest, and he drew in a long breath. The feel of her fingers was like a valuable gift that he had thought lost forever.

"Ruth . . ." He pulled her even closer. "Oh, Ruth, I want you so much."

"I love you, Paul," she said.

"And I love you, Ruth. More than you'll ever know."

Later, much later, when they had spent an hour as long as a lifetime in relearning each other, she sighed happily. "We're a family again, aren't we?"

"Yes."

"And everything's all right, isn't it?" She sounded like a little girl.

He kissed her forehead. "As all right as it can be."

PAUL and Josie sat holding hands, huddled together on a Naugahyde couch. Under the harsh light from the fluorescent strip hanging from the ceiling, their faces looked gray and haggard. Other anxious people had obviously waited here before them: The cheap table was dotted with cigarette burns, and the box of tissues on the windowsill was empty.

Every time someone passed the door, they tensed. "I can't stand much more of this," Josie said.

"I'm sure they're rushing the tests. They know it's urgent."

Josie glanced up as a white-coated doctor paused at the door, then continued down the passage. She leaned toward Paul. "Can you understand how desperately I want this to work? It'd be like making up for all the harm I've caused."

"Josephine, if you can provide a match for Will, that'd be fantastic. But that's not why we're so happy you're home. We love you because you're Josie. Our daughter. Remember, whatever you've done, whatever you do, we love you." Paul looked down at her hand, softly ran a finger across the knuckles. "You do realize that the chances of this working are pretty slim, don't you?"

Josie's face crumpled. She took a sharp breath and squeezed her eyes shut. "I don't want to think about that."

"If it doesn't work, it's not your fault. At least you tried."

"Dad, whatever the result, let me be the one to tell Will."

"Don't you think he'll know?"

"Just let me do this, Dad." She leaned her head against Paul's shoulder. He rested his cheek on her hair. They sat again in silence.

Another white-coated doctor stood at the door. "Josephine Connelly?" he said, looking down at his clipboard.

"That's me."

"If you'd like to come with me, Ms. Connelly . . ."

Josie stood up, her expression anguished. "Dad . . ."

"You'll be fine," Paul said.

She hesitated as though about to say something more, then joined the doctor. Paul heard their footsteps receding down the corridor. After a while he got up and walked slowly along the passage, looking in at the windows of the side rooms as he went. Halfway down, he saw Josie. She was listening to the doctor, her head bent, hands clasped tightly in her lap, as he pointed to a printout, tapping it here and there with a pen. Paul could not hear what he was saying.

But he knew anyway.

RUTH left Paul sleeping and went downstairs. There was a lingering smell of coffee in the empty kitchen. Early morning sun slanted through the windows, golden and hopeful. There were two mugs on the table and a milky cereal bowl.

"Will!" Ruth called. "Where are you? Josie?"

No answer.

"Are you okay?" She looked in the open door of Will's bedroom, went out to the porch. "Will? Josie?" Her voice floated up into the astringent sea-sharp air and was lost.

Slowly she went back up to the bedroom. She had been surprised at her reaction to the news. Having pinned all her hopes on Josie's tests, she had expected to be crushed if the results proved negative. Instead, her mind was already turning over possibilities that might remain. More chemo, a sudden match discovered on the register, another remission, a miracle.

On the balcony she lifted the binoculars she kept there, swept them around, across pale water and blue spruce. Out on the sea a lobster boat was pulling up traps. When she focused, she could see

Dieter Hechst at work. She swept the glasses around once more. There was nothing out there except trees, grass, boulders thrusting up from the ancient earth. And the sea. A couple of sloops lay at anchor, hardly moving on the still surface of the water.

Where would Will have gone?

She slipped the strap of the glasses over her neck. The children might not even be together. Perhaps Josie had driven off somewhere while Will decided to go for a walk.

A jolt of alarm shook her. Suppose he had collapsed, suppose he was lying somewhere, waiting for them to find him. She ran into their bedroom. "Paul!" She shook his shoulder. "Darling, Will's gone, and Josie."

Hearing the anxiety in her voice, he pulled himself up, swung out of bed. "Let's go look."

Ten minutes later, standing on the porch, binoculars around his neck, he said, "Do you think he's strong enough to take out the Beetle Cat on his own?"

"I don't know."

"Then let's go up to Caleb's Point." Paul put his arm around her shoulder. "Don't worry, Ruth."

Hand in hand they took the trail up into the trees.

The Hechsts' lobster smack had gone, but one little dinghy bobbed on the water. Ruth focused on the white sail. "There they are," she said, relieved.

The Beetle Cat skimmed along against the sky, its sail full of golden wind, a wake forming a line of white behind it. Small waves glittered. She could see Will leaning back in the cockpit, one arm spread lightly on the tiller. He was smiling at his sister.

"Paul"—she took his hand—"seeing them together again, our children . . . It's wonderful."

"A true miracle, darling."

In the little boat Josie was apparently exhorting Will, one hand slapping through the air as she made whatever point she was trying to convey. Will kept shaking his head.

"She looks well," Paul said. He raised his glasses.

Ruth looked through her binoculars. "She looks *lovely*."

"She always did. Takes after her beautiful mother."

Ruth laughed aloud. She leaned against her husband. Josie was back. "Aren't they something?"

The little boat tacked between pot buoys, then veered toward open water. It sailed between the wooded arms of the bay before turning and tacking back again, while brother and sister sat and talked. Beyond the trees rose the whale humps of Mount Desert Island.

"In spite of the test results, I feel happy," Ruth said. "Something's going to turn up. I just know."

"It's so peaceful up here." Paul sat on Josie's bench.

Ruth sat beside him. She closed her eyes, turning her face to the sun. The breeze brought the fresh tang of salt and kelp. Gulls screamed distantly out in the bay.

"Should we do something about this bench?" Paul asked.

"Leave it here?" Ruth murmured.

"As a reminder? That's right."

They sat quietly, hand in hand, the air between them rich with promise. Happiness filled her like water. Every now and then she lifted the glasses to watch her children talking while the Beetle Cat drifted gently between the pot buoys and the water danced. A yellow-gold light shone across the bay—the color of honey, the color of hope.

"I wish this day could last forever," she said lazily. "Just this part of it, with them out there and us here."

She lifted her glasses again. Josie had moved to sit beside her brother. She put her arms around him for a long moment, hugging him tightly. She rubbed her face against his, touched his cheek. Will took her hand and talked earnestly.

The little boat came in right below the bluff, so close that Ruth could hear the clunk as the boom swung over. She saw Will lean forward and kiss his sister. As they headed out again, Ruth's contentment began slowly to dissipate. What were the two of them discussing? Although the scene seemed idyllic, somehow something was dragging it awry.

Through her glasses she saw Josie speak and then turn away, her face grim. At the same time, Will let go of the tiller. He clasped the anchor against his chest, wrapped the chain around his wrist. He swung his legs over the side.

"What's he doing?" Ruth asked. A wave of fear engulfed her. "Paul, why's he holding the anchor like that?"

"Ruth," said Paul suddenly. "Ruth." He closed his hand tightly around her arm as Will slowly, slowly, slipped over the side of the boat into the sea. A silent splash of spray rose, sparking a brief rainbow as it caught the sun, and then he was gone. Disbelieving, Ruth watched him disappear beneath the surface of the sea, remembering the numbing water, cold that burned like fire.

"The water's so cold," she said in a reasonable voice while fear clutched her heart. "Why would he swim out there?"

Paul's grip on her arm was painful. "I don't think he's—"

"What's he doing?" Ruth cried. "Paul, why hasn't he . . ."

Paul stood up. "Oh, God," he said. "Oh, no."

Below them Josie resolutely sailed away from the spot where Will had disappeared.

"Where is he?" Ruth rose to her feet. "Why has she left him alone? Why isn't she helping him?"

Paul said nothing.

Ruth stared at the spot where she had last seen her son. Will did not reappear. Josie, her head bent, steered across the water toward the open sea.

Understanding finally came. And horror.

"No!" Ruth screamed. "Will . . . Oh, my God. Oh, Will, no!" The words flew across the water. "Will! I love you—"

She turned and began to run downhill to where the bluff grew less steep and it was possible to gain access to the beach. Paul ran behind her, calling her name, but she paid no heed. If she could swim out to the spot where he had disappeared, she could save him, her sad sick child. She could breathe life back into him, turn back the clock. Will . . . But even as she scrambled across the rocks, slipping on the seaweed—Will!—she knew it was useless.

One part of her mind insisted that this was not happening, that somewhere another Ruth still stood at the edge of the bluff and looked across to where a little boat bobbed and her children laughed together. As she plunged into the waiting sea, the only message her distraught brain could process was this: He had chosen his own path. There was nothing she could do.

She swam. She screamed Will's name, and the sea poured through her, swamped, deluged her. The gasp, the choke, clutching at water that slid through her fingers. She remembered it still—the panic of that long-ago moment when salt had burned the back of her throat and she had been aware of death, oblivion, nothingness.

Would you die for me? Would you give your life for me?

Encumbered by her clothes, heart bursting with terror, the answer was so blindingly clear that Ruth wondered why Josie had needed to put the question. Oh, yes, without any doubt whatsoever. If it was necessary, I would gladly give my life for you. For both of you. But neither of you ever asked.

SHIVERING, she stood passive while Paul silently removed her wet clothes and guided her into the shower. She felt his hands on her body, washing away the salt, washing away the sea. A cold numbness filled her, blotting out all feeling except grief.

Paul toweled her dry, found her robe on the back of the door, and wrapped her in it. He began to weep, and she took his head in her hands and held it against her breast.

"Paul," she said, tears sliding ceaselessly down her face, "this time we must treasure each other."

"Yes."

"Not be careless of the richness we have together." She bent her head over his and began to weep, her shoulders bowed over, sobs ripping her body.

He nodded slowly. He could not speak. Together they went downstairs to the kitchen, where Josie was sitting at the table, staring at her clasped hands. Seeing them, she hesitated, then got up and stood between them, touching them lightly on the shoulders, like a bridge. "He was going to die anyway," she said.

"But not like that. Not drowning." While Paul walked toward the back door and stood looking out, Ruth sank down on a chair and buried her face in her hands. Despair ate into her body: A skeleton of grief had formed beneath her flesh. "Will," she moaned. "Oh, Will."

Josie put her arm around her mother. "He said he was getting weaker and weaker. This morning he could hardly stand. He didn't want you to know, but he was afraid he soon wouldn't be able to get up. He said he was damned if he was going to spend a perfect down-east summer in bed."

"Oh, Will. My poor boy."

"I told him the results this morning. He'd already guessed. He asked me to take him out in the boat, and I knew he was planning something. I could see it in his eyes."

Sorrow pushed against Ruth's heart, cold as a winter sea. She felt as though she were going to suffocate. It was what he would do. What, somewhere in the very bottom of her heart, Ruth had always feared. "He was so young. . . ."

"He didn't want to live. He told me this morning. He was tired of being ill. He didn't want any more treatments. Just a few last days up here and then, finished, over, ended. The way he wanted to go." Tears gathered in Josie's eyes but did not fall. "We talked for hours this morning. I'm so glad about that. My poor little brother. He was just waiting for me to come back, so he could go himself."

"I thought he wanted to spend the summer here."

"He wanted to *die* here, Mom. He told me he had had a wonderful life and that he knew it wasn't going to get better, only worse."

"He's like you, isn't he? Both of you are so . . . strong."

"We get that from you." Josie put a piece of folded paper on the table beside Ruth's arm.

Ruth opened it, scarcely able to see the letters.

Mom, Dad, don't be sad. I couldn't take any more. I wanted to be in control, not like poor Michelle in the hospital.

Thank you for all the things you gave me.

I love you all. Please don't cry.

Your son,
William

Ruth thought of his swollen-knuckled fingers struggling to hold the pen to write the words. Grief welled up, then a sudden kind of peace. She rested her head on her daughter's shoulder. Heard her husband's footsteps across the kitchen and felt the comfort of his arms around them both.

THEY SAT ON THE BENCH AT Caleb's Point looking out to sea. Bertlemy's Isle lay on the water, the tips of the spruces at its center gilded by the setting sun. Out of sight, on the strip of stony beach below them, the sea whispered, sucking at the pebbles and falling away with a sigh. A single star was already out, low on the horizon.

Ruth stared at the place where she had last seen Will. I gave birth to him, she thought. I gave him life and raised him—my sunny, funny Will—and now there is nothing left of him.

"Mom," Josie said, "Will told me he thought you'd be happier up here than in the city."

"I think he's right," said Paul. His arm tightened around Ruth's shoulders. "We'll have to think about it."

For so long Ruth had not had time to consider the simple matter of happiness. Now, tentatively tasting the idea, she realized that somewhere, out beyond the edge of now, a kind of contentment waited for them. Along the way she would find it. Paul too. And Josie. The three of them.

"One of the awful things, when we thought you were dead," she said, "was that I couldn't talk about it. I tried to pretend it had never happened."

Paul tightened his hold on his family. "We mustn't do that with William. We have to tell you all about it. All the things he did and said while you were away."

Ruth looked across the water. One child exchanged for another. For the rest of her life, whenever she came up here, she would see, in slow motion, tiny and foreshortened, the figures of her children in the little boat out on the water. Her resurrected daughter. And her doomed son, bending, slipping slowly into the welcoming sea.

All her life she had feared death by water, but until that moment she had always imagined that the death would be her own.

SUSAN MADISON

The Color of Hope is the first of Susan Madison's novels to appear in the United States. A native of Oxford, England, she explained that the book's American setting is the legacy of her first marriage, to an American, and a ten-year stint in Tennessee, where she raised two of her three sons. It was a great place for boys, Madison recalls, "but I was terribly homesick." Eventually she returned to Oxford, although she confesses a secret ambition left over from her American adventure: "If I weren't a writer, I'd love to be a country-western singer, up there onstage in those glittering costumes, belting out songs for all the guys in cowboy hats." Her many new readers will be glad she made the choice she did.

To learn more about Susan Madison and *The Color of Hope,* visit the Select Editions website: 📖 **ReadersOnly.com** Password: *Life*

The volumes in this series are issued
every two to three months. A typical volume
contains four outstanding books in condensed
form. None of the selections in any volume has
appeared in *Reader's Digest* magazine. Any reader
may receive this service by writing to
The Reader's Digest Association (Canada) Ltd.,
1125 Stanley Street, Montreal, Quebec H3B 5H5.

Some of the titles in this volume are also available in a
large-print format. For information about Select Editions
Large Type, call 1-800-877-5293.

ACKNOWLEDGMENTS

Pages 6–7, 8: illustrations by Liz Pyle
Pages 146–147, 148: illustrations by Amy Guip
Pages 320–321, 322: illustrations by Phil Boatwright
Pages 440–441, 442: illustrations by Andrew Powell

The original editions of the books in this volume are published and copyrighted as follows:
Ghost Moon, published by Delacorte Press,
The Bantam Dell Publishing Group,
a division of Random House, Inc.,
distributed by Random House of Canada Limited at $35.95
© 2000 by Karen Robards
The Empty Chair, published by Simon & Schuster, Inc.,
distributed by Distican Inc. at $37.00
© 2000 by Jeffery Deaver
Hawke's Cove, published by Pocket Books,
a division of Simon & Schuster, Inc.,
distributed by Distican Inc. at $34.95
© 2000 by Susan Wilson
The Colour of Hope, published by Transworld Publishers Ltd.
© 2000 by Susan Madison